Black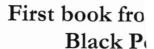

First book fro...
Black P... ...s

J P Ashman

Black Cross was awarded the 'Most Complex' award and chosen as a group
finalist in Mark Lawrence's
Self Published Fantasy Blog Off
2015

"The magic system is fascinating and very well crafted. This is quite an epic
saga, and surprisingly political. There are factions, and back biting, plenty of
twists and turns, violence and bloodshed – everything epic fantasy fans
enjoy."
www.bookwormblues.net

Black Cross
First book from the tales of the Black Powder Wars
J P Ashman

Cover art & series map by Charles Richardson

Edited by Jeff Gardiner
www.jeffgardiner.com

This, my first book, is dedicated to my wife, Cassandra, for encouraging me to chase my dreams and take up writing.

To Martyn, my brother and second pair of eyes, thank you for proof reading my work again and again since the very beginning. Your critique has been and will always be welcome and appreciated.

I have received support from many friends and family members, all of which have encouraged me every step of the way. I must give special thanks, however, to Robert Jeffries for his enthusiastic proof reading towards the final stages of the book, which, along with my brother, helped me clean up this lengthy project.

My editor, Jeff Gardiner, for coming into this late in the game, but making all the difference with your professional insight, enthusiasm and support. Thank you.

Any mistakes still remaining are my own.

A final thanks to my mother, Jan, for her support and for introducing me to fantasy, all those years ago. Without you, this would never have happened.

Prologue

Brisance
492nd year of the Alliance

With a cold wind at her back and the sun illuminating her solid frame, *Sessio* crashed through a large wave, the resulting spray raining down on a well-dressed merchant's agent.

'Sail astern,' came a call from above.

The large vessel creaked as she changed tack, her sails bloating in the strong wind.

Joinson turned and watched the ship's crew scramble about the rigging as they followed orders, whilst the first mate, a grisly fellow, looked up to the fortified crow's nest high above their heads.

'Ye see a flag, boy?' he shouted.

'Can't see none,' the boy in the crow's nest shouted back. 'They must've seen us, yet they're making no move our way.'

'Not pirates then,' the first mate said, to no one in particular.

Joinson sighed with obvious relief as he caught the first mate's comment. He'd been granted a great deal of trust by his employer with this trip, and had struck gold with his last find whilst in the south; a scroll he was sure his employer, Peneur Ineson, would agree made the trip worthwhile.

The agent jumped as the first mate roughly slapped him on the back.

'Don't worry none Master Joinson, we'll have ye home to Wesson fore ye can say 'morl's balls.'

Frowning at the blasphemous remark, Joinson glanced up at the captain, who, standing on the aft-castle above the two men, merely shrugged and indicated he hadn't heard the remark.

The boy in the crow's nest leaned precariously over the side. 'Sail's turned; now head'n away to the south.'

Joinson closed his eyes and released the breath he'd held, and the first mate gave a fresh order, which the crew attended to swiftly.

Looking to the sky, Joinson thanked Sir Samorl for their safe passage, and politely excused himself, moving to the aft-castle and his mundane quarters.

Before he could close the door, Joinson heard the boy from the crow's nest call out again.

'New sail on horizon! North this time… they're head'n straight for us!'

Swallowing hard, Joinson stepped back through the portal and looked up to Captain Mannino, who hadn't moved from the front rail of the aft-castle above.

The crew busied themselves around the rigging as Joinson watched on. The heavily tanned men and women scurried up and down ropes and across spars, up into the tall masts of the large, square rigged ship. This all made Joinson rather dizzy as he peered up at the swaying mizzen-mast which stood directly in front of him, his plump face a sour shade of green. He looked out towards the horizon, wishing for land to focus his sights on to settle his stomach.

'What's her heading, nest?' Although calm, Mannino's voice projected easily up to the top of the main-mast. It was the most Joinson had heard the captain say in hours.

'Still head'n for us cap'n.'

'Very well, keep your eye on the sail behind us as well. I don't want any surprises, boy.'

The boy pointed south. 'Aye cap'n, that one's still head'n away from us. Almost gone.'

'Ye heard the lad,' the first mate shouted, 'now bring her about. I want her side on wi' that ship up ahead.' The first mate approached Joinson, a wry grin spreading across his pock-marked face as he stopped next to the nervous agent. He slapped the man on the back in what could only be taken as a reassuring manner, before shouting up to the aft-castle above. 'Master Spendley, yer move lad.'

A young officer descended the aft-castle's steps quickly, making his way to the centre of the ship. 'Archers on deck,' he said to one sailor, who opened a hatch and passed the order on.

The helmsman started to bring *Sessio* around to her new heading, upwind of the target, a much safer, calmer position, allowing the archers a greater range and an easier platform from which to aim and loose their arrows.

A commotion erupted from below as over two dozen men with un-strung war bows climbed up ladders and piled out of trapdoors, followed by two men with large windlass crossbows. The latter hauled their weapons on ropes up the main-mast to the fortified crow's nest above. The archers swiftly climbed the steps of the fore- and aft-castles, forming rough ranks at the centre of each, and within seconds, had taken their wax coated hemp strings and strung their powerful war bows. They wore white linen bags full of arrows at their sides, and a variety of close combat weapons hung from their belts.

Sessio rode a particularly large wave before she finally came about to her new heading. Joinson stumbled, catching himself at the last minute by taking hold of the first mate's shoulder. The agent's cheeks turned from green to red as he noticed how not only the sailors, but the archers too, had hardly moved as the ship rolled over the large wave before settling down in her new position.

'Ye might be best in yer cabin, Master Joinson. Things might get nasty ye see,' the first mate said.

Joinson's eyes widened with fear at the possibility. He felt even worse as the churning in his stomach increased with the thought of a violent clash with pirates.

'Yes, I think you're right, Master Hitchmogh. I'll leave you gentlemen to your area of expertise. I don't want to get in your way, but... should you need

6

me… just—'

'We's know where to find ye, aye.'

The blushing man gave a shallow bow to Master Hitchmogh and hurried back into his cabin, closing the door behind him and sliding the bolt across as more yelling erupted on deck.

Not good, not good at all.

He played with the key around his neck whilst pacing up and down. As the shouting increased outside his cabin, he removed the now warm key, placed it into the hole of an iron padlock hanging from an ornate oak chest at the foot of his bunk, and turned it. He opened the chest and checked, for the hundredth time, the expensive, magical item inside, and stroked the ancient wrapping that held the magnificent scroll in the centre of the chest, before closing the lid and fixing the padlock once more.

The ship lurched suddenly and Joinson dropped onto the small bunk. He placed the key chain back around his neck and prayed that the sail coming towards them didn't belong to a pirate ship.

Then he heard the order he'd dreaded.

'Loose!'

Joinson closed his eyes and pushed away the sickly feeling as much as he could. He wringed his hands together as he tried to block out the noises coming from outside; the shouts of orders, the faint flutter of dozens of arrows leaving their strings, the creak of *Sessio* as she shifted in the water, and suddenly, the loud concussive crump of magic as the ship lurched violently.

Lord above. Theirs or ours? I didn't even know we had a mage on board… I pray we do?

A loud, stabbing crack to the ears then screams, distant, but far too close for Joinson's liking. He mumbled a prayer to ward off the magic as the fighting reached a crescendo outside.

On the deck? Please, no…

The clash of metal on metal sounded close, but he couldn't be sure if it was on *Sessio* or an adjoining vessel.

More screaming and one final thump of magic before all went quiet.

***

Joinson frowned as no one answered the door of the large house. Stepping back and looking about the windows, he saw no light inside and so set off up the dark street. He'd been assured by the Merchant Guild's clerk that Master Ineson was home, but clearly that wasn't the case.

He's probably out celebrating, and that's what I should be doing now, after that trip, with my share of the shipment's profits.

The streets were quiet, and yet, although a much safer district than his own, when Joinson heard, or rather felt, someone move out onto the street behind him, he couldn't help feeling more vulnerable than he had whilst aboard the pirate hounded *Sessio*. He quickened his pace, wheezing as he did so. Fumbling in the belt pouch which held his smoking pipe, the merchant's agent wished he carried more than the small eating knife on his belt, which he now fingered with his other hand. This was Park District though, no muggings happened around here, and the City Guard patrolled regularly, perhaps it was one of those that was now approaching at a quickened pace.

Can I hear, or feel it? I can't hear a damned thing over this wind.

Joinson's breathing increased and the first beads of sweat appeared around his head and neck.

Up ahead a park opened out, just three house lengths away.

Am I better near an open, dark park, or around inhabited buildings? The question was all he could think about. Unable to come to a conclusion, Joinson decided he would turn and look upon whoever was following behind. He quietly laughed to himself, quite sure all of a sudden that he was being paranoid.

A feeling I've had ever since buying that damned scroll for Master Ineson's client.

He slowed his pace and turned to look upon who he was sure would be a patrolling guardsman.

Joinson's body dropped to the floor, his lifeless eyes wide and his mouth open in a failed attempt to release the scream he had intended. The shadowy figure that had been following him disappeared into the park ahead, at a speed the large man could never have escaped.

Joinson's white silk shirt began turning crimson from a single spot on the left hand side of his chest, as his thick woollen cloak blew open in a gust of wind. Rain fell in sheets suddenly and washed the warm liquid down onto the cobbles, which quickly became slick with water and blood. Joinson's open mouth filled with water before overflowing and pouring down his fleshy left cheek, to add to the swirling mix of blood and water, whilst his foreign, light green pantaloons darkened with a mix of rain and piss.

Chapter 1: Cursed Wind

An uncharacteristically strong west wind for the time of year howled through the city streets as the day's light faded and distant thunder quietly rumbled out to sea.

'This is perfect,' remarked a tall, hooded figure. He stood in a window overlooking the distant harbour.

His silhouette seemed ominous to his attentive listener, who'd just entered the chamber at the request of the man standing before him.

'With these unusual gales, folk will fear curses and bad omens. We couldn't have asked for a more suitable cover for our experiment.'

'Lord Severun, I merely assist you in your work. The whole idea has been yours from the start and is yours still. It is your skill with magic that has brought this experiment so far. It is your experiment, not ours.'

Severun turned and looked down to the small gnome, who was playing with his unkempt, grey beard.

'Not at all, Orix,' Severun said, whilst removing his rain-soaked hood. 'I could not have worked through all the problems I encountered without such a dedicated cleric at my side.' Severun smiled at his partner, although Orix wouldn't have called it a partnership.

'You give me far more credit than I deserve, Lord Severun. If it is agreeable with you, I would like to oversee the enactment of the spell that will set this experiment in motion?'

'I'm afraid not, Orix, the spell will need my full concentration and I cannot have any distractions, no matter how small.' Orix frowned at the unintended pun whilst the wizard continued. 'I will perform the spell here in my chamber. Once enacted, you can deliver the vial and we can merge the two together and pass it to the courier for delivery.'

'As you wish, Lord Severun. Is there anything else you called me for?'

'Anything else?' The wizard looked aghast. 'I called you here to tell you that I've finally prepared everything needed to proceed, and you ask if there is anything else, Master Orix?'

The small gnome resisted the urge to roll his eyes and just shrugged. 'I thought you might have told me where you've been? What was so important to warrant holding up this experiment while you gallivant around the city in a blasted storm?' Severun attempted to respond, but the old gnome continued regardless. 'You told me recently that everything was set in place to carry out the experiment, that you finally had the magical item you'd been waiting for. The one that is apparently so important we could not proceed without. The one which also,' the gnome went on, flinging his arms up into the air, 'you don't seem to trust in me enough to see!' Severun again went to speak, but was dramatically cut off by Orix. 'But no, don't mind me, my lord Severun. I'll be on my way to await your next summons.'

Severun sighed heavily. 'Master Orix, please, you know how important you are to all of this, but I don't ask you every detail included in your potion, so I'll not bore you with every detail included in my spell and its preparation.'

'Very well,' the gnome said, unconvincingly. He turned to leave before hesitating to add, 'Please do be careful. You know the risks if you… or I, are not!'

'Don't worry, my little friend, I will be most careful indeed.' Severun turned then to gaze out over the ancient harbour once more, as Orix reached up and turned the cold, iron door handle, letting himself out.

Severun admitted to himself silently how he'd grown fond of the fussy old gnome during their work together. For that reason if no other, the wizard hoped the experiment would go exactly as planned. After all, if it went wrong and they both somehow managed to escape the king's punishment, they may themselves bear witness to the spell and potion's powers first hand, and that wasn't something Severun liked the thought of at all.

I'm doing the right thing aren't I? Someone needs to do something… As long as there are no more mishaps like tonight… but that was unavoidable, wasn't it? Yes, unavoidable. This experiment will save far more lives than it will destroy, and all thanks to the scroll.

The wizard stepped down from the window, removed his soaked woollen cloak and hung it and his hood over the back of a chair, before moving across his chamber to begin the enacting of the experiment's lengthy spell.

***

Easing himself out of bed, Orix pulled on his nightgown and cap, before padding across his room. He unlocked the chest below his window and stared down with mixed emotions at the contents; a simple vial. A strange magenta glow emanated from the glass bottle, and Orix frowned as he reached slowly for it. Although the liquid had been magenta on creation, Orix had never seen it glow before. It was as if it knew its time had come.

Fascinating…

Gently lifting the glass vial from the chest, he placed it into his nightgown's inner pocket and stood, groaning as he did so. *I'm feeling my age of late.*

Moving towards the door, Orix heard familiar yet slightly more exaggerated chants floating along with the equally familiar shadows, which flitted around in his periphery as if sentient.

Oh Severun, I do hope this works, or then again, do I?

Guilt, that's what I shall feel should we succeed.

The old gnome chuckled to himself and shook his head.

That's what I shall feel should we fail!

Orix shuddered before opening the oak door. He wandered across the hall to the steep, spiral staircase, which whistled and moaned with internal winds.

Reaching Severun's waiting room, he sat on a small rosewood chair built just for him. He wondered how many times he'd sat in that very chair, waiting for Severun to finish some spell or other, before his mind moved on to other things.

'I hope we're not set for a full blown storm.' He spoke this thought aloud, as a sudden deluge hammered against the room's window.

'I think we are, Master Orix.'

Orix jumped and instinctively raised his hand to his chest, where the vial was hidden in his inside pocket.

'Don't scare me so, Falchion, especially when I'm holding such a dangerous item!' Orix directed his outburst to a man stood in the shadowy corner of the room.

'Why couldn't you sit in the torchlight? Skulking in the shadows trying to scare an old gnome, it's not on.'

'My apologies, Master Orix, I didn't feel like sitting is all.' Fal, as he was commonly known, moved into the light, rubbing his tribal-tattooed face as he did so. 'I don't even know why I'm here at such an hour. I haven't been ordered to do anything but wait here for further instructions from Lord Severun. You mentioned a dangerous item?' he added quickly, before Orix could speak. 'Something he needs for his spell I presume?'

'Yes, for his spell,' Orix snapped, 'but no further concern of yours, Falchion. A sergeant-at-arms needs only to follow orders, not ask questions.'

'Of course, Master Orix. It was not my place to ask.' Fal bowed his head briefly, before leaning back against the wall besides the old gnome, his leather armour creaking as he did so. He looked down at his chest to see the coat-of-arms of the Wizards and Sorcery Guild; a blue and black split field, with a white crescent moon crossing the centre and a yellow crown above that. Looking back up from the heraldry that he was proud to wear, Fal asked another question of the master cleric sat beside him.

'For weeks, Lord Severun has conjured ghostly shadows and winds within Tyndurris, but never have I seen so many, right down to the lower levels. Do you think these uncommon gales are causing the increase in the spell's effects, Master Orix?'

'The reason for the increase is because Lord Severun is completing this lengthy experiment tonight. Gales from the west... south... or wherever, is a mere coincidence. You don't believe the rot about curses and bad omens being sent from other lands do you, Falchion?'

Fal laughed. 'Not at all, it's an unusual storm for this time of year, nothing more. I admit, however, that I know nothing of magic.'

'Well I'm glad you realise that whisperings about curses and omens are utter twaddle, Falchion. I took you for one of more intellect than that and as I thought, I was right.' Orix's grin was just visible through his wiry beard. 'Otherwise your next task might give you the creeps even more than I expect it will anyway.'

Fal's eyes widened a little.

'Well, I'm going to shut up now,' Orix said, hastily. 'Your orders will come soon enough from Lord Severun, not me.' *Thankfully.* Fal nodded to Orix and moved back to the shadows to lean against the wall and await his orders.

An hour or so went by before the winds died down, in the tower at least, for outside was quite the opposite compared to the now eerie stillness within Tyndurris.

Orix jumped when the door to Severun's chamber swung inwards with a bang. Noticing the lack of Fal's animation didn't help, and the gnome's cheeks flushed an even deeper shade of red than normal.

'Come on in, Orix, it's all going wonderfully. Now it's time to complete the task and add your potion.' The wizard's voice echoed around the stone walls as if amplified, but Severun himself wasn't in view from where Orix now stood. The old gnome noted Fal peering through the door from his position by the window, where he'd been watching lightening split the sky. As Orix looked at the sergeant, the man turned to meet his gaze, smiled and bowed his olive-skinned head. Orix nodded in return and entered the larger chamber.

Severun smiled broadly when he saw Orix, which, along with his flowing robes, made the wizard seem quite intimidating.

The hairs on the back of Orix's neck stood to attention. *I've felt like that often of late in here, especially since he came by that ornate chest. Makes the room feel... cold, dark even. Oh don't be stupid, it's an oak box you old fool.*

'Lord Severun, I pray the spell went accordingly? You do seem to be positively beaming, which I hope answers my question. You know my reservations about this experiment so I need not say any more about that.'

Orix looked away from Severun for the first time since entering the chamber and saw a room covered in scattered papers, fallen books, paintings from walls and all manner of debris.

By the gods...

'Of course it did, Orix. It went perfectly in fact. The wind blew my window open and caused all this.' Severun swept his arm around about him, gesturing towards the mess lying on the floor. 'Certainly not the spell, if that's what you were thinking, I assure you.'

That's exactly what I was thinking, and worse.

'Do you have the vial?'

Straight to the point, Orix thought. He fumbled through all his many pockets. After an impatient few moments which felt much longer, Orix remembered the new inner pocket he'd sewn into his night gown. He carefully retrieved the vial and looked up into Severun's eyes, just in time to have the vial plucked from his hand by the wizard.

'You're certainly eager to see this through aren't you?'

Severun didn't reply. Spinning on his heels, he strode across his chamber before stopping at a stone alter in the centre of the room.

Orix shook his head and looked about the chamber once more. Around the walls hung all manner of strange and foreign objects, from paintings, some of which seemed to have a great sense of depth to them, architectural plans and tall ornate mirrors, to outlandish carvings and ornaments, one of which Orix could have sworn blinked as he looked away from it. The walls were usually cluttered with many more such items, however, with most of the lighter objects now decorating the floor, the chamber walls looked almost bare compared to usual.

On the right-hand side of the chamber stood Severun's desk, littered with scattered papers from the wind that continued to howl through the open window.

Orix tutted. *This just won't do, damned wizard. Never seen him so distracted. At least his mind is on the spell… I hope.*

Orix hurried across the large chamber, cursing as his woollen slippers soaked up the rain-sodden floor. Reaching the opposite side of the room, he dragged the ornate chest under the window, his stomach twisting for some unknown reason as he did so. He never noticed Severun's sudden attention as he touched the chest, and so continued to reach up, managing with some effort to slam the window shut.

Turning from the window, Orix saw Severun turn away, before proceeding to pour the contents of Orix's vial and Severun's own magical potion into an empty wine bottle. A violent hiss and thick smoke poured from the bottle as the two liquids met, rolling across the floor and ceiling briefly before dissipating swiftly. The luminous magenta glow of Orix's liquid met with the luminous green glow of Severun's to create a… somewhat disappointing brown liquid, which the master cleric thought resembled ale. *How uninteresting,* Orix thought, frowning. He'd hoped for something a little more dramatic, and even the hissing sound and smoke had gone by the time the bottle was full. Orix wondered if Severun had planned it that way, so as not to draw attention to the bottle once it was being transported through the city streets. Orix began to worry as usual about the experiment. As they'd discussed it, the ghostly shadows seen earlier throughout the tower, would carry the potion's effects to their targets, and then Severun and Orix would record the results as they came in.

If they come in…

Orix was still unsure any of this would work.

Surely he's not expecting someone to drink the contents of the bottle?

'Here we have it.' Severun turned to face Orix, the unsettling grin still plastered across the wizard's face.

Orix frowned again. 'Yes I can see that. It doesn't look incredibly impressive though, does it?'

Severun walked towards the chamber door, laughing. 'Well of course it doesn't, we can't have Sergeant Falchion discarding a bottle of luminous potion in the city before walking off minding his own business, can we?'

'I suppose not,' Orix replied whilst shaking his head. He was at least satisfied that Severun hadn't decided to feed it to some street urchin or beggar in Dockside.

'Good evening, Lord Severun.'

Orix barely heard Fal's voice from where he stood on the farthest side of the chamber from the door. He hopped down off the chest and slopped across the chamber, whilst nervously playing with his beard and mumbling to himself about the cold and his wet feet.

'Good evening, sergeant,' Severun said. 'I trust you don't mind being called here at this late hour? I'd just prefer someone I can trust to see this experiment through, as well as someone who can look after themselves around Dockside at night.'

'Of course not, my lord. I'm honoured you thought of me, and I'm as ever at your service. Where exactly am I to go in Dockside?' Fal rested his hand on the single-edged sword at his hip as he thought of the dangerous district he'd be heading into.

Severun looked at Orix, lost for a way to explain Fal's orders. Orix shrugged and Severun turned back to Fal, answering in a very serious manner.

'I know you well enough to know you need no explanation of the task I ask you to perform, but respect you enough to tell you as much as I can, Sergeant Falchion.

'I wish you to take this bottle to the harbour end of Dock Street, but to stop before you reach the wooden jetty. Once there, I wish you to empty the contents onto the ground, taking care not to draw attention to yourself.'

Fal nodded and Orix rolled his eyes at the wizard's dramatic tone.

'After emptying the bottle,' Severun continued, 'you may see shadows like those you saw earlier tonight and on other nights when I have enacted similar spells. This is all part of experiment, and is nothing to worry about. As I'm sure you know, all our work here comes with the approval of the king himself, and I would never ask or order you to do anything that would have you break the law.'

It doesn't have the approval of the king yet though does it, Severun? Oh gods above, what are we doing? Just smile and keep quiet, it's too late for anything else.

Orix grinned suddenly, and both Severun and Fal looked at him, expecting an addition from the gnome. Fal never noticed the nervousness in Severun's eyes, but after a moment of Orix grinning at them, yet saying nothing, Severun continued and Fal looked back to him.

'After the potion is released, you are free to make your way home. Your work will have been done. I wish you to report back to me tomorrow, so I know everything went smoothly.

'Any questions, sergeant?' Severun held the bottle out to Fal, who took it gingerly, whilst shaking his head.

'None at all, my lord. I will see it done immediately. Good evening to you both, Lord Severun, Master Orix.' Fal turned and descended the stairs into darkness.

'Will Falchion not realise what he's released when people turn up dead in a few days' time, all with the same symptoms, and all over the slums of Dockside?'

Severun snorted. 'A mere coincidence is all he'll think. A few dozen people will not be missed, and as I said, this storm is a blessing, Orix. You know how folk gossip. People will claim a 'cursed wind' caused the deaths, by carrying whatever their imaginations can conjure from foreign lands. Sergeant

Falchion isn't the sort to listen to such nonsense, so I doubt he'll even entertain such rumours.'

Orix looked unconvinced. 'Maybe not, but he also has his wits about him. He didn't make sergeant-at-arms of such a prestigious guild without them.'

Severun laughed. 'You worry too much, Orix. Get some rest and we shall talk to Sergeant Falchion tomorrow, then you can hear first-hand exactly how simply it went.' Orix felt weary all of a sudden, so he didn't question Severun's admission of a few dozen, rather than the handful he'd previously been told would be involved.

'Very well,' Orix said, finally. 'I shall return to my bed and meet with you here tomorrow. Good night Lord Severun.'

Severun smiled, nodded and they both turned their separate ways, to retire to their rooms and beds for the remainder of the night.

Fal's night, however, had just begun.

Chapter 2: Dock Street

Fal waited in the doorway of a large outbuilding used for storage. He'd requested a guild coach to take him as far as Piper's Inn, half way down Dock Street, where he would continue down to the harbour on foot.

He checked again that the wine bottle Severun had given him was securely strapped beneath his waxed canvas cloak, and then moved his hand instinctively back to the falchion at his side.

The clattering of hooves and metal-rimmed wheels alerted Fal to the arrival of the coach as it rounded the base of the large tower, travelling from the stables on the other side of the courtyard. The black cab rocked on its springs as the driver pulled on the reins to halt the two bay mares. A familiar face peered from a low-pulled hood as the driver, Casson Bevins, climbed down from his seat at the front of the coach.

Fal pulled back his own hood and nodded to the driver.

'Good evening, sergeant, where is it you wish to go tonight?' Casson opened the coach door, wrestling with it against the wind whilst inviting Fal to enter the sheltered cab.

'Thank you,' Fal replied warmly, once inside. 'I'd like to be dropped off on Dock Street if possible, just by Piper's Inn.'

Casson looked surprised at the request, but shrugged, smiled and bowed all the same. 'As you wish sergeant.' He closed the cab's door, climbed back up to his driver's seat and with a jerk, the coach set off towards Tyndurris' double gates. Once through, the horses began to trot proudly through the deserted streets.

Fal rubbed his face and let out a groan.

Casson Bevins, of all the drivers.

What rumours would Casson spread tomorrow? He was notoriously nosy and as bad a gossip as the servants in the guild washroom and kitchens, and Dock Street wasn't the sort of place Fal wanted to be associated with.

After several streets and one large avenue, the area visibly changed as the coach proceeded onto and further down Dock Street. Although architecturally not all that dissimilar from buildings they'd already passed, those along Dock Street became untended and downright decrepit at times.

And so I come back to Dockside.

The number of people on the streets for such a late hour increased. Painted ladies stood on street corners despite the weather, offering themselves to passers-by, whilst groups of men stumbled up and down the street from one drinking hole to another. There were also children darting from shadow to shadow, looking for pockets to pick for their respective gangs, none of which was missed by Fal's trained eye.

The coach jerked to a halt. Looking across the interior of the cab and through the opposite window, Fal saw the inn's brightly lit bay windows. Silhouettes moved to and fro on the other side of the small glass squares, creating a jumble of figures with no features, whilst a rowdy chorus of laughter and awful singing emanated from within.

Fal stepped out of the coach's door before Casson Bevins had time to open it for him, and received a score of whistles, whoops and jibes from locals and sailors alike. Ignoring the comments, Fal spoke just loud enough for Casson to hear, but loud enough to be heard over the gusts of wind blowing straight up from the harbour further down the hill.

'Best be on your way, Master Bevins. I'd hate to have to explain to Lord Severun that I lost a coach… and driver tonight.'

The scrawny man's eyes widened at that.

'You don't have to tell me twice, enjoy your night, sergeant.' With a smirk and a wink from beneath his hood, Casson Bevins shook the reigns and the coach sprung into motion, turning a full circle in the wide street and heading back up Dock Street.

Turning to face the hecklers, Fal saw thankfully that they'd already moved on. Even the sight of an expensive coach couldn't keep them from their next drink.

After walking for what seemed like an age, Fal was regretting not putting extra layers on to counter the cold and harsh winds. He covered his face as much as possible with his hood, although his vision through the gap was still impaired by the fine rain collecting on his eyelashes, causing him to blink constantly. *At least my back will be to the wind and rain on the way home. I must be getting old, I used to patrol these streets in all weather and hardly feel it. Or so I remember. The mind dulls the past though, I'm sure of it.*

As he reached the end of Dock Street, the buildings fell away and the space opened up into Market Square. The centre of the square was raised, the road leading around the edge of an island of stone where crates, cargo and tied up stalls were left ready for the next day's trading. A couple of crates had collapsed in the wind and various items of cargo blew across the square, whilst the constant clanging of rigging on masts continued to play their tune.

I'd be surprised that cargo's still rolling around if it weren't in Dockside, Fal thought, knowingly.

Owned by various ship crews, guilds and surely even local gangs, the owners of the cargo controlled all manner of ways and means to pay back thieves, otherwise the produce would've been taken long ago.

Fal stopped as he reached the centre of the square and took a good look about the shadowy scene for any onlookers. It was clear. Taking a deep breath and wiping his face once more, he pulled the wine bottle containing the potion from his canvas cloak, which whipped out on the strong wind before he pulled it back close around his body with his free hand.

Despite his visual scanning of the square, the constant noise around the harbour masked any sound that could've warned him of the two figures stood atop large crates behind.

The men dropped towards Fal and hit the ground with the grace of oxen.

The smaller of the two managed to land on his feet, albeit awkwardly, whilst the other landed heavily on his shoulder after his leg gave way, right where Fal had been standing.

After heaving the other to his feet, the smaller man pulled a cudgel from his sodden, tatty cloak and started to advance slowly. Grimacing, the other pulled a crude looking dagger from his belt with his good arm and followed his young partner's actions, slowly starting towards the man they'd attempted to jump upon.

Fal's blade was held out behind him, hidden by his cloak which danced wildly in the strong wind. Shrugging off his hood he stared at the two men, snapping his water-filled eyes from one to the other. He still held the bottle tightly in his wet hand. In fact, it was the bottle that had saved him, along with the oil lamps surrounding the square, which rocked back and forth in the wind, causing shadows to jerk about all around them. If not for the bottle held up, Fal wouldn't have seen the reflection of the men as they leapt from the crates behind him. Surely noticing Fal's facial tattoos, the two men hesitated in their advance, looking at each other questioningly.

Ahh… you noticed, you bastards.

Seeing his marked face could have been enough to put most thugs off, but these two seemed determined, and moving to the left, the younger of the two motioned for the other to flank to the right.

Seeing no point in ceremony now, Fal threw the bottle to the ground at the feet of his closest opponent, keeping the lad back long enough to draw a bone handled seax knife from his boot with his now free hand.

A flash erupted as the glass bottle exploded on the stone floor.

Lightning was Fal's first thought – for the briefest of moments, before remembering that the bottle contained the potion.

Both attackers jumped back at the flash, which gave Fal his chance. Rushing at the larger man, Fal brought his heavy blade over in a controlled overhead chop aimed at the man's injured shoulder, water flicking from the blade in an arc over Fal's head.

The man jerked his shoulder and arm back to evade Fal's blade, and grunted in pain at the sudden movement, giving Fal the opening he needed from the feigned attack. Fal swiftly hopped forward and thrust the tip of his seax through flesh and ribs. The big man cried out louder, and before he could drop his dagger and bring his good hand up to the wound, Fal had pulled the seax free, moved past him and turned about to see the remaining thug swinging at him with his cudgel. Jumping back, Fal threw his falchion around in a sideways parry that connected with the oncoming weapon. Immediately switching his momentum, he stepped in close, knowing there was little danger from the smaller man's blunt weapon without a swing behind it. The young man tried to back away, but Fal was upon him, his seax drawing a deep red line across an outstretched arm, causing the lad to drop the cudgel and pull back further.

Fal's forehead connected with the bridge of the wiry lad's nose, flattening it to his face and decorating his wet clothing with blood. The momentum of the thug's attempted back step, along with Fal's impacting head and the rain swept stone, sent the lad crashing over backwards into a pile of small crates.

Fal, looking around quickly to make sure there were no more attackers accompanying the two men, caught a glimpse of movement from the corner of his eye.

Turning to see what the fresh threat was and wiping the rain from his eyes with the back of his left hand, Fal saw the same ghostly shadows he'd seen earlier that night in Tyndurris. One of the closer shadows seemed to hover over the larger of the two men, who rolled on the floor, clutching his chest and groaning. The shadow looked straight at Fal, although no visible eyes were apparent, it was more a feeling of someone, or something, watching him. Almost as soon as he'd seen it, it descended into the man on the ground.

Gods below…

Quickly turning to the lad, half covered in broken crates and out cold, Fal caught a glimpse of another shadow disappearing into the younger man's open mouth.

The wind remained strong and the rain swirled around the square. Other shadows followed the gusts, keeping to Fal's peripheral vision and flying just out of his direct gaze whenever he turned to look at one. The shadows were rising up high with the winds. He looked all around the square, trying to catch a glimpse of one fully, but they were leaving swiftly, following the westerly wind to blow high and far out over the city, until all were gone and there was no movement at all around him, apart from the rain, swaying masts of ships and the squirming of the larger man on the ground close by.

Although he knew it couldn't be anything sinister he'd just released, since his orders came from the guild master, he felt an unnatural chill on top of the wind and rain. He shuddered briefly.

Fal cocked his head as an unusual sound began to drift in over the din of the storm.

Singing?

Several voices in unison were audible, from further up Dock Street.

Sailors, he thought, *on their way back to their ships.*

Fal decided, against his natural sense of duty, to leave Market Square and the two men before the approaching group arrived.

Don't bring attention to yourself. Nice, Falchion, great job.

Cleaning his weapons swiftly on the young man's clothes before sheathing them, Fal slipped off into the shadows, away from the glow of the square's swaying lamps. He took a roundabout route back to Dock Street and avoided the group of sailors heading down to Market Square. Suddenly hearing shouts instead of singing, he knew the sailors had come across his downed attackers. He wondered then if the group of men would call for aid or strip the two of anything worth taking, leaving them to the elements.

The latter I'd wager.

Despite that thought, he heard the sailors raise the hue and cry not long after.

Wet hood back up, wind and rain at his back, Fal strode on at a fast pace up Dock Street, beginning his long walk home, his mind full of questions.

He never noticed the figure watching him from a dark alley. The same figure that had witnessed him dispatch the two men and release the ghostlike shadows into the city.

***

Crouching down on the blood and rain-slick cobbles to examine the obvious wound on the dead man's chest, the city guardsman spoke for the first time since arriving at the murder scene.

'Sword thrust is what I say.'

'What type of sword, Biviano?' the second, much larger guardsman said as he wiped the collecting rainwater from his thick, red beard.

'How the hell should I know, ye filthy lump? It's a deep hole, it's not sign posted,' Biviano said, before standing back up next to his partner, rain dripping from the rim of his iron kettle-helm.

Frowning, Sears thumped the smaller man on the shoulder and despite the maille covered gambeson, Biviano felt it.

'Ouch!'

'How'd ye know it's a sword thrust then and not a knife, clever dick? Ye didn't look at it for long.'

'Because it's a bigger hole than a knife would cause. It doesn't take much to work that out.'

'Could've been a seax or scramasax?'

'Nope, there's an exit hole in his back, and it's the same size as the entry hole in his chest. So it's a longer, thinner sword like a rapier or something similar. I'd wager on that!'

'Fair point,' Sears said. 'Not a ganger then. Not in this district and especially not with a rapier.'

Biviano scratched under his kettle-helm as he answered. 'Aye, someone with money methinks. We'll have to find out who this man was and what business he was in. Well-dressed, pantaloons too, clearly piss stained despite the rain, but nice all the same. Ye don't see them often do ye?'

Sears shook his head and looked up and down the lamp lit cobbled street, squinting against the wind and rain. 'He was heading towards the park, but from where? No taverns back that way, not close by anyway, only houses and big ones at that.'

'Wonder what shade of green they are when dry,' Biviano said, still looking down at the corpse.

'Eh?'

'The pantaloons,' the smaller guardsman said, scratching again under his kettle-helm. 'From the south aren't they? I bet they're quite fetching when dry; a real lady-puller.' He stopped then suddenly added, 'Damned sure I've

20

got nits.'

'They look like something a woman would wear under her dress.'

'Not in Sirreta, big guy, all the rage down there.'

'We're not in Sirreta. Anyway, keep yer mind on the job will ye?' Sears said, having a scratch under his own kettle-helm. *Bastard's got me doing it now.*

'Aye alright. So, we need a cart to take the body to the nearest infirmary. Let them have a look whilst we ask about. You stay here. I'll go fetch one.'

Sears grabbed Biviano by his rain slick, maille covered arm and tugged him back. '*You* stay here and *I'll* go for one, alright?'

Biviano sighed audibly and nodded, before flicking two fingers up at his large companion's back.

'Be back soon,' Sears shouted over the wind, as he headed off up the street.

Take yer time ye big ginger get, I'm going to take me another look at this poor bastard's pantaloons.

Chapter 3: The Report

The large chamber was dark, with only one window allowing insufficient light to chase away the shadows. As Severun closed the door behind him, he uttered an inaudible word and the torches and beeswax candles around the walls and furniture of the chamber sprang to life.

'Take a seat, gentlemen.' Severun gestured to two chairs over by his desk, which effortlessly slid out of their own accord to accommodate the man and gnome. Severun walked over and sat on his grand wooden spinning chair. Such chairs were extremely rare, and this was the only one Fal had ever seen. Trying to study the base of the chair to see how it turned so effortlessly, he realised all eyes were on him.

Shit.

'Lord Severun, Master Orix... I'm not sure what to tell you, other than I did as you asked and released the potion down on Market Square, by the harbour—'

Before he could go any further, Severun cut in excitedly. 'Did you see anything happen, sergeant? Were there any obvious effects, and were there any witnesses?' Severun leaned forward and placed his elbows on the desk, eagerly awaiting Fal's reply.

Good questions and not ones I'm looking forward to answering.

Fal grimaced and hesitated before replying. 'None that were in a fit state of mind to notice the effects—'

'Excellent, tell us everything.' Severun interrupted again.

Did he miss my meaning?

Fal went on to explain the events of the previous night, and to his relief and surprise, Lord Severun seemed to have no problem with the fight that had occurred, in fact he seemed quite pleased upon hearing that the shadowy spectres had actually entered the two men. Orix, however, fiddling with his beard, seemed to show no sign either way, apart from a frown when Fal said he'd left his attackers to the group of sailors, and again when he mentioned the shadows rising high across the city. In fact, after divulging what had happened, Orix failed to look Fal in the eye altogether.

'Excellent, Sergeant Falchion,' Severun said, clapping and then clasping his hands together. 'I appreciate your time and won't keep you any longer.'

Fal rocked back a bit at that. Surprised at the abrupt dismissal, he stood, inclined his head to both guild masters and left the room.

'I told you not to worry didn't I, Orix? All went well and we can await reports from your infirmaries,' Severun said, enthusiastically. 'There are definitely two affected already and it just shows it's working as planned. Those two men might have killed someone had Sergeant Falchion not been their target, and now they will get their deserved punishment, do you not think?'

Orix shook his head, his bushy eyebrows furrowed. 'I still don't believe it's our place to be magistrate and executioner, Lord Severun. I'm a cleric... a master cleric, and my place is in healing and preventing suffering, not causing it.'

Severun smiled genuinely at Orix. 'My old friend, you have a heart of gold and I admire you for your beliefs. I, however, have come to the conclusion over the years, that there are many in this city that do not deserve your worry, and certainly don't deserve to be treated fairly. They don't think about those they prey on, so why should we think about them? I assure you that the people in Wesson, be them humans, gnomes, half-elves or whoever, will be happier when the streets of Dockside become a safer place. Is it fair that one district suffers, while others live relatively safe daily lives? I think not.'

Orix sighed, clearly unconvinced, and slumped in his chair. 'What about Sergeant Falchion's report on the shadows travelling across the city? Maybe further than Dockside? They weren't supposed to stray further afield.'

Sitting back in his chair, Severun scratched his head. 'Again, I wouldn't worry about it, Orix, it changes nothing. It only spreads the effects throughout the districts. We'll just have to acquire reports from all the infirmaries and not just those in Dockside.'

'Very well,' Orix said. 'I will have my clerics report to me directly regarding any unusual illnesses and deaths that occur in their infirmaries.'

Severun nodded approvingly and their discussion moved on to lighter-hearted topics, after all, they both knew the effects would take a few days to show themselves.

***

High up in a majestic, ancient building, dimly lit by beeswax candles and a thin, arched window, lay a circular chamber. The incense burning in the clay oil burners on the large oak desk couldn't hide the musty smell from the years of dust that had gathered on the antique furniture. The large man wrapped in deep purple robes who sat in an old chair behind the desk, however, was accustomed to the smell. He clasped his hands together, fingering multiple jewel encrusted rings on stubby fingers. His breath rasped through a flat nose and his deep, penetrating eyes hung like lost souls under his wild eyebrows.

Another man stood in front of the large desk, waiting patiently for a response to the news he'd delivered. His hands mirrored that of the robed figure but behind his cloaked back, twisting a single silver ring around and around his middle finger.

The robed man slowly placed his hands flat on the desk in front of him, before replying in a broken voice. 'It is as we have suspected for centuries then, General Comlay. The guild cannot be trusted with such power and position in the kingdom. Whatever they are planning, or have already released upon us, is an unforgivable crime. We must act upon this news immediately. We cannot pander to the moods and whims of the lords of Wesson or King Barrison any longer. If we present the news to them and leave matters in their hands regarding such dark conspiracies, we will all fall to a world of demons and nightmares before they decide to call upon a council; a council that will include the very traitors you speak of.' The robed figure leaned back in his chair, which creaked under the strain, and clasped a hand around the lance emblem hanging from his thick neck. 'I want you to order your men to watch over the traitors, General.'

'I wouldn't dare question you, sire, but we don't have the resources to watch them all,' Horler Comlay said to the Grand Inquisitor. He moved his hands round to rest, one on the hilt of his rapier, the other on one of the two throwing knives sheathed across his abdomen.

The Grand Inquisitor scowled. 'I don't mean for you to watch every single one of them, General. I want your men to watch the highest ranks, the ones instigating this conspiracy against the kingdom. I also want you to watch the sergeant you mentioned. He clearly has a key role in this heinous crime.'

Horler's thin lips curled up to one side. 'Very well, sire, I will give the order to my finest and keep you updated. I take it we won't be informing the King's advisor, the Archbishop, of this?'

The Grand Inquisitor shook his head. 'No. For too long we have abided by the laws changed by a king long since passed, requesting permission before acting and often losing opportunities because of it. We cannot afford the delay, or their blind questioning of our current evidence when faced with something of this scale. We will move in silence and strike when it suits us, not the King or his council. Our work will be done before they have chance to question us, and our results will speak for themselves, thus heightening our status in the kingdom once again.'

'Very well, sire.'

'Oh and General Comlay...'

'Sire?'

'You never mentioned how you took care of the merchant and his agent?'

'Ah...' Horler ran a hand through his lank, black hair before continuing. 'I dispatched the agent in the street—'

'And Joinson's employer, Peneur Ineson?'

'Is dead, sire, but not by my hand.'

The large man's eyes widened for a brief moment. 'By theirs, General?'

'Possibly, sire, there were no visible wounds on Ineson's body.'

'Very well,' the Grand Inquisitor said as he leaned forward in his chair, offering his hand to Horler, who bowed and kissed it.

'You are dismissed, General Comlay.'

Horler Comlay turned and left the room, whilst the Grand Inquisitor sat back in his chair, pressing his fingers together to form a steeple as he slipped into thought.

They're covering their tracks; removing all who know about the scroll. All evidence. Well, apart from that captain and his crew. They'll not remove him, not with his reputation. Alas, there'll be no way of making him talk about his contract either, and so we must forget about Captain Mannino and Sessio, as much as it pains me to do so.

Chapter 4: Symptoms

Sav woke with a start as someone banged on his door.

Sod off, for crying out loud. Sod off!

The banging continued.

'Alright… alright… I'll be a moment,' the scout shouted as loud as he dared, the banging continuing in his head long after it had stopped at the door.

As he threw on a simple linen shirt and a pair of braes, he remembered starting the night before downstairs in the bar. How he'd ended the night was beyond him, but the way he felt this morning gave him a clue as to his night time activities.

Walking across his small room, he turned the key in the lock and opened the door a crack. To his dismay, Fal pushed the door open forcefully, laughing as he strode into the room.

'Good evening Sav,' Fal said. 'I gather you spent the day in bed then?'

Fal! Well I'll be flayed. He could be a little quieter though.

Sav's bloodshot eyes widened suddenly. 'Evening?' He looked completely confused as Fal, still laughing, nodded.

Looking over to the window blind, Sav realised no light shone through the gaps.

He collapsed back onto his bed and released a huge sigh. 'I thought it morning. I don't recall last night,' he said, his eyes tightly closed.

Fal leaned against the now closed door, grinning and shaking his head. 'When'll you learn that after two seasons in the wilds, you can't just return and drink the place out of ale and mead as if it's a nightly occurrence? It's been three days since I saw you last, and you're in no better state.'

Three days?

'Sorry, I didn't realise you'd adopted me and become my father, Falchion, sir!' Sav draped his thick, bow-strengthened right arm over his face, as if it would help relieve his hangover.

'You'd be in a lot more strife from me if I were your father, young man.' Fal held a stern look as best he could without breaking into a smile.

Looking up, Sav waved his hand dismissively at his scowling friend. 'Bah… you're not even funny. Why are you here anyway?'

'Oh, you don't recall inviting me round any time for a few drinks then?' Fal stuck out his bottom lip.

Did I? Sounds like me. Must have then, but the thought of…

'No… don't mention drink, I can't stomach the thought. And no, I don't remember because I wouldn't invite you, I don't even like you, especially at this moment in time.' After a brief pause, Sav grinned for the first time since waking, and threw his straw-filled pillow at Fal, which missed and hit the wall next to Fal's head before falling to the floor.

'I hope your aim is better with your bow, scout? Can't have people with such an awful aim patrolling our borders now can we?'

'Alright, enough,' Sav said, releasing another sigh. 'I'm defenceless to all this mocking. Can't you see how delicate I am at the moment?' Dropping his head back to the bed, Sav rolled onto his front and smothered his face in the covers where the pillow had been.

'Only one thing for that, Sav – hair of the dog,' Fal said, taking his friend's woollen tunic from the floor and throwing it over him. 'Come on, let's go drink and get some greasy food down you.'

Groaning, Sav rolled back over, swung his long legs from the bed and grabbed Fal to help himself up. After pulling on a pair of mix matched woollen hose from the floor, his boots and tunic, Sav pushed Fal onto the bed and strode to the door. As he opened it he paused, turned to Fal and said, 'Come on then, you can't lie in bed all evening, there's drinking to be done.'

Fal shook his head once more and watched his friend leave the room.

'How does he do it?' he thought aloud, before jumping off the bed and running after Sav, slamming the door shut behind him.

***

'Morri, Morri, come quick, we have another one with the same symptoms,' an elderly woman shouted up a simple flight of wooden stairs, stairs which led to the chambers of one of the infirmary's resident clerics.

A young man dressed in a dark green woollen nightgown came running down the stairs, clearly woken by the woman's shouting and not looking best pleased.

'What is it Midrel? I'm trying to sleep.' The cleric brushed a messy blonde fringe from his eyes and yawned as he entered a treatment room the old woman had hurried into upon his arrival.

'I'm sorry, Morri,' she said, as he entered. 'I thought ye should see this straight away. This man has the same symptoms as the two brothers who were arrested the other night and brought here. Ye know the two I mean, Llard and Bein?' she asked, talking slowly and loudly as if Morri's tiredness made him hard of hearing.

The cleric simply nodded his head whilst holding his oil lamp over the prone, unconscious man. 'Some blisters on the face and hands—'

'Also on the rest of his body,' Midrel said. 'I had a look. He's burning up too, and it's far from warm in here, that's for sure.' The elderly woman rubbed her arms as if to accentuate the point. 'The room's hearth's not been lit like the others, but I didn't want him put with anyone else whilst in this state.'

'You did the right thing keeping him separate,' Morri said, smiling at the woman. 'Hold this.' He passed her the oil lamp before continuing. 'His pulse is weak but steady, when did he come in and who brought him?'

'Dunno who brought him.' She shrugged. 'He sat in the entrance hall alone. When I heard him coughing I went through and tried to talk to him, he didn't reply… well, he passed out there and then so he never had the chance. I asked Orrel to assist me lifting him in here.'

'The guards didn't see anyone with him?'

Shaking her head, the woman looked a little guilty. 'I'm sorry, Morri, I was serving Orrel and his friend tea in the kitchen. I know they should be at the door, but it gets ever so cold in the dead of night.'

Morri smiled and held his hands up. 'Never mind that, the guards' main job is to protect us, so I guess there's no better protection than having them right by your side, is there?'

Smiling, Midrel turned back to the patient and her smile turned into a grimace. 'I didn't expect I'd see anyone like this after those two men the other night. I thought they might've been poisoned or drugged, being the sort of men the guards said they were. Maybe this fellow's a ganger?'

Morri looked at the man on the bed curiously. 'I have to agree I haven't seen anything like this before. And to have two separate cases within a week… unless this man has had dealings in whatever the other two have? Like you say, all three could be gangers and could easily have taken something, or been handling some dangerous substances from a ship. It's not our place to assume these things though.'

'It's not as if we can ask or even have the guards interrogate them though, Morri. Those two brothers are still out cold and looking worse by the day, no matter what we try. I'm really surprised the one with the knife wound survived at all, let alone this long.'

'Well, let's hope there are no more like this then, eh Midrel? I must speak to Master Orix personally about this tomorrow. Seek his advice on a cure if there is one, since any attempt at magical healing hasn't worked. Only recently he asked to be informed about any unseasonal illnesses. I doubt he had something like this on his mind, but I'll check with him anyway.

'For now,' Morri added, whilst rubbing his eyes, 'keep trying the same as you did on the other two, and ask your guard friend, Orrel, to watch over this one. If he *is* an associate of the brothers, we don't want him waking and setting about you, do we?' The young man placed both hands on his assistant's shoulders and smiled.

Her eyes widened. 'Oh no, we do not! I'd be sure to give him a good clout if he tried, mind.'

Morri laughed, took his lamp from Midrel and climbed the stairs back to his bed. Tomorrow he would seek an audience with the master cleric of his guild, and see if any of the other infirmaries had experienced anything similar.

Chapter 5: Visitors

Orix was reading a book written in Sirretan when he heard his name across the guild lounge.

'Yes, he's sat over there as usual,' a rather rounded female wizard said.

Morri walked over towards the old gnome with a worried look on his handsome face.

'Good day Morri,' Orix said, a smile peeking from beneath his beard. 'What can I do for you this fine day?'

The young cleric returned Orix's smile, although not whole-heartedly, Orix noticed.

'Master Orix, I wish to report a rather strange case at my infirmary,' he said solemnly.

Orix gestured to a chair opposite his own as his heart quickened, and the young man took a seat.

And so it begins. 'Tell me about it,' Orix said, placing his book face down on the arm of the chair and leaning forward to listen.

'Well, Master Orix, the first case, or should I say two, were admitted a few nights ago by the City Guard. Two men, brothers in fact, said to be known thugs of the area, had been beaten unconscious and found by a group of sailors in Market Square. One had been stabbed in the chest; lucky for him it wasn't fatal.'

Orix made an effort to look confused as he replied, 'Nothing out of the ordinary there for your infirmary, Morri?'

'Well no Master Orix, not at all, but the night after they were admitted, they both became feverish and one of the two men, shortly followed by the other, claimed to be exhausted and lacked any strength whatsoever. I could understand this after the beating they had taken, especially the one who'd been stabbed, but I couldn't explain the blister like boils on the skin of both men.'

Orix tugged at his beard and stared into space whilst nodding here and there. *Not quite how I thought it would manifest itself, but these two fit Falchion's description and so these must be the symptoms.*

'Fellow clerics I have spoken to,' Morri continued, 'and my assistant at the infirmary thought perhaps they had been poisoned during the fight somehow, but no poison we know of acts in this way. Nor could it be drugs after so many days, or none I know of?'

Orix made no move to offer any answers to Morri, and so the cleric continued.

'They're still very much alive, although very sick. They can speak quite easily about events, although the guards think the story about being attacked by sailors is false, created to hide what they were really up to or involved in. I see no value in any attacker poisoning them with something which leaves them able to bear witness to their attacker's identity though?'

Orix nodded his head as his cleric went on.

'I've also never seen an illness come on so fast and simultaneously between two patients.

'Adding to the mystery,' Morri said, just as Orix opened his mouth to speak, 'last night my night watch assistant, Midrel, woke me.' Orix nodded at the name, having met the talented – although not magically adept – woman several times. 'She showed me another man who'd been brought in unconscious, with exactly the same symptoms as the other two. Unfortunately, we don't know who brought him in, and he hasn't woken for us to question him yet. I currently have all three under guard and constant watch.' Morri leaned forward, awaiting some insight from the master cleric.

'Good,' Orix said, nodding, but not looking directly at Morri, something the young cleric found out of character for the old gnome.

After a long pause, Orix took a deep breath. He let it out slowly, nodded once as if to himself, and then continued, eyes now locked on Morri's. 'I want you to keep all three guarded at all times, and record their symptoms and progress. Have you tried any remedies, unguents or potions at all?'

'Well yes, Master Orix, I tried the usual for the fever on the original two men, as has Midrel on the third, but to no avail. I've also tried magical healing, but again it's had no effect. As for the strange boils, we're at a loss as they're not usual boils, pocks or mumps even. Hence my visit to you. You'd also requested reports on anything unusual.'

Orix nodded approvingly. 'I want you to stop any treatment, Morri. This doesn't sound like any normal fever we know of anyway and I want to see how it progresses.'

Morri's head rocked back slightly. 'But Master Orix, surely we can't just sit and watch? Should we not consult the other infirmaries and clerics of the guild? Perhaps have clerics search our archives to see if this has occurred in the past, or anywhere else?'

Orix shook his head and replied sternly. 'No, Morri. Leave it to me. Just record the symptoms as I said, and I will look into the archives. You have other priorities to tend to I'm sure, and I would like to have something to distract me from my usual routine. If I find anything helpful I will be sure to let you know immediately. Until then, keep the three patients comfortable and most importantly, guarded!'

'Very well Master Orix,' Morri reluctantly agreed, his disappointment evident in his expression. 'I'll be sure to record all happenings and have a messenger bring you the reports at the end of each day, if you wish?'

'Yes, that would be grand, thank you Morri. You may return to your infirmary now.'

Morri stood, bowed and walked out of the lounge.

Oh lad, you're too good sometimes, and certainly don't deserve this. I truly am sorry.

***

29

Sav woke to a beam of light shining on his face. No matter where he moved his head, the light seemed to hit him directly in the eyes. He sat up and swung his legs off the bed, rising to close his window blinds – blinds already closed. Quickly looking around the room, he again caught an intense bright light shining from the corner of the room. He lifted both hands to shade his eyes and jumped back, startled, nearly falling over his bedside chest as he saw the source of the light.

'Errolas! What are you doing here? Cut it out will you!?' Sav said, a mixture of surprise and annoyance in his voice.

Melodic laughter flowed from behind the bright light, followed by an equally melodic voice. 'Did I startle you, scout? Tut... tut... your skills are waning with all your drinking of ale and mead since you returned to your city. I apologise for the light, it seemed amusing to me. Still does in fact.' As Errolas spoke, the light blinked out just long enough to allow Sav to lower his hands, before flicking on again, shining into his eyes once more.

'Enough, enough... Yes, very amusing, now quit it and tell me what you're doing here in Wesson, not to mention my room?' Sav was now clearly more annoyed than surprised.

'Very well scout, as you wish.' The light once again blinked out. 'It's just a star stone,' Errolas said. 'I've had it since childhood, still amuses me though.'

'Yes, I'm sure it does,' Sav said, rubbing at his sleep filled eyes.

'I decided to visit your capital, is the answer to your question. So I thought I would drop in and visit you while I am here. You really should bar your window though. It is very easy for someone to open and climb through, especially when you sleep so heavily. I even had time to close it behind me, shut the blind, walk around your bed and tease you with the stone, all before you stirred.'

I only stirred because of the damned stone.

'Most people use the door and knock,' Sav said, whilst stretching. 'Anyway, how did you find out where I was staying? You've never been to Wesson as far as I know, so you wouldn't know where to start looking.'

Errolas smiled wryly, crossed the room and brushed the dust off a small stool in the corner, before sitting on it and answering Sav's question. 'I asked at the eastern gatehouse.'

'And they just told you?' Sav asked incredulously.

'Of course,' Errolas replied, still smiling. 'When someone of my race asks an honest question, people tend to give an honest answer.' As he spoke, Errolas brought his hand up to a soft leather pouch, hanging around his neck.

Sneaky bastard! Sav stood up suddenly, pointing at the pouch. He laughed. 'You used some fairie dust or something, didn't you? Didn't you Errolas?'

Feigning a look of horror, Errolas brought his hand quickly down from the pouch. 'I'm hurt you'd even think I'd use such a dishonest trick. Not that fairie dust would actually do that, but that's beside the point.'

Sav sat back down and shook his head. 'You're not hurt at all, and you're not a very good liar either.'

'You're right, I'm not,' Errolas said, another smile spreading across his angular face once again. 'How else would you expect me to find you in this jungle of stone and mortar?'

'Well, I doubt you could,' Sav said, 'but once you found me, you could've come through the front door, asked for me and knocked like a normal human being.'

'Ahh… but there you have it, scout, I'm no human being. And what I did was far more fun anyway.' Leaning back on the wall and crossing his arms, Errolas looked completely satisfied.

Sav sighed. 'What's the use,' he said, defeated. 'So you're here for a visit are you; a grand tour of our capital city? Well, you came to the right man, I can show you all the landmarks and all the best drinking holes too.' Sav grinned.

'That, scout, I'm sure you could. Alas, I doubt I will take you up on the latter as I'm not here completely on leisure, and so need to keep my wits about me, but a tour of your landmarks and your great city would be wonderful.'

Not here completely on leisure, eh, elf?

'Oh, I see,' Sav said, his eyes now boring into Errolas'.'

'You wonder what business could bring me here? Quite understandable. I am, after all, in your home, quite literally.'

Sav put his hands out, palms forward. 'That's your business, Errolas, not mine. I'm not asking a *ranger* to explain his mission to me.'

Errolas flashed Sav a genuine smile, stood, and turned to open the door. 'I shall wait outside while you change, then you can show me the city, and I may tell you the real reason I am here.'

'Alright Errolas you're on. Give me a few moments and I'll be with you. Prepare to be amazed by the largest, grandest city of the north.'

After the door closed, Sav dropped back onto his bed, letting out a long breath and wondering why he always seemed to be practically dragged out of it. 'After all, I only get several days here and there to sleep in a proper bed,' he said to himself, before climbing to his feet and moving to fill his chamber pot.

Chapter 6: The first deaths

Sav and Errolas had spent almost a whole day walking around Wesson. The elf had been shown everywhere from King Barrison's palace – only the outside, of course – to Tyndurris and the grand Samorlian Cathedral; and finally, after much persuasion from Sav – who insisted it was a famous landmark – the Coach and Cart Inn.

'Right then Errolas, you really want to see Dockside do you? Well I'm warning you, it isn't the best part of the city, by far, and you really won't find anything down there of interest, bar drunken sailors and merchant ships.'

Errolas smiled with his reply. 'Oh, I'm sure there will be something of interest to me at the harbour. I don't see many ships in the forest, that's for sure.'

Sav shrugged. 'I've already shown you the King's ships, why you want to see merchant cogs and fishing vessels I have no idea?'

'Just humour me, scout. You told me you would show me the greatest city of the north, and I want to see it all.'

Sav sighed. 'Very well,' he said eventually.

After passing Kings Square and entering Dock Street, Sav pointed out more ale houses and with a snigger a few whore houses too. Errolas merely smiled at Sav's crude mirth, and concentrated more on the people filling the streets.

Groups of sailors walked up and down Dock Street, with the occasional child darting from pocket to pocket. Errolas had heard such tales of the lowest district of Wesson, and cringed to think they called the city the grandest of the north.

What must other human cities be like?

Their coach finally pulled up at the side of a large square full of market stalls, crates and barrels. 'I take it this district is as dangerous as they say after dark?' Errolas looked around at some of the market traders packing up their wares and heading back up Dock Street, away from the harbour.

'Yeah, it can be,' Sav said. 'I used to work for the City Guard in this district. A lot of fun, I can tell you.'

'I'm sure,' Errolas said with a smile. 'So, this is Market Square?'

'Yup, it's where a lot of trade is done, hence the name. Stalls also set up along Harbour Way, but this is where the finer goods are sold.'

Errolas set off across the road, towards the centre of the square with Sav close behind him, talking about times he had to break up fights in the square when a guardsman. As Sav rambled on, more to himself in a reminiscent tone than to his companion, Errolas walked around the stalls and crates as they were being packed up and moved to the centre of the great square. He looked intently at the floor, smiling and nodding at merchants as they moved out of his way. At one spot, he knelt and held his hand just a few inches from the stone floor, his eyes closed in contemplation, a deep frown creeping across his face.

'Everything alright Errolas?' Sav finally realised he wasn't being listened to, and noticed the elf crouching close to the ground.

Errolas stood suddenly, Sav staring at him. He shook away the frown and smiled. 'Yes, sorry, must have been the effects of the wine. I might not have drunk a lot, but I don't think I'm used to human alcohol.' Errolas finished by rubbing his stomach.

'Ah,' Sav said with a wry smile. 'You're a lightweight, that's for sure! You'd need a lot more practice to come drinking with me properly. A good friend of mine would be glad to meet you; he'd look like a real drinker besides you.' Sav put his arm around Errolas's shoulder and walked him towards the great merchant ships swaying by the wooden jetties. He never noticed the elf's keen eyes darting from shadow to shadow as the sun sank towards the harbour's outer wall.

Eventually, the duo caught another coach back up to the Dutton Arms where Sav rented his room. Errolas thanked Sav for his excellent tour of the city and bade farewell, apologising for his swift departure, but explaining he needed to finish some important business before leaving Wesson. He gave Sav two shillings and told him to have a few drinks on him. Sav thankfully accepted, hugged Errolas – much to the elf's surprise – and said he hoped to see him when next on patrol around their borders. Once Sav entered the Dutton Arms to spend the coins he'd been given, Errolas slipped off into the shadows of the fast darkening city.

***

Morri stood by a closed door with loud coughing coming from the room beyond.

The three men's symptoms, Midrel told him, were worse. She'd not been happy when Morri had informed her of Master Orix's orders, and after Midrel had stopped treating the men's fevers, they'd become quite aggressive towards her, especially the one called Llard, who demanded to know why Midrel had stopped treating them. Midrel had rushed to fetch the two guards who should have been on duty at the room's door, and asked them to watch over the now locked room. They had, as usual, been in the kitchen drinking hot nettle tea Midrel had prepared for them.

After being secured, Midrel checked upon the patients an hour later whilst being accompanied by the two guards. She managed to calm the three men down, enough to tell them a cure was being searched for by the highest ranking cleric in Wesson, and they would need to rest if they wanted to receive the cure once found. Morri wondered who the third man was, but his elderly assistant told him the man wouldn't answer any questions in front of the guards, and she didn't want to enter the room alone to question him. It was clear, however, that he didn't know Bein or Llard, nor, Midrel had said, did the more vocal brothers know him.

Morri didn't bother to chastise her for dragging the guards away from their post. He preferred them to be close to her rather than guarding men too sick to attempt anything serious.

'Fair enough, Midrel, I don't want you in there alone anyway. The fact the third patient won't answer any questions about himself in front of the guards makes me think he's a criminal like the other two anyway, so you're better off staying out of there as much as possible.'

Another stream of hacking coughs came from the far side of the door.

'They do sound worse, don't they Morri?' Midrel sighed. 'Is there nothing we can do while Master Orix looks for a cure?'

I wish there were. 'No, I'm afraid there isn't. He was quite clear all he wanted us to do was record their symptoms and send the results via messenger to him each night.'

Midrel sighed again, slowly shaking her head, looking helplessly at the young man.

Morri smiled at her and gently placed a hand on her shoulder. 'You have a heart of gold, Midrel. All three men became aggressive towards you, at least two of them are known criminals, and still you wish to help them?'

She shrugged. 'It's just how I am, Morri, always have been. Whether a bird caught by a cat, or lads caught up in a tavern brawl, I always wanted to try and help fix them up... well someone has to eh?'

'Yes they do,' the young cleric agreed. 'Anyone who comes to this infirmary is very lucky indeed to have your excellent care and service. I couldn't ask for a better assistant.'

Midrel blushed.

'More the reason for you to leave them three alone as much as possible,' Morri continued, 'until Master Orix finds a cure. I don't want you coming to harm, whether it's by their hands or through catching the sickness.'

The guards either side of the door seemed to tense up and edge slightly away from it as Morri mentioned a risk of catching whatever the men inside the room had contracted.

Midrel chuckled. 'Don't worry lads,' the old woman said, 'I'm sure ye won't catch it through a solid door!' She reached up and pinched the closest guard, Orrel's cheek as she said it.

Both guards flushed slightly, yet they seemed to visibly relax.

No sooner had they relaxed, a crash of what sounded like breaking glass erupted from the patients' room and a painful cry had them both stiffening up again and spinning to look at each other, then the door.

Morri and Midrel were pushed and ordered away from the door and back down the corridor by Orrel, who pulled free a wooden cudgel from his belt. The guard on the right of the door fumbled for a key just as another cry – sounding like the younger brother, Bein – reached their ears. The guard with the key quickly placed it into the lock on the door and turned it until it clicked audibly. He looked at Orrel before gingerly reaching for and turning the handle. Just as he did so, a third, short gurgling cry rang out and he forcefully swung the door inwards.

Inside the room everything lay still. All three patients lay motionless, the two brothers in their beds and the unknown man on the floor by the broken window. Both guards crept cautiously into the room. After a moment taking the scene in, Orrel went straight to the body on the floor by the window and crouched down to check for signs of life, whilst the other guard moved from one bed to the other, doing the same with the two brothers.

As Morri and Midrel tried to enter the room, the closest guard held up his hand and gestured for them to stay outside. 'Back down the corridor, until we call you,' he commanded, whilst Orrel rose from the body at the window, shaking his head before peering out through the broken glass.

'All's clear out there, as far as I can see,' he said, without taking his eyes away from the opening. 'This one's dead for sure, his throat's been slit. How about those two?' he asked, finally turning and nodding his head towards the brothers lying still in their beds.

'Yeah, dead too,' the guard said by the beds. 'They've both got small throwing knives in their throats!'

Orrel shook his head and returned his cudgel to his belt as his companion shouted through the open door. 'You can come in now.'

Morri and Midrel both cautiously entered the room, a look of shock on both their faces.

'What happened?' Morri asked, his face pale as he looked upon the three dead men.

Orrel shrugged as he answered. 'Ganger hit by the looks of it, someone bloody good mind; to hit all three in such a short space of time.' He turned back to look out of the window again.

'Sounds about right to me,' the closest guard agreed.

Midrel rushed to the nearest bed where Bein's punctured throat leaked blood down to soak into the bed's sheets.

Morri crossed the room to the body on the floor.

'His throat's been sliced! How'd anyone manage to get in, do all of this and then escape before you two entered the room?' Morri stared up at Orrel standing over him.

'Through the window, I imagine,' Orrel said honestly. 'Looks like this one walked to the window, maybe he saw something outside? Then someone smashed the glass and slit his throat, all at the same time, I'd say. The other two must've sat up when they heard or saw the commotion, and were hit in the throat by throwing knives.'

'Very professional,' the other guard said, turning to the others. 'I'll go to the front door and check around the building with the guards there, if that's alright, master cleric?'

After a short pause and shake of the head in disbelief, Morri replied. 'Yes… yes of course, thank you, and have the morning duty guard call for someone to fix this window.'

35

'Of course, master cleric. I'll check back with you when all is clear,' he said as he left the room.

'I'll stay here, Master Morri, I don't like to leave you both in this room alone after what's happened,' Orrel said, whilst looking around at the three bodies.

'Thank you dear,' Midrel said, from across the room. 'Oh Morri, this is awful! This is a place for people to come and be treated, not executed.' Midrel walked over to Morri as he rose to his feet.

'You're right. I know we treat gangers who've been in fights, but to have them carry out a vicious murder like this on our doorstep is quite alarming, to say the least. Come now, we must leave everything how it is and send messengers to both Master Orix and your captain.' Morri directed the latter to Orrel.

'Of course, Master Morri,' the guard said, nodding once. 'I'll have one of the guards send word when the perimeter is checked, so someone can come and look at the scene, see if we can gather any information from it.'

'Thanks again Orrel, we'll be in my chambers if you need us. Come on Midrel, I think we need a drink and I have some spiced rum in my room.'

Midrel smiled weakly as Morri led her out of the room, whilst Orrel shuddered at the three bodies before following, shutting the door firmly behind him before having a good scratch under his arm.

***

A cloaked figure sat upon a roof not far from the infirmary. Everything to have taken place had happened within clear view from the vantage point, and the figure who sat there had been watching since before the attack. Two infirmary guards were now rushing around the building checking alleys, doorways and calling to a patrol nearby, the guardsmen of which were now running from street to street, raising the hue and cry with shouts and horn alike. This would make movement from the rooftop awkward at best for the rest of the night.

The event had confused the onlooker, who'd been watching the quiet infirmary for some time. Just moments ago, however, he heard stones tapping against one of the ground floor windows. Several moments later a very ill looking man with angry looking lumps marring his face and neck had appeared inside the window, clearly searching for whoever threw the stones.

Before the onlooker could spot where he'd come from, a rough looking man in dark clothes rushed up to the window, smashed it and sliced the throat of the sick man with a rapier, all in one swift motion. The attacker then sheathed his weapon, which he swiftly replaced with two small knives, both of which he threw through the broken window with obvious skill. The knives ended two more lives the onlooker reasoned, for why else would he have thrown them?

Almost as quickly as the attacker had appeared, he'd gone, and very soon after, a burly guard appeared at the window, first crouching to the victim there, and then peering out through the empty frame. It hadn't been long after, that the hue and cry had started.

It's going to be a long night indeed, the onlooker thought, whilst watching the activity in the streets below. *A long night on a cold, slate rooftop; a far cry from the trees of Broadleaf Forest.*

Chapter 7: The one that got away

Without warning, the door to Severun's chamber swung open and a loud voice called from within.

'Master Orix, come on in. How long have you been out there?'

Gods…

Orix jumped as the door opened. He hopped off the chair and hurried inside, closing the door behind him. When he turned, he saw the tall wizard stood by his bed, stretching and yawning.

'I knocked several times, Lord Severun,' Orix said, questioningly.

'I do apologise,' Severun said. 'I had a very late night last night and didn't get back to my room until the early hours. A deep sleep took me. I mustn't have heard you knocking. Do forgive me.' Severun walked over to his desk and sat behind it, beckoning Orix over to the seat opposite, which slid out of its own accord. 'Now, how can I help you?' the wizard asked wearily.

Orix pulled himself up onto the chair and started explaining frantically what Morri had told him in his latest report. Severun tried to interrupt a couple of times to ask questions, but the old gnome ranted on as if he had to get it all out in one go, otherwise he'd burst.

Finally, Orix finished. He slumped back in his chair and stared at the wizard, awaiting a response. Severun didn't return the gnome's stare. Instead, he looked passed Orix and stared at nothing at all, clearly deep in thought.

'Well?' Orix asked impatiently. 'What do you think this means?'

Severun looked back at the gnome as if seeing him there for the first time. 'I don't know, Master Orix, I really don't. Perhaps a ganger attack like the guards at the infirmary suggested. I can't see why at all it would be connected to us, or our work?' Severun slowly shook his head whilst talking, his eyes drifting off past Orix once again.

'But it was such a professional job by the sounds of it. Surely one, if not all of the three men must have been important in the criminal underworld to warrant such a professional assassination?'

Severun sighed. 'I don't know, Orix. All the subjects who are now, or who will become infected, will be criminals. It is highly likely at least a couple of those could be high status thieves or gang masters. Perhaps the third, unknown subject was one such character, and the other two merely got in the way, or were silenced so as not to give away the attacker's identity? Makes sense to me.'

Orix huffed. 'I'm not convinced. They were all seriously ill, anyone could have seen that. They had been in there for a couple of days at least. If someone wanted the man, or any of them, dead, then why not strike before last night?'

'Orix, I don't know. All we are doing, or can do, is speculate. I think we are worrying about nothing. It's a shame we haven't had the chance to record the effects through to completion on the first, and up to now only, subjects we've had, but there will be more and we will just have to make sure any we discover now are better protected, so we can follow the symptoms through to conclusion and stop any more ganger attacks, assassinations, or whatever, happening to our subjects once we have them.'

Subjects… thought Orix. *People, Severun, people!*

Orix didn't look convinced at all. 'I'm still not happy with all of this. It endangers my clerics and their staff at the infirmaries. I want extra guards, Lord Severun.'

'That would surely draw attention to all of this, would it not?'

'There has been a vicious attack at one of my infirmaries, I'm quite sure people will understand if we upped the guard on the rest.' Orix leant forward, expectantly.

With a smile, Severun nodded his agreement. 'Very well Master Cleric, send a request to the captains of the City Guard to up their patrols around the infirmaries at night and to station two more men to each infirmary throughout both the day and night. Sufficient?'

'Yes, Lord Severun, thank you,' Orix said.

'It will do for now, but if there are any further attacks I want battle mages as well,' he added, seriously.

Severun laughed. 'Battle mages? You'll be wanting crossbowmen on the roofs and men-at-arms along the walls next too.'

Orix's eyes opened wide. 'Oh… I may hold you to that, Lord Severun.' Both Severun and Orix managed to laugh, and the gnome lowered himself down from the chair. 'I'm going to send messengers now then, to the Constable of Wesson so it filters down to the captains properly, and to my infirmaries, to inform them of the step up in security.'

'Very well,' Severun said. 'Don't hesitate to let me know when more subjects have turned up either.'

Orix bowed his head with his reply. 'I will be swift with any more news, Lord Severun. Good day to you.'

'Good day Orix, and don't fret over all of this, there was bound to be teething problems on such a large scale experiment.'

Orix nodded again, although not very enthusiastically, and left the room.

Severun rose from his chair, crossed his room to the window and looked out over the city. He wondered where the other infected subjects were. Would most of them stay away from the infirmaries now, with added guardsmen on patrol in and around them? Perhaps this event had just made the experiment that bit harder.

Who had killed those men? Severun had lived in Wesson most of his life, had heard many tales of the underworld and ganger attacks on rival members, but never anything this professional, not in or around an official building anyway… not without it being the work of a large organisation or guild… the Black Guild?

Severun rubbed his face and let out a long, slow breath, before crossing back to, and dropping into, his swivel chair. The apparent absence of the agent who'd brought the scroll to Wesson worried him more. The agent who held the key to where the item came from and more importantly, who else knew about it.

Severun pulled an old map of Wesson from his desk drawer and pawed over it as he'd done several times of late, before taking an ink pot and feathered quill sat on his desk and marking another black cross on the map, not far from a previously added mark.

Where the blazes are you Master Joinson?

***

After a few minutes banging on Sav's door, then another ten minutes persuading him to go fishing and to get ready, Sav followed Fal and they both left the Dutton Arms and headed off towards the docks. They flagged a hire coach at the first opportunity and asked the driver to take them down to the docks near the prison. The rocks made for better fishing according to Fal. As did the lack of the busy markets, which didn't set up down that end of the harbour. Nor did the ships weigh anchor that far down.

The end of Sav's rod pulled down and sprung back up violently.

'Ooh, I have a bite, first one!' Sav pulled the rod back hard, and swiftly started pulling the line in.

'Don't rush it,' Fal said, 'you might snap the—'

As Fal spoke the words, Sav's line snapped, and the lanky scout toppled over backwards, narrowly missing the sharp edge of a rock.

Sav cursed as Fal pulled him to his feet.

'First time I get a bite and it snaps. This fishing lark sucks cronies' arses. I never was any good at it; you've caught three already.' Sav sat on a rock looking thoroughly pissed off.

Laughing, Fal retrieved Sav's rod and began attaching another line, tackle and adding some bait to the new hook. 'Don't worry Sav, there's plenty more fish in the sea.'

'Very droll,' Sav said. He stood back up, snatched the rod from Fal, who laughed even harder, and cast the line back out into the choppy water, before sticking it in the sand between the rocks.

'So,' Fal said. 'Who's this ranger bloke then?'

'Oh yeah, Errolas!' Sav's face beamed as he forgot the lost fish, and turned to tell his friend all about Errolas and the previous day.

They talked for a good while about Errolas and his tour of Wesson, Sav's latest scouting tour and elves in general. Fal was extremely interested in hearing all about Errolas and his kin, and Sav was equally enthusiastic in telling him all he knew.

More than a couple of times, Fal and Sav pointed out an inquisitive grey seal bobbing up and down on the waves not far from where they were fishing. It seemed very interested in the two fishermen, probably because of their cries of laughter and shouts of banter towards one another. Fal appreciated the wildlife and usually enjoyed sitting there watching the gulls, terns and occasional seals as he fished in peace, but with Sav as company, he didn't have much time between Sav's – often tall – tales to appreciate it.

When the sun hung low in a plumb hued, cirrus clouded sky, the two friends decided to pack up their fishing gear, Fal's seven sizeable fish and Sav's one, far too small to eat or sell, but which Sav refused to throw back in, it being his only catch of the day. He even refused to throw it to the grey seal when it had come in close as if expecting the treat.

They both headed back up Harbour Way and flagged down the first coach they could, before heading up to The Cartman via Fal's house to drop off the tackle and fish. Upon reaching The Cartman, they both ordered a meal and drinks, and the sizes and numbers of their catch grew each time they talked to the other regulars.

After closing time, both men walked to the Dutton Arms where they persuaded the landlord to have a lock in for the price of six fish – one Fal wanted to keep for himself – to be delivered by Fal the next day, and one very small and pathetic fish the landlord only took from Sav so as not to upset him.

Sav never mentioned to Fal once, for fear of being mocked, his feeling of being watched all day, and Fal failed to mention the very same thing to Sav for the very same reason.

***

'He escaped, General,' a man in dark, dirty clothing said in a southern Altoln accent. The man he addressed sat behind a metal mesh screen with naught but his silhouette visible in the small, dimly lit room.

'You mean you let him get away, Master Dundaven?' Horler Comlay said, dangerously.

The man addressing Horler visibly cringed at the harsh tone of the reply. 'General… they were difficult circumstances. The patrols in the area have been increased. The target ran, I pursued, but when a target runs towards four city guardsmen, I can hardly maintain my pursuit, can I? Not without questions being asked by the guardsmen. It isn't right, we should have the jurisdiction to pull people in, without pandering to the lords of Wesson.'

'Well of course, Master Dundaven, we all agree there, but nor should you let it get to a stage where a target gets away from you and manages to escape to the City Guard, whether they've stepped up their patrols or not. Could he have identified you?' The harsh tone from behind the screen didn't let up and the cowering man had to clear his throat before answering.

'No, General,' Egan Dundaven said honestly, 'I wore my hood low, and since I'm not from Wesson, I very much doubt anyone would know what I am around here, never mind who I am.'

'I would prefer it if you were certain, Master Dundaven, especially

41

regarding matters this serious, but you doubting it will have to do. Now get back out there and carry on with your assignment.'

'Yes, General, at once, General,' Egan Dundaven said, as he stood and turned to leave the small room.

'Not in Dockside though,' Horler said, from behind the screen. 'Swap with someone in another district. We can't risk you carrying on there after your failure.'

Egan bowed low as he replied, 'as you wish, General.' He then pulled his hood back over his head and strode from the room, careful not to slam the heavy wooden door behind him as he left.

A third voice, low and croaky, spoke from Horler Comlay's side of the screen. 'I thought you said your best men were on this, General?'

Horler bristled at the comment, but kept his temper. 'They are, sire. General Clewarth sent Egan Dundaven to aid me, claiming he is an exceptional witchunter in the south. However, he has never worked in Wesson before, or in any large city.'

'Then why use him?' the large man asked from the far corner of the room. 'It is imperative we do not make mistakes that could draw attention to ourselves, especially the attention of the City Guard and its captains.'

'I am using him, sire, because he is said to be one of the best witchunters in south Altoln; he is skilled and experienced and extremely loyal, and more to the point, is not known in Wesson as a Samorlian witchunter.'

'Very well General, I trust you know what you are doing and won't let mistakes like this happen again. Sort this one out yourself, this evening. I don't want this arcane magic spreading. We might not know what that unnatural guild is up to with these evil shadows, but we can certainly hinder it every step of the way, until we know more and can strike properly.'

'Very well sire,' Horler said, as he rose from his seat. He crossed the room, bent low and kissed the large man's outstretched hand. 'I will personally see to it straight away, as you wish, just as I did with the first three.'

'Good,' the large man said. 'Now be on your way.'

Horler Comlay left the room through the door on their side of the screen, and left the large man – who remained sat in the corner surrounded by tall candles – pouring over an ancient looking tome titled: *Sir Samorl, our Saviour.*

Chapter 8: No more beds

'Lord Severun, this is getting out of hand,' explained Orix. He looked very tired; his eyes shadowed with dark rings. 'My clerics are constantly contacting me, asking whether I have found anything, whether the bodies I have been performing autopsies on have yielded any information, and now Morri has informed me his Dockside Infirmary has run out of beds! It's been days since the release, yet the infected keep coming.' Orix slumped in his usual chair in the guild lounge, while Severun lowered his book to look at the old gnome.

'Good morning Lord Severun,' the wizard said, sarcastically.

Orix sighed. 'Yes, yes, good morning. Now what do you suggest? Should we set up extra beds in other city buildings and use them as makeshift infirmaries as we normally would in a large scale outbreak or disaster?'

'No, Master Orix, I don't believe that's necessary.'

Orix cut in rather sharply. 'Not necessary? Were you listening to me, Lord Severun? We have to do something. There are enough bodies being found in the streets as it is, without people being turned away.'

And I'm the one facing down my clerics whilst you sit there twiddling your thumbs.

Severun frowned. 'One, keep your voice down, and two, these aren't just people, they are criminals and there will only be so many affected; a good number have died already due to the spell, or murders—'

Orix flinched on this word.

'Oh stop it!' the wizard snapped in a hushed tone, glancing at the guild members sat closest to them.

Severun continued. 'They are criminals, and criminals murder each other all the time, it's nothing to do with what we're doing for crying out loud. It's just because we're keeping our eyes peeled and ears open that we're noticing more than normal. Now you told me late last night, subjects had started to die in a couple of the infirmaries. The number of fatalities will start to increase now, thus freeing up beds for others, and eventually they will all be dead and the experiment a success. We can then take it to the King and his advisers, and they will see for themselves what a wonderful service we can provide to make Wesson the safest city in the realm!' Severun raised his eyebrows expectantly, awaiting a retort.

Orix rested his head on the back of the chair and let out another deep sigh. 'Very well, very well. I hate to think of people, criminal or not, the way we're thinking of these "subjects" but I'm sure they have caused pain and suffering to innocents in their past and would again in their futures, had they not been sought out by the spell. I do, however, feel there are far more of them than you made out. Did you increase the number of carriers, Lord Severun?'

'No,' Severun said flatly. 'I didn't have a set number, but I didn't summon enough magic with the spell I used to greatly increase numbers. I guess every single carrier found a mark and we are unfortunately seeing just how many violent citizens we have out there. Quite disturbing really.'

'Well let's hope this first experiment has done such a good job, we won't have to apply this spell much in the future, at all,' Orix said.

'How have your findings been with the autopsies?'

'It's how I expected. The potion entered through the mouth of the subject by your carriers and absorbed through the subjects' lungs. The potion doesn't infect the respiratory system however, it merely uses it as an entry to the body, slowly breaking down and working its way through the victim's organs until it finally shuts them down. The boils just add to the illness' effect I suppose, so clerics and the public can see there's something wrong with the person, rather than their body giving up for no apparent reason.' *Although I didn't expect it to manifest itself quite the way it has, or be as prolonged within the patients like it has been.*

'Well, it all seems to be doing the trick and working extremely well, my old friend. All your hard work has paid off,' Severun said, sincerely.

Orix offered a tight smile. 'I shall continue to monitor things via the reports from my clerics and by carrying out random autopsies. The latest to die in an infirmary is being transported here as we speak, so I can perform the autopsy this afternoon.'

'Very well Master Orix, I will let you get on and I will continue with my book. Let me know of any changes. Not that I foresee any.' Severun raised his book and continued with his reading, whilst Orix hopped off his chair and walked towards the door, thinking how glad he would be when it was all over.

***

'Sire, there are too many,' Horler Comlay said, clearly annoyed. 'We have eliminated several as you know, yet the infirmaries are filling with patients all showing the same symptoms. We cannot risk another infirmary attack now they've increased the number of guards, and there are less and less of the infected on the streets. It seems word has got out they're being targeted, and so they flock to the guarded infirmaries to seek aid.'

Horler slumped into a chair in front of a large desk and rested his head against the hard, wooden back. He filled his pallid cheeks with air and let out a long, slow breath.

The plump man on the far side of the desk didn't answer immediately, but played with the heavily jewelled rings on his chubby fingers as usual.

'Very well, General,' he said eventually. 'Your witchunters have done well considering the attention the City Guard is giving the infirmaries and surrounding streets. We still don't know what the guild plans though, and this displeases me. I don't like being kept in the dark, especially in my own city.'

'Of course, sire, nor do I. If there were any way I could speed things up I would, but it is imperative my men work slowly, otherwise they may draw undue attention to themselves within the guild.'

'I am aware of that, General, but we do not have the luxury of time when pitted against the arcane, especially when wielded by such powerful foes.'

The large man shifted in his chair, which groaned as ever in protest under his weight. 'Tell your men to step up their efforts, to take chances! I want information and answers, General Comlay, and the risk of losing a few of your men doesn't concern me. The loss of the city, however, does. There will be casualties on our side during these dark times, and I am willing to accept their sacrifices for the greater good, so tell them to take necessary risks and get me answers before this city falls at the hands of our enemy.'

Horler nodded as he took in the orders. 'Of course sire, my men will be pleased to make progress and are quite willing to make sacrifices. They will not betray us to our enemy, I can swear on that.'

'Do not disappoint me, General.'

Horler Comlay stood, leant across the desk and kissed the rings upon the hand of the large man, before turning and striding from the room.

***

A black cart rumbled slowly through the large front gates of Tyndurris. Fal saw it from the tower's main door, and started down the steps and across the courtyard to where the cart had stopped, Godsiff Starks on his heels.

'Another body?' Fal asked the driver of the cart.

'Yeah, from an infirmary in Park District this time,' the young driver said.

Fal nodded towards the linen wrapped body. 'How many is it now then?'

'Not sure,' the driver said. 'I haven't worked the coach for a few days and I haven't spoken to the other driver yet, but I did hear there's been a handful since yesterday, all the same kind of deaths. Keeps us in business though. What with all these murders, as well as the illnesses, my father's in his element.'

Fal couldn't help but laugh, although he felt a pang of guilt as Starks cringed away from the body the driver and his companion had pulled from the back of the cart. Although covered up, the normally white sheets showed crimson marks here and there.

'That one of the murdered ones?' Starks asked, whilst half looking at, half looking away from the wrapped corpse.

'No, no,' the second undertaker said, 'those stains are from burst boils while she's been in transit.'

Starks turned round and threw up. The undertakers shook their heads and laughed before heading off to the cargo lift to take the body up to the tower's trade entrance.

Fal turned and placed a hand on the young crossbowman's shoulder.

'You alright, lad?'

'Ye... yeah, sorry Sarge, don't know what came over me.'

I do, Fal thought. 'First sighting of a body, I'm guessing? Doesn't matter that it's wrapped up either, it's the smell, and that one hasn't even been dead that long.'

45

'No Sarge, I've seen bodies before, just never a woman. Makes me think of my kid sister is all, scared me more than normal. Don't matter where you live at the moment does it? Murders and sickness all over Wesson, all stemming from that weird storm. All sorts of stories flying around at the moment about ghosts and such.' Starks wiped his mouth on his sleeve above his boiled leather vambrace, and headed back off to the tower's lift to escort the undertakers up and into Tyndurris.

Yeah, all since the night of the storm... Shaking his head back to the present, Fal turned and followed Starks to the lift, thinking all the way about the night he'd told himself to forget.

***

Biviano stared across at the gently swaying masts of the carrack moored up in front of him and his companion. He scanned from fore- to aft-castle and saw no one, nor anyone on the jetty. *Sessio* seemed abandoned.

Hah, not likely. Biviano turned to Sears. 'Well, that's that ain't it, big guy? No one here, might as well leave it at that,' he said, whilst scratching under his kettle-helm with one hand and down the front of his braes with the other.

'Cut it out will ye,' Sears said, 'and stop trying to skive off working. We ain't even been aboard her yet.'

'Go on then, I'll wait here, guard the ramp, ye see.'

Sears shoved his smaller companion onto the ramp with a growl.

'Request understood, on I go then,' Biviano said, before spitting at his feet.

'Not on this ship, shit for brains!' someone shouted from *Sessio's* main deck.

Try saying that fast when pissed, Biviano thought as he hopped back off the ramp. 'My apologies, captain, need words with ye is all,' he shouted, once firmly on the wooden jetty.

'I ain't the cap'n and I ain't talking to no law about nothing, so on yer way,' the voice said again, still no person visible.

'See Sears, not gonna get anywhere here, so off we go.'

Sears grabbed Biviano by his maille mantle and held him firm.

'Well where's yer captain then, sailor?' the large guardsman shouted, Biviano still tight in his grip. 'We needs words with him. Didn't say nothing about him being in trouble with the magistrates, just need to know about an agent sailed on yer ship is all. A Master Joinson we believe him to have been called, according to the Merchant Guild.'

A middle-aged sailor with a pock marked face popped up from behind the bulwark of the main deck. 'The cap'n ain't available for talking, so best be off.'

'Then maybe we can talk with you?' Sears' voice took on a serious tone and Biviano groaned audibly, before receiving a short but vigorous shake from Sears.

46

The sailor laughed and disappeared again behind the bulwark.

'That went well,' Biviano said, pulling his feet up and hanging from his companion's grip.

Straining with the weight, Sears dropped the smaller man – who grunted upon hitting the wooden jetty – and strode onto the gangplank, Biviano suddenly scrambling to his feet and following close behind.

The grisly sailor popped up again, a grin splitting his face. 'Got balls ain't ye?'

'Aye,' Sears said, upon reaching the main deck and turning to face the lone sailor, Biviano at his back, 'and you *won't* have if ye don't answer me damned questions, now!'

The sailor laughed again before whistling through the gap in his teeth.

'Err… Sears,' Biviano said, pulling on his partner's maille sleeve.

'I see 'em,' Sears said, as half a dozen sailors emerged from the open hatch in the centre of the main deck. 'All we wanna know is who Master Joinson were working for when aboard this ship?' Sears voiced the question whilst looking around at the crew who were slowly surrounding him and Biviano.

'We don't give out info ye see, so there ain't no point this going no further is there, Master Sears?' the pock-marked sailor said.

'Listen,' Biviano said in a pleading voice, a scratching hand under his kettle-helm once more, 'the agent were murdered, so we just wanna find out the name of his employer, to work out who done it. Clearly weren't you, so we'll be off as soon as ye tell us, no problems at all.'

'Unless they *did* do it,' Sears said, still looking around, 'then we'll have to take 'em in and hand 'em over to the magistrates after all.'

'Morl's balls, Sears, shut yer face afore we're fish food.

'Ha… ye got guts, Master Sears, I'll give ye that,' the sailor said, 'but it ain't enough. We ain't giving names and that's that. I'll give ye a count of three to leave the deck, or ye're going over it in that heavy chain armour ye're wearing!'

A lean, muscular sailor, his tanned skin tattooed with black spirals reaching from his waist to his neck, stepped up to Sears as if to show him the way off the ship.

The sailor's nose crunched as the large guardsman's knuckles spread it across his tanned face. Several sailors' eyes widened briefly as the bearded man struck their shipmate, and the first mate, who'd been addressing the duo, let out an appreciative whistle as his sailor hit the deck hard. Before Sears could react further, the first mate nodded slightly before stepping back. The rest of the sailors launched themselves at the two guardsmen.

Swiftly pulling free a wooden cudgel, Biviano ducked low, narrowly avoiding an incoming fist, before swinging the cudgel which connected with his attacker's closest knee. The man went down hard and Biviano wasted no time in leaping over the downed figure to thrust the cudgel at the next sailor's groin, who managed to spin to the side to avoid the contact. Biviano dived right, barely missing Sears who wrestled two sailors.

The tattooed and bloody-faced sailor who'd made the first move now climbed to his feet, ready to jump in.

Rolling once before coming to his feet, Biviano fended off two bare footed kicks from a female – or so he thought, but there wasn't much difference in appearance to any of the other sailors so he couldn't be sure – before striking her with a sideways blow to the head, which sent her down hard and cold.

Turning swiftly to take in the scene behind him, Biviano saw Sears throw clear one of the sailors, physically lifting the man and launching him at the first mate, who seemed to be watching the fight with an amused look on his marked face. The tattooed sailor started pounding on Sears' side with both fists, whilst Sears threw the other over the bulwark where he clearly hit the water after a loud splash.

Launching himself towards the first mate with a howl, Biviano passed a toppling tattooed sailor as Sears kneed him in the groin. As the smaller guardsman reached the first mate, his cudgel held up high, the gleaming blade of a cutlass appeared in front of him, stopping dangerously close to his face.

Teetering on the edge of an unbalanced foot, Biviano chose to fall backwards as he halted, rather than onto the deadly point in front of him, a point which followed him down and hovered in front of his left eye. He followed the length of the blade up to an ornate basket hilt, then further up a burgundy velvet dressed arm to the face of a well-groomed man, quite the opposite to any of the sailors on board so far.

'Enough,' the man said, his commanding voice carrying across the main deck with ease.

Biviano heard the renewed fighting behind him stop as the words left his mouth. 'I don't see I have a choice… Captain Mannino,' Biviano said, the sword point still his main focus.

The captain smiled, before handing his cutlass to his first mate and reaching down to haul Biviano to his feet.

'Err… thanks,' the wiry guardsman said, clearly confused.

'Impressive performance, gentlemen,' Captain Mannino said, flashing his smile again at both Biviano and Sears. 'Would you both care to join me in my quarters and I'll see if I can be of any assistance to your investigation?'

The two guardsmen looked at each other, frowning, before Sears grunted and nodded, and so they both, warily, followed the richly dressed captain to a door at the base of *Sessio's* aft-castle, before following him through into the dark passageway beyond.

Chapter 9: Trust

'Take a seat, gentlemen,' Captain Mannino said, as he took three crystal tumblers from a large cabinet.

'We'll stand if it's all the same, captain, and no drink neither, we're on duty,' Sears said, his eyes never leaving the first mate, who stood to the captain's right hand side.

Biviano licked his dry lips and nudged his large companion in annoyance.

'As you wish, gentlemen, but I will, if you don't mind?'

'Not at all captain, this is yer ship, after all,' Sears said.

'Aye, she is,' the first mate said, with a wink at the two guardsmen. Biviano bristled, but Sears placed a painfully strong hand on his partner's shoulder and the smaller man winced, but said nothing.

The finely dressed captain took a seat behind his desk before taking a quick sip of brandy. A pause in the cabin and Biviano, if no one else, felt more than a little awkward, so he decided to speak.

'We have questions and want answers, so don't be making this hard for yerself, alright, Mannino? We knows yer reputation!'

Sears rolled his eyes and moved his hands to his weapons in anticipation of whatever Biviano's words might bring, especially when the first mate's leering grin faltered.

'Of course, gentlemen,' the captain said, taking another sip of brandy.

'Well,' Biviano said, 'that were easy.'

'Will ye shut yer pock-marked face for two seconds and let me do the talking, gods below!'

'Alright, alright, calm down big guy, they're all yours. I'll take that seat after all, captain, cheers,' Biviano said. He slid out the nearest chair and dropped down onto it, one hand firmly wedged under his kettle-helm, fingers digging away at his scalp.

'By all means, now, what questions do you have for me? I'll answer what I can as fast as I can. I'm sure you're both busy men and I'd hate to keep you longer than needs be.'

Sears bowed his head slightly. 'Thank ye captain, most kind of ye. Our questioning relates to a murder we're investigating.'

'Wasn't us none, no sirs,' the first mate said, whilst packing tobacco into a short, ivory pipe.

'I'm sure that's not what the gentlemen are implying, are you?' Captain Mannino said, the slightest hint of annoyance crossing his relaxed features.

'No captain,' Sears said, 'we just needs to know about Master Joinson, who we believe travelled on yer ship recently?'

The captain's eyes widened and he put down the brandy, before leaning forward, both arms resting on his desk. 'Master Joinson is the victim?'

'How'd ye know that then, eh?' Biviano asked, before continuing, 'Never mind, we mentioned that didn't we? I remember now. Carry on.'

'Dick,' Sears said to his partner, before looking back to the captain. 'Yes, captain, he's the one alright, or so we've been informed, however, we ain't for knowing who he were working for ye see? His guild won't give much information out.'

'And ye think the cap'n will help wi' that do ye?' the first mate said, chewing on his unlit pipe all the while.

'Yes they do and yes I will,' Mannino said, much to everyone's surprise, especially the first mate's, who's pipe almost fell from his sagging bottom lip.

'That'd be appreciated, captain,' Sears said. 'Then we can be on our way ye see and leave ye to yer business.'

'Well, first of all gentlemen, let me say how sorry I am to hear of Master Joinson's demise. He was a quiet but polite fellow and I wish you all the luck in catching his killer, or killers, but all I know really is who he worked for. As for cargo, it's not our place to ask, so we don't, and so I can't elaborate, alas!'

Really, Sears thought. *Then why'd yer first mate just glance sidelong at ye when ye said the latter?*

'If you would be so kind as to enlighten us as to the employer's name and, perchance, abode then Captain Mannino?' Biviano said, who for some reason and unknown ability, had suddenly switched to a well-spoken, higher district accent.

The room fell silent and when Biviano looked up from picking at the hobnails on the sole of his left boot, he realised everyone looked at him. 'What?'

Shaking his head and muttering something under his breath, Sears continued. 'I stand by me partner's question, captain, if ye would?'

'Of course,' Mannino said, brows furrowed and eyes still locked on Biviano, who'd resumed his sole picking. 'I wouldn't normally, you understand, but since it is for a murder investigation…' He opened a worn ledger his first mate had reluctantly passed to him, and flicked to the last entry, crossed through in parts and blacked out all together in others. 'Ah yes, Master Peneur Ineson—'

'The importer?' Sears cut in.

Mannino nodded. 'The very same! He employed Master Joinson for the journey, who in turn employed us on Master Ineson's request and behalf.'

Sears and Biviano looked to one another, before Biviano spoke.

'He just got some big gaff didn't he, right near the scene of the murder?'

'Aye, that he did,' Sears said, and he turned back to the captain and bowed low. 'Captain Mannino, ye been of great service to both us and the city of Wesson. I thank you sir.'

Mannino flipped the ledger shut, swiftly finished his brandy and stood, as did Biviano. 'Thank you, gentlemen, for allowing me to help with your enquiries and for helping in our crew recruitment process.' The captain smiled and his first mate grinned and winked at the two guardsmen following his captain's comment.

Sears looked at a loss, but Biviano grinned knowingly in return, before bowing himself, albeit clumsily. 'Aye, they didn't quite cut the mark, eh?

'Right then big guy, off we go to that swanky gaff to do us some more detectivin' stuff.'

'Aye,' Sears said, rolling his eyes at Biviano, 'right ye are. Thanks again, captain. We'll see ourselves off the ship.'

'Take care lads, now off ye tot,' the first mate said, throwing a wink and a twist of the head their way.

'Keep us informed, gentlemen,' Mannino said, as the two guardsmen left the room.

'Will do, captain,' came Sears' reply from just outside the doorway, and then the guardsmen were gone.

Mannino sat back down and leaned back in his chair, looking across at his first mate, who'd now lit his pipe and moved across to the door to ensure the guardsmen really had gone.

'Did ye know he were dead, cap'n?'

'No I did not. Now have those two followed from now until I say otherwise. I want to know what in the depths is going on. Especially after the cargo Peneur Ineson had us bring up here.'

'Aye cap'n,' the first mate replied. He disappeared out onto the deck.

So, Master Joinson is dead; murdered, poor bastard. I liked him too. Never a bad word for anyone, not many like that around. Killed in the place he spent the whole damned journey wanting to get back to as well. The fool felt safer in Wesson than on our ship. He'd have been better staying aboard.

He wasn't right on the way back though. Something had him spooked, something he'd bought for Peneur Ineson and now he winds up dead. I don't like it, not one bit… especially if whatever shite Ineson has got himself into winds up back here…

Mannino laughed.

Already has! Those two guardsmen… not as dumb as they make out, especially the smaller one, and the switch in accent? Dropping an act? No… didn't seem like that. Taking the piss out of me? Possibly, but it didn't feel like that either and again, I don't think he's that stupid. Something strange with them two though, but damn me I like them. I just hope they're good enough not to wind up dead themselves with whatever the hell is going on. Damn your soul Peneur Ineson, you old fool, and damn whatever was in that blasted cargo!

***

Fal collapsed onto his bed and fell asleep fully clothed. After a long shift of escorting undertakers carrying bodies in and out of Tyndurris, Fal had promised himself a good night's sleep as soon as he reached home. He would wake a couple of hours later to undress, wash and eat, but now he wanted to clear his mind of speculations and worries, and to grab a couple of hours shut-eye.

Three loud knocks on Fal's front door startled him after just nodding off. *What now?*

He rolled out of bed and to his feet in one fluid motion, before reluctantly walking through to his sitting room and across to the front door.

Peering through the slightly distorted glass spy hole he'd had installed in the door, Fal could make out two tall figures on the other side.

'Who goes there?' He took extra care of late, due to the increased murders all over the city.

'It's me mate, let me in, I brought someone to meet you.'

Fal recognised Sav's voice immediately, unlocked the door and opened it to let Sav and his companion in. Both men entered the room. Sav found a comfy chair and took a seat while the second, hooded man, stood by the unlit fireplace. Fal closed the door and moved about the room lighting oil lamps and candles. The freshly lit room enabled Fal to take a good look at Sav's companion. As he did so, the man took down his hood revealing long, fair hair and slender porcelain features. Fal didn't need to see the man's ears to realise he was an elf.

'This,' Sav said, 'is Errolas, the elf ranger I told you about the other day.' Sav bore a grin so wide Fal thought it would consume his whole face.

'It is a pleasure to make your acquaintance, sergeant. Your friend here has told me a great deal about you,' Errolas said, bowing politely.

'The pleasure's all mine Errolas. Sav's told me about you also.' Fal returned the bow with one of his own. 'What brings you to my home at such an hour, Sav? Not that you aren't both welcome, of course.' Fal directed the latter to Errolas after realising his question may have come across a little cold. 'Oh and Errolas, make yourself at home, take a seat.' Fal gestured to the second comfy chair opposite Sav's.

'Thank you, Sergeant, but I prefer to stand.'

Smiling, Fal continued. 'Well I hope you'll excuse me if I sit, Sav never ceases to surprise me, and so I'll prepare myself for whatever he's about to say by sitting down now, and please, call me Fal.'

'As you wish, Fal,' the elf said with a smile of his own. Fal realised the elf knew what he meant about Sav, and had to conceal his amusement.

Sav sat forward, still beaming. 'If you've finished with all the pleasantries, I brought Errolas here because I knew you'd always wanted to meet and talk to an elf, and Errolas actually wanted to meet with and talk to you also. I know it's late, but I didn't think you'd be in bed already, so for waking you I apologise, but it's not my fault you're getting out of shape, tired and lazy, whilst working a static guarding position.' Sav seemed to impress himself with his joke at Fal's expense, and allowed himself a hearty laugh. Errolas merely smiled and Fal had to chuckle along with Sav, if nothing else, his laugh was always infectious.

'Well, Sav, we can't all be as capable as you, being chosen to work with our neighbours.' Fal nodded towards Errolas, the elf's smile turning into a grin.

'Ah, I see, the scout has been telling stories about our encounters,' Errolas said.

Sav flung his arms out wide as if surrendering before responding. 'I only mentioned we'd worked together once or twice, just in passing really.'

Both Fal and Errolas laughed at Sav's obvious play down of his story telling.

'And I'm sure you told Errolas you're the major fish catcher out of the two of us, eh?' Fal's eyebrows lifted, awaiting the answer.

'Oh, but is that not the truth?' The reply came from Errolas. Elves seemed to know sarcasm just as well as humans, Fal mused.

'Pfft... you're ganging up on me now. It's each other I thought you'd both be talking to and about, not me. I'm going to make some tea, anyone else for a brew?'

Errolas shook his head and raised his hand to decline the offer. Fal merely grinned, knowing Sav knew him well enough to know the answer.

'So Errolas, what brings you to Wesson? Sav said he'd taken you on a tour of the city.'

They both winced at the sound of Sav clattering around the small kitchen.

'I am tasked with checking up on the progress of something my council have taken an interest in here in Wesson. Whilst in the city, I decided to look up our friend in there, to take me on a proper tour, as he had offered should I ever visit.'

'Oh I see... a business trip! All going as planned I hope?' *And what would the elven council have business with in Wesson that a ranger would be needed for?*

'Yes, my report will show results my lords and ladies predicted.'

Something in the elf's eyes Fal couldn't read; he spoke about some unknown business, yet Errolas looked at Fal as if he knew of that business. Fal had never met an elf before however, and put it down to not knowing their culture and mannerisms. Strange though, Errolas had said his report *will* show the progress rather than *had* shown the progress. Sav said Errolas had left the city the night of their city tour.

'You must ride like the wind, Errolas. It hasn't been long at all since Sav said you'd left the city and headed back home. I'm surprised you managed the trip there and back so swiftly?' Fal tried not to sound suspicious or intrusive. The elves were a goodly race and had been Altoln's allies for centuries. He didn't fancy insulting the first he'd ever met by prying into his personal business. Suspicion however, was part of Fal's job, and it was hard to leave it at Tyndurris.

'Ah... yes, I had set off back when I received a message from home with an update to my task, and so luckily I have had the chance to meet Sav's most talked about friend. So I am happy to be here still and honoured enough to be talking to you, Fal.' Nothing but a genuine smile on the handsome face of Errolas as he answered Fal's almost prying question. Fal inwardly sighed with relief and chastised himself for his rudeness.

'Well the honour is both of ours then, Errolas. Now, tell me all about your adventures as a ranger? I'm sure there are many. Oh, and feel free to slip in any amusing anecdotes you have about Sav while you're at it.' Both Fal and Errolas laughed, and the latter launched into an animated conversation, filled with stories about monsters, goblin tribes and arcane wizards. Sav, after returning to the room with two steaming cups of tea, spun his own tales both Fal and Errolas took with a pinch of salt.

The talking and laughter continued late into the night. A warm fire glowed in the hearth, and Errolas sat cross legged on the floor in front of it, explaining how he and a unit of elven scouts had fought off a particularly nasty giant almost two hundred years ago. Fal and Sav replaced their tea with ale, and Errolas drank from an animal skin, apparently filled with elven wine.

'...and then, out of nowhere,' explained Errolas, 'a giant teratorn descended with the sun behind it so the giant couldn't see, and thrust its talons forward, one into each of the behemoth's eyes!'

'Truly?' Sav shouted with a slight slur. 'Where'd it come from?'

'The sky, Sav, ain't it obvious,' Fal retorted.

All three men laughed before Errolas continued. 'Some of our scouts are able to ride them. Reared and trained from a hatchling, the scout spends almost all of his or her time with their giant condor, creating a special bond. When our patrol hadn't returned the previous day, Riisoun flew out on her teratorn to search for us. I admit now, pure luck aided her in finding us in time. We may have injured the giant, but our arrows and swords would have proven too weak to pierce his hide deep enough to kill him. Flailing around blindly from the teratorn's strike, the giant's great size became his end. He stumbled and fell onto a thick pine tree, which skewered him like a piece of meat. Of course, we owed Riisoun and her mount our lives for turning up when they did. We had already lost the one poor scout, the one I told you about, and I feared we would lose more of our party before we caused the giant enough damage to escape.'

Errolas raised his wine skin. 'To comrades fallen!'

'To comrades fallen!' Echoed the toast, and all three men took the biggest swigs of the night.

'That's a lot've damn fine tales there, Errolas,' Fal said, before taking another swig of ale. 'I wish we had some for you that'd match 'em, 'part from your terrible losses 'course. Understandably we wouldn't want to match those.'

Errolas looked up from his bottle and smiled. 'Oh I think you do have at least one extraordinary tale, Fal.'

Confused, Fal turned to look at Sav, but the scout's head had lolled to the side. He began snoring loudly. Looking back at Errolas, the questioning look on Fal's face was all the elf needed to continue.

'The night of the recent storm, Fal... a most peculiar night, wouldn't you say? Strong, gale to storm force winds coming in off the sea for the time of the year, and strange, shadowy figures floating across the rooftops of your glorious city?' Although the questions being asked shocked Fal, it was nothing compared to the manner in which they were being asked. Fal felt sure Errolas knew what had happened, what Fal had released... or maybe the elf just knew Fal had released *something*, without knowing what exactly. The elf still seemed calm and completely relaxed, friendly even, in his questioning, which made it all the more uncomfortable.

Turmoil now raged inside Fal, between anger, guilt and fear, and the lack of response prompted Errolas to go on without any answers to his questions, whilst Fal's head and stomach spun from both ale and the questioning.

'Fal, I am no enemy, and after tonight I believe you to be an honest soldier doing his duty, and a great friend to Sav. I understand this is all a shock to you and you must feel betrayed by me...'

No shit!

'...coming into your home, socialising with you and then dropping these questions into your lap, but you must believe me when I say, I needed to find out your character for myself, not just through Sav's – often tall – tales. As we both know, they are hard to decipher between truth and fiction.' Still at a loss for words, Fal tried to force the hazy, dull feeling of the alcohol aside to take in all being said. 'I have seen for myself tonight,' the elf continued. 'You can be trusted, I can trust you, and so therefore I am explaining myself to you.'

Fal stood up, wavering slightly as his head spun tenfold. He fought the urge to throw up. After steadying himself, he noticed Errolas remained seated, making no defensive manoeuvres whatsoever.

Are his words genuine? I don't know... how could I? I hate this, this vulnerability, in front of a stranger and in my own damned home for crying out loud.

'I don't know what you want me to say or what you want of me? Wait...' *Gods below...* 'It's you! You're the one who's been watching me! All this time I've felt someone's eyes upon me, thought myself crazy, and it was you, Errolas, Sav's so-called friend!' His anger built, burned; urged him to pounce on the sitting elf.

I swear, elf, no matter your words, you make one false move and half-cooked as I am, I'll give you a thrashing before I go down. Waiting for a reply, his jaw tensing and his fists clenched tight, he urged himself to calm down, tried to push through the thick fog in his head, to see reason and await the elf's response.

Errolas looked down, as if ashamed and certainly not denying the accusation. 'You are correct, Fal, I have been watching you from afar. But please,' he raised his hands as Fal began pacing, the soldier's knuckles white, his teeth grinding. 'Let me speak,' Errolas said. 'I can explain my side, and then I hope, you can explain yours.'

Fal flipped at the latter.

Who The Three are you to order me around in my own home? He launched himself on top of Errolas, or so he thought. As he landed, he realised painfully he'd hit nothing but the rug covered stone floor. He quickly rolled over to find the elf stood in the corner of the room, hands out to the side.

'I won't fight you, Fal,' Errolas said, sincerely. 'I want to explain and talk this through. There are things we both need to know. Things that can save many lives!'

Fal pulled himself up and thought through the words. That night had haunted him for days and nights. Errolas could have easily restrained or even killed him, judging by the speed he'd just moved and the amount of alcohol Fal had drunk. Fal wanted answers, not blood, and so he dropped back into his chair and pointed to the floor in front of the fire where Errolas had been sitting. The tall elf warily walked across the room and sat back down, legs crossed and hands resting on his knees – a clear sign of co-operation, Fal understood.

'Explain yourself, elf,' Fal demanded, his hands balled and wringing each other to work his anger out.

'Very well,' Errolas said, a huge sigh leaving his thin lips. 'My lords and ladies have had your Grand Master under surveillance for several months.'

Fal moved to speak, but Errolas held up his hand again. 'Please, let me continue this tale as we have the others this night, and all will hopefully become clear to you.'

Fal, despite his anger, nodded and Errolas continued.

'Several months ago, our eldest mage sensed an arcane power emanating from the west, too far away for any of the younger mages to pick up. So he sent forth a scout party including one of his apprentices, to seek out this arcane magic, knowing they would pick it up the next time it happened if they were closer to its origin. The scout party spent several days travelling around North Altoln trying to find the source of the arcane magic. The party roamed somewhere slightly north of Wesson when it next occurred, and the mage who had been sent felt it emanating to the south, from Wesson itself. The scout party entered Wesson and waited. Within a couple of days the mage sensed the arcane magic emanating from the Guild District, specifically from the highest point in the district.'

Fal gasped, 'Tyndurris?'

Errolas nodded. 'Correct. Whoever used the magic did so from within the tower. The mage in the scout party knew of Tyndurris. Elf mages for centuries have made a point of knowing where their neighbouring magic users are and who they are led by. The mage knew Lord Severun to be the current Grand Master and a powerful wizard, although she had no way of knowing if he or one of his members enacted such a spell. The mage returned to our forest with two of the scouts, leaving the others to watch over the tower and its inhabitants. When the elder mage found out someone in Tyndurris enacted arcane magic, he ordered a ranger watch. A handful of elven scouts suddenly working around the Guild District would raise questions, but one elf isn't uncommon in such a large city. Plus, a ranger is more suited to espionage than a group of scouts. We didn't want our movements to be picked up by city guardsmen or their superiors and seen as a threat. We are your allies Fal, but we cannot let arcane magic go unchecked.'

'Why not inform our king?' Fal begun to sober up with the seriousness of the topic.

'They considered it, but surely the King would seek an investigation; an investigation that could cause whomever it was enacting arcane magic to fight, or worse still, go into hiding, gaining underground support before making a move.' Errolas shook his head slowly as he continued. 'No, we needed to assess the situation until we had hard evidence, so a lengthy investigation by your authorities could be skipped and a serious move made against the perpetrator could be carried out instead. That's where you come in, Fal. On the night of the storm, I had been watching Tyndurris after relieving the previous ranger. I saw strange lights in the highest windows of Tyndurris. At first I thought it the storm, lightning, but after almost four centuries I had never seen such strange flashes of light and I knew it to be magic. I could almost feel its chill within my soul. I kept a close watch on Tyndurris' doors and gates, waiting to see if anyone set out at such a late hour, hoping I would find a solid lead.'

'And out I came,' Fal whispered, all colour draining from his face.

'I'm afraid so. I had been told by the previous ranger about the guard routines, and thought it strange for you to be leaving Tyndurris so late, especially in civilian clothes. And to be granted the use of a guild coach? Stranger still.

'I managed to follow the coach's route by taking a course across the rooftops; very precarious due to the rain and wind, I assure you. I followed you all the way down to Market Square where I saw you dispatch, and skilfully I might add, your attackers.'

'Aye, thanks for the help.'

'I could not reveal myself then and I am sure I would have received the same welcome as those two thugs. During your fight however, I saw you throw down what I had previously taken to be an ordinary bottle, but when it smashed... those shadows... entering the men and rising, flying across the rooftops, across me! I thought it the end, but they passed right over me?

'I have since been back to Market Square, Fal; I could sense the arcane magic. It left an unnatural tremor in the earth. Even through the stone floor I could sense it.

'I managed to find out where those two men who attacked you had been taken, and watched from a roof as a lone man murdered them through a window he had broken at the infirmary they were in. I do not know his identity, but he had come for them specifically, and I suspect it was because of the illness they were suffering, not because of who they were.'

Fal's head pulled back a little, his brow creased, clearly unaware of the event.

Errolas continued regardless. 'Fal, I need to know what you released. After tonight I cannot believe you are a willing participant in all of this, but I need answers. Before you do, however, please know I was not the only witness. A hooded man stood on the far side of the square. I found it impossible, even with my eyes, to see what he looked like and by the time I made it across the square and back to the rooftops to follow you home, he had gone. I still do not know his identity, but I am sure he, or whomever he works for, is behind the recent murders and behind the infirmary attack. He may even have been the one I witnessed kill those men.'

57

Fal's head still spun, and less because of the ale. So much information all at once, about questions he'd wanted to ask and wanted answering for days. *Arcane magic though? Lord Severun and Orix... Master Orix...* he couldn't believe what he heard, and why should he? A strange elf arrives with tales of arcane magic and hooded men; this was all too much. How could he trust someone who'd been following him for... who knew how long? The elf could easily have attacked him or demanded information at sword-point though. After all, Errolas carried a sword Fal was becoming all too aware of, as well as at least two knives Fal could see, and an unstrung re-curve bow and full quiver of arrows, which rested in the corner.

Sav trusts him though, Fal thought, and he knew elves were known for being goodly folk. What choice did he have but to tell Errolas everything he knew. Fal needed to know; to know what he'd been dragged into and on which side he should be, not to mention how many sides there were, what with an apparent second stalker stemming from that night.

Fal looked at Errolas, who'd been patiently sat in front of the fire.

Here goes... 'I will tell you what I know, but this must stay between us, Errolas, until we both decide what step to take next. Do we have an accord, ranger?'

'Yes,' the elf said, 'I think it is only fair and I will not turn down the help of an obviously capable sergeant-at-arms, especially when the danger lies in your own city.'

Chapter 10: Answers

There were more than a few pairs of eyes on the duo as they approached the grand house in Park District, and they both knew why.

'Reckon they're not as comfy round here at the moment, eh Sears?'

'No, ye little weasel, reckon they ain't. Not used to murders and such in these parts.'

Sears stopped at a large door as Biviano stepped forward and hammered on it half a dozen times. His partner looked at him in plain disbelief as he stepped back alongside him.

'What?'

'Ye think he heard that?'

'I dunno, Sears. It's a big house, that's why I hammered on it so.'

Still shaking his head, Sears looked around at the passers-by, who'd all looked over at the noise.

'Ye think he's not in?' Biviano asked, impatiently.

'How should I know? It's early though, can't see him being out, not with no reason to be, but that knock might've just put the fear of The Three up him. He might not come to the door—'

Biviano stepped forward and hammered on the door again, this time for longer.

'Ye're addled, Biviano, I'm sure of it.'

'He's in there gentlemen,' a well-dressed woman said, from across the street, 'of that I am sure.'

The two guardsmen looked at one another, before crossing the street to talk to the woman.

'And who're you, milady?' Sears asked.

'A neighbour of the man you're looking for. I live here and I've not seen him leave since he bought and moved into the place. The shutters up top haven't been opened you see.'

Biviano turned and looked back at the large house, before turning back to the woman, a suspicious look plain on his pock-marked face. 'How'd ye know we're looking for him, eh?'

Again Sears looked at Biviano in disbelief. 'Because we knocked at his door I expect, ye damned fool.'

'No need for that, big guy, and don't be answering suspects' questions for 'em, can't question 'em properly if ye do that, can I?'

'Suspect?' the woman said incredulously.

Sears held up his hands to placate her. 'No, no, not at all, milady. My colleague here meant nowt by that.'

'I should hope not. Do you know who I am?'

'Well if ye'd answered our first question, we would, yes!' Biviano said, clearly pleased with himself.

'How dare you, both of you! I'll be having words with Captain Prior about this. Now go about your business, I'm done here,' she said, before swiftly repairing to her house and having a servant slam the door behind her.

'Ouch... what the heck were that for?'

'I know ye know, Biviano, and if ye don't know, I don't care, ye deserved it for a lotta things. Now follow me. We know he's in there and if he won't open the door, we'll have to let ourselves in.'

Rubbing his shoulder, Biviano suddenly perked up. 'Ooh... I can help there,' he said, darting ahead of Sears whilst pulling a small pouch from his belt.

'Great, this should be good.'

'Will be, aye,' Biviano said, dropping to one knee in front of the door's lock. 'I got skills!'

'Ye got fleas more than ye got skills.'

Biviano fiddled with some small wire implements and tried to poke and prod at the lock, his tongue moving back and forth on his bottom lip as he concentrated.

The snapping sound of whatever Biviano used was like music to Sears' ears.

'Great, ye put me off, ye ginger oaf. *Now* what do ye suggest?'

'Knocking again? He may not have heard ye the first two times, although that's unlikely.'

'I've a better idea.'

'Excellent, can't wait.'

Biviano stood, puffed out his small chest, turned and strode several paces back away from the door before turning back and then running at it full tilt.

Oh, this is going to make my week! Sears thought, folding his arms and awaiting the inevitable.

Rushing past at some speed, Biviano dropped his bad shoulder and crunched into the solid door, a sickening crack audible over his impact and immediate curse.

Ye stupid bastard! Sears attempted to suppress his laughter.

'Arrrgghhhh... me shoulder. I've bleedin' broke it, I swear.' Rolling on the floor in front of the unopened door, Biviano began visibly weeping.

'What the hell did ye expect, ye fool? Come here,' Sears said, lifting Biviano by his good arm.

'Get off... I'm fine... don't need yer help.'

'Course not. Now hold yer arm still while I get us in here.' Sears walked across to the large stained-glass window to the right of the door and put his maille covered elbow through it. The shattering green and red glass came second only to the noise of the cries of outrage from passers-by.

'Guard business, so mind yer own!' Biviano shouted, whilst gingerly trying to move his arm, wincing all the while.

'Now, get through the hole and get this door open.'

'Yeah yeah, always me having to go through holes and gaps and shit ain't it...' Biviano carried on mumbling, cursing and wincing as he climbed through the broken window, with an assisting shove from Sears as he was halfway through.

'I'm in, fat boy,' he shouted. 'Now quit pushing. I think me shoulder ain't broke ye'll be glad to know, 'cause it just popped back in.'

'Lovely, now open the damned door will ye.'

'Stinks in here,' Biviano said as he moved away from the window and into the house.

Not a good sign, Sears thought.

The door opened from within and the smell of decay turned Sears' stomach as he entered the house, despite the entrance hall's size.

They both took out their short-swords, not wanting to take any risks, and set out to check the rooms of the house. Sears shouted 'clear' as he moved from room to room, and Biviano shouted random farm animals whilst doing the same.

Biviano finally found the offending smells source in the master bedroom, whereupon seeing no immediate threat, he shouted, 'Goose!'

'You're not funny,' Sears said, entering the room; a garishly decorated affair with a grand four poster bed opposite the door.

'He's been here a few days by the looks and smells of it,' Sears said. 'Can't see how he were killed though, there's no wound; no finger marks by the neck to suggest strangulation… not even anything to suggest there were a struggle.'

'Apart from his shit and piss stained pantaloons… bollocks, does everyone have 'em except me now? I knew I should've taken Joinson's. Anyway, beats me, big guy. What about suffocation?' Biviano said, who stood by the door with one hand down his braes having a good scratch whilst testing his other arm's range of movement with his sword.

'Nah… Seen it before, this man's face don't show the signs. Ye'd be able to tell if he'd been suffocated, trust me.'

'Well, ye ain't exactly the best at postmortems, so we'll let the clerics decide, eh?' Sears snarled at Biviano, who grinned before continuing. 'Anyway, they're wanting to do autopsies on everyone at the moment.' Biviano laughed. 'Must have their work cut out lately is all I can say.'

'Too true,' Sears said, rising from his crouched position by the body and taking another look around the room, before moving to, unlocking and opening the window, sword still in hand. 'We'll send a message for them to have the body removed and checked over.'

'Strange though…'

Biviano frowned. 'What is?'

'Windows all around the house, and the door, none broken or forced like the other murders round here recently.'

'Apart from the one *you* smashed.'

Sears continued regardless. 'Makes me think Ineson knew the killer.' Sears turned to face his partner, a grim expression on his face. 'Makes it even worse that does, if ye ask me. To think someone ye know could end yer life when there's so many other crazy bastards out there who're capable of it.'

'Don't go thinking like that, Sears, it'll just get ye down and it ain't like ye. Ye sure this is Peneur Ineson then?'

'No I ain't sure and no it ain't like me, but there's something about all this; the killings, the illness affecting folk everywhere. It don't feel natural, Biviano... creeps me out.' Sears shuddered visibly.

'Don't get all superstitious on me now, big guy,' Biviano said, finally sheathing his short-sword. 'If ye start up about curses from faraway lands, ye're as bad as the sailors and drunkards in the tavs! Oooh... there'll be zombies walking the streets next.' Biviano shook his head, laughing, before turning to the door and leaving the room.

'Don't be stupid,' Sears said, whilst taking a final look at the dead body, 'as if I'd think such rot.' With a final shudder, he left the room with a quickened pace, to catch up to his partner.

Outside the house, both guardsmen had a good look up and down the street.

'So, we found Joinson up there, near the park,' Biviano said, pointing to their right.

'Aye, walking away from this place; reckon he did it? He knew Ineson!'

Biviano shook his head. 'Nope, don't reckon so. Hard to know where to look until we know how he were done in.'

'Asking about until then, I expect?'

Biviano nodded. 'Looks like. You go left, I'll go home?'

'Funny... Dick! You go right, towards the first murder.'

'Unless this *was* the first murder, Sears, then I'd be going towards the second murder,' Biviano said, at the same time as slapping his cheek then wincing. Sears just looked at him in disgust.

'Ye've got fleas, I swear, and now they're on yer ugly face.'

'Whatever, just go ask questions of whoever, and I'll do some too if it'll keep ye happy, alright?'

'Whatever. See ye later.'

'Aye, later, ye donkey's rancid arse!' Biviano ran a couple of steps out of Sears' reach as the big man swung for him, before heading off down the street to the left.

'Sears,' he called back, 'go knock on that lovely lady's door opposite, I reckon she'll be more than happy to answer some questions. Ha!'

Sears responded with two fingers and nothing more.

***

'Hi Sarge,' Starks shouted, as he walked up the street towards Fal. 'Late night last night? You look like shit!'

Fal raised his eyebrows in surprise. 'Yes it was and thanks, Starks, for making me feel a whole lot better.'

Grinning as usual, the young crossbowman walked past Fal and gave a salute before hesitating. 'Oh bollocks, I almost forgot,' he said suddenly.

Fal stopped just after Starks had passed and turned to face him. 'Forgot what? You *have* finished your shift I hope?'

Starks wasn't wearing his usual grin however, which worried Fal. 'Yeah Sarge, 'course, on my way home, but it's not me it's Sergeant Heywood...'

Fal suddenly mirrored the young man's obvious concern. 'Franks Heywood?' Seeing Starks nod, he continued. 'What's happened to him, lad?'

Starks looked like he didn't know how to say it. Franks and Fal had worked together for years. Shortly after Fal had been promoted and employed by the Wizards and Sorcery Guild, Franks Heywood had been moved in from the north wall as a fellow sergeant-at-arms, and they'd quickly become good friends. Franks always worked separate shifts to Fal, but it didn't stop them meeting up on the crossover of shifts or outside of work hours, whenever Franks' family and duty permitted.

'It's the illness, Sarge,' Starks said, solemnly. 'He took ill during the night. They said he's caught the illness filling up the infirmaries all over the city. Must admit, first person I know to have caught it.'

'Where is he now?' Fal tried to hurry Starks along with the information.

'Still in Tyndurris, Sarge, Master Orix is tending to him... Sarge?' Starks shouted, as Fal took off at a run in the direction of the tower looming above the other buildings in the distance. Starks stood on the spot, torn between chasing after his superior and carrying on home. In the end he chose home, thinking it unwise to interfere. There was nothing he could do anyway and there were others in Tyndurris who would be of more use than he in such a situation.

Fal ran as fast as he could, not even thinking about Starks as he left the young guard stood in the middle of the street. There weren't many people about this early, but those who were walking towards Fal swiftly moved out of his way, one cursing the 'painted foreigner' but Fal was in no mood to respond.

His head thumped from the previous night's combination of alcohol and revelations. Sav had still been sleeping when Fal left the house for work, but Fal had had little sleep himself, discussing what was going on in Wesson with the elf for several hours. His legs had felt like jelly when he started running, but now the adrenaline pumping through his body left the weariness behind.

Errolas had explained to Fal that he believed the illness sweeping Wesson was directly linked to the potion Fal released on the night of the storm. Great pangs of guilt had washed over Fal as he thought about all the people who had, or were still, dying... and now his friend Franks. Fal needed to get to Tyndurris fast to see how he was, to protect him in any way possible. Orix tended to him now according to Starks, but it was Orix and Severun who'd sent Fal on the mission to release the potion linked to the illness. He thought at the time they were his trusted superiors, but now... now he didn't know what to think; all Fal knew was his friend needed him there and needed it all sorting out before...

If he dies it's blood on your hands, Falchion... on your hands, you hear? You damned

63

fool.

Fal had left Errolas strict instructions not to tell Sav what they'd discussed; they needed to know more and he didn't want to drag his friend into the middle of a conspiracy. Errolas had wanted to come with Fal and act immediately, but Fal had disagreed. Promising he would discover more from within Tyndurris, he'd told Errolas to stay behind with Sav, to try and find out what he could on the streets, without raising the scout's suspicions.

Fast approaching the guild's entrance, Fal threw a quick salute in reply to those given by the two guards opening the gates for him. Once through and across the yard, he ran up the tower's steps two at a time and in through the front door.

'Where's Franks?' Fal shouted, as he approaching the porter's desk at a fast walk.

'Good morning Sergeant—'

'Where's Franks, damn it?'

The porter looked extremely shocked at Fal's out of character outburst. 'Downstairs sergeant, guards barracks with Master Orix.'

Fal took off down the curling stone steps as fast as he could without falling down them, until he came to the guard room. Upon hearing the commotion as Fal clattered down the stairs, three guards had taken up defensive positions. Two held up shields with their own falchions raised high and the third held a loaded crossbow at the ready.

Just before entering the room, Fal shouted, 'Lower them, it's Fal,' and the guards relaxed a little. On seeing him and knowing for certain it was indeed Fal, they lowered their weapons fully, and the one closest to the barracks door pulled it open. Fal ran through and into a large room filled with bunks, tables and chairs. At the far end, a basic bunk was surrounded by two white-robed humans and a gnome, the latter stood on a stool. All three looked from Franks, who lay on the bunk besides them, to Fal, who'd slowed again to a fast walk.

'Sergeant Falchion,' Orix said, with a curt nod.

'Master Orix, master clerics,' Fal replied, returning the gnome's nod to all three of the clerics. 'How is he?'

'He has the same symptoms as many lining the infirmaries throughout the city, sergeant,' the taller of the two human clerics said, rubbing his bald head in frustration, his sympathy evident as he looked at Fal.

'We're trying to ascertain how long he's had it'. This time the other cleric spoke; a young female with long dark hair tied up into a bun on the top of her head. She looked up at Fal with kind eyes before continuing. 'Up to now he isn't showing any physical signs like the characteristic boils, however, he does have a raging temperature and has been unconscious for hours. If the illness wasn't so widespread and the symptoms known to us, I would have suggested a fever, but we must fear the worst.'

Orix, Fal noticed, had turned away from him after the greeting, looking again at Franks, who looked pale and clammy, yet peaceful in his unconscious state.

'Master Orix, what do *you* think? No offence of course,' Fal swiftly added to the other clerics, realising how it may have sounded.

'None taken,' the female cleric said. They both smiled and moved away from the bed, to give their master and the sergeant some privacy.

I want to hear what you *have to say, master cleric.*

'I'm sorry, sergeant… there is no cure we know of at this time. The only thing I can say with certainty is Sergeant Heywood here will get steadily worse over the next few days, before passing away in his sleep.'

Like hell he will, bastard.

'All we can do is try and make him feel as comfortable as possible when he wakes and hope we find a cure beforehand, although I cannot give you false hope regarding the possibility of that happening within the time he has left, sergeant.' Orix didn't look at Fal while he spoke. He kept his eyes on Franks' wrist, through which he monitored the man's pulse, and he addressed Fal by rank – something the gnome didn't often do.

'I won't accept that, master cleric.' Fal's voice was steady, trying hard not to let his own guilt and anger show.

Orix looked completely surprised and put Franks' hand back on the bed before turning to face Fal. Although Orix stood on a stool, the small gnome still had to look up at the tattooed face of his sergeant-at-arms. 'This is a terrible tragedy, sergeant, and I feel for you and your men, but I must remind you I am a council member of this guild and you are to show me the proper respect.' Orix's cheeks flushed. He wasn't the sort to chastise anyone, but Fal knew there was more to the gnome's visible discomfort. The other two clerics moved across the room out of earshot, having a conversation of their own. It had become personal to Fal. A close friend was in danger and he suddenly agreed with Errolas; he wanted to act immediately, although he suspected the elf wouldn't be happy he acted alone.

'Listen to me carefully, Orix,' Fal whispered. He leaned in towards the old gnome, adding an aspect of intimidation over the cleric. Fal knew the other two were out of earshot, but he felt safer talking about such things in a lowered voice. 'I know the illness throughout Wesson is connected to the spell you had me release on the night of the storm!'

Orix leaned back at Fal's admission as if slapped, and nearly fell off the stool he perched upon. Steadying himself, he realised Fal hadn't moved an inch to stop him fall. Orix looked from Fal to Franks and back, his mouth half-open and his eyes wide. He stammered as he replied, 'I… I'm not sure what you mean sergeant? I think you're in shock.'

I'll give you a bloody shock, gnome.

Fal's nose wrinkled and his teeth showed as he finally revealed his true anger. He spoke very slowly, very steadily, yet sounded extremely dangerous. 'Don't lie to me! I know there's a connection. Many people are dying because of what *you* and Lord Severun asked me to release. I want answers, Master Orix… and I want them now!' Fal was hoping to appeal to the cleric's guilt.

65

He knew, or had always thought, Orix was a caring old gnome who'd trained many clerics because of his passion for helping others. He still hoped at least some of it was true.

'It's not that simple, Falchion.' The fact Orix used Fal's name and not his rank was a good sign. 'It's hard to explain as it may hurt you more, the more you know.' Orix flinched at Fal's reaction – a slight movement of his hand towards the hilt of his heavy bladed sword. 'I don't mean hurt you physically,' the gnome added hastily, fumbling with his beard, 'I mean knowing the truth! It may be upsetting due to your friendship with Sergeant Heywood.'

'Try me,' Fal said, leaning back away from Orix slightly, giving the gnome something in return for his admission of a connection.

'You cannot repeat this, Falchion, I beg you. Only Lord Severun and I know about all of this up to now, and until we know more and all of this is over, we can't risk anyone finding out and ruining all the work we've done before we've had a chance to present it to the guild, the King and his advisers personally.' Orix talked fast and breathed quickly as he shot the words out in a panicked torrent Fal only just managed to follow.

'You're *wrong*, Master Orix. *I* know, for one, and I'm not alone in my knowledge of your plans. I may not have all the details, but if *I* caught on to what you're both doing, others might as well, and they may not be as understanding or forthcoming with what they know as I am.'

Orix's face dropped even more and he started fussing with his robes, looking from Fal to the other two clerics across the room. 'Who else knows?'

'I cannot say for sure, but someone has been following me for a while now and I'm sure it has to do with all of this.' Fal pointed to his sick friend.

'This is bad, very bad,' Orix said, whilst shaking his head. 'We need to see Lord Severun, immediately—'

'No,' Fal said. 'I want to hear this from you first. My friend is lying here next to us dying, a soldier sworn to protect *you* and all the other clerics, wizards, magicians and sorcerers in this guild. Others are dying all over Wesson, and not just from this illness, but through murders which I believe are also linked. Help me by telling me what's happening to our city, and we can put it right together.' Fal relaxed a little, trying to calm himself, to let Orix know he wasn't a threat and to lead him into a confession.

The old gnome looked tired to Fal now, more tired than he'd ever seen him. His defences seemed to drop and he looked into Fal's eyes, a long sigh escaping his lips. 'Very well Falchion… I shall explain everything, but not here.' Hopping down from the stool, Orix walked across the room with Fal in tow. He asked the two clerics to keep watch over Franks, and then Orix and Fal both left the room. They crossed the guardroom beyond the door and climbed the stairs until they reached the seventh floor and Orix's private chamber.

'Take a seat, Falchion,' Orix said, panting slightly as he gestured to a wooden stool opposite the window.

Fal shook his head. 'I'll stand.'

'Very well,' Orix said. He crossed the room and sat on a small chair under the window. 'I shall start from the beginning, which takes us a fair few months back to when Lord Severun approached me regarding an experiment he wanted me to help him work on.'

Fal leaned against the wall and took in the floods of information. He realised the tension seemed to leave Orix as he opened up to him about the experiment; how he'd opposed it but decided eventually he wanted to help Severun keep it as safe as possible, and how he'd been scared Severun would go ahead with it anyway, even if he didn't help.

Orix explained all about Severun's plan to track down and wipe out Wesson's criminals; how after months of tests and smaller enactments of the spells used by Severun to release and carry the potion, they'd finally reached the time when they were ready to release the experiment and record the effects.

Fal could hardly take it all in. So he had released the cause of the illness spreading through Wesson like a disease. He voiced his concerns and Orix shot them down immediately.

'A disease spreads from person to person, Falchion. We released the potion with those ghostly shadows you saw, to be delivered directly to violent criminals and to them alone. It cannot spread! I must admit, there have been more victims than I thought, a truly scary revelation considering our infirmaries are full, and even the higher districts have had many people affected. Lord Severun assures me, however, that numbers will now be on the decrease as the subjects die off, so the experiment will be a success. We can then explain it all to the guild council and the guild itself, and then take it immediately to the King and his advisers. If this works, Falchion, it could make not just Wesson safer, but all of Altoln!'

Fal sat down on the stool and leaned back against the wall, his legs stretched out in front of him and his arms firmly folded. 'This is madness,' he said quietly, shaking his head. 'You cannot play magistrate and executioner, Master Orix. It's not your place. How reliable are the shadows Severun used?'

'Many tests were carried out by Lord Severun,' Orix said, 'and he was beyond certain the spell he used was sound. The shadows from the spell would search out the violent souls of evil men and women, and deliver the potion directly to them and them alone.'

'Are you trying to tell me,' Fal's anger rose again and he felt like screaming, 'Franks Heywood is an evil man?'

Orix looked scared. 'Falchion, I'm not presuming to know such things... but... but if he has the illness, if the shadows found and delivered my potion to him...' Orix let the implication hang a moment before continuing. 'How can we know a man's true soul, who he is when he is on his own in the city?'

'I can know, damn you!' Fal shouted. 'This isn't right!' He forced his voice down seeing the frightening effect he was having on Orix. He felt angry, extremely angry with the gnome, but Severun bore the brunt of his anger, for it was the wizard who created the 'experiment' and dragged Fal, Orix and all

67

the victims into it.

'Master Orix,' Fal said, and Orix nodded meekly, 'are you absolutely sure, no question whatsoever, this illness you created can't spread?'

'Of course I'm sure, Falchion. Diseases transfer in various ways from host to host. They can sometimes change… evolve to suit their surroundings, so to speak, but this isn't a disease. It was a magical potion, an illness I created to slowly shut down the body in a specific way.'

Falchion became increasingly frustrated. He knew little about diseases and such things, but struggled to believe Orix was right. There couldn't be so many people, all over the city, affected by a limited number of shadows released days ago, surely? It would have taken hundreds of the ghostly spectres. He hadn't seen that many when he'd smashed the bottle… far from it in fact. *Did Orix even have a hand in the distribution of his own potion, or did Severun deal with that alone?* Fal was now determined to press his previous point, if for no other reason than to prove Franks' innocence. His friend was not evil.

'Master Orix, you tell me a disease can change or evolve, which you seem to accept without question, because you know it; it is your field of expertise. I'm trying to understand how there can be so many people affected by your potion when it does not spread, even between 'evil' people, as you so simply label them.'

Orix flushed, wrung his hands and sighed heavily, but nodded all the same.

'Is there any chance that whilst your potion on its own would be as you expected, once combined with Severun's spell, it could become something completely different? Potentially gaining a means of passing from person to person?'

Orix went to speak, but Fal swiftly cut him off.

'After all,' Fal continued, 'Franks Heywood has only just contracted the illness… days after its release. I may be grasping for a solution here, Master Orix, but have you even looked into Severun's delivery spell and its effects on your potion, or have you blindly trusted in his work?'

Fal saw something click within Orix, and through his eyes he saw a sudden, dreadful understanding. He knew Orix believed Fal could be right, about what exactly – his potion evolving, or Severun's spell – Fal didn't know, but the gnome's obvious fear grasped at his stomach like a clawed hand.

'You haven't even checked for anything else, have you, Orix? You've just assumed it's your potion at work within the city and nothing more.'

Orix shook his head slowly, before leaping to his feet without saying a word. Falchion tensed, but the old gnome moved across to his bookshelf and searched frantically for something. Finding what he looked for, he pulled a dusty tome from the shelf and rushed to the door. Opening it, he turned to Fal and said, in a most terrified, yet commanding voice, 'Follow me!'

Chapter 11: Break In

The silence in Fal's living room was broken by the sound of Sav snoring and the faint crackle of glowing embers as the elf ranger, Errolas, lay curled up on the floor in front of the hearth, his breathing inaudible.

Sav had kept his eyes tightly shut in the earlier hours, listening intently to the conversation between his two friends. When they'd finally settled to sleep, he'd lain awake, his mind racing with all he'd heard.

Errolas had been in the city before coming to see him. *So had he wanted to see me at all? Or was I part of the elf's mission to follow and track the arcane magic released by Fal?*

Even at the end of their conversation, when Fal and Errolas were trying to figure out what steps to take next, Fal had asked the elf not to tell Sav when he awoke. Was it really for his protection, so as not to drag him into the conspiracy as Fal had put it, or did Fal not trust him? That thought had played on the scout's mind the longest.

Still thinking long and hard about all he'd heard, Sav had slumped back in the chair and fallen into a restless sleep.

Sav felt like he'd only slept for a few minutes when he woke, his snoring ending in a loud grunt that startled him. He looked across at the curled up figure of Errolas on the floor in front of the glowing hearth. Sav suddenly realised what woke him.

Someone's in the house?

Floorboards creaked from the room above Fal's, yet Sav knew it to be unoccupied. The owner was out of the city on business and wasn't due back for some time.

Taking his eyes from the ceiling, Sav looked again at Errolas. The elf looked back at him, a slender finger held to his lips. Without a sound, the elf rose to his feet and drew an elegant, curved sword with elven runes running the length of the highly polished blade. The small cross-guard, reaching out just enough to protect Errolas's hand, and the hilt, long enough for the elf to grip with two hands should he wish to, held a magnificently sculpted pommel.

Errolas stalked silently across the room to the front of the house. He peered into the morning light through the spy hole in Fal's front door, whilst Sav climbed to his feet as quietly as he could. He waved his hand to get the elf's attention.

Errolas turned to see Sav motioning through to the back of the house, before making a walking movement with two fingers, which he then walked up imaginary stairs. He finished by pointing up to the room above. Errolas understood the scout's signals – another staircase led upstairs.

Errolas followed Sav through to Fal's small kitchen and back door. They both held their breaths as Sav unlocked and slowly pushed the door open, worried an un-oiled hinge may give them away, but it opened in silence and they both passed through unheard. Sav had picked up his short-sword on the way out of the living room and slowly drew it from its scabbard as he reached the bottom of the external wooden staircase.

Leaning in towards Errolas, Sav whispered as quietly as he could, knowing the elf would pick up the slightest of sounds. 'The stairs creak. I've heard the man who lives above go down them before when I've been here, but there'll be no way in through the front door if whoever's up there has locked it.'

Errolas nodded and signalled for Sav to go back through the house and wait to catch anyone coming out of the front door.

Sav did as he was asked without question.

Errolas placed his feet slowly and carefully, feeling for support on the old wooden steps. He made his way up them without a sound, keeping one eye on his footing and one on the closed door at the top of the staircase.

Once he reached the top, Errolas realised the door couldn't have been the intruder's point of entry; even in his sleep he would have heard whoever it was climbing the stairs. The door would have had to be forced open too, but it remained intact. Whoever was inside must have entered via the front door or a window. It was clear to the elf the intruder was skilled, and so Errolas took no chances.

More movement came from the room above Sav, a faint sound he struggled to hear. Whoever was in there was looking for something, but a burglar would take what he could as fast as possible then leave the building. The intruder had been there a while now and made no attempt to leave. Sav kept his eye against the spy hole in Fal's door, his left hand on the door handle, ready to rush out should anyone try and exit that way. He'd already unlocked the door using the spare key Fal always left on a hook in the kitchen.

Errolas scanned the back door carefully, there was no way through, so the elf looked over to the window on his right. The window ledge was reachable, but he would draw a great deal of attention by smashing the glass to enter. He decided to try the roof. Silently sheathing his sword, he reached above his head and jumped. Catching the edge of the tiled roof, he pulled himself up and on to it. As quietly and carefully as he'd climbed the wooden stairs, the nimble elf walked up the side of the house, careful not to dislodge any roof tiles as he went. Upon reaching the slightly smoking chimney pot, Errolas saw the intruder's point of entry. Roof tiles had been pulled away one by one near the chimney until the wooden beams below were visible through a hole large enough for a man to squeeze through. Cautiously leaning over the hole, Errolas saw the room below.

Just then, a man with long black hair and dark clothes passed below Errolas.

The elf was certain the man below him was alone. As he thought this, the dark clothed intruder appeared below again and looked directly up, straight at Errolas, his eyes widening in realisation he was being watched.

Errolas was stunned. He hadn't made a sound, there was no way a fellow elf ranger could have heard him, never mind a human. The split second hesitation gave the man below a chance to act and with surprisingly fast reactions he threw a knife from his belt.

Errolas dived away from the hole. The knife barely missed as he tumbled sideways towards the edge of the roof. He struggled to catch a grip on the smooth tiled roof before he felt himself drop over the side, thankfully managing to grab the edge as he went. Cursing himself under his breath for the momentary lapse whilst over the hole, he pulled himself back onto the roof and ran towards the opening. As he reached it, the sound of breaking glass erupted from where he had pulled himself onto the roof.

Spinning on the spot, Errolas shouted, 'Scout! Out back out back out back!' before running to the edge of the roof where he'd nearly fallen. As he got there he saw a black figure disappear around the corner of a neighbouring building. Errolas jumped from the roof, aiming for a nearby wall as Sav came bursting out of the kitchen door, sword in hand.

'Where is he?' Sav shouted whilst running out of the yard and into the alley. He spun to face Errolas, sword held out defensively as the elf landed in a crouch on the wall above him. Errolas pointed in the direction of the intruder and ran across the neighbouring walls as Sav followed slightly behind him in the alley itself.

Turning the same corner as the intruder, both Errolas and Sav saw a deserted alley leading down to a busy street. Errolas jumped down from the wall and they both headed down the alley cautiously, checking behind barrels and crates as they went. Reaching the busy street, it was clear the intruder had fled into the crowd and escaped.

Errolas cursed and turned around. He stalked back to Fal's place, Sav close behind him.

'What happened?' Sav said between breaths. He sweated through the physical exertion and obvious hangover.

Furious with himself, Errolas snapped his response. 'I made a mistake; he got away.'

'Did you get a good look at him though Errolas?' Sav took long strides to keep up with the elf, looking at him from the side.

'Briefly. He wore black, no cloak but a light leather gambeson. I saw no sword, but he had knives, throwing knives, and long dark hair. Pale skin, gaunt even with a few days of growth on his face. The way he moved... I have seen it before, maybe *him* before.'

They reached Fal's backyard again and Errolas climbed the wooden stairs. 'We need to check inside, see if there are clues.'

Sav grabbed Errolas by the arm. 'You think you've seen him before?' Sav stared directly into the elf's eyes.

'I said I've seen the way he moved before. Perhaps him, I can't be sure.' Errolas pulled himself free of Sav's grip and went to move off again, stopping only for Sav's next words.

'At the Dockside Infirmary?' he said. 'The man who killed the sick men?'

Errolas paused before turning back to face Sav. 'You heard us?'

'Every word, aye.'

Errolas closed his eyes briefly and took a deep breath before continuing. 'He only wants to protect you by not telling you, scout; as do I.' Errolas' eyes showed nothing but the truth.

'I know. I had a long hard night to think it through and I know, but I don't need protecting. It's my city as much as it is Fal's.'

'That it is, scout... that it is. Come then let us search the place, I will show you how the intruder entered. He was very skilled, and this was no burglary.' Errolas turned again, reached the top of the stairs, pulled himself onto the roof and pulled Sav up behind him.

'It wasn't through that window then?' Sav asked, pointing to the smashed window to the right of the stairs.

'No, that was his exit. Follow me and keep your eyes peeled on the roof for a small throwing knife. If we are lucky we may find it.' Sav's eyes widened as he started to put together what had happened.

'So you think it could've been him then? The man at the infirmary?

'Wow!' Sav added, seeing the hole in the roof.

'Yes I do.' Errolas nodded once whilst scanning the rooftop. 'The throwing knives, the way he moved and dressed. It was him or an accomplice. This is all linked, scout, and this his entry.' Errolas pointed to the hole surrounded by loose tiles. 'He must have spent a long time moving them last night, carefully, so as not to make any noise.

Both men dropped down into the room. The place was not sacked as they'd expected. Nothing seemed out of place to them, although they couldn't be too sure since they'd never been there before.

'We will search around here, then outside for the knife, and then we need to inform the City Guard of the break-in.' Sav agreed and they both set about searching the rooms for clues as to what the intruder could have been looking for.

After an hour or so of fruitless searching for a knife, Errolas sent Sav off to the nearest barracks to report the break-in while he stayed at Fal's to await his return. The confrontation with the man in black, as well as his previous witnessing of the infirmary murders played through in his head. If it wasn't the same man, then they were of the same organisation, of that he was sure. It was clear there was a third party involved, and Errolas needed to know who they were before he could act on Severun and Orix. He needed to hear what Fal had found out at the guild, and hoped the sergeant would return soon with some much needed information.

***

The tall trees of Park District swayed gently in the cool morning breeze. The usual birdsong was punctuated occasionally by jackdaws squabbling in the treetops, and a large pond rippled as another small stone landed near its centre.

'I'm lost for what we do now,' Biviano said, as he picked up another handful of small stones from the path in front of Sears.

'Aye, that makes two of us.'

'No one on the street had owt useful to tell us,' Biviano continued, 'and the clerics don't know shit about how Peneur Ineson died.' *I almost feel like someone's purposefully hindering us on this one…*

Sears shook his head as Biviano cast another stone out into the pond.

'Ye don't skim 'em like that ye know?'

'That's 'cause I ain't skimming, ye nugget.'

Sears crouched down and picked up a fairly flat stone, before successfully launching it low, achieving seven bounces across the surface of the pond and almost clearing the other side.

Biviano threw the handful of stones he had into the pond and walked off, whilst Sears smiled broadly to himself. *'Course ye weren't.*

'Come on, fatty,' Biviano said, as he walked towards the park gate.

'Where to then? The infirmary again, see if they know owt new?'

'I dunno, Sears, but something'll come up won't it? Always does.'

Aye, pal, it does. We're lucky like that. Usually anyway… this investigation's taking its time however, and something about that doesn't sit well with me. Sears slowly followed his partner.

On the opposite side of the pond, shadows seemed to move, eventually revealing a black-clad man with a wide brimmed hat held in one pale hand, whilst his other rested on the hilt of a rapier.

Now now, gentlemen, you'd do best to let this one slide. Can't have you learning any more now, can we? Especially when you already know more than we'd like as it is.

73

Chapter 12: Outbreak

The fourth floor of Tyndurris split between a great library, the guild archives vault and the clerics' research chamber. The library took up most of the floor with huge wooden bookshelves reaching from floor to ceiling and rows upon rows of immense stacks divided the library into narrow passageways. Tall wooden ladders creaked as members of the guild stretched out from the top of them to reach for books long since read.

Orix thanked the magician who passed down a book he'd requested, whilst Fal stood by the library door, impatiently waiting as the gnome returned carrying a large, well-worn tome to accompany the other books he'd already collected. Fal's arms were laden with old, dust covered books, his impatience growing.

'Master Orix, we need to hurry. I don't see why all these are necessary for an autopsy?'

'Be patient, Falchion, we need to be thorough and I am no longer…' Orix looked around and dropped his voice '…looking for my potion's effects, or thinking of it as such. I am going to investigate this illness as I would any other. Therefore, I need references to various diseases and their symptoms. Now, this is the last book, so we can proceed to the clerics' chamber behind the archives vault.'

'Very well, do you want me to carry—' Fal took an unwilling step backwards as Orix reached up with the large book and threw it atop the ones Fal was already carrying.

'Thank you, Falchion, that one was quite heavy.' Orix trotted off through the library door and down a passageway past a heavily reinforced door, which was guarded by one of Fal's men. The old gnome stopped at another door, which was shrouded in shadow at the end of the passageway. He turned to wait for Fal, who staggered along behind him, barely managing an awkward nod to his guard, who tried to hide his amusement as he returned the gesture.

Fal knew the post on the archive door had not been a popular one amongst his men lately, and now he understood why. As Orix opened the door, the smell of death assaulted Fal's senses. He choked back a cough and followed Orix into the room, kicking the door shut behind him, which creaked eerily before closing with a loud mechanical clunk. Fal crossed over to the nearest desk and placed the books down, stifling a dust-triggered sneeze before turning to take in the room. Orix was moving around the room lighting more oil lamps.

'Come then, Falchion. Help me with the next victim. They are kept in this cold-room.' Orix trotted over to a large, stone door and pulled it open with great ease. 'Well-greased hinges, Falchion, as well as a little magic. Sometimes you have to use it on smaller things, or large in this case, especially when you're physically smaller than most.'

Fal smiled and followed the gnome into a cold, stone lined room. Icicles hung from the ceiling, and upon closer inspection – after almost slipping over – Fal realised the whole room was covered in a thin layer of ice. 'Magically maintained?' Fal asked, his breath clouding before him.

'Of course,' Orix replied, walking over to a sack in the ominous shape of an adult body. 'This one please, Falchion, if you could lift her onto the bench outside.' Orix tapped the body-bag and Fal crossed the room carefully, so as not to slip on the ice underfoot, before lifting the body up into his arms.

'Is this the woman we brought in yesterday?' Fal liked the idea of what was coming even less now.

'Yes. Not the latest body to be brought in, but I want to check them in chronological order of their deaths and I haven't opened this one up yet.' Orix left the cold-room and walked over to the desk where Fal had placed the books. Fal carried the cold, stiff body to a large bench in the middle of the chamber and lay it face up. He then turned and closed the stone door. He was shocked when he had to put his back into it.

'Alright then,' Orix said, without lifting his head from the book he'd opened. 'Remove the body bag and fetch my instruments from the cabinet over there.' Orix pointed, again without looking up from his book, to a simple, oak cabinet near the cold-room door. Fal removed the body-bag, his nose twitching in protest at the smell. He was thankful for the numerous oil lamps adding their mild smoke to the air and at least taking the edge off.

'Shall I open the window, Master Orix?'

'Yes if you wish,' Orix said, his head buried in the book whilst flicking pages over rapidly.

Fal walked over to the window and opened the shutter. A fresh breeze blew in immediately, followed by the sound of gulls. Fal took a deep breath, glad to smell the fresh air over the stale, death-ridden smog in the chamber. After taking his fill, he retrieved Orix's instruments from the cabinet and placed them on the bench next to the body, silently relieved at the faint sound of the busy city below as it stole away the near silence of the room.

'Thank you, Falchion. Now, you may take a seat and I will inform you of what I am doing.' Orix looked up from the book and across to Fal, who nodded and took the nearest seat to the window.

Stepping up onto a small podium on the far side of the bench, Orix looked over the body, took a scalpel and opened up the cadaver's chest. Fal sat in the chair watching Orix move from corpse to books, scratching his head and pulling on his beard.

Orix explained everything and Fal thought the gnome's knowledge of the human anatomy quite extraordinary. More than half of what Orix said was utterly wasted on Fal, but he didn't dare interrupt.

Then, after about two hours or so, Orix suddenly stopped talking; he stopped his running commentary and just stared through a strange contraption he called a *microscope*. He'd taken *cells* from the body and placed them on a *petri dish*, all unfamiliar terms to Fal, although he didn't dare admit it. Orix looked up then, his face suddenly pale. He ran across to the books and pulled out the third one down, ignoring the top two which clattered to the floor, shaking the dust from their covers. Orix muttered something about cleaning them before they came into the chamber, before falling silent again, his head buried in the book he'd taken. Fal got to his feet, eager and scared in equal measures to hear what Orix had clearly found.

'By the gods,' Orix said, finally stopping on a page a quarter of the way into the book.

'What is it?' Fal was now more scared than eager to hear the answer.

'It can't be, but… the symptoms now developing. All the warning signs though, hidden. Hidden from me by my own… my own stupid, stupid potion.' Orix was shaking his head, more colour draining from his already pale face.

'Master Orix, please?' Fal took a couple of steps towards the gnome.

'How could I have missed this? The buboes under the arms, on the neck, around the groin; I took them as being part of my potion's false symptoms. Oh Falchion, this is terrible.' Orix looked into Fal's eyes and pointed to the corpse. 'This woman had… I mean, the cause of death was a zoonotic disease.'

Fal felt sick when he heard the words and had to draw on his courage to ask the next question.

'Master Orix, what's a zoonotic disease?'

Orix swallowed hard. 'In this case, gods below… the King, he must be informed there's a plague in the city.'

Fal rubbed his hands through his hair and had to take a seat. He looked to the old gnome, who looked back, fear plain across his face.

'Falchion… it's the bubonic plague.'

***

The alley was quiet and dark. Large buildings either side stole the midday light and cast shadows over almost every inch of the narrow space. A tall figure stood with his back to one of the buildings, able to see from one end of the alley to the other; he was sure he was safe and free of his pursuers.

A sudden voice startled him. He thought he'd covered every possible approach to his shadow covered position and he was rarely caught off-guard. To this date there had only ever been a handful that had managed it, and only two – one being the elf who'd just discovered him, the other the one who now spoke to him – had lived to tell the tale, and the latter took great pleasure in telling it.

'You were almost captured just then, Master Clewarth, how unlike you.' The voice came from Exley Clewarth's left. He'd just looked left, then right and heard the voice. He didn't give the owner of the voice the pleasure of turning to face him.

'You never cease to amaze me, General. Sir Samorl must look upon you in great favour. I take it you had me followed?' Exley strained to hear the

General's breathing, but heard nothing except the slight sound of a distant coach rumbling up the main street further down the alley to his left. After a short pause that felt like a lifetime, Horler Comlay replied.

'Yes, of course I did, as I am sure *you* would were you in my position. After the failure of your, so called finest witchunter, Master Dundaven, how could I not?' The General's voice was closer now, right by Exley's head. He could just about hear the slow, calm breathing; *feel* the slow, calm breathing on the back of his neck. Exley turned at last to face the General by his side.

'I would indeed. I am the Witchunter General of the South, after all… Master Comlay.' Exley stared directly into his peer's eyes. Horler Comlay was the same rank as Exley. He was also right-hand man to the Grand Inquisitor, which Horler believed granted him a certain level of authority over his southern counterpart.

'Indeed you are, General Clewarth. Now, please, enlightened me where my witchunter could not. He watched from afar, my man, watched you enter a house at night via the roof. I like to see you haven't forgotten everything we were taught.'

Exley clenched his teeth and bit back a retort, allowing Horler to continue.

'But then,' Horler said, 'hours later, he saw you crash through the rear window of the first floor on your way out, pursued by two of the residents in broad daylight. Not, I would say, something *I* was taught.' Horler's mocking grin pulled at Exley's nerves, egging him to hurl a fist rather than a retort.

'Your witchunter saw much,' Exley managed through gritted teeth. 'He is a skilled man indeed. I *did* think he needed a lesson in concealment though, since I saw him watching me whilst I created the entry through the roof… at night… in the dark.'

Horler's smile slipped and Exley's replaced it. 'I only let him live because he is one of yours, not mine. *However…*' Exley raised his voice slightly with the last word; let his smile fade and moved straight to what Horler wanted to know before the banter turned sour. 'I *was* seen, yes, your man speaks true, although I disagree with his wording, for I most certainly was not almost captured. My pursuers… or rather the one who saw me anyway, was an elf, General Comlay, and a skilled one at that. Ranger, I believe I heard. Whilst in the house that is, listening in to Sergeant Falchion's cosy little conversation with his friends.'

Horler's eyes widened briefly then returned to his normal squinted glare, his cheeks flushing ever so slightly at revealing his surprise to his counterpart's words.

'You managed to listen in to Sergeant Falchion's conversation, a conversation about the guild's plans?' Horler's enthusiasm was barely concealed.

'Yes indeed. Plenty of worthy information for the Grand Inquisitor. Let's take it to him now shall we?'

'Of course, General Clewarth, exactly what I had in mind. We shall go and see him now, you and I.' Horler held his arm out as an offer for Exley to move on down the alley.

'Most kind of you General, but after you, I insist.' Exley held his arm out in the same way and Horler reluctantly strode away, his black cloak billowing out behind him.

Prick! Look at you, an exhibitionist to say the least, Exley thought, before following Horler Comlay down the alley to report his findings to his true master.

Chapter 13: Let them burn

Errolas paced Fal's living room. He hadn't wanted to leave in case Fal returned with news from Tyndurris, but now the elf felt useless. Sav had left a while ago to inform the City Guard of the break-in upstairs and seemed to be taking far longer than he should, and Fal could be hours if he worked his full shift at the guild. Surely Fal would return to inform Errolas should he have found anything? Errolas started to worry whether trusting the two humans had been the right thing to do. Elves rarely trusted other races with such matters. Yes, they shared an alliance and worked together to defend both of their realms, but regarding such dangers as arcane magic, the elves preferred to keep other races out of the loop, especially the humans of Altoln, due to its fanatical Samorlian Church.

Errolas stopped pacing.

The Samorlian Church!

He cursed himself for not thinking of it sooner. *The man I chased, he must have been a witchunter. It all makes sense.* They would want information about who was enacting arcane magic so they could hunt them down and execute them regardless of costs.

Errolas began to pace once more, his mind going over all the details. The murders around Wesson, and the three murders at the infirmary Errolas had witnessed – it was a witchunter who'd carried out the attack, he was now sure of that. They knew about Severun and Orix's experiment and decided it was up to them to wipe out the infected and find out who'd enacted the arcane magic, hence the reason for the witchunter in the room above Fal's. He wasn't stealing anything, but using the place to spy on Fal and listen in to their conversation.

How foolish I've been. I should have used a more secure location to discuss such a matter, and worse, I've put my friends in more danger by forcing Fal to divulge all to me here.

Friends...

That's what Fal and Sav were. He could trust them, he was sure of it and he needed them to know the Samorlians were involved. The witchunter had escaped and would surely inform the Grand Inquisitor, who would have the authority to go to the Archbishop; an advisor to the King. And the result... well... the result didn't bear thinking about.

Just then, a commotion in the street caught Errolas' attention. Moving swiftly to the window, he peered outside and saw Sav arguing with two city guardsmen. Opening the window slightly, the elf listened in.

'Sorry Sav, but we're busy,' a large guardsman with a black moustache and a gruff voice said. 'We'll check out the place when we can, but we've more pressing matters on our 'ands, mate.' The guardsman tried to move away from Sav after he'd spoken.

Sav stepped in his way.

'I know you're busy, Dale, but I believe this break-in is of the utmost importance… and it's above Fal's place. You wanna explain to him why his gaff isn't important?'

Dale sighed and shrugged. 'Sav, if it were up to me we'd check into it now, but a lot of guardsmen have been pulled down Dockside 'cause of the increased ganger activity. The murders may have died down in other districts, but Dockside has erupted wi' all kinds of shit. Gangs are openly fighting and people are panicking 'cause of this sickness everywhere. There're less of us in the other districts now so we need to check on things in order of priority, and the captain's keeping a close watch, not to mention the bloody Constable of Wesson himself. So please, mate, move aside and let me on me way.' Dale beckoned for his partner to follow and they set off down the street as Sav reluctantly stepped aside.

'Thanks for nothing, Dale!' Sav shouted, once the large soldier was out of earshot. He then walked across to Fal's door which Errolas opened.

Before Sav could explain, Errolas held up his hand to silence him. He told him he'd heard it all and it was no longer important to have them check the room above, but they needed to find Fal immediately, to inform him about the Samorlian Church's involvement.

Sav agreed, not at all surprised by the revelation. He then told Errolas they would have to go to Tyndurris to find Fal and risk facing Severun or Orix there. Errolas agreed it was worth the risk, so they both left the house immediately and headed as fast as they could towards the large tower in the distance.

***

Fal had been stunned when he'd heard Orix's words; a *plague* in Wesson. There hadn't been one for centuries and never had Altoln suffered the bubonic plague. It had spread through Sirreta a couple of hundred years ago, Orix told Fal, but had luckily been quarantined by their King at the time and never spread beyond their borders. That was exactly what Wesson needed to do and as fast as possible. Orix had sent Fal to the guardroom below the ground floor and ordered them to create a bonfire in the courtyard. When questioning the orders, Fal told Starks – who'd returned for his next shift in the time it had taken for Orix to perform the autopsy – to remember not to go above his station and to just follow the orders given. The young crossbowman looked confused and a little hurt, but had nodded and rushed off, taking two other guards with him to create the fire.

Fal then raced back to the fourth floor to find Orix standing over another body with two other clerics.

'This one died from the same symptoms, Falchion,' Orix said, as Fal entered the room. 'I want all the bodies burnt. Word must be sent to the clerics and guards throughout Wesson that all recent cadavers and any from now on are to be burnt. Black crosses are to be put on the doors of buildings where people have died, as well as the homes of those people quarantined in the infirmaries. Then we must seek an audience with the King as soon as possible. But first, you and I must speak with Lord Severun.' Orix stepped down from his podium, hurried over to a font of water and scrubbed his hands. He then walked over to Fal and beckoned for him to follow as he left the clerics' chamber and stepped out into the hall.

'Guard,' Orix said, to the man stood on the archive vaults door.

'Yes Master Orix?' The guard was clearly surprised by the uncharacteristic tone of the small gnome.

'Go into the clerics' chamber and assist the two clerics there with whatever they need. Don't worry about the archives vault, the sergeant here will assign a replacement. Your new task is much more important for the time being.'

'Of course, Master Orix,' the guard said as he passed them to enter the clerics' chamber.

Fal was equally surprised by the gnome's sudden air of authority.

Everything's happening so fast and I don't like it. I'm placing a lot of trust in you, Orix, and I hope I'm doing the right thing. For all I know, you're burning the damned evidence.

'What's happening exactly?'

'The bodies must be burnt, Falchion, and I need your guard to assist my clerics in taking the bodies down to it.'

'With all due respect, Master Orix, I'd gathered that, but why?'

Orix smiled realising he wasn't dealing with the average guard. 'The fire and its extreme heat is the safest, quickest way of destroying the disease. Even after a body dies, the disease it was carrying can be transferred to fleas on the body that might then spread it on and on throughout Wesson. That's usually how the bubonic plague spreads, by fleas, from human to animal and animal to human, and so on. By burning the bodies we reduce the risk, however it doesn't stop the spread, what with infected people coming into contact with one another throughout the city.'

Fal's stomach turned as he realised how fast the disease could spread, potentially out of the city.

I caused this... I smashed the bottle and I caused it, all by not asking what the hell it was I was doing; trying to be the good soldier as ever. I can't wash my hands of it because I didn't know. I should've made it my damn business to know. Gods below, enough have died already haven't they? And how many more before this thing is over... the way he's talking... the whole city, or even the whole kingdom. Gods above and below, if any of you bastards exist, help us now, I beg you!

'Can we cure it?' Fal dreaded the response.

'Yes and no. Through magic and potion we can perhaps cure or vaccinate a small number, maybe, but it will take time, which is something we do not have. Even if we were to come up with something right now... Curing or vaccinating Wesson as a whole? We cannot. A plague usually dies out, Falchion, although it takes huge numbers of people with it. I don't know how we can stop that from happening. Let's not think of that now. We need to stop it spreading, that's our main concern, but first we must see Lord Severun. We three need to talk about all of this. He needs to know what is happening throughout the city. Then we need to see the King and urge him to close the city gates and blockade the port.'

'Is it not wiser to have the city closed now, to leave Severun until after that?'

Orix shook his head. 'No, we need Severun with us on this if we are to go to the King. He is our Grand Master and the King will heed his warning. Of mine he may be sceptical.'

'Very well, Master Orix. Will Severun be in his chamber?'

'We can only hope so, Falchion.' Without another word, Orix rushed down the corridor to the stairs and Fal followed. They climbed to the top floor of the tower, crossed the waiting chamber and hammered on Severun's thick chamber door.

'Coming, coming,' Severun called from the far side of the door. Almost as soon as he'd spoken the words, the door opened. 'What's all the banging about Master Orix? Sergeant Falchion?' Severun sounded shocked, if not suspicious as he addressed the sergeant-at-arms.

'He knows,' Orix said as he pushed past Severun and entered the large room, 'but that isn't why we are here. We have a problem, Lord Severun.'

Severun's face dropped and for once he looked speechless.

'Lord Severun.' Fal bowed as he greeted the wizard. Severun nodded back and motioned for Fal to enter the room, noticing Fal's hand on the hilt of his sword. Fal passed Severun and crossed the room to stand beside Orix on the near side of the wizard's large desk.

'A problem, you say?' Severun's voice sounded shaky.

'A very serious problem, yes,' Orix said.

'With the experiment I take it?' Severun walked over to his desk and took a seat behind it, his eyes flicking nervously between Orix and Fal. 'Please, sit down, both of you.'

Orix climbed up into one of the two seats on his side of the desk and Fal remained standing. Severun didn't miss the implications of that.

'I'm afraid Wesson is in great danger, my Lord.' It was Fal who spoke this time, his voice strong and commanding as he addressed his superior. 'I think you should listen very carefully to what Master Orix has to say. Many, many lives depend on our actions at this point.'

Severun looked from Orix, to Fal and back. 'Please Master Orix... go on.'

'I have performed two autopsies today and have made a terrible discovery. I am ashamed to say, Lord Severun, that my potion, working along with your spell, has been concealing a true disease.'

Severun looked confused. 'Well isn't that the point?'

Orix shook his head. 'Not exactly no. I have told you before, the symptoms I created were to mask the death of the subjects. The potion itself caused their death... or so I thought, and the surface symptoms created a fake illness so people had a visible cause of death. Unfortunately, the potion has also been masking a deadly disease, the symptoms of which are very similar, although not entirely the same, as my potion.'

'I see no problem there Master Orix. As long as these criminals die and we rid ourselves of them, I don't see what difference it makes whether it's your potion or another disease doing the job?' Severun seemed to relax at this and sat back in his chair.

'You misunderstand, Lord Severun. This disease isn't restricted to the subjects. The numbers… there's too many. I can't believe they're all our subjects.'

Severun again leaned forward in his chair, his mouth slightly open and his face draining of colour.

'Do you know what this other disease is, Master Orix?' he asked eventually, although he looked like he didn't want to know the answer.

Orix looked up at Fal and then back to Severun. 'I'm afraid, Lord Severun, we have an outbreak of bubonic plague.'

Severun's mouth fell fully open as the words left Orix's mouth. He looked to Fal who nodded his confirmation.

'No, surely not. Are you sure of this? Are you certain Master Orix?'

Orix nodded. 'Without doubt, Lord Severun, and we must seek an audience with the King immediately. The city must be quarantined, the bodies burnt and vaccines produced for the royal family and nobles of Wesson if possible… for starters.'

Although staring directly at Orix, Severun seemed to be looking through the gnome.

Fal thought they were wasting time and so decided to speed things up. 'Lord Severun, we must act now. The city is in danger, the very city you were trying to protect and make a better place.'

No answer.

'Severun!' Fal shouted, and the wizard looked at him, his head bobbing slightly in a half-hearted attempt at a nod.

'Very well… very well…' he said eventually, 'we must face the King, explain all and help Wesson.' Severun looked unsteady as he rose from his seat.

'I know you were trying to help,' Fal said, 'that this was an experiment meant for good, my lord. I will explain that to the King. He'll understand. Our first priority, however, is Wesson and its people.' Fal turned and walked towards the chamber door, stopping when he reached it to turn and face the two mages. Orix climbed down from the seat and was following him across the chamber when an ear-splitting crack erupted from behind Severun's large desk. After the initial shock, both Fal and Orix looked to where the wizard had been standing, to see nothing but a hazy cloud, much like steam from a pot.

'Falchion,' Orix shouted, 'close the door!'

Fal obeyed immediately and swung the heavy door shut.

A muffled cry came from the door as it stopped halfway and bounced back. More steamy gas appeared by Fal's feet as Severun slowly materialised, lying crumpled in his purple robes on the stone floor. Fal reached down and grabbed the wizard by the throat, using his other hand to wrench Severun's right arm behind his back.

'Lord Severun, have you lost your mind?' Orix shouted. As he ran over to the two men, he continued his tirade, 'What were you thinking? Wesson is in need, it is partly if not wholly our fault and you try and run, to save your own neck. You coward, sir!'

Fal hauled Severun to his feet and held his throat and arm firm, thus breaking any concentration the wizard might need to cast another spell.

'I'm... I'm sorry... I'm scared... Orix... the Grand Inquisitor will... demand we burn for this.' Severun gasped for air as he tried to speak. Fal wasn't going to risk letting him go though.

'The Samorlian Church has no real authority any more, Lord Severun, you know that,' Orix said, his voice lowering and his eyes softening as his realisation of Severun's fears swept over him.

'But arcane magic... I have been so... so foolish.' Severun's eyes began to fill with tears. Fal felt for the wizard but maintained his hold.

'Arcane magic?' Orix said, taken aback. He shook his head then, knowing it wasn't the place or time to be thinking on that. 'Please Lord Severun, let Falchion release you. Give us your word you will not run. We need to inform the King, give him and his advisers all the information we can on what we have been doing. If we work together we may be able to help reduce the deaths caused by the plague, which can only help our cause with the King. We meant to do only good, he will see that, I am sure of it.'

Severun nodded slowly against Fal's grip. 'I give... you my word, sergeant... I will not... try anything again... I swear it.'

'I will hold you to that, my lord, I give you my word on that.' Fal slowly released Severun, but placed one hand on his falchion's hilt again and kept a close eye on the wizard for any sudden movements or silent mouthing of spells. Most sorcerers or magicians couldn't enact magic without verbal spells or magical items, but a wizard, especially a powerful one like Severun, could and that scared Fal. He had no choice, however, but to accept Severun's word.

Orix breathed a sigh of relief and Severun rubbed his throat and stretched the arm Fal had held back. 'I'm truly sorry, gentlemen. I panicked, truly I did.'

'Make it up to us with your actions from now on, my lord,' Fal said.

'Oh I will sergeant, I promise you,' the wizard said, his eyes darting for the briefest of moments to the chest by the window on the far side of the room, a look neither Fal nor Orix noticed.

'On we go then,' Orix said. 'After you Lord Severun. Falchion, you next, and off to the palace we go.'

The three companions descended through the tower, stopping here and there to pass on messages to clerics and orders to guards regarding the plague and what needed to be done. Messengers were sent to the infirmaries and extra guards were placed on Tyndurris' gates in case of attacks once the news got out. Mages were targeted throughout history for strange events, the ignorant always assuming disasters were brought on by gods or magic. Of course centuries of Samorlian preaching hadn't helped quell those theories. This time around, however, there was indeed some truth in those claims.

When they reached the courtyard, there was already an acrid smell of burnt flesh coming from the back of the tower, followed by thick black smoke. Godsiff Starks came running around from the back to see Fal, his eyes narrowing in suspicion as he saw the way Fal was watching the Grand Master of the guild.

'Sergeant Falchion, the bodies are on the fire. What now?' Starks' eyes hardly left Lord Severun.

'Thanks, Starks. Bring a coach and driver from the stable and one other guard, ask him to run a message to my house telling my two friends there to meet me at the palace. You shall accompany us there on the coach, riding crossbow.'

Starks nodded 'Yes, sergeant.' He ran off back the way he'd come.

'We will be on the move again when the coach arrives, my lords, and then I hope you can both persuade the King's men that we need an audience with him immediately.'

'Absolutely, sergeant,' Severun said, whilst rubbing his throat some more. 'Oh and thank you.'

Fal and Orix looked at each other before Fal answered, 'For what, my lord?'

'For stopping me at the door; should I have been left to flee in my panicked state, things would have become a whole lot worse for me as well as for the city, I am sure. I don't know what came over me and I apologise to you both sincerely.' Severun looked at both Fal and Orix and smiled. The smile was genuine; Fal could see it in the wizard's eyes.

'Then you are welcome, my lord. It was my pleasure, trapping you in the door and holding you there.' Fal's stern look broke slightly and the side of his mouth curled upwards into the slightest smile. All three allowed themselves a laugh, welcoming the brief respite.

A black glossed coach rumbled around the corner, Casson Bevins at the reins, with Starks sat next to him, his crossbow loaded and held aloft.

Fal smiled. *Casson, excellent. We need the news of what's happening to spread fast, and he's the perfect man for the job.*

'My lords. Sergeant,' Casson greeted, clearly intrigued as to what was going on as his eyes played over the three men. All three nodded to the driver and Fal opened the cab door, his hand held up to stop Casson climbing down from his seat.

'Master Bevins, to the palace. Ride swift and don't stop for anyone, that's an order,' Fal said. *That'll intrigue him all the more.* 'Starks, keep your eyes peeled for anyone looking to stop the coach and don't think twice about putting a bolt through them, understood?' Starks nodded, his jaw clenched with determination.

Fal quickly climbed into the cab. The coach lurched forward and through the opening gates, turning left onto the cobbled street heading towards Kings Avenue and on towards the palace.

***

Exley Clewarth had just finished explaining all he'd heard whilst above Fal's home, to the Grand Inquisitor, who sat behind his ancient desk like an overly-fed tavern landlord. Horler Comlay had tried to interrupt several times, just to be silenced by the Grand Inquisitor, who'd held his hand aloft, wanting to hear every detail of what Exley had to say.

Horler was furious, but didn't dare undermine the other Witchunter General in front of their master, especially when he seemed to be currently held in such high regards due to his findings.

After Exley's explanation of what he'd heard Fal and Errolas talking about, including the names of those responsible for the arcane magic – Lord Severun and Master Orix, much to the Grand Inquisitor's glee – the large man had only one thing to say, and he said it with a venomous tone, almost salivating at the victory he could now foresee.

'Let them burn!'

Both Witchunter Generals smiled.

Pleased with his findings, Exley Clewarth bent and kissed the hand of the Grand Inquisitor, before turning to leave. Horler Comlay, however, did not.

'You have more to add, General Comlay?'

Exley Clewarth clenched his teeth and gripped the hilt of his rapier. He knew Horler Comlay well enough to know the man would always try to upstage him in any way he could. Turning back to face the Grand Inquisitor, Exley hid his frustration well, and calmly awaited what his counterpart had to say.

'That I do, sire, although I fear it is not good news.'

Oh, perhaps this is worth hearing after all, Exley thought, a smile almost revealing itself.

'Continue, General Comlay,' the Grand Inquisitor said.

'One of my witchunters has been tracking two city guardsmen in Park District, who seem to be investigating the deaths of the merchant and his agent – the latter at my hand, as you well know, sire.'

The Grand Inquisitor's nostrils flared as his fat hands curled into tight fists. He paused for a moment before replying. 'You assured me your man in the City Guard had assigned *no one* to investigate those murders, General Comlay?'

Horler nodded. 'Aye, sire, that's true. However, the two mentioned aren't just any guardsmen, the two in question are...'

'Go on,' Exley said, enjoying Horler's discomfort.

Looking sideways at Exley with murderous intent, Horler Comlay continued. 'They're not your usual guardsmen, sire. They're never assigned duties, but choose their own, it seems. The witchunter who has been following them has made enquiries and it seems Captain Prior leaves them to their own devices.'

The Grand Inquisitor looked confused as he spoke. 'Why would he do that?'

'Because, sire, of their results.' Horler shifted uncomfortably. 'They choose their investigations themselves and they always solve the cases they choose.'

The Grand Inquisitor was growing visibly angrier and Exley Clewarth found it harder to hide his amusement and delight at his counterpart's plight.

'So you are telling me, General Comlay, the City Guard's two finest detectives are on the case of a murder you had a hand in, which is also linked to the dark deeds we are working towards thwarting without the City Guard's knowledge?'

'I wouldn't call them the finest, nor detectives—'

The Grand Inquisitor stood swiftly – for him at least – and slammed his meaty fists on the desk before shouting, 'And what *would* you call them then, Horler?'

Despite Horler's authoritative fear of the Grand Inquisitor, Exley could tell that, for the briefest of moments, the fat man standing opposite Horler had come as close as he'd ever come to death. Great restraint held Horler firm however, and he answered the question through gritted teeth.

'On all accounts provided to me, *sire*, they're nothing but damned and unbelievably lucky.'

Seeing the Witchunter General's anger barely hidden, the Grand Inquisitor, far from a brave man, took his seat once more. Dabbing his sweated brow with an embroidered handkerchief, he gave his final words on the matter. He wanted to correct the General, tell him there was no such thing as luck, that Sir Samorl had a plan for everything and he should know better, but since General Comlay was on the edge of violence as it was... and since he didn't fully believe his own dogma anyway, he let it go.

'Have someone deal with them, General Comlay, and make it happen before their *luck* leads them to you and *our* investigation.'

Horler Comlay simply nodded and left the room, leaving the offered hand of the Grand Inquisitor hovering.

Cursing *his* luck, Exley Clewarth crossed the room and kissed the bejewelled hand for a second time, before turning and following Horler from the room.

Chapter 14: Kings Avenue

From a narrow side street, a black carriage with the heraldry of the Wizards and Sorcery Guild clattered noisily across the dapple-shaded cobbles and out onto Kings Avenue. The black-cloaked driver cracked his whip and the young crossbowman next to him almost fell backwards as the coach accelerated. People stopped and pointed as the coach raced by at an unusually high speed compared to the other coaches and carts trundling along. One pedestrian cursed loudly as he jumped out of the way, whilst another shook his fist and shouted abuse at the driver.

The driver was following orders not to stop for anyone, although he didn't know why. He knew enough about his masters, however, to know they wouldn't give him such an order without good reason. He cracked his whip again and the two bay mares – muscles working harder than they were used to – surged on into a canter, striding towards the looming towers of the palace as their metal-shod hooves struck stone, echoing off the tall buildings to either side.

The driver's heart pounded as he steered the two beasts, his mind racing as he wondered why Starks, the lad next to him, had been placed as crossbow rider on a through-city route. Something was afoot, he was sure, what with the sickly smell of burning flesh filling Tyndurris' courtyard before the coach had embarked on its mad dash through Wesson.

Alas, before he could think anything else about the strange situation, Casson Bevins' fast beating heart stopped dead as a crossbow bolt thudded through his black cloak, his linen shirt and his chest, to silence the beating muscle inside.

Casson's body slumped to the side and he fell from the coach, his clenched fists taking the reins and whip with him. The horses swerved violently to the left and the two mares ploughed through an elderly couple walking down the path, their bodies causing the coach to buck wildly as it bounced over them.

The coach's front left corner, where Casson Bevins had been sitting, collided with one of the large oaks lining the avenue. Wood splintered and an almighty crash turned all heads in the vicinity towards the scene of destruction. Servants and residents rushed to their windows as the black coach crumpled into the ancient tree before flipping over onto its right hand side.

Starks was thrown clear of the wreckage as the coach flipped, and the two bay mares broke free of their harness, breaking into a wild gallop up the footpath and on towards the palace. People cried out and dived to all sides trying to avoid the large beasts. One man was knocked back and trampled under hoof as he failed to move out of the way in time. Others shouted at the sight and ran to the man's aid, whilst more people ran towards the couple who'd been ridden down before the coach had struck the tree.

They soon turned and fled however, as men in black cloaks ran from the nearest side street and more climbed from the doors of another coach opposite the wreck. They carried a mixture of crossbows and rapiers, with one man carrying both, his crossbow small and obviously intended for one handed use.

A young man still made his way towards the couple who'd been ridden down, despite the arrival of the men with weapons drawn. He refused to run away and leave the elderly couple who he hoped may still be alive. He was rewarded with a small bolt from the handheld crossbow which thumped into his back. The man stumbled and fell to his knees. He swayed briefly before slumping forward onto the mangled mess of the already dead man and wife.

Starks rolled around onto his back. One of his legs felt strange and his vision was blurred in one eye; the red blur and the dampness on his scalp indicated he'd cut his head badly. He looked around at the smashed coach on its side, shaking his thumping head at the destruction caused. Looking around further, Starks saw the men in black cloaks, their weapons drawn. He crawled desperately for his crossbow lying a couple of feet away. He prayed – although he'd never believed himself a religious man – his crossbow was undamaged.

His silent prayers were answered and the bow was remarkably still drawn, yet the bolt had flown from the loading groove. He quickly drew another from the pouch on his belt, fitted it to the crossbow and lifted the weapon, pointing it roughly towards the nearest figure, who was approaching him at speed.

Without consciously aiming, Starks squeezed the trigger underneath the crossbow and the weapon released the bolt with a crack. The white feathered bolt whipped out and plunged into the oncoming man's stomach. The black-clad man was propelled backwards, his rapier flying from his hand as he hit the ground hard. He let out a horrific cry, before rolling onto his side and curling up where, if unattended, he would die a slow and painful death.

Someone shouted and Starks noticed another man, dressed in black, point his way. He too had a rapier drawn, but the man he was shouting to held a crossbow similar to Starks' own.

Both Starks and the other crossbowman started to span their unloaded bows, ready to place bolts into the arming grooves. Starks panicked. His hands shook and he now saw the man who'd shouted the order to kill him running his way, rapier held at the ready. Starks managed to span the bow and fumble into place another bolt, just in time to release it with another *crack* into his nearest attacker's throat. The man gurgled for breath as he hit the cobbled floor hard. Starks rolled sideways in a rushed defensive manoeuvre, waiting for the dull thump of the iron tipped bolt surely speeding towards him.

A scream dared Starks to look back; his opponent with the crossbow had dropped to one knee, a long, white feathered arrow protruding from his back. The man tried to reach around, to grab at it, dropping his weapon as he did so, but it was wedged solidly between his shoulder blades. A few more grasps

89

at the long shaft and then he collapsed face down; crimson rivulets slowly spread out between the cobbles.

About a dozen men in black remained, including the downed and groaning man with Starks' bolt in his stomach. There was no one other than them in the immediate area now, as most of the people who would have been helping the coach had fled – all but a couple of onlookers who'd been shot by the attackers.

All of the men, bar two, looked around for whoever had shot Starks' opponent, forgetting Starks in the process. Starks took the opportunity to crawl painfully back to the crossbow he'd rolled away from as fast as his leg and dizzy, throbbing head would allow. The two men who weren't looking for the mystery archer rushed for the coach. They didn't try to get inside once there, but crouched to strike flint on steel. One of them was successful and lit a cloth-wrapped stick, which he proceeded to drag across the side of the splintered coach, attempting to set the cab on fire. As he did so, another long, white feathered arrow thudded this time into the torch wielder's head. Starks saw the arrow tip appear suddenly through the front of the man's face as he slumped against the coach, the torch dropping to the floor. As of yet, the coach hadn't caught light, but the torch still burnt on the floor and was lying by one of the large wooden wheels.

The second man at the coach dived for the torch whilst the others still shouted and ran around trying to find the hidden archer. Starks managed to reach his crossbow again and successfully spanned it. Placing another bolt on the loading groove, he lifted the weapon and aimed it as best he could with his impaired vision, at the man who grasped for the torch. He squeezed the trigger. As his crossbow *cracked* and the bolt launched from the groove, another long, white feathered arrow struck Starks' target, his own bolt hitting the torch wielding man just after the longer arrow. The man spun with the dual impacts before slumping dead over his companion, with both long arrow and short bolt piercing his side.

The attackers started to panic now as two more white feathered arrows killed another two of their number.

Two archers. There must be two archers. Starks knew archers were faster at loosing arrows than crossbowmen, but no one could strike two separate targets as fast as he'd just witnessed.

Fresh shouting, this time from down the avenue, drew Starks' attention. He saw two city guardsmen running towards the scene. *About time too,* Starks thought, as his leg began to throb in time with his head. He expected the unknown attackers to flee now, especially as another dropped with an arrow embedded in his face, but he was wrong. Two more men attempted to reach the coach and the flaming torch. They were determined, he gave them that.

The tallest man, wielding both a handheld crossbow and a rapier, managed to reach the coach. He sheathed his rapier swiftly and picked up the torch. His companion, just two strides behind him, took two arrows to the back. Whoever the archers were, they were good; very good. The tall man threw the torch into the window of the cab facing the sky, turned with his cloak spinning out behind him – which inadvertently caught another arrow in its folds – and ran for the coach on the opposite side of the street. That was the first arrow Starks had seen miss. The rest of the men fled for the coach as the city guardsmen – two of them – reached the wreckage.

'There's people inside the coach and a lit torch. Hurry!' Starks shouted.

One of the guardsmen climbed up on top of the coach, but as soon as he reached for the door handle, a crossbow bolt struck him in his leg. He fell off the coach backwards as he let out a cry.

The bolt had come from the coach on the far side of the avenue just before it pulled away, the driver clearly armoured under his heavy black cloak as a long shafted arrow glanced off his shoulder. He cracked his whip repeatedly and the coach charged off down the avenue, away from the palace. Two more white feathered arrows struck the coach as it left, but neither managed to penetrate the rear of the wooden cab.

Starks looked back to the coach wreck, where the second guardsman was attempting to open the door after climbing on top. He pulled away from the door's window as flames suddenly licked out at him.

Starks and the guardsman on the coach both gasped in fear for those inside.

As soon as the guardsman pulled back and Starks saw the flames, a loud *whoosh* erupted from the coach as a jet of water shot like a geyser from the door, extinguishing the flames within. The guardsman fell backward and only just managed to stay on top of the coach before regaining his balance and reaching for the open door. The water stopped as suddenly as it started and began to fall back to the ground as a light rain.

Someone else shouted then and Starks immediately recognised the name being called.

'Fal… Falchion?' An archer approached from across the avenue, yew bow in hand and a scout quiver of long, white feathered arrows on his back. Close behind him ran another tall figure carrying a re-curve bow and a similar quiver to the first man's, also holding long shafted, white feathered arrows.

Starks realised the second archer was an elf. The guardsman on top of the coach reached down into the cab and lifted out a small bearded gnome in sodden robes.

Master Orix. Starks sighed with relief.

Orix was passed down to the tall human archer who Starks now recognised as Sav, a border scout and a known friend of Fal's. Orix had a bright red face and seemed to be cursing and muttering under his breath. Sav climbed up on top of the coach and helped the guardsman lift out a similarly soaked Severun and Fal.

Fal quickly looked around and pointed to Starks as soon as he saw him. He said something to the elf by his side, who immediately ran over and knelt by the injured crossbowman.

'Are you hurt?' The elf's voice was soft and pleasant.

Starks shook his head, his mouth slightly open. He'd seen half-elves before, but although they occasionally venture into Wesson, he'd never seen a true elf.

'I'll take that as a no.' Errolas smiled as he moved to lift Starks to his feet.

'No, no, no, no, no,' Starks said quickly. 'My leg, sire, I think it's broken.' Starks patted his leg and immediately wished he hadn't. The adrenaline had clearly left his system.

'Just stay still and we will sort you out as soon as possible.' Errolas held out a hand to stay the young man. 'You did well today, I'd like to see you shoot when not blinded by blood and crawling about with a broken leg.' Errolas smiled again, stood and ran back over to the group at the coach.

Starks couldn't help but grin to himself despite the pain. He'd impressed an elf and was already thinking about how best to tell the story at his local tavern.

'Is everyone alright?' Fal looked around at the chaotic scene. 'How's Starks... the crossbowman?' he asked Errolas, as the ranger came running back to them.

'He has a broken leg and taken a bad knock to the head, but he should be fine. He saved your lives, you know? We would have been too late if he hadn't acted so swiftly.'

'I'll be sure to remember that, and thanks to you two, too.' Fal clasped both Errolas and Sav by the shoulders. 'I notice both your arrows around here.'

'We arrived at Tyndurris just after you left,' Errolas said. 'A guard on the gate told us where you had gone and so we made chase as fast as we could.'

Before he could reply, Sav dragged Fal to one side and swiftly explained what had happened that morning and who Errolas believed the attackers were. Lord Severun and Master Orix stood silently as they tried to listen in, but Sav managed to tell the story quickly and quietly, keeping out of their earshot as he had no idea what their involvement was.

Glancing between Sav and the two mages, Fal again started to look around the avenue, half expecting the witchunters to return. 'Guardsman,' he said. 'Stop a coach. We'll lift your partner and Starks into it and have the driver take them back to Tyndurris.'

'Yes, sergeant,' the guardsman said, before running down the avenue to flag down a coach that had stopped for the passengers to stare at the strange scene.

'What about us, are we continuing on foot?' Severun asked.

Fal thought for a second before answering. 'Yes, I don't fancy another coach ride. The palace isn't far now and our archers here can cover us as we go. Do you both feel up to running?' Fal asked Severun and Orix.

'It doesn't look like we have a choice,' Orix said. 'I can't run as fast as you though, long shanks.'

Severun just nodded.

'Alright,' Fal said, 'we'll head up now. Let's put Starks and the other guardsman into that coach first.'

Fal, Sav and Errolas lifted the wounded guardsman into the commandeered coach whilst Orix inspected Starks' leg. 'Now it may hurt when they lift you, but the clerics at the guild will have you fit in no time.' The old gnome held his right hand over the broken leg. 'It's a clean break, they will have no problem with it, but I have nothing with me to help you right now.'

'That's alright, Master Orix, I'll be fine.' Starks, fresh blood streaked across half of his face and matted in his hair, winced as the pain increased.

'Oh and Godsiff,' Orix said, standing whilst Fal and the others came over with the coach to load Starks into it.

'Yes, Master Orix?' Starks managed, through gritted teeth.

'Thank you. The elf said you saved our lives. We won't forget it, even if it is your job.' With a wink, Orix turned and headed over to Lord Severun.

Starks smiled to himself and then grimaced again as Sav and Fal lifted him into the coach.

'Good work, lad,' Fal offered, as Starks settled onto the floor of the coach besides the injured guardsman. 'That was some fine shooting, I hear. I owe you a drink, or several.'

Starks laughed as he replied. 'I'll hold you to that, Sarge, I have witnesses. Now get to the palace and do whatever's so gods-damned important you had to get my leg broken.'

Fal laughed back. 'What have I told you about getting above your station, soldier?'

'Alright driver, get these two to Tyndurris and make haste.'

The driver nodded and Fal closed the cab door, whilst the other guardsman climbed up next to the driver, holding on to Starks' crossbow. The coach rocked and turned in the wide avenue, heading back the way it had come, towards Tyndurris.

'Let's get moving shall we? It's not wise to hang around,' Fal said, as soon as the coach had set off.

'What about these people?' Orix motioned to the injured people scattered about the avenue.

'There'll be guardsmen and clerics along shortly no doubt,' Fal said, 'and the horses aren't here. They must've carried on down towards the palace where they would've been seen, so they'll have sent a patrol this way.'

'Well, let's move then,' Sav said, 'the faster we get into the safety of the palace the happier I'll be.' His eyes flicked from the rooftops to the side streets.

Errolas mirrored the scout's actions and nodded his agreement.

'Lord Severun, Master Orix, follow me. Errolas, Sav, keep your eyes peeled and I'll explain what's happening when we get to the palace.'

'Understood,' Sav said, before setting off at a dog trot behind the rest of the group, with Errolas at the front and the remaining three in the middle.

As they made their way down the road, people began shouting; asking what had happened and if all was well. Fal and the others tried to reassure people as best they could, and asked them to stay clear of the wreckage behind them so the guardsmen and clerics could do their jobs.

A troop of six palace guards met the group about halfway to the palace, so Fal stopped briefly to report to them, much to the relief of Orix who was quite out of breath.

Fal explained the situation, informed the guards of the casualties and asked two of their number to escort them back to the palace. The troop sergeant-at-arms agreed and sent two swordsmen to escort the group.

It didn't take long from where they met the patrol before they arrived at the palace. Two giant wooden gates housed in a huge stone gatehouse and flanked by thirty foot curtain walls barred their way.

A small door opened within one of the gates and the two palace guards led the group in.

Every member of the group let out a sigh of relief as they entered the palace courtyard. That relief faltered as a second group of a dozen men-at-arms met them with weapons drawn.

The group stood at sword point as a troop sergeant-at-arms informed them the King wished to see them immediately. They were ordered to disarm, which Errolas and Sav argued about briefly before giving in to the hard-faced men. They were then escorted into a drum tower a short walk from the gatehouse, where they were led up a curling stone staircase in single file and through a long, narrow passageway with no windows, arrow slits or décor to brighten the cold stone walls. Fal imagined they must be in the fortifications around the palace itself and heading towards an audience chamber.

He was right. After several minutes travelling through similar corridors, they reached a set of heavy wooden doors. Two King's halberdiers in polished plate and sallet helms stood either side. As the group reached the two guards, one of them turned and hammered on a large iron ring. The heavy thudding resonated through the stone corridor and the heads of everyone in the group.

The doors opened from within and a gruff voice called out.

'Escort them in.'

***

As the velvet dressed, voluptuous woman walked past two city guardsmen, she could have sworn she heard one of them call her a dog. She shook her head slightly, reassuring herself she'd misheard the wiry man, who seemed to be too intent on scratching vigorously at his maille covered neck to have commented on her.

'She looks alright to me,' Sears said, as the woman moved down the street away from them both.

'Eh?'

'Her,' the big man said, pointing to the woman, 'she ain't no dog.'

'Never said she was, ye buffoon.' Biviano switched to his other hand for scratching.

'Aye, ye did, I heard ye and pretty sure she did too. Anyhow, where ye getting buffoon from, doesn't suit ye?' Sears said, finally taking his eyes off the woman's swaying hips.

'Doesn't need to suit me does it? I was calling you a buffoon, not me, but enough of that. I was talking about a dog.'

'See, I knew it!'

'A dog, ye know woof-woof. Wasn't on about the woman, ye buffoon.'

'Ye're milking it now. Wasn't funny the first time ye used it, now ye're just milking it, and what ye harpin' on about a dog for anyhow?'

Biviano started walking down the street again, Sears hot on his heels.

'Well?' Sears said, when no response came.

'I'm thinking, Sears, stop interrupting it.'

'And here I thought I could smell burning.'

'Funny.'

'Thanks. Now come on, what dog ye talking about?'

'A hound to trace the killers from the house and street.'

Sears laughed heartily and slapped Biviano on the same shoulder he always did.

'Dick! Quit doing that will ye? I ain't talking no normal hound, I'm talking about Buddle.'

Sears laughter stopped. 'Ye mean Gitsham's mutt? Are ye crazy? We don't need to be bringing him in on this case, it ain't that big.'

'How'd ye bloody know, Sears?' Biviano stopped dead in his tracks, causing Sears to bump into him. He shoved the big man off him, who looked like he'd flatten Biviano, so the smaller of the two took a step back before continuing. 'Listen big guy, there's been two connected murders; one a stabbing, plain and simple, but one we've no clue as to how it happened, and I for one don't like that at all. Could be magic for all we know and ye know? I know! I feel it in me bones. So I reckons Gitsham and his hound is what we need for this, before the case escapes us completely.'

Sears sighed and nodded. 'Ye're right of course, I can't help but think there's something a lot bigger going on here. So aye, I agree with ye for once. Let's go see Gitsham and—'

Sears practically threw Biviano off his feet and to the ground before he finished his sentence, and a small black bolt thudded into the big man's right pectoral muscle.

Seeing his partner stagger back a step from the impact, Biviano quickly looked opposite Sears and saw a man in drab, black clothes re-loading a small crossbow.

Surging to his feet and drawing his short-sword and cudgel in one, Biviano sprinted towards the man as the crossbow came up, pointing towards him. Before the man could pull the trigger however, a wooden cudgel struck him between the eyes and he fell back, Biviano reaching him as he hit the ground.

A rapier swung out horizontally from the alley next to Biviano then and he threw himself to the right, narrowly avoiding losing his throat. Before he could stand, the cloaked figure was upon him, repeatedly slashing down with his rapier as Biviano struggled to block the attacks.

Where are ye Sears?

As if on cue, the witchunter – for surely that's what he was – dropped to both knees, crying out and swinging his rapier round behind him, trying to strike something unseen by Biviano, who took the opportunity to thrust his short-sword up into the man's ribs.

Coughing blood, the witchunter fell forward as Biviano rolled out of the way, pulling his sword free to see a small crossbow bolt embedded in the witchunter's back.

Sears stood over the witchunter, a grin splitting his red beard and blood oozing from a hole in his padded, maille covered chest.

'Stuck 'im wi' his mate's bolt, ha!' Sears slurred, before staggering and dropping to one knee.

Biviano jumped up and scanned the area, before looking to the unconscious crossbowman to make sure he was no longer a threat. Biviano rushed to Sears then, and hauled him to his feet with a grunt.

Everyone in the area had fled the scene and Biviano saw no movement from anywhere, so he pulled at Sears, struggling under the big man's weight.

'Come on… big'un, we need to be moving, and quick.'

'Aye,' Sears said, clearly slipping in and out of consciousness.

Biviano reached round the back of Sears' belt and fumbled in a pouch tied there, where he found a small flask of something potent. What it was, he had no idea, but he knew how strong it was from previous experience and so popped the tiny cork with his teeth and held it under Sears' nose.

The big man's eyes opened wide and he grinned, before coughing.

'Drink up, we need to move I'm telling ye,' Biviano said, holding up the small flask.

Sears let Biviano pour the viscous liquid into his mouth and he swallowed it in one, immediately staggering before straightening up, the sudden weight off Biviano's shoulder a huge relief.

'Alright ye big prick, let's get moving shall we. Need to get us to the wall and fast.'

Nodding, Sears stumbled into a run in the general direction of the city wall and its barracks.

Damn, Sears, that wound's not good. Biviano ran to the unconscious crossbowman to pick up his cudgel. Before he followed Sears, he thrust his short-sword into the man's chest and then ran to catch his friend up.

This ain't right and I knew it. Well flay me, but I'm swearing on all the gods above and below that we'll find the bastards that caused all this and when I'm through with 'em, they'll wish they'd never started whatever it is they've started.

Chapter 15: Marble and Gold

The room was dark as pitch. It felt like Fal's eyes were closed tight, although he knew they weren't. He'd felt a draft as the halberdiers opened the door and ushered him and the rest of the group inside, indicating a large space beyond. As soon as he'd turned to walk through the opening, his vision had gone. They now stood at one end of a large hall; Fal could *feel* a large open space, and although it didn't make sense to him, he felt crushed by that unseen void.

Gods, my eyes… is it just me? Fal thought, and then he jumped as a familiar voice whispered just behind him.

'A simple shrouding spell,' Severun explained. 'It shrouds the immediate area in darkness, but allows the caster and anyone else outside the shroud to see within. We are being observed by the King and his advisers.'

No one responded. The realisation the King was watching them stole any thoughts from their minds. They stood, motionless in the dark, awaiting the sound of their ruler's voice.

'It is quite a strong shroud, but not unbreakable,' the wizard continued. 'In fact, I imagine it has been cast by one of my own magicians, Ward Strickland, a highly respected member of the guild, hence his position in the King's court.' Severun's voice was growing slightly louder and he received a short sharp prod at waist height encouraging him to keep quiet.

'Lord Severun,' an amplified voice boomed from ahead of the group. It echoed off what could only be a high ceiling.

'Yes, Lord Strickland, it is I, as you can very well see. Greetings to you, and to you Your Highness.' Although none of Severun's companions could see it, he bowed deeply as he greeted Ward Strickland and the King. 'Bow,' he said under his breath, just loud enough for the others to hear. They obeyed, albeit awkwardly.

It was Ward Strickland, the magician and advisor to the King who addressed the group once again. 'I apologise for the shroud I have cast, my lord Severun, but it has been requested due to certain allegations brought to the King's attention. It is… as you well know, a matter of precaution and in no way meant as an insult to you or your companions.'

'Of course, we understand the necessary precautions,' Severun said. 'But I wish to declare we mean no harm and have indeed travelled to the palace to seek an audience with His Royal Highness regarding, I can only conclude, the same situation that has already been brought to his attention. I beg, however, that you first declare the allegations and allow us to present our defence.' Severun spoke humbly and bowed again, not wishing to seem arrogant in front of, not so much the King, whom he knew fairly well, but those surely present who held the King's ear.

'Lord Severun,' – there was a slight intake of breath from more than one person in the group as they recognised the strong, commanding voice of King Barrison – 'the allegations brought to my council are extremely severe. I *do* wish to hear your defence, but I am being urged to hear it whilst you are under the shroud created by Lord Strickland. This is the usual defensive measure I am advised to take when addressing potentially dangerous individuals or enemies, yet I do not,' the King seemed to direct the last to someone by his side, 'believe this necessary for the Grand Master of a royally aligned guild, especially one whom I have dealt with for many years. Lord Severun served my father faithfully, I remember as much from my youth, and I will not permit any more of this nonsense in my court. Lord Strickland, end the shroud immediately, this has gone far enough.' King Barrison had sounded strong yet cautious at first, now he just sounded certain.

'Sire, I must protest.' Neither Lord Severun nor any of the group recognised the third voice, even when the speaker continued. 'We have proof Lord Severun has enacted arcane magic, therefore he must be treated—' The third voice stopped suddenly. Severun imagined the King raising his hand to silence the advisor who'd spoken last.

'Lord Strickland, the shroud if you please,' Barrison asked once again.

'Certainly, sire,' the magician said, before mumbling what to most people in the room sounded like nonsense.

Everyone in the group blinked repeatedly as their eyes attempted to adjust to the brightness of their surroundings. Fal's eyes watered as he rubbed at them with his fingers, trying to force the sensation of blindness away.

A great, oblong hall slowly fell into focus. The group stood at one end facing a raised platform of solid marble with wide marble steps leading up to it. King Barrison sat on an ornate, walnut throne with patterns of intricately inlaid silver and gold decorating the smooth surface of the dark wood. He sat with both hands on the throne's arms, leaning forward slightly so his eyes could focus on the party stood at the far end of the hall. Along with his plain cream tunic and royal-blue hose, Barrison wore a simple iron crown, not the bejewelled golden crown he paraded about in during festivals and special events. The robust looking crown was half obscured by thick, grey hair, and his closely cropped and equally grey beard dressed his lined yet distinguished face and eyes well.

Eyes, Fal noticed, despite the distance, that were blue like a clear winter sky… blue and kind. Barrison looked serious, commanding and almost fearsome, yet his eyes showed a kindness his face could not betray, and Fal was thankful for that considering his current situation.

Current situation… and what's that Fal, you fool? Bringing possible traitors to your King or handing yourself over to him after releasing a deadly plague… and if the latter, well, I'm glad I saw those compassionate eyes, for they may just be my saviour.

…Saviour? Do I even deserve to be saved? I'm still not sure of that myself.

The group continued to blink as they took in their surroundings. Both Severun and Orix had seen the chamber before, yet they both followed the movements of their companions as they looked from the raised platform in front of them to the grand stained-glass windows running down both sides of the hall. Great twisting pillars of a rich marble sprouted from the floor to rise up and support the ceiling high above their heads; an impressive display with vines of pure gold cascading out from the centre, to twist and turn, finally wrapping themselves around the tops of the supportive pillars.

The colourful windows portrayed pictures of kings and queens of old, mixed with famous knights such as the revered and worshipped Sir Samorl. There was no other furniture bar the King's throne and four smaller, antique chairs, which sat two advisers either side of the King. Those advisers included the Lord High Chancellor, Ward Strickland, who held a title historically reserved for the Samorlian Church's representative up until Barrison's father's reign.

Also present was Will Morton, Duke of Yewdale and Lord High Constable of Altoln, the King's highest military advisor and commander of Altoln's armies. Will Morton was brother-in-law to and a close personal friend to Barrison, and was known for speaking his mind, even to the King himself.

Another chair was taken by Hugh Torquill, Earl of Royce, Lord High Treasurer and Lord Keeper of the Privy Seal, a man whose physical stature didn't seem to fit his many titles, although his burgundy stalked soft cap and matching tunic, along with multiple silver chains hung about his pale neck certainly made him look the part.

Finally, on Barrison's far right sat the Samorlian Church's highest representative and owner of the previously unrecognised third voice: Archbishop Corlen.

Severun was surprised to see Corlen in his chair. His place as an advisor to the King tended to be more of a tradition than a practice, yet he was known to attend councils regarding humanitarian and festival, or – as the group now realised – arcane matters.

Severun swallowed hard despite himself. He was no coward and had stood up to bullies as a child, and to foul creatures as a man, but the Samorlian Church scared him more than almost anything else. It was that fear, rooted in his past, that had caused his attempted escape back in his chamber, or so he imagined, since the memory of the event seemed vague to him with all that had happened in the short time since. The thought of facing King Barrison with what had happened had not scared Severun, indeed he knew it to be his duty and responsibility, but the thought of the Samorlian Church and its fanatical followers drove a fear so deep in the man it stole his breath and plucked at his nerves like nothing else. He now wished the shroud had been maintained by Ward Strickland so he wouldn't have known of the church's involvement. Had that been what the tall scout had pulled Fal to the side at the coach crash to explain, that their attackers had been Samorlian followers? Severun had no idea and it was too late to ask now.

By all that is magical and all that is not, I am sure the Archbishop is staring right at me, into me. He knows it all, he must, but how?

Lord Severun did his best to shake away the fear, ignore the Archbishop and look directly to Barrison, the man he knew.

As the group's eyes finally adjusted to the bright hall and its multitude of colours cascading through the stained-glass of the many windows, it became apparent there was a full unit of King's halberdiers and four crossbowmen in the chamber, as well as two knights wearing maille hauberks under long surcoats, which displayed the green and white quartered field of the Duke of Yewdale.

All weapons were trained on the group, bar the Duke's two knights who stood casually by pillars, one on either side of the group, their hands resting on the hilts of their sheathed swords.

Severun could understand the precaution, but it ate at him all the same, especially now he suspected the Samorlian Church was involved. He realised Barrison surely knew by now about the failed experiment, but he wished he'd been the one to explain it from the start, not those biased and twisted by their religious fanaticism.

'Lord Severun... all of you, please approach,' Barrison said, still leaning forward in his throne, clearly struggling to see the group in detail as he addressed them. Will Morton leaned across to whisper into Barrison's ear, but the King waved away whatever protest his brother-in-law had made.

Severun set off first, and slowly walked down the hall with the others following close behind, all bunched together like frightened children. Errolas was the most confident of them all, his race seemingly a shield of protection against whatever claims were being made by the King of Altoln and his advisers, yet the elf stayed respectfully behind the tall wizard as they made their way towards Barrison's throne.

Iron plate clanked all around the group as the heavily armed and armoured halberdiers followed the group up the hall, their weapons remaining levelled at the group. The crossbowmen also moved to keep the group covered, but Will Morton's two knights remained where they stood, seemingly unconvinced their services would be required, or more than likely unconvinced the group posed a serious threat to anyone in the room considering the number of soldiers surrounding them.

'Close enough,' Morton said in a gravelly voice, which matched a face criss-crossed with scars, one of which pulled at the right corner of his mouth giving him a permanent grimace. The Duke wore a knee-length green tunic with silver embroidered trimmings on both neckline and cuffs. Black and white striped woollen hose covered his thick legs leading to black, open topped shoes buckled in front of the ankle – which revealed the top of his feet – before ending in a ridiculously long point. Although he wore no armour, an ornate scabbard lay across the arms of his chair, within it a bastard-sword with an equally ornate cross-guard, hilt and pommel. The weapon was clearly old, a family heirloom no doubt, and Fal couldn't help but stare at the weapon appreciatively.

How many bastards have been created by that blade? Fal knew it wasn't the real reason for the name of that type of sword, but thought it might as well be.

Morton sat forward in his chair, but unlike Barrison's relaxed manner, the large man's hands wringed themselves eagerly in his lap as he stared at the group.

Aye, and you're ready and willing to use that on any one of us should we so much as look at the King wrong. Fal shifted his gaze up to Morton's stern face. *And I don't blame you, Lord Yewdale. Even I'm not sure what we're up against here and I'm part of it, flay my soul.* Fal struggled to keep his eyes on the older warrior, the Duke's rich and fancy attire doing nothing to soften the hard eyes that looked back at him briefly before moving on to Severun.

'No sudden moves and no silent mouthing of anything at all, wizard!' Morton's dislike of mages was clear as Lord Strickland, never mind Lord Severun, flinched at the words. 'We've been informed by sources I'm not willing to disclose at this time,' Morton continued, 'that you, Lord Severun, and you, Master Orix,' Morton pointed accusingly at the two mages as he spoke, his dark eyes flicking between them, 'have obtained, enacted and spread through the King's city of Wesson, illegal magic resulting in the deadly sickness now infecting all districts...' There was a dramatic pause in which no one dared make a sound. 'What say you both?'

Orix's mouth opened but Severun held up his hand to silence the gnome as he stepped forward.

Several of the halberdiers swiftly moved forward with their blades stopping dangerously close to the wizard's body, but surprisingly, the Lord High Constable waved them back.

And you two finally lifted your swords from their scabbards, Fal thought, glancing quickly between the two knights to either side, *even if it was ever so slightly.*

'Your Highness,' Severun said, his tone dire, 'what Lord Yewdale says, what you and your advisers have been told, is in effect true, sire.'

Barrison sunk into his throne, his eyes closing briefly and his hand moving up to cover his mouth before he composed himself and looked from left to right; to each of his advisers, all of whom showed mixed emotions. The Archbishop struggled to hide his elation at the admission whereas Ward Strickland looked mortified and could not compose himself enough, bringing both hands up to his face before letting them fall back to his lap. Will Morton showed no change to his hard, accusing stare, and Hugh Torquill seemed quite shocked indeed, looking from Lord Severun to the King and back again several times as if waiting for either of them to correct him on what he'd heard.

Severun had known all of these people for years, some more than others and some on much friendlier terms, but all of them nonetheless, and he was not surprised to witness their shock and horror at his blunt admission.

It was the King who spoke next, which surprised all in the room since it was Will Morton who'd opened his mouth to speak.

'Lord Severun, I must ask you to think about whatever you are going to say next very carefully indeed. You must know the consequences for such actions are of the utmost severity? You have, if your admission and our information is indeed true, committed grand treason towards the kingdom of Altoln, your home and birthplace.' Barrison paused to take a deep breath before continuing. 'You were an advisor to my father and have been a friend and mentor since my childhood. I do not want to see you handed to the Samorlian inquisitors, but should you admit your actions with no reasonable explanation, that will be the inescapable outcome.' Barrison leant forward in his throne again, eager for some scrap of information to explain why his known world was being torn apart by people he was sure he trusted and knew well. He swallowed repeatedly and his eyes bored into Severun's own.

Corlen stood up suddenly, his balding head flushing red as beads of sweat appeared. He turned his outraged face from Severun to the King. 'Sire, there is *no* explanation for such treachery, such *evil* debased and horrific deeds—'

'Sit down!' Morton bellowed, turning to face the Archbishop. 'Your King will *not* be spoken down to by anybody, least of all you, Corlen. Now be seated before I decide you need assistance in doing so.'

The Archbishop looked terrified of the warrior at his side and so swiftly took his seat, offering a muffled apology to the King from his bowed head. Fal noticed the Duke's knights on either side move briefly in his periphery, and assumed they were there to keep more than just Fal's group in check.

'Thank you, Will. Archbishop Corlen, please,' Barrison said with an exaggerated sigh, 'do not take it upon yourself to address me like so again, not unless it is clear I am in the wrong and we are in private council. Do I make myself clear?'

'Yes sire, my apologies, sire,' the Archbishop grovelled, his head remaining lowered and angled slightly away from Morton, who continued to glare at him openly.

'As I was saying, Lord Severun, please think about what you are to say next, because I am asking you now to explain yourself fully.'

Clearing his throat and holding his hands together tightly, Severun explained to his King and all present what he had planned all those months before. He asked if Orix was allowed to speak, to confirm his story and to fill in the blanks about the potion the gnome had created. Severun also admitted that although his intentions had been for the betterment of Wesson, unknown to Orix, the wizard had used the base spell of an arcane scroll shipped to Wesson from the far south.

From Orismar? Fal wondered, thinking back to his birthplace, if only briefly.

Severun explained how he'd believed he could harness the arcane magic to do the work of good, ridding Wesson and hopefully all of Altoln of its numerous violent criminals and gangs, thus making the King's lands a safer place for all.

Both Severun and Orix explained how Fal had been used to deliver and release the potion, but how he'd been unaware of the consequences of his actions, merely following orders.

So why do I still feel such guilt. Fal's heart pounded in his chest. *All the lives lost because of my actions, whether I knew it or not. And how many more will follow?*

'But who are the other members of your group?' Barrison asked, seemingly taken aback by the flood of information. 'You have an elf with you, who is he? Are the elves involved? I should sincerely hope not, Severun?'

Errolas was learned enough in court life not to open his mouth until asked to do so, even when his presence was questioned, and so he kept quiet.

Severun opened his mouth to speak, paused, and then continued. 'I admit, sire, that I do not know. I believe they are companions of Sergeant Falchion.' Severun indicated Fal before carrying on. 'It was he, in fact, who discovered what I had done, and so had been escorting me here when we were attacked on Kings Avenue by Samorlian forces.'

Corlen bristled, but a swift glance from Morton silenced him, before Lord Torquill asked Severun how he could be sure the attackers were Samorlian soldiers.

'It would be best my lord,' Severun said, 'if a soldier took over now. Sire, if you please, I would like you to hear from Sergeant Falchion and his companions.'

'Of course,' Barrison agreed. 'Sergeant, please proceed.'

Great! I'm addressing the King of Altoln… about who knows what, but I'm at the centre of it and everyone's looking at me now. Oh for all the gods' sake, Falchion, swallow it down and say something, damn you.

Falchion stepped forward and bowed deeply, his stomach churning as he looked up at his King. Despite those blue eyes kindly willing him on, he'd rarely known such fear.

'Sire, when I arrived at Tyndurris today, I confronted Master Orix regarding the sickness throughout Wesson. I explained my suspicions, suspicions proven the night before by Errolas.' Fal presented the elf stood at the back of the group, who now came forward. 'As an elf ranger, he'd been sent to Wesson to investigate arcane magic detected here.'

'Why weren't we informed?' Ward asked quickly.

Barrison held his hand up and asked the magician to hold such questions until he'd heard all of the details.

'Errolas told me,' Fal continued, upon the King's request, 'I'd been witnessed by both he and an unknown person on the night I released the potion. Since then I've been followed not only by him, but by Samorlian witchunters too.'

Go on Archbishop, just try and say something about that. I'd love to see Yewdale put you in your place. The Archbishop made no move, although Fal could tell he was strained not to, and so Fal continued.

'Sav, a border scout,' Fal presented Sav, who stepped forward, bowing his head as he did so, 'along with Errolas, have only this morning discovered a man in the room above my own. They gave chase, but he managed to escape them both, something Errolas assures us only a small number of humans could do. He recognised the man he chased as a Samorlian witchunter. Then again, when we were ambushed on the way to the palace, in which a guild coach driver and several citizens were murdered, Errolas confirmed those attackers to be witchunters too, and their acolytes of course.'

Barrison's eyebrows rose and he stole a sideways glance at Corlen.

'Is this true, Corlen?' Torquill demanded, catching the anger in Barrison's eyes and giving the King time to compose himself.

'I… I doubt it… I would have to ask,' stammered Corlen, as he looked everywhere but his fellow advisers and King.

Will Morton finally lost his patience. *'Is this true?'* he shouted, hammered his fist down onto his chair's arm, his sword clattering along the wood as a result.

'Yes, yes it's true!' Corlen snapped, turning finally to face both Morton and Barrison. 'The Grand Inquisitor gave the order to have the traitors torched before they reached the palace. He may not have told me himself, but I know he feared they were going to attack *you,* sire. It was done in the name of Altoln and you, my liege.'

Morton turned to Barrison, silently begging permission to strike the Archbishop from his seat, and Fal again noticed the Duke's two knights moving forward, their hands playing impatiently with their sword hilts. Barrison, however, gave the slightest shake of his head and Morton reluctantly sat back in his chair, clearly angered further. It seemed to Fal the Duke disliked the church more than he disliked mages.

I'm starting to admire you all the more, Lord Yewdale.

'I take it by your being here, Sergeant Falchion, the attack was a failure?'

Gods my throat is dry; of all the days. 'Yes, sire, but not through lack of effort on their part. After they shot our driver, Master Bevins, and the coach turned over, Godsiff Starks, a young crossbowman under my command, as well as Sav and Errolas here, kept the attackers at bay with bolts and arrows. One of the witchunters did manage to set light to the inside of the coach, but Lord Severun used magic to engulf the flames and us for a short time, with a sudden…' Fal struggled for a word, 'rush I suppose, of water.' *Which I could use now, to stop my voice breaking.* He cleared his throat and continued. 'It was Lord Severun and the bowmen, sire, that saved Master Orix and me. I don't believe Lord Severun or Master Orix to be evil, as the church claims, but misguided in their attempts to help their King and his kingdom.'

'Yes, thank you, sergeant,' Morton said. 'The King wasn't asking for your opinion. Facts man, that's all, facts.'

'It's alright, Will,' Barrison said soothingly. 'I appreciate the sergeant's honesty and input since he's been caught up in all of this more than any of us, and unwillingly as far as I see it.'

Thank the gods, no, thank the King!

'Thank you, sire.' Fal bowed again, relieved he hadn't overstepped the mark.

'It seems to me, Archbishop,' Barrison continued, 'that your Grand Inquisitor's attempts failed, and I am thankful of that. I am quite sure I can protect myself in my own palace from a small group of men without his help. Even if he'd given the order to burn these men for my protection, which I seriously doubt anyway, it is certainly not his jurisdiction. He should have notified the Constable of Wesson, Lord Stowold, immediately upon finding out this information, not taken it upon himself to execute people on my streets.' Barrison's voice had risen as he directed his words to the red-faced Archbishop, and it continued to rise and fall as he struggled to keep his own anger in check. 'Innocents have died, and yes, I am aware they are dying all over Wesson due to the actions of these two.' He pointed to both Severun and Orix. 'But I for one believe they did not intend it to happen like this. Your Grand Inquisitor, however, takes the law into his own hands and for his own reasons far too often for my liking. You will tell him I want answers for today's actions and *you* will bring me them, then the magistrates will decide if there is any punishment to be given out to his men. Those who survived the poor *attempt* at an ambush anyway.'

Fal was sure Severun had to fight to hide a smile, despite the consequences his actions would surely bring him, and Fal believed the wizard's turn would be next.

And what do I think of that? I don't know, is my true answer. Would I see them burn, as is the Samorlian way with arcane mages? No. Would I see them get away with what they have put the city and me through, no matter their reasons and intentions? I genuinely do not know…

'As for you two…' Barrison, obviously riled by the church's involvement, now turned on Severun and Orix. 'What you have both done, or rather what you intended, was no better than the church's interference in this matter. You planned to take the law into your own hands, becoming magistrate and executioner of *my* citizens. You obtained and used arcane magic to carry out your so-called experiment, which has caused countless deaths, seemingly ongoing. I cannot believe all the people who have been falling ill and dying in all districts of Wesson were violent criminals, and so I declare your experiment an obvious and absolute failure.'

Orix wanted to blurt out about the plague. He couldn't believe he hadn't mentioned it when given his chance to explain, but he'd been lost in the moment, too engrossed in the telling of the tale. He didn't dare interrupt the King however, especially with Lord Yewdale glaring at him like a hungry beast, and so he kept his mouth firmly shut, praying to multiple gods for a moment where he would be able to warn them all.

'As much as it pains me, especially since you Lord Severun have been a family friend my entire life, and you Master Orix have done so much for this city with regards to medicine, I find I cannot, for the sake of Altoln and its people, let either of you get away with this madness unscathed.'

The room became deathly silent again, except for the King's heavy breathing and voice, as he reluctantly read out the terms he believed were necessary.

'Lord Severun. As the obvious instigator and ringleader for want of a better term, you will be locked in the palace dungeons under battle mage guard until a verdict is determined.

'Master Orix. I understand you played more of a part in this to try and stop it getting out of hand. Well, I'm afraid you failed, master cleric. Do you have anything to say?'

For a couple of seconds that felt like hours in the oppressive silence of the great hall, Orix couldn't force a word from his mouth, but finally, he managed, and when he did, the words flowed in a jumbled mess of confusion and panic. 'Sire, so sorry must warn so bad... so very, very bad stupid fool of a gnome missed it... such danger... the whole city we need help not enough medicine or magic here is there? Not for this no, no not for this, for such—'

'Such what damn you?' Morton shouted, almost rising from his seat.

'Plague... my lords... it's the bubonic plague!'

'Oh my,' Ward gasped, followed by several sharp intakes of breath from not only King Barrison and his advisers, but the halberdiers and crossbowmen too. 'Sire,' the magician continued swiftly, 'if this is true and it certainly seems possible with the amount dead and dying all over the city, you can't imprison Master Orix. We need him.'

Barrison rose from his seat and so, mirroring his actions, did his four advisers. 'Lord Severun, Master Orix, follow us,' the King said, and without another word, the halberdiers raised their weapons and stood at ease, as did the crossbowmen.

Severun and Orix looked at each other, to Fal, and then to the back of their King who was striding across the marble floor to the side of the hall where a small, hardly noticeable door had just opened. Severun and Orix followed, swiftly walking, almost running to catch up as the four advisers followed them. Will Morton stopped only to whisper something to one of his knights who'd moved forward, before vanished through the same door as Barrison and the others, which closed with a slam that echoed throughout the hall.

Fal and his companions looked around at each other as the knight Lord Yewdale had addressed headed over to them. The man's thick surcoat reached just below his knees, quietening the sheathed sword knocking against his armoured legs as he walked. His bare hand rested lightly on the hilt of his sword, and compared to everyone else in the room, his expression showed nothing of the shock everyone was experiencing. He was accompanied by one of the halberdiers, who was clearly still trying to take in all he'd heard.

'Sergeant Falchion, you and your men are to follow this guard and await further instructions from milord Yewdale.'

'Of course, Sir..?' Fal raised his eyebrows in anticipation of the man's name.

'Merrel,' the knight said.

Fal smiled sincerely. 'Thank you, Sir Merrel.'

Sir Merrel offered a tight smile in return, nodded his head and set off across the great hall towards the remaining halberdiers and crossbowmen being formed up by Lord Yewdale's other knight.

'This way,' the halberdier who'd accompanied Sir Merrel said, before heading towards another hidden door, this one on the opposite side to the one the King and his advisers had used.

With a look of bewilderment from Sav and a sympathetic smile from Errolas, Fal merely shrugged and motioned for them to follow their armed and armoured guide out of the chamber, his mind racing as the sound of barked orders and marching men echoed from the hall they left behind.

Chapter 16: Condemned

Smoke, stale ale and sweat marked the aroma of Longoss' favourite establishment, but that certainly wasn't what had attracted him there. The warm, flat ale soothed Longoss' throat and he sighed with satisfaction. He figured it'd been far too long since he'd tasted the ale at his local tavern in Dockside.

'Not seen ye since last night, Longoss,' the innkeeper said, pouring another jug of ale for a large, heavily tattooed man stood opposite him.

Longoss just smiled, revealing a row of gold teeth.

'Thought I'd 'ave seen ye this morning?' the innkeeper added.

The poorly dressed Longoss shook his head and finished his jug. He belched before dragging over the newly filled one.

'Hey! That's mine, ye thievin' bastard.'

Longoss held both hands up immediately and turned to face the huge, tattooed man stood next to him.

'No trouble boys, I'm tellin' ye.' The innkeeper reached under the counter for a well-used cosh.

'Trouble's his, Keep, if he don't give back what ain't his.'

The tavern fell quiet and the fiddler in the corner began plucking an ominous tune.

Longoss didn't move, just continued to hold up his hands, before showing his gold teeth to the large man stood over him.

'What's he doing, Keep?'

'Holding his hands up and smiling, what's it look like? Now take yer bloody ale and throw me yer coin, before I bop ye both for wasting me time.'

The gold teeth still shone and the hands stayed high as the large man leaned threateningly across Longoss to take the jug.

Longoss' eyes moved from the other man's for the briefest of moments, to take in a particularly unique tattoo on his neck.

Holding the jug in front of Longoss for a moment longer than everyone in the room thought necessary, the tattooed man eventually, but slowly, slid the jug towards him, back to where it had been filled.

With Longoss' hands still held high and more than a few looks of confusion from around the small tavern, some clearly of disappointment, the fiddler stepped up his music again in realisation nothing was about to happen, and the patrons gradually began turning back to their drinks, companions and conversations.

The large, tattooed man slowly lifted his jug of ale and brought it close to his lips, glancing sideways at the still bared gold teeth and raised hands of Longoss, who, it was only now apparent from the smell, was literally pissing himself where he sat. That in mind, the man laughed directly at Longoss, before quaffing the whole jug in one. He finally took his eyes from the man he considered a loon as he heard him mumble some gibberish about a mark.

All seven tattooed feet of the man, jug and all, dropped heavily to the floor as a bollock dagger firmly lodged itself between his ribs and up into his heart; the grubby hilt left Longoss' hand only when the blade followed the body to the floor.

'Go on then, Keep,' Longoss said, turning back to the bar despite the sudden screech of the fiddler's bow on string, 'pour me another ale will ye?'

***

Fal felt as though he and his companions had been sat in the small, cold room for hours. They'd been brought to the windowless room via a passageway leading out of the great hall. Four torches lit the room where Fal, Sav and Errolas sat. There was a long bench curving around the circular room, a room housed deep inside one of the palace drum towers. The large wooden floor boards, sixteen in all – counted by Fal several times, he'd been there so long – had gaps in-between them in places and Fal could make out a faint light source from the floor below. What was down there he had no idea, but the sound of muffled voices accompanied by frequent laughter was apparent, so he guessed it was a guard room or something similar.

Sav and Errolas had asked Fal about what he'd found out at Tyndurris, about the plague and whether or not he trusted Severun and Orix. He'd explained all, including his thoughts and conclusions that, as far as he could make out, he truly believed both of the mages had good intentions.

Fal then moved the subject along to the attack on the coach, including the coach being set on fire. He told them the torch had come in through the sky-facing window and set the coach's curtains on fire as soon as it passed them. He went on to explain how Severun, panicked by the flame, had yelled out something Fal couldn't understand nor remember. Then, after Fal had tried to scrabble across the coach to throw the lit torch out, a rush of water had erupted from the ground-facing window, up through the opposite window and out of the coach like one of the fountains in Kings Square.

'It's a wonder you weren't drowned,' Sav had said, shaking his head. Fal couldn't make up his mind which would be worse, burning or drowning. He'd heard sailors claim drowning was quite serene at the end; how they knew he didn't know, but after what he'd witnessed in his past, he knew burning was the last way he would ever want to die.

Fire: we gain so much from its existence. We create it on a whim and some play with it like naught but a harmless toy, but it can kill; it can kill horribly and don't I know it.

Maybe I should burn, one day, for what I released... and more. Maybe I will, but by the gods there is no worse way to go, not in my eyes. And the fear in Severun's when the torch came through the window... I saw his soul in that moment and it mirrored my own. By the gods, he doesn't deserve that, no, no one does, and I don't care what's said otherwise, nor by whom... no bastard deserves that.

Sav had found it strange when Fal mentioned Severun panicking at the sight of the torch. He said he would have thought The Grand Master of the

Wizards and Sorcery Guild was made of sterner stuff and Fal was inclined to agree, although he flinched momentarily before saying so.

'He tried to escape back at Tyndurris,' Fal added a little later.

'Who did? Lord Severun?' Sav was obviously shocked and leaned towards Fal who was sat on the far side of the room. Errolas, who seemed to have drifted into a meditative sleep since the earlier conversation had stirred, opened his eyes and looked at Fal.

'Yes.' Fal nodded slowly. 'When Master Orix said we were to seek an audience with the King, I'd moved to the door to escort them and suddenly… poof!' Fal waved his hands in an explosive expression.

'What do you mean, *poof*?' Sav leaned forward even further.

'Well… he just vanished, right in front of my eyes. There was a cloud of smoke and Master Orix yelled for me to close the door. So I did. I slammed it, which caught an invisible Lord Severun between it and the frame. I grabbed at where I reckoned he was and – *poof* – he was there again. By then I had him in a hold.'

Sav's mouth hung wide open. He'd silently mouthed the words *vanished* and *invisible* as Fal had said them, and now he just stared unbelievingly at Fal. Errolas, however, smiled.

'You know what he did, don't you Errolas?' Fal was clearly eager to know, as was Sav, who spun on the elf.

'The wizard used what he would call a blinker spell. Not extremely hard for some mages, but it does need concentration before use, otherwise you could end up slipping out of existence.'

Sav's mouth, if possible, opened even more as he looked from Errolas to Fal and back.

'He was quiet as he was getting up to leave his desk,' Fal offered.

'That's when he was silently preparing the spell then,' the elf said. 'A mage, or rather some mages, find they can concentrate on a spot, not too far away mind, and it has to be in view. Then using their stored magic, they can actually move to that spot, swiftly, without anyone seeing them… well, it's not exactly that fast, it takes the same time as it would to run there. But the magic hides them from sight or sound by fading them out of this dimension, to put it simply…'

Simply? Sav thought. Fal thought the same.

'…and so it seems like they have travelled a few paces in the blink of an eye, hence it being called a blinker spell, by human mages at least.'

'So that's why he re-appeared when I slammed the door and grabbed out, because if he hadn't, he could've ended up disappearing forever?' Fal had worked around mages for a long time, but had rarely had the chance to hear about magic or spells in any great detail, and although a great uncertainty was hanging over the group, Fal wanted to know more.

'Well, not exactly,' Errolas replied. 'Once he has concentrated on making the move, the shift of his physical presence in this dimension only lasts until he makes the point he focussed on via the journey he planned. You, however, slammed the door, which must have caught him as his body was already returning to its solid form, and so the door hit him; you grabbed him and then he finally, fully reappeared.'

Sav had finally closed his mouth, but listened intensely, looking from Errolas to Fal, who looked back at him, then back to Errolas before finally asking a question.

'I understand him even less now,' Sav said. 'Because, if you believe Lord Severun meant only good by his experiment, Fal, then why did he try to escape? He doesn't strike me as the type who scares easily.'

'I think I can answer that as well,' Errolas said, to the surprise of both.

'How so?' Fal asked.

'I am not unfamiliar with Altoln history,' the elf said. 'In *thirty-nine-thirty-nine Landing*, the King of—'

'When?' Sav asked, looking to Fal – who shrugged – and then back to the elf.

'Ah, my apologies, I was using an ancient calendar,' Errolas said, before asking, 'Which calendar would you prefer, Altoln's founding, or the alliance?'

'Alliance,' Fal said quickly. 'The Samorlian's might not recognise it, but we do.'

Sav agreed.

Smiling, Errolas continued. 'In the year *four thirty-four Alliance*, the King of Altoln, King Barrison's grandfather I believe, allowed the Samorlian Church to begin an Inquisition throughout Altoln.'

Both Fal and Sav nodded their heads again, as the Samorlian Inquisitions were well known throughout Wesson.

'That Inquisition, as you know, was aimed by the King and the church at arcane magic users. Unfortunately, some elements of the Samorlian Church seemed to get carried away, for want of a better term, and thousands were killed, many burnt, throughout Altoln.

'During the winter of… *four thirty-five*, the Wizards and Sorcery Guild protested to the King that the Inquisition should be called off after many of their members had been targeted. The whole kingdom had gone through more than enough. So the guild council approached the King asking him… nay pleading with him, to call off the church; who were very much the King's puppet masters at the time.

'The King, alas, declined the request, and the two most passionate mages, a wizard and a sorceress, were tried by the Inquisition and burnt at the stake, leaving one child an orphan… his name—'

'Was Severun,' Fal whispered. He felt his heart drop as the realisation struck him.

Severun, whatever it is you have caused here, whatever pain and suffering now afflicting this city by your hands, I will always know the pain you have lived through, just as I lived through it myself, and know it has already been enough punishment. Gods only know how I hope you never witnessed their deaths.

'Gods below,' Sav said slowly. He ran his hands through his hair and leant back against the wall, staring at the torch-lit ceiling.

'That's why I believe he tried to flee and why he panicked when the torch was thrown into the coach,' Errolas went on. 'He was forced to watch both of his parents burn to death at the hands of the Samorlian Inquisition...'

You bastards. You vicious bastards. Fal closed his eyes and clenched his teeth at the thought.

'...and he fears he is going to follow their fate.' The elf's eyes showed his compassion, and the room fell silent for a few moments until Sav broke the silence with another question.

'Why wouldn't he want revenge? I'd want to pay back the church and...' Sav cocked his head to one side. 'Wait a minute, *four thirty-five*? That'd put him in his early sixties then wouldn't it? I know he's no young stag, but I thought he was younger by at least a decade or so.'

Errolas smiled again as he enlightened the two men yet more.

'Severun was in his teens during *four thirty-five*. As rangers, we are taught about him, because he is probably one of the most powerful wizards in Altoln at the moment. He is seventy four years old.' Errolas smiled even more as he watched Sav's mouth fall open yet again, but not before the scout let out a prolonged curse.

'That's impressive to say the least,' Fal said. 'I knew mages could live longer, Master Orix told me actually, but I had no idea Lord Severun was so old.'

'Hey!' Errolas laughed. 'You are hardly making me feel like I'm in the middle of my prime here, gentlemen!'

All three laughed before Errolas finally answered Sav's forgotten question about why Severun wouldn't want revenge for what the church had done to his parents. The returned subject swiftly dispersed the group's mirth.

'I imagine Lord Severun was deeply affected by what he witnessed all those years ago, Sav, and some people – yes, I can understand – would grow up with it eating away at them, driving them to seek revenge where others, Lord Severun in this case, are affected in quite the opposite way. He is clearly terrified of the Samorlian Church and at the thought of being burnt alive.

'What puzzles me, however, is why he'd use arcane magic in the first place, which is a sure way in this kingdom, in fact the only way, where the law states you must be executed through the use of fire. An ancient and archaic law but not one I would normally argue with since the users of arcane magic are usually twisted, evil creatures, no matter where they hale from.

'Lord Severun, however,' Errolas continued, 'does not strike me as such, and I do believe, as you say Fal, that he meant well, by unfortunately doing a great deal of wrong.'

Both Fal and Sav nodded and the room, once again, fell almost silent, except for the muffled voices in the room below and the occasional shifting of feet outside the closed, but not locked, door.

The quiet of the room was shattered a moment later as the door swung in and crashed against the wooden bench running right up to the stone arch of the doorway.

The door had been opened by a sergeant-at-arms in the King's livery – a crowned, white caladrius with sword grasped in its talons, was woven onto the man's short, red and blue halved surcoat. He wore a quilted gambeson under the surcoat, covered by tightly-knit, riveted iron links forming a short-sleeved maille hauberk which covered his torso and hung down to just above his iron knee cops. His head was covered by a maille coif and sallet helm, its point riding low at the back to protect his neck. Simple plate gauntlets sat atop maille mitons, a far simpler design than the expensive and sought after Sirretan fingered gauntlets worn by the wealthiest knights and lords. The sergeant's tanned leather boots were short and his legs were covered with a pair of woollen hose, one red, one blue, worn opposite to the colours of his liveried surcoat, which was secured with a brown leather belt, from which hung a long dagger on one side and a simple arming sword on the other.

He was an impressive sight indeed, especially considering he was only a sergeant-at-arms and not a knight. In normal circumstances Fal would have wished for such fine armour himself; which would surely cost him far more than he would earn in a year or more. It was the man's face, alas, not his armour the trio now stared at, for the sergeant wore a stern expression indeed.

'Sergeant Falchion?'

Fal stood as he answered. 'Aye that's me. What's happening?'

'I'm Sergeant Grannit of the King's Guard. The Lord High Constable, through Sir Merrel, has bid me deliver this message to you.'

'Go ahead, Sergeant,' Fal said. His fear for what that message would be brought bile to his throat.

Sav and Errolas stood now and walked to stand beside Fal as the palace sergeant delivered his message, read from an unrolled scroll bearing the waxed seal of the King.

'King Barrison wishes to offer you all, but especially Sergeant Falchion, his gratitude in your actions this day.'

Fal and Sav looked at one another, brows rising and the hints of a smile playing across their faces as the sergeant continued.

'He wishes you to know that Lord Severun and Master Orix have praised you all for your actions both on Kings Avenue, and Sergeant Falchion at Tyndurris, for confronting Master Orix and escorting Lord Severun to the palace, although King Barrison understands and believes both men came in of their own free will.'

Fal nodded.

'King Barrison also wishes you to know that the Samorlian witchhunters responsible for the attack will be dealt with accordingly, as will the Grand Inquisitor of the Samorlian Church.'

Fal smiled all the more to himself at that announcement.

'It has, however,' the sergeant continued, and Fal's face dropped at the tone, 'with the King's deepest regret, been declared that Lord Severun has been condemned to death at midday tomorrow, in Execution Square, by way of fire, as is the rightful punishment for the use of arcane magic within Altoln.'

Fal shook his head. *Lords no, what have you done my King? Severun, I'm so sorry. This is too much…*

Sav ran his hands through his hair and return to his seat, whilst Errolas' emotions were hard to see, but Fal believed he was no less shocked and saddened.

The room seemed to fall silent for a brief moment, a moment that felt like a lifetime, before Sergeant Grannit continued.

'Master Orix, however, has been ordered to work with his clerics to combat the plague effecting Wesson. King Barrison has ordered the city quarantined and no one is to enter or leave Wesson from this day until the King orders otherwise. After the plague has been destroyed, Master Orix will be confined to Tyndurris for the rest of his natural life as punishment for his part in this tragedy.'

Fal felt as if he was receiving blow after blow and he had to force himself to listen to Sergeant Grannit as the man continued to read from the scroll.

'The Lord High Constable has ordered Sergeant Falchion to report back to Tyndurris, as there are fears the citizens of Wesson will blame the guild as a whole for the plague. Therefore, greater steps for security are needed during this uncertain time. The Altoln border scout, Sav, is to assist Sergeant Falchion with security at Tyndurris, and the Elf ranger is asked to advise King Barrison and Altoln, as an ally, in this time of need.'

Errolas lifted his drooping head to look at the sergeant-at-arms. 'Am I to accompany you to King Barrison now?' he asked, clearly taken aback by the request.

'If you will, master ranger, yes,' Sergeant Grannit replied politely.

Errolas looked to Sav and then to Fal.

'Go on,' Fal said, 'do what you can to help us, for we're all trapped in the city with this plague now, and anything you may be able to help with will be needed. We'll see you again soon I hope.' Fal grasped Errolas' outstretched hand and Sav stood, walked over to him and wrapped the elf in a huge hug.

'Come to Tyndurris when you can,' Sav said, and Fal noticed tears in his friend's eyes; they'd been there since Sergeant Grannit had announced Severun's fate.

'I will scou… Sav,' Errolas said. After one last look at his two friends, Errolas followed the armoured sergeant out of the room and down the passageway.

As soon as their friend had left with Sergeant Grannit, Fal and Sav were escorted from the room by two more men-at-arms in the King's livery, all be it far less armoured than their sergeant. The soldiers led them down a curling staircase to the base of the drum tower, before exiting through a small door onto a large open courtyard where they directed Fal and Sav to the main gate. There stood a palace coach, waiting to take them to Tyndurris.

114

As the two friends climbed into the large, armoured coach, the driver told them he'd heard a rumour the sickness sweeping Wesson was in fact a plague, one caused by an arcane wizard and as far as he was concerned, it was only a matter of time before someone burned in Execution Square and the riots began. Fal clenched his teeth and along with Sav, said nothing to the driver, who merely shrugged, climbed up onto his seat and cracked his whip.

The bulky coach set off down Kings Avenue towards Tyndurris, which loomed in the darkening sky as a deep red sun sank low towards the sea on their left, bringing the terrible day closer to its end.

***

With nothing but torches and candles to light the long guard room, it was hard to make out the embroidery on the garment being handled, and so, eyes squinting, Effrin pursed his lips and then, finally, shook his head.

'No?' Bollingham said, sitting back on his bunk and scratching the back of his head in frustration.

'No,' Effrin confirmed.

'Why?'

'Because.'

'Just, because?' Bollingham held his hand out and Effrin threw him the garment.

'Yes, just because.'

'Ye can't be saying that mate, what's yer reason? I think she'd love it!'

'Oh yes?' Effrin said, moving across to his own bunk and dropping hard onto it. 'Well *you* would, you're trying to sell me the damned thing and for five pennies. You're a thief not a city guardsman.'

'Ha! That's a good one,' Bollingham said, holding both of his hands up. 'Ye got me, cleric, ye got me good. Take me to the magistrates now before I leave the city.'

'You can't leave the city, it's quarantined and you know it, they've just announced it not a moment ago,' the young cleric said, whilst plucking obvious bits of black fluff off of his white robes.

'Quarawhat?'

'Quarantined, Bolly, locked down, closed, shut—'

'Aye, I get it ye posh git, we don't all get schooled ye know.' Bollingham held the black garment to his nose and smelt it audibly. 'Mmm... still smells of her.'

Effrin's eyes widened as he sat up in his bunk and looked across at the man opposite. 'Its second-hand?' he asked, before screwing his face up in genuine disgust at Bollingham's grinning nod. 'And here I was thinking you were bad enough for wearing those green pantaloons.'

'He better be bloody joking, Bolly?' Biviano said, as he stumbled into the guard room, a clearly dazed Sears leaning heavily on his shoulder.

'Cheers Effrin, ye prick,' Bollingham muttered, before realising Sears was injured and not drunk. He jumped up to help his two fellow guardsmen, the cleric close behind him.

'Put him on my bunk, quick,' Effrin said, whilst pulling the ruffled sheet off to reveal a relatively clean straw-filled mattress below.

Biviano and Bollingham lowered Sears onto his back and Effrin swung the big man's legs up onto the bed. 'How long has he been like this?'

'Too long,' Biviano said. 'He was slipping to and fro on the way here, muttering shit as usual.'

'Stabbed?' Effrin asked, fingering the hole in the big man's maille hauberk, where something had split the links and pushed them through the padding below.

'Small crossbow bolt. He pulled it out himself.'

Effrin shook his head and crouched down to a small chest by his bunk. He opened it and rummaged inside before pulling out bandages and a pair of long nose pliers.

Bollingham screwed his face up. 'He was shot in Park District?'

'Aye,' Biviano said, crouching down to be level with his unconscious friend, 'bastard witchunters believe it or not.'

'Samorl's hairy balls,' Bollingham said, looking from Biviano to Sears' wound and back.

'Ye could say that, Bolly, there were two of 'em,' Biviano said, laughing at his own joke, before turning back to Sears. 'He gonna be alright, Effrin?'

The cleric was working on the wound, pouring something Biviano thought smelt like pig shit onto it, before reaching messily in with long nose pliers as he replied. 'Yes, he's healing already in fact and I'm yet to perform any healing spell, but I need to get any broken maille links out first. You give him something, Biviano?'

Biviano shrugged and changed the subject. Effrin wasn't surprised.

'I need Gitsham and his hound?'

'Ye take a knock to the head man?' Bollingham rapped his knuckles on Biviano's kettle-helm and Effrin smiled. 'No one can ever be arsed working wi' that man and his mutt. Flay me, but working and talking to him's like trying to get blood with a stone.'

'From a stone,' Effrin said, whilst holding his hand over Sears' wound and closing his eyes, satisfied he'd removed all the broken links.

Bollingham nodded towards the cleric. 'He's been schooled, ye know.'

Biviano smiled before pressing, 'So, where is he?'

'Gitsham?' Bollingham said. 'Out and I don't know when he's back in.'

'Good,' Effrin said, opening his eyes to look at Biviano, 'because this one,' he nodded at Sears, 'and you, need rest before you go back out, and especially if it's to do the sort of thing I can only imagine you two would be doing after something like this.'

Biviano shrugged. 'Whatever ye say, cleric. We can wait for Gitsham here, rest up and when we're ready, see what his hound can find. We won't act until we have something the captain can take to the magistrates, officially like.'

'Well good luck to ye both,' Bollingham said, moving back to his bunk and picking up a black garment of questionable description which he pressed to his face, 'because,' came his muffled voice, 'ye be going wi' out me, Biviano me boy.'

'Ye scared of the Samorlian's, Bolly?'

'No mate, I'm scared of the plague and I ain't leaving this damned room until it's gone, orders or no orders, otherwise I'd be right with ye both.'

Biviano nodded, knowing it to be true. His eyes suddenly widened as Bollingham's words sank in. 'Plague?'

'Aye, that's what they're saying the illness that's been knocking about is,' Bollingham confirmed.

Biviano looked to the cleric, Effrin, for real confirmation.

'It's just been announced, to us at least.'

Biviano stared at Sears and the cleric working over him, before sighing long and hard. His mind was racing as he climbed onto the adjacent bunk and laid back. 'Wake me if owt changes, Effrin, or if Gitsham comes in.' *I need to process what you both just said.*

'Will do,' the cleric said.

'Will do,' Bollingham muffled.

Chapter 17: Quarantine

The sun was close to setting on the horizon as it lazily dipped its bottom edge into the calm sea, bathing the capital city of Altoln in a hazy red glow. Thousands of starlings flocked together, swiftly twisting and turning to create ever shifting clouds as black as night, before suddenly falling to roost on the large warehouses along Harbour Way.

Several large bonfires had been lit throughout each of the city's districts, their columns of deathly black smoke reaching for the reddening sky. Anyone unfortunate enough to be within the immediate area of those bonfires could smell the stench of burning flesh as city guardsmen threw corpse after corpse onto the raging pyres. The guardsmen wore scarves over their faces in a feeble attempt to reduce the choking, acrid smell the burning bodies released. Others used brute force to keep families and neighbours back as their recently deceased relatives and friends were taken from their homes and thrown unceremoniously onto the fires.

Wesson's firefighters doused thatched roofs with water throughout the city in case burning embers landed on the highly flammable rooftops, and cart men brought piles of bodies from the infirmaries where many had been kept, awaiting funeral services that would never take place. Those infirmaries now closed their doors to anyone not infected, those with other ailments being directed to makeshift infirmaries in volunteer's houses.

Word had got out and spread fast that Wesson had the bubonic plague. Although most citizens did all they could to help the authorities, there were a great many who took the opportunity to vent whatever anger they had towards Wesson's City Guard.

Units of guardsmen were issued with shields as well as their usual batons to protect themselves and their colleagues from thrown missiles or actual attacks. The City Guard was well-trained in riot tactics and mounted men-at-arms patrolled the streets in small groups, ready to be called to aid should their colleagues on foot need it, which they frequently did.

The two great gatehouses of Wesson were closed, their portcullises dropped and their wooden gates firmly shut and bolted. Signs were hammered to the wooden gates informing travellers, merchants and visitors that Wesson was closed to all; anyone found trying to enter, leave or aid anyone in either would be arrested and hung for their efforts. Many had tried to flee when they heard the gates were being closed, but a shield wall of heavily armed men as well as crossbowmen had been placed across the roads leading through both gatehouses.

The King's navy took care of closing the port. Marines were positioned throughout the wooden jetties from the naval fort to Wesson's cliff-side prison. The King's men had their work cut out keeping large groups of sailors from their ships, but trained and experienced in pirate hunting, the hardened marines held their lines against the lesser armed and armoured sailors, who only half-reluctantly returned to the taverns and brothels.

King Barrison also released his most heavily built ships – cogs in most cases – which were ordered to blockade the mouth of the harbour, to stop any ships who attempted to make a run for the open sea. Messages were sent to any vessels attempting to return to Wesson, King's ships or otherwise, that the city had been locked down and they were to try and make port elsewhere until contacted.

It was during the first deployment of King's marines that Captain Mannino had realised – partly through having their movements followed – that the two guardsmen who'd visited him had been investigating more than murders alone, whether they knew it yet or not.

'How'd ye mean, cap'n? Ye think there's more to all these murders about the city?' Hitchmogh asked.

'Not quite how I put it man, but aye, there's more to this plague too. I'd wager *Sessio* on it.'

The first mate's eyes widened and he rubbed his stubbly chin, and rubbed it a good while before pushing for clarification from his captain.

'So, Master Ineson's and Master Joinson's murders,' he said, rubbing his chin some more whilst walking to and fro in front of the captain's desk, 'something more'n just someone thievin' coin then? Tied in to the plague ye thinking too?'

Mannino nodded, before delicately lifting the fine glass containing his port. He raised the glass towards his first mate before speaking.

'Care to take me on that wager?'

'Aye, and I'll cut me balls off too, just for fun, ye see.'

'I'll take that as a no then,' the captain said, before knocking back the port and wincing slightly.

Hitchmogh grimaced. 'Apologies, cap'n. Best port they 'ave around here. Ye can join me and the lads 'n' lasses for some rum, if ye please?'

'That won't be necessary, we'll be out of here and on our way before sunrise, so keep your wits about you.'

'And the blockade cap'n? They're setting up in the harbour mouth now. We'll need to get us a movin' if we're to make it out in one piece.'

Mannino smiled broadly as he poured another glass of port.

'Ahh... I see,' Hitchmogh said, scratching the back of his head nervously. 'I didn't think we'd be doin' that again in a hurry.'

'Nor I, man, but needs must eh? What!' Dropping his smile just enough to throw back another glass of port, Mannino winked at his first mate, before rising from behind his desk. He strode across to a small door which led to his bunk room. Turning before entering, he said, 'Wake me when it's time.'

'Aye cap'n,' the grizzled old man said, before grimacing and leaving the cabin.

Ah Master Hitchmogh, what would we do without you, eh? Mannino thought, as he patted *Sessio's* hull from within his bunk room.

Dropping heavily onto his hard bunk, he pulled off his polished boots and

119

placed them neatly to one side, before swinging his legs up and stretching back, resting his head on the down-filled pillow.

So, Peneur Ineson hires me at great cost to transport Master Joinson from Orismar, with little in the way of valuable cargo... but much in the way of magical value? Of that I'm sure.

Out of character for the man though and out of character for Master Joinson too. Experienced agent he may well have been, but that return journey he was different; skittish, afraid even?

If so, of whom... or what, I wonder?

What... aye, what, not whom; not directly anyway. That chest in his cabin. He was making sure I wouldn't look in that. Not that I would have. Probably should have? Aye, probably, but not my way, no, and Ineson knows that, or knew it. Ha! Clever bastard, well what good that did you, old boy, eh? Shame, I liked the old coot. Good at cards and always played fair too. Makes what happened to him all the worse and makes me wonder whether I shouldn't stick around to see what I can do, in his memory. Doesn't sit well sailing out on the old boy's death, nor before I find out how those two guardsmen are getting on, but needs must. Aye they do, and don't we always know it, Sessio?

As for this plague... hah, a plague – to the depths with me if that's not fishy. Coincidence is what it's not, I'm sure of that and I'm damned sure Master Hitchmogh knows too. I'd be more than surprised if he didn't, a man of his... skills. Then why'd he not mention it to me then? He'll have his reasons, sure of that I am.

Well, things will work out for the best. They always do, for us anyway, eh Sessio?

Patting the hull once again, Mannino rolled onto his side and closed his eyes, forcing his mind to quietude so he could grab what little sleep he hoped he'd get before making a run on the blockade.

***

As the sun sank deeper into the sea, eventually disappearing altogether, the red sky was transformed and the cirrus clouds slowly cleared. The full crescent moon shone like a tear in the sky, its neighbouring stars dancing across the vast blackness to shine down on the infected city below.

The disappearance of the sun brought an increase in trouble for the City Guard of Wesson, for night was the time when the gangs of Dockside operated.

Learning of the plague and the overly stretched City Guard encouraged the gangs to step up their unlawful activities and prey on the already terrified populace. As well as facing a deadly plague, the citizens of Wesson, but most of all Dockside, heard the calls of the gangs from the rooftops and alleys of the closely packed buildings. They knew, as did the guardsmen working across the dangerous district, that the gangs were calling their men to arms, to take their chance to loot, murder and rape.

Houses were being evacuated whenever someone died or fell ill, and their doors marked with the black cross of death. This made the empty houses easy pickings for the looting gangers, and if any guardsmen were caught up and killed in the process then that was all the better, for the gangers hated the soldiers that raided their hideouts and arrested their comrades.

Fal stood in Tyndurris' courtyard. He grimaced when a horn rang out from further down the hill, probably Dockside. He knew what that call meant. Three short blasts, to signify a unit of guardsmen needing urgent assistance. Another three blasts sounded soon after, closer than the last, but still a couple of miles away at least. There was no wind so the sound carried far. Lucky for those calling for aid, Fal mused. It also meant the fires burning the dead poured their smoke and sparks straight up into the starlit sky, lucky this time for the whole city, as just one house alight could spread rapidly, especially in the heavily built up district of Dockside.

Fal turned to look across Tyndurris' courtyard at the fire his men had built earlier that day. That fire glowed now, reduced to an under-lit black mess on the stone floor. Hardly anything remained; no recognisable logs of wood or bodies and no smoke save for a few wisps here and there, slowly drawing lines up to be lost in the blackened sky.

All the bodies the clerics had examined – except a couple they wanted to examine further – had been burnt. Those bodies, Fal had believed earlier, had all been violent criminals, but now he couldn't be sure. The plague had spread fast over the past couple of days, that much was now apparent and anyone could be a victim to its deadly grasp, whether violent or kind, young or old, rich or... well, mostly poor.

Always the poor.

Another three blasts from a horn, this one much closer than the previous two, sounded strange to Fal, as it seemed to come from within the Guild District, rather than Dockside, or at least on the edge of the latter.

The clatter of metal shod hooves on stone resonated around the street and guild gateway, as two mounted men-at-arms rode past the large iron gates of Tyndurris. They'd been visible for a brief moment, but Fal had seen the reflection of the gates' torches on metal. The soldiers were armed with blades, not batons. Something was clearly very wrong.

'To arms, to arms,' Fal shouted, as he ran over to the large gate. 'Bar the gate and double the guard, I want crossbowmen on the corner towers. No one is to enter or leave unless I give the order. Understand?'

'Yes sergeant,' two guards said simultaneously. They'd been stood either side of the gate in wooden guard boxes. One ran over to slam down a large bolt into a hole in the stone courtyard, locking the gates into place. He then clicked shut a large iron padlock that secured the sliding bar. The second guard ran down the inside of the wall a short distance and rang a bell until more men came running from both the large guild tower and a much smaller stone building next to the stables at the back of the courtyard. Some carried crossbows and climbed ladders to man the small guard towers in each of the four corners of the courtyard, whilst others ran to the gate with a mix of goedendags, arming swords, axes and shields.

This was more than one shift's worth of guardsmen for the guild. Upon returning from the palace, Fal had sent out messengers to call in all available men-at-arms and most had come. Some weren't anywhere to be found and Fal feared for their health, for their lives even.

'Riots?' a friendly voice asked, and Fal turned to see Sav walking across the courtyard with his yew bow strung.

'I think so, aye, and I'm not taking any chances. Word of the plague got out and spread fast so it's only a matter of time until this guild is named as culprits. I heard support requests from a horn first in Dockside and then closer, possibly within Guild District. They may be heading here?'

'You want me on a tower or by the gate?' Sav asked, his usual jovial character left behind at the palace, along with Severun, Orix and Errolas.

'No, you stay with me, I have crossbowmen in the towers, and I want someone I can trust completely at my side if this gets nasty.' Fal placed a hand on Sav's shoulder and smiled. 'It's been a good long time since we had to deal with a riot. It'll be like old times.'

Sav's returned smile was half-hearted, Fal knew the scout well enough to see that, so he didn't press the point. Instead, he turned his attention to the manning of Tyndurris' defences. A riot usually petered out after an hour or so, but something made Fal think this was going to be a long night, so he moved off to check his men and to re-affirm their rules of engagement.

Shortly after Fal and Sav had arrived at the guild, the Lord High Chancellor had ridden in on a grand white mare which held its tail high and walked proudly into Tyndurris' courtyard. After dismounting and greeting Fal, Ward Strickland had quickly entered the tower and called the guild council into meeting to explain everything.

The council, missing two of its members – one of them their Grand Master – once fully informed of the situation by Lord Strickland, addressed the rest of the available guild; all of which had been swiftly called back to Tyndurris from their homes and duties throughout the city. Many couldn't attend, however, needed as they were to assist the King's navy and City Guard, as well as the now heavily guarded infirmaries. A good number of mages were also spread throughout Altoln, working alongside the kingdom's many noble families, magistrates and sheriffs in matters of state and local law enforcement; some were further away, as always, on matters of private business, experiments or quests.

The guild members present had been shocked and many had cried out in both surprise and outrage as they heard about Lord Severun and Master Orix's experiment. Ward had pressed the fact the King himself believed both were attempting to act in the name of good, but because of Lord Severun's use of arcane magic, no matter what the reason, King Barrison was forced to declare Lord Severun guilty and the charge, as it would be for anyone else enacting arcane magic, was death by fire.

Ward had also announced Orix's sentence and advised all clerics present to await the master cleric's arrival, so they could all work on ways to deal with the plague under his supervision and expertise. Several clerics had muttered to themselves when asked to assist Orix and a few had outright scoffed at the idea after what had been revealed to them. Others, along with Ward, had swiftly chastised those clerics and made sure they understood their obligation to work with the most gifted cleric in the city; to come up with solutions to the epidemic threatening the whole kingdom.

Shortly after the guild had met, Orix had arrived under escort from Sir Merrel and a dozen of Lord Yewdale's own men-at-arms, who left after passing the gnome over to the guild's own soldiers. Orix hadn't been seen by Fal, as the gnome had been rushed to the clerics' chamber to start work alongside his fellow healers on ways to try and stop, or at best slow, the deadly plague's progression.

***

The smell of smoke filled the small hovel, its tendrils clinging to everything as it struggled to make its way through the small hole in the thatched roof. The smoke was a blessing though, since the smell of the sickness was the only alternative.

Elleth brushed her shiny, black hair from her tear-streaked face as she picked at the rat bones left over from a meal her mamma had made them only a couple of days ago. The pains in her stomach had subsided slightly as she pictured the bones to be a chicken. Oh, how'd she loved chicken when they'd been lucky enough to have one once, and although she'd been very young, she remembered that day well.

'I'm sorry there's no more for now, Elleth,' her mamma said, her voice hoarse from lack of water.

Elleth smiled sweetly at her mamma, who lay on the straw-covered floor by the pitiful fire in the centre of the small room. The faint glow revealed fresh purple lumps along her bare arms; some large, some small and tightly packed, but Elleth's young eyes saw them all. Her smile faltered for a moment as she thought of what those lumps had meant for her dada and baby brother.

'Oh, how that sweet smile of yours lights me heart, Elleth. Yer dada loved it so.'

Her mamma's eyes glistened then and a tear rolled down her cheek.

'Elleth my love, ye need leave me now. Ye're almost blooded and ye're a strong willed girl, ye'll be alright. Sir Samorl' watch over ye.'

The young girl shook her head and put down the bones immediately, not quite sure what her mamma meant by 'almost blooded'. She moved towards her.

The frail woman held up her lumpy arm, wincing at the pull it caused on the apple sized bubo consuming her pit.

'No darlin' no, ye stay away now and ye leave this place.' The tears fell freely now, as did Elleth's and she made to say something.

'No child, no more words,' Elleth's mamma said. 'Yer love is known to me as it was to yer dada and brother.' She nodded her head, leading her child to

123

do the same, before continuing. 'Take nothing from this house my love, it's all dirt of the sickness now and will do ye no good. Ye don't speak of it to no one neither; the words may bring it on to ye or make 'em avoid ye. I'll be happy to know ye live and that's all I can ask. Ye need to do that for me Elleth, can ye promise me? Ye'll live and live long?'

Elleth, her shoulders rocking with her sobbing, nodded strongly as her grey eyes held on her mamma's own.

'Ye're a good girl Elleth—'

Coughing wracked the woman then, followed by blood filled spittle, and again Elleth made to move towards her mamma.

'No Elleth, no,' she managed, wiping her mouth with the back of her hand. 'Ye go now, Ye do me that one last thing and go and live and don't ye ever come back to this place. It ain't our home no more my sweet girl. Now turn, turn and face the door and don't ye be lookin' back to me.'

Elleth struggled for a moment, then turned and placed her delicate hand on the door.

'Push darlin', push and don't stop walkin' until ye find somethin' better.'

More coughing came from behind Elleth, this time mixed with the sound of her mamma crying, and Elleth's black hair moved slowly up and down on her back as her head nodded.

She finally pushed and moved through the small doorway into the shadow of the narrow street beyond as she heard one last thing from her dying mamma.

'I love you, Elleth.'

'Love you too, mamma.'

***

Fal had been correct in his estimate of the horn blower's whereabouts. Fighting had broken out deep within Dockside where the streets were narrow and muddy, dismal places.

In the dark side streets and alleys of inner Dockside, the gangs ruled. Although a rough place during the day, Dockside at night was a violent underworld where normal people unfortunate enough to live there bolted their doors and barred their windows; closing shutters behind them and sleeping away the night, only half re-assured by their crude fortifications.

Burglars, muggers, protection rackets and all manner of violent criminals worked the narrow streets at night, most controlled by various gangs and or guilds, and those who weren't were either very good at their trade or very stupid, and both usually ended up being recruited or put out of business by one gang or another at some point in their lives, usually in a violent way.

The City Guard had been informed late in the afternoon of a whole block where people had died with symptoms matching the newly recognised bubonic plague. A patrol of guardsmen on foot had proceeded to check the row of closely packed hovels to discover their informer was correct and there were indeed a large number of corpses in the buildings. These buildings, unknown to the patrol, had been the working centre of an exceptionally violent gang known as the Constrictors. They'd earned their name after squeezing every last penny out of their unlawful fiefdom through violence and robbery. This row, it was said, housed the gang's womenfolk, which could easily have been true, since the majority of the bodies found by the guardsmen were indeed women, some as young as ten it seemed. The patrol had then proceeded to clear the houses of the dead and mark the doors with black crosses, before loading the bodies onto three hand carts to be pulled to the nearest bonfire, as their new orders demanded. Most of the guardsmen were vocal about how late it was getting and that their new orders should be left until the next day, but the sergeant-at-arms wanted to finish what they'd started, although he agreed it would be their last load before returning to the area at first light.

Once the carts were loaded and covered with sacks to hide the grotesque scene, the guardsmen made their way towards a large road separating Dockside from the Guild District. The unit made slow progress pulling the hand carts up Dockside, which was built on a natural hill, sloping down all the way to the harbour. Some of the narrow roads were in poor repair and quite steep in places. Most had turned to mud where the stone cobbles had been dug up and sold to the Masons Guild over the years by locals who needed money to pay the Constrictors. The climb took its toll on the men as the patrol pushed on.

An hour passed and the sun fell extremely low in the sky. The guardsmen grew increasingly nervous and replaced their batons with falchions and axes. Some people threw rotten vegetables and worse from alleys, whilst small children chose stones as their missiles. The gangs were hated throughout Dockside, but the City Guard was held with no higher regard, since they rarely set foot into the slums to help the people. Several times the carts had to be stopped whilst the patrol warded off angry locals, all of which took precious time.

The unit was nearing the edge of Dockside, but it had fallen dark rapidly, for the tall, closely packed buildings blocked the quickly dying light of the setting sun. Large shadows cast across each other to create areas as black as pitch, and just as one of the guardsmen walked past the opening of a blackened alleyway, he disappeared without a sound.

'Garl?' the sergeant-at-arms called, his stomach twisting all of a sudden. 'Where's Garl?'

Several in the unit shrugged, looking around, expecting him to jump out playing the fool, as was his nature, but Garl didn't jump out and the sergeant feared the worse. He ordered his men to leave the carts and check the two alleyways either side of the street. Two men checked each as the rest set their shields in a defensive line both front and back of the carts. The sergeant, with many years of experience, stayed in the middle with his horn, trying to follow all four of his men in turn down the two black alleys. His stomach continued to twist and turn and despite those years of experience, his hands grew slick with sweat. His head turned left then right and back again, straining to keep a visual on his men as his heart thumped in his chest.

The street's too damned quiet, where's the heckling? Where's the bloody shit and stones?

One of the men down the alley in which Garl had disappeared suddenly shouted something inaudible; he was clearly startled by something. A dog barked, to which a couple of the guardsmen in the rear shield wall laughed. The small mongrel ran out of the alley and away down the narrow street, its tail firmly between its legs. There was more laughter from the men in the rear shield wall.

The wily sergeant set his jaw firm.

A man screamed.

The scream was guttural and ended almost as suddenly as it sounded. Metal clashed against metal down the same alley and the rear shield wall turned to face the noise, unlocking their shields as they did so. As they turned, there was a strange snapping sound from above and two of the patrol dropped to the floor, struck by stones fired from powerful slingshots.

'On me! On me!' the sergeant shouted, and the front shield wall broke to reform around him.

The broken rear shield wall picked up the downed men who were alive but clutching bloodied cuts to their faces and heads, and rushed to their sergeant.

No men returned from either alley.

The horn called: three clear notes as the sergeant-at-arms emptied his lungs into the curved instrument.

As the notes echoed off the surrounding buildings and carried off down the streets, shouting started; heckling calls and wolf like howling from all about the lightly armoured men.

The sergeant was no rookie and recognised the shouts and howls as gang calls. He grabbed the closest man and dragged him along as he called for his men to retreat and follow him. The remaining guardsmen ran as fast as their legs could carry them up the steep, sewer-strewn street, leaving the carts and lost comrades behind. They knew the main street was not far and so they ran all the faster, but they also knew they were surrounded and the hornets nest had stirred.

As the tired, maille clad men made the top of the narrow street, their sergeant blew the horn again, praying for reinforcements to appear.

The last stretch was still sloping but much less than the one they'd just climbed, and so they ran all the faster. One of the men at the rear turned to look behind him and wished he hadn't, for there was a large number of people chasing them, most of which, in his brief glance, seemed to be carrying a weapon of some sort.

He'd just turned back to look where he was running when a door opened to his left and he was struck in the face with a plank of wood. His legs flew from under him and he hit the ground hard, his axe flying from his hand to clatter across the cobbled ground. His friends didn't stop. He'd been at the back and they hadn't seen or heard him go down over the calling of the gangers and locals. He tried to shout out but his mouth was full of blood and teeth. As he began to cough and choke, he looked up and saw a rough looking man with a gold-toothed grin.

The man slammed the end of a thick wooden pole down and the guardsman's face collapsed into his broken skull, its contents leaking into the helm, then over the ridge of the iron pot to mix with the mud and cobbles surrounding it.

Longoss grunted at the sight, before closing the door behind him and joining the passing mob.

The remaining members of the unit thanked whomever they prayed to as they ran out onto a large yet empty road.

'Keep going,' the sergeant shouted, as he turned to look at their pursuers, his lungs burning as he gasped at the cold air for breath. His pulse thudded in his ears.

He estimated at least thirty men and women were running up the street they'd just left. The crowd threw stones and insults and many carried weapons, some of them makeshift but weapons all the same, and so he ran on, following his men into the Guild District ahead, which was lined with larger buildings and set along wider streets. Here he felt safer and believed the gangers and their followers wouldn't travel far from Dockside for fear of greater reprisals by the City Guard.

Hah, let's see you bastards follow us now.

He was wrong.

The group of twelve gangers who'd originally assaulted the patrol had swelled to near fifty and more joined the frenzied charge. Men and women left their houses or ran down from other streets to join the mob who chased the patrol, and as they hesitated on the large street, which marked the border of Dockside, a man called out to them from his seated position on a rooftop, a man clad in black with a wide brimmed hat and a rapier resting across his folded legs.

'It's a plague!' The stranger shouted, and people looked up at his silhouette, confused. 'The sickness killing your families is a plague and it was created using arcane magic. Arcane magic sent forth from Tyndurris!' Exley Clewarth pointed to the silver lit tower scraping the sky.

The crowd screamed, they yelled and they cursed and they ran on, deep into the Guild District and on towards Tyndurris.

A horn sounded three times.

Chapter 18: Civil Disorder

Stars blinked in the cloudless sky and a light breeze made Fal shudder as the sound of clattering hooves on cobbled stone grew louder. The same two men-at-arms that had ridden past Tyndurris' gates just moments before now rode back, calling a warning to all as they approached.

'Lock yer doors, bar yer windows!'

The horsemen came to a halt outside the gates and Fal ran over to greet them, noticing their grim expressions as they neared the torch-lit gateway.

'What news?' Fal asked, Sav close by his side.

One of the riders, a broad shouldered young man with a closely cropped blonde beard and piercing blue eyes leant forward in his saddle to address Fal through the iron bars of the gate. His horse stepped sideways as he tried to steady it.

'Trouble from Dockside,' he said, and Fal noticed both he and the other rider looking back the way they'd come every few seconds. 'We were responding to the horn ye probably heard and so headed for that. We expected a riot. A few small ones have sprung up throughout Dockside and we're spread thin, but this one's made its way into this district,' – a few of Fal's men started mumbling to each other at the news – 'and it seems to be heading here.'

The mumbling increased and Fal had to hold his hand up high and cast a stern look their way. They soon fell quiet.

'You sure?' Fal asked, finally.

'They're crying out for the guild to be burnt; Tyndurris to be toppled. The unit they chased out of Dockside...' The rider looked ashen faced at his companion before continuing. 'They're all dead.'

Fal swallowed hard and Sav cursed under his breath.

'The mob caught them and we were but a heartbeat too late.' The mounted soldier's head dropped, and Fal could think of nothing to make the rider feel better and so kept his mouth shut.

'Tore them up they did,' the second rider said. His face was lined, showing his age, and Fal guessed he was much more experienced than the first. 'As we rounded a corner, they were hacking at the fallen men and dragging down the rest. We attempted a charge, blades drawn, but realised quickly there were too many; fifty of them at least. We turned the horses just in time to make it out of the street alive and so headed here, not what we're supposed to do as I'm sure ye know, but we needed to warn ye.'

'And I thank you for that.' Fal nodded to both men. He knew, as they suspected, that their job was to return to their captain with the news, to try and organise a force to turn back the rioters, and so was genuinely grateful they'd thought to warn him and his men first.

'We need to go now,' the younger rider said. 'They won't be far off. The horses only give us so much advantage on cobbles. We'll inform the captain and ask for reinforcements to aid ye, but there's plenty of us who haven't been seen for hours. Whether they're keeping doors locked to this plague, or worse... we don't know.'

'Sir Samorl be with ye, sergeant,' the older rider said.

'Sir Samorl...' Sav muttered. 'Those religious nutters are what—'

'Sav!' Fal sighed hard. 'Not now, mate.'

Shaking his head, Sav walked off to talk to the guild's men-at-arms who were anxiously discussing what they'd just heard.

'Forgive him,' Fal said, as both riders looked to Fal for an explanation. 'It's been a rough day for us all.'

'Not to worry sergeant,' said the older rider. 'I accept not everyone is of the same faith, but whoever ye do worship, I'd say a prayer now and may that god be with ye this night.' Both men turned their horses and spurred them off into the night.

Fal stood silent for a second, the question of faith sitting with him longer than he thought it would. He'd never been particularly religious, nor had his parents, but although the Samorlian Church had far fewer followers, he knew only the very brave spoke out against them, which was what shocked the riders about Sav.

Before his thoughts could carry any further, a shout echoed across the courtyard from the south western tower. Fal looked to Sav and the scout ran immediately to his side.

'They're here then?' Sav's usual humour was still vacant from his voice, even more so at the prospect of what was to come.

'Aye Sav, time to do what we're paid to do.'

'I'll be paid will I?' A smirk lit Sav's face briefly, before swiftly fading away again.

Fal rolled his eyes and didn't offer a reply. Instead, he put two fingers to his mouth and released two high pitched whistles just as the north western tower called out a warning.

A dog barked from the far side of the courtyard and then another. Sav looked across the dimly lit expanse to see three handlers running across from a small wooden building. Each man held three thick ropes, at the end of which pulled large wolf-hounds standing as tall as Sav's waist. The scout cringed. *I hate dogs.*

'I'll be in that tower.' Sav pointed to the last to call a warning.

'Oh no you won't.' Fal said. 'They're here to discourage the rioters, not you. Now stick by my side and keep that nasty bow of yours visible.'

'Yes Sarge, certainly, Sarge.'

'Keep them in view,' Fal shouted to the dog handlers. 'I want them visible through the gate, understand?'

Each handler acknowledged the order in turn and they walked their panting dogs over to the gate whilst Fal ran with Sav up to the tower that had called the last warning. Sav followed Fal up the narrow wooden steps to the small tower above, where one man-at-arms and two crossbowmen were peering over the wall at the crowd below. All three pulled back as a rock struck the wall just below where they'd been stood, and the shouting and chanting from the gathering crowd grew all the more.

'How many?' Fal asked, whilst stepping into the small tower.

'A good sixty to seventy, Sarge, and the mob's growing by the minute.' The man-at-arms had a heater shield strapped to his left arm and a mace resting on his right shoulder.

'Good lad, Berns, keep that thing visible, and the same with them.' Fal pointed to the two crossbows resting against the side of the tower's wall. The two crossbowmen picked up their weapons and made a point of aiming them at people, minus the bolts in their grooves.

'Be sure to remember the rules of engagement. I want no citizens shot at unless they are armed with bows, slings or crossbows, understood?'

'Sarge,' the two crossbowmen replied, as they continued to move their weapons around in a threatening manner.

'They're moving around to the gate,' one of them said.

'Alright, I'm heading back there now. Stay cool lads and I'll be back in a bit.'

'Cool as this rock wall me, Sarge,' one of the crossbowman said.

'Knob,' the other crossbowman said back to him.

Berns laughed before adding, 'You're both knobs. Now keep your eyes peeled, I don't want to take an arrow in the face because you two are having a lovers' tiff.'

Fal left them to it.

Sav couldn't fit into the small tower along with the others, so he waited on the steps; the increasing din gave away the picture from the other side of the wall though. People were shouting, cursing and some chanting about burning down Tyndurris and all inside.

'Back to the gate, Sav, come on.' Fal pushed Sav back down the stairs and across the courtyard.

Many of the guards were now in position between the tower's door and the large gate. Their heater shields were locked together creating a wall of men, wood and iron; ready to protect Tyndurris should anyone or anything breach the gate and head for the tower's entrance.

The nine large dogs were howling and barking as rioters appeared in the street. The people stayed well away from the iron gates where they could clearly see six crossbowmen in the courtyard, their loaded weapons pointing into the crowd. Stones were being thrown both over and at the gate, as people screamed and shouted abuse, calling for the mages inside to be brought out to answer for the plague.

'Stay your triggers,' Fal said, as he reached the gate and its crossbowmen. 'They won't be getting through or over that gate. As for the walls, I want one handler to keep his dogs here. The other two, take your dogs off separately on opposite sweeps of the inside perimeter. Take two men each and should anyone manage to come over the walls, detain them. Unless they make a run for the tower door, in which case take them down.'

All three handlers nodded and quickly decided which would do what. The two on patrol set off in their opposite direction, taking two men from the shield wall each, who hung a few paces behind the handlers and their dogs.

There was a wooden ladder to the left-hand side of the gate which was shielded from view by a small, wooden palisade. Fal made to climb up the ladder, until Sav caught his arm.

'What're you playing at? You'll be prime target if you pop up on top of that wall.'

'I need to address them Sav, see if I can persuade them to bugger off before the City Guard arrives in force.' Fal tugged his arm free and climbed the ladder.

'Your funeral,' Sav shouted, as Fal reached the top. 'Cover him lads,' Sav said to the crossbowmen. He nocked an arrow to his own bow and stood where he could aim through the bars, but far enough away from the barking wolf-hounds to his right.

'Listen to me,' Fal shouted to the crowd below. As soon as he did, he had to duck below the wall as a clay jug flew past his ear to smash on the stone courtyard behind him. 'Listen!' he cried again, and as he did, he saw a man to the edge of the crowd – just visible in the gate's torchlight – pull out and raise towards him an old looking crossbow. Fal ducked below the wall again and several screams followed. He couldn't stop himself looking back over the wall to see what had happened. The crossbowman was in the middle of a circle created by members of the crowd, who'd moved away from him as he lay flat on his back. He was clearly dead; one small crossbow bolt in his stomach, buried almost to the leather flights, and one larger arrow protruding from his forehead; the crowd edged further away from him. People shouted even louder, more chants erupted here and there and more stones were thrown.

'Hold,' Fal shouted to the crossbowmen below. 'Hold!' He swiftly climbed down from the wall to round the palisade, where Sav stood, another arrow nocked on his bowstring. One of the older crossbowmen was reloading his weapon.

Sav turned to Fal and shrugged. 'Told you so and before you say a word, that was according to your rules of—'

'I know, I know,' Fal interrupted, 'and before *you* say it, I've realised I'm not going to get through to them.'

'Glad to hear it,' Sav said, as a bottle with a lit cloth stuffed into it came over the wall further down the compound.

As the bottle smashed onto the stone floor of the courtyard, the liquid spread a few feet ahead of it and after a split second, there was a sudden flash as it burst into flames.

Another one of the crossbowmen stepped forward then and his weapon clicked as the short bolt whipped from the groove, through the bars of the gate and embedded itself into the bottle thrower's shoulder. The man, crying out in pain, was rapidly dragged away into the crowd by a group of men close by.

'Fire bottles,' one of the men in the shield wall shouted. They immediately split their formation apart, as taught by Fal and the other sergeants of the guild.

This isn't gang territory, Fal thought, *and they don't give two shits for any property or lives they destroy here.*

Fal turned to the crossbowmen. 'Take down anyone with a fire bottle!'

Sav and the crossbowman nodded and Fal ran around the courtyard from tower to tower giving the same order. After, he called for two of the stable hands – who were trying to keep the horses calm – to douse the thatched roofs of the outbuildings in water. Fal knew it wouldn't stop fire spreading, but it might slow it down. Buckets of water were also taken to each of the four guard towers in case their timber roofs were hit.

Two more fire bombs smashed on the stone floor near to where Fal was giving orders. There were screams of terror and outrage then, as the nearest tower's crossbowmen loosed their bolts, killing the culprits before dropping to one knee behind the wall to reload, covered by a heater shield held above their heads by Berns.

Fal realised this was no spur of the moment riot that would soon pass. These people wanted revenge for the deaths in their neighbourhoods. They'd clearly been told the guild was responsible for the plague and they were hell-bent on destroying the ancient tower and its inhabitants.

'We need a battle mage,' Fal shouted, as he arrived back at the gate.

'Finally,' the nearest crossbowman said, as he took out a man holding a slingshot.

One of the men who'd been in the shield wall, but who now stood in loose formation, ran up the steps and into the tower to request help. Fal hadn't wanted any mages outside during the riot, since he felt they would become prime targets, but with a very real risk of fire, he needed at least one here to douse any fire with water, just as Severun had done in the coach on Kings Avenue.

The rioters had lost their fear now and had stormed the gate, attempting to pull it down. The guild's men shouted warnings, but despite their loaded crossbows and drawn weapons, those warnings did nothing to hold back the fury of the citizens.

Every time someone tried to climb the gate, the two gate guards would shove the climbers off with the butts of their goedendags, rather than the spiked ends. The great wolf-hounds went berserk, pulling on their ropes and standing on their back legs, straining every muscle to get at the rioters who shook the bars of the gate and screamed in anger. The dog handler was doing all he could to hold the animals back.

'They'll have it down Fal,' Sav shouted, and Fal could see the large locking bars bow under the pressure of so many people.

'If they get in, we're all dead,' Sav added, in all seriousness.

There must have been close to a hundred people now; screaming, throwing missiles and working themselves into a frenzy. The weight of those at the front pressing and pulling on the gates offered a very real risk; if they broke through, Fal agreed with Sav, they wouldn't stand a chance and nor would the guild.

'Men-at-arms back. Handler…' Fal waited until Sav and the others were about ten paces back from the gate before he gave the next command, '…release!'

The handler turned to look at Fal and waited until his sergeant nodded before letting the ropes go. The three large dogs lunged forward as their ropes were released. They leapt at the iron bars and the people pressed up against them. The great hounds barked, snarled and bared their fangs as they snapped at the people through the gates. A couple of people were bitten and their screams of pain and terror caused those pressing on the gates to back off quickly. The dogs refused to release the two they held and the third dog snapped its strong jaws as it shoved its head through the gaps in the bars. The handler yelled a command and the two dogs holding the men let go, returning to snarling, barking and jumping up as they tried their very best to get at the now taunting crowd. The two bitten men, their arms a mess of blood and gore, disappeared into the still growing crowd who parted to make way for them, cheering them as they passed.

'Sarge,' the man-at-arms who'd gone to get help from the tower shouted. Fal turned to see Ward Strickland himself emerge, a dark cloak wrapped tightly around him. Fal waved the magician over and walked to the side of the gate, taking shelter behind the wooden palisade by the ladder as more stones flew through the air.

The crowd hissed, shouted curses and some chanted as more threw missiles. They'd clearly seen the mage appear in the tower's doorway. Ward was immediately surrounded by six shielded men-at-arms and walked to Fal's hidden position. As he neared Fal, another fire bottle flew over the wall above his head, the thrower realising the crossbowmen were out of sight because of the dogs.

Ward swiftly pulled a gnarled, wooden wand from his sleeve and pointed it at the flying bottle whilst uttering a string of words Fal hadn't heard before.

The bottle stopped in mid-air.

The magician uttered another word that put out the flaming rag stuffed down the bottle's neck and then, as he put the wand back into his sleeve, the bottle dropped harmlessly into his outstretched hands.

Now that's impressive. Fal struggled, but managed to keep the smile from his face.

Ward shook his head as he placed the bottle on the floor behind the palisade. 'I see why you called for a mage, sergeant. These people will have the whole place alight if they continue to throw these about and it just won't do. It's bad enough they blame the guild in general for what happened, but this is disgraceful. They know full well what fire can do to a city.'

The rioters carried on chanting whilst more threw rocks, empty bottles and anything they could get their hands on. One clay jug smashed as it hit a man-at-arms' shield held above his head, whilst another was less fortunate; there were oil lamps on posts as well as torches lit throughout the courtyard, but the sporadic lighting made it hard to see projectiles until the last minute, and one of the crossbowmen was hit in the face by a sharp stone which took his left eye.

The crossbowman, his face awash with blood, tried his best but failed not to cry out. He was quickly escorted inside and rushed down to clerics awaiting injuries in the barracks below the tower.

'Lord Strickland,' Fal said, 'this is getting out of hand. By the sound of it, the numbers out there are increasing. Our deterrents of dogs and crossbows will only last so long.' Fal was clearly agitated. Ward nodded, his eyes turning from Fal to look at the tower where the men-at-arms stood, shields high and weapons unsheathed; ready to protect the door should anyone break through the gate or climb over the walls. The dogs still barked and yet more howling and barking came from the back of the tower, out of view. Ward shook his head and sighed.

'I will address the crowd, sergeant, which will do one of two things, either antagonise them or disperse them.'

Fal sighed and shook his head. 'I've already tried, my lord.' Fal's patience was wearing thin. He was usually calm and collected in dangerous situations, but it felt like the whole city was against them and that scared him; more so because it was his home and these people his fellow citizens, not some unknown enemy.

'But you, sergeant, cannot do this.' Ward closed his eyes, took out his wand and muttered a few words under his breath. The wand's tip emitted a hazy azure mist which the magician inhaled. He smiled at Fal and began speaking in an amplified voice that made Fal, all of his men and the crowd outside, jump. The dogs fell quiet, both at the gate and from the back of the tower, and the handlers, along with their dogs and their escorts, came back around the tower to see who was addressing the crowd in such a way.

'Silence,' Lord Strickland commanded.

The mob outside obeyed.

The dogs whined and the handler by the gate took the opportunity to take hold of their loose ropes whilst the crowd was inactive. People looked all around for the source of the voice, but none dared utter a single word.

'My name is Lord Strickland, council member of this guild and Lord High Chancellor.'

Some people gasped whilst others raised hands to their mouths, all of them realising one of the King's own high lords was addressing them. A handful of young gangers tried to start a chant, but were silenced by deadly looks from the majority of the crowd.

'You have come here to seek revenge for the plague affecting us all. You may have lost neighbours, friends, even family members and you despair at what has befallen your home. Well hear this, citizens of Wesson, this is our home as much as it is yours. The mages of this guild work within the law and serve the King and his people, including all of you present tonight.'

'The plague was created by your mages!' an unseen man from the back of the crowd shouted. Fal motioned for Sav to keep his eyes out for ring leaders.

'A half-truth!' Ward bellowed, his voice echoing around both the courtyard and street outside. 'You have heard rumours of arcane magic and diseases, of evil wizards and plots against the people of this city, maybe against the King himself. Well, I am here, on King Barrison's own orders, to tell you otherwise.'

The crowd fell silent again, the only noise coming from boots on stone as feet shuffled, as well as the occasional whining of the wolf-hounds, now sat by their handlers' feet.

'It is true this plague has been brought to us unnaturally,' Ward continued. 'It has been brought to us through the use of arcane magic—'

The noise increased again as people began to whisper. The odd person shouted that the guild was indeed to blame, but all fell silent once more as Lord Strickland shouted out with his amplified voice.

'I asked for silence!'

He climbed the ladders and shrugged off Fal, who'd tried to discourage him. Fal motioned to his crossbowmen to move closer to the gate and stand ready.

People gasped and some, the closest ones to the wall, backed away when they saw the silhouetted figure appear where Fal had been just moments before.

Once at the top of the ladder, his body clearly halfway above the protective wall, Ward – wand delicately held in his left hand between his forefinger and thumb – inhaled more of the gaseous substance subtly emanating from the wand's tip. He addressed the crowd face to face, his voice now louder than ever; so much so that shutters opened on upper story windows of the surrounding buildings, allowing the residents to witness the unusual spectacle.

'Let me tell you the truth, citizens of Wesson, as the King wishes it. Not the babblings of drunkards in taverns or the gossips of coach drivers on the streets, but the truth; the facts!

'Lord Severun, The Grand Master of the royally aligned Wizards and Sorcery Guild has erred in his work. An error costing many, many lives and one that will cost more, especially if tonight's proceedings are anything to go by.'

Several people hung their heads in shame and some even laid down whatever weapons, makeshift or otherwise, were in their hands.

'His own life is now forfeit, for he has broken a most ancient law; the law regarding the use of arcane magic. The King and his advisors, including myself, have judged Lord Severun meant well with his experiment. He intended to rid the city of its violent criminals. Lord Severun worked these past months hoping to find a way to make each and every one of Wesson's

135

law abiding citizens safer in their homes, in their streets and wherever they may go in their city…' Ward let that sink in a moment, before continuing.

'Unfortunately, his ways were misguided and he failed, and through his failure he released this plague; something which he could not have foreseen and for which he is truly mortified.

'The King and my fellow advisors, after many, many years working with and as a friend to Lord Severun, have judged no matter the reasons, no man or woman… of any race, shall practice or use arcane magic in this kingdom. Therefore, Lord Severun is to be executed, as is stated by law, tomorrow in Execution Square at midday.'

There were several gasps from both the crowd and Fal's men.

Ward inhaled more of the gas from his wand as the noise increased. 'He is to be burnt at the stake by the Samorlian Church as is their duty, to protect the city under the King's orders from arcane magic and its users.'

Several people, upon hearing the facts and the outcome, shook their heads. One woman even sobbed, her head buried in her hands. Many cheered, however, briefly, but cheered all the same.

'It is with great regret,' Ward's voice boomed again, 'that we carry out the execution of someone who devoted himself to making life better for this city, nay this kingdom and its people, but the law stands and must be obeyed. This is why now, instead of tomorrow as was planned, I address you with the truth as declared by our King.

'So, citizens of Wesson…' Ward's voice, although still amplified, lowered to a calm, peaceful tone, 'I bid you go home. Do not cause any more suffering tonight. Allow the City Guard and the clerics of this guild to fight the real enemy, the plague stalking our streets and homes.'

'Yeah… home!' a stocky man with gold teeth shouted. 'To your homes people, there's no enemy here!' He bared those teeth and looked at the people around him in a challenging manner. No one argued. Throwing down a bloodied, thick wooden stick he'd been carrying, he walked away. The crowd parted as he went.

Many agreed and followed suit, throwing down whatever was in their hands; heads down or talking to their companions about what they'd just heard, they left the scene.

'I'll see revenge tomorrow at midday,' a woman shouted, her face streaked with tears, 'for the loss of my husband!' Another woman nearby put her arm around the first's shoulders and walked her away.

The street remained crowded, but people scattered slowly as they tried to find those they knew to walk back with. Some looked angry still and just stood, staring at the gates and the men-at-arms beyond. Fal decided some of these would have been the ringleaders; the gangers responsible for the original patrol's deaths, but he dared not act for fear of antagonising the dispersing crowd. He gritted his teeth and merely watched, albeit with a heavy heart, as those men eventually turned and left.

Most headed towards Dockside, but some Fal noticed walked the other way, and he was surprised other district's residents had been present at the riot.

Severun, what have you done to this city?

Ward slipped his wand back into his cloak, sighed and turned, looking down at Fal, his voice normal again as he spoke. 'We were lucky, sergeant. I feared that could have gone either way.'

'It worked, my lord, that's the main thing.' Fal allowed himself a genuine smile.

Ward climbed down from the wall and clasped Fal's shoulders with his hands. 'It's been a strange and no doubt hard day for you Sergeant Falchion, as it has for many of us and I fear it won't end here. You've done well today, for your guild and King, and he is truly grateful for your actions in bringing Lord Severun and Master Orix in, I promise you that.'

'They came in—'

'Yes, I know they came in willingly, but it was your persuasion and investigations, as well as that elf friend of yours, that stopped this thing getting any further out of hand; not that it isn't a disaster already, but at least we have Master Orix and his clerics working *against* the disease now.' Ward released Fal's shoulders and wrapped his cloak tight about himself once more.

'What's happening regarding Errolas?' Fal asked desperately, for he'd heard nothing of the elf since he'd been summoned by King Barrison.

'All in good time, sergeant. He is safe and well, that is all you need to know for now.'

'Very well my lord...' Fal paused before his next question. 'I feel for Lord Severun, to be burnt... it seems so wrong, don't you think so, my lord?'

Ward took a deep breath and let it out slowly. 'That it does, sergeant, but Lord Severun knew the risks when he delved into arcane magic. He may have meant well, but he knew the risks involved... not only to himself, but to the city too. Now,' Ward continued, managing a weak smile, 'I assume you will set a doubled guard or whatever you do tonight, and then get some rest? It may not be what you want and I am sorry to be the one to tell you this, sergeant, but you are requested to be at Execution Square tomorrow, at midday.'

Fal's face dropped, his stomach churned and it was all he could do not to allow his anger to show through. He wanted to argue, but knew it was pointless. So he swallowed hard and simply nodded.

And so I follow orders without question, as always.

'I'm sorry again sergeant, now go to bed, get some sleep and we will talk again tomorrow. You will ride with me to the palace in the morning and will, along with your scout over there, be amongst the escort taking Lord Severun through the city to meet his end.' Ward Strickland smiled sympathetically and then turned and walked back to the tower's door, the six shield-bearers surrounding him once again as he did so.

Elsewhere in the city, another horn sounded and Fal knew the night was far from over for most. He transferred command to another sergeant-at-arms and retired to the barracks. Sav had been unusually quiet whilst following Fal into and down through Tyndurris, always a pace behind, and no words were spoken between the two as they both dropped heavily onto the first available bunks. Despite their exhaustion, sleep didn't come easy to either of them. They knew what was awaiting them the following day and neither wanted it to come.

Starks, the young crossbowmen injured in the coach crash, an event that seemed so long ago, lay in the bunk next to Fal's. He was fast asleep, and in his inability to do the same, Fal looked across at the young man and made a note to formally commend him as soon as it was all over.

Whenever that will be…

***

The night held a chill that clung to Elleth's bones as she slowly made her way through the streets of Dockside. She knew where she was going and she forced the tears away.

The women at that place always looked so fine, with powdered faces, big hair and fancy, short dresses. Elleth thought there was no way they'd take her in with a dirty, streaked face. There was a horse trough round the side of the building they usually stood outside and so she decided to make her way towards that.

A girl's scream made Elleth jump. It came from an alley the other side of the small row of houses. She quickened her pace. The occasional horn or trumpet sounded, and shouting further away in the district had been going on for a while, as had the numerous ganger calls. But that scream was by far the closest she'd heard since she left her mamma.

'No tears,' she said under her breath, forcing the thought of her mamma away again and thinking only of the lady she would become.

She was close now; round the next corner and she would be able to sneak down the side, to the horse trough.

'Want to see somethin' that'll make ye groan, girl?' a man slumped in a doorway said, a black cross above his head, barely visible in the darkness.

She quickened her pace, as fast as she could without breaking into a run.

'Girl! I asked ye a bloody question,' the man shouted, whilst noisily getting to his feet. He started walking towards her, his heavy footsteps scuffing on the patchy cobbles.

'Ye leave her be, ye shite!' a woman on the corner shouted, and Elleth's heart skipped as she recognised one of the women from the place she'd been heading.

'Piss off, whore! I'll be to see ye later and ye'll watch yer mouth then.'

'Ye won't be seeing me, that's fer damned sure, ye black cross bastard,' the large woman said, loud enough only for Elleth's ears, who smiled as she saw the woman wink at her. Her mamma had said not to mention the sickness and so she wouldn't.

138

Elleth slowed down now, feeling safer already and didn't even look back to see where the man was. The woman held out a hand and Elleth took it.

'Aren't ye a pretty little thing, eh? Oh my, what a smile and what lovely grey eyes ye got there.'

Elleth smiled sweetly, yet cursed herself for not being able to think of anything to say in return.

'Ain't I seen ye about here before, my lovely?'

'Aye, miss.' Elleth's voice grated through her dry throat.

The woman pulled Elleth alongside and linked arms with her as she turned and walked her gently round the corner. They both moved slowly towards the tall building where Elleth had been heading. She saw another lady standing outside, this one pretty and slim, with green hair, and a dress that would surely keep none of the chill out. Elleth assumed that they couldn't afford enough of the fancy material to make their dresses any longer.

'So what brings a lovely out on a night like this?' said the woman walking Elleth along. 'There's a lot going on, dear, a lot indeed and it ain't safe in Dockside tonight.'

'Is it ever?' Elleth said, pleased at her swift response.

The woman's smile slipped slightly, but only for a moment before grinning all the more and looking down at Elleth.

'My oh my, ye're clever as well as pretty. Could do with some meat on those bones though, my lovely, fill yer breasts up a bit, and that cute behind. How'd ye like a good late supper?'

Elleth beamed at the thought and her stomach growled, although she couldn't understand what her breasts and bum had to do with anything, but if the kind lady thought it'd help her then she assumed she was right, and if eating food was all it would take, then Elleth could do that all night long.

'Come on then, dear. Let's get ye in from this night air and give ye a drink and a meal.'

'Thank ye, miss, I'd like that,' Elleth said as they passed the green haired woman, who smiled at Elleth with what looked to her like pity. Well, she didn't need pity now did she? She'd found a life, and a lady she would be.

Mamma would be so proud.

Chapter 19: High Stakes

With the faint glow of fires dotted here and there throughout the city, visible as it was from the jetties at the bottom of the hill Wesson clung to, Captain Mannino pulled on his ivory pipe, listening to the occasional horn and shouts drifting down to him from the city. He looked up at the lightening sky above the great east wall of Wesson, and then to the inky blackness above the western sea defences.

'Time cap'n?'

'Aye, Master Hitchmogh, ready as we will be.'

The first mate spat over the port side of the aft-castle before moving down the steps and across deck to the main-mast, where a young officer awaited him with a thick rope in hand.

'Make it tight, Master Spendley,' the captain said, his voice carrying down to the main deck despite him not raising it.

The young officer nodded at the captain and shrugged at Hitchmogh, who rolled his eyes and pressed his back against the thick, wooden mast, facing the aft-castle and his captain.

The ropes rubbed at his bare arms as the officer looped them round, tightened then looped them again, repeating several times.

'Tighter lad, ye don't want me getting out of these do ye?'

'No I do not,' Spendley said, in all seriousness.

'Nor do I lad, nor do I.'

Sailors scurried about the ship in preparation to launch, whilst two waited by the starboard side, reaching over suddenly to pull up a sodden woman, who flopped onto the deck gasping for air.

The two sailors who pulled her on board immediately moved off to continue their duties, and the female sailor – breath caught – finally rolled over and up onto her feet. She looked to the first mate – now securely tied to the main-mast – before climbing the steps to the aft-castle and the captain above.

'Cap'n,' she said, hands on hips as she panted some more, her clothes dripping on the deck by the captain's feet.

'That took longer than I thought,' Mannino said, pipe in hand.

'They're further out than ye thought, cap'n.'

He nodded and asked for her sightings.

'Dozen or so cap'n, all chained together across the way, as ye'd said they'd be.'

Mannino nodded again and turned to the stern, walking a few paces before stopping and turning back. He pulled on his pipe again and then walked back to the sailor.

'Ships?'

'Mainly horse transports cap'n, seems they don't want to use their others for a blockade.'

He nodded again. It made sense. Should any ship try and run the blockade and succeed, then what good would their warships be if they were chained together. The others must be further out.

'Did you see any ships past the blockade?'

'No cap'n, although I saw one try to get past, but it wrecked itself north of the horse transports; went too wide.'

Nodding again and taking another pull on his pipe, Mannino dismissed the sailor, who ran back down the steps to the deck and proceeded to climb the mizzen-mast.

We can get round, but we don't know their layout beyond. This new admiral is a clever soul. Never seen a blockade with horse transports before, but it makes perfect sense. Where, then, are their warships? There'll be more cogs than just the horse transports, and caravels for sure, but the carracks? Further out to sea, a third line of blockade? Possibly, I would if I was the admiral.

Mannino paced the aft-castle again and pulled on his pipe one more time before putting it in a pouch tied to his belt.

'Must get some tobacco.'

'Sorry captain?' Spendley said as he climbed the stairs.

'Tobacco man, you smoke it in pipes.'

'Aye captain. I'll have the men get you some from below if you've run out.'

Mannino's brow furrowed. 'Run out?'

'Of tobacco, captain.'

'I've never had any to run out of, man.'

Spendley's brow furrowed too, as his eyes glanced to the pouch that held the captain's pipe.

'Oh, there's nothing in it man, never has been. I just like the look and thought I'll have to try and actually smoke it one day.'

Spendley looked for something to say, but instead turned and pointed to the eastern horizon. 'The sun will be up soon, captain.'

'Aye, that it will. So let's make way then and let Master Hitchmogh do his thing.'

'Aye aye captain,' Spendley said, before calling the order to weigh anchor and set sail.

And we'll see where those warships are once we pass the chained cogs.

'One step at a time,' Mannino said.

'Captain?'

'Nothing man, nothing.'

***

'Marines on me!' an officer of the watch shouted, as a carrack started to unfurl sails and pull away from the jetty.

How'd they get on board? We've had this damned jetty on guard all night. Fought a few off of other ships aye, but no bastard stepped foot on that ship, nor was anyone on it when we arrived, I swear it.

Several armed marines ran down the harbour and noisily crossed the jetty to his position.

'That ship's moving off,' he said in surprise, to no one in particular.

The marines looked on in amazement as the square rigging on the carrack now pulling away from the jetty filled with a strong wind, which pulled the ship swiftly through the calm waters and out towards the naval blockade. As it got closer to the chained horse transports, the sun appeared over the city's eastern wall and bright rays of sunlight lit up the area it was heading for; the southern end of the blockade. The experienced marines knew the rising sun would blind the archers and crossbowmen on board the chained cogs, severely hindering their accuracy.

'They'll be away then,' one man said, after a long pause.

'They?' another replied. 'There was no bastard on board.' He looked to his officer.

'Never mind that,' the officer said, looking to the limp flags on nearby ships, 'there's no bloody wind?'

Every marine looked to the officer and then back out to the ship, which was now lost in the dazzle of sun on water.

'Did ye see its name?' a marine asked, and the officer nodded.

'*Sessio,*' he said, an audible sigh leaving his lips.

The marines turned and walked back down the jetty, one of them mumbling about how much he'd have bet on that being the name.

The others agreed.

***

'Morning, Sarge,' Starks said. The young man beamed at Fal over Sav's shoulder. Sav in the meantime, continued his shaking of Fal.

'Enough Sav, I'm awake already... my eyes are open—' Sav shook him again '—I'm looking right at you.'

'Fair point,' Sav replied. 'Muggins here wanted to see you.' He gestured to Starks' beaming face with his thumb.

'Morning, Starks,' Fal said, less irritated as he realised Starks was on his feet. 'You're up and about quick considering?' Fal sat up on the bunk and swung his legs out, forcing Sav to move aside.

'Aye Sarge, the clerics did a good job on me alright. Reckon I respond well to magical healing. Not all do apparently.'

Fal smiled at the young crossbowman.

'Oh, erm...' Sav looked down at the floor and Fal knew he had bad news. Starks' face darkened and he turned to sit on the bunk opposite Fal's. 'I'm sorry old friend... not quite sure how to tell you but...'

Tell me I'm wrong, please, Fal thought immediately. 'It's Franks isn't it?' he said, before Sav could finish. 'Franks Heywood?' Fal's heart felt like it'd dropped into his stomach and beyond.

Sav nodded and Starks looked away. Fal was sure he'd seen a tear on the young crossbowman's face. He wasn't far from it himself.

'I'm sorry Fal,' Sav offered. 'The clerics tending him reckon he had the illness longer than they'd thought, either that or it affected him worse than others and came on faster, they say it seems to take just two days in some people, three to four in most.'

'People are panicking,' Starks added. 'I heard some tried to get over the walls and escape. Most were stopped by the wall guards, but a handful managed to rope down and run... they were killed by crossbowmen from the walls and towers.'

'It's a scary time,' Fal said, taking a deep breath and letting it out slowly.

'What time is it?' Fal asked, looking about the empty barracks.

'It's mid-morning Fal. We let you sleep in a little.'

Shit!

Fal stood immediately. 'I'll be late! Lord Strickland said—'

Sav raised his hands to stop his friend. 'It's alright. I spoke to Lord Strickland this morning when I went to see how Starksy boy was doing—'

'He was in here last night?' Fal interrupted, clearly confused.

'I was moved out during the night for my final healing by the clerics,' Starks said, smiling again.

'Anyway,' Sav continued, 'Lord Strickland said we're all – now Starks has been healed – to meet him in a short while at the stables. We're to ride to the palace with him. Then we're to be among the escort for Lord Severun.'

Starks' smile fell away again.

'You're cutting it fine letting me lay in this late if we're meeting him soon, Sav,' Fal said, suddenly looking around for his boots and clothing.

'We got all your stuff ready, sorted the shifts and readied you a horse, and since Starks can't ride yet, he's riding crossbow on a guild coach. The King has allowed Lord Severun to use one you see, from the palace to Execution Square, rather than the usual prison coach.'

Small mercy, Fal thought, *but lets him keep some dignity. I understand, King Barrison, but it's a damned small mercy with what you've condemned him to.*

'You sure you're up to that, Starks?' Fal's concern was evident in his voice.

'Sure am, Sarge. Survived an attack when we were outnumbered, let 'em try when we're escorted by the King's men!' Starks was beaming again at the prospect of being part of a royal escort, until he saw Fal and Sav's expressions and remembered who they were escorting and why.

'Very well, lads,' Fal said, as he started to pull on his boots, then his shirt, which Sav had handed him. 'Keep your eyes open out there and stay close to that coach in case anything does happen. I'm going to get ready now, so go do what you have to do and I'll meet you both at the stables.'

Sav and Starks nodded in turn and both left to ready themselves. Fal stopped dressing for a moment, sat on the bunk when he was alone and let his mind drift, thinking about what had happened and what was to come. Things had a long way to go before they were back to normal, he was sure, and he prayed to whatever god may be real and listening, that something would save Lord Severun from the flames.

I don't know if I can do it, if I can watch anyone burn; let alone someone I know... not again.

***

Safely out to sea, heading in a southerly direction with Wesson and its blockade far behind them, Captain Mannino finally gave the order to release his first mate from the ropes binding him to the main-mast.

They had a good strong wind now and no King's ship in the area would catch them, especially the one that had appeared at the end.

Big bastard that was, slow, but drown me if its heavy load didn't scare the shit out of the lot of us when it came about and used them. I haven't seen anything like that since...

The captain's thoughts were interrupted when Hitchmogh slumped to the deck, after being released by the young officer who'd tied him there.

Crouching to check on the first mate, Spendley fell back as a fist came up and connected with his chin.

Rolling around, he cursed and spat blood.

'I bith my futhing thongue, you bathtard.'

The crew roared with laughter as their gnarled first mate unsteadily rose to his feet and stood over the young officer.

'Aye, and ye'll 'ave more in future if ye release me any sooner than that ye fool.'

'Capthains orders, whathma suppothed the do?'

'Order someone else to do it for ye, lad. Ha!' Hitchmogh bent and pulled Spendley to his feet, before pushing him away again to stagger across to a barrel of water he used to splash his bloodied mouth.

'Are you alright, Master Hitchmogh?' Mannino said, as the old fellow climbed the steps towards him.

The first mate revealed an almost toothless grin and turned to face their heading, standing next to his captain.

'Does it get harder, man?'

'Aye cap'n, this time, but not always, mind; there were a lot of folk to fool that time though and magic don't come cheap on the body, or soul for that matter.'

'Well your body was wrecked before you joined my crew all those years ago, man, and your soul. Well,' Mannino looked to his old friend and smiled, 'your soul doesn't belong to you now, does it?'

Smiling sincerely, Hitchmogh stepped back down to the main deck and began barking orders to the crew.

Captain Mannino wouldn't have it any other way.

***

144

Fal had ridden a large dappled grey gelding to the palace. He wasn't a great rider, but had learnt on his father's horse as a boy, and in recent years had ridden occasionally on escort duty for the guild. He didn't feel as comfortable as some in the saddle, but was sure he could fight from horseback if the need arose. Sav, however, was a border scout and an experienced rider. He'd sent a stable hand to fetch his own horse and looked at ease in the saddle atop his smaller built, but confident looking black mare. Ward Strickland guided his mount in-between the two friends whilst Starks rode crossbow on the black guild coach following behind. Two of the guild's men-at-arms rode behind the coach on large bay destriers. The hard-faced, armoured men were trained and experienced horsemen, mounted soldiers whose duty it was to escort guild members on journeys out of the city. They carried heater shields and maces, backed up by secondary weapons such as axes and arming swords strapped to their saddles; they looked ready and willing to use them.

Once the group arrived at the palace, they were greeted by a royal herald who informed Lord Strickland the King was in the stable with his horse.

Eight knights of the King's own retinue were already mounted and stood in perfect formation. Their destriers pulled at their reigns, just to be heaved into check by the heavily and expensively armoured knights they carried.

Fal and his companions had only a short wait before King Barrison rode from the royal stables on a great white stallion. He controlled it well and looked regal in his ornately carved saddle. He wore a heavy, purple cloak about his shoulders, with highly polished steel plate underneath; the King's own livery carved onto a rare breastplate. The cloak cascaded over the rump of the white beast, which lifted its head proudly as it walked to the front of the column of knights.

A large bang turned everyone's head in the yard.

Fal turned, following their gazes to see Lord Severun in drab, black robes being led from a side door in one of the outer wall's large drum towers: the entrance to the palace dungeon.

Two stocky men-at-arms wearing the Duke of Yewdale's colours escorted the wizard, who looked pale, tired and not at all his usual grand self.

Another wizard walked several paces behind Lord Severun and Fal recognised him as one of the guild's battle mages. He had a gnarled red staff and unkempt black hair. He was powerful, Fal had heard that much before and knew he was there to keep Lord Severun in check, or do his best to if the need arose.

The guild coach pulled up close to Lord Severun and he was prodded inside by one of the Duke's men. They followed him into the coach one by one, the battle mage climbing in last and closing the door behind him.

'Where are the other advisers my lord?' Sav asked Ward Strickland.

'They have duties to perform in this dire time, and so I will be the King's only advisor, oh... apart from the Archbishop, who will be at the square already, overseeing the preparation of the funeral pyre.'

Fal balked. 'Funeral pyre?' It was an execution, plain and simple. Lord

Severun would be burnt alive. It was no funeral pyre.

'I apologise, sergeant,' Ward said. 'This is hard for me to deal with, as I imagine it is for many of us. It's just my way of making it that bit easier to witness.'

Sav bristled at the mention of the Samorlian Archbishop and both Fal and Ward noticed, but decided to ignore it. Neither of them liked the Samorlian Church any more than Sav, but today was to be a horrific day as it was and neither Fal nor the magician next to him wished to make it any worse by encouraging Sav in his open hostilities towards Archbishop Corlen or his church.

'Here we go,' Ward said, as the King moved forward.

Hooves clattered on stone, armour on armour and the clanking retinue of the King followed close behind. Their horses' heavy trappers barely flapped in the wind as the knights spurred their powerful steeds on into a walk to follow their King. Every single knight was dressed for combat. Their lances held high; pennants flapping. They wore broad heater shields on their left arms, their personal heraldry displayed for all to see, the most recognisable being the Duke of Adlestrop, who led the King's retinue. Each wore an intimidating great or sugarloaf helm, which covered their faces completely. It was an impressive sight indeed and Fal couldn't help envying the highly trained and skilled warriors, hand-picked from the noble families to serve and protect the King himself. Their colourful surcoats, also displaying their individual heraldries, covered their thick coats of plate, whilst their arms and legs were encased in armour, from maille to articulated steel plate, which gleamed in the late morning sun.

'Fal, come on,' Sav said urgently, and Fal realised it was their turn to move on as Lord Strickland's escort.

Barrison rode from the palace courtyard and on to Kings Avenue, his retinue close behind, their helmets sweeping from side to side as their eyes peered through the narrow slits, scanning the gathering crowds starting to fill the edges of the tree-lined route.

Behind the Duke of Adlestrop and the other knights came three mounted drummers, slowly hammering a solemn beat on their goat-skinned drums. Following the drummers were three mounted trumpeters, their long brass instruments held at their sides like swords.

Ward Strickland came next, flanked by Fal on his right and Sav on his left with the guild coach that held Lord Severun prisoner close behind them. Starks scanned the rooftops and streets joining Kings Avenue, as well as the gathering and cheering crowds of people that grew rapidly. The coach was followed by the two hardened veterans of the guild guard, their maces visible to all. They too scanned the crowds for anyone who might attempt to assault the coach or anyone else in front of them.

The procession made it to and through Kings Square with no trouble and Fal was surprised that, whilst people – rumoured in their hundreds – lay dying across the city, so many others had made the time to stop and witness the procession of the King.

The noise of clattering hooves and scraping armour travelled the length of Wesson to reach Execution Square. No one had made any attempt other than verbal assaults on the coach as it was escorted to the "funeral pyre". Perhaps because many didn't realise what the procession was, since the coach Lord Severun was travelling in was not a prison coach. Fal thought the real reason was the heavily armoured knights of the King's own retinue, and the now dozens strong rear guard from Fal's own command, all of whom had followed on after the procession had passed near to Tyndurris itself. Over forty men-at-arms, crossbowmen and mages walked out into the road behind the black guild coach, following on foot all the way to Execution Square. At first, people shouted insults and screamed threats at the mages, but when they realised just how many armed men and spell-bound battle mages followed, they soon quietened down.

They want to see him burn, as if his death alone will rid them of this plague and bring back their friends, family… make right so many wrongs. Can I blame them? So little do they know, scraps of information, gossip; rumours from here and there, until the terrified man sat in the coach behind me becomes a faceless monster to hundreds if not thousands of people. Is death by fire his worse fear now, or is it knowing his name will pass down through generations as the man that brought a plague upon Wesson?

***

'They'll all be down there.' The green haired woman sat by the window in the small kitchen. Elleth gazed at her in awe, thinking about how amazing it would be to have hair like Coppin's.

Coppin, I like that better than Elleth; Coppin, a real lady, not like me, but a real grown up lady, like mamma.

Elleth's eyes glazed over and she bit back a sob at the thought of her family. It seemed so long ago now, yet it hadn't been long at all… so much had changed.

'The execution?' Elleth asked, although her voice broke.

'Oh Elleth, come 'ere,' Coppin said. 'Don't let Mother see ye cry, we need to stay strong, us girls. Stick together, that's what we do.'

Elleth nodded as she tried but failed to hold back the tears. She moved over to Coppin.

'Ye got me now, girl. The two of us, sisters, ye see,' Coppin said, smiling down at Elleth, who clung to her tightly.

'Wish I were more a lady like you.'

Coppin half-laughed and Elleth blushed. 'Oh no ye don't! Being a girl's the best thing ye could want, and ye hold on to it for as long as ye can, sis.'

Elleth smiled again, before continuing, 'But ye look so beautiful and Mother said how all the men love yer little waist and big—'

Coppin's smile slipped and Elleth stopped.

'Ye hold on to it, sis, I tell ye,' Coppin said quietly. 'Enjoy being you! Ye got the sweetest smile and biggest grey eyes, and ye know what?'

Elleth sat up a little, eyes widening in anticipation.

'I wish I were just like you, Elleth!' Coppin smiled fully again, stroking Elleth's black hair and pulling her close.

Both girls jumped then as Mother walked in.

'Coppin, put my lovely down and get yerself upstairs, girl. Someone here to play,' Mother said with a wink, as she crossed the kitchen and dropped onto a wooden chair by the fire. Her fat terrier snorted as it was shoved from its spot by Mother's large foot.

Coppin took a deep breath and stood then, lifting Elleth to her feet and patting her on the bum.

'Who's here to play?' Elleth asked, but before Coppin could reply, Mother did.

'One of her man friends, my lovely. Now set about yer chores to earn yer keep and let Coppin go earn hers.' The terrier snorted again, several times as it turned once then twice on the spot, before resting its head back on the floor. Mother leant back in her chair and closed her eyes.

Elleth looked as if she wanted to ask more, but turning from the doorway, Coppin shook her head, smiled and then disappeared into the hall beyond.

Elleth sighed to herself and prayed for the day she'd be a woman, so she could go up and play with Coppin and the other sisters upstairs, and perhaps even the men, although that thought was a little scary.

I don't even know how men like to play.

***

In the centre of the sun drenched, cobbled expanse, the usual gallows had been replaced by a great stake reaching easily twenty foot into the air. Logs and branches surrounded the stake, and Fal noticed most of the branches pointed to the sky, the Samorlian's alleged way of sending the damned up to meet Sir Samorl for judgement. Alas, Fal knew it was to inflict maximum pain. The vertical logs meant the fire would spread upwards and not outwards, thus burning the victims alive rather than choking them to death on the thick black smoke.

Bastards!

The crowd hissed and called out insults as the guild coach lumbered into the opening created by the City Guard. The drumming had changed beat and Fal felt like it was feeding the crowds' frenzy.

Around the back of the bonfire was a raised platform which the King, after dismounting from his noble steed, climbed to stand before a wooden throne. His heralds joined him whilst his knights positioned themselves around the square at evenly spaced intervals. Wherever a knight and his destrier stood, the crowd's volume dropped, and Fal could see people warily keep their distance from the powerful horses and their armoured riders.

The drummers kept up their new rhythm, still astride their horses standing in front of the raised platform, where the King had been joined by Archbishop Corlen and a large man Fal had never seen before, who dressed in similar robes to the Archbishop. The King said a few short words to the Archbishop, who in turn spoke to the larger man. The stranger frowned and descended the steps of the platform to stand at the bottom on his own. King Barrison clearly didn't like the man and so neither did Fal.

'He's the Grand Inquisitor,' Ward said, following Fal's gaze. 'He's not in the King's favour after the Kings Avenue attack on you, and so is not permitted to take his usual place by the King for the execution. I assure you, Sergeant Falchion, he will be punished further after today's proceedings.'

Fal merely nodded and turned his gaze to the black guild coach they'd let pass them. They followed it until it stopped on the far side of the pyre. The coach rocked on its springs as the driver hauled on the reigns to stop the two horses pulling it.

Two black clad men carrying rapiers moved from the side of the platform and opened the coach's door. Out came the Lord High Constable's men – swords in hands – followed by Lord Severun, which instigated a chorus of hisses and insults from the crowd. Finally, the wild looking battle mage climbed down from the coach and whispered into Lord Severun's ear. The former Grand Master of the Wizards and Sorcery Guild turned to the battle mage, a mixed look of surprise and fear evident on his face. He then walked to the foot of the platform to face the King. Severun knelt, his head lowered.

Fal, Sav and Ward all shifted in their saddles as the coach pulled away and the King stepped forward. Starks looked back at the kneeling wizard from his seat on the moving coach, a look of pure sorrow on his face as he disappeared from view behind the large bonfire.

The trumpeters sounded then and the drums stopped, and almost immediately the whole square, hundreds of people, fell silent. A child cried towards the back of the crowd and gulls circled above, their mocking calls irritating Fal as he stared at the King, awaiting the announcement.

One of the King's heralds stepped forward and unrolled a parchment from which he began to read. 'It is with great regret that our royal highness, King Barrison, as well as his royal advisors, declare the former Grand Master of the Wizards and Sorcery Guild, outlaw.'

People began to murmur and some shouted again before the King himself raised his hand.

Near silence fell across the square once more.

The herald, looking back down at the parchment, continued. 'Lord Severun has been found guilty of both the practice and use of arcane magic. He was brought to the palace for questioning and confessed to all. He had only one accomplice, who has been placed under lifetime house arrest and who will, by order of the King, remain nameless.'

The crowd stirred again, one man threw a bottle which fell short of Lord Severun. That man was swiftly dragged away by two guardsmen, one of which clamped a hand over his mouth to keep him from calling out.

The King raised both hands this time and stepped forward, gently moving his herald aside. The crowd quietened down once more as King Barrison spoke.

'People of Wesson, of Altoln, have I not always been a fair King where possible?' Many people called out their agreement.

'Then trust in me, in my judgement and that of my advisors. We have talked with the outlaw who kneels before us and we are convinced his accomplice attempted to stop Lord Severun's work many times, and only continued alongside Lord Severun in an attempt to make the experiment they were working on as safe as possible. He was unaware Lord Severun had used arcane magic in the process. He did, alas, work alongside the outlaw, and his work did allow the experiment to continue, thus has he been detained under house arrest for the rest of his years. The accomplice works for you now, the citizens of Wesson, he works to free us of the plague he helped release.

'As for the outlaw you see before you, he will pay the ultimate price. He meant only well for this city. I know this to be the truth. Although we all know his methods were misguided and have caused much suffering, his work with forbidden arcane magic was intended to help the city. It has, however, brought us closer to destruction than Altoln has known in centuries. By meaning only to do good, Lord Severun,' Barrison's eyes fell to the kneeling wizard, who raised his head to meet his King's gaze, 'all you have done is brought us suffering, pain and death. You may have meant well, but you practised forbidden and dangerous arcane magic, and that is why we cannot stray from this course of action.' The King pointed at the high stake, rising from the bonfire. 'Execution by fire, as set out by Altoln's protectors against arcane magic, the Samorlian Church.'

The crowd roared again and the King said something else to Lord Severun, but Fal was too far away to hear the hushed words. Severun stood then and the two black clad men, whom Fal recognised now as witchunters, lead the wizard to the bonfire.

They walked him to the top of the pyre and secured him to the great stake using chains.

Fal moved his horse a couple of steps closer and caught Lord Severun's eyes. The wizard looked back, tears streaking his cheeks as Fal mouthed the words, 'I'm sorry.'

Both Sav and Lord Strickland moved forward either side of Fal.

Severun nodded to Fal and briefly glanced at Ward, before looking back to where the King was now sat. Corlen stood on the King's left hand side, bending to whisper into his ear.

The drums pounded and the trumpets called out three long, hollow notes. The fire was lit.

Fal felt anger burn within him as he looked from Lord Severun to the King and back. He looked then at Sav who had tears in his eyes and was visibly clenching his teeth. His knuckles were white as he gripped his reigns.

The flames licked higher as the two witchunters lit more kindling around

150

the base of the bonfire. People screamed and jeered and one woman laughed. Fal cursed himself for the thought he briefly had upon hearing that.

Lord Severun was squirming now, the heat and smoke clearly getting to him.

The drums kept up their eerie tempo as the flames began to lick at the base of the stake Lord Severun was chained to.

Men of the City Guard shoved back the crowd as they tried to push forwards to get a better view of the execution. On one side of the bonfire – where the crowd became too rowdy and managed to force two guardsmen back – a knight of the King's retinue walked his destrier forward. He turned it about and lowered his lance towards the crowd. The great bay destrier reared and clattered its metal shod hooves on the cobbled stone. The people before it ceased their advance and pushed back again, away from the snorting animal and its faceless rider.

Fal's gaze was drawn back to the fire as Lord Severun cried out in pain. The smoke was enough to half hide the burning man now, but not enough to finish him off before the flames engulfed him. Fal turned to look at Lord Strickland, who, hidden by a long, voluminous sleeve, held one hand high whilst closing his eyes and whispering to himself. Fal thought it strange the magician might pray to a deity, but in such a horrific situation, people did whatever they could to ease the pain.

The screaming was raking at Fal like an animal now. He could see Lord Severun writhing in agony, thrashing around on the stake. His skin bubbled as his clothes burnt away and he blistered from feet to thighs.

Gods above, we commit a definite evil here and now, as justice to an act that is perceived as evil, but was not meant to be so. Does this right the wrong, or plunge us deeper towards the gods below?

Fal started, as Sav moved forward suddenly, his horse taking a few steps. Fal turned to see his friend quickly stringing his bow before pulling an arrow from a linen bag tied to his saddle. Fal kicked his horse forward and tried to grab Sav as he nocked the arrow and drew the bow, aiming it at the screaming wizard now being roasted alive.

'Sav, no!' Fal shouted, but before he could say another word, Sav was dragged from his saddle by two guardsmen and wrestled to the floor. Fal turned to call for Lord Strickland, just as one of the King's own knights surged across the cobbles on his warhorse and rammed his shield into Fal's face.

The pain was instant and his vision flashed white, but before he registered what had happened, Fal felt himself fall from the saddle and his world turned black.

***

Thick, black and tan fur became visible from under the low bed, as a large bloodhound appeared, sniffing at the floor all around the late Peneur Ineson's

151

bedroom.

'Long body ain't it?' Sears said.

Biviano nodded. 'Aye…' he scratched his left arm pit as best he could through his maille, 'and short legs for such a heavy looking hound.'

'Never seen another like him, that's for sure,' Sears said as he watched the hound, which seemed to be following a scent leading out through the bedroom door.

'Buddle's Sirretan,' Gitsham mumbled, as the three men followed the dog down the grand stairs of the house. 'They calls 'em chien de something I don't remember what, down there.'

'Long name,' Biviano said.

'Funny,' Sears said.

Biviano ducked out of the way of Sears' fist and grinned to himself in triumph when his friend winced, moving his hand to his chest and the small hole in his maille hauberk.

'Effrin and a night's rest seem to have got ye almost fighting fit again, big guy… almost.' Biviano awaited a retort, but Sears ignored the comment and nodded to the dog.

'Ye get him from Sirreta then, Gitsham?' Sears pointed at the hound and tried to act like he wasn't in pain.

'No.'

'From a breeder in Wesson?' Biviano asked, struggling to satisfy the itch under his maille.

'No.'

Talkative bastard this one, both Sears and Biviano thought.

'I hear he sniffs out all sorts, Gitsham, not just scent?' Biviano said, raising his eyebrows – just visible under the rim of his kettle-helm – in anticipation.

'Aye.'

Sears rolled his eyes before asking, 'Well, what kind of other things does Buddle sniff out then, man?'

'All sorts.'

Sears cursed and Biviano ducked. It hadn't been necessary, but his arm was throbbing as it was, so he wasn't going to take any more chances with the big guy, who'd been particularly angry since he'd woken up with Effrin hovering over him. The cleric had advised them against it, but as soon as Gitsham had arrived and Sears could physically stand, the trio and the bloodhound left the barracks and headed straight for Peneur Ineson's house.

Buddle stopped at the front door of the house, which was shut.

All three men stood and looked at the hound, which turned and looked back at them, wet nose glistening.

'What's he doing now then?' Sears said, looking from Buddle to Biviano and then to Gitsham, who stood picking his nose, paying little attention to his dog.

'Gitsham,' Sears repeated, 'what's the mutt doing?'

Buddle snarled at the red bearded guardsman and both Sears and Biviano stepped back a pace.

'Eh?'

'Yer lovely bloodhound,' Sears said, his frustration growing, 'what's he doing now?'

Gitsham looked to Sears, then to Buddle's drooping eyes before answering. 'He's waiting for ye to open the door and let him out.'

Biviano became animated at that and looked excited. 'To chase the scent?' he said in a high pitched voice that made Sears smirk despite himself.

Gitsham shook his head. 'To piss and shit.'

'Lovely.' Sears gingerly reached over the bloodhound and opened the door.

Buddle squeezed through the gap as soon as it opened, ran outside and started to do his business to the side of the doorway. The three men followed him out, closing the door behind them.

'Been too long to pick up the scent has it?' Sears asked.

'Nope.'

'So he *has* found a scent to follow then?' Biviano leant forward and rested his hands on his knees whilst staring at the dog, which was still crouched and hovering.

'He don't like being watched,' Gitsham said, his finger still prodding up his nose.

'Well I suppose not, I know I don't,' Sears said, turning away.

'And who watches you then?' Biviano asked, doing the same.

'You!'

'We watch each other's backs, Sears, it's what we do, ye big ape. Ye'd be squealin' if some ganger jumped ye mid-shit wouldn't ye?'

'Hardly going to happen now is it, ye dick?'

'Ye never do know, Sears, especially after what happened to ye in the street.' Biviano mimed the shooting of a crossbow. 'Be prepared, that's what me da always told me.'

'Ye never knew yer da.'

'Must've been yours then, all's I know is someone's da telling me so...'

'That dog finished yet?' Biviano added whilst looking up into the sky, watching a flock of pigeons pass over.

'Aye, finished just after ye both turned,' Gitsham said, sucking something slimy off the end of his middle finger.

Sears and Biviano spun around then, to see the dog just sat there looking at them.

Turning from the dog to its handler, Sears shook his head in disbelief. 'Why didn't ye say so then, ye fool?'

Gitsham pointed at himself. 'Me?'

'Never mind,' Sears said. 'What's he found then and why ain't he following it if it's a scent?'

Gitsham looked at Buddle and the dog tilted its head, before it yawned and lay down, licking its left paw. 'No point following no scent,' Gitsham said, 'culprit's no longer a threat.'

Biviano and Sears looked to one another, frowned and then looked back at Gitsham. Both went to speak at the same time, stopped then did exactly the same again, so Sears punched Biviano in the arm, grimaced at the pain the action caused him and then spoke whilst the smaller man cursed repeatedly.

'Explain what ye mean, Gitsham. Ye need to be more specific and maybe explain how ye seem to know anything at all from just looking at a damned dog.' *Gods only know,* Sears thought, *I wish I could talk directly to the bloody dog, I think I'd get a lot more back.*

Buddle raised his head and growled at Sears again.

Or not!

'He knew who done the killing as soon as he entered the house,' Gitsham said in his monotone voice, 'but the killer's no longer a problem to ye, or anyone else for that matter, so I guess we're done.'

'Woah there, sunshine,' Sears said, holding his arm out to stop Gitsham leaving, 'we certainly ain't done and I don't think ye know the meaning of specific.'

Gitsham sat down on the floor and scratched behind his ear repeatedly as he looked again at Buddle, then back up to Sears and Biviano, the latter finally standing upright again after being curled over in pain. The smaller guardsman glared up at his friend, before locking eyes with Gitsham, who sighed and continued.

'He's looking at the reason the killer's no threat right now, and it's behind ye both.'

Both men turned and looked up the empty street. There were black crosses on two front doors down the row of tall houses, and apart from a carriage in the distance near the park, there wasn't a soul in sight. More and more people in all districts were staying indoors, trying to avoid the now confirmed plague.

'What am I looking for?' Biviano asked, whilst still scanning the street.

'Up,' Gitsham said, returning to his nose picking.

Both men looked up and as they did, their eyes naturally followed the thick, black smoke rising from the north-west corner of the city.

'Smoke?'

'Aye, Sears,' Gitsham said, chewing on something, 'smoke!'

'What about it?' Biviano asked next. 'They're burning plague victims all over the city now, where ye been, Gitsham? Ye not heard? It's all been confirmed and announced.'

Buddle seemed to huff at that, and rested his head on his two front paws.

'But that ain't smoke from the fire burnin' *those* bodies. That's the smoke from the fire burnin' *his* body.'

'Whose?' Sears shouted, finally losing his temper and narrowly missing a fast side-stepping Biviano with his huge fist. He sucked in through his clenched teeth against the pain the movement brought to his chest.

Biviano's mouth dropped then and his eyes slowly moved to Buddle's as he spoke.

'The murderer's body?'

Buddle's head lifted and his tail started to wag.

Biviano looked up to Sears, who looked back whilst gently prodding at his wounded chest, frowning all the while. 'Lord Severun?' he offered, unconvinced.

Biviano nodded, eyes wide, and Buddle let out a single bark.

Sears' eyes widened too and he sat down suddenly, next to Gitsham, turning round once he had to look at the thick column of smoke once more. Biviano shrugged and followed Sears to the floor, removing his helmet and placing it in his lap, then having a good scratch underneath his coif; behind one ear, then the other.

After a couple of moments of them all sitting there and the news sinking in, Biviano looked back to Gitsham – who seemed to be in a world of his own – to ask another question. 'How do you, know that he,' Biviano pointed his chin at Buddle, 'knows that Lord Severun, Grand Master of the Wizards and Sorcery Guild, killed Peneur Ineson, a previously small-time trader of foreign shit?'

Sears added, 'And does Master Investigation know why the wizard did it?'

'As for how *I* knows *he* knows,' Gitsham said, without looking at either of them, 'I don't really know. I just do, and as for the why, that ain't for us to figure out, so no, we don't know, although it has something to do with this plague and that's all I can tells ye on that. I do know, however, that whatever it was the wizard killed the merchant over, well, it scared the shit out of me hound, and he ain't for sniffing out any more on this case.'

'Well the plague link makes sense,' Biviano said, 'seein' as that's why the church just burnt the poor bastard wizard, but ye see, Gitsham, that ain't good enough for us to—'

'For we need to know a motive,' Sears interrupted, 'as well as where and why all this started, for that's the only way we know how to get it sorted ye see?'

'Also,' Sears continued, 'there's another murder down the road there, by the park, so we need yer mutt—'

'Quit yer snarling!'

'So we need Buddle to sniff it out, as we believe they're both—'

Sears stopped as Gitsham held up his hand to stop him.

'That one was even easier for Buddle, and he had it when we passed the site on the way here.'

Sears looked to Biviano, who's eyes hadn't moved from Buddle's, looking for some sign of communication from dog to handler, but finding none as of yet.

'Go on then,' Sears said, rubbing his hands together.

'Witchunter.'

'What?' Biviano said incredulously 'A Samorlian witchunter killed Master Joinson, an agent for a small-time merchant of foreign shit?'

'Aye, Biviano, that's what I'm saying and after he came through *here* too,' Gitsham said, nodding to Peneur Ineson's large house. 'But got no answer he didn't, the witchunter, on account of Ineson already being dead.'

Sears stood then and pulled a wincing Biviano to his feet by his bad arm, whilst wincing himself.

'Right then,' the big man said, 'that's why the bastards attacked us on the street. I knew it and I don't care how Gitsham knows he knows whoever knows what and all that cock and bollocks, we can go off that can't we, officially like, for the captain and the magistrates?'

'Aye, we bloody well can,' Biviano said, grinning at Buddle, who he could have sworn winked at him.

'That means we can go back to the barracks then, lads? Leave ye to it?' Gitsham asked, climbing to his feet and groaning at the effort, Buddle doing the same. 'I don't like being in the streets with this plague afoot.'

'For now man, aye.' Sears patted Gitsham's back and moved to stroke Buddle. He stopped short at the bloodhound's bared fangs.

'Alright ye miserable dog, I'll leave ye be, because us two have business with the bastard Samorlians,' Sears said, a wicked grin splitting his red beard.

Buddle turned then and slowly plodded down the street, Gitsham in tow, his hand held up as a farewell.

'What a flaming strange old pair them two make,' Biviano said, whilst placing his helmet back onto his head and then scratching underneath it.

'Aye, that's true. Now come on, ye weasel, we've witchunters and inquisitors to interrogate. Ha!'

'Ha, yeah, ye laugh now Sears, until we end up on the other side of said interrogation. Any other guardsman would've left it be after hearing all that.'

'Any other guardsman would've shit it when they attacked us in the damned street, ye prick, so it's a good job for these two dead bastards they got us two on the case, eh?'

Sears pulled Biviano into a headlock and began walking him towards the great cathedral in the distance.

Bit late for them, Sears. It's us I worry after mate, but aye, we'll interrogate 'em alright and that's just for starters.

156

Chapter 20: In The Dark

The thick wooden door at the end of the darkened chamber crashed as it swung open and collided with the stone wall. Two tall figures strode into the room, one of whom had a black cloak billowing out behind him, which rested at the back of his legs when he and the other man stopped. They both nodded to the large man behind the ancient desk before taking a seat opposite.

'Were you born in barns, gentlemen?' the Grand Inquisitor said.

Neither man stirred at first, then they looked at each other before the taller of the two left his chair, strode across the room and slammed the door, causing the room's beeswax candles to flicker.

'Thank you, General Comlay. Now, I take it you and your southern counterpart have something you wish to discuss, or are you both in a habit of bursting in here unannounced for no apparent reason?' The Grand Inquisitor took great pleasure in watching the two warriors squabble like children, and so occasionally fed the fire of their mutual hatred for one another, rather than berating them as he supposed he should.

Horler Comlay took his seat and sighed, gesturing for the southern Witchunter General to speak.

Exley gladly took the rare opportunity of getting a free word in without Horler trying to stop him. 'Grand Inquisitor, as you know, Severun has been executed and the gnome, Orix, is under house arrest for the rest of his living days.'

'Yes… and?'

'Well sire, your Wesson General here insists not only do we break into Tyndurris and kidnap the gnome, to burn, but we also kidnap the sergeant-at-arms that released the plague and put him to the flame as well. May I remind General Comlay where that sergeant is and how difficult and pointless both exercises are?' Exley looked to the other General, but swiftly continued before Horler could interrupt. 'With the fate of both already decided by King Barrison, I don't see any point in taking this matter further. The enactor of the arcane magic which caused the plague is rightfully dead – a death dealt by fire; a fire that still burns as we speak no doubt, and the other two aren't likely to be a threat to this city ever again.' Horler went to speak, but Exley continued hurriedly. 'And that's not mentioning the fact King Barrison has ordered us to cease such activity in the city immediately, and to report to the Constable of Wesson before we take any actions in future.'

Horler Comlay rolled his eyes, and the Grand Inquisitor had to strain to hide a smirk.

'May I remind you, General Clewarth,' the Grand Inquisitor said, 'this is not your region of command, and what we decide to do here is our business not yours. You were ordered here to assist in the investigation of the guild's treachery, and up to now you've done your job well. We have dealt with the ring-leader of this attempt to overthrow the city, but as General Comlay has pointed out to you, there are at least two more who were involved, both of whom should also rightfully be executed.'

Exley Clewarth's mouth dropped open as he looked from the Grand Inquisitor to Horler Comlay and back. 'You agree with him?' Exley jerked his thumb at Horler, who now sat a little straighter in his chair and grinned. *You smug bastard*, Exley thought, irritably.

'That I do, General Clewarth, and I suggest you don't take that tone with me again. I want that shite of a gnome dragged from that tower kicking and screaming, and the sergeant killed using any means necessary. I don't see the use in troubling ourselves with burning him, so ridding Altoln of him is all we need do… filthy tattooed foreigner.' The Grand Inquisitor spat on the floor.

Exley Clewarth shook his head slowly before asking, 'Am I to return to the south then, or assist here, sire?'

The Grand Inquisitor slipped into thought for a few moments, twisting on his finger what looked like a new addition to his collection of rings. 'General Comlay,' he said eventually, 'you will rid us of the sergeant. General Clewarth, you will take the gnome from Tyndurris and burn him. Both of you will use any means necessary to get the tasks done. I don't want either of you in my sight again until both are dealt with. Am I understood?'

Aye, I understand, Exley thought. *I should've kept my mouth shut and perhaps I'd be back off down south this evening.*

Both men nodded and the Grand Inquisitor continued to read an old looking tome. Both General's took it as their dismissal and so strode from the room, saying nothing to one another nor looking each other in the eye. They had their orders and were determined to carry them out. If not for the Grand Inquisitor and Sir Samorl, then to best the other and get one step ahead in their constant fight for bragging rights and supremacy, and although Exley Clewarth didn't like the idea of what he'd been ordered to do, for many reasons, he was just as determined as his Wesson counterpart to succeed.

***

Fal opened his eyes. His head was thumping but he saw nothing. His eyes had definitely opened, but might have well stayed shut for all the good it'd done. Fal's nose twitched at the sudden and strong smell of excrement, and he reached up and felt his head for a blindfold, although it hadn't felt like there was one there. *Another spell like Lord Strickland used when we were brought in front of King Barrison?* He winced when his hand brushed a tender lump on his forehead. *What happened to me?* He couldn't remember how he got wherever he was or what had happened to get him there.

'Hello?' Fal called out softly, hoping for a reply from someone he knew.

'Fal?' a nasal but familiar voice said.

'Sav, mate, where are we? Where're you?' Fal was a little relieved upon hearing his friend's voice. He pushed himself up into a sitting position, his eyes still unadjusted to the darkness all around.

'We're in Wesson Prison, Fal. You were knocked unconscious, but I was dragged here fighting. Not much good it did me; bruised ribs and a flattened nose. Lost my pretty looks I suppose. Oh well, still have my charm.'

Although it was as black as pitch, Fal could hear the mirth in Sav's voice.

'Prison? Why the hell are we in prison? I've never even seen the inside of this place as a guardsman and now we're in a damned cell... not that I can see it.' Fal's eyes had started to adjust ever so slightly to the dark, but all he could make out was a hazy figure opposite him from where Sav's voice came.

'Well I think that's down to me, Fal,' Sav said, his tone dropping. 'I'm sorry, I just couldn't take it. I've seen executions before, hangings, but that... that was horrific. I couldn't watch it, especially after hearing about him at the palace, about his parents, his fears.'

Gods above, the fire... Severun... Fal's heart lurched.

'I strung my bow and tried to end it for him,' Sav continued, 'to stop him roasting alive, but I was dragged from the saddle and beaten. Next thing I know one of the King's retinue smashed you from your horse. It's been a fair few hours now, not sure exactly how long. I was worried you were going to sleep forever. Bet your head hurts, eh?'

Like you wouldn't believe, Sav, but more from what I'm starting to remember than the pain. Fal nodded, then realised it was pointless. 'Yeah, it's hammering a beat not too different from the drummers in the square. What's been said then? When're we getting out?' It was so quiet in the cell that Sav's gulp was audible.

Oh shit. 'Sav?'

'Well, that's just it isn't it? They haven't said anything about getting us out, as of yet anyway. They threw us in and all Sir Bullen told us was we'd be fed twice daily, and there's a small latrine hole in the corner. He also said to be careful it doesn't fill up and flood before it flows away.

'Great.' Fal let out a long, slow breath. 'What about Lord Strickland? He was there; did he say nothing at all to help us?'

'No, he had his eyes tight shut and kept mumbling to himself. I guess he couldn't stand the sight of his old friend burning. I wish he'd tried something though, I know it's the King's law, Fal, but come on, that's barbaric. Lord Severun only meant to do good.'

'I know, Sav, and I didn't like it either, but what could the King do?' Fal prodded tentatively at the lump on his head again as he spoke. 'There's been arcane mages burnt before in that square, not to mention witches and warlocks throughout Altoln, so how could he have one rule for one and one for another? The city is in a panic and rioting left right and centre... I guess as horrific as it is, Lord Severun's execution might calm them down; seeing the one who was responsible executed.'

Who am I trying to convince, Sav or myself? No matter what someone's done... death by fire? No. I've seen enough of that and I've seen its pain and the pain it leaves in those who've witnessed it. I don't care how they cheered in that square, their dreams won't let them

159

forget what we all witnessed.

Sav went quiet and the cold, black room fell silent. Fal couldn't see, but sensed the cell was small.

I feel exactly the same as you, my friend. Perhaps I've tried to justify it to you to make myself feel better. To make up for the fact I took Severun to the palace, that maybe it's because of me he died like that… that perhaps I could have done more earlier on, opened my damned mouth and asked more about what I'd been ordered to do instead of blindly following those orders. One thing I know is that the horror of what I… no, what we all saw out there, will be our punishment for the rest of our days, a punishment for me that only adds to that I already suffer for what happened all those years ago. A punishment I well deserve…

'I admire you for trying to stop it, Sav, more than you know.' *Part of me wishes I'd had the balls to try myself.* 'And no matter what comes from it mate, you tried to do the right thing and I should've supported you, not tried to stop you.'

'I guess,' Sav said sullenly. 'I've a bad feeling about all of this though, Fal. I think we could be made examples of. Attempting what I did in front of the King, undermining him, me as one of his soldiers standing against his law in front of the whole city, it doesn't bode well. You should be fine. I'm sure they'll let you go, but me? What will become of me?'

Fal shook his head again. 'I don't honestly know, Sav. People have tried, gangers mainly, to cut people from the gallows before they choke, but you're no ganger, you're an Altolnan border scout and a good one at that. I'm sure you'll get a slap on the wrist, a few lashes maybe and sent back out… your leave forfeit maybe?' *But in all honesty, I haven't a clue, Sav, and gods, if I'm honest, I'm a little fearful for you, for us both. But telling you that'll do us no good.*

'Great, my leave cancelled, no more ale or women for months, they may as well hang me.' Sav laughed, although it sounded forced.

Both men fell silent again then, escaping into their heads, thinking about what had happened and feeling their eyes slowly close, which hardly made a difference. After what seemed like hours, both men fell asleep on the straw covered, cold stone floor of their cell.

***

The tall, vaulted ceilings of the Samorlian Cathedral offered superb harmonics to the dozens of voices reaching up and out from the choir of monks and boys below. The sound was eerie as it slowly built from a low hum to a stirring crescendo that leant weight to the finale of Archbishop Corlen's sermon, a sermon that had followed on from the burning of Lord Severun and lasted hours.

'When's this shitting bollocks gonna end?' Biviano said, rubbing his chin and staring down to the pew in between Sears and himself, where they sat at the very back of the cathedral.

'Quit complaining and make yer move, we can't make *our* move until the

King and his lords have left, can we?'

Biviano slowly reached down and moved his small, black stone into one of the twenty four half holes carved into the pew itself. He then picked up a white stone and passed it to Sears, grinning all the while.

'Bastard,' Sears said, as he realised he was now losing stones from his mills.

'Shit!' Biviano froze, and Sears looked up to him from the game. 'What?'

'The sermon's finished, they're walking past us to get out of the cathedral!'

Sears didn't dare turn, for fear of the King's own eyes upon him. 'Where's the King?'

'He left already. Don't think he looked this way though, although one of his high lords has...' Biviano trailed off and held his breath.

'Who?' Sears asked, his tone hushed as he too froze in place, not wanting to turn around and take a look for himself.

Biviano stopped talking and smiled meekly to someone behind Sears. Taking a deep breath, the big man slowly turned around to see who Biviano was looking at. He saw a crowd of richly dressed people moving down the aisle to the main doors, and an angry looking Duke staring at them both, his gnarled left hand tapping on the back of their pew further down the row and his right gripping the ornate hilt of his bastard-sword.

Will Morton nodded towards the white stone in Sears' hand and then to the pew in between the two men as he spoke. 'Enjoy the sermon, gentlemen? Or was your game of nine men's morris more entertaining? Looks freshly carved that board... on that pew?'

'Erm, the sermon, milord. Arousing it was, milord,' Sears said, nodding, whilst Biviano closed his eyes.

Morton moved a step closer and leaned in to Sears. 'Arousing eh? Didn't know the Archbishop did it for you, Sears? He certainly doesn't do it for me I can tell you. In fact, I'd rather have been back here myself, watching Biviano here take your stones.'

Biviano dared a grin as the Lord High Constable stood back from Sears.

'Now, when you're done being beaten, get that bloody hole in your maille fixed, it looks awful, and no, I don't want to know how it happened... although I'll no doubt hear it from Stowold at some point.'

Sears brought his hand up to where the crossbow bolt had struck him and winced at the memory of the impact.

'Ha, arousing, classic!' Morton continued to laugh as he turned and walked back down the row, turning onto the aisle. Two knights wearing the Duke's colours awaited him. All three moved off with the crowd to leave the cathedral through the large, main doors.

'Ye dick,' Biviano said.

'I don't get what's so funny,' Sears said, picking up and placing all of his white stones into a pouch on his belt.

'And that's what makes it all the more funny ye fool.

'Speaking of fools,' Biviano said, nodding to the front of the cathedral. 'Let's us go speak to that fat fool up there, before he scuttles off into chambers beyond.'

Both men stood then and moved down the row to the centre aisle. Once there, they walked with menacing confidence towards the Archbishop at the front of the cathedral; a man who, until noticing the two experienced warriors – for surely by their stride alone, he knew that's what they were – had been feeling fairly confident himself. Not now, alas, for now it was all he could do not to void his bowels as the two approaching men drew their short-swords and locked eyes with him.

***

Fal woke with a start. There was a crash of steel on steel in the corridor outside the cell door and a man yelped, before hobnailed boots echoed as they scraped on stone away into the distance.

Fal felt the air in the small chamber shift then as Sav stood up next to him. He was so close Fal had no problem finding and using Sav's arm to pull himself up.

A loud thud immediately outside the door was followed by a groan and a jingle of metal on metal.

Keys? Fal held his breath and listened. *What The Three's going on out there?*

Both Fal and Sav clenched their fists and squinted in anticipation of the light that would surely spill through the door about to be opened. Several keys could be heard jingling and scraping on the door, one after another being tried in the lock.

Not the guards then, Fal thought, *but who? Witchunters back for more? Surely they wouldn't be so bold as to attack the prison?* Fal clenched his fists tighter still and widened his stance.

A loud metallic click signalled the release of the locking mechanism, and unoiled hinges screeched as the heavy reinforced door swung inwards. Both Fal and Sav had to raise their hands to shade their eyes from the bright star-like light that shone directly into their eyes from the doorway, and Sav laughed aloud as the light flicked from Fal to Sav and back.

'Errolas!' Sav announced in delight. Fal lowered his hands just enough to see the illuminated, grinning face of the elf, curved sword in one hand and a small glowing stone in the other.

'Greetings, gentlemen,' Errolas said, his brilliant white teeth shining in the star stone's light, and from behind him two more heads appeared at his shoulders. It was Godsiff Starks and a rather stern looking woman with short black hair and a scar running down her left cheek. Despite her hard appearance, she had a subtle attractiveness that Fal and Sav could hardly take their eyes off.

Fal spoke next, clearly confused. 'What's going on?'

'No time to explain,' Errolas replied hurriedly, as he looked back down the corridor to his left. 'We have to move, now!'

Errolas disappeared then, along with Starks and their female companion, who was dressed in fitted black leather armour and openly carrying two curved swords. Before leaving, she hesitated just long enough to gesture for the two captives to follow.

Fal and Sav looked at each other and Sav shrugged and then grinned. 'Better than swinging from a rope,' he said, before running from the room, Fal hard on his heels.

Chapter 21: Knockers

A bell rang in the distance. It echoed eerily through the prison's maze of passageways cut into the northern cliffs of Wesson. The group had been running for just a few minutes, but Fal's head was spinning from the blow he'd received in Execution Square, and Sav kept hauling him roughly along every time he stumbled in the dim light. Errolas was just in front of the two friends, shining his star stone ahead, just enough for the unknown woman to lead the way. Godsiff Starks brought up the rear, his crossbow slung across his back and a short-sword in his right hand. He kept stopping and looking back every so often, listening for following footsteps.

Fal was surprised at how well Starks' leg had healed, but not as surprised as he was to see the lad there, in the prison... not as surprised as he was to see any of them there in the prison.

As the group followed the woman around a corner and into an extremely narrow corridor lined with cage-like cells, a dozen grubby and boil infested hands burst through the bars to grab at the passers-by. Despite keeping quite a pace, the woman managed to shrug away the one hand that took hold of her arm. Another man tried to grab her behind, but cried out in pain as she turned without stopping to slice his forearm with her sword. As the man cried out, so did his cell mates, screeching like animals as they threw mud, stones and worse through the bars of the cells. A stone flew towards Errolas, which he batted away with his closed left hand, briefly causing the star stone's beam of light to cast across the cell.

Fal almost retched at the sight of the bearded men hunched over with wild unkempt hair, filthy boil marked faces and dead-looking eyes. The stench contributed to Fal's nausea; in the brief glimpse he caught, he saw piles of excrement mixed in with what looked like a rotting corpse.

'Keep moving. Hurry,' the woman shouted, and Fal realised he'd unwittingly slowed to take in the horrid scene. More arms reached for him from the other side of the corridor and he batted them away, as prisoners spat and threw more makeshift missiles his way. Fal didn't want to know what it was that hit his knee, for it was far from solid, and so he moved on as fast as he could in the dim light provided by the elf just ahead.

'Stay with us, Starks, don't drop too far back,' Fal shouted, as they turned another corner and left the grasping hands and screeching wastes of men behind.

'Right with you, Sarge. Glad to have you back,' Starks said, and Fal could hear the sincerity in the young crossbowman's voice.

Glad to be back lad, whatever 'back' means now we're fleeing the prison.

Fal quickly turned to look at the crossbowman, and as he did, he ran into Errolas in front, who managed to stay on his feet whilst Fal crashed hard to the ground.

Sav picked a cursing Fal up and they both realised the woman had stopped. She pulled Errolas forward and asked him to cast a beam of light down the corridor. None of the three men behind the front two could see anything but a dead end.

They took the opportunity – in what might only be a brief respite – to catch their breaths. Fal rested his hands on his knees and Sav leant against the stone wall. As he did, he jumped and pulled away from it. 'Eeuw… it's wet,' he said. 'We're not in carved corridors now, this tunnel's natural rock.'

Fal straightened and ran his hands across the cold surface of the wall, which was uneven and jagged in some places, yet smooth and wet in others. The floor, however, had been flattened, and Fal guessed the tunnel had been started but never finished.

'What now?' Fal wiped his wet hands on his woollen hose and looked to the group's leaders. Receiving no reply, he looked to Sav, who shrugged.

Errolas and the woman muttered to each other before she edged ever so slowly forward, guided by Errolas' light. She moved down the tunnel towards the far end – the dead end.

A bell rang again in the distance and although the crazed prisoners in the caged cells had quietened down, Fal could still hear the odd shriek and manic laugh, which sent a shiver down his spine.

Fal, along with Sav and Starks, stared past Errolas, following the elf's light and the woman's progress.

Not one of them dared speak until, with a loud crack and rumble, a section of stone ceiling gave way. Dust filled the tunnel as rocks crashed down between the woman and the rest of them. Fal and Sav looked at each other after ducking instinctively, whilst Starks spun round to face the way they'd come, a bolt now resting on the groove of his crossbow – which he'd taken hold of and made ready when they'd stopped.

'Don't panic,' Errolas said, his voice as calm as ever.

'But the lass?' Sav shouted, 'what if she's—'

'Boo!'

Fal and Sav both jumped.

The female voice came from beside Sav's head and he almost crashed into the low ceiling as he jumped. Errolas laughed and walked through what looked like a solid rock wall. Fal gazed mouth open, but before he could say anything, a female hand emerged through the liquid-like rock and took hold of his arm. He felt himself being pulled hard, and through the wall he went.

Sav looked to Starks and tried to compose himself, although his expression gave away his shock and embarrassment.

Starks turned, took the bolt off his crossbow, placed it in a pouch on his belt and relaxed the string. He strapped the weapon onto his back and laughed as he shoved Sav into the fluidic rock, before following him through.

Once through the liquid wall, Fal and Sav realised they were in what looked like an ancient mine shaft. Thick wooden beams held the ceiling and walls back, and Sav shuddered at the thought of how deep they must be. Only then did he realised they'd been running down slight gradients most of the way from the cell; constantly travelling deeper into the cliffs and the depths beneath the prison. The tunnel they now stood in seemed to continue where the other had ended, although it ran parallel to the other tunnel, as if the whole thing had shifted across to the side before it continued.

'An illusion barrier,' Errolas announced. 'It hides the true way from the last tunnel into this one.'

Fal and Sav still looked confused and so Errolas said, 'My explanation wouldn't do it justice, but the ceiling didn't really collapse… I'm sure you get the idea.'

Fal and Sav both looked at a laughing Starks, who shrugged and walked past them. He followed the woman who'd set off again down the tunnel, the star stone now in her hand, her swords sheathed at her sides.

'We explained it to Starks beforehand,' Errolas said. 'It took quite some time mind, but it is the only reason he didn't jump as high as you two. Now come on, we need to get going again and catch Correia up.'

Correia? Fal and Sav thought simultaneously, before setting off after Errolas, all three jogging a few steps to catch up to the two in front.

Whilst jogging, Sav asked the obvious. 'Who's Correia? How come she's helping us and what in the name of 'morl's wrinkled scrotum is going on?' Sav's curse made Fal grin despite the situation.

'Patience, Sav,' Errolas said. 'I'm sure you both have a hundred questions, but they can wait, I assure you. We will stop and rest when Correia says so and we will explain all that needs explaining then, I promise.'

Fal and Sav acknowledged that and they both stumbled on in the dim light to keep up with Correia, who seemed to navigate the twisting tunnels effortlessly.

***

Archbishop Corlen hadn't given Sears and Biviano any information, despite the man's obvious fear, and as much as they'd wanted to, neither guardsman had laid a hand on the Archbishop. They knew there was someone else they needed to question, someone in the inquisition. So, trusting the Archbishop's fear to stop him from doing anything stupid, Sears and Biviano had followed the man through a small door and down a stone staircase into the depths of the cathedral, a place both men had found fitting for the inquisitors.

When, however, the Archbishop had led them into a darkened room, slamming and then locking the heavy door behind them, they'd known they'd made a mistake in thinking fear of them alone would have manipulated the cowardly man.

'Ye stupid bastard, Sears,' Biviano said, as he turned and hammered on the door with the hilt of his sword. 'Let us out, Corlen, or it'll only get worse for ye!

'Gods below, it stinks in here.'

'I'm stupid? Why me?' Sears sheathed his sword and fumbled in the pouches about his belt, trying to find the flint and steel he knew he had.

'Because ye said to follow him, that he'd lead us to the Grand Inquisitor.'

'We both thought he would, ye dick. Wasn't just me, or would you have thought the puddle of piss would ever risk his fat neck and not do as we asked?'

A flick of flint on steel and the room was lit briefly. Another and Biviano noticed Sears moving slowly towards the wall to his right. Another and Sears was trying to light a torch on the wall. The next one lit the torch and the room revealed itself in an orange glow.

'Flay me, Sears… what is this place?' Biviano said, trying to comprehend what the torch was illuminating.

Sears turned to see what his partner was looking at. The big man drew his short-sword once more, his flint and steel held tightly in his left hand.

'Is he dead?'

'I don't know, big guy, but part of me hopes so. Look at his arms and legs… they've stretched the poor bastard.'

Through the gloom, they could both make out the elongated form of a naked man, his wrists bound above him and his ankles below. He lay on a large inclined wooden rack, the ropes linked to pulleys at either end.

'Shit! Literally, no wonder this place stinks,' Sears said, pressing the back of his left hand to his nose.

'Aye and I'm not surprised.' Biviano moved slowly towards the man on the rack, unable to take his eyes from the beaten and bloodied form. 'Bring that torch, Sears.'

Following Biviano, torch in hand after placing the flint and steel in his pouch, Sears lifted it high, its light fully illuminating the man on the rack.

Biviano recoiled slightly at the scene and for the first time, quickly cast his eyes about the room. 'It's a pissin' torture chamber, Sears.'

Sears did the same and saw a multitude of devices hanging on hooks, as well as tables littered with filthy and in some cases rusting implements and tools. 'Bastards,' he growled. 'Evil bastards.'

Biviano nodded. 'And under the cathedral too, of all places.

'This is where the inquisitors do their work then. And here I was thinking all that was in the past, that the inquisition and the witchunters' only role now was in hunting arcane magicians and the like. They're supposed to be here to protect the people, not cut the poor bastards up like the bloody Three, and for what, Sears?'

'I dunno, I really don't. But there's no way there's enough arcane magic about Wesson for them to need a room like this, to *ever* need any of this. Hunt 'em down and execute the evil shites aye, but torturing people, and for what, information? *We* didn't know this was here, Biviano, so who the hell knows who the inquisitors are taking and torturing? 'Cause I sure as hell doubt Captain Prior does, let alone the Constable of Wesson?'

The man on the rack groaned suddenly, and both men sucked in a breath

'He's alive.' Biviano breathed the words out as a whisper, sheathing his sword quickly and moving so he could lean over the man's face. Sears followed suit and held the torch over them both.

The man's eyes slowly opened and when he saw the two men above him, those eyes widened and his whole body stiffened; he cried out in pain.

'No, don't move,' Biviano said. 'We're here to get ye out; City Guard.'

The man was breathing hard, his thinly covered ribcage rapidly rising and falling as his bloodshot eyes remained wide with fear.

'Hold still,' Biviano said, 'we're going to cut ye free, but it's gonna hurt.'

Biviano moved to the ropes above and cut them with the bollock dagger from his belt. The man cried out as his arms slid helplessly to his sides. His whole body slumped down the rack and his legs folded awkwardly.

Moving quickly, Biviano cut the ropes attached to the man's swollen ankles.

'He's passed out,' Sears said.

Biviano looked to his friend. 'We need to get his arms and legs popped in, before he wakes then.'

Sears nodded and jammed the torch so it stood upright on the top of the rack.

Both men moved into position, their stomachs turning at the frailty of the man they now handled. They – from experience – shoved hard, pushing one arm back in before moving to the next to do the same. Both of them were surprised, but thankful the pain hadn't brought the man around.

After doing both arms, they struggled, but managed to do the same with both legs.

'He needs water,' Biviano said, looking about for a jug or bowl.

Sears had moved off, searching the tables. He pushed implements of torture over as he did, his anger rising as he saw more and more methods the inquisitors used to inflict pain on their victims.

'Pissin' cowards!' Sears threw a hollow box with a large screw passing through it into the wall on the other side of the room and kicked a large sack of salt over with force, scattering the granules across the dark floor.

'I know, I know,' Biviano said, moving to calm the big man whilst cringing inside at the cruel use the salt was surely intended for.

'Stay back for gods' sake,' Sears said, his breathing fast and his fists clenching over and over.

'Sears, ye need to calm yerself, it's me, just me. We can help this guy and be ready for when they come in, since the stupid bastard Archbishop locked us in with our weapons.'

Sears pushed over a tall man-sized chest, which opened to reveal metal spikes on the inside. The torches' light reflected off the ones that weren't caked in dried blood.

'Who thinks this shit up?' Sears shouted, as he kicked the spiked chest's door closed. He looked up then and saw a barrel in the corner nearest him. Moving swiftly to it, he dragged it into the dim light, water sloshing down its side as he did so. He dipped his finger in and brought it to his lips. 'Water!'

'Great, let's get it over,' Biviano said, moving to help shift the heavy barrel to the rack.

Once there, they both cupped their hands and poured the cold liquid over the blood-stained skin of the man, half expecting it to wake him, but again he remained unconscious.

Biviano grabbed a rag from nearby and mopped the man's brow, before working down his body, trying to clean him up as best he could. Why, he wasn't sure, it just seemed like the right thing to do.

'I hate to think what he's been through,' he said, gently scrubbing at the swollen knees of the man.

'Well think it, man.' Sears kept his voice low as he paced the room, his sword drawn again. 'Think it and think on it good, for when those bastards come through that door, I'm gonna rip 'em limb from fucking limb.'

'I will, Sears, I promise.' *Although I don't know what scares me more, the thought of what they did to this poor man, or the thought of yer voice lowering like that; the thought of ye going berserk...*

***

About an hour passed before the group entered what looked like a natural cavern. Errolas, who'd been handed his star stone again, shone it around the cavern, revealing a large heap of loose rubble a few feet away from the group. The beam of light broke on the pile of strange stones; shards of light cascaded up and across the high ceiling, which now resembled a clear night sky filled with stars.

Errolas gently rested the stone on a large, flat rock so the beam maintained the dazzling shower of light. Within seconds the room brightened with a spectacular show of illuminated crystal specs on a ceiling as high as Tyndurris, which carried on ahead of the group for at least as far again as the cavern was tall.

Sav whistled appreciatively and Fal turned to face his friend, adding his agreement before realising Sav was whistling at Correia, who was just a few paces away and bending down to tighten the leather thongs of her black riding boots. Fal nudged Sav to silence him, but couldn't help admiring the woman's figure himself, until she turned to look their way. Both men swiftly cast their gaze up to the impressive ceiling.

'Hence the name star stone,' Errolas said, as he walked over and sat opposite Fal and Sav.

'It's beautiful,' Fal said, as his eyes became accustomed to the new light, allowing him to fully appreciate the spectacular scene.

Starks found a place to sit next to Fal. 'That it sure is.'

Correia walked a little further down the cavern, seemingly oblivious to the star stone's effects and the cavern's natural beauty.

'Do you think she needs help with whatever it is she's doing over there?' Sav asked, peering across at her.

169

'She's fine,' Errolas said, glancing briefly at Fal to acknowledge the smirk on his face.

'Now I think it's time for some answers, Errolas, if you would?' Fal leant forward in anticipation.

Starks spoke up before Errolas could, the young crossbowman asking the elf if they were safe in the cavern. Errolas assured them they were, for the time being at least, and then explained what had happened leading up to their dramatic prison break.

After leaving Fal and Sav, Errolas had been asked to advise on Wesson's tragic situation. Errolas, the King and his advisers, had discussed options for several hours. Lord Yewdale, however, had been sent from the room to direct Wesson's quarantine, and to stop him attacking Archbishop Corlen, who'd been suggesting all kinds of useless options which had enraged the Lord High Constable and, it seemed, Errolas.

'It's not often an elf gets so angry,' Errolas said, 'not through discussion and debate alone, but that man, that ignorant so-called holy man is insufferable.'

Sav laughed. He clearly agreed with the elf, but had to be stopped by Fal before he began his usual tirade about the Samorlian Church.

Correia had joined them by this point. She sat quietly listening, whilst chewing on what looked and smelt like some kind of dried meat.

Errolas continued by telling his friends that Lord Severun had told the council all he knew about the arcane scroll he'd used, which he'd bought from a merchant called Peneur Ineson.

'That same merchant,' Errolas said, 'was found murdered in his home by the City Guard a few days ago. No wounds or cause of death had been found, but naturally, after hearing that, Corlen accused Lord Severun of the murder.'

'I hate that man,' Sav said, and Fal nodded.

Errolas took a deep breath, paused and then offered a sympathetic smile before continuing. 'Well... to everyone's surprise, Lord Severun admitted it.'

'No...' Fal protested. 'I know most of this is down to Lord Severun, but not murder? Did he give an explanation?'

'He didn't,' Errolas said, shaking his head. 'Apparently, if we can believe what he said, which I think we can, he remembers carrying out the murder using a spell from the scroll.' Fal shook his head in disbelief as Errolas continued to explain what he'd heard. 'Severun told us the scroll containing the shadow-distribution spell also contained some other arcane spells. Alas, he could not for the life of him remember travelling to the merchant's house, or why he'd carried out the crime, just that he had. Lord Strickland believed it to be the scroll protecting itself through Lord Severun, which has been previously documented regarding some magical items, but of that we cannot be sure.'

'That's creepy,' Starks said, and he shuddered at the thought of the scroll controlling such a powerful wizard.

That's an understatement, lad. Fal rubbed his face as he tried to digest the shocking revelation.

'Then it could've been the scroll,' Sav said, 'not Lord Severun who released the plague?'

Correia shook her head. 'I think not.' It was the first words she'd said since they'd entered the cavern.

'Why not?' Fal asked, a little sharper than he'd intended. He was annoyed she so flatly shot the possibility down.

'Because,' she continued, 'despite some arcane magic being known to protect itself... to actively release a plague, or influence a powerful mage to do so? No, you'd have to have the will and stupidity to do that yourself—'

'As far as you know?' Starks said in a surprisingly venomous tone. 'We'll never be able to ask him now though, will we?'

Errolas broke the awkward silence that followed, and continued his tale. He told the group that after Corlen's outbursts towards Severun, King Barrison had lost his temper and ordered the Archbishop out of his sight until further notice. It hadn't been until Corlen had stormed from the room however, that Correia had entered the chamber.

Fal and Sav turned to Correia. Sat under the seemingly star-filled sky of the cavern, they awaited an explanation.

'I guess it's time for an introduction, good elf. Will you do me the honours?'

'My pleasure,' Errolas said. 'Fal, Sav... Starks you have already been introduced, but not formally. This is your King's Spymaster, Correia Burr.'

Sav stood and saluted the woman and the other two followed suit.

'It's a pleasure, gentlemen, now take a seat,' she said, a rare but beautiful smile gracing her face and betraying her stern visage.

'The pleasure is ours. We owe you our lives,' Fal said, realising their situation must have been dire indeed for her to feel the need to break them out of the King's own prison.

'I wouldn't have said that.' Errolas smiled. 'Neither of you were in any immediate danger, certainly not from the magistrates anyway. You were to be released in a couple of days with a stern warning and ten lashes each, not that that is pleasant, but there were other dangers lurking in your shadows and we needed you both out, and more importantly, we needed you with us for our mission.'

Fal and Sav looked confused and both mouthed the word "mission" at the same time.

Before another word was said, the companions tensed as a faint but distinctive sound of stone knocking on stone came from the tunnels they'd just left. Starks moved to pick up his crossbow resting next to him, but Errolas raised his hand to stay the young soldier. The elf rose to his feet without a sound, Correia following his move almost as silently.

The knocking grew louder and Errolas motioned for them all to stand, placing one finger to his lips so they would do so quietly.

Correia pointed to the far end of the cavern and began pacing slowly in that direction. Errolas moved to recover the star stone and Fal, Sav and Starks followed Correia as quietly as possible. All three wondered who or what was making the noise, and why the other two weren't drawing their weapons.

The light dimmed again as the star stone was moved from its place on the rock, and the star-like lights on the cavern ceiling died slowly away, making it again hard to navigate the loose stones and rocks underfoot.

The knocking continued and then another, almost identical sound came from the corner of the cavern close to where they'd been.

Starks stumbled forward then and collided with Sav who cried out in pain as he fell and hit his elbow on a rock, a string of curses flowing effortlessly from his lips.

Both knocking sounds stopped dead and Correia shouted one word.

'Run!'

Chapter 22: Pursued

The Castellan of Wesson's prison was young and fairly inexperienced considering his position within the city. He'd been brought up far from Wesson; his parents, the local Baron and baroness of a farming community, had raised him as a devout Samorlian. At twelve years old, he was accepted as another lord's squire. At nineteen years, he'd successfully saved his liege lord's life in a terrible fire, a fire which left the older man severely burnt, but alive. The older man's command had been Wesson Prison, but due to the terrible injuries he'd suffered, the post had been passed on in genuine gratitude – along with the approval of the King – to the young squire, who was knighted and appointed the prison's Castellan.

That had happened less than three years previously. Since then, the running of the prison had continued in its historically efficient manner... until the escape of two prisoners, alas.

The Castellan's muscles grew tense as he stood outside the very cell that had held the prisoners in question. He felt the icy stare of a fellow Samorlian, one whom he'd always hoped he would never have the misfortune of meeting. For this man, as well as his companions, brought fear and doubt to the minds of anyone whom they questioned.

The tall, black-clad figure turned then, looking back out from the cell he was inspecting. He glared at the young knight, who stood rigid in the doorway. 'They were let out, you say, Sir Bullen?' Horler Comlay asked for the second time.

The Castellan bristled under the Witchunter General's cold gaze. He'd not been a knight for many years, but the title alone usually commanded respect from anyone the Castellan encountered. The witchunters of the Samorlian faith, however, although lacking the power they once had, could still bring about an inquisition if they so chose. Since the Castellan had been brought up by strict Samorlian parents, he knew full well what horrors that could entail, especially if any 'evidence' of arcane magic was found. He clenched his teeth and steadied himself before replying humbly.

'Yes, General, it seems the two men being held in this cell had three accomplices who managed to enter the prison unchallenged, assault two of my guards in this very corridor, steal the keys to this cell and make off with the prisoners.

'Where they went, none of my men seem to know. They were last heard passing through the lower chambers and have since... vanished.' Sir Bullen cursed inwardly, wishing he hadn't used that word.

Horler's eyes widened momentarily and he lifted his wide brimmed hat to scratch at his greasy scalp before replying in a mockingly astonished tone. 'Vanished?'

Truth be told, Horler was relieved the prison's Castellan seemed not to have been told about the Samorlian Church's cessation of investigations, as per the King's orders, which made the Witchunter General's life much easier indeed.

Sir Bullen clenched his fists behind his back before remembering there were two more witchunters in the corridor behind him. 'Yes, General, vanished, in the sense that they are not in my prison to be found. I have had guards search every level, as well as every cell, and there is no sign of the escapees or their accomplices. My guess is they somehow made their way back out into the city during the confusion.'

'That's what you guess is it, my lord Castellan? Well then, I guess my men and I will have a look around the prison. Not that I think your guards have failed to do their job properly, but, well, they have haven't they, if we are to be honest?'

Sir Bullen bristled visibly this time and Horler had to hide his satisfaction at the young knight's lack of discipline and control.

'Very well General, I will have my men show you down to the lower chambers, to see if your expertise can be of more assistance than my guard's knowledge of their own prison.'

Horler pulled off his hat, swept it out wide and bowed mockingly as he replied. 'I am grateful to you, my *lord*. I do hope my skills can be of assistance and we can have your prisoners, plus their accomplices, in your custody before long.'

'So do I, General, so do I,' Sir Bullen said, moving aside as the Witchunter General strode from the room. The Castellan motioned for his two guards to lead the witchunters down to the lower chambers, before calling out to the back of the three black-clad men. 'And what shall I tell the Lord High Constable is the interest of Wesson's Witchunter General in this matter… when I offer my report later today?'

All three witchunters stopped at those words. The two at the rear parted as Horler Comlay turned to face the stern faced Castellan – who was now thinking the mention of Altoln's highest ranking commander might be an aid if the witchunters decided to drag the prison into an inquisition.

'Tell the Duke, I am further investigating the sergeant-at-arms who instigated the damned situation Wesson has found itself in, and if he has a problem, to see the Grand Inquisitor himself. Is that satisfactory, Sir Bullen?'

Horler didn't await a reply, but merely turned back and stormed down the dark corridor in pursuit of the two prison guards sent to show him the way.

Sir Bullen, swallowing hard before licking his dry lips, turned and headed back towards the prison's barracks, his brow beaded with sweat and his heart only now starting to slow back to its usual rhythm.

***

The knocking sound, which had started again, echoed around the large cavern, making it sound like the group's pursuers were coming from every direction.

The ground was rocky in places, but criss-crossed with what seemed to be man-made paths. Those paths cut through the jagged stalagmites which increased in size the further into the cavern the group ran.

At first, from the viewpoint where Fal had first taken in the amazing sight of the cavern, it had seemed as if the natural space was about as long as Tyndurris was tall. Whilst the group ran and delved deeper into the fast growing forest of stalagmites however, Fal swiftly realised the cavern was much larger. It seemed to stretch for at least a mile into the darkness. Even the light from Errolas' star stone could not penetrate its farthest reaches.

The elf shone the beam of light at the ceiling whilst he moved, which cast thousands of dancing bands of light back down to roughly help the group navigate the dangerous terrain.

No one had asked what the noise was or who or what was making it, there was no time, and as soon as the King's Spymaster ran, so too had the others. She seemed to know where she was going and who or what was following them, and so they chased after her without question.

Fal wished he'd his falchion with him or at least his seax knife, and could only take comfort in the fact he still wore the maille and boiled armour he'd ridden out of Tyndurris in; apart from his padded arming cap, maille coif and mitons. Where they were, he had no idea. He brought up the rear of the group, but had no trouble in keeping up with the others despite his heavy, constrictive maille hauberk. They wouldn't let him fall behind anyway, he was sure.

The knocking sound was constant now, as were the sounds of falling stones and occasional rocks. The path the group ran curved round to the left, behind a giant stalagmite which almost met an equally large stalactite.

As Fal ran around the large formation, a small stone clattered off his right shoulder. He'd made it around the corner just in time to avoid a shower of similar sized stones raining down behind him. He didn't dare look up in case he caught one in the face, so kept his head down and continued to follow Starks who was in front of him. The young crossbowmen carried his crossbow in his hands, but the bow was not spanned, nor was a bolt loaded. Fal was pleased to see how far the young man had come, for if Fal had been running in front of Starks or any other crossbowman for that matter, he surely wouldn't appreciat a loaded weapon being jerked about behind his back.

'In here,' Correia shouted from ahead, her black armoured back speckled with rays of light cascading down from the ceiling.

More stones rained down then, several smaller ones hitting Sav, Starks and Fal as Correia and Errolas ducked into a small, natural looking tunnel which led off to the right.

Fal had no doubt Correia had known exactly where the opening was, and as he ducked into the dark hole in the cavern wall, a large rock smashed into thousands of pieces behind him.

Gods that was close. Fal's heart raced.

The group didn't stop there. Correia kept on running after taking the star stone from Errolas and shining it down the small tunnel. The rough stone walls either side were damp and smelt salty as the group started to descend down the tunnel.

The knocking sound seemed a long way behind them now, and without warning, Correia held her hand up, giving the order to halt.

Starks almost careered into the back of Sav and only just managed to avoid tangling his crossbow up in the scout's long legs.

There was just enough room for Fal to push past and he made his way to Errolas and Correia, whilst Starks – no order needed – bent down and spanned the bow cord of his weapon before fitting a bolt and turning to aim it back down the tunnel. Sav leant forward and drew Starks' short-sword from the kneeling crossbowman's scabbard, ready for any sudden attacks at close range.

'What was that all about?' Fal demanded, as both Correia and Errolas turned to face him.

'Kobolds,' Errolas said, who along with Correia, was hardly out of breath. Fal suddenly felt unfit in comparison, despite the heavy maille he was wearing, which restricted his chest as he sucked in another lungful of cold air.

'Kobolds?' Fal had never heard of such things before.

'It's the true name for knockers, sergeant,' Correia said impatiently, and Fal recognised the name from childhood stories; very small goblin folk, known to infest mines and cause havoc when disturbed. 'We really should move on,' she continued, 'they don't take kindly to their territory being disturbed. Your loud friends back there were probably the reason they attacked.'

'I'm no fool, Correia,' Fal said. 'You obviously know these tunnels well, so why did we stop if we were in danger?'

'They've never bothered me before, sergeant. Then again, I usually pass through here with pathfinders, rather than men who seem incapable of travelling discreetly, so until today, I didn't even know it was knocker territory.'

'Enough,' Errolas said. 'We're not your pathfinders, Correia. These men are good soldiers, but you can't expect them to act like pathfinders when they have never been trained to do so.'

'You're right, Errolas,' Correia said, sighing heavily and rubbing at her face with her free hand. 'My apologies, Sergeant Falchion, but we must move on. Knockers aren't dangerous in small spaces like this, but out in the cavern we would've had hails of stones, crystal-tipped darts and spears raining down on us. They shouldn't pursue us in here though. If they do, however, it's their damned knocking that'll be our downfall, attracting who knows what else from deeper caverns.'

'Shhh,' Sav hissed from behind. Everyone fell silent.

Correia pointed the star stone's light down and passed it back to Errolas, so it dimly lit the area in front of them, but not much beyond.

Fal crept back to Sav and asked as quietly as he could what he'd heard.

'Scurrying sound,' Sav said, 'back down towards the cavern.'

Errolas was behind Fal and he whispered for them both to keep quiet and for Starks to stay his weapon unless told otherwise. The nimble elf blinked out the star stone and crept back down the passage ever so slowly in the darkness.

Without warning, the elf – a little ahead of the group – shone the star stone at the floor in front of him.

A terrible grating shriek burst from the mouth of a strange looking goblin creature, as it covered its large black eyes with small hands. Errolas leapt forward and grabbed the kobold by the neck, hoisting it up at arm's length. He quickly moved to stand behind Starks, who re-raised his crossbow and aimed down the tunnel.

The kobold shrieked louder then, and the faint, intermittent knocking from the cavern back down the tunnel increased once more.

'Take the light,' Errolas said hurriedly to Sav, 'and give Starks something to aim at if more come up the tunnel.'

Sav pointed the star stone's beam past Starks, who watched carefully for any movement that might provide a clear shot.

'Don't shoot unless they come close and present a danger,' Errolas added. 'We're in their home remember.'

Correia rolled her eyes behind him.

The kobold had quietened now and Errolas whispered into its drooping ears. He placed the creature on the floor and let go of its neck, much to the surprise of both Fal and Correia, as well as the creature itself, whose head reached to the elf's knee and no higher.

Trembling, the kobold slowly brought its hands away from its black, bauble like eyes and peered up at the now crouching elf. It shifted nervously and its miniature coat of plates rustled as the orange crab shells it was made of rubbed against its dry, grey skin.

Errolas leant down and whispered into the kobold's ear again and it nodded meekly before reaching up on tiptoes and whispering back to the elf, who smiled. The kobold shrugged, bowed low to the elf and looked up at Fal and Correia, its fear plain to see.

Fal managed a smile, although he had no idea why, and so too – much to Fal's amusement – did Correia, although hers looked much more forced than his own.

'Let him pass,' Errolas said, and Starks lifted his crossbow to point at the ceiling. 'They won't bother us now,' the elf added.

The small kobold crept cautiously past Sav and Starks, pulled a stone from beneath its coat of plates and hurried off down the tunnel back towards the cavern, hammering the stone against the wall as it went.

The knocking sound from the cavern stopped and Errolas laughed quietly to himself.

'What did you say and how do you speak knocker or kobold or whatever?'

Sav asked, clearly impressed.

'I told him that if his tribe let us be, I would return one day with a crystal the size of my head, and would also ensure every time Correia here passed through the cavern with her pathfinders, they too would bring a gift.'

'Great,' Correia said under her breath. 'Let's just hope they haven't already alerted anything else as to our whereabouts,' she said to the group. Without another word, she snatched the star stone from Sav and set off down the tunnel again.

'Guess we should follow her,' Fal said, as he pushed Errolas on down the tunnel. 'Full of surprises aren't you, elf?'

Despite the confusion and questions Fal and Sav still had, they managed to push them to one side until they were in a safer spot to talk. They also managed a genuine and hardly controllable smile as they glanced at each other, their imaginations racing with the possibilities of what the mission they found themselves on could be and where it would lead.

Chapter 23: Reconnaissance

Elleth woke with a start and immediately cringed as she felt the dampness between her legs.

'No, no, no. I haven't done that in years,' she whispered to herself. *What will Mother think?*

She cast her eyes about for signs of the woman in the dark room. The faint orange glow from the small hearth provided just enough light for her to see she was alone.

Elleth let out a relieved sigh, before realising something wasn't right with her. The wetness between her legs felt different. Elleth's heart rate increased as she quickly climbed to her feet, her eyes adjusting further to the gloom. She looked down at the thin, straw-filled mattress on the floor of the kitchen where she'd been sleeping and at her linen night dress, which she pulled up and out in front of her.

Her breath caught in her throat.

That's too dark for wee, she thought, but before she could think on it any more, the shrieking laughter she now realised had woken her, drew her attention upstairs.

Was that laughter?

She'd heard a fair bit of laughter from the floors above since arriving at the large house, a fair amount of all sorts of noises whilst the ladies and men played, if she was honest.

'Bastard!' Mother's muffled shout came from above. 'Get the hell out of my house. Ye don't pay for that ye freak!'

Elleth held her soiled dress tightly as she froze, listening to a man's cursing, before someone stomped down the stairs. Another person followed the first, but only halfway down.

Mother's voice shouted out again. 'And don't come back, ye black cross bastard!'

The front door opened then slammed shut, and a torrent of abuse poured from a man's throaty voice in the street beyond.

'Elleth?' Mother shouted from the stairs.

Slightly stunned at what she'd woken to, Elleth didn't respond.

Mother almost screamed this time. 'Elleth! Wake up and bring a cloth and hot water to Coppin's room, now!'

Eyes now wide and hands releasing her nightdress, Elleth managed to shout that she'd heard. She looked around quickly for a cloth, instantly forgetting worries about herself, what with the mention of Coppin's name and all. She quickly padded across to the hearth and jumped as Mother's terrier yelped.

'Sorry doggy,' she said, realising she'd trod on its tail. She also realised she'd never been told its name. 'Remind me to ask Mother your name, alright?' she whispered, as she leaned over it to grab a cloth hanging on the back of Mother's wooden chair. Quickly dunking the cloth into the small pot hanging over the glowing embers of the hearth, Elleth immediately pulled it out and wrung it, eager to get upstairs to see if Coppin was alright.

She ran across the kitchen, cloth dripping, and pulled the door open. Oil lamps in the room beyond dazzled her for a moment. Quickly composing herself and covering her right eye with her free hand – which helped reduce the brightness – she turned left and up the flight of stairs. She passed one shut door and ran into the open one she knew to be Coppin's.

Elleth froze as soon as she entered the room. The hand shielding her right eye lowered slowly as she took in the shocking scene.

Coppin sat up in the large bed, her green hair a mess and her eyes streaked with tears. That wasn't what stopped Elleth in her tracks though, for Mother was leaning over the young woman, holding a blood soaked sheet against Coppin's left breast, dabbing the bloody mess that had once been her nipple.

A rush of thoughts and emotions ran through Elleth then.

'Elleth, for Samorl's sake bring that cloth, the bastard bit her—'

Mother stopped short as she looked at Elleth properly. 'Well that's some good news at least,' she said, nodding towards the blood stain on Elleth's night dress. 'Ye're finally a woman.'

Elleth looked down at the stain, her fears of it being blood confirmed in the room's light, but confusion as to why that made her a woman took precedence.

When she looked up, her stomach lurched to see Coppin's tear-filled eyes looking back at her. When those eyes met, Coppin smiled at Elleth the same way she had when Elleth had first arrived at the house, a smile full of sympathy.

'Oh, Elleth,' Coppin said. She started to cry all the more.

***

'There's no way in bar a full-frontal assault, General,' Egan Dundaven explained. His reconnaissance role on Tyndurris for the southern Witchunter General was a blessing after his failed attempt to execute an infected citizen a few days before. The anger of Wesson's Witchunter General, Horler Comlay, had convinced Egan he was going to be stripped of his position and banished to some far off monastery in the Chapparro Mountains. Exley Clewarth, however, was much more understanding, if not any less ruthless than his Wesson counterpart, and demanded the return of Egan Dundaven to his ranks since he was, after all, one of his men. Egan thanked Sir Samorl again for the opportunity to prove himself to the Witchunter General who'd vouched for him and saved him the humiliation of being stripped of his rank; a rank he'd fought hard to earn during a decade of dedication to the order.

It was understandable then, that when Exley Clewarth frowned at the news Egan presented him, the witchunter's stomach churned as he realised his opportunity may have slipped away before his very eyes with another failure.

'You are certain, Master Dundaven, that there is no other way into Tyndurris other than a full-frontal assault... against mages backed up by experienced men-at-arms?' Exley tapped his fingers on the railing he leant against as he waited for the witchunter's response.

They were in a shadow filled alley three blocks from Tyndurris, and Exley, although seemingly alone, was surrounded by witchunters and warrior monks, all hidden by the evening shadows.

Egan hesitated before answering. Searching his mind for an answer other than the one he knew his General would not appreciate, he finally replied. 'General, I have watched Tyndurris from rooftops on every angle during the day. I have travelled around the walls of Tyndurris looking for back gates, doors or weakened stones in the wall. I have dressed as a beggar and in that guise I have approached the iron gate to check the locking mechanism, and after all that, as well as questioning our two men on the inside, I have found no way into Tyndurris that does not result in us being seen. It is heavily guarded and patrolled by soldiers and dogs, as well as magic. If we are not seen, we will be detected by the dogs or some form of magic, I am sure. I see no other way in.'

Exley snorted at the explanation and Egan's heart sank and his stomach lurched.

'Very well, Master Dundaven,' Exley said, his tone far lighter than could have been expected. 'I appreciate your thoroughness in the reconnaissance of the tower and its surroundings.' Egan relaxed visibly and the Witchunter General hardly managed to keep the amusement from his face as he went on. 'It is fortunate for us that we have found another way to enter Tyndurris and access the gnome, without resorting to a disastrous overt assault on the outside of the building.'

Egan's confusion showed as plain as day, so the General let the awkward pause drag out a few seconds longer, wondering if the witchunter had the courage to ask how and from whom they'd found such information. When Egan continued to look shocked yet intrigued, but failed to ask, Exley continued.

'If you were wondering how we came by this information, Master Dundaven,' Exley teased, causing Egan to wince in the realisation he should have had the courage to ask, 'we recently requested the company of a palace aid, one who has worked as a royal scribe for well over twenty years. During his current... visit to the cathedral, our lord and master the Grand Inquisitor, along with two of his most talented inquisitors, put the scribe to the question.'

Egan shifted uncomfortably, knowing full well how the inquisitors put people to the question. It wasn't a thought he relished and so he pushed it to the back of his mind. He'd fought, killed and burnt arcane magic users and vile creatures many times, yet the thought of torturing an innocent citizen purely for information didn't sit well with him. He swiftly composed himself under the gaze of his superior and nodded approvingly, or so he hoped, as

Exley continued.

'During the questioning, the scribe uttered a riddle of sorts. He'd memorised this riddle from old writings that haven't been seen for decades… possibly even centuries. He admitted finding this particular writing in the royal library's archives. Ancient scripts and scrolls are housed in those archives, Master Dundaven, and I am certain the one he spoke of holds clues to help solve our predicament. Understanding it may well lead us to a way into Tyndurris itself.' Exley grinned wickedly before going on.

'The Grand Inquisitor had the riddle written down, and Inquisitor Makhell handed that writing to me personally, so we could use it to carry out our mission.'

'Did the scribe not know the meaning, General?'

Exley laughed heartily at the question. 'If he did, Master Dundaven, he would have told us. Believe me, the inquisitors stretched their resources to question that man. However, I am sure that between us we can figure it out, do you not think?'

Egan nodded as he saw the parchment brought forth from a small pouch on Exley's belt. The Witchunter General unravelled the parchment and read it aloud, his voice barely more than a whisper in the quiet alley.

Egan's brow creased as he listened to the words. He prayed he would be the one to solve the riddle and find the way into Tyndurris as he felt, in all honesty to himself, this was his last chance to save his career and maybe even his life.

Exley read the words effortlessly as if for the thousandth time and Egan knew the Witchunter General had already tried to solve the riddle and failed. His chances were growing with each line Exley read out, as his mind started to find the meaning behind the puzzle of words.

> *Few know the true source of His light, its new weakness fewer still*
> *Stone protects all, it has oft been said; hidden in view of the sea*
> *Beware the darkness of the ground, through it the light could cease*
> *We will, all of us on that day, fall to darkness, as it was before*
> *As long as the source stands tall in its succour, light will always be*
> *Best it remains forgotten, unlike the memory of He*

Egan stared at nothing in particular as his eyes flickered, his mind working fast.

Exley leant forward in anticipation. He'd saved Egan from his Wesson counterpart, who was prepared to strip the man of his rank and banish him to some far-flung place, but Exley knew that where Egan had failed in one area, he would not fail with this.

Egan Dundaven had been set to be a scholar in Royce until his parents were slaughtered by a crazed warlock. Following that, he'd taken to the Samorlian faith and the witchunters' order like a vulture to a corpse. Exley Clewarth had always admired the man's intelligence, and had no doubt Egan would succeed in this task.

He was right.

'General, I think I have it,' Egan said finally, the elation clear in his voice.

'Well, Master Dundaven, I have always known you to be a clever man, but I couldn't have hoped for you to solve it so fast. It seems you have redeemed yourself.' Exley slapped Egan on the back. 'Come now my friend, we shan't discuss the meaning here.' Exley placed the parchment back in his pouch, fastened it securely and strode off down the alley, a beaming Egan at his back.

When both men had left the alley, the shadows moved and a dozen black clad witchunters and warrior monks left their covert positions to take up new positions on the streets around Exley and Egan, as they made their way to the Samorlian Cathedral to discuss the riddle and their tactics for using the answers it had revealed.

Chapter 24: The Pathfinders Cave

Smoke, dust, blood and a number of other unsavoury smells thickened the air of the dimly lit chamber. Biviano sat on a bench opposite the tortured man – who'd yet to awaken. His skin had been cleaned and he was now wearing some blood-stained rags Biviano had found on a table, as well as Sears' padded gambeson for warmth.

'How long ye reckon we've been here?'

'Dunno, Sears,' Biviano said, as he rubbed his face with one hand and spun his kettle-helm that sat beside him with the other.

'I'm starved.'

'Well, think how he feels.' Biviano nodded towards the torture victim, who looked like a child in Sears' large gambeson.

'I'm trying not to, ye dick, it'll set me off again.'

'Aye, there is that.'

Sears was hidden in the darkness of one of the chamber's corners, where he'd been for quite some time.

'Ye think they're waiting for us to fall asleep?'

'Sears, I have no idea mate, so stop asking what I think they're thinking or planning or doing, will ye?'

The darkened corner growled. Biviano sighed.

'Well stop spinnin' yer damned helmet then if ye want me to stop asking ye questions.'

Biviano spun it all the more, but before Sears responded, the torture victim stirred with a cough.

'Sears, water, now!' Biviano left his helmet and rushed to the man. Sears emerged from the corner and moved swiftly to the barrel of water next to the rack – which they'd pulled flat like a bed so the man could lay properly.

Biviano stood over the man as Sears passed him a small cup of water, which he held to the man's cracked lips, carefully pouring it into his open mouth.

'Not too much,' Sears said.

'I know, I know.'

Suddenly, the man went rigid and his eyes opened wide, looking from Biviano to Sears and back.

'It's alright, sir, we're guardsmen,' Biviano said, but the man still looked petrified.

Biviano pointed to his chest then, which displayed the coat-of-arms of the City Guard. The man visibly relaxed, albeit slightly. He tried to talk, but coughed instead.

Once the coughing passed, Biviano pressed the water to the man's lips again.

'Take yer time,' Sears said quietly, 'there's no rush.'

The man nodded slowly as he gulped at the water, the cup draining quickly.

'Not too fast, sir,' Biviano said, passing the empty cup to Sears, who refilled it and passed it back. The man coughed again and winced at the following pain. He sat up then and rubbed at his wrists, his face creasing up with every movement.

'Take yer time, sir, like Sears says. Ye been through hell and no mistake, but we'll get ye out of here, that's me word.'

Looking up into Biviano's eyes, the man nodded slowly again and accepted the cup of water offered to him. He slowly brought it up to his lips and began to sip at the water, his eyes moving between the two guardsmen as he did so.

'In yer own time, tell us yer name, friend. Mine's Sears and this is Biviano.'

Biviano waved at the man and then reddened as Sears looked at him as if he was stupid.

Finishing the cup of water, the man finally spoke in a horse voice. 'Frane, Ellis Frane. I'm a royal scribe at the palace,' he said, managing a weak smile.

'Well Ellis Frane,' Biviano said, smiling back at the man, 'me and Sears here'll get ye outta this shit-hole soon enough, and ye're going to be just fine.'

Ellis Frane nodded and smiled again, before filling the two men in on what the inquisitors had done to him.

When he finished, Biviano told Ellis Frane to get some more rest. The man didn't take long to fall asleep. It was only then that Sears fully let what he'd been told sink in; it was Biviano's words alone that calmed Sears enough to allow him to return to his dark corner without tearing the chamber apart.

***

The tunnel extended into darkness whenever the light of the star stone didn't shine down it. The group had been travelling for a long time, although Fal had no idea how long exactly. All he'd been doing since the knockers attacked was concentrating on putting one foot in front of the other. He was glad when Correia stopped to talk to Errolas. She held the star stone cupped in her hands, both her and Errolas' faces illuminated eerily in the dimmed light, their hushed tones drifting back to the men behind them.

'What's she saying?' Sav whispered, whilst Starks turned, crouched and again aimed his crossbow back up the slight gradient of the tunnel they'd travelled down.

'I can't make it out,' Fal said, whilst bending forward and resting his hands on his knees. 'It's quite clear it's not for our ears though.' His head still ached from Execution Square, and his lungs burnt along with his thighs, but he knew they would be pushing on again soon and so did his best to make the most of the short reprieve.

The Spymaster had stopped every so often to talk to Errolas, and Fal had failed to hear any of what had been said. He'd asked once, but had given up after receiving a deadly look from the hard-faced woman, and so it genuinely surprised both Fal and Sav when she suddenly turned and motioned for them

185

to approach.

Both men looked at each other in anticipation before walking up to Correia and Errolas, leaving Starks as rearguard.

'Ready to tell us your little secrets now are we?' Sav asked, moving forward and smiling wryly.

Correia quickly reached out and thumped Sav on the elbow he'd banged in the cavern.

Sav grunted, grabbed his arm and stepped back.

'You can go back and stand guard with the lad for that,' Correia said calmly, not a trace of amusement on her face.

Sav looked to Errolas for support, but the elf just shrugged. Cursing to himself, the tall scout plodded sulkily back to Starks' position. Once there, he mumbled something to Starks, drew the crossbowman's short-sword, and took up the defensive position they'd assumed every time the group had stopped since the cavern.

'Sergeant Falchion, we'll soon be meeting up with some of my men; pathfinders, who have both you and your scout's weapons.'

Fal looked both relieved and confused at the same time, but when he attempted to ask the Spymaster how her pathfinders had his and Sav's weapons, he was silenced by the same look she had used on him before. Fal held his tongue and merely hoped for more information.

'At the end of this tunnel,' Correia explained, 'is a sharp bend to the left, which opens out into a coastal cave. That's where my pathfinders will be. They left the prison with your weapons shortly before we rescued you and were ordered to wait for us there.'

'Why there?' Fal managed to ask.

'Why there and not the cavern?' Correia said, elaborating on Fal's question.

'Yes, why not the cavern where we first stopped?'

'The cave we are about to enter is used only by the King's special forces, and is a highly guarded secret. If you were to show up there unannounced, then whoever's in there wouldn't think twice about gutting you before you could say 'morl's balls. Therefore, I sent ahead with your weapons a small pathfinder group as an advanced warning of our arrival. The men I sent are well known in the cave and bay surrounding it. They will have no problem entering and announcing our following arrival, should there be other forces operating in the area.'

Fal merely nodded as he took in the information thrown at him. It was not hard to believe the King had forces operating secretly, but Fal hardly thought he would ever hear anything factual about them, let alone meet some of them and maybe even, if this mission they were on was as serious as Fal thought it must be, work alongside them.

Correia's attention was drawn to Sav as the scout looked back to the group, then leaned down and whispered something to Starks. The two men laughed at whatever it was Sav had said.

The Spymaster rolled her eyes, sighed heavily and turned back to Fal. 'Even with me leading your group, sergeant, I would appreciate it if you told your men back there to keep their mouths buttoned as we approach and enter the cave. The only one doing any talking shall be me, understood?'

Fal nodded. 'Yes ma'm.'

'Very good, now go back, inform them two and then follow us in.' Correia looked to Errolas who nodded his understanding, and the two slowly made their way down the tunnel once more. Fal quietly called for Sav and Starks to follow and whispered a brief explanation as they headed towards the end of the damp tunnel.

The rock wall finally curved to the left after several minutes, and its glistening surface reflected orange as it gave away the setting of the sun. A fresh sea breeze hit the group as they reached the end of the tunnel, and Correia shouted out to announce their arrival.

Nothing…

Correia shouted a second time and a man shouted out, clearly in distress.

A shriek like nothing any of them had ever heard before followed, resonating off the tunnel's walls. Correia looked back at the group and Fal saw she was as equally shocked as the rest of them. Even Errolas seemed confused at what they'd just heard.

'Pathfinders on me!' a man hidden just around the corner shouted, and almost immediately afterwards, a bloodied soldier in a dark green gambeson stumbled around the bend and into the tunnel, clutching his right arm. He looked startled when he saw the group, until he recognised Correia, who dashed to his side.

'Mearson, what's happening?' she demanded.

Before she received an answer, the shriek ripped through the tunnel again. Errolas doubled over, his hands either side of his head.

Two more soldiers wearing dark green ran into the tunnel then, and one raised a yew bow before hearing Correia cry out an order to stay his weapon. The two men quickly took in the group, their eyes settling a moment longer on the elf doubled over before them. Fal rushed to Errolas' side and tried to help cover his friend's ears.

The sound erupted again and Errolas dropped to his knees, his sensitive ears taking in even more of the painful din than the humans around him.

Correia threw the star stone to Fal as he crouched by the elf, who was now rocking back and forth on the wet floor. The Spymaster drew her slender swords and turned back towards the cave and her men. 'Explain?'

'I don't know, ma'm?' the man with the bow said. 'Like nothing I've seen or heard of before; it came from the sea. The *Norlechlan's* been testing her guns out in the bay with two carracks as escort.'

Correia gave the soldier a dangerous look – one Fal didn't miss – and the soldier carried on with a guilty look on his face. 'Shortly after the last tests, there was an eerie sound in the water. A couple of marines posted here were swimming in the bay. They said it sounded like whales, but it's no whale ma'm—'

The terrible screech echoed through the tunnel again and the soldier raised his hands to his ears. Once it passed, he lowered his hands.

'Go on Tom,' Correia said, nodding to the archer.

'The marines shouted to us about the noise and we ordered them in—'

Another screech.

'They never made it ma'm,' Tom said, shaking his head. His companions nodded solemnly. Correia urged him on and he took a deep breath. 'As they reached the shallows and began wading in… they were torn to shreds.' He looked back over his shoulder to the cave's entrance again before continuing. 'Great claws erupted from the sea, snapped one marine clean in half they did. We ran down to the beach, loosed a few arrows at it as it emerged, but it's armoured—'

'Like a giant lobster or something similar,' another soldier added.

'Where's the others?' Correia was clearly worried.

Both the pathfinders in front of her and the one slouched and clutching his bleeding arm – now being attended to by Sav – shook their heads.

'It's fast, ma'm, very fast,' Tom continued. 'Its legs are like tree trunks but it moves with such surprising speed. It can't fit too far into the cave, but it was snapping its claws in at us. We tried more arrows to its face, tried to aim under its armoured shell, but we've had no luck. We had to retreat in here.'

'I'm going to take a look,' Correia said, and Fal stood to follow. Fal had wrapped Errolas' cloak around the elf's head to try and block out as much of the noise as possible, but the elf was still down, rocking slightly as the beast in the cave screeched again.

'Stay there sergeant,' Correia ordered.

'My weapons?' Fal asked, directing the question to the pathfinders. They looked to Correia and she nodded reluctantly.

'In the cave,' the burliest pathfinder said, 'towards the back. We may be able to get to them but it's risky and they'll do no good anyway.' His black, boiled leather armour and dark green gambeson were smeared with blood and grime, and he carried a fresh wound running through one ear, almost dividing it in two.

'With all due respect, ma'm,' Sav said, from the wounded pathfinder's side, 'if I can get my bow, I may have a better chance. No disrespect to you, lads,' he added swiftly.

'None taken. Try away,' Tom offered. 'If you can get to it that is.'

'Sav, you stay here, we'll fetch your bow,' Fal said, and Sav nodded. It was the time to take orders from appropriate ranks and Sav knew it. Friendship didn't come into it.

Correia moved forward into the orange light of the setting sun, her shining swords held defensively. Fal followed close behind, refusing the offered axe from the pathfinder with the torn ear. He wanted to get to his falchion and Sav's bow fast and unhindered.

They turned the corner and saw the beast. Its armoured body was the size of a large coach, with eight long, jointed legs supporting its bulk. It shifted forward and back surprisingly quickly for its size. Two blood-red claws were held high above its head – a head which looked like a mess of rigging and spears as its arm-thick antennas probed the inside of the cave's opening.

As the two companions stepped into the orange light of the cave, they noticed jet black eyes the size of bucklers, and both instantly knew the orbs would have to be Sav's targets.

The beast screeched again and Fal felt the two pathfinders close behind him.

'Tom, Gleave, back in the tunnel,' Correia said, and both men reluctantly obeyed.

Rocks fell to the ground as the beast smashed its huge armoured claws into the side of the cave. It lunged forward, its large armoured shell colliding with a low rock formation on the cave's ceiling. It screeched again, its antennas whipping around in a frenzied attempt to feel for threats.

It lurched one of its large claws at Correia as she and Fal made a dash for the weapons. As the claw came in, Correia dropped into a roll and at the same time, thrust her trailing left sword into the joint of the creature's open claw. It shrieked terribly, far louder than before. Errolas cried out from within the tunnel.

Grabbing Sav's bow and quiver, Fal ran for it. He leapt the last few feet into the arms of the two pathfinders, as the creature's other claw smashed into the floor behind him.

'Sav, your bow, quick,' Fal shouted, as he and the two pathfinders stumbled backwards.

Sav hurried to the opening and snatched his bow. He strung it immediately with a spare hemp string from his pouch and nocked one of his long, ash-shafted arrows.

Correia jumped back into the tunnel then, closely followed by another earth shuddering blow from one of the beast's claws. She was pulled out of the way by Fal, as Sav stepped forward with his bow. He immediately drew the inside of his right hand to his cheek. The broad headed arrow he'd chosen glinted in the fading light as he loosed, hardly a second to aim as his natural skill and years of training took over.

The creature screeched again, more of a scream this time and Sav jumped back as a rock the size of his head fell just in front of him; the creature smashed the roof of the cave as it reared up on four of its eight main legs.

The broad head had churned its way into one of the baubles that were the creature's eyes, cascading liquid down to the cave floor as the shaft sank in as far as the white fletching.

Sav nocked another broad headed arrow to his string and as he loosed, the creature came crashing back down onto all eight legs. The arrow glanced off the hardened shell above its face.

Starks rushed forward then, dropping to one knee with the butt of his crossbow firmly resting on his shoulder. He swiftly aimed before squeezing the cold metal trigger with his thumb, which launched the weapon's bolt into the cave.

Fal missed stopping the young crossbowman and was glad he had, for the bolt that had launched from the steady weapon disappeared into the creature's other eye.

The sudden blindness sent the giant crustacean into a frenzied whipping of antennas, claws and legs. One antenna lashed out, its very tip no larger than a reed of grass. The weapon like appendage caught Sav on the mouth, splitting his bottom lip. He fell back, spitting blood, and was caught by Correia who immediately dropped him when he looked up at her and grinned, his teeth covered in blood.

Fal patted Starks on the back and dragged him from the tunnel opening as the creature thrashed around the outside of the cave. It rocked from side to side and turned to reveal a fanned, armoured tail which slapped the ground, lifting stones and dirt into the air.

As the sun dipped behind the sea and the light finally faded, those of the group who risked stepping into the cave – Fal, Correia, Tom and Gleave – saw multiple flashes of light out to sea followed by a loud rumble. It could almost have been mistaken for thunder, but this thunderous sound was immediately followed by large balls of iron that smashed into the creature and cave alike.

The large beast exploded in a shower of blood, innards and pieces of armoured shell, one of which practically decapitated Tom, his head lolling as his lifeless body slumped to the floor.

Fal grabbed Correia as she screamed, swiftly dragging her back into the tunnel. Gleave followed close behind them as shrapnel tore up the cave and rocks fell to the ground.

***

Mother had wasted no time in explaining to Elleth she was now a woman. She told her she would have to learn to play with the men who came to visit, and after sending Elleth off to the room next to Coppin's, with strict orders not to disturb her sister, Mother took payment from the first man to walk through the door.

'At least he's a handsome one,' Mother said under her breath, after explaining to the man how he could tell the girl was untouched – for he'd paid extra for that, once presented with the option.

Climbing the stairs to the first floor and counting along to the third room, the young man took a deep breath and turned the handle, before walking confidently in.

His breath caught at the sight of the girl sat on the bed in front of him. He took in her silky black hair as it fell across her delicate shoulders, her small yet pert breasts that lifted her linen nightdress slightly, and those oh-so-innocent eyes. It wasn't until she smiled the sweetest smile however – albeit a nervous one – that he smiled back at her. Taking a deep breath, he closed the door behind him.

She's nervous, that's a good sign. It seems Mother was telling the truth.

Neither of them said a word as the man walked slowly towards the bed.

'Stand up, let me see you,' he said softly, and after hesitating, the girl climbed off the bed and stood just out of arm's reach. He looked her up and down, taking in her slim figure as she wringed her hands together in front of her flat stomach.

He pointed to the low ceiling and slowly moved his finger around in a circle.

After a moment, the girl seemed to realise what he meant and blushed slightly, before slowly turning around. He licked his dry lips as he took in the cute bumps of her behind. Swiftly taking two steps forward, he came up behind her and put his right hand over her eyes as his left wrapped around her waist.

The girl gasped and then giggled ever so slightly. 'Is this part of the game?' she whispered.

Smiling to himself, he whispered back. 'Yes. Have you played before?'

She shook her head and he smiled all the more.

'Keep your eyes closed,' he said into her ear. He felt her tremble as he slowly moved his hand down to her breasts. He moved his other hand up so he could cup them both and she giggled again as he caressed her.

As he grew stiff, he pressed himself against her cheeks.

'Turn around slowly, but keep your eyes closed,' he said, his voice naught but a whisper.

She obeyed. Her hands remained clasped in front of her, whilst his moved down to the outside of her thighs. Once facing him, he lifted her night dress by sliding his hands up from her thighs to her waist and further still, hindered only by her hands, which hadn't moved at all.

He noticed her swallow hard, and her breathing quickened as he leaned in close to her lips.

'Move your hands and let me take this off,' he said, pulling the dress up.

'Do we take our clothes off in this game?' she said shakily, frowning as she hesitated to move her hands.

'Yes. First you, then me.' He pulled at the dress again, this time successfully as the girl's hands and arms moved to allow him to pull it up and over her head.

'Do you want to see me without my clothes?' he said, throwing her night dress to one side. His eyes followed his hands, which moved round to her backside as he turned her sideways.

'I guess,' she whispered, her hands back to her front.

'You guess?'

'I mean, yes,' she said, smiling, although not convincingly.

'Sit on the bed then and watch.'

She yelped as he slapped her on the bottom and gently pushed her towards the bed.

Slowly, she ⟍ down and turned, her eyes widening as he pulled off his shirt. Her eye ⟍widened more and she giggled again as he pulled his braes and hose down ⟍ one, revealing himself.

Her ⟍ce screwed up for an instant as her eyes settled below his stomach.

'N⟍er seen one before?'

⟍ne shook her head. 'Not... pointing up, like yours.'

'Let me show you what it's for then,' he said, moving confidently towards her whilst she slid back further along the bed.

'I know what they're for,' the girl said, screwing her face up without taking her eyes from it, as he climbed up the bed towards her.

'Not that, silly. What it's used for in our game.'

Head tilting slightly, the girl cried out playfully as he grabbed her by the ankles and pulled her towards him, opening her legs at the same time.

'You going to play nice and let me do what I want so we can play the best games?' He held her legs apart, and despite being extremely nervous, she nodded, her eyes not leaving his.

He wet his middle finger in his mouth, smiled at her and then moved his hand between her legs, pressing his finger into her slowly as he did. She squirmed slightly and bit her bottom lip, her brow furrowing as he probed deeper. Suddenly, she winced and tried to close her legs. He stopped and removed his finger slowly, smiling all the more as he muttered something about someone telling the truth. Before the girl could question any of it, he pulled her down the bed until her legs were along the outside of his.

He pressed himself down and into her then. She gasped with a mix of shock and pain as he slowly pushed deeper.

'Trust me,' he whispered, brushing the hair from her face with one hand and holding her firmly by the waist with the other.

He took in a deep breath and started to roll his hips more, pulling out and pushing in slowly but constantly. The girl took a deep breath of her own and clenched, trying to stop him going any deeper.

As he started to make a little noise, his hand tightened on her waist and his other moved down to her right breast, squeezing it a little too hard. The girl went to say something, but he thrust deep as she did, causing her to cry out, a sound he mistook for pleasure; he thrust all the harder for it.

As they both cried out in a final few spasms of pleasure – on his part – she felt him throb inside her. He collapsed on top of her then, his damp chest heaving to match her own.

Groaning and rolling away, he lay next to her, his eyes closed as his right hand traced the side of her body.

As he lay there, his breathing eventually levelling out, she moved her hand between her legs and prodded gently at the wetness. She winced at how tender it all felt. She brought her hand up then and looked at the sticky, bloody mess on her fingertips.

After a while, the man rolled off the bed and onto his feet. He pulled on his clothes and looked her up and down. As he smiled and left the room, Elleth curled up, thought of Coppin, and cried.

Chapter 25: Coincidences

Orix had been pouring over corpses for more than a day with little sleep. His face bore more lines than ever and his eyes were shadowed, making him look ghostly in the dimly lit clerics' chamber. The old gnome had called for Morri soon after being placed under house arrest. He and the young cleric, along with two others, had been examining plague victims new and old, relentlessly searching for the link between the gnome's potion and the current epidemic.

'I see no connection, Master Orix,' Elloise said, her blonde hair tied back to keep it away from the samples in front of her. Elloise was an expert on diseases and had said the very same thing several times. 'It seems the earlier subjects died from your potion, which although unethical, is very impressive I might add.'

Orix's brow creased and an uncomfortable silence followed.

Elloise swiftly continued. 'What I mean is the first victims died from the potion, and were, as far as we have been informed by the City Guard, criminals. The later victims died again of the same potion; however, they had also contracted early stages of the bubonic plague, whereas more recent victims like this one here,' she indicated a corpse, 'died of the plague itself, but had no traces of the potion whatsoever.'

The clerics looked at each other, whilst Orix stared at the body on the table. He seemed to mutter to himself and no one dared ask what he'd said.

Morri walked over and looked at the samples Elloise had been testing. 'Could this mean the plague is a terrible coincidence?' He glanced towards Orix to see the old gnome's reaction. When Morri had heard what had happened, what his old tutor and the guild's Grand Master had done, he'd been shocked, but had swiftly defended Orix from those who'd spoken out against him.

Master Orix, I fear you will forever hate yourself for what happened in this city, and yet, as far as I am concerned, the blame lay with Severun and no other; although he met an end I would not wish on anyone, no matter their crimes.

Orix looked up. He dared not let himself hope Morri could be right, but he wanted to hear what the other clerics had to say. It was a terrible plague and on that day alone hundreds of bodies had been burnt and more and more houses had been condemned; black crosses painted on doors and families locked inside. There was no more room in the infirmaries and the King had made, with the help of his advisers, the terrible decision to lock residents who showed signs of the plague in their own homes.

'It's possible it's a coincidence, Morri,' Elloise said, who again looked at the samples in front of her, 'although I can't say for sure. It is extremely improbable, but not impossible. It could have arrived on a ship perhaps, but... surely it would have been that ship's crew who showed signs of the plague before anyone else? The first to contract the plague, alas, seemed to have been those who were infected with the potion.'

Morri looked down, his eyes unfocussed; he was clearly deep in thought. Orix felt proud of the young man before him. *Oh lad, you shine now, in our hour of need…what example have I been to you of late? A poor one I fear, to say the very least.*

'Who's checked the carrier of the potion?' Morri said eventually. 'The arcane magic itself… the scroll?' He looked at Orix and then to the other two clerics.

Elloise shrugged and Orix looked none the wiser. 'I've hardly left this room as you well know Morri. I've been concentrating on the plague and the disease. Other clerics are working on a vaccine and cure for the plague, but I don't know if anyone has looked into the carrier, despite that being Sergeant Falchion's original, uneducated guess?' Orix suddenly sat a little straighter on the bench he was perched on, as his conversation with Fal came back to him. *Falchion questioned Severun's spell, not my potion…*

The fourth cleric pulled at his grey beard – not too dissimilar to Orix's – as he said, 'Lord Strickland told me he was going to look into it and have wizards, sorcerers and magicians do the same.'

'But no cleric has searched the scroll's writings?' Orix asked.

The old cleric shook his head and headed for the door. 'I'll see to that myself.'

'And I'll join you,' Orix said, as he hopped down from the bench and hurried after his colleague. 'Stay here and see if you can find out more,' he added to Morri and Elloise. 'We'll come back with anything we find.'

The metallic rustling of maille followed Orix down the corridor, and Morri's heart sank to think of the old gnome being escorted everywhere he went by the guild's own guards.

'You really think there could be something in that?' Elloise asked Morri, a hint of annoyance in her tone. 'Orix seems to have gotten his hopes up,' she added, gesturing with her thumb towards the door.

'I hope there's something in that, Elloise, because we're getting no further here and we need answers. And I say hope, because I don't actually believe the plague *is* a coincidence, but neither do I believe from what we've seen here that it's a mutated strain of Master Orix's potion either.' Morri sighed heavily. 'We'll carry on looking here and who knows, they may find something on Severun's scroll.'

Elloise nodded unconvincingly and continued checking her samples.

Morri silently hoped again for there to be an answer within the writings of Severun's arcane scroll, for Orix's sake if no others.

***

Elleth wept into Mother's arms as the two of them sat by the glowing fire in the kitchen, a steaming pot of dandelion tea hanging above the embers.

'But why?'

'Because, my dear, it's how we live. Some folk bake bread, some butcher animals; others pick pockets or even kill for a living.'

Elleth's head lifted then, her tear streaked face turning towards Mother's, who nodded.

'Oh aye, assassins, guardsmen, knights even. They're all paid to kill ye see. People need money or trades to eat; to have a roof over their heads. And for us dear, we spend time with men, sometimes other women, and fulfil a role and a service they greatly desire.'

Elleth's head shook slowly from side to side as she spoke. 'But ye said it'd stop hurting me down there.'

'And it will, my lovely.' Mother stroked Elleth's black hair. 'Was that man not better than the first?'

Elleth moved to shake her head then stopped. 'A little, but he was younger and not as…'

'As what dear?'

'Big, ye know, with his thing,' *and I'm still hurting from the first. It's not been long since him, so how could the second be better?* Elleth didn't dare say that out loud.

Mother laughed and Elleth pulled back a bit. 'Ye'll learn there's benefits, my lovely, to all kinds of things. Look at the girls up top floor…'

Elleth noticed a change in tone then, as well as Mother's mirth falling away, but only for a moment.

'…they learnt… have learnt to know exactly how to please a man, but more importantly, how to get pleasure from it themselves, no matter who they're entertaining.'

'I don't think I can, Mother. I just don't think I can.'

Mother's grip tightened on Elleth. 'Ye will girl, I tell ye, ye will. Did I not give ye two handsome men as yer first ones?'

'Handsome? Is that pretty?'

'Aye lass, for men it's pretty. Did I not though?'

Elleth nodded.

'Then count yerself lucky, girl, it's only because I love ye I do that for ye. Some of the other girls don't get that from me when the men come.'

'Like Coppin?' Elleth's intense, grey eyes locked with Mother's.

'Don't question me, girl,' Mother said, and it was clear the question had angered her. 'Did I not throw him out and tend to yer sister miself?'

'Aye Mother, ye did, but—'

The slap shocked Elleth. Mother hadn't shown her such anger in the days she'd been there. She'd shouted, sure, what mother didn't, but this? Mamma would never have hit her. She pulled from Mother's grip then and stumbled backwards into the room, facing the older woman with raw determination, Coppin's voice in her thoughts.

'Dear, I—'

'She told me!' Elleth shouted. 'She told me they pay ye, pay ye to hurt us! Told me before it happened, for I ain't seen her since, have I?' *Yet I couldn't believe it, not then… Coppin, I'm so sorry.*

'Ye don't listen to that bitch.' Mother stood and her face darkened, and for the first time, Elleth knew she'd seen Mother's true face; her true feelings for

196

her girls were showing through.

Backing away slowly towards the kitchen door, Elleth continued. 'Is that what's happened to me? These pretty handsome men have paid to hurt me between me legs, instead of bite me tits?'

'Stupid girl, that's just sex. Ye wait till one really wants to hurt ye and I'll damned well let 'em do it for no extra if ye carry on.'

Elleth's stomach twisted then and her heart raced as the truth of it all sank in. She turned quickly, pulled the door open and ran for the front of the building.

Mother followed noisily.

The fat woman wouldn't be able to catch her though, Elleth knew that much... until she reached the locked door; a lock requiring Mother's key.

'Think ye can run, Elleth? Ye be smart and realise how to embrace it like those girls up top did.'

The girls upstairs!

Elleth hadn't met the girls upstairs, but Coppin – who'd been sent on an errand hours ago according to Mother – had always said they were like true big sisters, who taught her tricks of beauty and hair, amongst other things. Elleth now knew what sort of other things Coppin had been talking about, but one thing Elleth was sure, the girls up top would protect her, or so she hoped, for it was her only option now there was no way out of the bolted door in front of her.

Just as Mother reached Elleth, the girl ran for the stairs and moved as fast as she could up to the third floor, which was richly decorated with thick rugs and papered walls. None of the usual sounds came from the rooms. No giggling, laughing, shrieking or grunts, but knowing how slow Mother would climb the stairs, Elleth stopped and knocked on the first door. She didn't want to get whoever was inside in trouble if they were entertaining.

'Hello,' Elleth said in a hushed tone, her heart racing. 'It's Elleth, from downstairs. Mother's angry and I need yer help. Please.'

No answer.

'Please,' Elleth said again, fear rising within her as the lower stairs creaked. 'Open up, please...' She knocked again and then tried the handle, hoping whoever was inside was asleep.

The door opened slowly and quietly, revealing a green papered wall, leading to a large four poster bed with...

Elleth screamed.

On the bed lay an emaciated girl with purple and black spots covering her bare arms and large tumours here and there about her neck. Her red rimmed eyes moved to Elleth's and widened as she tried to speak through dry, cracked lips.

Elleth was stunned. She recognised the sickness for what it was and fear gripped her heart like a clawed hand, squeezing as she tried to take a step forward. Nausea threatened to double her over.

'I can't,' she whispered, sorrow pushing tears from her eyes. She turned

197

suddenly and rushed to the next room along, bursting in and finding the same scene, albeit surrounded by different décor.

The next two doors held similar scenes, but these girls were dead, one of them looking like she'd been there for quite some time.

Elleth slumped to the floor then and sobbed, despite hearing Mother reach the top of the stairs. Looking up, she caught Mother's eyes, eyes that held no love as far as Elleth was concerned.

'They'd black cross the door, my lovely,' Mother said quietly. She slowly moved past each door, closing them in turn. She eventually reached the girl on the floor, whose thin arms were wrapped around her knees. 'It'd be the end of us. No one would come, Elleth, and we'd starve me and thee. Our only hope now is those grey eyes of yours, that shiny black hair and that innocent smile. Even Coppin lost her appeal; her breasts ruined, and no, despite what she said I didn't let that bastard do that to her, not that.'

Elleth's crying came on all the more at the realisation Coppin was gone.

'She made us a lot of money by going, dear. Let's us eat a few weeks with what he paid for her.'

Elleth's swollen eyes widened as she took in the words and watched Mother crouch down beside her. 'Ye sold her?' Anger rose in her again and her sobs turned to heaving breaths as she suddenly surged to her feet, knocking Mother over in the process. She stood over Mother then and went to hit her, something she never thought she'd want to do until this moment.

An iron grip caught her wrist as she swung down, and the much larger woman pulled Elleth to the ground and held her there.

'You ungrateful bitch. There's only a couple of ye left. These one's up here're dead or as good as and I ain't for letting 'em black cross me door and close me down, so ye'll have to work for yer keep girl and work hard like the others. No more pick of the bunch for you! Next bastard comes through that door is yours and the next and the bloody next.' Mother stood and hauled Elleth to her feet easily, dragging her literally kicking and screaming behind her.

'Ye think I ain't been through it all miself? Ye think I ain't had men beat me, shaft me however they please and wherever they please? I did me time and I worked for this bastard place and no little bitch like you is gonna ruin it and take it from me!'

Elleth had been dragged down the stairs to the floor below, where Mother managed to throw her into a room before pulling the door shut and bolting it from the outside.

A door further down opened and a woman with blonde hair looked out, before pulling her head swiftly back in at the sight of a raging Mother.

'Ye'd do best to stay in there, Aynsa, if ye know what's good for ye!'

Mother turned back to the door in front of her and leaned against it. 'Elleth?' she called softly.

Silence.

'Ye do good in that room and ye may be able to heal the wound ye caused between us, ye hear? Ye try to get out or do anything stupid,' the woman's voice raised again as she went on, 'and I'll offer ye up on the street and believe me, that's far worse than in that room, for there'd be no break between the bastards who come a-calling!'

Elleth didn't even make the bed before she fell and curled up, her returning sobs racking her body as she gasped for air between them. Her life had been destroyed by the plague, but she'd been lucky enough to find a new family, or so she'd thought. This hell, however – for surely that's what it was – made her wonder whether the sickness would have been better for her; to die in her mamma's arms, with her dada and brother beside her.

Oh Coppin, where are ye? I hope it's better than here. It just has to be.

***

'You left them in there armed?'

'Yes, inquisitor,' Archbishop Corlen said to the tall man stood opposite him in the corridor. 'I panicked, but I knew the Grand Inquisitor didn't want disturbing, so thought it best to lock them up until you were available.'

Speaking slowly and emphasising each word, the inquisitor said, 'With... their... weapons?'

The Archbishop's jowls wobbled as he nodded swiftly, swallowing hard at the same time.

'Then we shall leave them a while longer, I want them tired and hungry when I finally go in there.'

'Surely not alone though, inquisitor?' Corlen said, his face flushed and his hands wringing together in front of him.

What a pathetic excuse for a man you are, Corlen. How you ever made Archbishop is beyond me. 'Yes, alone,' the inquisitor said. 'There's no reason to antagonise them and I am confident I can handle two guardsmen should I need to, or do you doubt me?'

'No, Inquisitor Makhell, of course not. It's just...' the Archbishop looked around for the right way to put his thoughts into words, 'they seemed very... capable.'

'Trust me, Archbishop, capability is something I have often found the City Guard lacking. Now be on your way and make no mention of this to the Grand Inquisitor or the witchunters, for your own sake as well as mine.'

Corlen nodded and thanked Inquisitor Makhell, before shuffling down the corridor towards his private chambers.

Snorting his disgust, the inquisitor turned and walked confidently in the other direction, all the while mouthing prayers to Sir Samorl and slapping his wooden rod into his open palm.

***

Fal slowly opened his eyes and blinked immediately as dust and grit stung them. He tried to raise his hand to rub at them, but it was snagged under something by his side. It was dark and through his obscured vision, he couldn't make anything out.

The last thing he remembered were lights out to sea, thunder and then an almighty explosion as the cave erupted with flying debris. He tried to pull his hand free again as someone groaned next to him. Fal's hand slid free as the weight was removed and the end of his fingers began to tingle. He managed to sit up whilst moving his fingers to get the blood flowing again.

Someone shuffled beside him.

'Who's that?' Fal asked. He managed to stifle a cough as he wiped at the dust on his face. He winced as his eyes stung again. *Blink blink blink…* he thought, although he did more rubbing than blinking.

'It's Correia. Is that you, Sergeant Falchion?'

'Yeah it's me. Are you injured?' He tried to wipe away the tears so he could make out the woman beside him. Although the sky was clear and the moon bright, it offered little light in the tunnel at the back of the cave.

'Not really,' she said. 'Bruised in places, but I'm alright. What about the others?'

Fal thought he could make out her faint outline now.

'I'm fine, thanks,' Sav mumbled. 'My bloody lip hurts though.' No one replied and Sav sighed. 'Get it, bloody lip? I split my lip?'

'Yes we got it,' Correia said, 'now shut up if you're not hurt, and help us find the others and Errolas' star stone.'

Fal imagined Sav rolling his eyes and smiled to himself. He could always count on the lanky scout to try and boost morale, even if Correia didn't appreciate it. He slowly pushed himself to his feet and felt a slender yet firm hand on his arm as Correia pulled herself up next to him.

'Mearson?' Correia shouted. 'Gleave?'

'Starks, you there?' Fal asked as loud as he dared considering his head was still tender from Execution Square. 'Errolas?'

The sound of someone moving came from Sav's direction and then the scout cursed. As he did, someone else grunted and then moaned.

'Who's that?' Fal asked, 'Starks?'

'It's Mearson.'

'Sorry Mearson,' said Sav, 'I think I trod on you.'

'It's not that, it's my head, it's banging. It felt like half this flaming tunnel came down on us. Ma'm, you injured? Where's Gleave and Tom?'

There was a pause before Correia replied. 'Tom's dead and we can't find Gleave. He was near us before the cave-in…'

Mearson fell silent for a few moments before grunting and muttering something about his arm. 'Cave-in? It was that bloody ship—'

'Mearson!' Correia hissed and the man held his tongue fast.

'What's he talking about?' Errolas' voice came from Mearson's direction.

Correia's feet shifted audibly. 'Errolas, you're not hurt, thank goodness,' she said, clearly avoiding the elf's question. 'Do you have the star stone? We need to find Gleave and the crossbowman.'

'Starks,' Fal added.

'Starks, of course, we need to find him.'

'I have the stone here, Correia, and you shall have it when you explain what your man meant?' Errolas' voice was deadly serious, and Fal wished the elf would shine the stone so they could see Correia's expression.

There was silence for a few moments and then Correia sighed. 'Very well elf, if I must. We are currently testing a new type of ship off this shore. Its presence may have attracted whatever that thing was that attacked my men... and brought this tunnel down on top of us.'

'You think whatever you're doing out there may have attracted that thing?' Fal asked, incredulously.

'Well, it could be a coincidence of course,' Mearson said. Correia shifted again, as if wanting to shut the pathfinder up before he gave anything else away.

'What are you testing, Correia,' Errolas said, his tone as deadly as before, 'that could bring such a creature from the depths? For in all my years I have never heard such a sound, and my bleeding ears are testimony to that.'

'I need your stone, Errolas,' the Spymaster said, clearly losing her control. 'We need to find the other men. We have a mission to press on with and we don't have time for a debate. I've already lost damned good men here today and we're not even away from the bloody coast yet.'

'This is no debate,' Errolas said quickly, ignoring her attempts to shut him up, 'nor is it a coincidence as your pathfinder claims.'

Both Fal and Sav were shocked to hear the elf sound genuinely angry.

'They're testing cannons, elf. Now give me your stone or light this tunnel up yourself, either way we need to find my pathfinder and the crossbowman and move on with our mission. I've lost too many, Errolas, I'm not losing another under this rubble.' Correia's temper was rising and Fal could sense her impatience.

'You mean a bloody ship blasted this cave to bits around us?' Sav shouted.

'Yes, it seems they did,' Correia said, a heavy sigh leaving her lips.

'Sound travels far in the sea, Correia, and many creatures communicate or navigate using it. The repeat firing of cannons in this bay most likely drew that creature from the depths and enraged it!' Errolas was furious and everyone in the tunnel knew why.

The humans of Altoln, Sirreta and Eatri had signed a treaty centuries ago regarding black powder and black powder weaponry. After all, humans had not developed it; the dwarves of the Norlechlan Mountains had.

The elves had fought a long and hard war against those dwarves. Their blatant disregard for nature and their use of black powder weapons had sparked the war in the first place, and the elves feared that in the hands of humans, the use of black powder would prove far worse. Therefore, the treaty to never experiment with or trade in black powder or black powder weaponry was created and signed. Until now, that treaty had never been broken, overtly at least. The Samorlian Church and its holy warmongering centuries ago had seen to that when they chased all the dwarf traders, merchants and residents from Altoln. Since then, the elves had thought themselves safe in the knowledge that the dwarves, who could hold a grudge like no other, would never again trade with not only Altoln, but any of its neighbouring human nations.

'Where did they come from?' Errolas demanded.

'I don't have to answer, elf. This is the King's business and I think you have asked enough questions. Now hand me the stone or light this tunnel.' Correia was seething, and Fal had no idea what would happen next.

'I will ask one more time, Correia… I think it slips your mind I have no problem seeing you in this dim light.'

Fal took that as a threat and wasn't going to take any more. 'Errolas,' he said in a calm tone, 'light the stone, please, we need to find the other two and tend to everyone's wounds.

'Correia,' Fal directed to his side, 'answer the damned question. He knows now, we all do, so you might as well tell us everything. If this mission, whatever The Three it is, is going to work, we all need to be honest with each other from the start.

'And Sav,' Fal added swiftly, 'say nothing, before you start them off again.'

Sav started to say something, but wisely thought against it.

The tunnel fell into silence for a few moments; moments that felt like an eternity, before a bright light blinked on from Errolas' direction. The beam of light pointed to the rough stone of the ceiling, illuminating the tunnel in a ghostly silver glow.

'Thank you, Errolas.' Fal looked around and let out a relieved sigh before continuing. 'Sav, Mearson, tend to our companions. Correia, answer the bloody question and we can move on with this mission of yours.'

Sav and Mearson – the latter still clutching his bloodied arm – wasted no time in scrambling over to Starks and Gleave, who were both slumped by the tunnel's entrance to the cave. Their groans indicated to all they were alive, and they came round with splashes of cold water from a deerskin on Mearson's belt. Loud coughing followed. Rubbing at their dust-filled eyes, they eventually accepted a drink offered by Mearson, before taking in the destructive scene, whilst Sav checked them over for wounds.

'Tom?' Gleave asked, seeing a body part covered by rubble nearby.

Mearson nodded once and sat next to his friend. They said nothing more, falling into a companionable silence. Sav slumped down next to Starks and the two of them mirrored their new companions as they let what had happened sink in.

Despite the hard reality of what had happened, Correia finally answered Errolas' previous question, albeit through gritted teeth. 'Dwarves, Errolas,' she said, holding the elf's gaze, 'Prince Edward managed to trade with the Norlechlan Dwarves.'

Chapter 26: On With The Mission

The thin, almost brittle girl breathed hard, her heart pounding away, as did the grubby man on top of her. She fought not to wince and instead somehow managed to feign a pleasurable moan – something she hoped she was becoming better at, despite the short amount of time she'd been practising. He grunted through his final, jerking thrust, before rolling away.

He sat on the edge of the bed then, his broad and scarred shoulders lifting up and down as heavy breaths left his gold-filled mouth.

She'd noticed those teeth as soon as he'd entered the room, not to mention the faint aroma of urine, and wondered how, or by whom, he'd had his original teeth knocked out.

She pulled the cover back up over her legs, but left her small breasts visible. They seemed to like that, the men, after they'd finished. She'd learnt the hard way – despite there only being a few – that covering up completely, angered some of them. They could see covered women without paying, so why whilst getting dressed, shouldn't they be able to see what they'd just paid for and used. She could understand that. Didn't make it any easier though, being thought of as something to be bought.

'Ye'll get used to it,' Mother had said. Well, she hadn't yet had she, and the witch had sent enough through since their fight. She had to admit the pain wasn't what it had been though, but that was because she felt almost numb to most of them now… most of them.

The man stood and pulled up his braes, before doing the same with his filthy hose, which he tied to his belt before turning to face the girl, who arched her back and smiled sweetly back at him, cringing inside.

'Ye enjoy that, girl?' Longoss asked.

She fluttered the lashes over her large, grey eyes and nodded, her smile staying the same, almost too sweet to be true.

Aye, and that's it ain't it, lass, too good to be true, that's you, because it ain't true is it?

'Don't lie to me girl,' he said, pulling his baggy shirt over his head, but not before noticing her flinch at his words. Head through the hole, Longoss noticed the cover being pulled over her cute breasts. Her knees following the cover up as she swallowed hard and looked away from him, clearly searching for the right answer.

'I won't be hitting on ye, girl, that's me word and I don't break me word.'

She looked to him then and he sat on the end of the bed, facing her. She pulled her legs back a little more and looked to the door briefly, before looking back into his eyes.

'Others hit on ye, girl?'

She hesitated, before nodding.

'Aye, that they will. Cowards, ye see. Reckon they'd hit on the likes of me?'

She shook her head.

'Hah, no, 'course not. Cowards they are,' he said again. 'Well as I say, girl,

I'd never hit on ye.'

She smiled ever so slightly, like she'd think he'd want to see, but he knew the truth in that, and it was only then, when he looked at her properly, that he noticed the bruises here and there.

'I ain't saying this to own ye neither, girl, nor for any free favours. No, I'm saying this because I won't hit on no woman and that's the truth of it. A man? Ha, oh aye, I'll kill any man and worse, because they probably deserve it for something or other and if they don't, well, their fault for not being tougher, plus, I get paid for it ye see; well for most of 'em, and paid well.'

Just like Mother said, some people get paid to do this and some people get paid to kill. Well Mother, since ye locked me up in here, I'm for thinking the latter is the better way to be… but I don't think that do I? Not really, because if I did, I'd figure a way to kill the witch and I'd feel no badness in doing it neither. So why the hell can't I? Instead, I've already started learning to give men what they want and for what, to end up like Coppin… to end up sold? No… to hope they don't beat on me, like the third one did.

He was still looking at her she noticed, but his eyes met hers and hadn't wondered lower, not once. Wasn't normal that and she wasn't sure if it made her feel less, or more, afraid of him.

'Ye're safe whenever I'm here. Not that I promise to be here often, but when I am girl, ye'll be safe wi' me. I give ye me word there. No reason ye can't enjoy yerself once in a blue moon, eh?'

She smiled a little more and nodded again.

'I ain't no looker, 'morl's balls that's true, but ye tell me what ye want next time I'm in and I'll try to do as good by ye as ye did me. How'd that be sounding to ye?'

'Aye,' she said sweetly, her voice barely audible.

'Aye,' he said, nodding, 'and I tell ye, any man hits on ye again, ye tell me next time I'm in, girl, agreed? For I'll kill any man as I telled ye, and any man hitting on a cute little thing as you, ain't no man at all, but a rat and rats are for killing, ain't that right?'

Nodding again, she looked to speak and then stopped herself, smiling sweetly again.

'Go on, speak it.'

'Ye've killed men before?'

Gold teeth shone.

She relaxed ever so slightly then, yet she didn't know why.

'Aye girl, many men and one woman,' Longoss said, his smile slipping at the end.

Her legs tensed once again, with her arms wrapped tight about them.

'An accident?' she asked, barely audible over Longoss' heavy breathing.

He shook his head and for the first time, his eyes dropped, but not to her body; to another place entirely.

She cursed herself, knowing then she'd pushed too far, at least, that was until he smiled sincerely – no gold – before answering her question.

'No lass, not an accident, least not the way me da told it. Killed me ma, ye see. First person I killed, me own ma.'

She swallowed hard and for the life of her she didn't know why, but she asked how.

Longoss looked to her grey eyes again and shrugged. 'Don't remember. What's yer name?' he said quickly, raising his eyebrows a tad with the question.

'Elleth.'

'Is it short for owt?'

She shook her head and for the first time, he noticed how shiny her black hair was as a few strands fell across her face, before she brushed them aside with delicate fingers.

'Well Elleth, I don't remember killing me ma, 'cause I were being pulled from between her legs at the time. But me da never let me forget it and he would beat me proper for it year after year. Her *deathday* he called it, not me birthday, like the other kids in the keep, but me ma's *deathday*... the day I killed her.'

Elleth had relaxed fully at this point, and although there were no tears on either side of the bed, her eyes at least, felt moist. She smiled sympathetically; the first genuine smile in a long while.

'No pity though gir... Elleth, no pity. The bastard's dead now. He were the second I killed ye see, and I might not remember me ma, but I remember me da, and oh did that bastard squeal when I stuck him wi' his own sword.'

Swallowing hard again, Elleth saw the two men Longoss could be, and as much as he scared her to the core, she couldn't help hoping she'd see him again, even if it was just to hear his calming voice; a voice that wasn't demanding anything of her, calling her all sorts or threatening the worst.

'Anyway,' Longoss said, as he stood, 'questions like this of other bastard men will get ye hit on, or worse! And I'm telling ye for the last time, Elleth, and I mean it now, any of those shites do anything that makes ye feel like sticking 'em wi' a blade, then ye tell me and I'll do it for ye, understood?'

'Aye,' she said, a little more confidently this time. 'Aye, I will at that too.'

They both shared a sincere smile and Longoss picked up the rest of his things and moved to the door. He turned just before opening it and looked upon Elleth.

'Pull yer cover up, girl, I can see yer tits, and I'd much rather look at yer eyes when we're talking.'

She hadn't even realised the cover had fallen so she looked down, blushing slightly – for reasons she couldn't fathom after what they'd just done together – and when she looked up, cover back where it had been, Longoss was gone.

The smile on her face then was the most genuine she'd had in a long time and despite herself, she thought she would look forward to Longoss' next visit, even if only for the fact he'd talked to her as a woman, not a possession.

***

It had been almost as dark as the tunnels whilst the group recovered what was left of their belongings at the back of the rubble- and meat-strewn cave. Correia had advised against lighting the star stone in case, for whatever reason, the *Norlechlan* opened fire on their position again. She also recommended moving on swiftly before a landing party of King's marines arrived to assess the damage to their cave, and to examine whatever had attacked them. Although they were all part of the King's forces, except Errolas of course, Correia did not want the inconvenience and wasted time that would come with explaining all that had happened, or as much as she felt necessary, to a ship's officer… or worse, the prince himself.

The group had swiftly worked out if there were any serious injuries – fortunately there wasn't – before heading out onto the shore and north along the beach.

Fal had been pleased to find his seax knife along with his falchion. His maille coif and mitts, alas, had not been picked up by Correia's pathfinders when they collected his weapons. Sav had found his short-sword and so was fully equipped with that, his yew bow standing almost as tall as his shoulders, and a near full quiver of his own broad headed arrows.

The pathfinder, Mearson, had an open wound across his forearm, but Sav had bound it well and Mearson insisted he was fit for action, despite the dubious looks from Correia, who, after her argument with Errolas, was in a foul mood indeed. Neither her, nor the elf, had broached the subject of dwarven weapons trade and broken treaties since the cave, and everyone in the group was silently thankful of that.

Gleave and Mearson had briefly argued with Correia about their fallen comrades, but the Spymaster had inevitably won and the two pathfinders conceded the point that they didn't have the time, or light, to find and bury their friends, or what was left of them.

Fal felt for the two men, and Correia when he thought about it, realising it would be like leaving Sav or Starks behind without a proper burial. He also realised, however, that whatever the mission was, it was extremely important to Altoln, and if the two pathfinders and their commander could stoically accept their friends deaths and soldier on, then so too could he if the horrific situation arose.

As they'd left the cave – travel sacks stuffed with whatever supplies they could find – Errolas had heard the sound of oars in the water, so the group had swiftly made their way along the rocky shore, where they could creep away from the landing craft of the King's marines unnoticed.

The voices of the marines carried on the sea breeze for a while after coming ashore; their gasps, curses and shouts evident of their discovery of what was left of the monster and its victims. Eventually those voices died away as the group forged on, following Gleave blindly as he searched for an apparent route up to the cliff-tops above. Starks brought up the rear with his crossbow, whilst Correia and Errolas kept a wary distance of each other, making light, whispered conversations with anyone close to them, to try and hide their anger and frustration with one another.

'We'll stop when we find a safer spot, and I think it will be time then to explain our mission,' Correia announced, to Fal's surprise.

He hadn't expected her to offer any more information after events at the cave and her argument with Errolas about the ship, which he still couldn't quite believe. He certainly hadn't wanted to broach the subject with her or Errolas, and assumed her pathfinders, as friendly as they seemed, wouldn't offer any information without her say so.

'I'd be lying if I said I wasn't looking forward to hearing what it is we're all up to,' Fal said eventually.

'It is of the utmost importance to both Wesson and Altoln, sergeant, and so is a serious business indeed.'

'Absolutely, ma'm,' Fal replied, intrigued all the more.

As the group walked on, watching their footing on loose stones and slippery rocks, all those behind Errolas noticed the elf suddenly stop dead. He turned his head slightly as if listening to something, and then held his hand up. All those behind stopped. Gleave looked back just a few heartbeats later and he too stopped, motioning for Sav and Mearson to do the same. Both pathfinders drew their weapons ever so quietly, as did Errolas, Correia and Fal. Sav swiftly and silently strung his bow and nocked an arrow to the hemp string, whilst Starks turned and crouched to assume the same defensive position he'd been adopting throughout the journey from the prison.

Just as he did so, a grey seal called out and slid from the water – which was coming in quite close to the group at that point – before shuffling behind a large rock they'd just passed.

Errolas held up his hand again and walked slowly towards Starks, who'd lowered his crossbow and was looking on – along with the rest – to catch another glimpse of the creature.

Before Errolas reached Starks, a handsome, naked man with an extremely toned physique, long silver hair and ocean blue eyes strode from the same rock the seal had shuffled behind.

Starks nearly fell over backwards and in doing so hit the crossbow's trigger, which sent the loaded bolt skipping across the rocky floor, barely missing the shocked man, who covered his face and ducked instinctively. Fal rushed forward as Starks scrambled back and drew his short-sword, dropping his crossbow as he did so.

Errolas spun to face Fal, both hands held out, his curved sword in one – which no one had seen him draw. 'Hold!' he said swiftly, and Fal skidded to a stop, turning to see the group's reactions. Sav was reluctantly easing the string of his bow, whilst Correia and her pathfinders stopped dead in their tracks. They too lowered their weapons.

'I'm sorry, Errolas,' the naked man said in a strange accent none of the humans recognised. His arms still covered his head.

'It's alright, Furber. I'm sorry you almost got skewered, but I failed to inform anyone you may be paying us a visit once we hit the shore. We have had quite the journey so far.'

Everyone relaxed a little more now, and Fal, to show he meant no harm to the strange man, slid his falchion back into the scabbard at his side.

Errolas lowered his arms and nodded to the naked man. 'How about covering something else, my good friend, it's not a custom here to walk around naked.'

'Oh… of course, I do apologise good people. I did not mean to startle you.' Furber ducked back behind the rock and came back out wearing wet, mottled-grey seal fur around his waist.

Starks' brow creased as he looked around to Fal and then to Errolas. 'He killed that seal?'

Errolas laughed out and shook his head. 'No Starks, he *is* the seal.'

Starks gasped. 'Shape shifter!' he shouted, startling them all.

Correia shook her head and sighed. 'There's no such bloody thing as a shape shifter, don't be so stupid.'

Sav frowned, adding, 'After what we've seen tonight, Correia, I'd believe anything.'

'You would,' Correia said, and Sav blushed.

'Furber is not a shape shifter… well, not as such anyway. He's a selkie,' explained Errolas, as Furber nodded and bowed low, his fur slipping slightly, much to the amusement of Sav and the apparent appreciation of Correia.

'Fin-folk,' Gleave said, almost growling. 'I know of your kind.'

It wasn't hard to hear the venom in Gleave's voice. Everyone in the group turned to him. Furber swallowed hard and his attractive, innocent smile slipped slightly.

'You come ashore to take men's wives and daughters,' the stocky pathfinder continued, 'to drive them away from their husbands and fathers.'

All heads turned back to Furber and the selkie seemed to shrink under their probing eyes.

Before he could speak, Correia turned back to Gleave and scowled at him. 'Back on point, Gleave, I don't remember relieving you of that duty. This is of no concern to you. Furber is clearly an informant for the ranger.'

Gleave looked like he'd been slapped, but nodded slowly all the same. He turned away and only Errolas heard him mutter something about Correia 'changing her tone' as he made his way a little further up the shore.

'It does happen,' Furber said regrettably, once Gleave had gone. 'Your friend is right enough there, but not all of us are like that. Although, it's not really our fault human women find us so appealing. It's the same with human males and our females.'

'I bet it is,' Sav said, and he whistled at the thought.

Starks stifled a laugh and Correia glared at them both. 'Don't worry Furber, Gleave has a temper, it's nothing personal.'

Fal found it amusing how the selkie had softened the hard warrior woman more in a dozen heartbeats, than he believed it would take a human male to do in a lifetime.

'Thank you, you are too kind,' Furber replied, bowing again.

'Starks, pick up your crossbow,' Fal ordered. 'Find that bolt, stop staring at the man and take rearguard. I think Furber needs to talk to us, am I right?'

'Yes, please let us sit.'

Fal ordered Sav up to Gleave while Correia ordered Mearson down to Starks. The rest sat on whichever rocks were flat enough to do so.

Errolas told them he'd asked the selkie to watch Fal in the early stages, before the plague, and it was then Fal remembered the grey seal whilst he and Sav had been fishing. Furber smiled innocently and Fal laughed, asking if he'd scared Sav's fish away or whether the scout really was that unlucky with fishing. Correia had silenced Fal with one of her looks for that, and then taken the sudden silence as an opportunity to ask Furber all about himself and his people. Fal and Errolas both rolled their eyes. Correia caught their expressions and swiftly changed tack, asking about the news Furber had of Wesson.

'It is bad,' the half-naked selkie said, and Fal again noticed Correia's eyes slipping below Furber's as the man spoke. 'Two more ships attempted to leave port early this morning. Both were intercepted immediately at the blockade, one of them wrecked.

'People are dying by the score and I can smell it on the air when I enter the harbour. Columns of smoke reach high as Wesson burns its dead. You need to move fast before your efforts are in vain.'

Fal cringed at the thought of his home being ravaged by the disease, one that he'd released, or at least might have released.

'What of the rumours,' Errolas asked, and Fal was quick to notice Correia turn suddenly to the elf.

'What rumours?' she asked, and Fal found it amusing the King's own Spymaster didn't know something a half-naked selkie did.

'Rumours from the south,' Furber confirmed. Correia's eyes turned swiftly back to him. 'I met a dolphin today that had travelled with his pod from the Chriselle Coast. He encountered strange ships down there, of a build he has never seen before. He witnessed a battle between two of these ships and a Sirretan merchant cog, and so assumes they were pirates from the Tri Isles, but I am not so sure. There are rumours of Sirretan soldiers from coastal keeps along the Kaja Strip going missing and then turning up mutilated.' Furber glanced at Fal, but continued before Fal could think why. 'No word on who or what is doing it though, but it *is* being noticed. Over five hundred Sirretan soldiers were seen marching the coastal road just two days ago.'

'A defensive manoeuvre,' Correia said, 'but against whom, Orismar?'

Fal flinched. *Ah, that's why you glanced at me.*

'We don't know,' Errolas said. 'Rumours are all we are hearing. I have been away from home some time however; there may be more to be learnt once we arrive there.'

'Home… our mission lies in your homeland?' Fal said, both stunned and excited at the same time.

All three turned to Fal then and Furber was clearly surprised Fal didn't know. Errolas smiled as Correia nodded.

'I can't wait to tell Sav,' Fal said, the biggest grin for days playing upon his face despite the unusual and worrying news Furber had brought.

***

A flock of pigeons lifted from their roost on a nearby building as the black carriage rounded the corner, its driver cracking his whip over four chestnut geldings. The street was clear, as were many in the city. Most of the population were hiding away from the plague, suffering from it, or already dead, and so the driver cracked his whip again, enjoying a rare chance to send the carriage clattering down the cobbled street at speed.

A figure stepped out in front of the carriage without warning. The driver's shock was evident in his lack of action to halt the horses bearing down on the person.

The driver closed his eyes and gripped the rail behind him.

Nothing happened.

Opening his eyes and seeing an empty street once more, he turned to look back as he slowly pulled on the reigns. He could have sworn he saw the carriage door close from the corner of his eye. He listened for a shout from the man inside, but nothing came, so he turned back, cracked his whip once more and shook his head, muttering to himself as he did so.

Inside the carriage, a slender, richly dressed man wearing horn-rimmed spectacles read a small, black book. Pursing his lips, he closed the book and peered over his spectacles to the man suddenly sat opposite him. The only sound came from hooves and wheels on cobbles, as well as the heavy breathing of the gold toothed man staring back.

The well-dressed man placed his book down beside him, removed his reading spectacles, cleaned them thoroughly with a velvet cloth and placed them in a soft leather pouch, which he withdrew from a side pocket in his immaculate coat, before placing the encased spectacles back in the same pocket. Finally finished, he looked up and smiled at his visitor.

The coach rounded a corner then and both men leaned into the turn. Once levelled out, the slender man spoke in a soft tone, but one that hinted of a confident capability his appearance seemed to contradict. 'Master Longoss, what a pleasant surprise.'

The gold teeth revealed themselves fully.

'I wasn't expecting you so soon.'

'Don't like to hang about, Master Son,' Longoss said, slouching back into the carriage's comfortable chair.

'Of course, of course and what an impressive entry you made,' Poi Son said, trying to hide his disgust at the almost overpowering smell of urine.

'Aye,' Longoss said, grinning again.

'I take it you have completed your last two tasks then, Master Longoss?'

'Aye and don't I always?'

Smiling, Poi Son nodded slowly, before continuing. 'Excellent, Master Longoss, simply excellent. Your pay will be at its usual place tomorrow. I have but one more question.'

'Go on,' Longoss said, through the fingers of his left hand whilst biting his nails.

'The riot, Master Longoss?' Poi Son let the question hang for a moment, seeing how his visitor would react.

'Which one?' Longoss said, continuing to bite his nails.

'The one you attended of course, to Tyndurris.'

'Oh aye, what of it?' Longoss moved to the nails of his right hand.

'I heard—'

'What?'

Poi Son flushed at being interrupted, for he certainly wasn't accustomed to it, especially by someone who knew who he was. 'I heard, Master Longoss, you killed a city guardsman during that riot.'

'Aye.'

'Right outside the door of your second mark?'

'Aye, he ran into the door, stupid bastard.'

Poi Son winced at the curse. 'Language, Master Longoss. We're not in the habit of that kind of language now are we?'

Longoss sighed before muttering an apology.

'We're also not in the habit of killing outside of our contracts, are we? I thought you understood after the last incident.'

No reply.

'Master Longoss, do we have a problem here?'

Longoss sat up then, stopped biting his nails and looked directly into the cat-like eyes of the man sitting opposite him. He thought for a second of how easily he could physically crush the man, by simply leaning over and squeezing his scrawny neck, but as Poi Son smiled, Longoss shook his head and apologised again.

'Apology accepted, Master Longoss, but let us not have it happen again, dear fellow, eh? We walk a fine line the likes of you and I, and we cannot afford undue attention from the City Guard. It's lucky for us, I believe, that the current… situation in Wesson, is distracting any attention to normally fall our way when contracts outside of Park District present themselves.'

Longoss' eyes widened and he sat up that bit more, awaiting instruction.

Poi Son was pleased Longoss was now taking matters seriously, for what was worse than an uninterested listener during matters of such importance?

'We have ourselves such a contract you see, Master Longoss, one which shall present itself to us in the near future. And I would like you, Master Longoss, to accept that contract. Our organisation will have a lot riding on this, a lot indeed, and so I need to gauge your interest so I can make plans.'

I know ye know me name, so quit saying it every other pissin' word, ye pompous prick. 'Why me, Master Son?' Longoss said, trying not to smirk. 'Ye have a lot of others ye could call on, Master Son, so why me, Master Son?'

'Yes, Master Longoss I do, *many* others…'

The threat was not lost on Longoss, but he let it slide, eager to hear what the stuck up bastard had to say. Also, knowing as he did, just how dangerous Poi Son was, he decided mocking the man may not have been his best idea ever.

'However,' Poi Son continued, 'how shall I put it…?' Poi Son paused briefly, searching for the words. 'Ah yes, as rough and ready as you and your methods may be, Master Longoss, you have never failed us or passed on a contract. Nor have you ever been implicated as a suspect to one of your marks by the City Guard, or, which is even more remarkable I have to say, has anyone ever hinted at any connection between you and our organisation… ever, despite your countless and quite often overt contracts over the years. And so it is for that, Master Longoss, as well as your reputation amongst your peers, that I will, when it comes through, offer the contract to you and you alone.'

Longoss' eyes widened again, as did his grin, the thought of the gold, for surely it would be gold, exciting him. *Ye can say me name as much as ye want, Poi Son, if it means gold.*

'I take it you're interested then, Master Longoss?'

'Oh aye, Master Son, I'll take whatever it may be, as I always do… as long as it's a bloke and not a woman, as ye well know.'

'Well let's not be hasty, I wanted your interest, not your agreement. We haven't even been offered the contract as of yet, nor have I negotiated a sum for the mark. And as for details, they will come later.'

The coach rounded another corner and then came to a stop. The driver noisily climbed down from his seat and opened the carriage door. He jumped back as he saw the golden grin facing him, and his eyes darted to Poi Son, who snorted and waved the man away.

'I shall be in touch, Master Longoss.'

'And I'll be waiting, Master Son,' the assassin said, as he climbed out of the carriage.

'Oh and Master Longoss?'

The assassin leaned back into the cab.

'I shall expect you not to mention this to anyone of course, not even your fellows in the guild; it is of the utmost import you do not in fact.'

Longoss raised his eyebrows, but nodded his agreement, before turning to walk away.

'One last thing, Master Longoss.'

Sighing, Longoss stopped, but didn't turn round.

'Was she good?'

He turned around, his brow furrowed at the question.

'The whore?' Poi Son had a wicked grin upon his face. 'I hear you visited a new whore at Mother's tonight, and wondered what you thought? You see, our watcher said you looked quite content upon leaving. He even said he may

212

visit her himself. Shall I pass on your recommendation to him?'

Longoss swallowed hard, before bearing his gold teeth, turning and stalking off. The thought of anyone from the guild touching Elleth pulled at his nerves more than he would have thought... for reasons beyond him.

After the assassin had left, Poi Son's grin fell away and an altogether more sinister smile presented itself. The master of the Black Guild considered the emotions he'd just witnessed in one of the most vicious men he'd ever had the pleasure to do business with.

Now that reaction may prove useful indeed...

Chapter 27: Bookworms

Not knowing why, Longoss knocked on a door he'd left only a few hours before, a door he didn't think he would be walking back through for at least a week or so. Waiting for a response, he cast his eyes around the empty street. He was used to crowds of people milling about; pickpockets, thugs, gangers and the scared residents of Dockside all, but very few ventured out now. There were the occasional riots, big and small, when guardsmen attempted to take bodies or black cross doors in gang held areas. That always drew the people out, giving them something, or someone – the City Guard – to vent their anger on, but apart from that, very few made journeys that were unnecessary.

A key in a lock and a bolt being slid across brought Longoss' attention back to the door in front of him, just in time to see a large woman with a surprised look on her face.

'Longoss... ye're back far sooner than I'd have thought,' the woman said suspiciously.

'Aye, that I am,' Longoss said, flashing Mother a golden smile. 'Decided to come see that girl again, Elleth.'

The woman smiled, but didn't invite Longoss in. 'Elleth's busy my dear, how about Aynsa, the blonde? She has a lovely—'

Longoss pushed past Mother and made for the stairs, just in time to hear a cry of pain from a room above.

Mother attempted to latch on to the man's thick arm whilst he passed. 'What ye think ye're doing, Longoss?'

Dragging her along briefly before shrugging her off, Longoss took the stairs two at a time.

Receiving no answer, Mother shouted after the man. 'Ye don't disturb when other clients are in, Longoss, ye know that, ye dumb bastard!'

The scream from the room Elleth had been in stopped Longoss' planned reply, and he continued to the top of the stairs and along the corridor swiftly.

'Please,' Elleth said. Her eyes were red and swollen from crying, and her fat lip throbbed as the man thrusting himself into her slapped her across the face again, before spitting on her stomach and laughing.

She cried all the more then, her chest aching from the hacking sobs pulling at her throat. The large man thrust harder and harder, before grabbing her by the throat and squeezing hard. 'Stop crying bitch!' he shouted, spittle flicking from his thin lips.

Why me, why me, why me, why me...? Elleth thought, over and over, praying for anything to make the horror she was going through stop. *Coppin, help me, please, where are ye?*

The crash of an opening door released the man's vice like grip from Elleth's delicate neck. She coughed hard, sucking in stale air between coughs as the man attempted to twist around on top of her to see who'd entered the room. His forceful thrusts finally stopped.

Not caring what had made him stop, Elleth rubbed at her throat and thanked Sir Samorl as the man suddenly – and unbeknown to Elleth, fearfully – pulled himself from her and threw himself off the bed, to the side where he'd left his clothes and dagger.

She closed her eyes then, dizziness taking her as she concentrated on breathing whilst massaging her bruised neck. She thought of Coppin's sad smile as she forced herself to calm down and take in the noises she was now hearing; grunting, cursing and metal on metal.

Longoss lunged for the naked man – who was slightly larger than him – with a small eating knife. The sweating man moved his red, heaving chest out of the way of the lunge just in time to bring his dagger up to meet the small blade.

Blades clashing briefly, Longoss pulled his knife back and threw his left fist at the man's head.

He missed.

Think, ye fool, calm down and think. Longoss barely missed being gutted by the dagger his opponent thrust his way.

A sudden scream from the bed drew Longoss' attention. He saw Elleth's bruised face take in the scene of flashing blades and swinging fists. The momentary distraction cost him as the other man's dagger slid across his left arm.

'Bastard!' Longoss jumped back a step, narrowly avoiding the dagger coming in further towards his neck. The man was good and Longoss knew it. He needed to concentrate to win here, and for reasons he couldn't fathom, the girl was breaking that concentration in a way no one had ever managed to do. He side-stepped another lunge from the naked man's dagger, and then his heart lurched as the man turned and jumped towards the bed.

Elleth screamed again and rolled off the other side, escaping the grasping hand that had reached for her.

Longoss rushed forward then and slashed down, slicing across the calf of his opponent as he scrambled across the bed towards Elleth, who was pressing her naked form into the corner as much as she could.

Crying out in pain, the man kicked out at Longoss and connected with his leg just above the knee, which dropped the big man to the bed.

Elleth cried all the more then as blades flashed and blood spilt across the linen. She made for the door, but the gap alongside the bed was blocked suddenly as a large, bloodied body fell into it. Stunned to silence and immobility, Elleth looked down, frozen by the sight at her feet; a sight she couldn't have envisioned in her worse nightmares, for the man lying there, his face torn to shreds, was split from groin to chest, his innards steaming as they hung from the open cavity.

She noticed then, that even if he could have survived the butchering he'd received on the bed, he could never again have raped a woman.

Elleth turned then and took in the room. The door was splintered but still hanging from its hinges and there was blood everywhere; on the bed, floor and walls alike, even some on the ceiling. Finally looking up to the bed's headboard, Elleth saw Longoss, breathing heavily and clutching – knuckles white – a small eating knife covered in gore.

Body trembling, Elleth climbed onto the bed, amongst the blood. She crawled next to her saviour, whose eyes had not left hers since she had looked at them – despite her lack of clothes. The smile he showed her revealed no gold whatsoever.

Elleth wrapped herself around Longoss and, showing more fear than he had during the fight, the big man finally relaxed and wrapped himself around her too, gently rocking her as he rested his head atop hers.

Longoss noticed Mother at the door then, her eyes wide as she looked around the room, finally meeting his. She swallowed hard, turned and disappeared back down the corridor and stairs.

Elleth clung to Longoss, her eyes closed tight as she sobbed. Her head shook slowly every so often, and soft mumbling of what sounded like a girl's name came from her buried head.

'Ye can't stay here, Elleth,' Longoss said, surprisingly softly. 'I'll take ye with me if ye like? No strings, just away from here. What ye do then, where ye go and who with, will be up to you. I won't make ye do anything ye don't want, ye have me word and I never break—'

'Yer word,' finished the girl, as she finally looked up into his eyes. 'Ye never break yer word?'

He shook his head. 'Never!'

Elleth nodded then and he tilted his head, looking deep into her eyes as he waited for her to speak.

'I'll come with ye,' she said, and even managed a brief smile, 'but—'

'Anything,' Longoss said eagerly, the whole situation running away from him and confusing him. All he knew was that nothing had mattered to him in his life until now, and whether he understood the reason or not didn't matter.

Her eyes moved to the rest of the bed then, to the blood, the torn linen and then to the knife in his hand, and his slashed arm, which still bled freely. Looking back up at him she said, 'I don't want ye to kill again, ever—'

Longoss made to speak, but Elleth placed her delicate fingers on his mouth and continued.

'For us to be together, ye need to swear it. Ye may think ye can't ever save me if ye can't kill, but ye done that already, ye done all this.' She waved her other hand around the room at the horrific scene, 'and I don't want any more of that 'cause of me, ye hear? I don't. Ye saved me and I'm yours.'

'I didn't do it for that, Elleth... to own ye.'

She smiled again. 'I know ye didn't, but I'm yours, and you're mine.'

A gold-less smile and Longoss nodded, his heart fluttering in a way he'd never felt before.

'Ye swear it though, never to kill another man, not for me nor anyone or anything?'

Taking a deep breath and grinding his teeth for a moment, his eyes drifted past Elleth's own. Finally, he nodded. 'Aye, Elleth, me word. I'll never again kill a man, but I swear this to ye too, I'll do all I can to protect ye, all I can without killing a soul.'

'Thank you,' Elleth said, and despite her swollen lip, she leant up and kissed Longoss on the cheek.

Blushing slightly, Longoss unwrapped himself from her and climbed from the bed. 'We need to go now,' he said, but Elleth shook her head.

'Not without Coppin.'

'Who?'

'My sister,' she said. Her large eyes held Longoss' in such a way he just nodded, knowing that for this girl, he would do anything.

'I'll go get her then. Which room?'

Elleth's head was shaking before he even finished. 'She's not here. Mother sold her and I need ye to find her for me, 'cause I ain't leaving without her and that's the truth.'

Longoss climbed back onto the bed then. 'Ye're not staying here, Elleth, ye're just not. I'll find yer sister, but not if it means leaving ye here.'

'Mother knows who took her and I don't think she'd dare send anyone else to me now, eh?' She glanced at the body by the side of the bed.

Longoss took hold of both delicate shoulders and held her firm, gentle, but firm. 'I don't care, ye can come with me. We'll find her together.'

Elleth shook her head again. 'Find her and bring her to me, Longoss, then we'll both go. I can't risk ye not finding her once ye have me away from here. If I'm here, I know ye'll find her and quick, to get me out.' *Oh Elleth, what're ye doing? He'll take ye away, right now, away from all this and from Mother; without Coppin though? No, she needs me, she needs him. I'm already saved, now I need to be a strong, brave woman and let him save her, and this is the only way I can be sure he will.*

Longoss sighed and rubbed the back of his head. Pulling his hand away, he noticed fresh blood there too. He wiped his hand on a part of his shirt that wasn't already bloodied, and leaned in to Elleth, kissing her on the head and then nodding his agreement.

'If ye're certain and it's the only way to get ye to go with me, then I'll find her and bring her here, then we're all out of here. Do I have your word, Elleth?'

She smiled and nodded, then wrapped him in a tight hug before kissing him fully.

Standing, Longoss tore a strip of linen and tied it about his bleeding arm, before telling Elleth to stay in the room. He explained to her Mother was unlikely to enter such a scene, and certainly wouldn't send any punter in to witness it. She swallowed hard, but nodded and agreed.

Longoss moved to the door and took hold of the handle. He turned to look upon Elleth and smiled. As he did, Elleth said, 'I don't know what we are, Longoss, but it may be we end up loves like me mamma and dada were, and I think I'd like that.'

Nodding, but saying nothing for fear of his voice breaking, Longoss turned and carefully closed the damaged door behind him.

Elleth could have sworn she saw a tear in his eye.

***

Egan Dundaven had been pouring through ancient books and scrolls throughout the night. He was searching for answers to what he believed was the meaning of the riddle brought to him by Exley Clewarth, which he'd laid out in front of him.

> *Few know the true source of His light, its new weakness fewer still*
> *Stone protects all it has oft been said; hidden in view of the sea*
> *Beware the darkness of the ground, through it the light could cease*
> *We will, all of us on that day, fall to darkness, as it was before*
> *As long as the source stands tall in its succour, light will always be*
> *Best it remains forgotten, unlike the memory of He*

So far he'd found nothing describing what he was looking for in enough detail, and he, along with the monks who'd been assigned to him, were becoming extremely frustrated as the Witchunter General stalked the cathedral's library, asking question after question.

'Well, you're the bloody bookworms, brothers, not me,' Exley had said, when one of the monks had suggested the Witchunter General looked for himself if he was unhappy with their progress.

Egan, however, was determined the 'light' in the riddle referred to magic, rather than Sir Samorl's divine power, much to the disgust of Exley and many of his acolytes who had naturally assumed the latter.

Reluctantly accepting Egan's theory, a witchunter had suggested the 'source' must therefore refer to Tyndurris' magically gifted residents. Egan had agreed and then pointed out the 'stone' the light was encased in, its succour, must mean Tyndurris itself, which indeed rose into the sky, and with its subterranean levels, reached down into the ground. That, Egan had stated, was the tower's weakness, as mentioned in the riddle itself. Therefore, Egan had swiftly surmised the way into Tyndurris lay beneath the ground.

That being the case, Egan had then requested as many plans of the city as possible. Following that, Exley had demanded, failed and then politely requested – much to the amusement of Egan – the assistance of the resident monks. All of whom now looked through countless plans of the city, searching for underground tunnels that would lead to the lower levels of Tyndurris.

'Perhaps there are tunnels from here within the cathedral,' one monk wondered aloud, but an older monk pointed out that with such historic hostility between the church and the guild, it was unlikely there would be any tunnel built from one to the other, by either side. He went on to say that he failed to see why the guild would purposefully add tunnels which presented a weakness to their defensive capabilities.

Egan nodded his agreement. 'Surely that means the tower was built over said weakness unwittingly. Or at least to a point that at the time of building, whatever was below Tyndurris, be it tunnel or chamber, it didn't pose a threat to them.'

'Could that mean they might not know of the lower entrance, even now?' Exley asked excitedly.

'We don't even know if there *is* an entrance,' Egan said, whilst flicking through pages of ancient sewer mapping. 'It could be a tunnel leading close to one of the lower floors.'

A young monk pointed to the sewer maps. 'What about those?'

The eldest monk looked up from a book and shook his head. 'No, the sewers are only three hundred years old, much too young to be connected, and the guild has royal approval, so it would have had the power to stop the sewer system from running close to any of its underground chambers. They probably have a system of their own which runs into the main system via unpassable pipes.'

Egan sighed and slumped back into his chair. He rubbed his tired eyes and strained to think of another way. Maybe he was wrong about the riddle, he hoped not for his sake, but it was a possibility.

'What about older tunnels?' Exley asked, as he moved to stand behind the old monk, whom he realised was probably the most knowledgeable about the city.

The white haired man paused for thought. He'd not asked why the witchunters wanted this information, but he was no fool and so, imagining the possibilities, had decided not to bother asking, for it was better in his mind not to know. 'It is a possibility,' he said eventually. 'Wesson is thousands of years old. The city hasn't always been this large—'

'Obviously,' Exley muttered, but the old monk carried on regardless.

'—and the palace, which is the natural fortress of the city, has not always been where it is now, at the southern end of Wesson.'

Every head in the chamber looked up from whatever they were reading, and Exley sat down on the bench next to the old monk, his attention well and truly captured.

'Go on,' the Witchunter General encouraged, as Egan moved to sit opposite the man.

The old monk laid down the book he was holding and looked around the room at the intrigued faces. 'The palace where King Barrison resides was commissioned way, way back in *three seventy-four Altoln* by the King at the time. It wasn't finished, however, until *three eighty-five Altoln*, after which the commissioning King had unfortunately died. Murdered actually by the queen, a sad affair in which—'

'The point?' Exley demanded. Many of the monks in the room scowled at him before turning back to the old monk.

'If you will let me continue then I will come to the point, *young* Master Clewarth.' The Witchunter General scowled, but kept quiet. 'Now where was I… ah… yes, the King who'd been murdered, as I previously said. He had a son, and it was his son, I believe, that once the castle was complete, moved into it. He left Wesson's original castle as no more than a military barracks, to defend the northern end of the rapidly growing city.

'Many, many years later,' the monk continued, 'centuries in fact, the King of the time… early *eighth century Altoln* I believe it was, decided the northern city barracks were far too large, and were hardly being used by the troops based there. So, he commissioned the conversion of those barracks, the original Wesson Castle, into Wesson's—'

'Prison,' Egan finished, realisation flooding his face.

'Precisely,' the old monk said, a smile creasing his already lined face.

'I don't understand the relevance?' Exley asked irritably.

'General,' explained the old monk, 'it was written… where I read it I cannot remember, alas… that there was an ancient network of tunnels built deep under Wesson; tunnels travelling from the old castle to the new – to what is now the palace.'

Again, Egan's face lit up with realisation. 'General, do you see what this means?'

'Of course,' Exley lied, and to his relief, Egan continued regardless.

'The riddle talks about 'light's succour' delving deep into the ground, which we have already established as being the lower levels of Tyndurris. Now, we've been searching for tunnels that meet one of those lower chambers, rather than—'

'Tunnels the lower levels met themselves,' the elderly monk said. 'An ancient tunnel the builders of Tyndurris could have come close to breaching; the tower is situated between the prison and the palace.'

'Exactly.' Egan nodded to the old monk and smiled. 'You're a credit to your order, brother.'

The old monk smiled, nodded in return and rose from the bench before saying, 'It is time for my bed, gentlemen. I am glad to have been assistance, may Sir Samorl be with you all.'

'And with you, brother,' Exley Clewarth replied, although his eyes were staring into the distance as he began to work out his plan to enter those tunnels, a plan that would lead him on a course following his counterpart and rival Horler Comlay; into Wesson's prison.

***

On his way out, Longoss had warned Mother not to allow anyone into the building, even to see the other girls. He'd also threatened to burn the place down if she didn't tell him who'd bought Coppin.

Mother, however, had laughed that threat off, telling him she knew he'd hurt no woman because he'd told her so previously. Shrugging that off, Longoss had threatened instead to stand outside and kill any man who tried to visit, something he knew she knew he was capable of. Of course, she didn't know he'd sworn to Elleth not to. 'After all,' he'd said to her, 'if I did that, what man would wanna risk visiting yer girls then?'

Eventually and reluctantly, without Longoss laying a finger on her, Mother told him who'd bought Coppin and where she was, although she warned Longoss he was making a deadly mistake in going there.

Fear of other men, however, was not something Longoss often felt, whereas fear of losing Elleth, a girl he'd just met, was all too real.

He'd set out across the city on foot, moving as quickly as he could without draining himself of too much energy, for he knew he'd need to be prepared to fight for Elleth's sister, and fight all the harder if he was to do it without killing anyone. He'd given his word and breaking that was not an option, especially to her. Why? He didn't know, but whatever these feelings for the girl were, he'd never felt anything so strong in his life, and that was worth fighting for, he was sure of it.

As he walked down a long, narrow street towards the edge of Dockside, a lone figure wearing a smart, knee-length coat stepped out of a doorway and into Longoss' path.

Longoss stopped and quickly glanced behind, noting another man wearing similar – albeit cleaner – clothes to him.

'Longoss, me old mucker, long time no see,' the man in the coat said as he walked towards Longoss, finally stopping just outside of arms reach. 'Ye look a state,' he added, looking Longoss up and down and taking in the blood stained shirt, hose and braise, the latter stained with piss as well as blood.

'Aye, long time. Now out of me way, Bill, I need to move on.'

'What, no golden grin? Very serious that is, eh Kerril?' Bill said to the man who'd moved up behind Longoss.

Longoss flashed his golden teeth and moved to pass Bill, who held up his hand – which held a scroll sealed with black wax.

'Ah-ah, I need to pass this on, Longoss. The mark Poi Son mentioned, ye see? Needs yer signature on this it does, before Poi Son will release any more details.'

'Tell him no,' Longoss said, pushing past Bill and continuing down the street. Two pairs of footsteps followed, closed in and then Bill overtook Longoss and turned to face him once more. Longoss stopped and quickly checked Kerril's position behind him again.

'Longoss wait, the mark's here and it's a big one, I know that much. Don't be silly mate, just sign it. It ain't a woman, Poi Son wouldn't do that to ye so what's yer problem, ye never turn marks down?'

'Well I am now, from now on in fact, so move Bill, I don't wanna hurt ye.'

Longoss placed a hand on Bill to move him to the side, but the man didn't budge. They locked eyes and Bill shook his head.

'Longoss, listen, we won't mention this, but ye turn this down and Poi Son will have yer head and ye know it. Just take the damned mark and be done wi' it, man.'

Longoss shook his head in return.

'Just bloody take it so we can go. It'll be worse for ye if ye don't,' Kerril said from behind Longoss. Bill closed his eyes and sighed as Longoss spun round and knocked Kerril out cold. Longoss then managed to push past Bill and continue down the street, shouting behind him as he went. 'I'm done, Bill. Tell Poi Son will ye?'

'He'll gut ye like a fish, Longoss, I seen it done.'

'Not yer concern, Bill, and if he tries, tell him I'll ram a fish up his arse and we'll see what he'll do about that, eh?'

Longoss continued to walk down the street despite the threats now following him from Bill about the whole guild coming after him.

'That not bother ye, Longoss? The others? Ye think it'd bother yer new girl?'

Longoss stopped dead and turned, slowly, to stare back at the man he'd called friend.

'Aye, we seen ye go there twice, Longoss. Ye never go the same whore's twice so close together. Slut must be good.'

Clenching his teeth and fists at the same time, Longoss started walking back towards Bill.

'So this is why ye're refusing the mark, for a pissin' whore?' Bill laughed.

'I gave ye a chance to leave, Bill,' Longoss said, as he picked up his pace.

'And I gave you a chance to take the mark after refusing it. I shouldn't do, it's my head as well as yours if Poi Son found out.'

'I'll spare ye now, Bill, but ye touch the girl and ye're a dead man.'

Bill produced a long-sword from his coat and took on a defensive posture as Longoss closed on him. 'No, Longoss, *you're* the dead man. I can't give ye any more chances and ye know the penalty for refusing Poi Son when he's this insistent.'

'Aye, and you know the penalty for drawing a weapon on me, boy,' Longoss said, as he reached Bill and drew his knife.

Bill lunged forward immediately, his long-sword far outreaching Longoss' small blade, but despite that, the knife scored a red line across Bill's cheek. Cursing, the younger man jumped back and swung his sword across towards Longoss' neck; a desperate move to keep the big man back.

'Leave, Bill, I don't want to kill ye,' Longoss said, as he circled the other man.

Bill spat, then shouted. 'Well that's a first, not wantin' to kill a man!'

'Aye, it may be, but that's me now.'

The long-sword came in again, this time at Longoss' stomach yet he managed to parry the thrust with his knife. Bill smirked as he rolled his wrist and nicked Longoss' ear with the tip of the blade.

'Ye'll have Poi Son after ye, ye know that don't ye?'

'Aye lad,' Longoss said, 'I know it.'

'And he'll have the bitch raped before he kills her.'

Longoss threw himself at Bill then, stabbing repeatedly and swiftly for the man's face. Every blow was deflected just in time as the young man struggled to back step away from Longoss.

Managing to create a gap between them – using the prone Kerril – Bill reached into his coat and drew a second, shorter sword with his free hand.

'They touch her Bill, I'll bring the lot of 'em down, I swear it; the whole fucking guild!'

Bill swallowed hard, rapidly breathing as sweat beaded his brow. 'Ye're serious aren't ye?'

'I just swore it didn't I, lad?'

Bill nodded his head. 'Aye, ye did, me old mucker, ye did.' Bill turned and ran, looking behind him one last time as he headed down the deserted street, past the black crossed doors and eventually round a corner.

I liked ye, Bill, and not many men can say I liked 'em, not many at all.

Sighing hard, Longoss kicked the stirring man on the ground back to unconsciousness before turning and continuing on his way.

After walking out of Dockside and well into the Park District of Wesson, Longoss looked up at the ornately carved, cliff-like sides of the Samorlian Cathedral. His mind raced at all that had happened to bring him there. His physical journey across the city was a blur after the brief fight with Bill.

So, yer sister's here is she, Elleth? Well, I'll keep me word to ye and get her out… somehow.

As he looked on, Longoss wondered how he'd manage such a thing, especially if he couldn't kill. *That's gonna do me no good, Elleth. Why couldn't ye've made me swear to it* after *I got yer sister from these bastards?*

Sudden voices drew his attention to a large contingent of monks leaving a side door halfway down the cathedral; armed monks, followed by witchunters, all of which headed away to the north.

Well, at least I won't face those bastards in there. Longoss made his way towards the door the group of men had just left.

***

The library in Tyndurris was crammed with books new and old, of scrolls native and foreign and of some artefacts that required jars and tanks to preserve their contents.

Morri had been sent by Master Orix to see a young sorceress by the name of Cullane. The oil lamp she sat under illuminated her deep blue robes and her mousy brown hair, which she wore down over her shoulders. She had her head buried in a large book, and jumped when Morri spoke.

'Good morning, Cullane.' Morri pulled up a chair and sat opposite the young and attractive woman.

'Hello, Morri, good to see you,' Cullane said. 'You're looking well, which is a rarity within Tyndurris these past few days.'

Morri beamed at the compliment. 'As are you,' he swiftly replied, a little too swiftly he thought to himself. He'd held a torch for her since their days as students at the guild, and had been extremely disappointed when Cullane's skills had pushed her towards sorcery rather than medicine and healing. Since then, they'd seen little of each other and so Morri relished the opportunity to work with her again, albeit on the awful subject of the plague, or rather the cause of the plague.

Two clerics on duty in the city had also fallen victim of the plague and Morri had been most upset to hear of the death of Orrel, the guard at his infirmary who'd been a good friend to Midrel. Shaking away the awful thought, he smiled.

'You're here to see if I've found anything in these books I take it?'

'Yes. Master Orix asked me to come down this morning after a quick nap, not that it was much of one mind, we're all so busy trying to find as much as we can. I can't seem to sleep for long at all, even when I have a rare chance to.'

'I've only just been assigned to this,' Cullane said, a sympathetic smile gracing her pretty face. 'I was working on a long term project, but volunteered my services and this is what I've ended up with: book duty.

'Good job I have this little fellow.' Cullane grinned and nodded towards the pages of the book she held open in her arms.

Morri jumped as a long, sickly yellow worm emerged from the liquid-like pages of the book. The worm seemed to look up at him, despite its lack of eyes. Turning to Cullane, it whistled and clicked before squirming its way across and into the opposite page.

'What the...'

Cullane chuckled.

'It's a bookworm,' she said, trying to straighten her face.

'It's a what? Bookworm's a term, Cullane, not an actual creature, or so I thought?'

'Where do you think the term bookworm comes from, silly?'

'Well I... I don't know, but not from whatever that was,' Morri said, shaking his head and still staring at the flat pages of the book, waiting for something to happen.

'It's not corporeal; not a real worm. I summon it when I want to search large volumes and tomes. It travels through the contents of the book without physically disturbing the pages, taking in the information as it... well... burrows through the written knowledge, I guess? I don't have a complete knowledge of how it works, just how to summon and converse with it. That's what the whistling was.' She smiled at Morri again and he smiled back at her in amazement.

'What did it say?'

'It hasn't found anything yet, but I only just conjured it, so it'll be able to search for a good few hours. Until lunch at least.'

'Well that's great. Not sure what good I am then.' Morri's eyes dropped to the book again, just in time to see a tail flick out of the side of the book, before sliding back in again. Morri shuddered at the sight and Cullane laughed.

'You've been told what to look for?' Morri asked, finally able to drag his eyes away from the book in her arms.

She slowly moved her head from side to side, one cheek raised. 'Sort of, we're looking for references in ancient recordings of diseases, for any unnatural causes, carriers and the like, but like I said, we've just started.

'Any luck with Master Orix and the old Grand Master's room?'

Morri shook his head. 'Not as of yet. It seems Lord Severun destroyed or hid everything he was working on and he's no longer here to ask...' Morri looked down as he continued. 'I know what he did was awful, Cullane, but I think it wasn't the best course of action, what they did, to say the least. The execution I mean; a brutal affair if you ask me.'

Cullane reached across and squeezed Morri's arm.

They both fell silent for a while then, until Cullane's bookworm popped out of the book, whistled, clicked and dragged itself down and into a small, red-bound book on the table next to her.

Cullane closed the large book, placed it on top of a couple of others and dragged an even larger, more ancient looking tome off a precariously high stack. Once open in the middle, she placed the small red book onto the open pages of the tome and the bookworm slid from one to the other.

Morri's mouth dropped open again and Cullane laughed, pulling out a smaller book and handing it to Morri.

'Come on then,' she said, as he took the book, 'let's get reading. We've a long day ahead of us and answers to find.'

Chapter 28: Sea Of Gold

Biviano was struggling to keep his eyes open as he took the first watch of the door.

'Blind me, this is boring,' he said to himself, for Sears and Ellis Frane were fast asleep.

Deciding sitting was worse than standing when trying to stay awake, he donned his helm and climbed wearily to his feet. Quietly, he made his way around the torture chamber, taking in all the vicious devices and tools used by the inquisitors to torture their victims.

Aye, victims... poor bastard victims of murderers who think they've a damned right to do it in the name of Sir Samorl. Pretty sure that hoary bastard would run the lot of 'em through if he were still about to witness this shit.

Picking up a particularly nasty looking tool, with barbed hooks and a long, needle-thin spike, Biviano's nose twitched as a slight breeze crossed his face. He returned the tool to the desk he stood by and turned towards where he thought the breeze had come from. Moving slowly, short-sword now in hand, he held his free hand up to feel for any shift in the air as he moved slowly down the wall next to the bench.

'There,' he whispered to himself. He pressed his hand against the cold stone of the wall and to his amazement, the stone he pressed moved. Pressing harder, a mechanical clunk echoed through the chamber and the sound of gears and pulleys whirred as a section of the wall in front of Biviano slid back and then to the side, revealing a small, pitch black void beyond.

The void reeked of death.

'Sears,' Biviano shouted, without turning around.

'I see it,' Sears said, who was awake and already crossing the room towards his friend.

'What is it?' Biviano asked hesitantly. *I'm not sure I want to know the answer.*

Ellis Frane's rough voice turned both their heads then, as he answered their question. 'It's where they keep them.'

Biviano and Sears looked to one another and then back to Ellis Frane. 'Where they keep who, Ellis?'

'The girls, Sears, it's where they keep the questioned girls.'

Biviano looked to Sears quickly and could have sworn he saw a flash of red in the man's eyes. 'Keep calm big guy. Go grab me a torch and I'll go check it out.'

'The Three ye will. I'm going in there, Biviano, and I'll be flayed if ye're stopping me.'

Swallowing hard, Biviano ran across the room to grab a torch from the wall as Sears disappeared through the gap.

'It won't be nice, whatever you find,' Ellis Frane said, and Biviano knew him to be right.

Following Sears, Biviano entered the small room on the other side of the wall. Torch held high, its flickering light danced across dozens of stacked, naked bodies, all of them female.

'Some of these are kids,' Sears said, his voice strained. His jaw muscles bunched under his red beard as he pointed to a small body off to his right.

Biviano, stomach churning, cast the torch about from the doorway. 'She's no more than ten.' He closed his eyes tight.

'Fucking ten!' Sears' eyes glowed suddenly, like hot coals in the dark room.

The lock of the torture chamber door turned then and Ellis Frane called out a warning.

As sick as this is, it couldn't have come at a better time. Biviano looked at Sears' eyes, before swiftly turning and moving back into the main chamber.

Sears was hot on his heels.

Biviano's first sight in the chamber was of Ellis Frane, hiding behind the rack he'd previously been tied to. Biviano then looked past the frightened man, and at the same time, felt Sears push past him to run full tilt towards the chamber door.

Oh shit…

As Sears reached the door, it began to open. The big man kicked it with such force it split the frame and smashed it down and outwards. The resulting cry made it clear to all that it had flattened whoever had been opening it.

Biviano ran towards Sears as two warrior monks burst into the room. One swung a mace at Sears as the other ran at Biviano with a cudgel held high.

Roaring again – eyes now ablaze – Sears reached up and grabbed the mace as it came in at him, his other hand closing on the monk's throat and crushing it easily. The body crumpled to the floor as Sears was rocked back by a thrusting blow from a wooden rod. As the big man stumbled to the floor, eyes flaring, an inquisitor stalked into the room, wooden rod tucked neatly under his right arm.

'Gentlemen,' he said, addressing Biviano – who'd just run through his attacker, and Sears, who was picking himself up off the floor. Inquisitor Makhell's eyes scanned the room for Ellis Frane.

'Gentlemen?' Sears shouted. 'Ye won't be saying that when I tear ye to bloody pieces for those girls in there!' He pointed to the hidden chamber, eyes flaring once more.

Hold big guy, just hold, this one's dangerous, Biviano thought. His palm felt slick with sweat, and he gripped the hilt of his sword all the tighter for it.

'I suggest you calm down soldier, otherwise I may see fit to—'

The inquisitor stopped then, as he finally settled his eyes on Sears' own. 'What on Samorl's earth…'

Biviano smiled as he saw the genuine fear in the inquisitor's eyes. He thought of the girls in the chamber then and of Ellis Frane and what he'd been through at the hands of these men. *Ye've done it now, ye sick bastard. Ye've got him so angry even I can't stop him.*

'Red sky, inquisitor,' Biviano said, grinning.

The inquisitor tore his eyes from Sears' glowing orbs and looked to

Biviano then, whilst backing away from the red bearded guardsman.

'He was born of a red sky?' Inquisitor Makhell's ashen face looked back to the burning eyes of Sears.

'Aye, but not during a red night, inquisitor, or morning for that matter; Sears was born in-between ye see. In-between a red night and a red morning... for Sears was born under a blood red moon...'

Upon hearing the words, Inquisitor Makhell turned to run for the door.

Sears roared and his eyes flared as a rush of flames burst from his open mouth, flowing like liquid to engulf the doorway the inquisitor had intended to use. The flames inadvertently swallowed another warrior monk who was running to the inquisitor's aid.

Inquisitor Makhell turned then, just in time to deflect a blow from Biviano's sword, as a lunge followed from Sears' blade.

The warrior monk ran screaming from the room as the flames engulfed him.

The three men lunged, parried and swung at each other in a rapidly moving blur, as the two guardsmen forced the inquisitor round towards the rack.

Biviano knew the inquisitor was dangerous, but not only that, he knew he had to try and keep Sears away from him if they were to find out where the Grand Inquisitor was. He needed the inquisitor alive.

Inquisitor Makhell expertly side-stepped and twisted to avoid several sword thrusts and overhead chops, whilst jabbing and striking back at the two men whenever possible. He struggled to pull his eyes from those of the large guardsman, fearing the beast would open its mouth and spit flame once more.

Biviano stepped in close then and thrust his sword towards the inquisitor's right leg, hoping to incapacitate him long enough for them to pin him down.

The thrust was stopped dead by the skilled man, who stepped forward and wrapped his arm around Biviano's, bending it back until Biviano had no choice but to drop his weapon, and all the while the inquisitor fended off Sears' attacks with his wooden rod.

Stamping down hard on the inquisitor's soft-booted foot, Biviano managed to break free, just in time to see Sears launch himself at the man.

Inquisitor Makhell cracked his rod across the side of the big guardsman's head, which seemed to have no effect as the fire eyed monster wrapped him in a bear hug and squeezed, roaring as he did so.

Inquisitor Makhell's eyes bulged as the immense pressure cracked several ribs.

Sears threw the man onto the horizontal rack and Inquisitor Makhell took in a lungful of air that stung his chest and caused his vision to blur and swirl. His arms were pulled roughly to the side and he realised he was being bound to the rack. He managed to raise his head and spat a painful curse as he saw Ellis Frane tying his feet.

'Sears,' Biviano shouted, 'the door!'

Sears nodded his acknowledgement. His eyes had calmed, but not enough

228

for the fire to die. He ran to the door and the sound of approaching footsteps. Biviano winced as his friend left the chamber and roared once more; an orange glow lit up the doorway.

Screams followed.

'Demons!' Inquisitor Makhell shouted, although doing so pulled at his face from the pain it brought to his broken ribs. 'You shall burn for this, all of you!'

'And what of you?' Ellis Frane shouted in return. 'You tortured me *and* those girls! Dozens of girls! Raped them too, you monster!'

Before Biviano could say anything, Ellis Frane had picked up a blood stained instrument and jammed it into the inquisitor's right thigh.

Inquisitor Makhell screamed as the tool was twisted and then pulled back out.

'It's my turn to put you to the question, inquisitor,' Ellis Frane said, as he moved to the handles that operate the pulley system of the rack.

Biviano looked on as the previous occupant of the rack began to slowly turn the handles.

Mechanical clunks accompanied Inquisitor Makhell's screams.

'Where is the Grand Inquisitor?' Ellis Frane demanded, turning the handles with every word.

'You will all die,' Inquisitor Makhell shouted at them, despite the pain

'Fuck you!' Sears yelled, as he re-entered the room.

'Out,' Biviano told his friend, his heart racing as he did so, 'out!'

Sears pulled a table over before returning to the corridor.

'Where's the Grand Inquisitor?' Biviano shouted then, slapping the man on the rack hard across the face.

Ellis Frane repeated the question and Inquisitor Makhell cried out as the rack pulled him taught. Fire like pain seared his ribs.

Biviano wasn't surprised how little the inquisitor had taken when he quickly told them where the Grand Inquisitor's chambers were.

'Ellis, wait here and guard him. Use him as a hostage if more come, and do what ye will with him, but wait here, damn it, and barricade the door. We'll come back for ye.'

Ellis Frane nodded and thanked Biviano. They both jumped at the sound of Sears roaring further along the chamber, shouts of alarm following from several voices.

With Inquisitor Makhell's screams filling the chamber behind him, Biviano headed out of the broken door and chased after his friend, who was tearing a bloody, burning path through several cathedral guards.

***

The sky in the east began to lighten as the last remaining stars faded from sight. To the West, over the horizon, the sky was still a deep blue, speckled by stars, but the group had their back to it now as they swiftly walked across green fields full of grazing sheep. The young lambs bleated and kicked their back legs, unsure on their feet as they scattered away from the group. Their mothers lazily raised their heads from grazing before continuing regardless.

Furber had left the group as they reached a low dip in the coastal cliffs. He'd been amazed to hear about the monster that had attacked the group in the cave, and had told them about some of the strange things, of all sizes, that lived far out to sea and in the deep trenches, rarely if ever seen even by his kind. He offered to accompany them further inland, much to the annoyance of Gleave, who would not accept his presence at all. Errolas however, turned down the offer, claiming it wasn't safe for Furber to leave his seal coat on the shore in case it was discovered by anyone who may be following the group.

A selkie's coat is its source of magic, Errolas had explained to the group; a strong bond allowing it to return to seal form whenever it slipped into the fur. Some humans, both male and female, had been known – once realising their new partner was a selkie – to find and hide the selkie's coat, therefore trapping the creature in human form and binding it to the holder of the coat. Errolas didn't want that fate for his friend and so sent him back out to sea after thanking him for his assistance in passing on his news.

Since leaving the coast, the group had walked for hours, passing across seemingly endless fields whilst being assured by Correia and her two pathfinders that they knew the way to the nearest village.

'Are we nearly there yet?' Sav asked, for what seemed like the hundredth time.

Correia held no hint of amusement in her tone as she replied. 'Yes we're there now, Sav, can't you see the houses you walk past even now?'

'Oooh… touchy,' Sav said, before grinning, much to the further annoyance of the King's Spymaster.

'Hold your tongue before I remove it, scout,' she said, and Sav laughed heartily, although Fal and Starks exchanged worried glances, both of them wondering if it was a meaningless threat or a promise.

A fresh inland breeze brought the scent of manure to the group and Starks' face screwed up as he brought his hand up to cover his nose.

'What the bloody hell is that smell?' he asked through his hand.

'Manure. You never been in the countryside, Starks?' Sav asked, surprised.

Starks shook his head, his face screwing up even more as another fresh breeze brought a stronger whiff of the fertilizer along with it.

'I don't see why I would've wanted to if it smells like this.'

Gleave laughed. 'We're getting close to crop fields, manure is what they use to fertilise the crop, lad. Bet you won't enjoy bread and the likes in the same way now, will you? Knowing where it came from.'

'They don't grow bread, I'm not stupid,' Starks replied, and half the group laughed.

'Starks, don't listen to them,' Fal said. 'Bread is made from ingredients grown in fields, that's all.'

'Well I don't think I'd let that stop me eating some bread right now, I'm starving. When can we stop to eat?' the young crossbowman moved his hand from his nose to rub is belly.

'In Hinton,' Mearson said, from the back of the group. 'It's only a mile or two now I reckon.' His bandages were caked in blood, but it was all they had. Correia had said they would be able to get fresh ones from the village, so until then, he had to make do.

'Wow, look!' Starks said, as the group passed over a low rise in the field. At the end of the field they were in, which looked almost black in the dim light, a hedge ran across their view. Beyond, as the first rays of the rising sun cascaded over the distant horizon, a sea of yellow spread as far as the eye could see.

'Rape seed,' Sav said, and both he and Starks stopped to admire the view. The sun seemed to pop all of a sudden, its light illuminating the crop, causing it to glow like a sea of gold; the fields seemed to rise and fall like giant golden waves.

The rest of the group carried on after briefly taking in the stunning view, heading for a wooden gate in the thick hedgerow.

'Come on you two,' Fal shouted, as they slowly left the two appreciating the view behind.

'Wonderful isn't it,' Sav said, and Starks nodded to show his appreciation. 'You'll be seeing much more wonderful things where we're going, I'm sure.'

Starks looked up at the tall scout and grinned.

'Come on then, mucker, let's catch the others up and hope Hinton is on the other side of that field, my stomach's beginning to sound like a waking beast.'

Sav and Starks ran to catch the others. They all climbed over the wooden gate one at a time, which proved easier than trying to open the old, rotten latch.

On the other side, they pushed on through the tall rape seed. Fal noticed the pathfinders scanning the horizon constantly, and as the group reached the top of the rise they were climbing, they saw the thatched rooftops of a dozen small buildings about half a mile in the distance. Sav and Starks grinned at the prospect of hot food and the group carried on down the gradual slope towards the village.

Once they reached the edge of the village, where the smell of wood smoke hit them, Correia held her hand up to stop the group before turning on them, a stern look upon her face.

'This is Hinton, it's not on any main road and its people aren't used to strangers. It's a small farming village with a very small inn, usually only used by the locals and an occasional patrol of the local Baron's men. So keep it quiet. No rowdy behaviour.' Her eyes lingered on Sav a little longer than anyone else. 'And keep your weapons sheathed. No one needs know why we're here, where we're going and especially where we've come from. If anyone asks, which I don't think they will, we're from a King's ship anchored to the north west of here whilst hunting smugglers. They hate smugglers around here as they bring unwanted trouble, so they won't mind us, I'm sure. Do I make myself clear?'

'Ma'm,' the two pathfinders replied in unison. The others nodded.

'Very well, now follow me in and keep quiet.'

The group opened the small gate at the edge of the village and passed through, wincing as its hinges screeched. A dog barked nearby and Sav tensed, wondering how big it was. The track through the centre of Hinton was muddy, despite the lack of recent rain, and the group's boots, all but Errolas' it seemed, squelched as they walked through the stinking black mess.

A small thatched building with a faded and unreadable wooden sign outside stood at the end of the path, and Fal guessed it was the village inn. As they approached, the door creaked opened and a large, red haired man in a dirty white apron strode out, before freezing under their gaze.

'Oh... erm... 'ow do?' the man greeted, and Correia suddenly transformed her hardened expression into a surprisingly sweet and innocent one. She fluttered her lashes at the burly man and smiled sweetly, before gracefully walking up and holding out her hand, which he shook cautiously.

'Hello, master innkeeper, could we possibly purchase some of your fine ale and food this morning?'

Fal had to stifle a laugh as he noticed Sav's jaw drop.

'Well... erm... yeah, don't see why not, come in. Not much room like.' The man's eyes dropped to the weapons on each member's belt, so Fal made an extra effort to smile at the innkeeper and nod as he passed by him to enter the dimly lit building. He didn't fail to notice the extra cautious look the large man gave when he looked Fal in the face however, and Fal was surprised at first, before realising the village was unlike the city he was used to; the man had probably never even heard of an Orismaran before, let alone seen one, or his tattoos.

The sun outside was already shining brightly, but the inn had small slits in its walls instead of windows, which failed to let much of the morning light inside. The group sat clustered around two small tables in the flickering glow of a crackling fire pit, which sat in the middle of the room, as well as several tallow candles set here and there. The smoke from the fire lifted lazily to a hole poked in the thatch above it, little of which actually escaped the room, leaving a thick, cloying atmosphere hanging like a fog about the group.

Correia had remained at the small bar and slid four shillings across it, much to the sudden delight of the innkeeper's wife, who'd appeared behind the bar as the group entered.

Fal strained to hear what Correia was saying, but the murmuring of the others sat around him drowned the woman's hushed tones out.

Correia returned to the bar and shortly after, the innkeeper and his wife brought over a large clay pot of small-beer, which they dished out to each of them, much to the delight of Sav, who quaffed his share immediately.

Within half an hour, each member of the group tucked into their bowls of sop in wine – which Sav announced was his favourite breakfast, much to the amusement of all but Correia – and a large wooden plate piled high with black pudding.

Fal laughed along with the others as Errolas cringed at the greasy food.

'What's black pudding?' the elf asked, prodding it with his eating knife.

'Clotted pig's blood, amongst other things,' the innkeeper said, and he too laughed heartily when Errolas paled.

All eyes were on the elf as he cut a small piece and forced it down his throat. The group laughed again when his eyes lit up. He tucked into the steaming pudding with enthusiasm then, a new delicacy clearly discovered.

The group wolfed their breakfast down, especially Sav, who easily talked Errolas into giving him his wine soaked toast. Whilst the men finished off their clay pots of small-beer, Correia rose and crossed to the small bar. She again talked in hushed tones to their hosts, who'd been staring across at Fal more than any of the others, even the elf. Fal shrugged off the scrutiny, and considered asking Errolas what they were talking about, since he knew the elf could hear the conversation. Fal thought better of it though, deciding the elf would tell him if he needed to know.

There I go again, cracking on with the mission without knowing the full story. Ask no questions. That's right, Fal. Blindly follow your orders as usual.

'Does it not bother you, Fal?' Mearson nodded towards the innkeeper's wife, who was staring at Fal again.

'What do you mean?'

'People staring, because of your tattoos?'

Fal shook his head. 'I'm different is all, can't blame them for being curious.'

Mearson seemed to accept that with a half-hearted nod as he turned to the bar eagerly upon hearing Correia's question.

'Do you have an outhouse for my companions and I to use, before we set off again on our journey?' she had said, loud enough for them to hear. 'I very much doubt their bladders can contain that small-beer once on the move. It's like travelling with children.'

The innkeeper's wife laughed heartily. 'Of course, it's just out back. Careful though,' she said to Correia, who was heading out to use it, 'it's not been emptied for a while and is close to full, so you do right to use it first.'

Everyone else in the group suddenly looked around at each other, and after a pregnant pause, followed by a scraping of stools and chairs they raced as one for the door.

After the group had done their business, Correia told them to prepare to move out whilst she popped back in to thank and tip the couple inside for their hospitality.

Once inside and away from the others, Correia did as she said she would, but also asked, in a very specific way, for the recipe to a dish a friend of hers had recommended as a speciality of Hinton. The innkeeper's wife nodded knowingly before hurrying into the kitchen to retrieve a scrawled copy of the recipe. Both women knew it meant more than that, and the woman nodded once more to Correia as she handed it over. A look passed between them that the innkeeper didn't notice and Correia felt safe in the knowledge her order had been understood. She smiled, thanked them both once more and left.

By the time Correia came back outside, Sav had re-dressed Mearson's arm and the group was ready to move on. Starks complained about getting no sleep and was silenced with one of Correia's looks, her visage returning to normal after the sweet display in the inn. The group set off then, following a rough track heading east out of Hinton, surrounded on all sides by a brilliant sea of gold.

***

The dark walls felt oppressive in the small chamber, the ceiling too, and as Coppin attempted to hold her breath instead of smelling the awful breath of the large man pawing over her, she realised everything about the room and the man felt oppressive.

Her skin crawled as he ran his fat fingers up the inside of her robe, licking his lips as he did so, his eyes not once meeting her own.

She sat on the Grand Inquisitor's desk, wearing a simple brown woollen robe his inquisitors had given to her. The wool was course and itchy. Oh, how she wanted to scratch a dozen places at once, but her hands were bound tightly behind her.

Pinching the soft, pale skin of her inner thighs, the Grand Inquisitor suddenly looked her in the eye and sneered.

'You make me sick,' he said, quickly removing his hands and dropping heavily into the chair opposite her.

Coppin said nothing. She tried to move her knees together, but before she could, the wheezing man picked up a wooden rod and tapped her on each knee, shaking his head. She opened her legs fully again, and again he licked his lips, lowering his head slightly to try and see up her robes in the dim light.

Hissing, he sat up straight again, locking eyes with her once more.

Coppin stared back at him defiantly.

'You're a witch, admit it? The hair is a giveaway and there's no mistaking the charm you're attempting to work on me, to seduce me for Sir Samorl knows what vulgar pleasures.'

Coppin tried to speak, to deny the accusation, but the rod cracked off her left knee painfully and she had to stop herself from crying out.

Leaning forward, the Grand Inquisitor prodded at her with the rod, pressing it against her stomach, shoulders and then once on each breast, his small eyes lighting up at the movement his prodding caused.

'My inquisitor's tell me you have but one nipple, witch?'

Coppin nodded, but said nothing.

'Taken in a ritual no doubt, an orgy of witches and warlocks,' he said, sliding the rod up her dress and lifting it slightly.

She dared not respond and she knew doing so would be useless anyway. She was his now and there was nothing she could do about it. In her experience, playing along was the safest option.

'I shall have to put you to the question, witch. You see, we need to know what others there are, so we can protect Wesson from the evil that girls like you bring to its streets.'

Coppin shifted nervously as he stood once more. He leaned in close as he whispered into her ear, his left hand pulling at her green hair as he did so.

'You're going to tell me where your coven is, witch. You're going to tell me anything I want you to and If you don't, or maybe even if you do, I'll pass you down then,' he pulled hard on her hair, forcing her head back as he licked her neck, 'to my inquisitors, so they can finish you off.'

Coppin tensed, her eyes welling despite her attempts to stay strong.

'You didn't think you'd walk out of here did you, whore? You're evil, bred for nothing but dark deeds; I cannot allow you to walk free.'

Coppin struggled against the ropes binding her wrists. The Grand Inquisitor smiled wickedly as he stood back and watched.

'Bastard,' she said finally, stopping struggling and looking him in the eye. 'Nothing but a cowardly, fat bastard—'

The rod struck her across the side of the head and she fell sideways onto the desk. Her vision blurred slightly before the throbbing pain kicked in.

'Any more, witch? I want you to talk, but not if you have nothing of use to say to me, and not until I ask a question, understand?'

Coppin tried to move, to sit back up, but with her hands behind her back she struggled.

'Answer me!' he shouted, his reddened face inches from hers.

'I understand,' she whispered.

'Louder, whore.'

'I understand!' she shouted, bursting into tears.

'Tears? Weak child, I had thought you would fight the questioning, put up an interesting struggle. Alas, perhaps I was wrong.'

Coppin felt his hands on her then as he pulled her roughly round onto her stomach, her feet dropping down to the cold floor. Still crying, her mind racing for any way for it not to happen, her head banging where he'd struck her and her eyes now tightly closed, she tried to think of a better place as the Grand Inquisitor pulled her robe up high and proceeded to cane her with his wooden rod.

She fought not to cry out as the pain worsened with every blow. Instead, she continued to cry quietly, but as he hit her again and again, she eventually cried out despite her best efforts not to.

'You think that hurts, witch? How do you think your wicked ways hurt the good people of Wesson when you bewitch and ensnare them? I will show you such pain girl, and then so shall my inquisitors when I am done.'

Coppin cried all the more at the sound of him unbuckling his belt, and when the Grand Inquisitor took the buckled end of that belt to her back, she screamed; all the more when he forced himself into her.

She wished she was a witch then, a powerful one, so she could curse the man that was surely more evil than anything else in Brisance, and after the things she'd experienced at Mother's, that was saying something indeed.

'I hope ye… rot in yer own… piss and shit, ye… fat… fucking… bastard!' she shouted, as he pounded against her, whipping her all the while. She blocked out the chanting that came in between his gasping breaths and concentrated now on the pain, holding onto it and wishing for a way to turn that pain back upon him.

Chapter 29: Smoke

On the western horizon, a column of thick, black smoke rose lazily into the partially clouded sky. As the sun reached its zenith, skylarks sang and butterflies twirled above the slightly swaying, golden crop of wheat below.

Correia dropped back as the rest of the group pushed on through the field to the east. She stood, staring back at the black smoke, her hands resting comfortably on the hilts of her swords as they hung at her sides.

Turning to see why Correia had stopped, Gleave called for the rest of the group to halt.

'What's wrong?' Starks asked as he brushed his hands across the tops of the wheat.

'Smoke,' Fal replied, 'and I don't think Correia likes whatever's caused it so neither do I.'

Errolas set out for Correia then and Fal followed, holding his hand up to stay the others, who turned separate directions to scan the undulating horizon around them.

Correia met Errolas and Fal half way, and with Starks chatting to the others a little way away, she explained her fears.

'Warning signal,' she said, as she pointed back to the black smoke.

Fal's hand moved instinctively to his sword. 'From who?'

'Hinton,' Errolas said, looking to Correia for confirmation, 'the innkeeper and his wife?'

Correia nodded. 'That puts whoever's following us about half a day behind, at most.' Her eyes flicked to the horizon behind them. 'Assuming they aren't on horses. We've set a good pace since Hinton, but it's all for naught if they're mounted. I planned on us picking up horses at a village not far from here, but we may be caught before then if we don't find anywhere closer.'

'Leave that to me,' Errolas said, as he rooted in a soft pouch on his belt. He pulled out what looked like a short section of a very thin water reed, lifted it to his mouth and blew through it gently. Correia and Fal looked at each other in confusion as the reed made no sound. That confusion intensified as the sudden lack of bird song became apparent.

Sav held his hand up and Starks stopped talking. They all looked around then, expecting an attack due to the sudden silence. They moved to draw their weapons until Fal waved to them that all was well. The four men frowned but obeyed, although they kept their hands on their weapons just in case.

Errolas blew again on the whistle that seemed to make no noise at all. This time however, a tiny bird appeared in the distance, bobbing through the sky towards them. Errolas grinned and held his hand up to receive the tiny wren, which flitted in and landed on his index finger. It bobbed its upturned tail as its head turned from side to side to take in the trio.

Correia and Fal exchanged surprised glances and looked back at the little wren, which looked up into Errolas' eyes. The elf lifted the whistle to his mouth again and blew a number of short silent notes in a sequence the wren seemed to understand. It jumped into the air and flew a short way to his shoulder before leaning into his ear, chittering ever so quietly.

Errolas' eyes widened. He nodded gently before smiling and replying with the whistle.

The wren, without warning, took to the sky and flew off in the direction of the smoke, until the speck that was the bird disappeared into the distance.

'Well?' Correia asked.

Fal managed to close his mouth before Errolas explained.

'Jenny there, the wren that is, told me there is a column of humans about half a mile to the south east. She said they have horses—'

'Wait… Jenny?' Correia looked at Errolas sceptically. 'You mean to say that bird is called Jenny and she told you all of that? I know elves have powers, but that all seems a bit… never mind, who am I to question it if it gets us moving.'

Errolas smiled. 'She said the column is heading north towards a small village. The one you were thinking of?'

Correia nodded.

'If we hurry we could rendezvous with them,' Fal said quickly.

'Hopefully,' Errolas replied, 'and with Spymaster Burr with us, acquiring mounts for the rest of the journey shouldn't be a problem.' Errolas looked across to the forward group, all of whom were staring back. It was clear they wanted to know what was going on.

'Your confidence in me is flattering, elf. Now let's move on.'

Errolas smiled again and motioned for Fal to return to the others, and so he did, with Errolas and Correia in tow.

'Oh I sent Jenny back to see who is following us,' Errolas said as they reached the others. 'It might take her some time to pass the message back to us, but it is better to know eventually than not at all.'

Gleave looked back past the trio. 'Who's Jenny?'

Correia rolled her eyes. 'You don't want to know, Gleave, you really don't. Now come on, there's a column of…' Correia paused and looked to Errolas, 'of what Errolas? Troops maybe, a caravan?'

The elf shrugged. 'Humans.'

Correia sighed and looked back to the others. 'A column of people with horses, and if we want to mount up and make haste, we need move now.' Correia squeezed past the group of men and began pushing ahead through the wheat as fast as she could without breaking into a run.

The rest of the group looked to Fal, who shook his head and shrugged, before pushing past and following the Spymaster's lead. As he strode on, Fal couldn't help but laugh as he wondered why Errolas hadn't called upon a falcon, pigeon or even a duck. *'Morl's balls, elf, anything would've been faster than a wren?*

Errolas motioned for the rest of them to follow Correia and Fal. 'Keep

238

your eyes peeled, gentlemen, and be on your guard. It seems we are being followed.'

Despite their curiosity, the remaining men set out without question.

The group pushed on across the fields for a while longer, until they saw a tall windmill on top of a hill to the east.

'Make for that,' Mearson said, pointing to the crooked structure. 'It'll be next to a road.'

The group set out towards the windmill without question.

***

The spiral staircase favoured the defenders as the shield-bearing cathedral guards took blow after blow whilst hacking back down at the two city guardsmen trying to assault their position.

Sears parried one overhead blow from an arming sword as he managed to thrust his short-sword past the shield and across the unprotected shin of its bearer.

The man cursed as he fell back, lowering his shield to protect himself and leaving the man next to him exposed.

Biviano darted past Sears and hacked downwards, breaking the toes of the exposed man's left foot with his now blunted blade.

Falling down besides the first guard, the second was swiftly dispatched by Sears, whilst Biviano fended off the desperate attacks from the prone shield bearer.

'Hold them off!' Biviano shouted, as the three guards left standing surged down the stone steps towards the duo. 'Think of... those raped... and tortured... kiddies, Sears,' he added between lunges, slashes and parries.

Sears roared and so did the flames that engulfed the three guards above him. They screamed as they thrashed about, the iron links of their maille hauberks welding to their skin since the woollen gambesons beneath had already burnt away in the intense heat. It wasn't long until they dropped to the steps, their blackened forms crumbling as Sears ran through them, scattering their smoking armour and weapons down the stairs.

Biviano had finished the shield bearer the moment Sears had unleashed hell, and so he followed his friend onwards and upwards.

Reaching the top step, Sears looked left then right, down corridors that looked identical. 'Which way?'

'Left.' Biviano pushed past and headed that way, blunt sword leading.

'How'd ye know?' Sears shouted from behind, as he chased the smaller man.

'I don't, I guessed.'

'I'm in no mood for ye to piss me off.'

Biviano halted then and held up his hand. Sears stopped behind him and whispered between heaving breaths. 'What is it?'

'A scream, a girl's scream.'

'I don't hear anything,' Sears said, moving to push past Biviano, who held one side of his kettle-helm up, tilting his head to listen. He waved his sword in front of Sears to stop him passing. Sears punched him in the arm and Biviano almost dropped to one knee, biting back a curse as a woman screamed further down the corridor.

'I heard it,' Sears said. 'Came from inside a room, I swear it.'

Arm throbbing, Biviano took off again, heading further down the dark corridor until he came to a studded door.

Sears caught him up and moved to the far side of the door. He looked his friend in the eyes.

Biviano stared back at Sears and was thankful to see his friend's eyes were still glowing, if only faintly.

The muffled voice on the other side of the door sounded like a man's then, followed by a woman cursing.

'She'll end up like the others,' Biviano whispered.

Sears' eyes flashed so bright Biviano had to look away. Before he could look back, Sears threw him across the floor, turned and kicked once, smashing the heavy door from its hinges.

Another scream, this time a man's although it wasn't dissimilar to the first.

Biviano surged to his feet and tried to follow Sears through the door. He didn't notice the large man swiftly approaching him from behind until the smell of urine hit him, but by then it was too late.

'Help!' Coppin had bindings around her wrists that had been looped over a hook on the wall. Hanging naked, a patchwork of bruises and bloody welts criss-crossed her back. She desperately tried to spin to take in the scene behind her, but the movements proved incredibly painful.

A knife came round and pulled tight against her throat then, breaking the delicate skin slightly as it did so. She held her breath and closed her eyes tight, ready for the end.

'Stay where you are,' the Grand Inquisitor said. He held his knife to the green haired girl's throat whilst looking towards the approaching guardsman.

Sears hesitated, his heart pounded and his entire body shook with fury.

Biviano breathed hard as he walked slowly into the room, a small but sharp eating knife held across his throat.

'All of ye stay still,' Longoss said as he turned the man in front of him to face the others in the room.

Biviano shook his head slightly as Sears' eyes flared, and despite his rage, the big man managed to calm himself, knowing no good would come from rash actions or rage.

Everyone in the room, bar Coppin who couldn't, looked from man to man, with the further exception of Biviano, who looked from Sears to the Grand Inquisitor and back, several times.

A pause followed, as everyone tried to work out what was going on and how best to proceed.

Sears clenched his fist with one hand and squeezed the hilt of his sword with the other. He clenched his teeth and breathed slowly, trying to hold the rage inside him. It was rare his birthright would present itself and he was rarely able to control its manifestation when it did. He usually had Biviano for that, but in a situation like this, staying in control was proving harder than ever.

'What's up wi' his eyes?' Longoss asked, and the Grand Inquisitor flinched then as he too noticed the burning embers of Sears' eyes for the first time.

'Long story,' Biviano said, the knife grazing his throat slightly as he did so. 'Ye'd be wise to drop the knives, both of ye, before we all go up in flames.'

'Longoss?' Coppin managed, the sound of his voice familiar to her.

'Aye lass, long time no see. Ye've looked better.'

'Cheers,' she said sarcastically, resulting in the Grand Inquisitor tightening his grip on her.

'Quiet! All of you!' he shouted, his reddened face screwing up in disgust. 'A witch and a demon in my own chamber... what evil is this? What scheme to overthrow me?'

'I'm here for the girl, nothing more,' Longoss said, nodding towards Coppin. 'Elleth sent me to get ye out.'

Coppin's eyes welled up then as she thought of Elleth and what the poor girl must have been through since she bled. 'Is she well?'

'I said quiet!' the Grand Inquisitor shouted. He pulled the knife away as he turned and struck her with the back of his hand.

Biviano took the opportunity and nodded to his friend, despite the knife's bite.

Sears threw himself at the Grand Inquisitor, who managed to dive out of the way just in time.

Realising in an instant the two city guardsmen were no threat to Coppin, Longoss threw Biviano to the ground and jumped over him, making for Coppin's bindings with his knife.

The Grand Inquisitor scrambled to his feet around the back of his desk and ran for the door. Sears pulled himself up and followed.

Biviano had just managed to stand when the Grand Inquisitor barrelled him over and ran from the room. Sears stopped and pulled his friend to his feet at the sound of multiple boots approaching, followed by shouted orders from the Grand Inquisitor.

'Help us,' Longoss said, from the corner of the room. He'd cut Coppin down and wrapped her in a hug, covering her naked form.

'We need to chase that bastard down.' Biviano looked from the man who'd held a knife to his throat, to the girl and then to Sears' settling eyes. The big man shook his head and nodded to the couple in the corner.

Sighing hard, but nodding, Biviano turned to them. 'Throw something on her. We're getting her out of here.'

Coppin broke down with relief as Longoss pulled her across the room to where a brown robe lay on the floor. He lifted it over her head and she let him, hardly able to contain her gratitude for the rescue he'd performed, and for what reason? He was a selfish, viscous bastard as far as the stories Mother and the other girls had told her, but somehow, Elleth had managed to persuade him to come here and get her out. Before she could hold back the sobbing long enough to thank him, Longoss pulled her across the room by her arm, which caused the woollen robes to scratch painfully across her damaged skin.

'Stay behind us,' Biviano said, 'and when we get outta here, I wanna know who the hell ye both are and what's goin on. Agreed?'

Longoss flashed his gold teeth and Coppin nodded.

'Alright, Sears, time to light the bastards up!'

Sears nodded once and moved to the door, but not before all in the room saw his eyes burn bright.

***

Old blades creaked as the wind turned them in a slow arc and the gears inside crunched as the mill stone ground the windmill's contents. Starks screwed his face up as he reached the open door of the mill. 'Another foul smell, and I thought Wesson was bad.'

'Horse fat, lad,' Gleave said. 'They use it to lubricate the gears and it smells like they've been mixing some recently.'

'No one about though.' Mearson had popped inside to check.

The column of smoke was still visible in the distance from the hill where the windmill stood, but only just. A rough, beaten cart track wound away down the hill through the wheat fields, running from north to south.

'The column will pass here if heading north, we should wait,' Errolas said.

Starks sighed in relief at the prospect of resting his legs and having a bite to eat.

The rest of the group sat on whatever they could find as Gleave headed to the highest point on the hill to look back towards the smoke.

Starks barely managed to take a few bites of the bread Correia had bought from Hinton's inn, when the sound of hooves beat the ground. Everyone stood then as Gleave ran back to the windmill.

'Scouts,' Gleave shouted. 'Stay your weapons, they're ours.' *I think.*

Sav cursed whilst unstringing the bow he'd only just strung, and Starks relaxed the cord on his crossbow whilst the others sheathed their half drawn weapons.

The sound of hooves grew louder as three scouts rode over the hill. Upon seeing the group, all of whom had raised their hands in a gesture of peace, the scouts pulled on their reigns and the horses slowed, trotting proudly up to the windmill.

'Who goes?' the lead scout said, from under his boiled leather skull cap. He wore pouldrons similar to his cap and a dirty white tabard over a short, maille hauberk and padded gambeson. His bare hands were clenched tight, one on the axe at his side and the other around the horse's reigns. He was clearly the lead scout, for the other two, although wearing the same white tabards over their padded jacks, wore no armour at all, not even boiled leather.

Correia stepped forward, her hands held high. 'Greetings scout master, may I ask whom you serve?' she said in the sweetest voice. Sav rolled his eyes and shook his head.

'Answer me first and then I'll tell ye.' The scout master's horse shifted nervously as he tried to hold it steady.

'My name is Correia Burr, Spymaster to King Barrison,' she announced regally, lowering her arms finally and saluting in the customary fashion.

The scout master and his two companions returned the salute, but all three looked sceptical.

'Am I to take yer word, milady?' the scout master asked, his eyes searching hers for a hint of a lie.

Sav tried to hide his amusement. *Milady? That's hilarious.*

'I would be disappointed if you did.' Correia slowly reached into a pouch on her belt and retrieved an extremely small, rolled and sealed scroll, before passing it up to the mounted scout.

As he reached for a bollock dagger on his belt, Correia shook her head. 'Ah-ah...' she warned, 'that's not for your eyes, scout master, but look at the seal and recognise the King's very own mark.' His eyes widened and he looked around the group quickly before nodding to his men.

'Return to Baron Brackley and tell him to hurry, we may have help here.' The two scouts kicked their horses on and rode down the road before Correia could stop them.

'Help with what?' she asked, as dust from the hooves of the two horses enveloped the group.

'The fight, milady. The Baron of Ullston is marching north to head off a large group of goblins that've come down from the mountains. They rarely push this far, but something's spooking things lately and there's strange folk about; hooded travellers and shadows in the night sky.'

The group murmured as they heard the strange news and Fal asked, a little too urgently he later thought, about the shadows.

The scout master rocked back a little when he saw Fal's tattoos, but he composed himself quickly and explained what he'd seen. 'Couple of nights ago, out patrolling I were, looking for this goblin tribe we're marching on when I saw it, high up. Blacker than night it were, blotting out the stars as it passed from cloud to cloud. Sent a shiver down me spine it did.'

'gryphon maybe, or a teratorn,' Sav offered, 'although you don't usually see them around here.'

The man shook his head. 'No, I've seen gryphons before and it were bigger, so bigger than a teratorn too. Just a large condor that ain't it?'

Sav and Errolas both nodded.

'So no, none of those and it were nowt else I've seen either. Dragon I'd say if there'd been one in Altoln in the past thousand years.'

'Dragon?' Gleave could barely hide his amusement.

The scout master frowned. 'Listen, I don't knows what it was, but it weren't no gryphon or giant bird that's for sure. All I knows is we're off to wipe this goblin lot out before they reach the village up ahead—'

The sound of drums interrupted the man, followed by the two scouts riding back in. They nodded to their scout master as they passed, and headed back to the north.

'Here's the Baron now.' The scout master side-stepped his horse off the road as a column of men-at-arms, archers and light cavalry headed towards them, including a couple of poorly armoured knights at their head.

The Baron of Ullston, who rode in front of them all, wore a dirty white surcoat over an old maille hauberk. His horse's trapper matched the scruffy attire of its rider, and the Baron's maille covered arms led to a pair of dented and rusted mitten-style plate gauntlets. A chewed and scarred white heater shield with a black hart in its centre hung from one side of his saddle, and a broadsword hung from the other, its blade the only clean thing about the Baron. He wore a rust-stained arming cap under his maille coif and his dark eyes gazed out at the group.

'Greetings, milady,' Brackley said, bowing as best he could in his high fronted saddle.

Correia bowed in return. 'Greetings, my lord Baron, it is a pleasure to make your acquaintance.'

Brackley grinned, showing teeth about as white as his surcoat.

A young squire sat on a smaller horse next to the Baron. He carried his lord's black lance, the fluttering pennant of which repeated the black hart on a white field, which was present on most of the Baron's mounted men, and some of those on foot.

'Sire, fresh smoke!' The squire pointed north and everyone followed his finger with their eyes.

Brackley turned to the scout master and the man shrugged.

'They weren't at the village when we were there, milord,' he said, shifting in his saddle. 'They must've moved in fast.' Without another word, he turned his horse and sped off in the same direction as the other scouts.

The two drums of the column pounded once again and Brackley turned in his saddle to face his men. 'Form a line, form a line!' The men-at-arms and archers began to fan out immediately across the fields surrounding the windmill.

Slightly hunched archers, their drawing arms large and their backs broad, ran to the front and strung war bows that stood as tall as most men. Men-at-arms tightened the straps on their shields and shoved their blades into the ground, dirtying them before the fight. The twenty or so light cavalry and two knights; maces, swords and axes held at the ready, stayed in a column behind their commander as he turned back to face Correia.

'If ye are who the scouts said ye are, then I need yer pathfinders help, milady. We need to re-take the village and its lands ahead, and drive these damned retches back to the mountains from whence they came. Or preferably slaughter the bloody lot of them here and now, damned sacks of putrid shites that they are.' The large framed Baron spat on the floor and then frowned, as Correia shook her head and looked apologetic.

'My apologies, Baron Brackley, but I cannot. We are on a mission of the utmost urgency for the King himself, and I need seven fast horses to get us on our way, as even now an unknown enemy pursues us from the west.'

The Baron's eyes strayed in that direction briefly before returning to Correia's gaze.

She showed him the seal on the scroll the scout master had passed back to her.

The veteran soldier sighed and looked back at his cavalry, rubbing his face roughly and leaving fresh marks from his rusting gauntlets.

'Very well,' he said, without argument. 'I realise ye wouldn't ask, especially now, if it weren't as urgent as ye say it is. Ye say ye don't know who follows?'

Correia shook her head and Brackley sighed again.

'If I survive what comes, which I will,' he said with a wink, 'then I'll imprison anyone else who crosses me on the path ye take.

'Seven from the back, to me!' he shouted.

The rear most seven mounted men kicked their horses forward through the wheat at the side of the road.

'I need you seven to join the infantry line on the left, yer horses are forfeit in the name of the King,' Brackley said, no sign of apology in his tone.

The seven riders looked furious as they dismounted and handed their reigns over to the strangers by the windmill, before running off to get into line, much to the amusement of those already on foot, who hooted and jeered at the new arrivals, hoisting their weapons – some makeshift, as was often the case with local militia – high as they did so.

Correia mounted the dappled grey horse she had taken. 'We owe you a great debt, Baron Brackley. The King himself will hear of your generosity and service.'

'Yes yes I'm sure. Now away with ye all and have done with whatever it is ye need do. I have goblin arse-wipes to kill.' Brackley winked at Correia before turning to his mounted column behind.

'What are ye waiting for, ye bastards?' The Baron of Ullston dug his spurs into his destrier's flanks and the beast snorted and then surged forward. The Baron's remaining cavalry cheered, formed into a double line and followed him, trampling the crops either side of the road as they went. The archers and men-at-arms on foot followed at a dog trot, as the whole line advanced, drums beating and horns blowing.

Correia's group looked to one another, soldiers all, and none liked to leave fellow warriors to face the likes of goblins, but on they needed to go and so on they went. They kicked their horses on, and the road's dust rose from their mounts' hooves as they cantered off to the south, a large skirmish already developing behind them.

It had been a hard-fought escape from the cathedral, with guards, warrior monks and two more inquisitors attempting to stop the group. The Grand Inquisitor hadn't been seen again and Biviano cursed their luck at finally finding and then losing him.

In the bright light of an open street running alongside the cathedral, the handful of passers-by quickly dispersed as three armed and injured men and a woman with green hair piled out from a side door.

'We need to keep moving,' Sears said, breathing heavily and prodding an open wound on his right thigh.

'Aye, thanks.' Longoss headed off towards Dockside, Coppin in tow.

'Woah, no ye don't.' Biviano caught up to the two of them, Sears close behind. 'Ye owe us an explanation.'

Longoss knew he couldn't fight the two men off, not after giving his word to Elleth and not after seeing them fight, especially the bearded one, and so he nodded reluctantly. 'Not here though.'

'Agreed,' Biviano said. 'We'll go to the barracks. The captain needs to hear what's really goin' on here and inform the Constable of Wesson, and this girl can help us tell him about it.'

Longoss laughed. 'I ain't going to no barracks to be strung up, and that's that. I need to get this one back to Mother's—'

Coppin pulled away from Longoss then and stumbled towards the two guardsmen, a sneer upon her face. 'Ye said Elleth sent ye, not Mother?'

Sears and Biviano moved either side of the girl to protect her.

'And she did, Coppin, she did, but the stubborn girl won't be leaving the damned place without ye, so I need ye to go back with me, so we can get her outta there... both of ye outta there.'

Coppin looked unsure and looked to Sears, then Biviano.

'Ye don't need to go with him, not if ye don't want, lass,' Sears said, and Biviano nodded.

'I do if he's tellin' the truth,' she said eventually. 'I can't leave Elleth there, not if there's a chance she can be free of the place, although I'm not sure being with you, Longoss, would be any better for her?' She stared directly at Longoss when she said the latter.

'This is ridiculous,' Biviano said, rubbing the weariness from his eyes. 'With what we've just seen and done, Sears, we need to get the hell outta here and get to the barracks. Take these two in. Then we can get back here with the captain and more men.'

Longoss held his hands up. 'I told ye, I ain't going to no barracks and there's a girl needing me help, and yours, right now. I can make it worth yer while. I'll owe ye big for this.'

'Biviano,' Sears said, looking into his friend's eyes, 'this Elleth girl needs our help, and this one's scared to go along with him alone.'

Biviano sighed. 'How will *you* owing *us* be of any use, eh?'

Longoss' nostrils flared and his jaw bunched as he rubbed his face and looked to Coppin, then Biviano. 'The Black Guild is planning a high status mark, something real big. How's that for starters?'

Coppin's eyes widened. For all she'd heard of Longoss and known from her own experience with him, albeit a brief one in the past, the man didn't do anything to risk himself, certainly not to expose himself. So why was he doing all of this for her? *No, not for me, for Elleth...*

Biviano scratched his behind as he looked from Longoss to Sears, noticing Coppin's reaction to the man's words at the same time. *This guy's serious.*

Sears looked to Biviano and shrugged.

'And how do ye know such a thing, eh, Longoss?' Biviano said finally.

Sighing hard and looking off to the side, before looking back at Biviano, Longoss simply said, 'because I'm one of 'em.'

'Oh, Longoss.' Coppin shook her head. 'They'll kill ye for this.'

Gold teeth flashed. 'They'll try.'

Gods above, if this guy's only half serious and I reckon he is, we can't not get him onside, Biviano thought, as he looked to Sears. The big man nodded and so did he.

Turning to Longoss, Biviano held out his hand. 'We'll help,' he said.

Longoss took the offered hand and shook it. 'And I'll do all I can to help ye with whatever ye need when we get Elleth out. I give ye me word!'

Chapter 30: Confrontation

Despite holding onto a spark of hope, Elleth didn't really believe Longoss would come back, especially with Coppin, however, since he'd left, Mother had sent no more men to her room to 'play games'. How silly she felt about it all now.

Huddled in the corner of the room, for she didn't wish to lie on the bloody bed, Elleth thought about how much had changed, how much *she'd* changed in such a short amount of time. It didn't seem long at all and in truth it wasn't. Not long since she had been cuddled by her mamma. She began to cry again, before slamming her fist on the floor and cursing herself.

Ye're a woman now, she thought, fighting to control her churning emotions. *All this crying, I can't be doing it, I can't be showing I'm weak. Not to the men and certainly not to Mother.*

Elleth had heard her door being locked shortly after Longoss had gone, and she knew if he broke his word and didn't return for her, it wouldn't be long until Mother was shoving in the next man who showed her his coin.

Well, after the dead man's been taken away. She struggled against looking across that side of the room. Swallowing hard, she tried to block out the things that had happened to her. The pain between her legs flared then as her mind touched upon it and before she could even shift to ease the discomfort, someone hammered on the front door of the building.

Longoss?

She wasn't even sure how she'd feel if he did come back. What if he came back, but hadn't found Coppin? She would have no idea whether he'd even looked for her. Could it all be just another game? She fought the tears back again as the sound of raised voices came from down stairs.

'Just another guy wanting to buy a girl, no doubt,' Elleth whispered, bitterly. 'And if Longoss wants to buy me?' She didn't even know how to feel about that. He'd been the only one to talk to her as a person and he seemed to mean it. Would it be so bad going with him? He wasn't handsome pretty like some of the other men, but perhaps that didn't matter if he treated her better; better than Mother had, but that wasn't exactly hard, she saw that clearly now.

A scream... Mother's scream.

Elleth stood and stared at the locked door, her hands wringing themselves as she chewed her bottom lip.

More screaming, then glass being shattered; someone was smashing things downstairs and Mother was screaming for them to stop. A dog yelped and then Mother went mad. She shouted curses and from the sounds of it, threw things at whoever was down there.

Silence...

Please be Longoss... with Coppin, please.

A few moments passed that felt like an age, then a heavy thud; two, three and splintering wood.

Another scream; Elleth recognised it as Aynsa's from two rooms down.

Elleth looked to the body in the room. So much blood had come from that man and Elleth couldn't help but think about how it must have hurt him, to be stabbed so many times. She also thought about how quickly it had happened and how still and peaceful the man now looked.

Footsteps in the corridor outside and the next door was kicked in, followed by furniture being turned over and more things breaking, yet still Elleth stared at the body.

Will that be me in a moment? Despite her fear, she felt suddenly calm. *It's Longoss who's in the house, or it's not. Either way, I may die, like that man, or I may not and my life will continue like this and there's nothing I can do about it, nothing at all. My life is not my own anymore and I'm not even sure it ever was.* The sudden realisation of her helplessness, for reasons she couldn't fathom, allowed her to look at the door, lower her hands and walk forward, accepting her fate. For nothing could be any worse than the life she'd fallen into. In fact, death suddenly seemed an easy way out.

As she crossed the room, wood splintered and the door caved in. Despite her resignation to whatever may come, Elleth flinched at the sudden sound and violent entry. Then she stared at the elongated white mask of the man who now stood opposite her.

The masked head tilted as the man looked her up and down. She looked down at herself, at the stains of blood on her night dress and then looked back at the man, who slowly entered the room.

Turning to look at the bloodied bed behind her, heart racing, Elleth moved to it and sat down, giving in to what was to come, but hoping whoever this man was would make it quick.

He stood in front of Elleth now, looking down at her, the mask hiding his features and expression as he spoke in a surprisingly soft tone. 'I'm going to ask you a question, girl, maybe more than one and I need you to be honest with me.'

'Or ye'll kill me?' she said flatly.

The mask turned briefly and took in the gutted man on the floor. Looking back to Elleth, the man nodded before responding. 'Did Longoss do that?' He jerked his thumb towards the corpse.

Elleth simply nodded.

'Did he talk to you whilst here?'

She nodded again.

'What did he say?'

'That he would do that,' Elleth pointed to the dead man, 'to any man who beat on me.'

The mask tilted again, before nodding ever so slightly. 'Interesting,' he said eventually. 'Well, I won't beat on you girl,' he said after a moment's pause, 'I give you my word.'

'So did Longoss.' Elleth heard the man swallow at that and her spark of hope returned as she realised he feared Longoss.

Checking over his shoulder suddenly, the masked man asked, 'Where is he now?'

Elleth shrugged.

'What did you talk about?'

'Doing things to please me next time he's here.'

He laughed. 'Are you sure we're talking about the same Longoss here?'

Elleth opened her mouth to answer, but the man held up his hand.

'Did he mention anything about what he does to make money? About any plans he has?'

'Like what?'

'That's what I'm asking you. Now answer the question and quit stalling. He isn't coming back here for you, you know that, don't you?'

'It doesn't matter whether he is or not, I'll be dead before he gets in this room, so there's no point telling ye any more.' It was unnerving not seeing any reaction to her words. She'd got so used to seeing men's anger, but this, this mask made it almost impossible to read the man stood in front of her. She expected him to react to what she said, but he just stood there, staring at her. He crouched suddenly and that made her rock back a little.

Face to face with the blank mask, she couldn't help but notice his grey eyes through the oval holes, eyes so like her dada's. Elleth suddenly had to fight back the tears again and she felt her eyes moisten at the thought of her dada, the thought leading on to her mamma and brother.

'I'm going to ask you one last question.'

Elleth breathed hard as the mask came closer, its elongated tip almost pressing against her chest. His eyes didn't blink as they bore into her.

'Did Longoss swear anything else to you?'

What a strange question? She didn't quite know what to say, but found herself nodding.

'What was it?'

'He swore to me he wouldn't kill,' she whispered, without really intending to.

The mask moved away suddenly and looked up to the ceiling, and then the man stood, before bursting out laughing.

Elleth flinched at the outburst and then again as he dropped back into a crouch in front of her.

'You have no idea what you've done, do you girl? He'll keep that promise, you know that? The stupid bastard will keep that promise, because he never breaks his word. Never! You've just killed him.'

Elleth's heart sank as the words hit her. All of what Longoss had said to her came flooding back in that moment and the sincerity in his voice; his eyes as he'd given his word to her, twice, struck her far worse than anyone else had ever done.

Why? Why did ye do that for me? He says I've killed ye and his eyes don't lie. Ye would have saved me, truly, but I've just killed ye by making ye swear to me and by telling him that ye did. I didn't even put up a fight, I was so ready to die, but I didn't think of you… Longoss, I am so sorry. Elleth couldn't stop the tears then and she let them flow freely as the masked man stood again, grabbed her wrist and pulled her to her feet, before turning her round to face the bed.

'Close your eyes,' he whispered into her ear, his mask pressing against the back of her head.

Elleth did as he asked.

***

The small chapel stood on the edge of Hinton. It had a spire no taller than a large oak tree and a small bell that hardly ever rang. As the trio of black-clad men crossed the golden field of rape seed, heading towards the iron studded door of the chapel, its small bell rang in what could have been misconstrued as a warning signal. It was in fact a coincidence that the approach of the men had coincided with the marriage of a young couple.

The groom's father, a local farmer called Mickel, stood proud as his son took the hand of a beautiful young woman from Hinton. He'd known the girl's father all his life and it pleased him to know her family was well liked in the village.

It was annoying then, when the small chapel's door swung open and a tall, hard looking man removing a wide brimmed hat strode into the ceremony unannounced. The bride and groom turned as the stranger sat on a stool at the back of the chapel and waved them on, as if it was he, not the bride-to-be's father that was giving her away.

Mickel turned back to the front and pushed it from his mind, happy again to see the frail old priest bless his son and new daughter. The ceremony ended with a cheer from the gathering, and two small children ran giggling down the aisle, throwing bluebell heads as the newly married couple strode down the aisle after them, their faces beaming at all who'd witnessed their joining.

Horler Comlay stood, bowed and smiled, although the expression was not obvious, appearing more as a grimace than a smile. The bride curtseyed to the stranger and the groom offered a quick bow as they passed, their postures tensing slightly as they saw the Witchunter General's rapier at his side. Both of their fathers nodded as they passed, their faces set like stone. The rest of the guests hurried after them, out into the sunlight and away from the chapel as fast as they dared without looking suspicious to the two witchunters who stood outside the arched doorway.

Horler walked casually up the aisle towards the old priest. 'Good day, Father..?'

'Farrely. Good day to you too,' the priest greeted, his arms open wide to welcome a brother Samorlian.

The two embraced, although Horler had to bend almost double. The old priest beckoned for the Witchunter General to follow him through a small door into a back room. Upon entering, Horler was amused to see how fast the elderly man had crossed the room and collected two goblets, and was even now reaching for a dusty bottle.

'Would you care for some elderflower wine, General?' Father Farrely asked, and Horler was even more surprised his rank had been so obvious to the little man. He could easily have been a normal witchunter; he wore no symbol to advertise otherwise, yet the priest, who was pouring the wine into both goblets before Horler could accept or decline, had noted it with ease.

'Thank you, father,' Horler said, as he took the goblet. The priest motioned for him to be seated on a rather grand looking chair whilst the old man sat on a very basic stool, swatting away any attempt Horler made to swap seats.

'How may I be of service to your order, General? I take it this isn't a social visit?' Beady eyes raced around Horler's face as if reading him like a book and Horler couldn't help but smile.

'Nothing would escape you now would it, father? I shall be frank. I respect you far too much not to be.'

'I expect nothing less, General. This is my chapel after all.' He grinned then, revealing several missing teeth.

'My men and I are in need of horses. Hinton unfortunately had none for our use and we are on a desperate mission to track down and apprehend a group of dangerous arcane mages.' Horler added an ominous tone to the latter. *Well, not exactly mages…*

The old priest didn't seem surprised at all and merely shrugged before asking a totally random question which threw Horler completely.

'How's the old goat at the cathedral in Wesson these days? Still overweight and in need of some good hard work I'm sure our Lord Sir Samorl could prescribe?' Again Father Farrely grinned at Horler, who couldn't have expected anything like what he'd just heard.

Does he mean Corlen or the Grand Inquisitor? I assume the latter, that he's referring to my order. Horler found himself smiling back; his usual instinct to threaten or strike whoever might have insulted the Grand Inquisitor immediately draining away under the amusing grin of the old man.

'Now now, Father Farrely, it's not my place to say. If you'll please advise me on my predicament, I would like to be on my way, to capture those whom Sir Samorl would want capturing, and leaving you to the work you must surely have to do after such a lovely ceremony.'

The priest's grin slipped slightly at the realisation the General was serious about not wanting his time wasting. He sighed openly.

'Very well, General, we all have our own paths to take and yours must be leading you somewhere important indeed for you to need to tread it so quickly. Go back out of the chapel and head north for an hour or so, maybe less with your long legs. There you will find a farm. I say a farm because it's made to look like one, but it's not. Within that farm is the best chance of finding the horses you need, maybe even more men should you need them.'

252

'What is this place you speak of?'

Father Farrely shrugged and then drained his goblet in one go, wiping his mouth with his sleeve. 'I don't know what goes on there, General, I'm not a scout. What I *do* know is they pass this chapel on horseback often and the locals don't go near. If they are brigands then maybe a visit from you will not go amiss. If they are goodly folk though General, be warned,' the old priest slammed his goblet down suddenly and the small table next to him shook. He pointed a bony finger at the dangerous man in front of him before continuing. 'I will *not* tolerate bloodshed in my parish for the sake of horses, arcane mages or any other cock and bull witchunter wild-goose chase. We may share the same faith, but that doesn't mean we share the same views on that faith. Do I make myself clear, General?'

Horler rocked back in his seat as if struck. It had been a long time indeed since anyone had dared raise their voice to him and yet, although frail and hardly able to defend himself, the old priest had done just that. After a brief moment, Horler merely stood, raised his goblet and then drained it in response, unsure what else he could do. He gently placed the goblet on the table, nodded his thanks to Father Farrely and left the small chapel, unsure whether to laugh or curse.

Once outside, without a word spoken to his men – who knew better than to ask where they were going – Horler Comlay set out for the place where he would shortly be acquiring horses, by whatever means necessary.

***

The cell was cold and damp despite the warm spring day outside, and the man lying on the floor grunted as a heavy set guard kicked him in the ribs, forcing him to roll over and curl up in a whimpering ball.

'That's enough,' Sir Bullen ordered. 'I don't think he knows any more. Take him back down and bring up the next one.'

The brutish guard turned to face the young knight leaning against the cell's door frame. 'We could torture him properly sire, he'd talk then, I swear it.' The guard prodded the prisoner with his foot.

'Yes, I'm sure we could and I'm also sure he'd talk... about whatever we wanted him to. I've told you before, torture, to the degree you're talking about anyway, is pointless. Push a man too far and he'll swear blind he's a dog if it will stop the pain. No, I don't see the point. We'll give them a thorough questioning, the fear of torture should get the truth from their lips and... well, this one needs to go to a separate cell from the others now doesn't he? Otherwise he'll tell the others there's no need to talk because we won't torture them.' Sir Bullen sighed and rubbed the back of his head repeatedly. 'Find another cell for him, and tell the men in his previous cell this one's been strung up.'

The guard grunted as he lifted the stinking, flea-bitten man to his feet with one hand.

Moving from the doorway, the prison's Castellan looked on as the guard dragged the prisoner past and headed off down a gently sloping corridor. Pressing his hand to his mouth, Sir Bullen yawned. *When did I last sleep? It seems an age ago.*

Footsteps echoed down the corridor from the opposite direction as soon as the guard and prisoner had left. The well-dressed knight turned to see another guard walking quickly towards him, a worried look upon his face.

'Milord,' the guard said as he approached.

'Yes, what is it?' Sir Bullen replied irritably. There had been no rest since the prisoners had escaped, and even less since the disappearance of a Samorlian Witchunter General. Sir Bullen had been questioning prisoners from the lower levels ever since, and had received numerous letters and messengers from various lords of Wesson, all demanding to know what was going on in the prison.

He had even – much to his annoyance, wishing he'd had it sooner – received a letter from the Duke of Yewdale himself, stating the Samorlian Grand Inquisitor no longer held any jurisdiction anywhere in the city, or kingdom for that matter, without the signed authorisation of a high lord or the King himself. Oh, how Sir Bullen would have loved to have waved that order in the face of Horler Comlay when he'd stormed through the prison before disappearing.

The bastard's lying dead in some prisoner's cell I'd wager.

The guard who stood biting his lip in front of Sir Bullen looked worried, the Castellan's mood not helping matters, and so Sir Bullen made a point of visibly relaxing before asking again, in a calmer voice, 'what's the matter Andrel?'

'It's the Samorlian Church, milord.' The young guard shifted from foot to foot, nervously twisting his hand around the hilt of his sheathed falchion.

Sir Bullen felt his temper rise again and took a deep breath before continuing. 'What about them?' he asked, as politely as he could.

Andrel seemed to relax slightly before continuing.

'Well sire… they're here, at the prison gate.'

Sir Bullen looked away for a second, brow furrowed, and then back again, not sure what he was hearing. 'They're *here?*'

'Aye, milord.' Andrel tensed again upon seeing his lord do the same.

'Well who, the whole bloody church? What do you mean "they're here?"'

'About forty of 'em, milord…'

You couldn't count to forty.

'…witchunters, warrior monks, the lot. There's a Witchunter General asking for you personally. We told him to wait outside while I came to fetch you.'

Sir Bullen swallowed hard. He was afraid of no fight. Well, that wasn't true. No sane man was fearless before or during a fight. It was fear that gave them the energy, courage and strength to do what was needed, but Sir Bullen would never back down from one, he had proved that time and time again.

Alas, the Samorlian witchunters were another matter, and he'd seen them in action in his home town years before. His father had called them in to deal with a werewolf when his own retainers had failed. The witchunter, a single man, tore the beast to shreds. Sir Bullen didn't see it happen of course, but the man had brought it with him after he'd killed it, to prove the deed was done. It wasn't that which had bothered the young man though. It was the family the witchunter had taken to the inquisitors afterwards, claiming they were in league with the werewolf. The family never returned to their home and were never seen again. Even his father dared not call upon the witchunter to explain himself, and it was his father's fear that had scared Sir Bullen the most.

'It's different here,' Sir Bullen muttered.

Andrel looked confused, but didn't dare ask what his lord meant.

'The letter sent to me by Lord Yewdale, take it to the main gate immediately and await me there.'

Andrel nodded swiftly before running back up the corridor.

Sir Bullen set off at a fast pace and then hesitated at a junction in the corridor. Instead of going directly to the gate, he took a longer route via his chamber, where he ordered the guard by his door to help him on with his harness of armour.

Blued steel pouldrons on his shoulders linked to articulated plate arms and fingered gauntlets. He pulled on a padded arming cap and his maille coif which the guard tied down to his coat of plates, now hidden beneath his knee-length, thick woollen surcoat. The surcoat was bright and the stitching was of the top most quality, bearing a black gryphon rampant on a yellow field.

The guard crouched then, and strapped on Sir Bullen's articulated leg armour.

Articulated plate was the most sought after armour from the master smiths in Sirreta, and all the lords and knights who could afford it – and even some who couldn't – spent months of wages or loans on the custom made steel.

Lastly, the guard fitted the young knight's long, pattern stitched sword belt; with Sir Bullen's scabbard hanging down from the left hand side. He sheathed the fine blade passed to him by his former liege lord, the last Castellan, and was finally ready. Ready to meet the force stood at his prison's gate, and if needs be, to defend that gate, his men and his honour.

Sir Bullen padded across the stone floor in soft leather boots, his maille rustling against his plate as he walked to the main gate. He'd ordered his room guard to follow. Having donned all of his wealth, there was no reason for his room to be guarded.

I've a feeling I'll need every one of my men for this encounter.

***

It was a long walk through the streets from the Samorlian Cathedral to

Mother's, which lay in the heart of Dockside. The small group had avoided a patrol of city guardsmen upon Longoss' request, much to the annoyance of Sears and especially Biviano, but both of them knew they needed to help the man rescue Elleth and they didn't want to do anything to risk that, never mind finding out about the Black Guild's latest mark.

They hadn't seen many people about and knew most were either hiding away from the plague, or already locked away behind black crossed doors along with the rising number of dead.

After barely entering the district of Dockside via a narrow alley, Biviano suddenly stopped.

'Shit!' he said loudly, half turning to look back the way they'd come.

Sears turned to him, immediately recognising the genuine look of shock on his friend's face.

'What's up?' Sears said. Longoss and Coppin stopped and all three looked upon the small man, who looked back at them. He shook his head and brought his hand up to scratch violently under his kettle-helm.

'Ellis Frane,' he said, all colour draining from his face.

Sears closed his eyes tight and dropped into a crouch, pressing his large hands against his face and rubbing hard.

'We forgot him, Sears.'

'Who's Ellis Frane?' Coppin shared the guardsmen's concern, but didn't know why.

Biviano looked from Sears to Coppin and explained.

'Ye need to go back for him,' she said, before Biviano had even finished.

Sears stood then and looked around the group, finishing on Biviano. 'I'll go. You stay with these two and help this Elleth girl.'

Biviano was shaking his head as he replied. 'Ye can't, big guy, not on yer own. We barely made it out the four of us. I'll go fetch Captain Prior and more men, and get him out with a show of force, it's the only way. These two and Elleth need ye, Sears. Ye'll serve 'em far better than I will.'

Despite his reservations, Sears knew it to be the only option, but it didn't make it any easier. He stepped forward and wrapped Biviano in a huge hug, squeezing the man until his friend repeatedly punched him to let him go. 'You be safe, Biviano. No heroics without me, understood?'

'What were that for, ye fat shit? I'll be fine, just help these two and get the hell outta Dockside with 'em as fast as ye can. Ye leave Ellis Frane and the cathedral bastards to me. I'll be just fine with two dozen guardsmen at me back.'

Nodding, Sears pushed Biviano on his way and the little man ran back out of the alley towards Park District.

'He'll be fine,' Longoss said, confidently.

Sears nodded and turned back the way they'd been heading, walking fast as the other two caught up.

'I'll lead,' Longoss said, 'ye don't know the way.'

'True that.' Sears looked behind him one last time before dropping back to keep Coppin between the two of them.

As they walked out onto an uneven, patchy cobbled street with poorly maintained town houses to either side, Sears noticed Longoss looking to the rooftops again, as he'd been doing the whole way.

'Ye think we're being watched?' Sears said, looking up.

'Aye, all the way from the cathedral.'

Coppin started looking about then, her nervousness plain to see. 'The Black Guild,' she whispered.

Sears' hand moved to his short-sword. 'Ye thinking they'll make a move?'

Longoss shrugged.

'Reassuring,' Sears said.

'I told 'em I don't want to work for 'em any more.'

Sears barked a laugh. 'They're not a fan of retirement then?'

A flash of gold teeth. *I like this one.* 'Just keep walking,' Longoss said, turning a corner and continuing down another alley.

Coppin's eyes darted everywhere as she walked. 'Should we not stick to the streets?'

'Would make no difference,' Longoss said, 'and I just wanna get there as quickly as we can.' His pace quickened then and the other two followed suit, keeping up as Longoss almost jogged down another alley branching off from the one they were on.

'We're close,' Coppin said, beginning to recognise the area.

'Close to what exactly?' Sears moved alongside the girl. 'What is this Mother's place?'

'A brothel,' Longoss said.

Coppin turned and looked up into Sears' eyes; her own a depth of sadness. 'Elleth didn't choose to be a whore, Sears, nor did I.'

Sears nodded once. 'We'll get her out,' he said firmly, 'and ye won't be going back there, I promise.'

Smiling and nodding in return, Coppin moved ahead of Sears before the kind guardsman could see the single tear rolling down her cheek.

After three more turns and an exceptionally long, narrow and winding alley, Longoss stopped at its end, looking across the street at a large house opposite.

Without realising, Coppin found herself holding on to Longoss' arm as she stared at a place she knew all too well. Her heart thumped in her chest and her stomach churned. A mix of emotions ran through her, from fear and loathing to excitement at the thought of seeing Elleth and her other sisters again. Steeling herself against the fear of facing Mother, Coppin made to move out of the alley, but Longoss held his arm out to stop her.

'I'll go first,' he said to Coppin, before looking to Sears, who nodded. Stepping out onto the street, Longoss looked about for any signs of sudden movement before walking confidently across to the house. He heard Coppin and Sears follow and felt a little better knowing the powerful guardsman was at his back. Not being able to kill had allowed a small knot of fear to lodge itself in his gut and that fear had grown as he approached the house, especially after Poi Son's comment about Elleth – all be it not by name – sprang to mind. *Ye wouldn't dare*, Sears thought, although he couldn't hide his own doubt about that.

Reaching the door, Longoss tried the handle, not wanting to knock unless he had to. It wasn't locked. Looking back at Coppin and Sears, Longoss opened the door slowly. He listened for any sign of movement on the other side.

Silence...

He stepped inside and quickly looked both ways, before quietly moving towards the kitchen.

Coppin held her breath as she awaited an outburst from Mother, but nothing came as Longoss disappeared into the kitchen and so she followed, Sears close behind her. Before she could pass through the door, Longoss came barrelling out past her, literally pushing her to one side as he ran past Sears and up the stairs.

'Elleth?' he shouted, clearly in panic.

'Stay here.' Sears ran after Longoss.

Coppin looked at the kitchen doorway and took a deep breath, before stepping inside.

She sucked in another breath as she saw the destruction all about her. The table was turned over and broken glass and crockery littered the floor, all of it mixed in with the blood of both Mother and her dog. Coppin brought both hands up to her face as she took in the scene, looking from the open throat of Mother to the bloody mess of the small animal by the woman's side. Shaking her head slowly, torn between the feelings of final release from Mother's grip to one of horror, she jumped suddenly at Longoss' cry of pain from above.

Moving fast and forgetting her own fears, Coppin raced out of the kitchen and up the stairs. She ran along the corridor to where Sears stood looking into the third room along. Its door, like the two Coppin passed as she ran, had been kicked in, and when she reached Sears, who held his head low, she had to force herself to move past him and enter the room.

There, on a blood soaked bed, sat Longoss, cradling the still form of Elleth. Her open throat still leaked her life's blood, which now ran onto Longoss' chest as he rocked her back and forth. His eyes streamed as he rubbed Elleth's back over and over again with his right hand.

Coppin dropped to the floor, stunned into silence at the vicious scene.

Sears stepped into the room then, looking about, taking in all the details. He breathed heavily and his eyes began to darken. A pinprick of light appeared in the centre of those eyes, gradually increasing in size and intensity. Slowly, they began to burn like the embers of an intense fire.

Coppin, her face ashen, looked up to the guardsman stood above her and she found the strength to stand. Turning to him, she placed a hand up onto each shoulder, feeling the cold links of his maille on her palms.

He looked down into her sad eyes.

Coppin shook her head, her face literally aglow under his intense stare. 'Not now,' she whispered. 'Save it, Sears, save it.' She could almost feel the battle raging behind those eyes. The man was tense, his beard moving as he ground his teeth. His right hand squeezed the hilt of his sword and his left clenched repeatedly. Slowly he began to calm, to win the fight within him and store the anger, locking it away to be used upon those who'd killed the young girl being cradled by Longoss opposite him. His eyes dimmed and finally returned to normal.

Coppin fought her own battle, holding back her tears and grief, staying strong for the two men present. They'd done so much for her and now it was her turn to be there for them.

'I'm going to Longoss now,' she said softly. Sears nodded.

Removing her hands from his broad shoulders, Coppin moved across to Longoss and sat beside him on the bed, her eyes settling on Elleth's empty grey orbs as she leant in to the big man and wrapped her arms about him, pulling him close. He wept all the more then and rested his head on Coppin's. She could feel his breaths shudder as he fought to control his emotions.

'Let it out,' she whispered. 'Ye need to let it out now, Longoss. It won't do you, nor me any good when we step out into that street.' She squeezed him tight as he cried all the more. 'They did it to her, didn't they?' she said. 'The Black Guild?'

Longoss nodded. 'Because of me,' he said between breaths. 'She died because of me.'

'No,' Sears said. He'd moved round to check the body next to the bed. 'She died because of *them*, Longoss, don't ye be telling yerself any different.'

Wood creaked outside of the room and all three fell silent.

Longoss tensed and Coppin released him, but not before Sears had crossed the room, short-sword at the ready. He stood to the side of the door, listened again for any sign of movement before rushing from the room, sword held defensively.

'Clear,' he said, before moving back into the room. 'There's no one there, but I'm going to check upstairs then we need to leave.'

Coppin nodded.

'Longoss,' she whispered.

'Only one to ever smile at me and mean it,' Longoss said, eyes closed as he laid his head back on Elleth's.

Coppin took a deep breath and pulled at Longoss, a man who until today, she would've said had no emotions whatsoever. 'We need to go, before they come back.'

'They *can* come back!' he shouted, turning and glaring at her. 'I told 'em, touch her and I'll bring the fuckers down, the lot of 'em. I swore it to 'em, stupid bastards.'

Coppin had jumped at the outburst, and Longoss' eyes softened then. 'Sorry girl, but I gave Elleth me word and I let her down.'

Shaking her head before Longoss finished, Coppin said, 'Ye saved *me*

259

Longoss, ye swore to her ye would and ye did. Ye saved me and that's what Elleth wanted.'

The words did nothing to take the pain from Longoss' eyes, but he nodded all the same.

'Now to keep that word, ye need to get me out of here, safe. Ye can pay the guild back, but now ain't the time and ye know it.'

He nodded again and looked down at Elleth's still form, stroking her black hair as he finally laid her besides him on the bed.

Heavy footfalls on the stairs drew their attention and Longoss rose then, standing in front of Coppin before Sears entered the room.

'The top floor,' the guardsman said, pointing up as he did so, 'they're all dead.'

'Bastards!' Longoss shouted.

Sears shook his head and spat on the floor. 'Plague, Longoss. They've all died from the damned plague. This Mother woman must've kept 'em up there and kept it quiet. We need to leave, now.'

Coppin's eyes glazed over then as she held her hand up to her mouth. 'I had no idea,' she said, more to herself than anyone else. 'How could I have not known... my sisters, all of them.'

Longoss pulled Coppin into a hug and she pressed her head against his shoulder, her eyes staring at nothing in particular as she kept repeating, '...all of them...'

'Longoss, we need to move,' Sears said again, and Longoss nodded reluctantly. 'We'll head to the barracks.'

'No! I told ye, no.

'Longoss, my captain will protect ye from the magistrates, I'm tellin' ye. Ye said ye had information about a mark, what is it?'

Longoss looked away from Sears. 'I don't know.'

The guardsman cursed and his nostrils flared, as did his eyes, briefly.

Longoss looked back at Sears and held his hand up to placate the man. 'But I can find out. *We* can find out when we take the bastards down.'

Coppin stepped forward and looked at Longoss, then at Sears, her face hardening. 'I want in,' she said, in all seriousness.

'No,' both men said, Sears adding, 'I'm not even sure *I'm* in, because it's a dumb idea to say the least.'

'Look at what they did!' Longoss shouted. He turned and pointing at Elleth's bloody body. 'We go for 'em now. Then we can both find out who the mark is and take revenge for Elleth at the same time.'

'Bring them in,' Sears said. 'I'm not going on a killing spree if I can bring them in to face the magistrates.'

Longoss laughed. 'Ye think ye can bring in Black Guild assassins alive, ye fool? And ye think ye can hold that rage in check the minute ye see who slit her throat?'

Chests puffing out, Coppin could see the anger building in both men.

'I told ye to save that rage,' Coppin said, staring at Sears and taking a step forward. 'Save it for them, both of ye. But not now,' she said, turning to Longoss. 'We need to wait. Neither of ye are fit enough to fight much more, especially against assassins.'

'She's right.' Longoss let out a deep breath of frustration. 'We'd be lucky to make it to your barracks and captain, even if I was willing. We need to get out of here and hide, in Dockside.'

'In Dockside?' Sears looked at both of them with incredulity.

'We wouldn't make it out of Dockside,' Longoss said.

'We made it in,' Sears countered, but Longoss shook his head.

'They *let* us in, Sears.' Longoss knew it to be true. If gangers could stop a full patrol from leaving Dockside, then the Black Guild would have no problems stopping two men and a woman.

Sears closed his eyes and leaned back against the wall as the realisation struck him. 'They wanted ye to see this?'

Longoss nodded. 'Aye, I think they did. They don't take kindly to people turning them down. They owned me and I walked away, for her.' Longoss nodded to Elleth's body and he visibly hardened himself to the returning emotions, waving off Coppin's hand as it rested on his arm.

'I thought they'd come for me directly though, I never thought they'd do this, Coppin.' He turned and looked upon the green haired girl, who nodded before moving towards Sears.

'Then let's go hide and keep them from doing it to me.' She felt selfish, but knew Longoss, if not both men, needed something to stop them going off on a berserk rampage. Sears nodded and when Coppin looked to Longoss, he did the same.

Sears motioned for Longoss to lead. 'Where to then?'

'I have a place,' Longoss said, stopping one last time to look at Elleth. *I'll protect Coppin, my love. I gave ye me word on that and I won't be breaking it.*

'We can't take her with us,' Sears said softly, hating himself for being so cold, but knowing it was needed.

'I know.' Longoss allowed himself to be led from the room by Coppin, who couldn't bear to look upon her little sister's body any longer.

Chapter 31: Beresford

Another scream erupted from the throat of Inquisitor Makhell, as Ellis Frane dragged a sharp hook across the man's ribs. The hook caught on each one as Ellis Frane dug deeper down the side of the inquisitor's torso.

'Oh, that hurts does it, inquisitor?'

Fast, heavy breaths were the only response as Ellis Frane withdrew the hooked blade.

'You know, I would never have thought I could do this to anyone.'

'But you want revenge,' the inquisitor managed, his voice hoarse from screaming. He turned his eyes upon his torturer as he hung from the rack he'd used on that very same person.

Ellis Frane nodded slowly as he moved to a table opposite the rack, where he rummaged through a wooden box. 'Not wholly for me though, inquisitor, you see, when you last passed out through the pain of being stretched... oh that is an awful feeling, isn't it?' Ellis Frane turned his head to look upon the inquisitor before continuing. 'I didn't know if I could continue, I thought you'd suffered enough—'

'But?'

Ellis Frane smiled. 'But then I decided to look in the room where you and your order keep the bodies of the girls you rape and murder—'

'Question!' Inquisitor Makhell shouted, his face screwing up with the pain his outburst caused.

'Whatever you choose to call it, my point, inquisitor, is that in seeing the bodies of those girls, and I say girls, because some of them are just that, children... I have a daughter, you know?' Ellis Frane lifted a particularly vicious looking barbed spike from the box and held it up for the inquisitor to see. 'She's twelve years old, about the age of some of those girls in that room, and older than others. You see it was looking upon them, seeing their lifeless corpses that gave me the strength to come back into this room, wake you and continue with what you feel is acceptable to do to others.'

'We have our reasons,' the inquisitor said, his voice little more than a whisper.

'And you truly believe that do you? That Sir Samorl, hero of Altoln who gave his life to save a nation, would want you to carve up little girls, after raping them?' Ellis Frane shouted as he rushed back across the room to the rack. 'Is that what you believe?'

Inquisitor Makhell cried out as the barbed spike plunged into his left shoulder, snagging and jolting all the way. He screamed all the more when Ellis Frane removed it slowly.

'I hate you, all of you!' the royal scribe shouted. 'For what you've done to them, to me... for what you've turned me into!' He stabbed the inquisitor again, several times in the same shoulder as before.

Tears running down his face, Inquisitor Makhell coughed repeatedly, struggling to take in a breath.

Ellis Frane stepped back, breathing heavily as he looked at the mess he'd made of the man's shoulder; shredded muscle and tendons barely allowing the arm to hold onto the body which hung from it.

'Why would you want ancient riddles about the Wizards and Sorcery Guild's tower, Tyndurris? What could it gain your church?'

The inquisitor said nothing as his head hung low, his chest rising and falling with the ragged breaths he was drawing in after his coughing fit. He jumped, however, when Ellis Frane stepped in close and flashed the spike across his vision.

'Access,' he said, almost as quiet as a breath.

'To what? Tyndurris?'

Inquisitor Makhell nodded weakly.

'For what purpose?' Ellis Frane shouted. 'You stretched me for a damned riddle... why?'

'You think,' the inquisitor said, struggling to lift his head as he spoke, 'any of this will make a difference? That those guardsmen will come back for you? That my men won't break down your barricade first and rip you to pieces for what you've done to me?'

Ellis Frane glanced to his hastily erected barricade across the door then, his thoughts switching to the two men who'd said they would come back for him. He'd heard fighting for quite some time after they'd left the room, but it had seemed like a lifetime since they'd gone and he genuinely feared the worst for them.

'They're dead, you fool,' the inquisitor said, a leering grin stretching his bloody mouth as he stared at the royal scribe, who's fears were plain to see. 'It won't be long before I am missed and my men break through here, and when they—'

The inquisitor gurgled and then tried to cough as the barbed spike was jammed into his throat.

'And when they do,' Ellis Frane whispered, his face almost touching Inquisitor Makhell's, whose life was draining from his open throat, 'they'll see what revenge looks like before they take me.'

***

A bloody corpse in a yellow gambeson with a black gryphon rampant emblazoned on its unmoving chest lay on the cold stone of the main archway into Wesson's prison. A bell rang, its clear tone sounding twice, then pausing before sounding twice again as it called the internal guards to the main gate. The sound of metal on metal ringing out and echoing around the stone walls of the courtyard accompanied the sound of the bell.

A young runner who'd brought a letter to the prison's Castellan from the Lord High Constable, faltered as he reached the prison's external gate, a small crossbow bolt embedded deep in his right thigh. The young man collapsed after bravely struggling on two or three steps towards the freedom of Executioners Square, beyond where he'd hoped to rouse the City Guard.

He nearly passed out as he pulled the bolt free from his leg. Doing the best to cope with the agony the action caused, he attempted to crawl onwards, dragging a dark red stain across the cobbles as he went.

As he struggled to pull himself through the opening, using the weight of the slightly open gate to drag himself across the hard ground, another bolt slammed into the back of his head, splitting the links of his maille coif and his skull after that.

The witchunter responsible turned to find a new target to loose his small but deadly bolts at.

Sir Bullen had been summoned to his prison's gate, where a Witchunter General stood with a small force of Samorlian warriors. It had been the second Witchunter General in as many days. The first had come in search of an imprisoned sergeant-at-arms from Tyndurris, just to find the guild's sergeant had escaped hours before and so he, with two of his men and two more of Sir Bullen's, had disappeared down the same tunnels as the escapees and never returned.

Sir Bullen had sent men down to search for the witchunter and his men, but had known it was hopeless. He'd done the same after the sergeant-at-arms' escape, and now... now he had another jumped up Witchunter General stood in his courtyard with a large group of men in tow. He'd hoped that, with the recent letter sent from the Duke of Yewdale, he would have been able to turn away the Samorlians without the use of force.

Alas, the letter had failed and the Witchunter General had insisted, quite aggressively, that he had a mission to carry out and no one was to stand in his way. Sir Bullen and his men, however, had done just that, and for that the young knight was proud.

Sir Bullen's crossbowmen and men-at-arms had initially dropped eight Samorlian warriors as they stormed the archway that opened out into the main courtyard of the prison, but the skirmish had swiftly changed direction for the worse.

Sir Bullen now stood with the last six of his men, young Andrel amongst them, their backs to the outside of the prison's door as the Castellan faced the Witchunter General himself.

'Stand aside, Bullen,' Exley Clewarth said. His face was spattered with fresh blood, and his right hand brandished an equally soiled rapier.

Sir Bullen spat at the Witchunter General's feet. 'It's Lord Castellan to you, witcher!' His six remaining men took heart at the act of defiance. Sir Bullen was counting on it.

Exley Clewarth grinned viciously as his men slowly moved forward. 'Very well *Lord Castellan*, I would rather not shed any more blood, but you leave me little choice.'

The young knight shook his head and pointed his broadsword at his enemy. 'The Lord High Constable gave me strict orders not to admit any more witchunters or their men, and I will stand by that order to the end.' Sir Bullen shifted his weight from one leg to the other and hefted the heater shield he'd been handed by his squire just before the fight broke out. The thirteen year old squire now lay dead in the middle of the courtyard, a rapier wound across his throat.

'To the end it most certainly will be.' Exley snarled as he and his men lunged forward as one.

A witchunter scored a deadly hit on the prison guard to Sir Bullen's far right, the man's padded jack offering little protection against the sharp blade. The body slumped heavily to the ground as the witchunter quickly withdrew his rapier from the dead guard's chest.

Sir Bullen parried an overhead blow from the Witchunter General with his shield and lunged forward with his broadsword in retaliation.

Exley easily side-stepped the lunge as he skipped across to swing his rapier in again, this time towards the knight's leading leg. He found his mark but the blade clanged and vibrated as it connected with Sir Bullen's plated knee. The Witchunter General cursed the armour as Sir Bullen came forward again, crunching his heavy shield into Exley's shoulder and almost knocking him from his feet. Exley regained his balance just in time to parry another lunge from the much stronger knight.

A cry rang out as two of the prison guards attacked a witchunter that had just shot another of their number with a handheld crossbow. One lunged low as Andrel swung in at head height, his aim proving true as the witchunter attempted to parry the lunge aimed at his stomach. Andrel's falchion cut roughly through the witchunter's cheek and deep into his collar bone, dropping the choking man to the floor. The guard who'd lunged, quickly changed direction with his short-sword and thrust it into the fallen man's chest, before pulling it out to deflect an incoming blow from a warrior monk's mace.

Sir Bullen pressed Exley while he had the advantage, raining blow after blow towards the Witchunter General, who staggered backwards under the force, his arm growing numb. Fear that his rapier might break under the force of the heavier weapon was almost all he could think about. He took one tremendous blow which forced him to one knee, but managed to use the low posture to roll sideways away from the knight, who stumbled forward after attempting a downwards chop leaving him unbalanced.

Exley kicked out with his metal studded boot and connected with Sir Bullen's right knee, which buckled under his own weight. The young knight crashed to the stone floor just as a crossbow bolt took another of his men behind him. The man didn't scream, for the bolt had lodged in his throat, which gurgled with blood and air as he dropped his axe to bring both hands up in a futile attempt to stop the bleeding. The guard slid down the rough stone wall and was dead before he hit the ground. Three were left, their backs to the door, hoping for reinforcements from within.

None would come.

Exley jumped to his feet and brought his rapier down hard at Sir Bullen, the knight's shield taking the blow just in time. Sir Bullen thrust at Exley's legs with his broadsword to no avail, whilst the Witchunter General rained blows down upon the splintering shield.

A warrior monk ran into the fray by the door, spinning around a witchunter who tried to find a weak spot in a guard's defence. The witchunter parried a weak blow coming from a shocked guard with an arming sword and buckler, as the warrior monk crunched an ugly looking mace into the guard's hip, crippling the man and folding him double. The guard cried out and dropped heavily to the floor, whilst the witchunter in front of him easily parried the short-sword of the downed man's companion, who tried to defend his fallen comrade. The warrior monk lifted the heavy mace and brought it smashing down onto the fallen guard's head, rendering him unrecognisable.

Sir Bullen managed to smash away a blow from Exley with enough force to throw the Witchunter General away from him, giving him enough time to roll and push himself to his feet, just before another swipe came in towards his head. He parried with his broadsword this time and almost stumbled as his knee gave way. Two warrior monks appeared by Exley's side then, and Sir Bullen readied himself for their attack.

Remember your training, he thought, tightening the grip on his shield and rolling his sword arm. Thinking back, he could hear the former Castellan's voice in his head. *Don't overstep, look to their posture, to their eyes, they'll give themselves away… you should be able to take each one in no more than three moves, you've done it countless times before.*

A horrific scream erupted from behind.

One of the prison guards had managed to thrust his short-sword into a warrior monk's groin – the one who'd dispatched his fallen companion with the terrible mace blow to the head. The monk dropped, screaming like a child, and the satisfaction lit up the guard's face, until the blade of a witchunter's rapier split his skull in two.

Andrel died quickly then, overpowered by relentless blows from witchunters and monks alike, as their brother monk lay howling in a rapidly spreading pool of blood.

Sir Bullen knew he was surrounded as the Witchunter General visibly relaxed. The young knight had nowhere to turn, each movement he calculated left him open to attack. Although fighting the very people who called themselves *His* warriors, Sir Bullen said a silent prayer to Sir Samorl and charged forward, ignoring the pain of his right knee. He smashed his shield into the nearest monk's chest, sending the man skidding over the blood slick cobbles and backwards to crack his un-armoured skull on stone. The blow might have been lucky and one to add to the stories of the local bards, but Sir Bullen would never have the chance to tell of his first real battle, the one where he'd killed more of the Witchunter General's men than any of the prison guards put together.

266

Sir Bullen's sword found its place in the stomach of another warrior monk as he fell forward, his knee giving out once more.

Exley Clewarth took his opportunity and swiftly surged forward to sink his rapier deep into Sir Bullen's neck, the point breaking the links of the knight's maille coif to find the flesh and bone beneath.

After a brief flare of agony, all fell silent for the young knight and Castellan of Wesson's prison. His blood pumped out of the fatal wound and onto the cobbles of his prison's courtyard, but not before he'd felt pride, in both himself and his men.

***

A multitude of lights flickered from lamps, fires and torches, casting a hazy orange glow beneath the forming clouds now filling the dark sky. The sources of those lights were hidden behind twelve foot high stone walls, which enclosed the river town the humans called Beresford.

Overlooking the ancient, walled town, a larger than average leucrota sniffed the floor by its master's booted feet, the animal held firm by a thick rope collar and lead.

Leucrotas were strange creatures, more akin to large cats than dogs, although their heads were unmistakeably canine, despite them lacking any recognisable teeth whatsoever. Their slim yet muscular feline bodies gave way to thick set heads, much resembling the hyenas of the Mhvari Desert. What made the leucrota different, however, apart from their feline bodies, were the bone-like ridges lining the inside of their mouths.

Although leucrotas were naturally carrion eating scavengers, goblins favoured them over dogs for their ability to instil fear into other beings from afar. Their otherworldly chatter was said to sound like the whispering of the dead. Goblins used leucrota at night to spook everything from cattle to humans, because once confusion and fear set in, it gave the goblins a much needed advantage to their raids. Alas, that tactic would not work on Beresford, the river town's protective walls would see to that.

Greater numbers and fire would be needed to bring Beresford to its knees, and the goblin chief who led the approaching war band was confident that, after the victorious battle over the last humans he'd encountered, he could do just that. By morning, the chieftain would be relishing the sound of screaming humans; their men dead, chopped and fed to the leucrota, the children dined on by him and his followers, and the women – the younger prettier ones – brought to him for his pleasure. It would be a good night indeed for his tribe, and he felt safe in the knowledge his force had left the only threat for miles around butchered in the golden fields not half a day's ride to the north west.

***

Despite a near miss with a group of what Biviano could only imagine were

267

gangers, he'd finally managed to make his way out of Dockside and into Park District, where he'd swiftly found a patrol of city guardsmen.

He'd briefly told them enough of what had happened so the sergeant-at-arms agreed to escort him to Park District's barracks. Once there, Biviano requested an audience with the captain of the guard. It was with understandable shock he learnt Captain Prior had been taken ill with what was thought to be symptoms of the plague.

With no one to take the captain's place, Biviano learnt the Constable of Wesson himself was dealing with all of the captain's duties.

Sometime later, after lots of worrying on Biviano's part, he was finally granted an audience with the Earl of Stowold.

'If what you're telling me is true,' Stowold said, his eyes boring into Biviano's for any sign of a lie, 'then we need to act immediately.'

No shit. 'I agree, milord.'

'I don't give a rat's shit-hole whether you agree or not, Biviano,' the Earl snapped. 'We have enough going on in this city, and almost a third of our own men, in this district alone, are dying or already dead from the plague and resulting riots. If what you say is true though, and I've no reason to believe otherwise, then I need to see it for myself.'

Biviano's eyes widened, but he managed to keep the smile from his face. *And here I was hoping to be backed by the captain of the guard, never mind the bloody Constable of Wesson.*

'The Samorlian Church has been ordered to halt all activity by the King himself, and I for one, aren't going to let the fact they're ignoring that slide.' He pulled a thin chain on the wall which rang a bell elsewhere. Both men stood in awkward silence for a few moments before Stowold continued. 'I'm surprised you left your partner, Biviano. Especially since I hear the captain has never managed to separate the two of you.'

Biviano's obvious relief at the constable's agreement to act on his news fell from his face as the words left the Earl's lips. He nodded slowly and scratched under his arm, wincing as he did so before answering. 'Aye, well Sears wanted to go, sire, and we both knew he was this Elleth girl's best bet.'

'Split up over a whore,' Stowold said, clearly amused, 'and here I was thinking you two were lovers, by all accounts from Captain Prior that is.'

Biviano bristled, despite it coming from his superior.

'There's no ulterior motives with the lass, sire. Sears is saving her as I would've done, nothing more. It is also leading us to information regarding the Black Guild, as I already informed you,' he said, the latter in an upper district accent.

'Yes, I'm sure it is,' Stowold said, clearly unconvinced and not missing the accent change either.

'As for Sears and I,' Biviano continued, 'that is absurd! Anyhow, even if I were into blokes,' he added, back to his lower district accent, 'ye think I'd want that hairy bastard?'

Stowold laughed and then shook his head in disbelief, never quite knowing what was going on when he was hearing about or dealing with Biviano and Sears. *Where are you from anyway Biviano? Come to think of it, I don't even remember when either of you were recruited by Captain Prior, never mind from where, or who trained you?* Before Stowold could voice his questions, his squire appeared at the door.

'You called, my lord?' the squire said, replying to the bell Stowold had used.

'Prepare my armour, weapons and have the stable prepare my horse.'

'Destrier or town horse, my lord?'

'Destrier,' Stowold confirmed.

The boy nodded and turned to leave, stopping just long enough to hear Stowold's last words. 'Oh, and send a messenger to Lord Yewdale. Inform him I'm marching on the Samorlian Cathedral, in person.'

'My lord,' the squire acknowledged, before leaving the room.

This time, Biviano couldn't help but smile, and the constable threw him a wink before dismissing him.

I may be over the bloody moon and grateful for ye marching on the bastards, Stowold, but don't be getting no funny ideas, Biviano thought with a shudder. He left the Earl's room swiftly.

***

Fal and the group had arrived at the walled town at dusk. They'd slowed their horses after a good hour or so of pushing them hard, knowing the poor beasts needed rest, and so had continued the rest of the way to Beresford at a fast walk.

Fal and Sav had protested bitterly about leaving Baron Brackley and his men to face the goblins alone, but had given up after being shot down by Correia time and time again. Even Errolas agreed with the woman, and that, in the end, was what silenced Fal and his friend. They both knew that although not of their species, the elf would never leave anyone to face such vile creatures unless he had no other choice, and the importance of their mission was such that he, nor any of the group, had that choice.

The rest of the ride had been spent discussing whether the elves would have the means to, or even agree to help Wesson with its plague. Errolas hoped they would, but admitted he didn't know enough about such things to be able to say for sure. They also discussed who might be following them after the smoke signal Correia has spotted. Sav had named the Samorlians immediately, to which all in the group had agreed was quite possible.

The entrance to Beresford was large, nowhere near as large as either of Wesson's gates, but big all the same. It was straddled by a stone gatehouse which housed two large wooden gates. A small door stood in the corner of the left hand gate and a smaller hatch in the top centre of that. The gates had closed as dusk fell and as the group arrived. Gleave dismounted, walked to the door and hammered on it with the haft of his axe. The hatch opened inwards and a dirty, wrinkled face with blood-shot eyes peeked through. 'What?'

Sav chuckled.

'Kind gatekeeper, do bid us enter. We are of the King's own forces and require shelter for the night.' All but Correia and Mearson were surprised by Gleave's polite manner.

The gatekeeper looked around at them all suspiciously in the dim light. 'A few weirdoes round here of late. Ye not be of them lot are ye?'

Gleave shook his head. 'No master gatekeeper, we are King Barrison's subjects and loyal citizens of Altoln.' Gleave managed a very regal bow.

'Hmmm… less of that here or the locals will think ye're a weirdo.' The man burst into a cackling, rather high pitched laugh and slammed the hatch shut.

Gleave turned to the group and shrugged.

'Like bloody children,' Correia said, walking her horse a little way from the group.

'Great. Well done Gleave.' Mearson clapped his hands towards his friend. 'What The Three was that bowing shite about, eh?'

Before Gleave could respond, the creaking, clunking sound of large bolts moving on the inside of the gate brought a smile to his face. 'My charm, you see.'

Everyone laughed heartily, bar Correia, who rolled her eyes as she rode back over.

The large gate on the left swung in then and two lightly armoured ashmen walked out, spears in hands as they beckoned the riders in. Once inside the gate, the group were told to dismount. Their mounts, they were told, would be taken to the central stable and their weapons to the neighbouring armoury.

'Our weapons?' Fal asked, confused.

'Aye, yer weapons, Earl Beresford's law,' the older ashman said, his tall ash-shafted spear shifting in his hands as he leant on it lazily.

Fal looked to Correia and was surprised to see both her and the two pathfinders unbuckling their weapon belts and handing them over.

Mearson pointed two fingers at the man who took his weapons. 'Got my eyes on you, ashman, and I'll remember who took these, you can be sure of that.'

The old gatekeeper, who stood to one side, bottle in hand, coughed as his cackling laugh erupted once more.

The younger ashman reddened as he took Mearson's weapon belt. He placed it on a cart next to the inside of the gatehouse and then moved on to Errolas who handed over his unstrung bow, arrow-filled quiver and sword. Fal noticed none of them had handed over knives or daggers and so he unbuckled his belt and handed over his falchion, leaving his seax knife in his boot. Sav and Starks did the same and the group set off into the town, Correia leading the way.

Starks asked what they were to do next and Correia told them all they were to take their much needed rest in an inn she knew near the river, before crossing in the morning. Their horses and weapons would be walked across by ashmen and could be picked up at the eastern gate once they left that side of Beresford. Sav's face lit up at the mention of the inn and Fal admitted he couldn't wait to get his dry mouth around a good tankard of ale.

Before the group made it halfway to the inn Correia was raving about, the first fire arrow fell from the sky.

Chapter 32: Wesson's Bowels

Taking the rest of the prison had proved quick and easy for the skilled witchunters and warrior monks. Almost a third of the prison's guards had fallen ill with the rapidly spreading plague and a handful were already dead. The bell – rang by a terrified young boy – served Exley Clewarth and his men, as it brought the remaining guards to the main entrance in small numbers. As soon as they ran into the main entrance hall they were cut down by hand-held crossbows, rapiers and maces until there were none left to come to the call of the chiming bell, or none that dared.

It had been some time since the last guard had been slaughtered, and Exley had led his men through the lower levels of the prison shortly after. The Witchunter General had ordered the release of any prisoners they passed who looked capable in a fight. Those men were given a choice by the Witchunter General. 'Return to your cell to rot,' he'd said, 'or fight for us. When this is over, you will be free to go, with no questions asked by me or my men. All I ask is, you follow my orders and ask no questions in return.'

One ganger had immediately asked where they were going. He received a swift cudgel blow to the back of the head by a warrior monk for speaking out, which left the man unconscious in the narrow, damp and foul smelling tunnel. The last witchunter to pass the prone figure thrust his rapier into the man's back to make sure he wouldn't get up again, whilst the steadily increasing group carried on deeper and deeper into the prison's winding tunnels.

Egan Dundaven shoved a prisoner from his path as he approached Exley Clewarth. 'We could be searching for hours, if not days, General. Samorl be with us… even weeks at this rate. Is it not wiser to split up?' Egan had hung back in the initial fight at the prison's gate. Not through fear, but through the distaste he had of murdering fellow Altolnans for no better reason other than their getting in the way of the Witchunter General's goal. He'd shot one guard who'd attacked him directly, but apart from that his sword was clean and his crossbow bolts almost fully stocked.

'You're right Master Dundaven, we could, and if that's what it takes, that's what we will do. Or do you fancy informing the Grand Inquisitor of our failure?'

Egan shook his head. 'No, General, of course not.'

Exley disagreed with the mission as much as Egan, but he couldn't show that in front of the men, after all, many of them were Horler Comlay's not his. He knew there would be at least one that would run squealing to Horler upon his return, or to the Grand Inquisitor himself. Exley had argued against the mission and would have preferred to travel back south, where he could continue his command and not risk being strung up by Wesson's magistrates. The Grand Inquisitor had ordered the capture and burning of the traitorous gnome, however, and so that was what he was going to do, no matter how long or what it took to do it.

Exley headed down another stinking corridor as Egan asked, 'How about the prisoners down here then, we could ask them if they know of anything? General Comlay was said to have entered here in pursuit of the sergeant-at-arms from Tyndurris and hasn't been seen since. For all we know, he found the tunnels and has chased the sergeant through them. Wherever he's gone, some prisoner must have seen or heard something.'

The General stopped, almost causing Egan to crash into his back.

The whole column of thirty or so men behind the General stopped too, with witchunters and monks slapping prisoners who started to ask questions.

'I don't give a shit where he's gone, where he is or if he's still alive, Master Dundaven.' Exley closed his eyes and sighed heavily. *Well done pushing me into that outburst, Dundaven, it will likely cost me once Horler hears of it.* Exley paused, took a deep breath and turned on Egan, who flinched instinctively. 'That being said, Master Dundaven, you may be right about the prisoners knowing something.' Exley turned to face those behind him. 'Who knows these tunnels?' he shouted. 'Anyone?'

'I do, sire.' A barrel chested man with a bald head and hands like shovels pushed his way to the front.

'Good man,' Exley said. 'Do you know anything about what we were just talking about? A Witchunter General who passed through here and never came back out?'

The large man nodded. 'There were rumours, sire. They went down to the north east tunnel. Goes by the nutters' cells! You think it stinks here, wait until you smell it down there.' The large man grinned and Exley beckoned him forward. Egan had to squeeze against the cold stone wall whilst the large man pushed past.

'Can you guide us? You'll be rewarded,' Exley said, placing a hand on the man's shoulder in a show of friendship. Egan tried not to laugh out at the poor display, but the brutish man grinned again and seemed to buy it.

'Sure I can, we can get to it this way, won't take long at all to get there, then down, down into the prison's bowels and past the nutters, although I dunno what's down there, never been that far down before see, for I ain't no nutter. Ha!'

'Yes, funny… now on you go,' Exley said, handing the man a burning torch. 'Take this and keep me informed where we are and what you're doing.'

The passages were lit with the odd oil lamp or torch, but it was still extremely dark and so a handful of Exley's men had lit extra torches to help them find their way.

The heavy set prisoner – stripped down to his waist and wearing only a pair of linen braes – had been true to his word. Not long after he'd taken the lead, had he taken them to the 'nutters' as he called them, and beyond. The prisoners down there didn't dare reach through their bars at these men though, not after the first one lost his hand in an attempt. The stench was awful and all the witchunters, bar the General, lifted their scarves over their faces to try and block the smell of human excrement, sweat and blood.

As the last of the column passed the nutters' cages, the large man at the front halted and shrugged, before turning to Exley. 'Dead end, sire,' he said, pointing to the end of the tunnel, the light of his torch revealing a solid wall. 'Guess we'll have to head back?'

'It doesn't make sense,' Egan said, from behind the General. 'Why would they build a tunnel leading nowhere?'

Exley's mouth had stretched into an uncontrollable smile. 'Because it leads somewhere, Master Dundaven, I'm damn sure of that. Search the wall,' Exley shouted, as he pushed past the large man in front. He felt his way down the rough stone looking for some sort of lever, trigger... something to give away a hidden entrance.

Many of the men looked at each other with confusion before running their hands across the walls either side of where they stood.

The large prisoner at the front followed Exley, as did Egan, but they didn't go as far as the General.

Without warning, a loud rumbling stopped everyone in their tracks.

'Whoa... stop there, General,' Egan said, looking up at the rough stone ceiling above.

Exley took a couple of steps forward, daring himself to touch the wall of the dead end despite the noise and Egan's warning. When he did, an incredibly loud splitting groan and rumble announced the following collapse of the roof.

The Witchunter General dropped into a crouch and wrapped his arms about his head, knocking his hat askew in the process.

As the noise abated and the dust settled, Exley realised he was trapped; cut off from the others in total, dusty, silence.

Climbing to his feet, the Witchunter General looked around and saw nothing. He had no torch and even though his pupils were dilating as he strained to look around, there wasn't enough natural light to make anything out in the black tunnel. He pulled up his scarf and pressed it against his mouth to avoid breathing in the dust filled air.

He began searching around behind him for the fallen rocks of the cave-in. *No rubble?* Scrambling across the floor, he found nothing but small stones.

His knuckles scraped against a rough wall then, much the same as the one in the tunnel he'd just been inspecting. He put both hands on it, palms forward as he felt around the rough, but clearly cut stone wall.

How is this possible?

There had been a cave-in, no doubt about it, yet there was a solid, rough, but flat wall where he thought he'd come from. He called out then, not too loud for fear of another cave-in. There was no reply. He frantically ran his hands all over the wall he couldn't see; searching for a crack, a hole, anything that would signify the wall was some kind of door, but there was nothing, nothing but the occasional smooth line running in seemingly random directions and...

Patterns?

The smooth lines were runes, but from what language he had no idea. He searched on, the fear building inside him as he pictured himself trapped, starving to death, dying alone in the dusty pitch black bowls of Wesson.

***

Egan Dundaven hit the deck, his hands over his head as the roof caved in. The large prisoner just in front of him did the same and almost every one of the thirty or so men behind them dived to the floor; over each other and some back up the tunnel.

Dust filled the air and coughing erupted throughout the column. One man cried out, his leg pinned to the floor by a rapier; the prisoner had thrown himself onto a witchunter who'd hit the floor first. A swift crack to the head ceased the man's whimpering and Egan just managed to see one of the warrior monks standing up, fresh blood staining his mace.

'Is everyone well?' a witchunter from behind Egan asked. 'Except for the obvious,' he added under his breath.

A chorus of confirmations followed and Egan turned back to make eye contact with the witchunter. He beckoned the man to him and both of them made their way forward to the rubble littering the tunnel.

'Help us dig,' Egan said, as he turned to the large man who'd led them there.

The man was sat on the floor rubbing his head, and merely grunted at the request. 'What's the point, he's a dead man and so will we all be if we don't get out of this old tunnel. The whole bloody lot could come down. There're other lower tunnels, you know? Whatever you're looking for could easily be down one of them.'

Egan caught something in the man's eye when he mentioned the other tunnels, and it struck him as strange that a prisoner would know so much about the prison's layout.

'Help us dig,' the second witchunter said. 'It wasn't a request.'

The prisoner felt the presence of someone behind him. He looked up and saw a large warrior monk brandishing a blooded mace. The prisoner nodded reluctantly and pulled himself to his feet with the hand of a young witchunter who'd come forward with the warrior monk.

Before anyone knew anything of it, the large man pulled a dagger from the witchunter's belt and jammed it into the monk's throat. Gurgling, the monk dropped to his knees, his mace clattering to the ground as he tried hopelessly to fend off his attacker with half-hearted slaps. The large man quickly withdrew the dagger and the Monk pressed his hands to the wound, desperately trying to stem the flow of blood, before slumping helplessly to the ground.

Half stunned at what had just happened, the young witchunter fumbled for his rapier as he saw the prisoner turn on him with the blooded dagger.

An audible thud caused the prisoner to jerk forward as a crossbow bolt plunged into his back, and a heartbeat later another found the back of his skull. He was dead as he crashed to the ground over the outstretched legs of the dying monk. The young witchunter who's dagger the prisoner had stolen looked up thankfully to his two comrades. Face flushed, he nodded before turning back to the other prisoners. He swiftly gave orders for them to move forward and help shift the rubble, for it was too late to do anything for the now dead monk.

No one else tried anything, and as they came forward to move the rubble, Egan realised the large man he'd just killed was probably a prison guard. He imagined he'd been trained to lead anyone looking for the hidden tunnels on a wild-goose chase around the prison until the City Guard could arrive. He felt a fool for following the man, but it'd been Exley who'd ordered the man forward and so Egan felt embarrassingly satisfied in the knowledge no blame could come his way. Egan wasn't even sure Exley was alive to chastise him for anything at all anyway.

With that in mind, Egan Dundaven turned back to the rubble, and if he hadn't, he may not have believed what he saw then. The first prisoner to try and lift a stone fell straight through it and hit a solid wall on the other side. The whole cave-in flickered like a candle then and blinked out, replaced by the same wall Exley Clewarth had reached before the ceiling had fallen in.

***

After entering the deserted street outside Mother's brothel, it wasn't long until Longoss led Sears and Coppin into the back door of a house; a door marked with a black cross.

Despite both Sears' and Coppin's protests, they followed Longoss in, neither of them wishing to linger on the streets longer than was necessary. Both were relieved to find, once inside, that the house was uninhabited and the black cross had been painted there by Longoss himself, shortly after he'd learnt what it meant.

Sears peered through the gap in the window shutters. 'And no one knows this is yer place, Longoss?'

'Can't guarantee that,' Longoss said, as he painfully sat in an old, wooden chair.

'Then we move on,' Sears said forcefully, looking across the small room at the man who was now staring at the floor, clearly still in pain over what they'd found at Mother's.

'Ye both need time to rest and heal before we move anywhere else.' Coppin said, noticing both men were shying away from contact with various parts of their bodies. 'Neither of ye're in any fit state to move, let alone fight should the need arise.'

Stepping away from the window, Sears reached behind him, wincing as he did so before pulling forth a small flask. 'I may have something for that,' he said, holding his meaning up for them both to see. Longoss looked up, lips pursed and brow furrowed as he took in the small flask.

'What is it?' he said eventually.

'Honestly? I'm not sure, but it works wonders; fixed this up in a matter of hours.' Sears poked his finger through the hole in his maille hauberk.

Longoss' eyes widened. 'Then it must be good.' He held up his hand and Sears threw him the flask, after taking a huge swig for himself and replacing the cork.

'Great, there'll be nowt left...' Longoss stopped what he was saying when he realised the flask was full. Looking back to a grinning Sears, he pulled the cork with his gold teeth and knocked back what he imagined was the whole contents. The bitter taste almost made him gag and Sears laughed as he held his hand out for the flask, which was already re-filling itself.

'Magic,' Sears said, catching it and placing it back in his pouch.

'Literally,' Coppin said, eyes wide.

'Sorry lass, ye could do with a nip yerself, methinks.' Sears held out the flask and Coppin took a quick swig, followed by a string of curses.

'Ha! Good girl.' Sears took the flask back from Coppin and returned it to its pouch.

'That'll sort ye out, Coppin.' Longoss showed his teeth, before literally pissing himself where he sat.

'Longoss!' Coppin was disgusted, but not surprised. 'Mother said ye're known for doing that. It's disgusting.'

The big man looked to her, confused.

'I know why he does it,' Sears said, sitting on the floor opposite Longoss.

'Why I do what?'

'Piss. Your. Self,' Coppin said, pronouncing every word and pointing at Longoss as she did so.

Sears nodded. 'Quite clever really. It's a diversionary tactic. He does it to throw his opponents in a fight. Last thing they'll think about someone who's pissed themselves, is they're a real threat, am I right?' Sears smiled at Coppin and looked to Longoss expectantly.

Longoss frowned. 'Never thought of it like that,' he said in all honesty.

'Then why?' Sears and Coppin both asked.

'Weak bladder,' he said, rubbing his stomach. 'Plus, I've never had anyone else but me to think of, so why bother making the effort to find somewhere to go, when here will do just fine, same as any other animal.'

Coppin's face screwed up as she moved across the room and sat on the floor next to Sears. 'But ye're not an animal, Longoss.'

Longoss merely nodded, his eyes drifting away from them as he took a deep breath.

'Longoss, ye're no animal,' she said again, staring right at him.

He looked back at her eventually and smiled; no teeth. 'I held it once ye know, me dick. I held it hard and long, not wanting me da to find me pissing miself. Ye know what happened?'

Coppin shook her head and Sears just looked on.

'I pissed miself anyway, but instead of piss, it were blood.'

'Longoss, that's awful,' Coppin said, but the big guy just grinned gold.

'Not what me da said, beat me silly that night he did. Still, he never lasted long after that.

'I am an animal though, Coppin, we all are. Just some act it more than others is all.' *And if I'd been less of one and never joined that guild, then Elleth would still be alive.*

'This is all lovely,' Sears said, much to Coppin's annoyance, 'but I'd rather hear about the Black Guild and whatever it is they have planned.'

Longoss nodded. 'Aye, I imagine ye do, Sears, and I'd be telling ye if I knew, but all I know is there's something big coming; to be doing all of this to me for turning down one mark…' Longoss looked up at the low ceiling, lifting his hands to his head and rubbing hard.

'This has been extreme then, even for them?' Sears asked.

Longoss nodded again. 'Even for them. They don't take kindly to assassins turning down marks. They'll even kill one to prove that point, but that's rare indeed for one with my experience. All of this though…'

He was becoming animated and clearly agitated as he thought about what they'd done to him; to Elleth.

'It's alright, Longoss,' Coppin said.

'It's not though is it?' Longoss shouted, surging to his feet.

Sears stood too, and held his hands out in front of him. 'Calm down big guy.'

Coppin followed them both up.

'If I'd taken the mark, Elleth would still be alive, but I'd have broken me word to her not to kill. I was damned either way, but least she'd be alive.'

'Alive in that shit-hole,' Coppin said, tears wetting her eyes. 'That was no life, Longoss, trust me. She's gone, aye, but I'm not and I need ye to be strong. I need ye to train me, like you.'

Both men looked at her then.

'Why is that so hard to believe? That I want to be able to fend for miself?' She crossed her arms and raised her eyebrows.

'There's fending for yerself and then there's what I do… did,' Longoss said. 'Sears here would do better for ye than me.'

'Well it ain't Sears that swore to Elleth to rescue me, and that means more than dragging me from that bastard in the cathedral and dropping me in the middle of Dockside being hunted by the Black fucking Guild!'

Longoss stared at Coppin, as did Sears.

Coppin forced herself to calm down. Wiping her tears away she looked at both men. 'I'm a distraction to ye both and if they come, Longoss, ye can't kill, ye can't break yer word to Elleth. Let me help. Let me fight. I deserve that, after what they did to me, to me sisters, I deserve to pay the bastards back miself.'

Sears' smile at Coppin was one of sympathy as Longoss spoke. 'I can't train ye to do anything in the time it might take 'em to come, Coppin, I just can't. It takes years to train, to reach a level needed to beat the likes of those they'll send.'

'So ye've done it before? Trained assassins?' Coppin asked, hope lighting her face.

Longoss dropped back into the chair and nodded. 'Aye lass, one – a girl much like yerself.'

'Lovely,' Sears said. 'I bet she's a peach.'

Ignoring Sears' comment, Coppin continued. 'If it's time we need, then we'll move again, now. Hide somewhere they can't find us until we're ready for 'em.'

'What happened to us not being fit enough?' Sears said, rounding on Coppin.

'The way ye both surged to yer feet a moment ago and the already fading bruises on yer faces tells me yer magic juice works well enough for ye both to move again. I can certainly feel it working on me. Anyway, I ain't suggesting we go looking for no fights, I'm suggested we go deeper into hiding.'

Longoss was shaking his head to match Sears. 'It's no good Coppin, we can't hide forever and they'll be looking for us even now. I wouldn't be surprised if they knew we're here in fact.'

'Great,' Sears said, moving back to and looking through the gap in the window shutters again, one hand on his short-sword.

'So, what would ye do if they burst in now, Longoss?' Coppin said, moving to stand in front of the man. 'Ye can't kill 'em, can ye? So what then? Ye just watch me die whilst ye tickle the bastards?'

'Ye're being stupid, girl.' Longoss rested his head in his hands.

'And ye're being stubborn,' she replied, dropping down so she was face to face with him. 'Ye want to take the fight to them don't ye?'

Longoss looked up into her eyes and nodded once.

'Well so do I, damn ye, but I need yer help to do it and ye need mine—'

'And I need answers about this bloody mark,' Sears said, turning to face them both. 'I didn't send my partner off on his own so I could sit around discussing shit and bollocks.'

'Nor did ye do it so ye could get killed by assassins in the street,' Coppin said. 'But that's what'll happen if we go for 'em now, or try and get out of Dockside, isn't that right?' She aimed the latter to Longoss, who reluctantly nodded.

'Then what're we gonna do?' Sears said.

'We do what I say and we move. We go deeper into hiding and ye both do all ye can to train me to fend for miself.'

Neither man said a word, but both stared at each other. Coppin turned back to Longoss, placed a hand on each knee and looked into his eyes. 'Don't leave me,' she said, her bottom lip trembling ever so slightly.

Longoss sat straight and leaned in towards her. 'I won't, Coppin, I ain't going nowhere.' *And I almost gave ye me word, but I'm not sure I can do that no more, for I don't know if I'll break it.*

'Well *I* am.' She sprung to her feet and made for the door.

Sears rushed forward and barred her path, shaking his head as she looked at him.

'I'm going and if ye ain't for leaving me, ye best be with me, both of ye.'

Both men looked at each other and both men sighed.

'Ye won't let up, will ye?' Sears said.

Coppin shook her head. 'Would you? If it were yer brother or sister they'd killed?'

Sears' mind drifted immediately. *Biviano… ye better be safe, ye little weasel, and gods I hope ye got to Ellis Frane in time. What sort of men are we, forgetting him like that; too caught up in trying to save this lass. Wherever ye are Biviano, I can't help ye now, old friend, for if ye're too late for Ellis Frane and I don't do all I can to help this one, then it were all for naught.*

'No,' Sears said eventually, 'I wouldn't let up.'

'Then help me.'

Sears nodded. 'Alright, lass, I'll do what I can.'

They both looked to Longoss, who sat in his chair and stared back at them.

All I can do now, Elleth, Longoss thought, *is my best for yer sister.*

'As will I,' he said finally, standing and moving towards them both.

Sears wrinkled his nose. *I'll tell ye what ye could do Longoss, change those stinking braes.*

***

Exley Clewarth slumped against the solid wall, his hands grazed after what seemed like hours of running them along the rough stone, searching for a way out of the pitch black and silence assaulting his senses.

Silence? No… not any more.

There was a noise, very, very faint, but there was a knocking sound coming from…

'Shit,' he whispered, as he realised he couldn't pinpoint the direction of the knocking.

He gently banged the back of his head against the stone wall in time with the knocking, his wide brimmed hat lost somewhere in the darkness. As he continued to bump his head against the wall, he whispered a prayer to Sir Samorl. When he finished reciting the prayer, he realised the knocking was growing louder, ever so slightly, but definitely louder.

He strained his ears to listen for a direction, but it was hopeless. Could it be the others, trying to hammer through the wall behind him? Exley turned then and pressed his ear against the cold stone, praying to hear a voice or anything that would let him know they were close. All there was, was the knocking… over and over again, growing louder but only slightly, as time dragged on by.

What seemed like another hour passed before he could determine where the sound was coming from; it wasn't the wall. He tilted his head and slowly drew his rapier, wincing at the sound it made as it scraped from the scabbard. He climbed to his feet for the first time in what felt like an age, and held his breath to see if his movement had changed anything. The knocking continued, and so finally he dared, in the blackness, to venture forward, his left hand outstretched while his right held up his rapier defensively.

Exley shuffled his feet forward bit by bit, aware of the stone walls surrounding him. He worried about walking face first into one, and so he crept on, ever so quietly towards the sound that continued to come from... where? In front of him?

After a dozen or so pounding heartbeats, he suddenly felt unsure about leaving the wall behind. It was his only anchor to his men and the potential way out. Shaking his head, he steeled himself and shuffled his feet forward a little more.

His leading foot hit something, something soft. It made him cringe as his imagination threw all sorts of images at him. Exley Clewarth was no coward. He'd faced everything from goblins and hobyahs, to werewolves and vampyrs, but he'd always had light; a torch at least, to show him the way; show him his enemy. His keen senses helped of course, excellent hearing and smell, but his eyes were his tools in a fight and he found himself sweating profusely at the thought of being attacked whilst effectively blind.

It moved. *Oh, Sir Samorl, no,* he thought, as the soft... whatever it was... at his foot moved; not much, but enough for him to realise it was alive. He slowly and silently turned his rapier point down and then thrust hard.

The scream was a terrible assault on ears that had heard nothing but a faint knocking for who knew how long. He stabbed again and again until his rapier repeatedly struck stone.

The screaming stopped... as did the knocking.

Chapter 33: Fire & Ice

Night had fallen completely across Beresford as the arrows fell; some lit, some not and it was those invisible missiles falling from the black sky that kept most of the townsfolk inside their homes.

The men-at-arms and crossbowmen on the town wall cringed behind the ramparts as deathly whispers emanated from the darkness; the voices of the dead come to haunt them in their walled town.

A large ball of fire whooshed through the air – over the cowering men on the wall – to crash into a thatched roof, sending sparks high into the night sky. People screamed from within and a man ran from the front door. As soon as he set out, an unlit arrow slammed into his chest, sending him crashing back into the blazing inferno.

It didn't take long before fires jumped from building to building, despite the few townsfolk who braved the arrows to rush around with buckets of water. Those who managed to avoid being struck by arrows still failed to slow the spreading flames, which easily caught hold on the wood and thatch of the closely packed buildings.

People screamed and bells rang all over Beresford.

A stone church to one end of the town opened its doors to let flocks of people through until it could hold no more. The keep, which stood just a couple of hundred yards from the northernmost point of the town, opened its doors too, but filled much quicker, for the squat stone tower had nowhere near the space needed to give its townspeople refuge. Many more people piled across the wide stone bridge leading to the east side of the River Norln. That press of people hindered the soldiers who attempted to cross the bridge the other way, to reinforce their comrades on the wall.

'Watch out,' Fal shouted, as a ball of fire crashed into a building nearby, sending burning debris scattering through the air.

Starks fell back and pressed himself against the wall of the bakery they were using as shelter, its overhanging first floor protecting them from the falling arrows.

The group had almost reached the inn Correia had spoken of when the warning bells had begun to chime. The first fire arrows had fallen in the north of the town, almost half a mile away, but it didn't take long for the bells to ring and the people to react.

It hadn't been long before they realised the town's attackers were the goblin force the Baron of Ullston had ridden against; his bloodied head had landed at their feet along with his squire's and several others, clearly launched by some sort of catapult.

Before the horror of it could sink in, Fal had called for them to head to the wall, to reinforce the defenders there.

Correia grabbed his arm as he set out, and hauled him with surprising strength back under the bakery's overhang, as did Gleave with Starks.

'We'll do no good here, sergeant,' Correia shouted over the din, and Fal glared at her angrily.

'So we leave again,' he snapped, 'to run and hide like before? Leaving good men to die? Do you know what the goblins will do should they breach the wall Correia? Do you?' He wrenched his arm from her grip and punched the wall beside him.

'We all bloody well know,' Mearson shouted. 'The women and children will get it the worst. You ever seen what they do, Fal? 'Cause we have, alright, and it ain't pretty. But Correia's right, we can't do any good here, not a handful of us verses a tribe. The wall can hold if more troops arrive from the other side of the river, and then they'll have a good fighting chance of awaiting true reinforcements. This town has stood for centuries, I'm sure it can hold out to a few goblins.' Mearson leant back against the wall and knocked the hilt of his sword against it, his eyes avoiding Fal's, who wondered who the pathfinder was trying to convince.

'Falchion,' Correia said calmly. 'We have a job to do, a mission from the King himself and it will affect far more lives than those in this town if we fail... if we fall in battle here tonight. Wesson is relying on us, hell, the kingdom is relying on us. Do not think we enjoy walking away from a fight, Fal, nor do it lightly.'

Fal nodded slowly and looked to Starks, who was staring at the sky, his eyes glazed over.

Another ball of fire smashed into the middle of the street in front of them and they all turned and threw themselves to the ground as flaming shrapnel scattered across the area.

'Is everyone alright?' Errolas shouted.

Everyone *was* alright, physically, but far from alright with regards to leaving the town to fend for itself.

'We need to make for the bridge,' Gleave said, pointing the way, just as a hail of fire arrows struck the buildings around them. People screamed and dogs barked, one ran into the street and was struck by an unseen, unlit arrow that killed it instantly.

'The horses... our weapons,' Sav said, his voice utterly dejected, 'they won't have been taken across yet.' He too had witnessed farms overrun by goblins, had witnessed what they did to people, to children, and he fought against the memories as the thought of leaving these people behind weighed on him tremendously.

'I'm staying,' Starks announced. 'I can man the wall with my crossbow, it's far better for the town's defence than in the field.' He looked around for someone to agree, to give him leave to run to the wall; to aid the men who were screaming orders and crying out in pain. They were easily heard, even from so far away.

'No,' Correia said, surprising Starks. 'You were assigned to me and I want you with us. You're a brave soldier, Starks, and I might not be one to normally say it, but I feel safer with us all together. That means you too.'

Starks might have felt pride if he didn't feel so torn between the group and the town he so wanted to defend. In the end he merely nodded, resigning himself to a mission he'd accepted back in Wesson.

The warning bells changed suddenly, rang faster.

Gleave cursed and looked about the group. 'They're in!' He took a step forward to scan the streets towards the wall.

'Surely not already?' Fal mirrored Gleave, searching the flickering orange light of the streets for signs of none human movement. The occasional townsperson ran past, some with buckets of water, but the fires were spreading too fast for that now.

'The Earl of Beresford is in Wesson,' Correia said. She too was scanning the darkness. 'He was there with a large contingent of men when the King ordered the quarantine. It will have seriously depleted the garrison here,' she explained, answering the question of how the goblins could have breached such a well defended town. 'We need to move to the bridge and quick.'

'We need our weapons,' Sav protested, and Correia hesitated.

'To the armoury then. It's near the bridge anyway. Hurry!' she shouted, after looking back down the street they'd travelled. She'd seen a man with a water bucket run between two buildings before being hit by a fire arrow in the back. The arrow had come from ground level.

'Shit! Move, quick,' Gleave shouted, and the group bolted with nothing but knives and daggers in their hands.

Mearson led the group past the inn they'd been heading to, down a side street and out onto a wider street. They looked down it, away from the bridge and towards the wall where they saw strange looking dogs running in and out of buildings not yet alight.

Over a dozen ashmen ran into the street further up from the group then. They set their long spears towards the wall. One row stood, whilst the others knelt in front, creating a linear schiltron across the street. A crowd of goblins, the tallest no more than four and a half feet, came screeching round a corner from the direction of the main gate. The goblins loosed their small, wood and bone re-curve bows and three of the ashmen in the defensive line dropped immediately, one rolling and crying out from the arrow embedded in his leg. The other two were dead.

The goblins, small as they were with beady eyes and greasy pock marked skin, bared their crooked teeth at the ashmen before surging forward. Many of them leapt without any sense of self-preservation onto the bristling wall of spears. Several were skewered, but more came on, throwing hand axes and loosing their short arrows at point blank range. The ashmen fought well, but without shields to defend against the missiles, they took serious losses. After using their spears to kill the first wave of goblins, the half dozen ashmen who still stood drew axes, short-swords and small maces, ready for the next group that were even now charging down the street, howling like banshees.

The goblins stopped then as a line, throwing insults and missiles alike at the remaining ashmen. Laughing and pointing, jumping up and down, they suddenly howled to the sky as a dozen pigs appeared, pushing their way out from the centre of the goblins. Not wild boars, but simple farm pigs, squealing and kicking as a handful of goblins prodded them forward with crude spears of their own.

The pigs, which had the light of the burning buildings glistening off their wet hides, charged forward to escape their tormentors. The ashmen, as nervous as they were at the loss of their companions, looked to each other in confusion.

From the line of goblins, two small archers stepped forward with fire arrows nocked on their bowstrings. They loosed their burning arrows at the pigs then and the creatures erupted into flames, squealing insanely as they bustled into each other, spreading the fire across the oil painted over their bodies.

The ashmen broke, running for the cover of open doors and side streets as the crazed animals crashed into buildings and ashmen alike, desperately trying to escape the searing flames blistering their skin. The houses nearby went up like bonfires and the soldiers and families within screamed as the goblins lurched forward again, laughing and howling to the sky in triumph.

The foul creatures smashed windows and doors, piling into the few buildings yet to catch fire on the street, but many more headed for the bridge.

Fal's group, hardly believing what they'd just witnessed, ran on as fast as they could. They continued to follow Mearson, and eventually, as a group, burst through the door of the armoury by the river, but not before they noticed the crowd of fleeing people blocking the bridge to the other side.

***

Poi Son looked long and hard at the elongated white mask sat on the table in front of him. The mask's wearer sat opposite him as a lithe woman in tight-fitted, boiled leather armour paced the richly decorated room.

'Is he still in Dockside?' Poi Son asked, still looking at the mask.

The female assassin stopped, her plaited golden hair swaying at her back as she turned on the guild master.

Without looking up, Poi Son nodded and said, 'I take it from that look of annoyance at my question, Terrina, he is?'

'Well give us some bloody credit. You did say have him watched,' she said, before continuing her pacing.

The usually masked assassin opposite Poi Son failed to hide his amusement at the woman's tone.

Poi Son looked up, one eyebrow raised as he began to pluck a single string on the black lacquered lute in his lap.

'Well come on, Master Son,' the handsome assassin said, folding his arms across his chest under the guild master's gaze, 'she's hardly going to be pleased about this mark, is she?'

The plucking stopped.

'You've both taken marks on fellow guild members before.'

Both assassins glanced sideways to one another briefly then, neither of them knowing the other had killed a fellow guild member before.

'But, Longoss?' the man sat opposite Poi Son said eventually, his head subtly tilting so Terrina was never out of his sight.

'He refused a mark, an important mark.' Poi Son resumed the plucking of his lute. 'And that holds consequences.'

'Aye, Master Son, for a street-assassin maybe, but Longoss?' The male assassin shook his head. 'No. One mark passed isn't worth losing him over. He's too great an asset to this guild and you know it.'

'I would normally agree, Blanck, but this time I cannot allow it to go unpunished.'

'So he's offered to the both of us as a mark, just like that?' Terrina said, moving behind Blanck, much to the man's annoyance.

Poi Son shook his head. 'To most of the guild,' he said flatly.

Blank stood up then and moved away from the chair, clearly outraged, although both Terrina and Poi Son realised it was partly so he could keep the female assassin in his sights.

'That's unheard of.' Blanck did well to keep the anger from his voice.

'It's bollocks is what it is,' Terrina said.

Poi Son looked to both assassins whilst saying in a most serious manner, 'The mark Longoss has turned down is of such a status, of such import to me – to this guild – that I need him and his companions silenced immediately. He was offered a second chance if that satisfies you both, but turned it down. Not only did he turn it down, but he threatened this guild and all of its members, you two included. So yes, I have offered the mark to all available assassins.'

'You threatened his girl,' Blanck said. 'That'll be why he threatened the guild. She was likely the first one to ever like the ugly bastard. Gods, she even managed to have him swear not to kill for crying out loud!'

Terrina laughed. 'You killed the whore, Blanck, so don't go bleating about threats made by Master Son to some bitch Longoss was shafting and paying to do so.'

Poi Son winced every time Terrina swore whilst Blanck raised his middle finger towards the woman, who mimicked licking it, to which Blanck couldn't help but smile.

Poi Son twanged a string on his lute, bringing both their attentions swiftly back to him.

'Both of you listen,' he said, suddenly sounding very dangerous indeed. 'There is more than both of you can imagine riding on this mark, and as I just said, I need Longoss and his companions, whoever they are; whore, guardsman or god I don't care, killed and killed yesterday. As you just said, he swore not to kill again and we all know Longoss' word is final. So no, he is no longer an asset to this guild. He is a liability and nothing more. Do I make myself clear?'

Both assassins nodded their heads and neither commented on – then or at any time in their futures – how scared Poi Son had looked, despite his attempts not to, whenever he mentioned the importance of the mark.

'We'll find him,' Blanck said, and Terrina nodded her agreement as she moved across to the table, lifted the white mask and threw it to her brother.

As the siblings were both leaving, Blanck turned and from behind his mask asked one last question. 'Do the other masters agree on this, Master Son?'

'They don't know about this, nor shall they. Am I understood, Blanck?'

Was that fear in your eyes again, Poi Son? The white mask nodded, although the assassin behind it balked at the depth of Poi Son's answer. *How has he ensured that? Mind you, there's no way either of us would betray a guild master, even to another, that's a sure way to end up with a mark on your own back.* His mind drifted to his new mark then, as he left the room and followed his sister down the corridor.

Longoss, you fool, you had it made in this guild, why throw it all away for a whore? We may not have told the old coot in there, but we know where you are old boy and we're coming for you, whether you, or we, like it or not.

***

The goblin chief grinned as he strode down a wide street, before having two young, smoke blackened human girls thrust at his feet. He looked around at his bodyguards, and made a crude gesture towards the girls that they all howled and laughed at.

He was in his element. His tribe's numbers had grown considerably as he'd travelled down from the Norlechlan Mountains just days ago; travelling fast towards this very goal. He remembered a most vivid dream then, of this very scene playing out before him, which proved all he'd been told was indeed true. A voice had boomed in his head, telling him to march south, amongst other things, and upon waking the next day, two whole tribes had come to pay homage to him. Where they'd come from he hadn't bothered to ask. Why question a gift from the gods below? So he'd called the camp to break and march, to march for victory against the humans of Altoln.

They called him The Red Goblin, a simple but effective name, for he'd been born with crimson skin, unlike the usual greyish-green skin of his people. Thanks to that simple fact, he'd been revered as a chief sent by the Blood God himself.

As The Red Goblin stood overlooking the sacking of one of the largest northern towns of Altoln, he grinned and silently thanked the voice that had spoken to him in his sleep; the voice had since sent the emissary, Dignaaln, to him in person, a powerful emissary that had imbued upon him an incredible gift from his new master.

Master... He snarled as he said the word in his head.

He hadn't relished the thought of serving another, not after his success as

287

a chieftain, but he knew without doubt it was his new master that had allowed him to come this far; a master that asked only enjoyable things of him. A master none would deny.

Despite the latter, The Red Goblin laughed aloud, triggering more of the same from the goblins around him. His mirth came easily since the gifts he'd been given, and the pleasure he would take in carrying out the simple tasks his master required of him promised more to come.

Taking a deep breath and enjoying the smells of a dying town, the goblin chieftain thought back to his victory over the human army that had marched against him. He grinned again, knowing his master would be pleased with the outcome, as he would with the goblin horde ripping through the town of Beresford; murdering, raping and doing whatever they wished to its occupants.

Chaos is what he wants and chaos is what I do best.

The Red Goblin left his thoughts behind and nodded to the two young girls – who were crying hysterically and hugging each other tight at his feet – then to two of his personal bodyguards.

Two large hobyahs, encased in pieces of crudely forged, red iron plate, carried the screaming girls away to a large building near the breached gate, which The Red Goblin had taken as his own. Normally feared by goblins due to their size and cannibalistic tendencies, the chieftain's hobyahs had been trained to protect him until death, and extremely loyal they were, especially since he'd started feeding them goblins that he suspected of treachery, or ones that merely annoyed him.

Rolling his shoulders and then snarling at those closest to him, The Red Goblin set off down the street and continued with his inspection of the town's sacking. He smiled to himself as he witnessed the unfolding destruction and horrors his tribe was capable of, and wondered all the while what else his master would do for him as he continued to carry out the enjoyable tasks bestowed upon him.

***

The long guard room of the barracks was full of noise as two dozen guardsmen readied themselves to march on the Samorlian Cathedral. Many were sharpening blades or repairing damaged links in various pieces of maille, not wanting to leave anything to chance in a possible face off against witchunters and warrior monks.

Biviano was pacing the length of his bunk as he thought about Ellis Frane, Sears and everything that had happened. He hated himself for leaving the royal scribe behind and hated himself more for leaving Sears in Dockside, although he knew Sears wouldn't be able to live with himself if they'd left Ellis completely, nor could he if he was honest with himself.

Hold on Ellis Frane. Hold on the both of ye.

He looked up then, disappointed at the small number of men available to them. So many had failed to report for their shifts and everyone in the room feared them dead or dying, be it from the plague or the recent crime wave.

'I see ye're still not moving,' Biviano said to Bollingham, who was still lying on his bunk, but now wearing fancy green pantaloons – something Biviano hadn't missed.

'Nope, nor will I,' Bollingham said, without raising his head from his thin pillow, 'especially not to assault the bloody Samorlian Cathedral, ye crazy bastards.'

'Nor to help Sears?' Biviano prodded Bollingham's bare foot with his finger after moving across to the man.

'That's not where ye're going though, is it?'

'No, but it's helping Sears, by helping another.'

Bollingham spun on his bed and stared at Biviano, clearly confused.

'Sears stayed on in Dockside on the understanding Ellis Frane would be rescued. He'll be destroyed if he returns and we failed, Bolly.'

Effrin walked up to stand next to Biviano. 'He's right and you know it.'

'Don't you start, ye posh prick.' Bollingham dropped his head back to his pillow.

'Too late,' Effrin said. 'We need you, Bolly, as much as I hate to admit it, but we do.'

'Listen lads, ye know I'd be there, all the way, but this plague, there ain't no fighting it is there? People are dropping dead all over the show and I ain't one for dying from no plague.'

'Is anyone?' Biviano asked.

'Ye know what I mean.'

'No, we don't,' Effrin said. 'People *are* dying all over the city, Bolly, in the damned palace of all places. Even Captain Prior has it, yet you think yourself safe in this shit-hole?'

'Ooh, you've got Effrin swearing now, Bolly.' Biviano grinned and Bollingham couldn't help but laugh as Effrin looked at them both, far from amused.

'Anyhow,' Biviano said, 'ye owe me for the pantaloons.'

'What?' Bollingham's mouth hung open as his brow furrowed.

'Ye knew I had me eye on 'em and ye took 'em from the infirmary anyway.'

'I never went to the blasted infirmary.'

'No, you had me bring them to you,' Effrin said. Both sets of eyes turned to him.

'Snitch,' Bollingham muttered, as Biviano thumped the cleric on the arm.

'Ouch! You're not Sears and I'm not you!'

Bollingham laughed and both turned back to him. He changed tack quickly by commenting on how long Lord Stowold was taking.

It seemed to work.

'Too pissin' long,' Biviano said, kicking Bollingham's bed.

'He has a lot to sort out for something this big and well, let's face it, unheard of… taking on the Samorlian Church?' Effrin took a deep breath and let it out slowly.

Biviano cursed and took another look at the guard room and its occupants. 'Maybe, Effrin mate, but the longer we wait for Lord Stowold to sign gods know what scrolls and shit for the scribes at the palace, one of their own is waiting for us to rescue him, before he's gutted by the shite he's hopefully stretching as we speak.'

No one replied to that, they just considered the implications of not reaching Ellis Frane in time.

Bollingham was the first to speak. 'I'm surprised all this is happening for one man anyhow. Not like the nobility to push the boat out like this to save one bloke, is it?'

Biviano snarled. 'And is that wrong, that we're actually doing that for once?'

'No,' Bollingham said, holding up his hands, 'course not. It just ain't, is it, mate? One of *us* trapped and nowt would happen is all I'm saying. A royal scribe though…' Bollingham believed he didn't need to finish and so left his meaning to sink in, but Biviano wasn't having it.

'He may be one man, Bolly, but he's been fucking stretched and gods know what else. He looks like he's been seen to by the bloody Three, think on that.'

Bollingham grimaced at the thought.

'Apart from that,' Biviano went on, 'those bastards have been raping and torturing young girls and whoever they damned well want and it's that, not Ellis Frane poor bastard, that the constable is having us march to fix, get it?'

'Aye, Biviano, I get it.'

Effrin put a hand on Biviano's shoulder after glaring at Bollingham to keep his mouth shut. 'He'll be alright, Biviano.'

'Sears?' Biviano looked sidelong at Effrin.

'I meant this Ellis Frane character, but yes, Sears too.'

Biviano nodded, although not all that convincingly.

'Where's Gitsham and the hound?' he asked suddenly, looking about the guard room again.

'Who gives a—'

'Out,' Effrin interrupted, and Bollingham flicked him two fingers, 'not sure where, he just took off all of a sudden, led by Buddle.'

Biviano scratched under his arm, wincing again as he did so and nodding all the while, before moving off without a word towards his own bunk, where he picked up his short-sword and wet stone.

Effrin's eyes followed Biviano, and Bollingham knew the cleric well enough to recognise the concern on his face.

'What's up, Effrin?' Bollingham asked, as the sound of Biviano sharpening his blade added to the noise of two dozen guardsmen preparing for a fight.

'Nothing,' Effrin said, before moving back to his bunk too.

Liar! Bollingham closed his eyes and tried to ignore the thought of a faceless stranger being tortured by an inquisitor.

***

Beresford's armoury was empty, with no soldiers and very few weapons. Most had probably been handed out to the town militia as the bells first rang, but luckily the group's weapons had been thrown in a corner and wrapped in linen bundles. Mearson pulled them open and handed out the various swords and bows, as well as their quivers full of arrows and Gleave's hand axe, as the din of a town being sacked assaulted their ears. More people screamed and loud crashes signified the collapsing of roofs as the goblins ripped their way through Beresford with vicious enthusiasm. Some men-at-arms, archers and ashmen still stood against them, but they couldn't hold the high numbers of goblins back as they ran through the streets, dragging cowering people from their homes and butchering others where they found them.

A dog barked and then yelped just outside the door. Gleave, who'd just left the armoury, popped his head back through the open door, clearly worried.

'They're close, hurry,' he shouted over the increasing noise of the people trapped on the bridge near to the armoury.

The towns folk's rush to cross the bridge had stopped the soldiers on the far side from coming to aid their comrades. As the group buckled and looped their weapon belts and strung their bows, the last of the town's soldiers and militia on the western bank fell to the onslaught creeping even closer to the bridge full of people, and the armoury where the group were finally ready to move on.

Gleave made way as Sav, Starks and Errolas piled out of the armoury into a savage scene. The whole area seemed ablaze and the sound of crackling fire, weakened wooden beams breaking and now horses crying out as the stables caught fire was deafening. People pushed to try and force their way across the bridge, causing others to fall from the sides into the cold water quickly flowing down from the spring melt in the mountains. A line of ashmen with a couple of archers at either side made a rough defensive line by the bridge, hindered by small groups of people who pushed their way past the spears and into the panicking crowd.

Sav, Starks and Errolas loosed their weapons as goblins raced down the street opposite them. As the two arrows and one bolt left the bows, both Errolas and Sav were knocking, drawing and loosing another shaft whilst Starks nocked the release mechanism's nuts on his crossbow, put his foot through the loading hoop and hauled the cord back, lifting it to fit another bolt to the groove. The two archers had loosed, made their targets with deadly accuracy and nocked another shaft each on their hemp strings as Starks loosed his second bolt in time with the scout and elf ranger's third. Eight goblins had dropped by the time Fal, Mearson and Correia left the armoury.

Sav and Errolas loosed again as Starks loaded and every time they did they scored a hit, dropping a goblin and sometimes knocking them clean off their feet. The bullish archers over by the line of ashmen did the same with their tall, immensely powerful war bows and yet still the goblins came on.

'No way across, ma'm,' Gleave shouted. 'Bridge is blocked and all the boats have crossed already.' He pointed to small wooden jetties laying empty by the river's fast flowing waters.

Mearson looked back to the approaching goblins again. 'Can we cross the river?'

Gleave shook his. 'Too deep here, the current would sweep us away for sure and we're wearing maille, mate.' Gleave managed a grin as the realisation of that sank in with Mearson.

'Oh aye, forget I said it will you.' Mearson managed a nervous chuckle. Both men were seasoned veterans, but neither could see an immediate way out and they could see it in each other's eyes. They set their jaws firm and looked to Correia for an order to attack or stay on guard, hoping she had the answer.

Before she could say anything, however, more than a score of goblins raced out from behind a nearby building and came straight at them. Three dropped immediately as Sav, Starks and Errolas planted shafts deep into them. Errolas even managed to successfully loose another swift arrow almost immediately after the first, which took the closest goblin clean off his feet, flipping him backwards into another that was running close behind.

Fal roared as he stepped forward and swung his falchion into the neck of an oncoming goblin, its head lolling as its body fell past him. Fal didn't stop, taking another two steps forward, he pulled his seax knife from his boot and thrust it sideways into another goblin's side as it tried to pass him and attack Starks, who was reloading his crossbow.

The goblin dropped at Starks' feet and he kicked it in the head before lifting the weapon and loosing its bolt into the next goblin's face.

Sav loosed another two arrows before throwing his bow back and drawing his short-sword, as did Errolas, his curved blade slashing across a goblin jumping at him, teeth bared and rusting cleaver held high.

Correia and her two pathfinders ran forward then, Mearson's arm holding up just enough to parry a blow with his dagger before thrusting his sword into the attacker's chest. Gleave punched one goblin in the face, smashing its jaw as he kicked out at another on his right. He sliced a deep red line across the one he'd punched and hacked into the other with his axe. Correia turned, quick stepped and spun as if in a dance, her curved blades leaving opened goblin stomachs and faces wherever they struck.

More goblins came down the street, their near-useless armour allowing the group to cut through them like a ship through water. Upon seeing the group's success, the line of ashmen nearby ploughed forward, ramming their spears into oncoming goblins as the broad shouldered archers hung back a pace or two, loosing arrow after arrow. To draw a war bow was akin to lifting a prone man from the ground with one arm, and so the muscular shoulders, backs and arms of the two archers burnt under the strain of drawing their bows time and time again.

Goblin after goblin fell as they came on, either to a swift sword, arrow or a thrust of an ashman's spear, but it was not enough. A horrific sounding horn blast erupted from the end of the street and the ground rumbled as the fire lit space filled with a mass of glistening, squealing pigs, some being ridden insanely by goblins wielding meet cleavers and axes. As they neared, the fire arrows flew and almost two dozen pigs lit up like a forest fire spreading out towards the defending men and woman. The people on the bridge that had begun to calm at the sight of the warriors to their rear panicked again, scrambling to cross the bridge, some even jumping into the cold, black water below.

The pigs came on, leaving no building safe as they ploughed through opened doors and lit up the interiors. Some careered off down side streets, but most came towards the bridge and armoury, several dropping to arrows or the flames eating through their hides. Even the handful of goblins riding the beasts were alight now, screaming as they held on for dear life, seemingly eager to make the human lines before they perished. One fell to a bolt from Starks' crossbow, but it was far from enough.

'In the river. Take your chances, but strip your armour quick,' Gleave shouted, as the group backed up rapidly towards the fast moving waters behind the armoury. They started to untie leather thongs and undo buckles on various pieces of armour that would surely see them drown if left on.

As the first pig reached the line of ashmen, it was impaled and pushed aside by two spears, but the next – goblin on its back – halted suddenly at the sight of the sharp spears, dropping exhausted to burn to death as its rider was launched forward, flames following, onto the ashmen in front. The crazed goblin, barely still alive, chopped down with two cleavers, one striking home and cleaving an ashman's unprotected head in two.

As Fal turned to make for the river – trying to pull his maille up and over his head at the same time – he caught a blacker than black shadow pass across the side of a flaming building. A cloaked figure ran then, from the shadows and into the middle of the street. Raising both arms, the figure let out a sudden rush of energy that enveloped almost all the incendiary pigs charging towards them. The energy rushed around the street and enveloped almost everything else too. The ashmen were knocked from their feet and the light of it forced Fal and everyone else watching to turn away. As the reflection died on the water, Fal turned back and saw – once his eyes had adjusted – all the fires in the immediate area were no more, and in their place lay a white blanket of what looked like snow. Icicles clung from what was left of rooftops and frozen pigs and goblins alike scattered the street almost all the way down to the end.

The small number of remaining ashmen and archers climbed to their feet, shivering as their visible breaths clouded the air about them.

The people on the bridge cheered, jumping up and down and whooping into the night sky.

Fal looked to the others and saw Errolas looking back, a mischievous grin spreading across his face, whilst Correia winked at Fal. Gleave and Mearson laughed out, slapping each other on the shoulders and jumping along with the crowd on the bridge. Sav and Starks stood with jaws hung low, looking to each other, then to the hooded figure and back again.

Fal took a step forward and the figure turned, lowered his black hood and bowed slightly to the group by the armoury.

Fal gasped. 'Lord Severun?'

Severun simply nodded.

Chapter 34: Hold The Bridge

Exley Clewarth felt deafened by his heartbeat, his breath rasping through his dust-filled throat and the slightest of sounds made by his shuffling feet whenever he moved. He slowly crept backwards bit by bit, straining his eyes to see anything in the lightless tunnel. The strange knocking sound had stopped and all was silent; any movement he made now assaulting his ears.

He started at a sound ahead of him. He couldn't make out what it was, but he'd definitely heard something over the din of his beating heart. He waved his bloodied rapier around to the front, hoping he would hit anything that came forward before it reached him.

A loud crack echoed off the wall to the side and he jumped away from it, cursing as he crunched into the opposite wall. Another crack and then another as something skipped across the floor and hit his leg. He stumbled backwards and fell hard as a hail of small stones rained down onto and around him from further down the tunnel. He waved his rapier around whilst covering his face with his other hand, tucking his legs in and trying to make himself as small as possible. He cursed again as something sharp caught his bare hand, blood running warm as it dripped from the cut.

'Away,' he yelled, waving his rapier even more fiercely than before. He pushed himself to his feet as stone after stone struck him from head to toe. Exley dived backwards as a large rock crunched down in front of him, breaking into several pieces. How he'd known to move he had no idea, perhaps it was Sir Samorl looking down on him. He backed up further and further until he found the solid wall, where he felt vibrations running through the thick stone. He crouched again, giving up on his sword and instead wrapping his head in his folded arms, screaming for whoever or whatever was attacking him to leave him be.

The wall behind him almost bounced, time and time again. It felt alive as it vibrated and shuddered.

Without warning, the blade of a miner's pick burst through the stone inches from Exley's head. He looked sideways and rolled away from the metal spike as it disappeared back into the hole, a thin beam of flickering, yellow light streaming through.

'General?' someone called, muffled by the wall and the constant barrage of stones and rocks. One struck him on the side of the head as he let his guard down to shout back through the hole. He touched his cheek, feeling the wetness of blood on his fingers before shouting back.

'In here, hurry!' He started waving his rapier about in front of him again and his confidence grew; he'd heard Egan Dundaven's voice.

'Stand back, General,' Egan shouted, and the Witchunter General leapt back as two more pick blades punched through the stone, letting more flickering torchlight escape into the previously light-less tunnel. Exley's eyes began to adjust, taking in a faint outlined scene ahead of him and around him of a floor littered with stones, small crystal tipped spears and the bloodied body of a goblin-like creature.

'Knockers,' he whispered with vehemence, shaking his head as more stones clattered towards him. He was thankful there had been no one present to witness his distressed actions and now embarrassment.

More stones fell from behind Exley as a large hole appeared in the wall, letting a lot more light pour through, which caused the thrown stones to stop as the kobolds backed off down the tunnel. The small creatures knew they were no match for armed humans in low and narrow tunnels and so, in the time it took the large group of men to fully break through the wall, the kobolds had disappeared completely, leaving nothing but a stone littered tunnel floor and the corpse of one of their own behind.

'General,' Egan Dundaven greeted, as he squeezed through the man sized hole he and the prisoners had created. Egan had ordered Monks to take some of the prisoners and find whatever they could to smash through the wall, and to his delight the picks were what they'd found.

Exley scowled at the men. 'What took you so long?' he said, before breaking into a huge grin and slapping Egan on the shoulder.

'It was a set up from the start, General. The large prisoner was no prisoner at all and had led us down here to be trapped.'

'Makes sense,' Exley said, looking at the crumbling wall behind Egan. He prodded tenderly at the cuts on his face as he continued. 'I don't think they would bother to build such a trap without a good reason, and so it is, Master Dundaven, I think we have found our way under the city.'

Egan's eyes widened as he looked around. He reached back through and was given a torch that, when brought into the narrow tunnel, showed the runes Exley had felt before the kobolds' attack.

'Do you know what they are?' Exley asked, as another witchunter clambered through the hole. 'Bring the rest, we may have found the tunnels,' Exley said to the second witchunter, who shouted back through for the rest to follow.

'I'm not sure,' Egan said. 'They're old, very old, but I don't know what language. I suspect they may be magical, perhaps allowing the reader to pass through? This could be an ancient, secret way in and out of Wesson's original castle.' He ran his fingers over the indented runes.

'More over here, General,' the second witchunter said, after taking his torch further down the wall, 'this area here.'

Exley and Egan walked over to look at what their brother witchunter was pointing at. Sure enough, there were more runes of a similar design on another section of the wall.

Exley grinned and looked back at the prisoners who were coming through the hole, picks and shovels in hands.

'Break it down,' he ordered, pointing at the section of wall with the second set of runes.

'There're bodies over here,' a warrior monk shouted, after venturing a little further down the tunnel. 'Looks like two prison guards, killed with a rapier I'd say.'

Exley snarled. 'Horler Comlay.'

'He had them two guards show him the way through it seems.' Egan nodded appreciatively. 'Clever.'

Exley scowled at Egan before snatching a pick off one of the prisoners and hacking into the runes and wall himself.

***

The star-filled sky above Eatri seemed depthless as Cheung looked up into it, listening to the cicadas surrounding him, their whispering song bringing a sense of calm before a storm.

Taking in a deep breath of the cool night air, Cheung finally rose from his cross-legged position. He twisted slowly to the left, then to the right, before bending double and touching a middle finger to the tip of each soft soled boot. His loose robes made no sound as he moved. Cheung smiled inwardly, enjoying the feel of the material on his pale skin; a stark contrast to his black robes and hair.

After finishing his series of stretches, Cheung walked silently along the rooftop he'd been waiting on for three days and three nights. He carefully rolled the sheet of brown canvas at one end of the flat roof, which had been his only shelter from the day's sun and night's chill. Once rolled tight, he weighed one end down under a large potted succulent, before sliding a long satchel from behind another.

The satchel, once opened, revealed a pair of bone handled kamas, their black blades almost invisible as they absorbed the light of the moon above. Taking a bone handle in each henna tattooed hand, Cheung lifted the weapons. He stood and looked to the sky again, holding the weapons at his sides as he walked slowly towards the edge of the roof. Once there, he looked from the stars to the alley below, where a well-dressed woman escorted by two burly bodyguards walked. Blocking the sound of the cicadas out, Cheung lifted his kamas and carved three short red lines across his heavily scarred face, before stepping off the roof.

No cry of warning came from the first bodyguard as the points of two black bladed kamas punctured the top of his skull. The head jerked back as the wielder of the kamas used the weapons anchorage to swing his feet into the small of the victim's back. As Cheung's back touched the ground, he used the weight of the dead man's backward momentum along with an explosive kick with both legs, to throw the corpse over and behind, withdrawing the kamas as he did so.

Springing back to his feet, Cheung leapt forward, bringing the inside curve of one of his blades around and across the throat of the second bodyguard, which spun the choking man to one side. This left the woman seemingly defenceless as Cheung, already past his second victim, reached his mark. He

297

suddenly knew better however, and crossed both kamas in front of him in time to parry a blow from the woman's naginata. How he hadn't seen her carrying the long weapon he had no idea, but vowed he would punish himself later for his poor observation.

The woman, despite her cumbersome dress, came at Cheung swiftly, moving the blade at the end of her naginata swiftly in confusing circles, slashes and lunges Cheung deftly avoided or parried. He found little opening to lock either of his kamas onto the haft of his mark's weapon; the blade at its head was long, so he resigned himself to a series of defensive manoeuvres until he could find an opening in the well trained woman's attacks.

For several minutes, both Cheung and his mark danced about the alley, the blade of the naginata flashing occasionally in the bright moonlight whilst the twin blades of the kamas soaked it up. It was that in the end, that gave Cheung his chance. He noticed the woman's eyes being drawn to his blades more than once and the next time she did – his weapons held high – Cheung spun low, taking the woman's legs from beneath her with a sweeping kick. Before she could react, Cheung had moved inside the danger of her naginata and thrust the tips of his bone hilts hard against her shoulders, pinning her to the ground.

To his surprise, his mark made no sound as he crunched his head into her delicate nose, stunning her before she could make any move against him. Head next to hers, Cheung finally whispered to her his guild master's regards, before quickly lifting his right kama from her shoulder to bring it point first down through her chest and into her heart.

The only noise was the cicadas as Cheung climbed the side of the building next to him. He walked the roof under a star filled sky and collected both his canvas and satchel. He stopped only once before leaving the roof, to admire the potted succulents and the male cicada sat atop one of the smooth leaves, playing its calming song.

***

An intense white light shone up from the area of Beresford's bridge like a reversed ray of moonlight. The Red Goblin snarled as he saw it. Pointing a clawed finger, he howled into the night sky and jumped onto the back of a large brown boar with blood stained tusks, which grunted and scraped the ground with its front right foot. The red skinned chieftain kicked the boar's sides and drew a crude looking sword that glowed in the flickering light of the surrounding fires.

Six large hobyahs clad in spiked, red plate held large cleavers and axes high as they trotted after their chieftain, his boar bouncing off down the street in the direction of the strange illumination.

The air chilled as the chieftain rode closer. Humans were cheering now and he knew it was not a good sign. *Always better screaming humans are, always better screaming.*

298

More goblins rode out from side streets upon boars almost as big as their chieftain's. They were followed by many more goblins on foot, brandishing everything from spears and hatchets to human swords and crossbows, which looked comical, since many of them were too big for the goblins to wield. Their shrieking and whooping made for a bloodcurdling sound, especially when mixed with the chattering and whispering sounds of their leucrotas.

Two women ran out of a burning building and into the street. They soon fled at the sight of a red-skinned goblin in black plate armour riding a large boar and wielding a glowing blade; hobyahs loping along at the side of him, weapons held high and jaws snapping at any goblin venturing too close.

An unfortunate man who'd followed the two women froze at the nightmarish sight, just to be ridden down by The Red Goblin and his boar, before being hacked to pieces by the following horde.

As The Red Goblin rounded the last corner to Beresford's bridge, a line of ashmen ran out into the street, stopping to set their spears into the ground whilst archers stood to either side. They were clearly attempting to block his path from the dwindling crowds of people finally managing to make it across the river.

The goblin chieftain saw another small number of soldiers amongst the people on the bridge, trying to make it to the other side of the Rive Norl. Two had bows and The Red Goblin could have sworn one was an elf, but before he could confirm it, he and his horde had reached the line of ashmen and two archers.

His lead hobyah was hit with two arrows, both of which the creature snapped off before careering into one of the archers responsible. It literally tore the man limb from limb.

As the hobyah turned to another human, The Red Goblin's boar slammed into the line of ashmen, their spears knocked aside by other boar riders as they ploughed in to their deaths ahead of their chieftain.

The glowing blade of the howling red goblin sliced effortlessly through padded jackets, maille and iron helmets with its shamanistic charms. He cleaved one ashman's head from his body as his boar thrust both of its tusks up into another's stomach, disembowelling him before he landed lifeless on the frosted ground immediately under the beast's heavy head.

Hobyahs smashed and slashed wildly, killing almost as many goblins as humans as they swept their way through the defensive line, leaving little to do for those behind. One of the larger hobyah's turned suddenly, biting off the arm of a passing boar rider, causing the boar to buck and smash through the goblin ranks as the rider shrieked and let go of the reigns, gripping his bloody stump with his one good hand.

The Red Goblin glared at the hobyah, who looked down for a second, clearly hurt by its master's disapproval, before it continued across the swarming mass of goblins towards the remaining humans on the bridge.

***

Every sound tore at Ellis Frane as he stared at the barricaded door of the torture chamber. He'd stared for a long time at the dead inquisitor on the rack; the mangled corpse he'd created from a living, breathing man. After squatting in a corner for some time, rocking slightly whilst trying to force the horrors he'd inflicted on the inquisitor from his mind, Ellis Frane had managed to find enough blood-soaked rags to cover at least the face and torso of Inquisitor Makhell, although it hadn't really helped.

The royal scribe had then paced the room, occasionally stopping – as he was now – to stare at the barricade; awaiting the painful death those outside would surely visit upon him.

'I hope you escaped,' he whispered to himself, thinking of the two guardsmen who'd set him free and given him the chance of revenge upon Inquisitor Makhell.

Revenge? Was that what it was…? Murder, I should think, which makes me no better than him.

He glanced over to the half-covered body, but only momentarily before straying to the secret room's entrance in the wall. Ellis Frane shuddered as he remembered what was behind that wall. He looked back to the dead inquisitor and nodded slowly.

Revenge for them more than me, now that's *worth seeing your bloodied face in my dreams, even if it were for a thousand years, you bastard. Although at this rate,* he thought, looking again to the barricade, *it won't be another hour.*

The silence was deafening as he strained to hear footsteps, voices, raised or otherwise. There was nothing, nothing for what seemed like hours if not days. His eyes felt heavy and his belly empty and although he knew his luck had gone, he hoped again to see or even hear the two men who'd saved him once, here again to save him a second time.

***

The people crossing the River Norln screamed and cried out again as they witnessed the slaughter of their protectors, whilst the soldiers on the east side of the bridge attempted to organise a defensive line, despite the crowds pushing past them.

Fal looked back from his position on the bridge, and his stomach lurched as he saw the ashmen and archers ripped apart. The moving mass of goblins, boars and leucrota, not to mention the six tall and fearsome hobyahs, closed in on the now undefended opening of the bridge. The western stone towers on either side should have held crossbowmen to defend the bridge, but those crossbowmen had been called to the wall during the early stages of the goblin assault on the town, and now the towers lay empty, allowing the blood crazed enemy to advance unmolested.

Sav and Errolas found room to loose arrow after arrow into the heaving throng of advancing goblins. Every shaft found its mark and several goblins were thrown from their war boars and trampled under the mad stampede that followed.

'We can't hold them,' Sav shouted from his position on the side wall of the bridge. 'We need to get these people across this bridge, and fast.'

Severun jumped up onto the wall alongside Sav and cupped his hands in front of his mouth. 'Move the people on, clear the bridge, clear the bridge!' His voice drowned out any other sound, despite the ear assaulting din all about him.

The soldiers on the other side, rather than stare astounded at the cloaked man addressing them, nodded quickly and started picking up children and the elderly to hurry them along.

Correia's group was almost fully across as the goblins, a red skinned heavily armoured boar rider at their head, made it onto the bridge and began to charge across. Both Errolas and Sav loosed more arrows, whilst half a dozen crossbow bolts whipped down from the towers on their side of the river. Starks shot one hobyah, but the bolt seemed to have no effect. Roaring, the creature shrugged off the wound and plucked the iron tipped bolt from its shoulder, charging all the faster for it.

As Correia's group made the other side, the townsfolk fled towards the far gatehouse, eastern keep and the tougher looking stone buildings of the armoury and smithy nearby.

Fal turned then and joined the ranks of the ashmen and shield bearing men-at-arms as they formed two lines across the opening of the bridge.

Correia stopped and pulled on him to follow.

'These men need our help,' he shouted, over the continuous noise.

Balls of burning pitch – amongst other things – were still being catapulted over the distant walls across the river, and buildings were flaring up here and there whenever one of the flaming missiles struck them. The flames licked at the sky as some buildings collapsed, creating flickering reflections on the fast flowing water cutting through the town.

'We need to go while we can, Fal. We have to complete our mission. Now come on… now!'

Fal shrugged off Correia's grip.

Starks and Sav stood in the defensive line too, as did Gleave and Mearson, to Fal's surprise. Correia screamed at them all, but none of them moved. They set their feet and hefted their weapons ready for the incoming charge to hit. The goblins were half way across the bridge now, several of them dropping every few heartbeats as arrows and bolts slammed into them, but never enough to slow the oncoming tide of blades, tusks and teeth.

The man-at-arms to Fal's left dropped to his knees suddenly as a crude goblin arrow glanced off an ashman's kettle-helm in front and struck him in the eye. He fell forward then and the arrow shaft snapped; the noise was somehow audible over everything else. For some reason, the sound affected Fal more than anything he'd seen or heard since the town's assault had begun.

He knelt quickly, pushing the sound from his mind as he retrieved the dead man's wooden heater shield, quickly strapping it to his left arm and lifting it to protect himself from incoming missiles.

'Hold!' Fal shouted, suddenly aware there seemed to be no officers in the ranks. 'Hold!'

The men in the line strengthened, and as the goblins closed on the tensing soldiers, Correia pushed in next to Fal, her swords held in a defensive posture and her jaw set firm. Fal allowed himself a sideways glance, but Correia's eyes were set on the oncoming horde.

Fal looked back to the shrieking goblins, towards the red skinned, black armoured boar rider leading the charge. He'd almost forgotten Severun's mysterious return, until, from the corner of his eye, a black cloaked and hooded figure ran across and in front of the spears of the ashmen.

Surrounded by what looked like the shimmer that rose from the land on a hot summer day, Severun released the build-up of tension and rage he felt within. The wizard shuddered violently and threw his arms – almost his whole body – forward, unleashing an almost invisible wave of energy that crackled, rippled and ripped through the oncoming mass of goblins, throwing them far back and into the air. Many of them flew over the side of the bridge and plunged into the fast flowing water to be swept to their deaths, whilst others flew back into their kin, skewering themselves on the oncoming wall of weapons. Others were crushed as heavy boars slammed into them, whilst the large hobyahs flattened goblins here and there, the smaller creatures falling under their cannibalistic cousins' feet and blades.

Not much more than a dozen heavier set goblins remained standing, along with just two hobyahs and their red skinned chieftain, who, head down and glowing blade held forward, crashed into Severun, sending the wizard flying back amongst the ashmen's spears.

There were gasps and cries at the sight of the wizard going down, but as Fal feared for Severun's life, he saw the man stand, seemingly unharmed.

More shouts from the humans, this time of hope and encouragement, as Severun drew a gleaming sword from naught but thin air.

The Red Goblin kicked his boar forward again and Severun ran headlong at the beast as it came on, arrows whipping past the two as they collided.

Sparks flew and lights flashed as enchanted swords clashed high and low. The boar attempted to ram its tusks into Severun's long legs, but the experienced wizard leapt to the side, thrusting his blade towards the goblin chieftain as he landed. Releasing a haunting choir-like sound, Severun's sword illuminated the whole area briefly, before crunching through black iron plate to pierce The Red Goblin's heart.

The townsfolk, many of which were hanging out of windows watching the spectacle, cheered and clapped, and the closest ashmen rushed forward and thrust their spears into the large boar's neck, pinning it down.

Thrashing, grunting and fighting to break free from the spears holding it, the mighty boar eventually died in a final spasm of defiance that tore a spear from one of the ashmen's grip, leaving him defenceless.

Fal swiftly pulled the ashman back as the two remaining hobyah came on, several goblins close behind. Most of the leucrotas ran back across the river, their eerie chattering fading as they escaped, but others remained, snapping their bone ridged jaws at the defenders as they closed in rapidly.

The ashmen lurched forward as the gap closed; the men-at-arms and Fal's group close behind as they passed Severun to slam into the remaining enemy.

Errolas and Sav managed to drop the lead hobyah before the ashmen's spears reached it, and the other red armoured brute, along with the remaining goblins, were impaled on the long ash-shafted weapons before being hacked to pieces by angry men with swords, axes and smashed with maces, fists and feet.

Fal, Correia and the two pathfinders put their worth in, tackling the last hobyah as it fought on with an ashman's spear protruding from its chest. All four scored hits on the creature, but it was Mearson in the end that thrust his sword into the hobyah's roaring mouth, the bloody tip emerging from the back of its head before it slumped heavily to the ground.

With another cheer from the onlookers and the surviving soldiers, the bridge was finally won and the eastern side of Beresford saved. Alas, there were still many goblins visible on the far bank, but Correia couldn't allow the group to stay any longer. She ordered them to her side and they obeyed, satisfied they'd helped defend the bridge and pleased they'd witnessing the raw power of a high wizard in action. Severun looked exhausted, but pushed away helping hands, insisting they listened to Correia and moved out while they still could. King Barrison had secretly spared him, but that was because he had a city to save, and that was Severun's and the group's first priority.

This time, they all agreed.

Chapter 35: Vulnerable

A light breeze blew the last wisps of a smouldering campfire across half a dozen sleeping men. Two men-at-arms stood watch over the camp, or rather played nine men's morris; their board carved into the top of a wooden barrel.

To the edge of the camp lay a deflated balloon, its canvas envelope not dissimilar to a ship's sail, whilst its large circular basket housed a strange mechanical contraption suspended on chains in the centre.

The sleeping men wore padded jackets under maille hauberks, their arming swords kept close besides them as they slept. Two large windlass crossbows were propped against wooden barrels whilst one man, a knight, had much finer armour laid out by his side.

The sleeping knight and his team had been patrolling the borders between Altoln and Northfolk when they'd spotted a goblin tribe on the move. The goblins had already sacked several hamlets and seemed intent on continuing their destructive march south. Upon landing back at their encampment near Hinton, the balloon commander had sent dispatch riders to the local Baron, warning him of the threat to his lands. Since then, the balloon had been taking daily flights to monitor the progress of the goblins. Upon seeing them destroy Baron Brackley's force, the balloon commander had sent more riders out to call for reinforcements; to assist the defenders of Beresford. Alas, no reinforcements seemed likely for some time since Wesson had closed its gates and the next nearest forces were days away.

With the camp's riders away trying to encourage neighbouring barons to march to Beresford's aid, the camp had been left with just the balloon's crew and two men for guard duty. Those two guards died quickly, as expertly shot crossbow bolts tore into them simultaneously. They both slumped over the barrel where their nine men's morris stones scattered, and after that there was near silence, apart from a tawny owl which screeched in the distance as three shadows moved quickly and quietly across the camp.

The man to the sleeping knight's left, who lay curled up on his woollen cloak, was the balloon's battle mage. His powers did him no good as his deep sleep left him open to the blade that sliced through his throat. He gurgled slightly as he died and the knight to his right stirred before having his own throat cut by the black clad man who knelt beside him. The rest of the balloon's crew had their lives taken in the same way, bar two, who were clubbed across the head before their hands were tied roughly behind their backs.

Horler Comlay grimaced at the sight of the dead men and shook his head, mouthing a silent prayer for their loss as his two companions did the same.

***

Morri and Cullane sat slumped amongst piles of ancient books and scrolls as they slept. They'd searched, with the help of Cullane's bookworm, which had now dissipated, through volumes and stacks of material on illnesses, epidemics and cures. They'd also been allowed access to the *Arcane Listings* in a hope to find something similar to what Severun had used to create the spell that had caused the plague.

Only a couple of other mages sat in the great library, and they smiled at each other as they rose wearily to leave, looking across at the young cleric and sorceress asleep against the stacks of books.

As they reached the door of the library, what sounded like a distant explosion came from below. They could have sworn they felt a vibration through the wooden floor, but neither worried, there was always some experiment or other going on in the deep vaulted chambers of Tyndurris, and so they carried on, leaving the library before heading up the winding stairs to their bed chambers.

Morri stirred, his eyes slowly opening to a blurry scene of dusty books, scrolls, parchments and then, as they cleared, to a beautiful face opposite his. He smiled as he looked upon Cullane. He moved to wake her, to tell her it was about time they made their way to their beds as a distant rumble caused her to open her eyes.

'What was that?' she said, her eyes flitting around the library.

'It'll be an experiment in the basement.' Morri stretched away some of his weariness, finally rubbing his eyes. 'The cheek of them at this time.'

'You're probably right. I've been a bit on edge since the whole Lord Severun using arcane magic thing.' She too stretched and they both yawned.

A bell rang on a lower floor and then another on a floor above. The two young mages frowned as they looked at each other.

'Another riot?' Cullane said, frowning.

Morri shrugged. 'I don't know, let's go see shall we?' He pushed his chair backwards and stood, swaying slightly as his head rushed with the sudden movement. Cullane giggled and walked across to the library door as another explosion echoed through the tower. She turned and looked at him with a worried expression. More bells began to ring, followed by heavy footsteps on the stairs. She looked out into the corridor as two men-at-arms ran past, hurrying towards the lower levels.

'Guards,' she said back to Morri, and he hurried over. 'Let's follow them down, come on.'

Morri nodded and had to hurry as Cullane shot off at great speed.

Bells seemed to ring on almost every floor now and raised voices came from both below and back above them on the stairs. Mages were coming out of their bed chambers on the higher floors and hurrying down to see what was happening.

'Hold the gate,' someone out of sight shouted, as Cullane raced into the entrance hall, Morri close behind her. They saw six fully armed, shield bearing guardsmen pile out of the front door and into the courtyard beyond.

'What's happening?' Cullane demanded of the duty sergeant-at-arms, who was fastening his sword belt around his waist.

'Not sure yet, milady. Bells ringing from the courtyard and shouts about fire-bombs. I think we've another riot on our hands.'

Cullane looked back at Morri.

'Is there anything we can do, sergeant?' Morri asked, but the sergeant shook his head, still looking down at his belt as he finished looping the tip down the back of the buckle.

'Not at the moment, master cleric,' he said finally. 'Just be ready to treat injuries if ye please.'

'Of course,' Morri said, as more mages reached the bottom of the stairs. He ran across to them to explain what was happening as the tower shook with the largest explosion yet.

The sergeant ran outside shouting orders and dogs started to bark.

'Of course, Master Orix,' Cullane heard Morri say. She turned to see the old gnome hurry back up the stairs.

'They are off to collect some equipment and want us to go and prepare the barracks below. Come on.' Morri hurried past the young sorceress and she followed swiftly as the tower rocked once more. She thought it strange and a little frightening that the rioters' fire-bombs could cause such explosions.

***

Sears hit the straw covered ground hard as Coppin used the large man's weight and momentum to throw him off her.

'Good,' Longoss said, moving round the two in the small room.

'Aye, bloody brilliant.' Sears rubbed his left shoulder as he climbed to his feet. *Is that how Biviano feels every time I thump him?* he thought, suddenly wondering how his friend was getting on. His stomach knotted at the thought of Ellis Frane being left by the two of them. Shaking it off, he forced himself back to the moment, to concentrate on the task at hand; helping Coppin learn to defend herself and ultimately finding out who the Black Guild's mark was.

Coppin beamed at Longoss' praise. 'I had no idea I'd be able to do that to anyone so fast, let alone someone like Sears.'

'What's that supposed to mean?'

'Fat,' Longoss said.

'No,' Copping protested quickly, 'just big-built I meant, with chain armour on too.'

'Maille,' Longoss said.

'Of course he's male.' She rolled her eyes.

Both men laughed and Coppin kicked out at Longoss – the closer of the two – who grabbed her bare leg and pulled, dropping the woman to the ground and inadvertently causing her robes to ride up high.

'We need to get ye some clothes,' Sears said, blushing slightly. Coppin nodded, quickly pulling her robes back down as Longoss seemed to revert back into himself, taking a seat and looking away from the green haired girl.

'I'll say it again, Longoss,' she said, taking Sears' offered hand as he pulled her to her feet. She clenched her teeth as the course material of her robes rubbed on her wounded back, which hadn't healed as quickly as the men's wounds. 'Ye did all ye could for Elleth. Not many men would've even *thought* about freeing her, or me.'

Sears cleared his throat.

'Present company excluded of course,' she said.

Longoss nodded slowly. *Aye lass, not many would, and that's partly why I made a career of killing the bastards, but all those lives I've taken and I fail to save just one.* He sighed heavily and looked back to Coppin, offering her a weak smile.

'Where's the gold in that?' she said.

Longoss smiled again, gold teeth shining and Coppin laughed. 'That's more like it, now climb to yer feet and show me how to take Sears down some more.'

'Grand,' Sears said.

'Yer back's bleeding again, Coppin, ye need rest.'

Coppin waved Longoss' concerns away. Knowing what it was like to soldier on in times of adversity, the former assassin stood and continued her training.

Whilst Longoss went through some more defensive moves with Coppin, using Sears as a sparring partner, he thought more about the word he'd given to Elleth and about how easily he'd given it. He hadn't thought about the consequences, hadn't thought about much really, apart from making the young girl smile and getting her out of that place, that life. Where they would have gone he had no idea. Would she have even wanted to stay with him? He doubted it, but gods how he'd hoped so. He knew he would have done anything for her, but why? Because she smiled sincerely at him once or twice? No, there was more to it, he was sure. More than his head could make sense of though, but enough for his heart to have known that everything he did for her in that short amount of time was worth anything... including his life.

But Coppin's life, yer sister? Longoss thought heavily. *Have I doomed her by swearing to you, Elleth? I won't kill because I won't break me word to ye, yet in not doing so, I got ye killed and now I've dragged Coppin into a shit storm with the Black Guild. I can't even fight effectively to protect her...*

Longoss was snapped back to reality by the thud of Sears hitting the ground.

'How was that?' Coppin asked excitedly, as she struggled to pull Sears back to his feet.

'Aye, lass,' Longoss said, nodding, 'that was good.' *And it's gonna have to be a whole lot better,* he decided, *for I ain't letting ye go through life a victim no more. If there's one last thing I can do for Elleth, it's to train Coppin like I once trained—*

'No shit, Longoss,' Sears said, breaking the former assassin's thought. 'She's a quick learner is Coppin, I'll give her that.'

'Ye reckon ye can train me to do more, Longoss?'

'The last lass I trained was one of the best warriors I ever fought once I'd finished with her,' he said, smiling sincerely for the first time since they'd found Elleth murdered.

'Oh aye and who was she?' Sears asked, his chin lifted in anticipation.

'None of your beeswax, guardsman. Now, ye alright for her to continue, or are yer wounds playing merry hell with ye, fat boy?'

'I'm good to go,' Sears said. 'You?'

Longoss nodded once. It was only then he realised how physically well he *did* feel. *Well 'morl's brass balls, Sears, that juice of yours is something else.* He prodded the areas where he'd received wounds during the fighting retreat through the cathedral. No pain, none at all. When he looked back up at Sears, the guardsman winked at him, before swiftly sidestepping Coppin's thrown fist.

Longoss laughed despite his grief and Sears joined him, whilst opening Coppin's fist and tapping his finger on the palm of her hand, finally advising her that using that would save her breaking her knuckles on his or anyone else's face.

Coppin, ye'll do just fine. A sudden rush of nostalgia rose within Longoss regarding the woman he'd trained all those years ago.

***

'We're nearly through, General,' the young witchunter said, as a row of prisoners behind him hacked at the rock with picks and shovels. Rubble littered the ground around their feet in the torch-lit tunnel.

Exley Clewarth and his men had travelled for hours down a long, ancient tunnel before awaiting a sign from above. One warrior monk, the youngest and fastest, had been sent back to the surface by Exley, to inform men he had in place there that the Witchunter General had found the tunnel and now was the time to make their move.

Egan Dundaven had worked out the approximate distance to the area where Tyndurris stood, but not exactly where to dig up from, and had been worried they could end up breaching the main sewer pipe, or dig up for weeks just to come out in the middle of a road or another building.

As they'd waited in the small, torch-lit tunnel, the ceiling above and behind a spot they'd passed earlier had begun to shake, releasing earth in clouds and clumps alike. Exley had prayed for it to be the lowest subterranean floor of Tyndurris, for he'd previously given an order to his men on the inside of the guild – once they received the signal – to create as many explosions as they could in the lowest level, which he'd hoped would allow him to dig up from the correct spot in the tunnel.

It had worked well, and his planned riot had not only worked as a signal to his men within Tyndurris, but had kept the guild's men-at-arms at bay whilst his insiders did what was needed in the lower chambers.

Exley had been informed by those on the inside that the lower chambers had no defensive spells to stop anyone from breaking in, so once he'd heard several explosions and was sure they were where they needed to be, he'd ordered the prisoners to dig up and into Tyndurris.

A shard of light broke through the ceiling suddenly and one of the prisoners fell away, only to be covered in falling rubble. Exley gave an order and the rest of the prisoners – picks and shovels in hands – clambered up and over the half-buried man, entering the lowest chamber of Tyndurris.

Two young guardsmen stood grinning at them as they climbed through the hole, their faces black with soot as a handful of pots lay smoking on a thick table in the centre of the room. The hole had opened up just to the side of the table, and as Exley came through, the young men bowed low.

'You have done well, both of you,' their Witchunter General said. 'I had feared you would be captured once you started, but you proved me wrong. Sir Samorl be with you both. Now lead the way, gentlemen, we have His work to do now.'

Both of the men – the guild's livery emblazoned on their padded gambesons – opened the bolted door of the lower chamber and raced outside, swords drawn.

'What's happening in there?' a man outside asked, but instead of an answer from the two men in the guild's livery, the magician who'd asked the question had two short-swords thrust into his stomach. He collapsed to the floor writhing in pain before Exley Clewarth, striding out of the chamber behind the two impostors, finished him off.

'On me!' the Witchunter General shouted as he followed his two insiders up the stairs. They both hesitated before the next floor, but after a brief pause and a nod to one another, they burst through the door and instantly threw themselves to the ground.

A young magician dropped a book as the two men crashed through the door and hit the floor hard. He ran over to them immediately, crouching to see if they were alright, but he never got back up after Exley ran from the darkness of the stairwell and thrust his rapier into the magician's back.

Exley's two men shoved off the dying man and continued through the novices training chamber and on to the next door, which led to a set of narrow, winding stairs.

'Is this chamber clear?' Exley demanded, as he looked around at the other doors around the room.

'Yes, General. He was the only one working down here tonight. The next floor is the treasury though and heavily guarded, although some of the guards went to assist with the riot outside.'

Exley nodded. 'Very well, let's mob them on the next floor. Master Dundaven?'

Egan Dundaven came forward, pushing past the prisoners on the stairs. 'Yes General?'

'I want the prisoners up ahead, behind these two.' Exley motioned to the two men-at-arms at the door.

'Very well, General.' Egan moved back and shouted for the prisoners to come forward. Once they'd filled the novices training chamber, Exley addressed them himself.

'This is it, you dogs, your chance to win your freedom. We want the next floor taking, and let me tell you what floor that is…' he left a dramatic pause before continuing. 'The treasury.'

The prisoners' eyes widened and more than half grinned wickedly, some rubbing their hands together at the thought of what lay in wait above.

'I won't lie to you, it'll be tough going to get in there, but *when* you do, whatever you find is yours.' The prisoners started to cheer and Exley hissed at them to shut their mouths, and then motioned for them to follow the two men in front, adding, 'Do whatever it takes, boys… whatever it takes.'

The two traitorous men-at-arms ran up the stairs with the prisoners – picks and shovels still in hands – seemingly chasing them. They burst through the doors onto the treasury's floor and called frantically for aid.

The treasury's outer chamber tapered to a narrow doorway on the right, with an open door straight ahead which revealed more stone steps. The two crossbowmen facing up those steps turned then, surprised at the sudden outburst behind them. Upon seeing the prisoners chasing their fellow guards, they instinctively loosed their deadly bolts, taking down a prisoner each. It wasn't nearly enough though and before they could even reach for their swords, they were overwhelmed and beaten to the ground.

The slits in the tapered walls snapped with the sound of loosed bolts as the crossbowmen behind them shot two more prisoners who were battering the fallen guards.

Exley's inside men ran to the treasury door and hammered on it as the prisoners advanced, but the men inside had strict orders not to open it to anyone once the outer chamber was breached. The two young men, although technically on the same side as the prisoners, were hacked down mercilessly as the group of murderers, thieves and rapists attempted to batter the door down with picks, shovels and the swords and crossbows of the dead.

Exley stood in the shadows of the stairwell and grimaced at the loss of his two men, but swiftly pushed it from his mind as two more prisoners fell to bolts coming from the arrow slits in the tapered walls.

Exley pointed and two witchunters moved forward, drawing hand-held crossbows before running up to the slits where the men inside were reloading. A heartbeat later and the guild's crossbowmen were dead, a small crossbow bolt buried in each man's head. The two witchunters who'd killed them quickly reloaded and peered back through the arrow slits to see if anyone was trying to take up the positions of the fallen men inside.

As expected, two guards ran forward from behind the slits to drag the fallen crossbowmen back. They too fell as the witchunters loosed their reloaded weapons through the slits once more. Six loyal guards had died in that short space of time; two in the outer chamber and four behind the supposedly protective wall. The two witchunters reloaded their crossbows a second time and looked on again through the slits, waiting for anyone else who may be foolish enough to try and relieve the dead guards' posts.

Nodding his approval of his witchunters' success, Exley pointed to the door opposite him. Two warrior monks rushed forward and took up positions either side of the open door in case anyone came to assist the treasury from above.

The treasury door was made of heavy oak, reinforced with iron studs as well as magic and so the prisoners picks, shovels, swords and crossbows made no marks whatsoever as they hammered on and rebounded off the now blue-shimmering door.

'Tell them to try the bloody walls,' Exley said, and Egan raced forward to give the order. A few prisoners carried on at the doors whilst the rest started on the walls. The stone chipped away and Exley laughed. How stupid the guild was to reinforce a wooden door and then assume the ancient stone would do fine on its own. He knew it would take time, but his men on the inside had informed him that any casualties from the riot would head to the barracks on the floor above, where clerics would treat them, clerics such as the damned gnome this whole mission was about. He would allow these men their treasure and then they would assault the floor above, take the gnome and retreat back through the tunnels, saving Exley and his men the trouble of fighting through floor after floor to find what he'd come for.

Almost an hour had passed by the time the prisoners smashed through the thick stone and into the treasury's middle chamber; there was another reinforced door between that room and the treasury's vault.

The first prisoners through the hole died as two remaining guards cut them down with sword and axe. Numbers soon overwhelmed the guards and they were hacked down as more and more prisoners pushed through the still-crumbling hole.

Once the guards' screaming had stopped, another scream of pure terror followed, soon accompanied by more of the same. Exley, from the outer chamber of the treasury, looked around to his fellow Samorlians, who were clearly as confused as he was. He moved quickly then, climbing through the hole as some of the prisoners tried to push back out again.

A tremendous roar shook the room then and more men screamed and tried to scramble back out of the hole, but Exley forced them back with the point of his rapier. Two witchunters followed him through as more prisoners ran back from around a corner, trying to hide or push towards the hole. Exley strode past them all as a near deafening roar echoed around the middle chamber.

Exley almost fell back as his unbelieving eyes took in the scene. Several prisoners lay burnt on the floor as a blood-red fire drake sat on its haunches on the far side of them, the back of its body hidden behind another corner.

How big is this place? Exley wondered, trying to map it in his head from what he'd seen in the outer chamber.

Lurching forward suddenly, the beast's teeth filled maw snapped at a cowering prisoner who pissed himself whilst pressing himself against the far wall. Roaring, the fire drake shifted its scaly bulk and Exley just managed to jump back as a rush of liquid fire engulfed the cowering prisoner. His pick clattered to the ground as he rolled screaming in agony, before dying horribly as his skin charred and curled.

'Is that what I think it is?' the young witchunter behind Exley shouted.

The beast roared again.

Exley tilted his head briefly, before shaking it and laughing. 'No.'

After another burst of fire, the Witchunter General stepped out from the tapered wall and charged the snorting beast. He ran straight past the drake's head – which seemed unusually slow in its reaction to his movement – and around the next corner.

A shrill female scream rang out and the red scaled beast shivered, faded slightly and then disappeared completely, leaving nothing but the smouldering corpses of those it had burnt behind.

Exley strode back around the corner with a freshly blooded rapier. He grinned to the prisoners who stood mouths open in awe at him.

'Sorceress,' he said, laughing. 'It wasn't real, you fools. Now come on, we'll take the floor above and find someone who can get this door open for you... oh, and if you find a gnome up there, save him for me.'

The prisoners cheered their new found hero, who unbolted the middle door to let them back into the outer chamber. Exley Clewarth's two witchunters grinned back at him as they followed the prisoners out.

The awaiting Egan Dundaven wore a mixed expression of intrigue and confusion as his companions emerged.

Chapter 36: Deals

The rising sun was swiftly lightening the pale blue morning sky to reveal a patchwork of white clouds. Birds sang and dew glistened on the grass of the balloon crew's camp.

A bucket of cold water brought the remaining two crew members around with sharp intakes of breath. Their heads thumped behind their eyes, which blurred as another bucket was tipped over them. They sucked in the cold morning air again as they looked around, trying to bring up their hands to wipe their faces, before realising they were bound tightly behind their backs.

As their vision cleared, they saw the three dark blurs in front of them change into men; black clad and cloaked with wide brimmed hats and rapiers at their sides.

'Wakey-wakey, gentlemen,' the witchunter to the left said. One of the others sniggered.

'What's going on?' one of the captives asked, his long blonde hair matted across his handsome features as water dripped from his chin.

'Shut your mouth, *elf*,' the middle witchunter said.

The witchunter on the left held up his hand, silencing the speaker. 'No...' Horler Comlay said slowly, his voice little more than a croak. He crouched down to face the two men as he continued. 'This one's a half-elf.'

'An abomination then,' the witchunter in the centre of the trio continued, and Horler held up his hand again, throwing the man a vicious look.

'Don't listen to him, my friend,' Horler said, with a poor attempt at a genuine smile. 'He speaks without thinking. He is ignorant is all.'

'He's from the south, it's understandable,' the human captive said. 'Don't suppose you have many half-elves down there do you?' He was clearly trying to pander to the men that held them hostage.

'Precisely, my good friend. I recruited him from an old friend of mine, the southern Witchunter General.' The two witchunters hid their sniggers as both knew of Horler's hatred for Exley Clewarth. 'This is all a huge misunderstanding,' Horler continued. 'We stumbled across your camp in the night. Filled with goblins it was, with you two bound and tied and your companions... well... I'm afraid they'd already been killed.' Both men looked around, eyes wide, in an attempt to see their fallen comrades. 'We took the liberty of burying them after we chased off the little green bastards.' Horler smiled tightly this time, attempting to look sympathetic.

'Dead... all of them?' the half-elf asked with incredulity. He looked sideways at his one remaining companion before clenching his jaw and straightening his posture. 'Then why are we still bound, Master...?'

'Master Comlay at your service.' The Witchunter General stood and bowed. 'We didn't want you to wake and attack us thinking we were your enemy of course. Here, I'll untie you now.'

Horler pulled a knife from his belt and knelt to cut the ropes at the men's backs. He hesitated as the knife touched. 'We would ask for a deal, if it isn't too much trouble of course, for your freedom. It is of the utmost urgency and a matter of great importance to Altoln's safety.'

Both men looked at each other again, struggling to come to terms with the news they'd just received.

'A deal?' the human asked, suspiciously.

'Well, I say deal, but obviously I am going to cut your bonds anyway.' And so he did. 'So it's more of a favour, for those who have helped you.'

The half-elf looked to the human, his worry clear to see, but the human merely shrugged and nodded his agreement to Horler. He stretched his arms out in front of him and rubbed his wrists.

'Excellent,' Horler said, standing once more and pulling both men to their feet. He clapped the half-elf on the back. 'We will show you to your friends' graves should you wish to pay your last respects, and then I will explain our request.'

Both men nodded again, continuing to rub their wrists as they followed Horler to the mounds of fresh earth at the far side of the encampment. As they followed, the other two witchunters fell in behind them and snarled at the thought of working with a half-elf.

***

The small room had fallen quiet as Coppin's training petered out; the woman clearly shattered and in need of food and a drink.

When did any of us last eat or drink anything? Sears thought. He looked to Longoss as the man's stomach growled audibly, and couldn't help but laugh at the timing. Longoss looked back at Sears and nodded, whilst rubbing his own belly.

'She needs food,' Sears said. 'We all do.'

'Aye,' Longoss agreed, 'and she needs clothes.'

Coppin looked up from where she'd rested her head on the side of Longoss' chair. 'Did someone say food? I don't remember the last time I ate.'

'Nor do we,' Sears said. 'I think I need to go find something—'

Longoss held up his hand. 'I'll go.' He waved away Sears' attempted protests and pushed himself to his feet, using one of the chair's arms to do so. 'I know Dockside better than you, Sears, and ye know it. I also know what to look for with regards to the bastard Black Guild.'

Sears looked unsure, but nodded all the same.

'Ye won't be long, will ye?' Coppin asked, concern evident in her voice and expression.

Longoss shook his head and smiled a gold-less smile before moving to the door.

'Don't stray too far,' Sears said. 'Ye're vulnerable on yer own now, Longoss.'

'Don't I know it,' the big man said. 'But I'm still a mean bastard,' he

314

added, winking at Coppin, who nodded and smiled before rising and moving towards Sears.

Unlocking and opening the door a crack, Longoss peered outside and then moved swiftly through and into the street beyond, closing the door behind him, which Sears moved across to and locked.

'He'll be alright, lass.'

Coppin nodded, but looked unconvinced as she settled next to where Sears had been sitting. The big man walked across and sat beside her, hoping he was right.

Longoss checked the rooftops as he walked swiftly down the deserted street. Despite the rising sun, dark shadows clung to the narrow street's edges, and as he walked past several black crossed doors, he made a point of heading towards those shadows, intent on outing whoever may be using them as cover.

No shadow he passed through bore any hidden agent of the Black Guild, but as Longoss turned a corner, making his way towards a baker he knew of nearby, he walked almost fully into an elongated, plain white mask. The grey eyes behind the mask widened briefly as they took in Longoss' own.

The two men jumped back a step, both equally startled and unused to being taken by surprise.

'Blanck,' Longoss said, his voice rasping through gritted teeth.

The assassin – his posture now defensive – rose both of his empty hands slowly, palms forward. 'Longoss,' the assassin said, his voice betraying his genuine surprise at bumping into his intended target, for although Longoss was exactly who Blanck had meant to find, the assassin had believed him to be in a hideout nearby, not wondering the streets. Blanck made a mental note to punish the watchers who'd been assigned to Longoss should he survive his encounter with the renowned assassin. Smiling behind his mask suddenly, Blanck remembered that Longoss had given his word to the whore, and that word was to never again kill.

As Blanck's posture relaxed, Longoss spoke slowly to the assassin, whilst risking the occasional glance about the area for signs of other threats. 'Do not mistake my word not to kill as a sign of weakness, lad. For there're many things I can do to ye without taking yer life, should the need arise.'

Blanck's defensive posture, although extremely subtle, returned. His hands, however, stayed high, away from the cloak that hid his weapons. 'Undoubtedly,' he said, his tilting mask muffling his words ever so slightly. 'There's no reason to prove that though, Longoss. I sought you out to talk, nothing more, although I admit I didn't expect to see you out and about.' The mask tilted back the other way, its jerking movements intended to distract.

Unaffected by Blanck's methods, Longoss glanced quickly about the place again, but saw nothing but a couple of children playing in the gutter further along the street he'd been turning from. *Watchers.*

'I'm alone,' Blanck said, finally lowering his hands, but keeping them out to the sides.

'Sure.' Longoss balled his fists as he squeezed them tight, eager to wring the scrawny neck of the man opposite him. 'I know exactly why ye were coming to see me, Blanck, and it weren't for no talking, not if Poi Son sent ye, just like he sent Bill, although *you* might not be as lucky as he was.'

'Aye, maybe, but I'd rather talk to you and sort this shit out, Longoss, that's the truth.'

'Ye're wiser than ye look then,' Longoss said, hinting he knew the face behind the mask.

Blanck didn't miss that comment and it unnerved him as to how the former assassin could know what he looked like unmasked, something very few knew indeed.

'Come back, Longoss. I can talk to Poi Son. This mark, it's important to him; to the guild. He wanted you, no other. He'll make exceptions for that, I'm sure of it. Don't throw it all away over some girl.'

Longoss bristled, but kept his anger in check as he thought about the mark, knowing that finding that out, and telling Sears, was a damned sure way to hurt Poi Son and the guild as a whole. 'Who's the mark, Blanck? Tell me and I'll reconsider.'

Female laughter from above Longoss lifted his head, revealing an attractive face and long, golden plaited hair hanging down from where the woman crouched on the edge of the roof.

'Terrina what a pleasant surprise,' Longoss said, stepping away from the building and moving so he could keep both assassins in his sights.

'You're a fool if you think Poi Son has told *him* the mark, Longoss. Something this big, that for whatever reason he wants only you to take on, and you think he'd entrust Blanck?' She laughed.

Blanck raised two fingers towards her without taking his eyes from Longoss.

'And you?' Longoss asked.

Her laughter stopped.

'No, I didn't think so, lass.' It was Longoss' turn to laugh. 'In fact, I'm glad he hasn't told either of ye, for I want to pry the answer from Poi Son miself when I next see him. Ye see, kids, I gave me word that should anything happen to Elleth then I'd bring down the Black Guild miself. My only mistake was to think my threat would be enough to save her.'

Terrina laughed and Blanck shook his head, a deep sigh only just audible behind his mask. 'What happened to you, Longoss?' Blanck said as his sister dropped lithely to the street.

'A moment of clarity, that's what, brought to me by an innocent girl.'

'A whore.' Terrina smiled as she saw Longoss' reaction. She turned to Blanck then. 'The whore who's throat you cut, brother.'

Longoss' head snapped to the white mask as Blanck leapt backwards, hissing at and cursing his sister as he did so.

'Oops,' she said, laughing and running around the side of Longoss as he

316

charged the masked assassin, a roar of anguish tearing from his gold filled mouth and a small eating knife appearing in his hand.

As soon as Blanck had landed his backwards leap, he rolled to one side, coming up into a run whilst drawing two daggers. He parried the small knife that came in at him as he passed Longoss, and scored a hit on the big man's thrusting arm at the same time.

Longoss cursed and spun away from the wounding blade, just in time to deflect a lunge from one of Terrina's stilettos. She followed up with a high kick, which Longoss barely managed to avoid as he ducked away from the woman, finally holding both assassins in his sights once more.

'She was no fucking mark!' Longoss shouted, his anger aimed at the white mask facing him.

Blanck shrugged. 'She was to me, Longoss. You've taken enough out yourself to know that's all they are, that it's nothing personal.'

Terrina laughed. 'Oh, but it was so much more, Longoss. Blanck couldn't wait to play with your little whore—'

Terrina dived to the side as Blanck swung for her. 'That's all you are now, Longoss – a mark,' she said, winking at her furious brother as she tried to move around her target.

'Not such a big one if you two're all Poi Son sent.' Longoss backed away from Terrina and subtly moved towards Blanck.

'Ah, but you assume much,' Terrina said, playfully skipping further around Longoss, placing him between the two assassins, 'to think we're the only assassins to be offered you as a mark.'

Without replying, Longoss ran at Blanck, his sudden explosive motion clearly shocking the masked assassin, who only just managed to side step the attack. Longoss, however, had anticipated Blanck's reaction and his trailing, open palm slapped against the assassin's mask, knocking it askew as Longoss turned and kicked out, connecting with the man's closest leg.

Blanck allowed his knee to give way, saving it from breaking and allowing him to drop to the ground and roll, away from Longoss' next attack and towards his swiftly approaching sister, who leapt over him to lash out at Longoss as she landed.

Two red lines appeared across Longoss' face, opening his cheek as Terrina's stilettos continued down, scoring shallow cuts across his outstretched arm.

Longoss cursed and spun to face the female assassin, parrying and barely avoiding a barrage of double lunges, slashes and kicks as she came at him, her features lit with glee.

Stepping back again and again, leading Terrina on, Longoss chose the moment of Blanck's renewed attack to throw himself at the woman, allowing her blades to rake his ribs as he smashed his head into her petite nose. Blood showered her lips, which let out a cry of pain and shock as her head snapped back.

Blanck's attack had missed, but he came on all the faster upon seeing the danger to his sister.

Aye, lad, now it's your turn to lose it. Longoss turned from the reeling woman and stepped in towards Blanck's hasty attack.

The assassin drove one of his daggers into Longoss' left shoulder – as Longoss had allowed – and as the blade sank to the hilt, Longoss dropped low, curled his thick right arm around the assassin's legs and sliced across the back of Blanck's knees with his eating knife.

A muffled scream erupted from behind Blanck's white mask as his legs gave way to the sliced tendons. The dagger sucked from Longoss' shoulder as Blanck held onto it before hitting the ground hard, thrashing about and finally dropping both daggers to paw at his near useless legs.

At a shriek of anger, Longoss jumped to the side, barely missing Terrina as she came in at him fast. He dodged two more kicks, but a third struck him where she'd sliced his ribs and Longoss fell back, rolling across the floor as the woman thrust her stilettos towards him, her brother screaming on the floor beside her.

'I may have given me word not to kill, Blanck,' Longoss shouted, regaining his footing and blocking out the pain, 'but I also swore to bring the Black Guild down, and you two shites are Black Guild!'

'You'll be dead before then,' Terrina shouted, lunging at Longoss again. He avoided her lunge, and the next, his gold teeth flashing as he used the woman's anger against her, opening himself up again for her to step in close, anticipating a killing blow. Before she could plunge her leading stiletto into Longoss' heart though, the man dropped to the floor, taking the woman by surprise, her forward momentum tripping her over the prone man as he rolled towards her, taking her legs and dropping her hard to the filthy cobbles. She managed to bring her trailing hand down to slow her fall, but the impact audibly cracked her wrist. Terrina cried out in pain.

Longoss wasted no time and threw himself back at the woman, lashing out with his fist and smashing her already broken nose. Despite her head rocking back, she recovered quickly as her watering eyes searched for her attacker. She saw only the blade that slashed across her pretty face, which scored a deep line across both cheeks and her flattened nose. Screaming all the more, Terrina lashed out with her foot, connecting with Longoss' jaw as he came at her again with the small knife.

Longoss took the blow to the jaw and the next to the chest. He ignored the pain and continued to slash at the woman kicking him. Her legs were cut to ribbons as he ran his knife across them again and again, eventually pressing his weight against the attack, forcing her leg down and pinning it as his free hand held her broken wrist to the ground. She cried out all the more as he pulled the knife across her forehead, carving up her smooth skin and ruining her face.

Longoss rolled to the side as Terrina managed to bring her good hand round, taking his left ear with the stiletto she gripped tightly, although she never saw the strike, since her eyes were filled with her own blood and tears.

318

She coughed several times before passing out from the pain.

Pressing his hand against the bloody hole where his ear had been, Longoss finally stood. He looked down on the mutilated woman. *I never wanted any of this, ye fools. I just wanted to walk away, with Elleth…*

He looked across at Terrina's brother then, who was crawling across the street, a trail of blood stretched out behind him. Longoss staggered across to the man. Crouching in front of him, he smiled gold despite his injuries.

'Even unable to kill, I will bring the Black Guild down. Do ye see now, Blanck?' Grey eyes flinched as the white mask pulled back from Longoss' knife, which flashed across in front of it.

'But you, Blanck… you took Elleth away from me personally.' The mask shook and Longoss could hear Blanck mumbling. 'Yes,' Longoss said, nodding, 'personally.' He leaned in closer and sneered at the man behind the mask. 'You made it personal, Blanck, you. Poi Son might have ordered it and he'll pay for that, believe you me, but you're the cunt that did it, sliced her throat, and there ain't no excuse for that. I may have killed many in my time Blanck, but not like that, not a defenceless girl, and for that ye'll suffer the most.'

Blanck screamed and his white mask shed red tears as Longoss took the assassin's eyes.

'It's a shame ye'll never get to see the only woman I ever truly fucked up; yer sister over there.'

Blanck screamed even more, in pain and anger, and thrashed about on the cobbles as Longoss moved about him.

'She was a pretty one yer sister, a real pretty one in fact, but then again, so was Elleth.'

'Please,' Blanck managed, after coughing on the blood running down the inside of his mask.

'Please?' Longoss said, almost whispering. 'Ye better be joking, Blanck, asking me for mercy? Ye better be fucking joking!' he roared, as he pulled the assassin's braes down just enough to slice away his manhood.

Blanck's scream caused pigeons a block away to lift into the sky, and then the assassin threw up behind his mask.

Longoss pulled the mask free as Blanck spat the blood flecked vomit across the ground.

'Can't have ye choking now, can we, lad? I gave me word not to kill, ye see?'

Rising to his feet after cleaning his blade on Blanck's cloak, Longoss took one last look at the butchered siblings, before grimacing at the pain now flooding his body from his many wounds.

I'll be needing some more of that juice, Sears, but not before I get us some food, drink and Coppin some clothes. Then we'll be on our way, for I think it's safe to say the Black Guild knows where we are, and I reckon I've just shat in the bloody hornets' nest.

Shaking his head at it all, Longoss continued on his way down the street, towards the bakers he knew.

***

As the riot continued outside Tyndurris, another bloodied guard was rushed into the barracks where both Morri and Cullane attended to a man who'd been hit by an old, blunt crossbow bolt. Luckily for him, his thick padded gambeson had taken most of the impact and the bolt tip had only slightly pierced his skin. The impact itself, however, had left him with a fractured rib, and the guard struggled for breath.

'You'll be fine,' Cullane purred, trying to calm the man down as Morri cleaned the wound and rubbed a balm into the skin surrounding it.

'Now, I can't bandage this wound tightly,' Morri explained, 'as I don't want to injure your rib any further or cause you to suffer fluid on your lungs. So once in a while you will have to brace yourself and take a couple of deep—

'What was that?' Morri looked up at Cullane, and then round to Orix and the other clerics tending to the newest victim of the ongoing riot.

Elloise tilted her head. 'It sounded like it came from the floor below… there, again.'

Orix – who was standing on a stool to reach the man he and Elloise were tending to – merely shrugged at the blonde woman next to him.

'There was some kind of experiment in the lower chambers earlier, I heard the explosions,' Morri said.

'Perhaps that's it,' Cullane said, clearly unsure, 'but it sounded like the floor below and it was no explosion—

'There it was again. It sounds like a beast's roar?'

Master Orix shrugged and waved his hands for the clerics to get back to work. 'It'll be that young sorceress showing off to the soldiers,' the old gnome said, as he struggled to mop blood away from the guard who was being held down. 'Will you be still, it's not even deep and you're just making it worse.'

The guard on the bench blushed at the realisation his injury wasn't bad.

A few moments passed before Cullane asked, 'There's no way anyone could have got down to the treasury is there?'

One of the older clerics shook his head. 'We would hear the guards outside this room if they had, no, the treasury is quite—'

The cleric was cut off by a shout outside the door and a clash of weapons. Everyone in the room looked up at each other and paused, whilst the two guards on the benches looked across worriedly to one another.

A bell rang twice before ending suddenly and then someone released a guttural scream from just beyond the closed door to the barracks.

'Weapons,' Orix shouted as he hopped down from the stool and pulled a curved knife from his many pocketed robe, surprising everyone. The two wounded guards swung their legs from the benches and hopped down, both wincing with pain as they did so, but managing to draw their short-swords that lay in scabbards on a table nearby. Both Cullane and Morri, as well as the other clerics in the room, ran to a weapons rack on the wall and pulled off a

320

short-sword each as Elloise took a goedendag and began spinning it with surprising skill.

One of the guards rushed forward and threw a catch on the door before stepping back to join the ragged line stretched loosely from one side of the chamber to the other.

More clashes of metal came from the other side of the door and Cullane muttered something about not having any combat spells prepared. As the words left her mouth, the door itself shook, clearly struck on the far side with something heavy. The people in the room looked around at each other again, wondering how the rioters could have managed to breach both the gates and the tower's entrance, especially through all the men-at-arms currently standing guard outside.

'Almost all of our men are in the courtyard,' the guard with the broken rib said, his breathing shallow and ragged. 'How could anyone get through? They never have before and no one out there's called for battle mages as far as I know? It wasn't that bad out there, no worse than the last riot.'

The door shook again, dust lifting from its hinges.

'Don't wait for them to get too far in,' Orix said. 'As soon as the door opens we attack, understood?' No one replied but everyone nodded as they tensed in anticipation.

'The horn!' the bloodied guard said, as he hobbled over to an old dusty horn sat on a wall bracket. He wiped the mouthpiece quickly before taking a deep breath and blowing long and hard into the curved instrument. The sound was strange, like a hundred strong male choir all humming at once. The note reverberated off everything and everyone in the room.

The banging on the door stopped for a second and then resumed at a higher rate. The guard blew again and the whole room shook; hairs on the back of everyone's necks stood high as the sound struck deep into their ears.

Renewed shouts came from the other side of the door and another man briefly screamed out in pain. Fresh clashes of weapons sounded and the banging on the door stopped. The bloodied guard shoved the thin end of the horn through his belt and came to rejoin the defensive line across the barracks as everyone looked at him in appreciation.

'I don't know if it's ever been used before, but it's supposed to rally every guard and battle mage on station to this point. Let's hope it—'

He was cut off as a large explosion and shouts of terror erupted on the far side of the door.

'Battle mage,' Cullane said, and several of the others nodded, involuntary smiles spreading across most of their faces.

Just then, the door rocked on its hinges and crashed open. A filthy looking man fell to the floor with a pickaxe in his hand. He looked up and snarled as two more similar looking brutes piled through the door past him. A fireball slammed into another man somewhere behind them, clearly cast by the battle mage who was out of sight.

Cullane screamed at the sudden entry – or rather squeaked as her voice rose too high – and the injured guard with the horn rushed forward before Orix could say anything. He was flattened by the ham-like fist of the biggest man, who came quickly for the group before bouncing off what looked like a vertical sheet of water that had suddenly appeared.

Elloise let out a sigh of relief as her defensive spell worked. The three attackers looked furious. 'I can't hold them for long,' she said, as the men swung their picks and shovel at the barrier, its liquid like surface splashing less with every impact.

The sound of someone calling for crossbows to be used came from outside the room, followed by another fireball that briefly lit the open doorway.

'Do something,' Morri said to Cullane.

'Why me?'

'Because the rest of us are clerics and you're a sorceress, you must be able to conjure something up, literally?'

The barrier began to fail.

'I'll go,' the remaining guard said, his free arm cradling his ribs.

The older cleric grabbed the guard by the arm, who winced instantly. 'I get the point,' he conceded, looking at the cleric, who nodded in return.

'Get ready,' Elloise said, as the last strike from a pick caused no more than a ripple in her rapidly fading barrier.

Another cry of pain echoed through from the far room and two of the three men hammering on the barrier glanced back, clearly worried.

'On guard,' Orix cried, his defensive stance a strange sight to his fellow clerics and an amusing one to the three brutish men, who laughed and jeered at the small gnome.

'Ooh…' Cullane looked pleased with herself, but before anyone could ask, her eyes closed, opening a heartbeat later to reveal white, pupil-less orbs. Morri looked at her, full of hope for what she might conjure.

As the barrier fell, the man in the middle – shovel in hand – lurched forward suddenly, before crying out in intense pain. His eyes rolled back and his body jerked in spasms as he raised the shovel and spun, wrapping it round the nearest man's head, surely killing him with the bloody strike.

His remaining companion jumped back, horrified as the shovel wielding brute swung at him wildly. The clerics and remaining guard looked on dumbfounded as the larger of the two men dodged another swipe from the shovel before stepping in and striking his attacker in the side with his pick. The distraction opened up a chance for Elloise and she lunged forward, taking the heavy man's legs from under him with the stave of her goedendag.

Both men hit the ground at the same time, and as the crazed shovel wielder crumpled, Cullane dashed forward and held out her hand. Cullane's pallid bookworm emerged from the man's head and crawled into her palm, whistling and clicking all the way.

Both Morri and Orix laughed out loud as the other clerics and injured guard kept the remaining man at bay with their weapons.

'That was amazing,' Morri said, beaming at the young sorceress.

Whilst her bookworm gradually faded from existence, Cullane blushed. 'It's all I could think of.' She smiled back at Morri.

Another man's scream carried through the open door followed by the sound of more armoured men.

'Listen?' Orix said. They all strained to hear over the shouts and clashes of weapons. 'Whoever it is, they're being beaten back down, not up?'

'Well, of course,' Morri stated matter-of-factly. 'The battle mage and guards will have come down from the riot in the courtyard.'

Orix shook his head and the older cleric looked at the gnome as the answer dawned on him too. 'The first support should have come from the treasury, on the floor below,' the white haired man said, who now held a short-sword to the surviving prisoner's throat.

Orix nodded. 'Correct. The first to attend should have been the treasury guards below, who are, or should be, closer than those outside in the courtyard or on any floor above ground level.'

The two guards in the room nodded slowly in realisation, the one who'd been floored finally coming round and being hauled carefully to his feet by Morri.

'That means they came from below,' Cullane wrinkled her nose in confusion, 'but how? We're already underground, so how could anyone get in a lower chamber? Not through a portal, I can vouch for that,' she added firmly.

Orix shook his head. 'No, Cullane, not a portal. There have long been rumours of underground tunnels though, dating back centuries or more. They may have come through them? Those explosions we heard earlier, and that roaring, from the treasury you thought?' Orix shook his head as it all became clear. Cullane slowly nodded her agreement. Orix pointed to the three men on the floor, two with pools of blood spreading from their still bodies and one whimpering under the gaze of the mages. 'Look at these men, they look like prisoners.'

The others noticed the binding marks on their wrists for the first time.

'But the lower chambers are reinforced with strong magic,' Morri said, and again Orix shook his head.

'The lower chambers are protected from within,' the gnome said, 'to stop magic, explosions and the like from damaging Tyndurris. They have never been protected against anyone breaking in, Morri, not to my knowledge anyway?'

Several in the room shook their heads in disbelief as it all became apparent. The fighting went on outside, seemingly descending the stairs as they fought on.

The guards demanded the remaining prisoner tell them what was happening below, but he refused, and Orix forbade them from harming him to get the truth.

Too many have died and suffered at my hands already, he thought, taking in the bloody scene on the floor of the barracks and the wounds of the two guards, *and it seems they still are…*

***

Managing to force down the last of his stale bread and cheese, Biviano looked again at the barracks door, hoping to see Lord Stowold striding through. The door remained closed and Biviano cursed under his breath before taking a swig of his small-beer.

'There, finished,' he said, looking across to the cleric, Effrin, who'd ordered him to eat and drink like the rest of them. 'Where's the pantaloon thief gone?'

'To relieve himself,' Effrin said.

Biviano rolled his eyes. 'Just say piss for once, will ye?'

'Piss.'

Biviano grinned. 'There, wasn't so hard now was it?'

Effrin laughed and then nodded towards the door at the end of the barracks, which opened, causing Biviano to jump to his feet.

Bollingham walked in and Biviano swore, before turning and kicking his bed.

'Kicking yer bed again?' Bollingham said, as he reached and dropped onto his own.

'Sod off, Bolly, I'm not in the mood.'

'Oh, ye're in a mood alright.'

As Biviano turned towards Bollingham, a retort almost leaving his lips, the barrack's door swung open again and a barking voice called all to attention. Biviano spun full circle and stood at the end of his bunk, biting back a smile as he caught Bollingham in the corner of his eye leaping to his feet and doing the same.

Bagnall Stowold strode into the room with his squire at his side. Both were armoured head to toe, although the squire wore far less than the Earl, whose blued steel plate carried decorative carvings of various battlefield scenes. The squire held Stowold's open faced bascinet, its riveted-maille aventail draped over his arm as the boy followed a pace behind his lord. Stowold was walking down the barracks briefly inspecting each guardsman he passed, prodding some with the shaft of the war-hammer he carried.

When he reached Bollingham, he took a double take. 'Nice pantaloons,' he said, one eyebrow raised as he looked the man up and down. One of the guardsmen opposite Bollingham winked at him and laughed silently.

'I saw that, Jay Strawn,' Stowold said. Jay's mouth hung open as he looked from the back of the constable's head to the men around him. Several of them shrugged.

'Are we ready, milord?' Biviano asked, unable to hold off any longer.

Stowold spun on his heals to face Biviano, and Bollingham sighed with relief.

'Aye, Biviano, we're ready,' Stowold said, turning to face the room. 'Alright lads, I'm sure you're all aware of the King's order for the Samorlian Church to cease all activity in the city with regards to its so-called witch hunting.' Several guardsmen nodded. 'Alas, it has been brought to my attention that they have not. In fact from all accounts… well, Biviano here,' Stowold pointed at Biviano with his war-hammer, 'they've been torturing innocents and are currently holding a prisoner, Ellis Frane, who has been tortured by their inquisitors.'

No one stirred, as all had heard the story.

'It is because of this, that we're to march on the Samorlian Cathedral. Now I understand some of you will follow the Samorlian faith, and so I say this to you…' He paused, looking around at the eyes of every man before continuing. 'I couldn't give Sir Samorl's hairy cock what you believe right now. Your faith is your own, but these bastards have been doing gods-know-what to whoever they want for however long and right under your damned noses!' Stowold's voice rose as he spoke, his maille coif covered head turning as he continued to look everyone in the eye. 'City Guard, ha! You've allowed innocents to be taken from all over the city, from this very district no doubt; to be raped, tortured and butchered in the cathedral that sits in the centre of your district, and I, for one, want revenge if nothing else. What say you all?'

The guardsmen voiced their anger as one.

Stowold nodded, a smile pulling at the corner of his mouth before he continued. 'Our main aim is to rescue Ellis Frane from the torture chamber below the cathedral and to arrest any and all witchunters, warrior monks and inquisitors we encounter. As well as this, I want the Grand Prick. He is my main target.

'Now, it's obvious we may receive strong resistance by skilled combatants and I am aware our numbers are depleted of late. Quite frankly, you dogs, I don't give a putrid rat pup's arse about those facts. All I require is for you lot to go in there hard and fast. You feel threatened and unable to take anyone alive, you have my support in running the murdering shites through. Do I make myself clear?'

Again the men shouted their understanding as one, Biviano loudest of them all.

'Excellent, now make your way to the stables, we're going in mounted,' Stowold said, to which almost every man cheered, before moving swiftly to the door.

'Not you, Biviano, you're riding with me,' Stowold added swiftly. Biviano nodded and glanced to Effrin, who nodded once to him before following the others from the room.

As they turned to leave, Stowold turned back to Bollingham, who still stood by his bed. 'Problem, Bollingham?'

How does he remember all our names? 'I thought it best someone stayed to guard the barracks, milord, if it's emptying of men.'

Stowold looked to Biviano, his eyebrows raised. Biviano snarled at

Bollingham, and the constable turned back to the pantaloon wearing guardsman. 'You do, do you?'

'Aye, milord.' Bollingham chewed his bottom lip.

'Well, I think it best someone else rides with me, eh Biviano?'

Smiling wide, Biviano nodded. 'Oh aye, milord, I think that's exactly what's needed.'

Bollingham closed his eyes and released a heavy sigh, before nodding and voicing his acknowledgement. As Bagnall Stowold laughed and headed for the door, Biviano and his squire in tow, Bollingham moved to follow.

'Ah-ah,' Stowold said, without turning round, 'not before you change those ridiculous pantaloons. And be quick about it, man.'

Biviano smiled all the more.

***

Exley Clewarth had successfully taken the outer barracks of Tyndurris, and although the three guards in that room had fought well, his prisoners had finally outnumbered them, leaving his witchunters and warrior monks – his rearguard – completely unharmed.

Despite the good fortune, the Witchunter General had snarled when a strange horn sounded twice from behind the locked door to the inner barracks, of which several prisoners had been pounding on with shovels and picks. Within seconds of the horn being blown, two more of the guild's men-at-arms had come clattering down the stairs to be struck down by the two warrior monks positioned either side of the stairwell. Those two monks had fallen almost immediately after, as a battle mage seemed to float down the stairs at such a speed the monks had been given no time to react. The red-robed mage had dispatched them swiftly with a wooden wand which instantly grew as long and sharp as a stiletto, and one of the monks had released a brief, stomach churning scream as the wand plunged into his eye. The mage had then thrown his free hand towards the nearest group of prisoners to him, all of which exploded in a ball of fire. As quickly as the fire had engulfed them, it had dissipated, leaving naught but ash on the stone floor.

Exley had shouted for crossbows then, and several had been loosed at the red-robed mage, who'd managed to leap back into the stairwell in time to avoid being struck, but not before he'd released another fireball.

At that very moment, the prisoners at the door had smash through to the room beyond.

The fireball had engulfed a prisoner in front of Exley as he'd given the order for the rest to charge the stairwell. The Witchunter General had been more than surprised when the prisoners had obeyed, and so he'd taken that opportunity to run for the lower stairwell, barrelling down and taking Egan Dundaven and two more witchunters with him. A warrior monk had followed them down and all of them had landed in a great heap of waving arms and kicking legs whilst renewed fighting had been heard above.

Exley had been pulled to his feet immediately, and ordered the guarding of the stairwell door at the same time, which had been slammed shut by Egan. Exley had then barred the door and ordered all of his men with crossbows to aim for it, telling them to fire only when they saw a target, to aim true and to make sure, 'It's that bloody mage in red!'

It had all seemed like a rushed blur to Egan, and as Exley had slumped against the wall and slid to the floor, kicking a prisoner who came too close, Egan had asked his General what their next move would be. The look he'd received had told him the Witchunter General wasn't in the mood to answer questions.

Exley sat for what seemed like an age after the sounds of fighting above them faded, trying to think of a way to rectify the problem when, without warning, a hollow image of that same red-robed mage fell through the ceiling to stand in the centre of the room. One of the witchunters instinctively pulled the trigger on his crossbow, sending the bolt through the flickering image and into the leg of a prisoner who dropped to the floor screaming. Everyone jumped except Exley, who raised his head and released a long sigh as he looked upon the image that now turned to him.

'Take him in the back and sort that leg out,' the witchunter who'd shot the prisoner said, and two others followed the order without question, dragging the crying man into the middle chamber of the treasury where the charred corpses of those who fell to the sorceress' conjured fire drake still lay.

'Who is in charge?' the broken, crackled voice of the red mage's image boomed.

Exley stood.

The image frowned at the Witchunter General. 'What is your business here Samorlian? You have broken the King's law entering this tower by force and we must ask you to surrender, although I'd much prefer it if you didn't, so I could finish you myself.'

Exley laughed and rested his hand on his rapier's hilt. 'I am here for the gnome called Orix. He is a traitor to Altoln for his dealings with arcane magic and must be dealt with accordingly. Hand him over and we shall leave. A simple deal I think. No more trouble for the life of a traitor?'

The red-robed mage glared at Exley and eventually shook his head. 'We do not bargain with those who assault our guild and home. You are criminals and will be tried by the King and his magistrates. It is not for you, Samorlian, to decide who is guilty and who is not; who should be executed and who shall not.' The battle mage was clearly furious and his image shivered, almost blinking out as his rage boiled within him.

'You have a wonderful collection in the vaults down here, mage... it would be a shame to see it all burn, that which doesn't fall into the hands of the gangs of Dockside that is.' Exley turned and winked at the few remaining prisoners. They looked from Exley to each other, grinning and rubbing their hands together in anticipation.

'Do not threaten me, witcher!' the mage's image shouted. 'I won't have it, not in my home. You will not—'

The image flickered as the mage was interrupted by another, fainter voice to his side, and when he continued, his voice was barely audible as he spoke through clenched teeth. 'Master Orix asks you not to touch the relics in that vault. He said he values them far more than his own life, and so he wishes to speak with you alone in the stairwell between these two rooms.'

Silence followed, broken only by the occasional whimper coming from the middle chamber of the treasury where the prisoner with the crossbow bolt in his leg was being treated.

Eventually, after Exley looked to Egan and his other companions, he answered. 'Very well, you will send the gnome onto the stairs where he will knock on this chamber's door. I will then wait a random length of time before opening the door. Any tricks and whoever is stood on the stairs, the gnome or not, will die.'

The battle mage snarled. 'You are to come unarmed.'

Exley laughed. 'You think me a fool? No, I don't suppose you do, you're too intelligent to be ignorant enough to think a Witchunter General a fool, so I will take off my rapier, put down my crossbow and hide a knife, as always, somewhere on my person, just as you would expect of me, just as your gnome will no doubt do as well.' He grinned at the flickering image then, as the battle mage's face turned almost puce with rage. The mage looked to the side and closed his eyes for a brief moment, before nodding his agreement.

The image disappeared.

***

A not too displeasing tune was being plucked on the strings of a lute, as two children stood opposite the man playing the instrument. Poi Son glanced up at the filthy boys, one eyebrow raised, as he stopped playing and placed the instrument on his lap.

'You are sure it was Longoss?'

'Aye, Master Son,' the taller of the two boys said, both of whom had recently been playing in the gutter of a street in Dockside, 'big man, with gold teeth.'

Poi Son ground his own teeth as he looked across to a wiry man stood in the corner of the room. The man swallowed hard and averted his gaze.

'And you say he bested them both, at the same time?' Both boys nodded. 'But they're still alive?'

'Aye, Master Son, but in a bad way,' the boy who'd spoken before said. The other nodded his agreement.

'Elaborate,' Poi Son said. When the boys looked to each other, confused, the Black Guild master added, 'Explain what he did to them.'

'Oh...' The taller boy's eyes showed his fear as he thought back to what he'd witnessed. 'After the fight proper, he sliced up the lady... mainly her legs and face, and then moved to the white mask man.' The boy paused, looking to his friend and wrung his hands together.

'Go on.' Poi Son began plucking the strings of his lute again.

'Well,' the taller boy continued, 'he took the man's eyes, from in the mask see, and then...'

'Yes?'

'He cut off his willy,' the boy said. His friend smiled before the memory of it returned and a disturbed look crossed his face.

'I see,' Poi Son said, looking again to the man stood in the corner, then back to the boys. 'Where are my assassins now?'

'We ran and got help from older watchers, Master Son, and they took the man and woman to a safe-house nearby, where they said they'd tend to 'em.'

Poi Son was nodding as the boy spoke. 'Very well, you've done well bringing this to me, very well.' The boys smiled at each other and beamed all the more when the man in the corner stepped forward and handed them a small bag of food each. 'Now off with you,' Poi Son said, 'and don't be speaking of this, understood?' Both boys nodded and the fear in their eyes told Poi Son enough to know they'd keep it to themselves, after all, it wasn't the first time they'd acted as watchers for him and they knew the rewards, as well as the risks should they fail.

After they left the room, Poi Son turned to the man in the corner, eyebrows raised.

The man stepped forward. 'Do you want them taken care of, Master Son?'

'The boys?'

The man shook his head. 'No, sire, Blanck and Terrina. For failing?'

Poi Son pursed his lips and thought for a moment before replying. 'You think you'd have done better against him, Pangan?'

'I never said that, but then again, I haven't taken him as a mark, have I?'

'No, you haven't, have you, despite most of the remaining guild members that aren't dead or dying from this damned plague taking it on. Why is that?'

'Because I'm no fool,' Pangan said flatly.

Poi Son laughed. 'And the siblings were?'

Pangan tilted his head, considering his answer. 'Not necessarily, but as good as they were alone, or together, they were a distraction to one another and Longoss knew that, because he knew them. He knows all of us, for Samorl's sake! All that matter anyway, so we have no advantage over him.'

Nodding, Poi Son plucked away some more at his lute, before looking back to the man. 'I don't want any more public displays like today, do you hear me, Pangan? I stressed how important this mark is to the guild and those two idiots went at Longoss in broad daylight, which is exactly what we don't need right now.'

'Understood.'

'Is it? I'm not so sure, but I want it understood and I want Longoss and his companions silencing. I certainly don't want them leaving Dockside, that's for sure. What's your opinion on how to handle it?'

Rubbing his unshaven chin, Pangan looked past Poi Son. 'Numbers,' he said, finally. 'Longoss knows us all as individuals too well and going at him one or two at a time, despite his word not to kill, won't cut it. We need to hit him in force, especially if he has assistance.'

'Very well,' Poi Son said, nodding. 'Make it so and deal with the siblings too.'

'You want them both dead?'

After a moment's pause, Poi Son shook his head. 'Not both, just Blanck. He's useless to us without his eyes, but his sister once recovered will be more useful than ever.'

Smiling at Poi Son's reasoning, Pangan nodded, turned and left the room.

Poi Son sighed heavily and drew a scroll from the drawer in his desk. He read it for the umpteenth time and then considered the offer from the Assassins Guild in Eatri.

'If things carry on like this,' he whispered to himself, his eyes pouring over the scroll in front of him, 'I may have to take their offer of service after all.'

***

Fields gave way to various copses of trees by the winding River Norln, thickening in places to form small woods as the rough cart path wound through and under a mix of oak, birch, ash and beech trees, to name but a few.

Errolas felt extremely relaxed around the trees. Although he almost always seemed relaxed to the humans, the last few days had left him feeling genuinely concerned and almost anxious for a number of reasons. The open spaces and the abundance of life about him now, however, helped strip those feelings away and add perspective to it all. *Is it the lifestyle of the humans that has brought me so low? I cannot be sure, a lot has happened and a lot leaves me unsure about the near future. But out here, out here I can feel like an elf again.*

Sav visibly relaxed too, constantly breathing in the fresh woodland air, a smell he could only describe to the others as 'green' much to their amusement.

A kingfisher darted across the river, a flash of blue and shimmering orange as it landed on a low, overhanging branch, the rushing water close to its tail as the thin branch bobbed up and down with the added weight. Various birds sang throughout the wooded areas; 'the dawn chorus' Sav had called it and Errolas had nodded his agreement.

The group made to leave Beresford early in the morning, with no sleep and no food in their bellies. As they were leaving, however, the townsfolk had pushed bundles of food into their hands in thanks for helping them safely cross the bridge the night before. The remaining garrison had told the group that riders had been dispatched to call for aid as far away as Rowberry, so help would arrive. When, they didn't know, but they were confident it would arrive eventually.

The goblins would not attempt a crossing during the day the group knew, and so Fal had finally agreed it was time to leave, knowing as he did that their mission needed to be completed. They'd collected horses from the eastern bank's stables and Correia had paid the owners handsomely, knowing the money would go towards rebuilding the western side of the town.

They'd been walking and cantering at intervals for the past couple of hours, heading south along the river, waiting for Errolas to give the order to head inland towards his homeland. Until that order came, the group enjoyed a pleasant ride through the countryside on the eastern shore of the Norln, which provided the first proper chance to catch up with Severun, about his 'execution' and where he'd been since.

'I was really there, it was no Illusion,' Severun corrected, as Starks scratched his head.

'But you're not burnt at all. Oh, Lord Severun it was awful, I feel ashamed I didn't try to act like Sergeant Fal and Sav did,' Starks said, nodding towards the two men riding on the other side of the cloaked wizard.

Sav leaned forward in his saddle and looked across to the young crossbowman. 'Oh no, Starksy lad, Fal was trying to stop me save Severun, not help me.'

'Thanks, Sav,' Fal muttered.

Severun laughed. 'Don't think more of it, gentlemen,' Severun said, finding mirth for the first time since he'd re-appeared. 'I wish I could have told you, but King Barrison wanted no one to know, no one but Correia, Errolas and his high lords of course.'

'So that's what Lord Strickland was doing,' Fal said in sudden realisation. 'He was casting a spell?'

Severun smiled and shook his head. 'No, he was preparing a spell and then *passing* it to me, for want of a better word. I then enacted the spell when the flames rose around me, which was extremely close since I'd been keeping them just far enough away to save my skin, literally. Although I am sure it looked like I was cooking on that pyre. The clothes really started to burn though and I don't mind saying, I was terrified. Once the spell had been passed to me by Lord Strickland, however, I was able to use its stored magic, along with my own magical reserves, to transport away from that place; out of my burning clothing and into a nearby building. It takes a lot of magical and physical energy to transport, as well as time to prepare, hence Lord Strickland's preparation for me, as well as the safe-house he'd organised. Once my 'execution' was over, he came to me with fresh clothes...' Severun looked down and sniffed the black robes and cloak he wore and grimaced. 'Not very fresh now mind. He then helped me out of the city.'

Starks beamed at the wizard. 'That's truly amazing.'

'It is pretty impressive,' Fal said genuinely, a smile lighting his face, 'and I'm sure I speak for us all when I say we're glad you're alive and well.'

'I thank you all, gentlemen, but I'm far from well. Oh, physically yes, but what I've done to Wesson... it hardly leaves me feeling well, or even that I deserve to be alive.'

'Hush now,' Correia said from behind. Her horse moved forward, between Severun and Starks' and she leaned over and laid her hand on the wizard's. 'We have much left to do and we cannot afford for you to think like that. So be glad King Barrison spared you, to put right what you, unknowingly at the time remember, did wrong.'

Severun managed a weak smile and nodded to the woman at his side. 'Thank you Correia, you have always been a good friend to me, and your family to mine before me.'

The others looked at each other surprised and more than a little intrigued, but shrugged it off as Errolas motioned ahead for them to take an upcoming path east.

The group rode on, moving away from the River Norln and through the small wood they'd entered, heading further inland, further to the east and closer to the realm of the elves.

Chapter 37: History Lesson

Sears and Coppin had both been sleeping – despite Sears' attempts to stay awake – when a knock at the door woke them both. Climbing to his feet and drawing his short-sword in one move, Sears crossed the small room to the door, Coppin's worried eyes on his back.

The knock came again and Sears pressed his ear against the door. His look of relief was obvious to Coppin as Longoss declare himself on the other side. The large guardsman held his hand up to stay Coppin whilst he opened the door to the former assassin.

'Shitting hell,' Sears said, as Longoss staggered through the door, a bundle of blood stained clothes and another bundle of what looked like food cradled in his thick, bloodied arms.

Coppin gasped and Longoss' gold teeth flashed before he dropped the bundles and fell to the straw covered floor. Sears missed catching the man because he'd quickly peered outside. Hearing the thump behind him, he closed the door and locked it.

'Sears, help me,' Coppin said, after rushing across the floor to Longoss.

Dropping to one knee, Sears instinctively reached back for his flask, which he brought round to Longoss' lips.

The former assassin shook his head, attempting to wave his companions away as Coppin pulled at his torn, blood soaked shirt to see the wounds beneath – especially the shoulder.

'We drank it all,' Longoss managed through gritted teeth, his eyes on the flask Sears was holding to his lips.

'And it replenishes, Longoss, ye've seen that already.' Sears flashed a worried look Coppin's way.

'Oh aye,' Longoss said, before allowing Sears to pour the bitter liquid down his throat.

Coppin managed to lift Longoss' shirt enough to see the open wound of his shoulder. 'We need to get this bandaged.'

Longoss coughed and his face screwed up at the taste of the tonic. Sears laughed.

'Black Guild,' Longoss said eventually.

'Ye don't say.' Sears shook his head and looked at the various wounds about Longoss' arms and torso. 'Ye take a knock to the head on top of all this?'

'Not that I recall, but me head's fuzzy and everything sounds dull.'

Coppin's eyes suddenly widened as she pulled Longoss' hand away from the side of his head and saw his left ear was missing; a bloody streak stained his head and neck. Knowing the shoulder wound was the worse of the two, she continued what she was doing and looked him in the eye whilst wrapping a strip of Longoss' own torn shirt around his shoulder. 'Ye killed them, the attackers?'

Longoss shook his head. 'Worse.' He flashed gold again.

'I don't wanna know,' Coppin said, looking back to her bandaging.

Sears had moved to the small window and was looking out into the street through the blinds whilst putting his flask back into its pouch. 'We need to move, don't we?'

Longoss nodded. 'Aye, and fast.' His eyes remained on Coppin as she suddenly looked at him again.

'Ye can't move anywhere.' She prodded him on the bandaged shoulder, to which he winced and bit back a curse. 'See?'

'It's his shoulder, Coppin, not his legs,' Sears said, still looking outside. 'He'll start healing soon and can still walk. His shoulder—'

'He's exhausted, Sears,' Coppin cut in, but Sears continued as if he hadn't heard her.

'His shoulder will be the least of his, or our worries should the Black Guild find us here.'

'They know we're here, they'll be converging on us as we speak,' Longoss said, smiling at Coppin and removing her hands from the bandage she'd finished tying. He used her to climb to his feet, much to the woman's annoyance.

'Where will we go?' she asked quietly. Her mouth opened and her nose wrinkled slightly in confusion as Longoss pointed to the floor.

Sears looked across and knew what Longoss intended straight away. He sighed heavily before speaking. 'He means the sewers.'

Coppin's nose wrinkled even more.

'We need to get out of Dockside, Longoss, I'm telling ye, get to a barracks and we'll be safe.'

Longoss was shaking his head before Sears finished. 'They won't let us out of Dockside for that very reason, Sears. We need to hold up somewhere, just for now.' He held his good hand up to stop Sears from talking whilst he explained. 'They know I know about this mark that ye wanna know about and they'll assume ye both know about it now too—'

'Ye said ye didn't know about it?' Sears said, nostrils flaring. Coppin's confusion returned as she tried to get her head around what Longoss had just said.

'I don't, big man,' Longoss said, sighing hard. 'I know of it, not about it, I told ye that, but I can find out, it'll just take time.'

Knuckles white on the hilt of his short-sword, Sears gritted his teeth but nodded, knowing somehow the former assassin was telling the truth.

Longoss looked to Coppin, rolling his arm slowly, his right eye twitching at the pain it caused. 'I brought ye clothes and food, although the clothes are men's and bloodied from me carrying 'em. Sorry.'

Coppin looked to the bundles on the floor and then to her brown robes. 'Anything's better than these, thank you.'

Longoss nodded and looked to Sears. 'There's a passageway beneath this room, under the hearth rug, it's narrow, but I've squeezed down it before. We can get to the sewers without leaving the building.'

'Great.' Sears rubbed his face with his free hand. 'Wait,' he said suddenly, 'I didn't think there were sewers in this area?'

Longoss had moved to the rug and rolled it up with his good hand. 'There aren't for these houses, but there's main sewer pipes running through Dockside to the harbour, and this tunnel will lead us to them.'

Sears took one last look out the window and then crossed to where Longoss was struggling to move a wooden trapdoor. 'Here,' he said, placing his sword on the floor and lifting the door clear. 'Gods below… that is small.' *And blind me does it stink.*

'Aye and it stinks too,' Longoss said, grinning at Sears, 'but nowhere near as bad as when we're down there.' He looked back then to tell Coppin to hurry, but the words stuck in his throat as he saw the woman's robes fall to the floor, revealing a back full of recently healed scars. He tried, but failed to avert his eyes as she quickly pulled on the braes and hose he'd brought her, tying the latter to the thin belt he'd found. She turned to scoop up the shirt and caught his eye. She smiled sincerely and nodded her thanks for the clothes.

Longoss' cheeks flushed. He looked back to the hole next to him as the woman pulled the bloodied shirt over her green hair, picked up the bundle of food by her feet and moved to join them.

'Well, down I go.' Sears lowered himself down and once his feet touched the damp ground beneath the house, he lifted one arm high, kept one low and shuffled himself through the gap, his maille hauberk rustling and bunching on the edges as he huffed and cursed his way down.

'Won't they realise we've gone down there?' Coppin said, as Longoss motioned for her to go next.

'Aye lass, but there's countless places this leads to and it's a damn sight better than staying here and waiting for them. They could bust through that door at any moment.'

Eyes wide, Coppin turned and took one last look at the door, before nimbly dropping down and through the hole.

This is gonna hurt. Longoss swung his legs around and into the hole, lifting his good arm as Sears had. He pulled his other arm in tight and rocked from side to side as he worked his way down. He could feel Coppin's hands on his legs as she tried to help. Grimacing against the pain of his shoulder, not to mention that of his missing ear, sliced ribs and various other cuts and bruises that rubbed on the sides of the hole, Longoss finally managed to squeeze through and into the dark space below the house, where the only light came from the open hatch above.

'How will we see?' Sears said, his faint outline just visible on the far side of Coppin's.

'We don't, not until the sewers, where I have a torch hidden.'

'Lead on then.' Sears brushed at his face as he moved from Longoss' path. 'Damned cobwebs.'

'Cobwebs?' Coppin strained to see Sears' face as she passed him. She followed Longoss on her hands and knees, the bundle of food tied around her.

'It ain't spiders ye need worry about, lass,' Longoss said from the darkness ahead, 'it's the big bastard rats ye get down here.'

'Great,' Coppin said. 'I've gone through all of this to be eaten by rats.'

Sears laughed from behind and Longoss followed suit. Before long, all three were laughing.

Despite the laughter, Sears' thoughts drifted to Biviano. He hoped his friend was faring better than they were as he cursed again, another web clinging to his face. *How is it that it always happens to me, even when people, two in this case, are in front of me? Bloody spiders!*

***

With the spire of the Samorlian Cathedral visible in the distance, the few people that dared the streets moved aside, watching with a mix of awe and concern as the armed and armoured men approached.

Bollingham cursed as the skittish chestnut gelding beneath him tossed its head several times. All around him, the sound of metal shod hooves echoed off the surrounding buildings as two dozen mounted guardsmen followed Lord Stowold. Alongside the constable rode Biviano, who was looking across to the green trapper of the destrier his commander rode, wondering about the Earl's coat-of-arms.

'Is that a snake, or an eel, milord?' Biviano asked.

'What?'

'Yer coat of arms?' Biviano pointed to the imaged displayed on both trapper and shield.

'Ah,' Stowold said, one eyebrow rising, 'interests you does it, heraldry?'

Biviano shrugged. 'No, not really, I just wondered if yours is a snake, or an eel?'

'Which do you think it is?'

Biviano sighed and scratched just under his left eye. *Why can't people just answer questions, instead of answering with one of their own?* 'I'm not sure, milord, hence the question.' Glancing up at the constable and seeing his stern face, Biviano decided it prudent to guess. 'But if pushed, I'd say snake,' he said, thinking it the better of the two.

Stowold frowned slightly and shook his head.

'Eel?' Biviano did his best to hide his amusement.

'Wrong again,' Stowold said, as he threw a wink Biviano's way.

Wish he wouldn't keep doing that.

'It is in fact a sea serpent.'

Eyes wide, Biviano looked back at the destrier's trapper, which offered the best view of the Earl's heraldry. Tilting his head slightly and frowning, he tried to work out what it was the sea serpent was coiled around. His eyes suddenly widened again. 'Ah… it's a drum tower.'

'Ha, good man,' Stowold said. 'A serpent coiled around a drum tower upon a green field, it is indeed.'

'What for?' Biviano asked, cringing inside as the constable pursed his lips and locked his eyes on Biviano's before answering.

'Many years ago,' Stowold said eventually, 'an ancestor of mine successfully besieged a sea fortress. The forces he commanded surrounded it and cut off all supply and aid. Eventually, the garrison commander surrendered, knowing they were beat.'

'Impressive,' Biviano said, before his eyes were pulled forward to a man walking out in front of them.

'What's your business?' the man asked, the cathedral rising high behind him.

'We ride to the Samorlian Cathedral, good sir,' Stowold said. Biviano was pleasantly surprised the constable offered a reply at all, rather than forcing the man from their path. Bagnall Stowold went up in Biviano's estimation considerably at that moment.

'Good!' the man shouted. He wore a cloak tightly about him, but his hooded mantle hung back, revealing gaunt features and pale skin. 'It's what they deserve. Luck be with you all!'

Stowold nodded and waved his appreciation as they approached the man, but something in the stranger's posture didn't sit right with Biviano once they drew near. Before he could call out a warning, the cloaked figure produced a small crossbow and aimed it at the constable. The bow twanged and the bolt left the groove with tremendous speed, heading for Stowold's chest. Realising the threat at the last moment, but without time to bring about his shield, Stowold twisted in his saddle and the bolt struck his right pouldron, glancing off the smooth steel and skittering across a wall on the far side of the street.

'On guard,' Biviano shouted, drawing his short-sword and pointing it to the man in front. He kicked the flanks of his horse with his heals and the horse surged forward. Biviano leaned into the charge, deftly using the reigns to aim the animal at the attacker.

More bolts flicked across the street then, as the men everyone had taken to be random passers-by suddenly drew crossbows. Even those without the ranged weapons charged the riders with other weapons drawn.

Hooves pounding the cobbles and nostrils flaring, Biviano's horse reached the cloaked man, who managed to jump to the side just in time. Not quick enough to avoid Biviano's sword though, the flat of which caught the man on the side of the head, fracturing his skull and dropping him heavily to the ground where he lay still; unconscious or dead, Biviano would never know.

Gently slowing his horse, but hearing hooves coming up fast behind him, Biviano turned in time to see the green livery of the Earl of Stowold pulling alongside. The constable looked across to Biviano as he drew his maille aventail across his face, looping it over and fixing it in place on his bascinet. Retrieving his war-hammer from the saddle loop and pointing it ahead,

Stowold shouted, 'To the cathedral!'

Biviano couldn't help but grin as the men behind cheered.

Many of the attackers had been ridden or struck down, and despite losing a couple of men, the rest of the guardsmen charged after their commander, weapons held high.

As the horsemen rode on, more attackers emerged, including a warrior monk who ran from a side street. He swung his heavy mattock at the knees of the nearest horse, which buckled under the impact, throwing the rider to the floor as the horse cried out in pain.

Effrin coughed hard as the wind left his lungs, and the pain of both of his palms burnt terribly as his skin was left behind on the cobbles he'd slid across. He knew he'd at least bruised ribs in the fall, but knew that to survive, he needed to move, and quickly.

As he managed to roll sideways, the heavy mattock that had unhorsed him cracked off the cobbles where his head had been. His heart thudded in his chest and still he struggled for breath as he looked upon the grimace of the man trying to violently steal his life away.

That grimace would haunt him, he knew, as it suddenly twisted into a sneer of disbelief and pain. A sword tip erupted from the monk's chest. Blood spattered Effrin's white robes as Bollingham's face appeared behind the collapsing man, who dropped the mattock and pressed his hands against the wound. Bollingham's sword disappeared as quickly as it had appeared and the monk slumped heavily to the ground.

'We need to move,' Bollingham said, looking across the street to where more cloaked figures were fighting with two mounted guardsmen. 'Everyone's riding on.'

Effrin nodded at his friend whilst painfully being pulled to his feet, and silently thanked Lord Stowold for forcing Bollingham to come along. Staring at his skinless palms, the cleric stumbled as Bollingham pushed him towards a chestnut horse. He looked back then and his stomach turned as he saw the dead animal he'd been riding, its face bloodied and its front legs clearly broken.

'The bastards need pay for this,' Effrin said with vehemence. He started as Bollingham burst out laughing.

'That's humans for ye,' Bollingham said. 'Ye can wipe out a bunch of folks, but one animal dies…' He began laughing again whilst pulling Effrin up onto his horse.

'It's not funny, Bolly,' the cleric said, whilst doing his best to hold onto the man in front of him.

'No, Effrin, it ain't, but if ye don't laugh at it all, ye'd bloody well cry. Now hold on!' Bollingham snapped the reins and the chestnut gelding shot forward, rocking the two men back slightly as it accelerated towards the Samorlian Cathedral in the distance. Another mounted guardsman fell in behind them as a couple of small crossbow bolts whipped past.

At the head of the column, the main doors of the cathedral grew larger as the riders approached at speed.

'There's a side door,' Biviano shouted, noticing the main doors were unusually closed.

Stowold shook his head. 'Main door, main door!' he shouted, before roaring a battle cry, his war-hammer held high.

Risking a quick glance behind, Biviano wondered where Bollingham and Effrin were, but was heartened by the sight he saw; well over a dozen armed, armoured and mounted guardsmen rode hard behind him, their stern faces set and their weapons – some bloodied – drawn. Nodding with satisfaction, Biviano turned back to the cathedral and began to pull on his reins as the enormous building loomed high above, its stone grotesques and gargoyles staring back down at him.

Stowold rode his destrier up shallow steps to the double doors of the cathedral and hammered his weapon on the wood three times, denting it where it struck. 'This is Stowold, Constable of Wesson. Open your bloody doors and bid me and my men entry, or we will enter by force!'

As the sound of hooves gradually quietened and the remaining riders arrived at the cathedral, Biviano looked across with concern as he noticed Effrin sat behind Bollingham. Effrin waved back and it wasn't hard for Biviano to see the bloodied palms of the cleric's hands.

'No answer, Biviano,' Stowold said, from behind his maille aventail. 'It seems the Samorlian Church does not want us to enter.'

'Perhaps ye didn't knock hard enough, milord?' Biviano grinned at the Earl, who laughed heartily.

'Then I shall indeed knock louder, man. Wake the raping sacks of dung up.' Stowold turned back to the doors of the cathedral and heaved on his destrier's reins. The beast rose onto its back legs and snorted as it smashed its two front hooves into one of the doors. The guardsmen – who'd moved into a defensive semi-circle around the steps – cheered as their commander had his warhorse pound on the doors again and again. Although the oak doors splintered on the surface, they held strong, so Stowold turned to Biviano, shaking his head. 'There's nowt for it, we'll have to use ropes and axes.'

Biviano nodded and turned to give the order. Those riding the largest horses came forwards, as the rest continued to watch for further attack. Ropes were pulled from saddle bags and tied to the handles of the large doors, the other ends threaded through the harnesses of the horses. Dismounted, the guardsmen urged their horses to pull, whilst on either side of the door, others took hafted-axes to the hinges.

With a sudden loud crack of wood, one of the doors gave way. It clattered down the cathedral steps as the three horses pulling it took off across the street, their handlers trying to slow them whilst riders pulled alongside the bucking animals. The dismounted guardsmen had no time to re-mount before Stowold reared his mount once more. He roared and charged into the cavernous building, Biviano and the rest of the mounted men close behind.

The racket the hooves caused on the stone tiles of the cathedral stunned those inside, despite their awareness of the force trying to gain entry. Those moments allowed the constable and his men to close quickly with the defenders. Several cathedral guards fell under the kicking hooves of Stowold's destrier in the moments following his entry. His horse, once in the middle of a unit of armed men, kicked and bit, whilst Stowold himself brought his wicked hammer down on helmeted heads, the iron pots little defence against the crushing blows the experienced constable dealt them.

Biviano kicked out at a warrior monk who ran at him from down an aisle. The large man fell back, cracking his head on the end of a pew, before a dismounted city guardsman reached and finished him off. Biviano kicked his horse on, noting how far ahead Stowold had got and worrying about his lord being overrun.

'In the name of the King,' Stowold shouted, between colourful curses and triumphant roars. He weathered several blows from arming swords, which glanced off his decorative harness of plate. An inquisitor made to attack Stowold from behind, but just before Biviano reached the man, Stowold's destrier kicked with both hind legs, launching the inquisitor across the floor with what Biviano swore he thought was the sound of breaking bones, despite the clash of metal on metal and hoof on stone.

'Biviano,' Stowold shouted, as Biviano dropped from his horse, preferring to fight on foot. He ducked as soon as he landed, barely missing a slicing swing from a cathedral guard's sword. 'Bit busy, milord,' he shouted back, parrying another attack from the same man, before lunging and swinging in return.

'Make for your prisoner!' Stowold kicked out, breaking the jaw of one man whilst stabbing the top spike of his weapon through the face of another. 'I'm for the upper levels and the Grand Bastard. First unit with me!' he shouted, 'second with Biviano!' He kicked his destrier towards the back of the cathedral and several still mounted guardsmen surged forward, following their commander through the defenders.

One guardsman was knocked from his horse by a poleaxe, and before he could climb to his feet or be rescued, he was run through. Grimacing at the sight, Biviano shouted, 'with me!' and ran for the side door he knew would lead them to the lower levels. He was pleased to see both Bollingham and Effrin in his unit – the latter doing his best to avoid combat, cradling his hands and looking extremely worried.

'Stay close to us, Effrin,' Biviano shouted. The cleric nodded, his eyes darting here and there as men yelled in anger and pain. 'We make for Ellis Frane and it's then we may need ye,' Biviano said as he plunged through the door. *Although I hope to the gods we don't.*

***

The sun sat high in the sky, its bright light warming the tired group as their horses carried them further to the east, away from the winding River Norln.

The sparse woodland had been left behind and the group's horses now walked a narrow path through vast wetlands fed by large lakes to the north. A warm breeze rustled through the reeds flanking the narrow path of dry ground, as dragonflies and warblers flitted from reed to reed.

A low, eerie booming began not far from where the riders travelled.

Starks, who'd been nodding off, was clearly startled by the sound. He spun left and right in his saddle, looking for the source.

'Nice of you to join us,' Sav said, who rode behind the young crossbowman.

'What's that noise?' Starks looked around, fumbling with his crossbow as Sav laughed.

Errolas appeared on foot at Starks' side, leading his horse and smiling up at the young man. 'It's a bird, Starks. Don't mind, Sav, you weren't to know. Caught you dozing did it?'

'Yeah, sorry, Errolas, I haven't slept in days, but I suppose you haven't either. It won't happen again... A bird you say?' Starks let his crossbow down so it hung from the saddle again as he looked around once more, trying to see where the deep booming sound was coming from.

'Don't apologise,' Fal said, 'you're not used to travelling is all, but you're reliable in a scrape and that's all that matters.'

'He's right Starks.' Errolas patted Starks' horse on the neck as he walked along. 'You get some sleep while you can and as for the bird, it's called a bittern and it's harmless. You won't see it though. They live deep in the reeds.' Errolas waved his hand across the expanse of wetlands surrounding them.

The bittern boomed again.

Starks smiled and looked out anyway, his eyes flicking from small birds to insects as they darted around in the sun. 'I ain't half hungry,' he said, turning to rummage in his saddle bags.

'You can't have eaten your supplies already, surely?' Sav laughed and Starks reddened.

'I'm a growing lad, ain't that right, Sarge?'

Fal laughed before answering. 'That's dead right, Starks. Sav, give him some of yours for winding him up.'

Starks heard Sav sigh from behind and turned to tell him it didn't matter, just as a lump of bread was thrown at him. He caught it quickly and smiled as Sav winked at him, stuffing some into his own mouth.

The group had pushed their horses hard after leaving the riverside and wooded areas, until they'd reached the wetlands and reed beds where such speed could prove fatal to their horses.

'We will be getting close to my forest come evening, but it would be best to stop and camp, and finish the journey in the morning I think. Give the horses a rest... and us.' Errolas moved up to walk next to Fal.

'I've got to say, Errolas, I'm looking forward to seeing your home. It's something I never thought I'd see.' Fal was positively beaming at the thought.

Errolas smiled in return. 'It still surprises me after so many years. It is quite a remarkable place I must say, the way most of the realm would still be if... well...'

'If it wasn't for humans?' Fal asked knowingly.

'Yes. No, I don't mean that... well, not all humans are like you and your friends Fal. Some are bent on destroying woodland and nature itself, for no better reasons than self-gain and profit. You have to work *with* nature for it and you to prosper, it's the only way. Yours is a young race in the grand scheme of things. I'm sure humanity in general will learn.'

'Like the dwarves learnt?' Fal smiled at the elf.

Errolas laughed. 'I see your point. Well, I hold out more hope for your kind than theirs. They don't care for much other than their own wealth, at all.'

The reed beds thinned out considerably on the group's right then as they walked on, and opened up to fields of tall grass, bushes and the odd gnarled tree. Sav rode up to Fal's left and Severun to the elf's right. Errolas mounted the horse he'd been leading and all four rode abreast.

'What're you talking about?' Sav asked nosily, and Fal rolled his eyes.

'Have to be a part of it, don't you eh?' Fal said. Sav grinned and motioned for them to go on. 'We were talking about Errolas' home, about nature and the lack of respect for it by us humans, and dwarves, but I'm sure you know about all that, eh?'

Sav nodded. 'See it all the time, people trapping animals for fur, don't even eat the meat half the time. Loggers cut down trees with nothing to build, in a hope to sell the wood. Have to make a living I suppose, but Altoln could manage it in better ways I'm sure.'

'There are many things we could change to improve things for ourselves,' Severun said. 'I just wish I'd devoted myself to something worthwhile.' The wizard sighed heavily, his head held low.

'Now now, Lord Severun,' Sav said, 'we all know you thought you were doing good. Let's just leave that subject for now shall we?

'As for the Samorlian Church,' Sav added. He snarled. 'Their fabricated shite concerns me much more; a law unto themselves that bunch.'

'That they may be, but it's far from made up what they believe,' Severun said, surprising Fal and Sav both. 'It may be twisted to suit them, but it's not that far from the truth.'

'I always believed there was probably a knight called Sir Samorl,' Sav said, 'and he most likely did fight in a large war against someone or other, but... snake people?' Sav laughed. 'I mean, come on? That's ridiculous. I've never heard of the... what do they call them, the Naga?'

Severun nodded. 'Yes, Sav, hence Naga Pass.'

Sav conceded the point, but continued all the same. 'Well that may be, but I've never heard anything about them after the time in which the Samorlian story is set, and I've certainly never seen one, how about you Errolas?'

Errolas glanced at Severun as Correia turned in her saddle and looked at both the elf and wizard, but it was Fal who spoke next, surprising Sav. 'I

342

have,' he said, matter-of-factly.

'You have what? Seen one of these Naga?' Sav asked, unconvinced.

Fal shook his head. 'No, but I've heard of them, when I was small. Scary stories told to keep the children out of the jungle in Orismar, or so I thought, until my parents brought me to Wesson and there was a whole religion based around a war against them. Makes me wonder if the stories back home were true?' There was no hint of amusement in Fal's voice or expression and Sav knew him well enough to know he was telling the truth. Correia and Errolas shot each other worried glances that Fal noticed, but he said nothing.

'So the Naga were real and still are?' Sav asked, to anyone who might give him a straight answer.

'Oh, they were real enough,' Severun said, 'I'm not sure about now, but—'

'They're still alive, yes, in the east,' Errolas said, cutting the wizard off, 'on the open planes where they originally came from.'

Severun looked to Errolas, clearly surprised. 'I thought all the Naga were wiped out during the final battle, when Sir Samorl was killed?'

Errolas shook his head. 'Not all. Most, yes, but several hundred returned home under our protection.'

'What?' Sav looked stunned. 'As I remember it, from what I've always been told about that damned religion and their beliefs anyway, the Naga invaded Altoln and we fought running battles until, eventually, a mighty Altolnan army faced them with the help of your people. So why The Three would you then help the survivors escape?' Sav seemed quite offended by the idea which surprised Fal, who knew how much the scout hated the religion from whence his information came.

Errolas allowed Sav to finish before correcting him. 'Again, you know only what the Samorlian Church bands about with its writings of events, twisted and changed over two millennia. We know exactly what happened because we recorded it and have never changed what was written. We also have two living elders who were there when it all happened.' Errolas smiled at the reaction to the latter.

'Two who're still...' Fal didn't feel the need to finish what he was saying and instead started to say, 'They must be—'

'Over two thousand years old, yes,' Errolas finished, 'and extremely old even for my kind. They are siblings, brother and sister and powerful arch mages too. They fought in the final battle against Crackador and his terrible Naga army.'

'Crackador, the black dragon?' Sav was clearly more than a little sceptical. 'The one they say Sir Samorl killed with a bloody wooden lance?'

Errolas sort of nodded although his eyes flicked briefly to Severun, who snorted at the statement. Everyone looked to the wizard who sighed before continuing the history lesson.

'Crackador was a rare great-dragon, a huge beast, but rarer still, as you said Sav, he was a *black* dragon. However, lucky for us at the time, he was young, for a dragon anyway, and rash. The Naga were, or are still it seems,' Severun looked to Errolas, who nodded, 'an unnatural race. They were human once, much like us until Crackador, who commanded immense arcane abilities, cursed their entire nation. Hundreds of thousands of humans were cursed, creating the mutations that were, sorry are, the race we call the Naga. He wanted, we can only assume, a nation of acolytes to worship him, pander to him, bring him wealth to store at his feet... it isn't beyond reason to assume he wanted to be thought of and treated as a god—'

'And then he invaded us?' Sav blurted.

Both Severun and Errolas shook their heads.

'No,' Errolas said. 'That is where the Samorlian Church twists the story and most of Altoln's history on the subject.'

Severun turned to the elf with the others, wanting to hear the elf's version.

'Some of what I will tell you,' Errolas explained, 'Severun and his guild already know, for they recorded it all as well as we did. It was the Samorlian Church's interference that stopped them teaching the truth, but the church has never had any power over us.' Errolas smiled, knowing he had all three – as well as Starks who'd moved his horse closer – hanging on every word. The elf continued then, his voice rising and falling melodically as he told his tale. 'After the entire nation on the Eastern Planes had been mutated, transformed, whatever you choose to call it, a large number of them, well, small in comparison to the rest, rebelled against their black dragon overlord. They were outraged at what he'd done to them and their people, and outraged at how they were now treated; no better than slaves in their own cities.

'The rebellion was swiftly put down, however, and so they fled. They fled their homeland and headed west in a desperate bid to escape their tormentor and his loyal – probably through fear more than anything else – Naga. The rebels travelled down through the Moot Hills and south of our forests, but not through them, and so we watched the strange creatures we had never seen before rather than engaging them.

'Into Altoln they then travelled, and before long they were met by a human army who attacked without question. The Naga, wanting to put as much distance between themselves and Crackador's armies as possible, fought back against the attack. After winning the battle, they attempted to move on through Altoln, but although Altoln was a relatively young nation at the time, it was still far larger than the Naga could have anticipated.

'More armies were thrown at the Naga and more armies fell, but every time they were attacked, the Naga were pushed further north, first between Knipewood and Broadleaf Forest and then further still, never able to cross the River Norln. Once past the wetlands and the lakes of this area,' Errolas waved his arm to encompass all that lay around them, 'the Naga encountered the largest human army ever to have formed in Altoln.

'The rebels were trapped,' he went on, 'and to make matters worse for everyone, Crackador had arrived with tens of thousands of his own loyal Naga. They came through the very valley your army had pushed the rebels into. Because of this, the rebels took up defensive positions on either side of the valley, hoping your army would not follow. But after human scouts reported a larger host of Naga approaching from the east, entering that very valley, the King of Altoln gave the order to advance.'

'Well, he wouldn't have known any better,' Sav said.

'When the King gave the order, he didn't,' Errolas agreed, 'but my people did. We had learnt the true nature of the rebels shortly after Crackador's forces had been spotted, and so moved swiftly to inform the humans. We also managed to make contact with the rebel forces on either side of the valley, declaring our intentions and offering our aid to them. The Naga thankfully agreed, so we stood and fought shoulder to shoulder with them as Crackador's loyal Naga marched through what is now Naga Pass and ploughed into the Altolnan lines. The humans fought bravely, taking losses in the tens of thousands, whilst both the rebels and the elves attacked the enemy's flanks.'

'Then Sir Samorl killed Crackador?' Starks asked excitedly, but both Errolas and Severun shook their heads.

'Not quite,' Errolas said. 'It was the combined magic of the human mages and the elf mages that turned the tide in the end.' Severun nodded proudly as Errolas continued. 'A group of human mages realised their occasional bursts of magical attacks from different positions within the valley were not enough to defeat Crackador, who continued to slay hundreds of men as the battle raged. The mages hoped that if they concentrated their combined powers, or what remained of them, along with their elven comrades', and locked that power into the lance of the King's champion, Sir Samorl, they might stand a chance against the powerful beast.

'Sir Samorl knew then what was needed of him and rode forth with hundreds of knights and men-at-arms at his back. They smashed into the ranks of the Naga and caused such destruction it was hoped it would attract the attention of Crackador himself… It did.

'Brave bastards,' Sav said, and everyone nodded.

Errolas nodded along with the rest before he went on. 'Since I am lucky enough to have been told by our elders who witnessed the act, I know for a fact that when Crackador flew down to wipe out the knights of Altoln, Sir Samorl stood in his stirrups at the front of the continuing charge, raised his lance high and plunged it deep into the wyrm's chest; an act of true heroism, that much is clear. When that lance and the offensive magic locked into it pierced the great-dragon's thick scales, the beast is said to have killed many more men and elves with his skull-splitting roar of pain. Despite that, it is said Altoln's remaining army's cheer was almost equally as loud. It was then that Crackador, in his last defiance against his victors, tore Sir Samorl from his horse, crushing him in his mighty maw and throwing him across the valley. The great-dragon somehow then found the strength to limp away on torn wings, away to the south where he was seen, as recorded by my kin, passing over the very forest where we are heading.'

'He survived?' Sav blurted.

'No one truly knows,' Errolas admitted. 'He was seen leaving the battlefield by all who still lived and fought on, for the battle raged on for several hours thereafter. He was seriously wounded by the enchanted lance though, that much is known. Sir Samorl died as the legend said, but Crackador most certainly did not, not then anyway, as your church has had people believe ever since.'

'Not my church,' Sav muttered, and Fal couldn't help but smile.

Errolas hid a smirk of his own. 'And so it was the joint effort of the earliest and founding members of your Wizards and Sorcery Guild,' he said, nodding to Severun, 'as well as Sir Samorl, his knights and all who fought that day, including the rebel Naga, that allowed us to succeed. Not just Sir Samorl himself as the church has always portrayed. Hence, Sav, the reason we escorted the rebel Naga safely back to their rightful home, the Eastern Planes, where we know they still exist and thrive to this day.'

'Truly amazing,' Starks said, and the expressions on both Sav and Fal's faces mirrored the crossbowman's sentiment.

'That's why the Samorlian Church and the Wizards and Sorcery Guild don't get along,' Severun said. 'What a shame all they have done over the centuries almost ruins the efforts and sacrifices of three nations joined together to face one evil.' Severun shook his head. 'That's the version, the truth that should be taught and written throughout Altoln, not their self serving propaganda.'

'You're right there,' Fal agreed, and the group fell silent, each contemplating what they'd heard as they rode on in the sun, a bittern booming from the reed beds behind them.

***

Darkness strikes such fear into the bravest men, and it was just that, after all he'd been through, that tore at Ellis Frane's reserves as the final torch died. He'd torn cloth and rags to keep them going as long as he could, but with no oil anywhere in the chamber, whatever he used had burnt quickly.

The last thing he'd looked at was the barricade as the last of the light faded. He was still surprised no one had come, not to save him for he'd given up on that a long time ago, or so it felt. No, he was surprised no one had come to kill him, or worse.

Why has no one come to find you, Inquisitor Makhell? I hear voices now and then, albeit from far away down the corridors, but not this one, not down here. Could it be that those two guardsmen, Biviano and Sears, did something up there? Drew everybody away? How could I know? Hope is all that is, I fear. Fear… of the dark, yes, It brings out the worst in all our imaginations. I have read enough in the palace libraries to know that. Every thought, every horrific thought is manifest in our minds, made all the more real by the lack of other things to be seen, real things. But what is reality, truly? Whatever we believe it to be I suppose. You—

Ellis Frane laughed.

You? I talk of a body I created, from a living man. I talk of him as if he can hear me, even after I stole his life for attempting to steal mine, for stealing that of those girls in that room. Well he, he believed Sir Samorl was real and so to him he was, as real as this floor I sit on. What do I believe is real? The bodies I can't stop imagining walking, the dead coming to tear me to pieces. It plagues the back of my mind because I don't want it to, because I have nothing to see with my own eyes; nothing to see that is real, so my mind makes my thoughts real. Fear is doing this to me, because I have no other options but to sit here in the pitch black of this torture chamber where horrors are brought to life and my biggest fear, the walking dead, comes to me as my eyes search anything to take my mind from that which my mind thinks I want to see. Well I don't want to see them. Fear makes me think of scary things, it doesn't mean I want to see them.

Ellis Frane sighed, rubbing at his red, smoke irritated eyes. He felt moisture there.

Pull yourself together man. You've been through all this and for what? To fear that which you've feared since you were a boy, just because the damned lights went out.

He laughed again.

The ironic thing is, that which I want most of all right at this moment, light, if I did see it now, if I got what I crave, it'd most likely be them, *coming to kill or torture me... t o r t u r e... again...*

Images flashed across Ellis Frane's eyes of dead bodies, of *his* dead body, *Inquisitor Makhell*, rising from the rack, tearing the ropes free and staggering towards the corner where the royal scribe sat huddled. Ellis Frane shuddered and rubbed at his eyes some more.

'Leave me alone!' he shouted into the darkness. Silence was his only reply. 'No, not silence,' he whispered, as he heard what he thought was raised voices, although he couldn't be sure any more. 'Are the bastards coming? The bastards *are* coming; the bastards are coming, the bastards are coming, the bastards, the bastards...' Climbing to his feet and keeping the cold wall to his back, Ellis Frane caressed the bloodied spike he'd not been able to cast away after he killed the inquisitor. He took deep breaths, trying to steel himself for what was to come. *I will fight back, I will go down fighting like Biviano and Sears likely did.*

Laughing out again, he shook his head, knowing he wouldn't last long. Every muscle tensed – most painfully – at the sounds of clashing metal. *Fighting? Who would be—*

'Ellis Frane?' someone shouted, from somewhere outside the room. 'We're coming to get you out!'

Ellis Frane's heart raced. 'Biviano?' he thought aloud, whilst shaking his head from side to side. His breathing was swift and shallow as he saw the flicker of torchlight through the gaps in his barricade. More clashes of metal and men's voices. One cried out in pain and then fell silent.

A curse and a crash of metal on wood.

'Ellis Frane, it's Biviano, I'm here with Lord Stowold and the City Guard. Are ye there?'

More crashing of wood and several streams of dust swirled light poured

347

into the room.

'I'm here,' Ellis Frane said, his voice no more than a horse whisper. *Is this real? Is it still dark? My mind… whatever the mind wants you to see is real. This isn't real, this isn't real this isn't real…*

'Ellis!' Biviano shouted again, 'Ellis Frane?'

'Shit!' a voice Ellis Frane didn't recognise shouted, as yet more unknown voices came from the corridor.

'We'll take 'em,' someone else said. 'You two get him out.'

'Cheers, Bolly,' Biviano said, or so Ellis Frane thought, still shaking his head and not wanting to believe what he was seeing and hearing, in case it was his mind and not reality.

Not real, not real, not real…

Wood crashed down and light flooded into the chamber, silhouetting two men, one holding a short-sword and wearing a kettle-helm, one in long robes.

'There he is,' the armoured one said. 'Effrin, we need to get him out.' Both men moved forward, one either side of the rack.

'Back!' Ellis Frane shrieked, pointing the bloody spike towards the men as someone screamed in the corridor and more weapons clashed.

'Ellis, it's me, Biviano.'

An outstretched hand and, finally, a face he could see was real. 'Biviano,' Ellis Frane blurted, his words erupting along with uncontrollable sobs. He dropped the spike and fell painfully to his knees as the robed cleric rushed forward, wincing as he grabbed his arms and began pulling him back to his feet. 'You left me,' Ellis Frane said between sobs. 'You left me.'

'I know…' Biviano reached out and took a fist full of the padded gambeson Sears had given Ellis Frane to keep him warm. 'I know and I'm so, so sorry.' Pulling Ellis Frane in close, Biviano wrapped his arms around him. His tears joined that of the man he held and as much as he wanted to magic the man away to safety, keeping him from any more bloodshed, he knew he had to keep moving, he knew they had to fight their way back out.

Pulling back suddenly, Ellis Frane looked at Biviano, eyes wide. 'The tower,' he said, his face streaked with tears.

Frowning, Biviano looked to Effrin and back. 'What tower?'

'The Wizards and Sorcery Guild's, that's why they wanted me. They're attacking Tyndurris!'

Biviano was shaking his head as the man spoke. 'It's a riot, but it's in hand, we've heard about—'

'No, I worked it all out. They're attacking from underneath, the church is attacking Tyndurris from underneath!'

Looking swiftly to Effrin, who nodded and took Ellis Frane by the arm, Biviano rushed to the doorway, taking in the scene outside as Bollingham walked back up the corridor, the last surviving guardsman of Biviano's unit.

'The others?' Biviano asked, fearing the answer.

Bollingham shook his head. 'An inquisitor.'

Biviano closed his eyes briefly. 'We need to go, Bolly. Now.'

Bollingham smiled, his teeth bloodstained. 'Typical, and here I was beginning to enjoy myself.' He turned about and headed back down the corridor, a bloodied sword in each hand.

***

Edging up to a black crossed door on a deserted Dockside street, Rapeel glanced sideways at his two companions, who were mirroring him on the far side of the door they were sure the renegade assassin was hiding behind.

Never thought I'd be taking you down, Longoss, but a mark's a mark, so here we go. Rapeel nodded to his companions.

Both burly men stepped away from the wall. They looked to one another and nodded, before stepping forward and kicking the door in simultaneously, swiftly stepping away from the splintering wood in case any missiles came out to meet them. They rushed in when it seemed clear to do so, a hafted-axe held by one of the men, a scramasax by the other.

'Empty!'

Rapeel frowned and hesitated. He pictured the siblings after their run in with Longoss and knew the man's word not to kill meant nothing, for there were fates far worse than death.

Steeling himself, he walked through the doorway, again noticing the black cross on the door now hanging from its hinges. *I hope you painted that on yourself, Longoss.*

The small room was almost bare. Two chairs, a woollen robe and some bloody rags were the only thing to draw the eye, apart from the hearth rug, which was rolled up on the straw covered floor to one side of a small opening.

Sewers, what a surprise. Rapeel grimaced at the thought. *At least you'll smell at home down there, you ugly bastard.* Hooking his two identical hand axes in his belt and looking to his men, he pointed at the hole. 'Check it,' he said, as he crouched by the rags to see how fresh the blood was. It was still sticky, but only just.

'Clear,' one of Rapeel's men said, as he stuck his head down the hole.

Lucky for you, you dick! Rapeel shook his head as he stood and moved back to the door. Looking outside, he whistled down the street and almost immediately a young boy with an extremely large black rat on a chain came running from an alleyway not too far away. Once the boy and his pet had arrived, Rapeel crouched and held the rags out to the rat, which held and sniffed at the offered clothing, before entering the house and pulling the boy along with it.

Sneering at the rat as it passed and dropped into the hole, boy in tow, Rapeel's two men looked to him for orders. They frowned and looked to one another as the street-assassin pointed to the hole and smiled.

This should be good. Rapeel watched his broad shouldered men squeeze their way down into the passage below.

'On second thoughts,' Rapeel said to himself. He leaned back outside as grunts and curses came from the hole. He whistled again, this time for longer, and three more boys came running down the street. Chests puffed out, they slowed to a swagger, a mix of crude looking daggers and knives in their hands as they approached the street-assassin.

'The rat's on the hunt with your brother,' Rapeel said, leaning against the splintered doorframe. 'Follow them and my men and I'll be close behind.'

'Who're we after, boss?' the oldest of the group asked, although he was no more than fifteen years.

'A bad man. Now hop to it you little shites, or I'll have your eyes like the bad man had Blanck's.'

The cocky demeanour of the boys never faltered as they grinned at Rapeel and ran into the house, wasting no time climbing down the dark hole.

Walking across the room, Rapeel took one last look around before following the boys down.

Ready or not Longoss, here we come.

Chapter 38: Negotiation

The heavy wooden door creaked as Orix opened it. He, along with everyone in the room, winced, not wanting to give their enemy any prior warning of the master cleric's approach. Morri, along with the battle mage, other clerics and the newly arrived sergeant-at-arms who'd managed to make it away from the continuing riot above their heads, had argued against Orix's decision to go, but the old gnome had insisted. He'd made it clear how devastating to both the guild and city it would be if but a quarter of the artefacts and knowledge held in the vaults were to fall into the Witchunter General's hands. And so in the end, knowing him to be right, everyone in the room had reluctantly agreed to let Orix go.

The small gnome tiptoed down the stone steps, jumping slightly as the door behind him quietly squeaked and clicked shut; his whole body went rigid as he expected someone to grab him from the darkness below. He had naught but a small candle in his hand, and when he reached the door at the bottom, he knocked swiftly before turning to run half way back up the steps.

He was too slow.

As soon as he knocked on the door and turned, it opened. A strong, pale hand gripped his arm and dragged him through. His candle fell and broke on the corner of the bottom step, blinking out as he was dragged into the torch-lit room. He tried to cry out, but a hand clamped tight over his mouth, making it hard for him to breath. He kicked wildly with his short legs, causing an outburst of mocking laughter from the men surrounding him, and before he could think of anything else, a sharp pain stung the back of his head and the room fell away into darkness.

***

The smell of smoke, sweat, blood and piss filled Biviano's nose as he stepped over the dead bodies of numerous cathedral guards and two city guardsmen. His stomach twisted at the sight. He could hardly believe how many had been lost in the assault, including all of the men in his unit bar Effrin and Bollingham. These bodies, however, were those of Lord Stowold's unit. They lay at the base of the stairs leading up to the Grand Inquisitor's quarters.

All had been quiet in the small corridor, so the sudden sound of footsteps descending the curling stairs caused Biviano to hesitate at the first step. He looked to Bollingham and held up his hand. Bollingham turned and motioned for Effrin to move back with Ellis Frane, who was staring at the bodies littering the floor, mouth open and head slowly shaking.

'Armour,' Bollingham mouthed. Biviano nodded, for it was now clear whoever was approaching them was wearing at least maille armour, possibly even plate. Bollingham held up one finger, cocked his head to the side and then held up two. Biviano shrugged, unable to tell how many there were. As the footsteps drew closer, Biviano breathed a sigh of relief; a familiar voice echoed off the stone walls and then another replied.

'Lord Stowold?' Biviano asked loudly.

'Aye, it's me,' the constable said as he rounded the curve in the stairwell. 'How fair you, Biviano?' Stowold was clearly injured, although not badly. He was carrying his shield arm awkwardly across his chest whilst his squire, who appeared behind him, deftly carried his shield and helmet, as well as his own bloodied arming sword.

'We have Ellis Frane, milord, but we lost many.' It pained Biviano to say it out loud and that pain was mirrored in Stowold's eyes as he nodded.

'Aye, me too, man, and no bastard Grand Inquisitor to be found.'

Biviano sighed hard, sheathing his sword. 'I'm sorry, milord. I'd hoped he would've returned.'

Stowold shook his head as Biviano spoke. 'I'll have none of that. We needed to show them they weren't above the law whether he was here or not, and we have.'

Biviano and the others nodded, but their faces betrayed their frustrations.

'Are all lost, my lord?' Effrin asked, of those who'd accompanied Stowold.

'No, cleric, I lost the two at your feet, my remaining men are securing the upper levels. I need three to secure the main door though and you three are it.'

'We have news though,' Biviano said, nodding back to Ellis Frane, whose eyes remained on the dead men.

'Go on.' Stowold motioned for all to follow as he moved back towards the cathedral proper.

Biviano continued whilst walking at Stowold's side. 'Ellis Frane has warned us that the witchunters are to assault the Wizards and Sorcery Guild from ancient tunnels below Tyndurris. They must be warned, milord, and I must make for Dockside and Sears.'

'Must you?' Stowold raised his eyebrows as he stopped and looked at Biviano.

Swallowing hard, Biviano nodded once, holding the Earl's gaze.

Wiping the sweat from his brow with his good wrist, Stowold breathed hard and shook his head slowly. 'I'm sorry, Biviano, but I don't have the men. We need to hold this building and there're few of us as it is. If we lose it, we'll lose far more men having to re-take it again.'

Biviano looked around, trying to think of a solution. 'Milord, I understand that, but the guild needs warning and we need reinforcements. I can head to Dockside on my own, after taking Ellis to the clerics at Tyndurris? They can call for aid on your behalf from there, for your own retainers or even from the Lord High Constable?'

'Ye've no chance on yer own in Dockside, Biviano,' Bollingham said, stepping forward. He looked from Biviano to the constable, and all present new it to be the truth.

'He's right, even if I were to let you go.'

'Then I'll go in without my uniform, sire. I can't leave Sears, not like we left Ellis Frane.'

The royal scribe looked up. 'You did what was needed, Biviano, I'm sure you did.'

Biviano nodded to the man and smiled with appreciation before continuing. 'Aye, maybe, although I'm not so sure, but either way I still need to go back for Sears, whether I'm allowed or not, milord, I'm sorry.'

All eyes – wide eyes – were on Lord Stowold, and the man blew out a long slow breath. 'You're treading dangerous ground there, Biviano.'

'It's what I do, sire. It's what we all do when asked.'

Nodding slowly, the Earl hooked his war-hammer onto his belt and stepped forward, whilst drawing the broadsword that until now had been sheathed at his side. 'You're a brave and loyal man, Biviano. I admire that and I admire the lengths you've been willing to go to, not only in saving this man here,' Stowold pointed his sword to Ellis Frane, who nodded, 'but in every case you've taken on whilst under Captain Prior's command, despite he nor I knowing where you and your partner are half the time.' Stowold paused for a moment in contemplation. 'Kneel,' he said finally, in all seriousness.

The squire's jaw dropped, as did most others.

Hesitantly, whilst looking from Stowold to Ellis Frane – who nodded and smiled sincerely – and back, Biviano knelt before the Earl.

Sword raised, Stowold spoke slowly and carefully. 'I, Bagnall, Earl of Stowold, Constable of Wesson and Watcher of the Deep, hereby knight thee, as is my right of office, on behalf of King Barrison,' he touched the sword to Biviano's right shoulder then moved it across to the left, 'Sir Bivi—'

'Stop!'

Stowold rocked back on his heals as Biviano held up his hand, shaking his head and looking up into the shocked face of his lord constable.

Whispers of disbelief from the lips of more than one trailed off as Stowold's face reddened.

'I'm sorry, my lord,' Biviano said in an upper district accent, holding up both hands and standing, 'but you cannot knight me, although the sentiment overwhelms me.'

Brow furrowed, albeit hidden under his maille coif, Stowold licked his dry lips and nodded once to Biviano. 'Explain.'

Taking a deep breath, Biviano looked about at the stunned eyes staring back at him, before scratching under his kettle-helm and then removing it. He held it at his side as he spoke, noticing Stowold's white knuckles as he gripped his broadsword tight. 'I am already a knight, my lord, or rather I have been knighted already,' Biviano announced, his upper district accent remaining, 'although, I have not classed myself as such for a long, long time.'

'That's horse shit!' Bollingham blurted, although it was clear by his face he hadn't meant for it to come out.

Stowold glared at the man, but looked back to Biviano before continuing. 'Do go on,' he said, somehow accepting Biviano's words easily, or so it seemed to all present.

Scratching his lower back, or attempting to through the iron links of his hauberk, Biviano told the men his story and as remarkable as it was, they believed him, which saddened him all the more being that the story he told them was a lie. He knew, however, the truth was far more dangerous than the lie, and in the end, when he'd finished, he held on to the fact that although the story he'd given them was false, the outcome was the same. They knew he wanted to be treated the same as before, as Biviano the humble guardsman and not as a knight, despite that being almost exactly what he had been... almost.

After Biviano's story, Bagnall Stowold had agreed that Biviano could head to Tyndurris with Ellis Frane, as long as he requested Stowold's own men-at-arms and further reinforcements from the Lord High Constable before any attempt to enter Dockside in search of Sears. After a moment's pause, Biviano had agreed and just minutes later, had ridden from the Samorlian Cathedral with Ellis Frane clung tightly to his back.

***

After reaching the end of the black tunnel, Longoss had felt around and located his torch, as well as pieces of steel and flint which he used to light the torch. Once in the main sewers, all three had to bend double in the low tunnels. Their backs rubbed on the stone ceiling – painfully for Coppin – as they sloshed through sewerage that stung their eyes with its overpowering smell.

Eventually, Longoss led them to a chamber via a series of turns and one smaller pipe that required all three to crawl on their hands and knees. The sewage had almost reached Coppin's elbows, and the smoke from Longoss' torch had thickened the air, making it even harder to breath. The chamber itself had a taller ceiling, along with a raised platform either side of the half-pipe that ran through its centre.

Climbing up onto one of the raised platforms, Longoss lit three more torches. It was obvious he'd been there many time before.

'Cosy,' Sears said, looking about the chamber. He took in the scattered blankets, as well as several small crates and barrels stacked in a corner. 'Although yer bedding needs its current occupants removing before we can use it.' He nodded to a couple of blankets which accommodated a family of brown rats.

Coppin stepped closer to Sears and Longoss moved across to and scared the creatures away, all of which jumped into the sewer pipe and swam back the way the trio had come, squeaking all the while.

The smell, although still horrific, wasn't as bad up on the raised platform, but with clothes dripping with all sorts, none of the group could escape it until they changed.

'I feel sick,' Coppin said, one hand pressed against her stomach. 'Do ye have any spare clothes here, Longoss?'

'Aye, lass, but not much.' He kicked a few of the blankets about, picking one up and shaking off the rat droppings. Eventually, he found a bundle of clothes mixed in amongst a pile in the corner, opposite the crates and barrels.

Coppin held them up after Longoss had thrown some to her. She grimaced at the filthy garments, before looking down at her sopping shirt which clung to her breasts, a single erect nipple visible through the thin linen. 'Well, anything's better than these,' she said, beginning to take off the shirt.

Sears quickly turned around, facing away from Coppin whilst Longoss did the same. She couldn't help but smile at that, unused to men not taking advantage of her at any given opportunity. *I don't care if there are assassins after us or not, I don't think I've ever felt safer around men in my life.* Dropping the wet clothes to the side, she picked up a stinking woollen blanket covered in rat hair and cringed as she quickly dried off as best she could. As she pulled the blanket round her back and moved it from side to side, she clenched her teeth at the pain it caused. She did her best not to cry out, for many of the cuts had been reopened during the crawl through the sewers. Once as dry as could be, she brushed herself down with her hands and cursed as she found a flea on her leg. She plucked it from her skin and squeezed it between the nail of her fore finger and thumb. Slicing it in two left a tiny smear of blood, which she wiped on the blanket, before quickly pulling on the huge shirt, braes and thick woollen hose Longoss had thrown her. She tied the braes as tight about her waist as she could and rolled up the long pair of hose at her ankles, before throwing another blanket over her shoulders like a cloak.

'I'm done,' she said eventually, moving over to the crates and inspecting them.

'Food,' Longoss said, nodding towards the pile. 'Mind you, salted or not, it's been there a long time, so it's probably a good thing we ate what we had back in the first tunnel.'

Nodding, Coppin turned and sat down, gingerly leaning back against the crates as she rested her head back and closed her eyes.

Sears removed his arming belt and bent forward. He shuffled until his maille hauberk fell forward over his head and then to the ground with a rustle of iron links. After that, he too swapped clothing and wasn't surprised – due to the similar size of the man – that Longoss' clothes fit. He rolled his eyes as he pulled the previously white braes on however, noticing the yellowing stain across the front of them. When he looked up, Longoss was facing him, gold teeth bared.

'How safe are we here, Longoss?' Coppin said, without opening her eyes.

'No one knows of this place.' His voice was muffled as he pulled on a musty padded gambeson that looked suspiciously like those worn by city guardsmen. Sears let it pass.

'No one knew of the last place though,' she said, eyes now open and fixed on the former assassin.

'I never said that.'

'Then why'd we go there?' Sears asked, moving across to sit next to Coppin.

'I couldn't be sure they'd come for me,' Longoss said, shrugging, 'but now I know they are, nowhere is safe. Although down here is safer than up top. There's no bursting in here.'

'Oh, no? I couldn't believe that,' Sears said, resting his head back and closing his eyes like Coppin had. 'I mean, with such a lovely smell pervading the air and such finery to be found and worn by all, I wouldn't be surprised if every man and his dog turned up to join us.'

Coppin smiled and so did Longoss.

'Aye,' Longoss said, 'well let's just hope it's not until we've rested and healed up some.'

'Or died of infection from that water,' Sears replied.

'That's a fair point,' Coppin said, suddenly worried. 'We're all carrying open wounds and that can't be good?'

Longoss shook his head slowly. 'It ain't, so let's do something about it shall we?' He walked over to the other two and pushed them apart, reaching behind them to bring forth one of the small barrels.

'What is it?' Coppin settled again once Longoss had stepped back.

'Rum,' Longoss said, gold teeth flashing.

'We need to keep our wits I'd have thought,' she said, rolling her eyes disapprovingly, tongue firmly lodged in cheek.

'He means for the wounds,' Sears said, looking to Coppin. 'It'll help clean 'em and it'll hurt like a kobold's rock, but it's what's needed.'

I hope he said rock? Longoss thought, his hearing muffled after the loss of his ear.

A hollow pop and the barrel's cork came free. Longoss spat the cork across the chamber and gritted his teeth before tilting his head to the right and pouring the alcohol onto the earless side of his head. Sucking in air through his gold teeth, he stopped pouring and shook his head, making a quiet roaring sound as he stepped from one foot to the other.

'Let me,' Coppin said, using Sears' knee to push herself up. 'Ye'll waste the lot doing it like that.' She took the barrel from Longoss and looked about. 'Do ye have any clean cloth?'

Sears barked with laughter.

'Point taken,' Coppin said, as Longoss prodded the side of his head with filthy fingers. She slapped his hand and shook her head. 'How've ye survived so long?' Longoss feigned confusion, much to Coppin's amusement.

A tearing sound turned Coppin's head to Sears, who'd torn off the cleanest part of the shirt he wore. Holding it out to her, she soaked the linen and proceeded to clean the wounds on Longoss' arms. After that, he removed his shirt to reveal his scar covered body, the freshest of which Coppin cleaned too. The three companions helped clean each others wounds then, before agreeing to have one last swig each from Sears' flask. He warned them it wasn't wise to have too much, for fear of addiction, but after screwing her face up at the taste, Coppin assured him that wasn't possible.

Aye, but I know better, lass. I might not know exactly what's in this stuff, but I do know what it can do to folk, Sears thought, as he returned the flask to its pouch at the back of his belt, which sat around his waist again, his sword close to hand.

After all three had finally settled next to one another, with blankets gathered in one spot to create at least a little comfort – despite the cloying stench that hit them every so often – Sears sighed heavily and looked across Coppin's green haired head to Longoss, who felt the guardsman's eyes upon him and so looked back.

'This isn't looking good,' Sears said flatly.

'Course it ain't, it's a sewer.'

'Excellent, Longoss. Points for observation, but that's not what I mean and ye know it.'

'Do I?'

'Aye, ye do. We're on the run. We've had to flee one place and skulk in the sewers of Dockside whilst we heal and rest up, again. All the while the Black Guild carries on with business whilst we're stuck doing nothing about it. Gods, Longoss, ye ran into two assassins and came back in a shit state—'

'Oh and you'd fair better would ye, Sears?'

'Please boys,' Coppin said. 'Let's not, eh?' She picked up the rum and took a swig, closing one eye tight and pulling her head to the left with the strong taste. 'Rum?' she blurted. 'Ye sure?'

'Ha, good stuff, eh?' Longoss said, appreciating the distraction.

Sears reached across and took the barrel, as well as a swig for himself. He coughed and the other two laughed. Taking a second swig, he passed it across to Longoss, who nodded his thanks to the man.

'All I mean, Longoss, is if it's such a struggle against two assassins, for either of us, how'd we expect to find anything out about this mark that's supposed to be so damned important by assaulting the whole damned Black Guild?'

'The siblings.' Longoss looked back at Sears whilst giving the barrel back to Coppin. 'They knew it was big, I could tell, and the fact they didn't know more confirms it. As for how we'll find out, I'll pry it from Poi Son's lips miself.'

'That's just it though,' Sears said, his voice rising angrily, 'we can't take the damned Black Guild can we? Not the two of us!'

'Three,' Coppin said.

'Two,' Sears and Longoss said together. Coppin took another, longer swig of rum.

'Anyway,' Sears continued, 'if we know nothing about this mark, who's to say it ain't too late, that Poi Son has had some other assassin kill whoever he or she may be?'

Longoss was shaking his head as Sears spoke. 'He, not a she, of that I'm sure and nope, they won't make a move whilst we're alive, not now they know we know what they know.'

Coppin looked from the barrel to Longoss and back, blinking several times.

'We don't know what they know though, do we?' Sears said, exasperated.

'We know enough as far as they're concerned, Sears. They wants us dead or pinned down in Dockside at the very least, where they think we can do no harm. The place is lawless with the plague afoot. Fires have gutted whole blocks, looting and worse are rife at night—'

'No change there then,' Coppin muttered.

'And they know,' Longoss continued, 'should they fail to kill us, at least keeping us here will stop us informing the City Guard.'

'Ye already did inform 'em,' Coppin said, laughing and prodding Sears on the arm.

'Ye know what I mean. They know if Sears gets clear of Dockside and reports all this to his captain, who in turn goes to the Constable of Wesson, then coming from him it could very well cause some serious shit for Poi Son, who will be aiming outside of Dockside with this assassination and needing the attention of the authorities anywhere but on the guild.'

'How'd ye know it'd be another district without knowing the mark?'

'If it's so big, Sears, it's hardly to be a gang master or such is it? So it must be someone in an upper district, see? Another higher guild's master or one of Wesson's high lords even?'

Sears took a deep breath and nodded. 'Aye, I guess so.' After a few moments pause, where no one spoke, Sears' eyes lightened and he asked another question of Longoss. 'Can we not leave Dockside through the sewers?'

Longoss shook his head immediately as Coppin said, 'I ain't crawling through that shit, literally, all the way out of Dockside.'

'Besides,' Longoss added, 'we'll get to Poi Son and we will get answers, as well as payback for Elleth.'

Despite their scepticism, both Sears and Coppin saw the raw determination in Longoss' eyes as he spoke, and neither denied the feeling the former assassin would pull off what he intended. When that would be, however, was a different matter and it was that which worried Sears the most.

Coppin's thoughts lingered on the prospect of revenge after Longoss' words. *I hope ye right Longoss, for I want that for Elleth as much as you do.*

'Well we can't wait for ever,' Sears said finally.

'No Sears, we can't,' Longoss agreed.

'Then we better continue my training then, eh lads?'

Both men looked to Coppin, the slightest of smiles appearing on both of their faces.

***

Exley Clewarth ran down the twisting steps, a small bundled figure over his shoulder as his remaining witchunters and warrior monks followed close behind. A couple of prisoners tagged on as well, but most stayed behind, trying all they could to break into the vault while two more stood guard on the door to the upper levels. Exley didn't expect they would last long once the battle mage realised something was wrong and there were no negotiations in progress, but the prisoners would slow down the battle mage and the men-at-arms, and that was all that mattered.

As he reached the bottom floor, Exley moved aside to let the two remaining warrior monks down in front of him. He passed down the unmoving gnome and dropped down into the ancient tunnels below, before taking the gnome and lead once more, his men close on his heals.

After twenty or so minutes, Exley passed the gnome over to one of his witchunters rather than pause to catch his breath. He had no idea how soon he would be pursued and so wanted to keep moving until he reached the prison. From there he would make for the cathedral where he would finally be safe and he could present the traitorous gnome to the Grand Inquisitor.

He couldn't help but smile as he thought of the victory, more over Horler Comlay than the guild he'd assaulted. He had no care for what the gnome had done. As far as he was concerned the real perpetrator had been the wizard, who was nothing more than ash at the bottom of a pyre in Execution Square, but the victory over Wesson's Witchunter General would be sweet indeed.

A monk who'd taken over leading the group coughed and spluttered as he ran through a spider web. Exley made a mental note not to take the lead through the tunnels again and so dropped back slightly, letting everyone but Egan Dundaven pass ahead of him as they ran exhausted through the darkness.

'I can hardly believe we managed it,' Egan said, panting, and Exley's smile widened.

'You did well in finding these tunnels, Master Dundaven. You're a credit to the order.' Exley couldn't see how the witchunter took the compliment, but he was sure the man would be ecstatic. It wasn't often the Witchunter General dished out praise, after all.

The tunnel was narrow in places and the group spread out into single file. Exley shuddered when he realised he was at the back, half expecting some thunderbolt or ball of flame to strike him from behind. He shook the thought away as his rasping breath struggled with the dust filled, stale air of the damp tunnel.

And then there it was, a deathly scream and a flash of light from ahead.

Exley couldn't see the monk leading the group, but as the flash shot down the dark tunnel, an image of the man doubled in pain almost burnt into Exley's retinas. He turned away, blinking repeatedly.

The familiar clicking of crossbows caused Exley to look back. He saw two of his witchunters crouch down whilst reloading their weapons. The two remaining prisoners turned to run back towards Exley, before being thrown with an invisible force past everyone in the group. They landed in a crumpled heap, far back into the darkness, their cries of surprise and fear ending suddenly as they landed.

The second warrior monk jumped up and lurched forward, his torch bursting to life again with the renewed movement and its flickering light briefly revealing a cloaked figure up ahead, just within Exley's range of vision. The warrior monk covered the distance swiftly, jumping at the end and striking the figure square in the chest with his raised foot, throwing the man down onto his back. The monk hefted his mace quickly and swung it down to strike the fallen man, who rolled to the side, the mace thumping the ground close to his head. A foot shot up and connected with the monk's groin, causing him to bend double just before a knife like wand thrust up into his chest. A loud crack from the wand launched the monk into the ceiling of the tunnel where he stayed as if pinned to the stone.

Three crossbows clicked then and Exley realised one was his own. He'd loaded and loosed the bolt automatically, without thinking. Both his and the other two bolts, one from Egan to his side and one from another witchunter further up the tunnel, spat forth towards their attacker. As they reached him, the body on the ceiling fell and took all three bolts. A cry rang out and all three witchunters knew they'd just hit and killed their brother monk. Exley roared in outrage.

Another bolt clicked from the final witchunter up ahead, but his bolt turned violently to the side at a wave of the magician's hand and a flick of his wand, shattering the bolt on the stone wall.

The cloaked figure ran forward then with great speed, somehow dodging another bolt loosed by Egan before reaching the two forward witchunters. Exley could just see the bundled gnome on the floor, his unmoving form caught in the flickering light of a torch thrown down by one of the witchunters now engaging the magician. They drew their rapiers and moved together to defend themselves and block the tunnel to where their General stood.

'Master Dundaven, get the gnome, drag him back here. I'll cover you,' Exley ordered, as he took Egan's loaded crossbow from him and deftly loaded another bolt onto his own.

Egan rushed forward as the sound of steel rang on steel. As he ran, he could make out the cloaked magician fending off the two witchunters' rapiers with a short-sword of his own, which hummed with every connecting thrust and parry.

Exley tried to get a clear shot with one of the crossbows but it was impossible. His two witchunters twisted and turned around each other in an almost perfect fighting harmony, but left no room for a bolt to safely pass between them. Now Egan too blocked the way as he ran back down the tunnel with the unconscious gnome over his shoulder.

As Egan reached his Witchunter General, so did the sound of death as one of the witchunters fell to a sword that now seemed longer than it had before, and of course it was. The magician had thrust with his short-sword causing the now dead witchunter to back away, leaving just enough room to stay on balance. The sword, however, had reached out further still, growing to the size of a long-sword to pierce the witchunter's heart. The black clad man fell dead immediately and the shock to his fighting companion left him open to attack. He jumped backwards and somehow managed to avoid the swinging blade, but not the magician's wand. Its sharp point entered the witchunter's brain through his eye, unleashing a scream that curdled the blood of the two remaining witchunters.

A light erupted then, from the back of the man's head before he slumped to the ground. The brightness of it blinded Exley and Egan briefly, giving the magician time to reach them before Exley loosed the two crossbows. The first bolt hit the ceiling, the wild shot wasted as the Witchunter General's blurred vision distorted his aim, but the second struck, a lucky shot but a true one and the resulting thud and grunt pleased Exley as the bolt found flesh.

A dull pain racked the Witchunter General's head and threw it back then as he felt his nose flatten and crunch under the unseen, invisible assault. He dropped to the floor and stifled a cry of pain as his eyes blurred even more.

'Hold!' Egan Dundaven shouted, and all went quiet and still. All except the harsh, dust filled lungs of the three heavily breathing men. 'Move and I'll slit the gnome's throat, I swear it,' Egan said in all seriousness.

Exley grinned to himself, feeling the hot, wet blood of his nose dribbling over his lips and teeth. He rubbed his eyes and they began to clear, revealing their attacker, who stood half bent as he pressed on his thigh where the flight of Exley's bolt was visible – his sword was gone. His other hand held the bloodied wand, its tip pointing at Exley, whilst Egan held a knife to the gnome's throat.

'If Master Orix dies, then so do you both and it won't be pleasant, I assure you,' the cloaked magician said, his voice calm despite his wound and the situation.

'Ahh... Lord Strickland, a pleasure to finally meet you.' Exley spat a mouth full of blood at the magician's feet.

'The pleasure is mine, General...?'

Exley sneered. 'Clewarth,' he said, eyes boring into the magician's, 'General Comlay is out of town on business and so I have been tasked with Wesson's necessary work in his absence.'

'Oh I see, General Clewarth, you're his replacement whilst he tends to more pressing matters. I do rather think he would have pulled this off without such, well, absolute failure, but you're new to this I'll—'

'Enough,' Exley said, his barely contained anger clear in his venomous tone. Ward Strickland smiled as Exley continued. 'You will let us past, magician. Otherwise Master Orix's blood will be spilled here as well as all of theirs.' Exley waved his hand and the empty crossbow towards the witchunters and warrior monks lying broken on the tunnel floor.

'So you can burn him like you did Lord Severun? Do you not realise this cleric is working towards a cure to the plague? If you kill him, how many

361

more would die before the remaining clerics find a cure?'

'He shouldn't have started it then should he?' Exley said nasally, his newly broken nose throbbing all the while.

'He didn't, you fool. This plague is a co-incidence, or at worse a piggy-back disease that attached itself to the arcane magic used by Lord Severun, not Master Orix. He did all he could to make sure this kind of thing wouldn't happen, but we now believe it was part of the spell Lord Severun used, not the potion Master Orix created. He had only just discovered this before your attack and now you have dragged him away from work that could save us all.' Ward was breathing heavily now, the wound in his leg and his magical exertion taking its toll.

'I'm not for believing the likes of you, magician. You weave spells and bewitch people, ensnare their minds and corrupt. How can I know releasing this gnome wouldn't cause more pain from more experiments and potions gone wrong? Now step aside man, otherwise he dies here and now and you will have no chance to free him.'

'Is it true?' Egan asked suddenly, and Exley turned to him surprised. 'Is what you say true? Could he stop the plague?'

'Master Dundaven, I think you should keep your mouth—'

'Yes,' Ward said, nodding. He looked deep into the eyes of the witchunter, whose hold on the knife at Orix's throat relaxed a little. 'If he is returned now, he could very well end all this suffering, all this death. And he has already been dealt his punishment. He is under house arrest for *life*, as ordered by the King, your ruler, not the Grand Inquisitor.'

'Kill him now,' Exley said, eyes boring into the witchunter.

Egan looked horrified. 'What?'

'Kill him now,' Exley said again, his voice low and dangerous, 'before he spins more lies. Kill him, Master Dundaven, that's an order!'

Egan's grip on the knife tightened once more. 'But the people, General… we follow Sir Samorl for his sacrifice to save the people of Altoln, and this gnome can help them.'

'I said kill him!' Exley shouted, and Egan jumped at the sudden outburst, the sharp blade touching Orix's neck and leaving a line of blood across it in an arc. He dropped the knife then and fell back shaking his head and muttering to himself. 'This isn't why I joined; this isn't what we're supposed to be about.'

Orix fell to the floor alongside the knife, and Exley threw down the unloaded crossbows and drew his rapier. He thrust it first at Lord Strickland, who fell back away from it, and then he raised it high and brought it down swiftly towards Orix's prone body.

Before the blade struck, the Witchunter General jerked violently to the side. His rapier fell from his hand and landed harmlessly on the gnome. Exley stumbled sideways then and fell to the ground, a dull pain spreading across his body as he probed his bloodied side with his fingers. He gasped in disbelief as he felt the gaping wound leaking his life's blood across the tunnel floor. Shallow breaths slowing, Exley Clewarth turned his head to his remaining witchunter, Egan Dundaven, before the light dimmed and his eyes closed; the fixed expression upon his face was one of shock and disbelief.

A blood-soaked rapier fell from Egan Dundaven's hand. Tears filled the man's eyes as he mumbled to himself repeatedly, 'This isn't why I became a witchunter; this isn't what we're supposed to be about.'

Chapter 39: Can't See The Wood For The Trees

Shite-filled water lapped around Rapeel's legs as one of the wiry lads he'd sent ahead returned down the sewer tunnel, eventually moving into the orange glow of the small torch one of his men held out ahead of him.

'Boss,' the boy greeted. He nodded as he reached the street-assassin, who motioned for him to continue. 'We think there's an opening ahead. We've seen torchlight, although it's through a smaller pipe.' His eyes flicked briefly to Rapeel's two large men.

'If Longoss can fit through it, these two can,' Rapeel said. 'I trust you were discreet?'

The boy nodded. 'Aye, boss, we don't got no light do we.'

Rapeel's brows lifted.

'And we was quiet too.'

Nodding, Rapeel asked about the large rat.

'The rat were pulling for us to head that way, so it's where Longoss went, I'd wager on it.'

'Any idea of his whereabouts with regards to up top, should our mark make a move from the sewers to the surface?'

The boy grinned. 'Reckon so, aye.'

'Good lad,' Rapeel said, slapping the boy on the arm. 'Head back up top as soon as you can then and get word for others to mark the exits. I don't want the bastard escaping us after we've tramped through this shit, understood?'

The boy nodded eagerly and immediately squeezed past Rapeel, heading back the way they'd come.

Once out of sight, one of Rapeel's men turned to him, clearly concerned. 'How're we gonna get in there, against Longoss of all people?'

'Suck it up, you soft sack of shit. We'll send the rat and the boys in, then we'll follow.'

Teeth clenching, the large man nodded and moved forward, wrinkling his flattened nose at the fresh stench the movement caused, whilst Rapeel motioned for the other to follow.

Keep moving, halfwits, Rapeel thought, as he followed his companions and tried to imagine the space into which they'd be assaulting Longoss. Several rats swam past him then, squealing as they went, with gods knew what swirling about in their wake. *Not sure if I'd rather the bastard stays down here or makes for the surface, after all.*

***

As soon as the lake had passed, along with its wetlands and uneven, dangerous paths, the horses of the group were again worked hard. They galloped for a while before slowing to a steady canter. Starks suffered the most, having hardly ridden before, but everyone in the group spurred him on and they silently acknowledged his efforts to prove himself to the more experienced and older warriors in the group.

'Wait up, Starks, we're not all as young and fit as you,' Sav shouted from the back of the group, causing both Starks and Fal to erupt with laughter.

'It's all that ale you drank in Wesson,' Fal called back from just ahead of the young crossbowman.

'What?' Sav asked, and Fal laughed again.

'You heard… you're getting fat.'

Starks laughed whilst turning in his saddle to grin back at the lanky scout, who could easily have ridden down the younger man. It was good for morale after everything the group had been through, and Fal was happy Starks was being accepted by the hardier men in the group.

He's endured more than most these past few days. Fal knew how little of the world Starks had experienced up until now.

The sun had started to sink to the west, where the sky took on an orange haze as the giant orb neared the horizon. The wind was almost still and the warmer air across the meadows felt silky as it blew across Fal's face, his horse working hard below.

Errolas' hand went up then, and one by one the horses slowed as their riders pulled on their reigns. Starks almost shot past Fal, before hauling on the reigns harder than the others, his horse coming to an abrupt stop, almost throwing the young crossbowman over its head. Fal and Sav laughed again as Starks clambered back towards his saddle, grinning at the others.

'Think we're dismounting, gents,' Gleave said, before sliding from his tall, bay mare. 'It'll give that horse of yours a rest after working her like that, Starks.' It was said in jest and Starks took it so, grinning back to the pathfinder as the hardy soldier walked his horse ahead to talk to Mearson, whose arm was considerably better since Severun performed some sort of spell on it shortly after leaving Beresford.

'I'm no cleric,' the wizard had said, 'but this should help a little.' And so it had. Within an hour, Fal had noticed Mearson waving his arm around, amazed at the recovery, and Fal had smiled to himself, glad to have the powerful wizard with the group.

'Make camp by those trees,' Errolas said, his voice carrying easily as he dismounted and walked his horse over to a small copse of trees to the group's right. They'd long since left any known path and so had to rely on Errolas' sense of direction to find Broadleaf Forest. Sav had sworn he could find it, that anyone could find it if they headed east from their position, but they let Errolas lead regardless, wanting to waste no more time and knowing that finding it was one thing, but entering it was surely another.

Once they'd tied up their horses, they lit a small fire and with what provisions they had left, Sav cooked up an evening meal accompanied by a small amount of mead Correia had been given in Beresford before they left. Sav, to everyone's surprise, passed on the opportunity, claiming he never drank when in the field.

'That's why he drinks so much when back in Wesson,' Fal said, laughing, and Sav nodded his agreement, followed by a broad smile and a wink.

'Well, you can count me out of that.' Gleave took a large swig from the deerskin. 'Warms you up it does, that's for sure. Here, Starks, get some down your neck.'

Starks thanked Gleave and took a swig himself, sighing with appreciation at the sweet taste, before muttering something about Sav drinking in Hinton, which should be classed as in the field.

'We can't be far now can we, Errolas?' Sav asked, ignoring Starks' comment as he drank from a skin of water.

'No, not far now; the Woodmoat is in sight.' Errolas pointed to a faint outline of trees in the distance.

'Woodmoat?' Fal asked. 'That's your wood then, them trees?'

All were listening now including Correia and her pathfinders. They knew the lay of both north and south Altoln well, but none of them had ever stepped foot across the tree line they were all looking at, understanding it to be the realm of the elves and not somewhere you ventured without permission. Errolas shook his head though, surprising all.

'No, the Woodmoat isn't part of our realm. It is a defensive moat, of sorts.'

Starks frowned. 'A moat of wood, how would that stop anyone, or do you mean a palisade?'

Errolas laughed softly, but realised then that everyone, not just Starks, was looking to him for an answer. 'It's not a moat as such, not like your moats of water. It *is* a barrier though and it surrounds Broadleaf Forest, although it won't show on any map.'

Errolas paused whilst the group leaned in or shuffled closer to the fire, where sparks reached for the darkening sky from the fresh logs that crackled and burnt there. Once settled, the elf continued.

'There's a wide band of flat, solid ground surrounding our forest, and running around the outside of that, over there,' he pointed to the distant tree line, 'is the Woodmoat. The Meadow Guard sit in the Woodmoat and act as our eyes and ears. Highly skilled warriors, they are excellent marksmen with the bow and well trained with both sword and spear. They protect the Woodmoat and call for assistance if needed. Anyone attempting to enter our forest, be it foolish goblins or whomever, think they are actually attacking or entering our home, rather than our woodland defences.

'Should they get past the Meadow Guard in the Woodmoat, however, they then realise they haven't entered the forest at all and now have to pass the meadow itself. Fast and highly skilled cavalry units patrol the meadow in groups of a dozen or so. Those mounted warriors are lethal with both lance and bow, and should they catch anyone in their meadows, then they know the trespassers have surely killed elves to get there. It also leaves any intruders open to volleys from units of archers, scouts or rangers that would have come to the call of the Meadow Guard's horns. As you can see, it would take quite a force to breach both the Woodmoat and the meadows beyond.' Errolas smiled as he looked around at the group who sat in silent awe of the elf's explanation.

'Amazing,' Starks said – a word he'd found himself using more and more since leaving Wesson – and Fal nodded as he looked across and strained to see the dark tree line of the Woodmoat in the failing light.

'Why, if we're so close, don't we head straight there now?' Mearson asked, before taking a swig of mead.

Errolas smiled as he replied. 'I don't think it wise to approach the Meadow Guard with darkness closing in on us, especially when I am one elf and you are many humans.'

'But we're allies,' Gleave said, a little affronted.

'Yes we are, but does Wesson not close its gates to anyone at night; elf, gnome or even human?' Errolas' smile remained.

'Fair point,' Gleave said, as he reached for the mead again.

'I can't wait to see your home,' Sav said, and several of the group nodded.

'Well tomorrow you will.'

'It shall be a sight I never thought I'd see a couple of days ago, so it makes it all the more wonderful to me.' Severun's face dropped as he looked westward towards the rapidly shrinking sun.

Errolas followed the wizard's gaze and then stood up.

'What is it?' Correia asked, she too standing and straining her eyes to see.

'I'm not sure, I thought it was my old eyes playing tricks at first, but...' Severun pointed and the rest of the group turned to gaze at the small circle that ever so slowly grew in the distant sky.

A tiny point of light flickered from its base.

Errolas squinted. 'I'm not sure what it is, but it's getting closer, slowly, but surely it is.'

Sav walked across and picked up his bow then, stringing it without a second thought and on seeing him do so, Starks walked over to where his crossbow was propped against a tree.

'There again, a light came from it, only briefly mind.' Mearson stood on tiptoes as if it would help him see further.

'There's only a light breeze,' Correia said, 'and it's more from the east than anything else so it's not moving closer on the—

'It's a balloon!' she said suddenly. All heads turned towards her.

Errolas looked back towards the strange shape in the sky. 'A what?'

Sav's face relaxed in realisation and he de-strung his bow and leant it back against a tree. 'One of the King's reconnaissance balloons,' he said reassuringly. 'It's alright Errolas, they're ours.' Sav sat back down by the fire again, craning his neck to glance briefly at the growing, dark circle in the sky.

'I saw one once,' Starks said, 'down Dockside. It took off from the naval fort and headed out to sea. Never seen one up close though. Do you think it's looking for us on the King's orders?'

'Could be,' Gleave said. 'It's possible the plague's been sorted out by our lot, and that thing's tracked us from Beresford.'

'Well, let's hope so.' Fal crossed his fingers. 'I still want to see your home though,' he added, looking to Errolas. Most nodded their heads in agreement, but Severun and especially Errolas didn't seem to be as relaxed as the others now were.

'We don't know for sure it's ours,' Severun said, but no one seemed to take the warning seriously until Fal turned and saw the seriousness in the wizard's face.

'Maybe Lord Severun's right, we should stay on guard. We can't risk the mission on an assumption,' Fal said, and without another word Starks lifted his crossbow back into his arms. Fal smiled inwardly at the young crossbowman's initiative.

'Ahh, come on Fal,' Sav said, 'who else has balloons except the dwarves, and they're not going to be this deep into our territory or so close to the elves are they?' He glanced back at the now rapidly growing balloon.

Fal shot him a look and Sav sighed before climbing to his feet, walking over to and re-stringing his bow again.

'You should never assume, Sav,' Fal said, a wry smile appearing on his face.

'Because it makes an ass out of you and me, yeah, yeah, I know.' They both laughed briefly over what could only be an old joke between the two of them.

'They're right, it's best to be on guard. You heard him lads,' Correia said, and Gleave and Mearson drew their weapons without question.

'Should we put this out?' Fal asked.

Errolas shook his head. 'No, keep it lit, we're probably being over cautious, but if we *are* attacked, it will draw the eye and those in the shadows won't easily be seen. Sav, Starks and Lord Severun with me, Gleave and Mearson, you stay by the fire with Fal and Correia, but be ready, understood?' All four nodded and Fal drew his falchion and seax before moving to the farthest side of the fire to the balloon, which was now creeping very close, the slight sound of its clicking dwarf built propeller reaching the ears of Errolas for the first time. Severun, Sav and Starks rushed into the copse of trees and readied their weapons whilst Fal, Correia, Gleave and Mearson acted calm, which wasn't hard since they were convinced the balloon wasn't a threat.

***

Rapeel's boys did all they could not to gag as they crawled slowly through the pipe towards the flickering torchlight ahead. They knew that to stay low to the water whilst they followed the large rat, and to move slowly, meant less of a chance of their approach being heard or spotted by their target. The tunnel lay in darkness as the torchlight from the opening they were drawing closer to cast across but not into the pipe they travelled, and the small torch their boss's man had been carrying had long since been extinguished in the waters behind them.

The large rat's body twisted slowly from side to side as it quietly swam towards the end of the tunnel. It dipped below the surface of the sewer filled water just before reaching the flickering light of the torch. Grimacing yet determined, the youngest of the group – the rat's handler – held his breath and followed his rat, pulling himself along just below the surface and out of sight.

Rapeel watched from the back as the other boys did the same, making their way further into the chamber as he and his two men reached the edge of the pipe and torchlight, weapons ready. He noticed the man in front grab a floating turd, before smearing it across the blade of his scramasax. He had to bite back a laugh as he thought of the weapon biting into Longoss' flesh. *If we don't kill you straight away and you best us, Longoss, you'll die a slow death for it.*

Reacting to the sudden explosion of water as his boys erupted from the surface within the chamber, Rapeel shoved the man in front and he, along with the other, burst from the mouth of the pipe. They charged up and onto the right hand side platform. A torch lit part of the chamber, but cast black shadows into the corners where three blanket covered forms lay. It was those areas the boys and men rushed towards, believing them to be the sleeping forms of Longoss and his companions.

They were wrong.

As the first of the boys reached what he thought was a huddled form, he felt his lead leg snag on a thin cord stretched taut across the chamber. The pulling of that cord yanked the single, burning torch from the wall, dropping it to the sodden, oil slick floor.

The large rat squealed and dived off the platform and into the water as Rapeel fell back and under the water's surface, an explosion ripping through the chamber and his group. Disorientated, Rapeel thrashed about and almost choked on the mouthful of sewage he took in. He managed to lift his head from the water then, only to crack it on the stone of the tunnel that the sewer flow had carried him back into. Gagging, he splashed out into the chamber again, only one of his two axes in hand. Wiping the stinking sewerage from his face with his free hand, Rapeel looked about as three figures thrashed around on fire, one of them large, the other two small. He looked to the water further along the half pipe and saw the youngest boy floating face down in the sewage. The ongoing fire's reflection lit up the surface of the water around the boy, which suddenly erupted as Rapeel's remaining man emerged, standing tall. The hafted-axe-wielding man looked to the screaming, burning forms thrashing around on the raised platform of the chamber, and then to Rapeel, who roared Longoss' name with anger and frustration at the realisation of what had happened.

The burning bodies finally lay still as Rapeel approached the man opposite him. Through gritted teeth he said, 'Grab the rat's chain and find the nearest way up top for 'morl's sake.'

The red faced man's mouth curled in a sneer as he nodded and turned to

369

retrieve the rat, which was cowering in the mouth of the pipe leading out of the chamber.

'And watch where you're stepping will you, there might be more traps,' Rapeel said, moving back to the original pipe to search the sludgy bottom for his other axe.

You think you're so clever, Longoss, burning a couple of kids and a dumb bastard? I'll show you clever when I ram a shit covered axe into your ugly, stinking face.

'The rat's got a lead down this pipe, boss.'

'Then get down and follow it, for crying out loud.' Rapeel finally fished out his second axe and turned to follow the black rat and his man. He pushed past the corpse of the rat's previous handler as he went. *Sorry kids,* he thought, taking one last look at his dead boys, *we all have our time, but by the shitting gods it ain't mine.*

***

The light of the camp fire burnt bright as the dark shadows of night fell almost completely over the land. The light breeze blew softly in the faces of the five men who stood in the balloon's basket. It was hard to see far from the fire, but the half-elf informed Exley there were four figures in the camp and at least two had just disappeared into the darkness of the trees behind the fire. Exley nodded and readied his small but deadly crossbow, as did his two companions, whilst the half-elf readied a windlass crossbow that he rested on the basket's sturdy wicker side. The other crewman, the human engineer, worked the dwarf-built propeller that directed the large balloon whenever there was insufficient wind to carry it in the right direction. He fired the balloon one last time as it dropped down towards the camp, the burst of fire giving it just enough lift whilst he halted the propeller, switching it briefly to reverse. The action dramatically slowed the balloon's progress until they were at a near hover above the camp.

Exley Clewarth aimed his crossbow at one of the silhouetted figures in front of the camp fire. 'This is it, men, these are the fugitives. Take no prisoners, they certainly won't.'

The half-elf swallowed hard, far from comfortable with his orders from the Witchunter General.

'Ahoy there, captain?' a female voice from below shouted. This stayed the half-elf's crossbow as he moved to pull the trigger.

'Don't listen, just shoot, damn you,' Exley said quickly, knowing his small crossbow had a lesser range than the half-elf's, and since they were still out of accurate range, he didn't want to waste a shot.

'Spymaster Burr here,' the woman shouted. 'I have pathfinders with me on an important mission. What news of Beresford?'

Both the half-elf and the human engineer looked suddenly to Exley, who cursed and nodded to his two witchunters.

The half-elf opened his mouth to shout a warning, but was cut off as the

370

witchunters swiftly shot him and the human engineer point blank.

Just then, a way off from the camp and unheard by the humans, a small hedgerow bird dipped up and down on furiously beating wings, screeching its tiny heart out to warn the elf who'd spoken to it the day before. The elf's ears pricked at the warning coming from Jenny Wren, and before the witchunters could reload their crossbows, an elven arrow, followed by another arrow and a crossbow bolt erupted from the shadows of the trees and headed straight for the balloon.

Those around the fire ran at a warning shout from the elf.

Exley had no time to move as the arrows and bolt travelled towards him. Unbeknown to him and his men, however, he didn't need to. As the three shafts reached the basket, they slowed, twisted and launched back into the trees from whence they came. A cry sounded from the shadows and Exley laughed out loud.

'The balloon's charmed, it's protected,' he crowed to his witchunters, as they reloaded their crossbows and loosed again, this time down at the four figures that rushed towards the safety of the trees. Both bolts missed in the dark and Exley realised the balloon was dropping still lower.

'Turf them out,' he shouted, and his witchunters heaved the dead bodies over the side. The balloon lifted suddenly as a ball of green fire burst from the trees, before arcing off away from the balloon and high into the sky. Exley laughed again and loosed his crossbow blindly into the trees from where the green fireball had originated.

'They have a mage, it seems,' one of the witchunters said, and the other looked to Exley, a grin on his face as he handed a clay pot to the Witchunter General.

'What's this?' Exley demanded, unimpressed.

'They call them grenados, General. Gnomes make 'em. Seen 'em used down south for mining, here.' The witchunter held the grenado's wick over the dwarf machine in the centre of the basket, the flickering flames lighting the end of the wick easily. He threw the clay pot out into the trees and within heartbeats a mighty explosion flashed and boomed within the small copse. Exley grinned and held out his hand for another as he lit the first he'd been given and threw it, whooping into the sky as it exploded.

'We need to hover here. How did he do it?' Exley asked, as the balloon continued to drift over the camp, now skimming the trees their targets had entered. Both witchunters shrugged, but before Exley could curse, one of his men pointed to the far side of the copse they were now fully drifting over. The pounding of hooves met their ears and a small number of riders left the dark copse at a gallop. Another horse whinnied below them and so Exley swiftly lit another grenado and threw it down into the shadows below. The explosion shook the basket of the balloon and Exley looked at the two witchunters with a mischievous grin.

'Oops, bit close then.' He laughed hard and his companions joined in.

The horse below had stopped whinnying, but the riders who'd left the trees were heading to a distant tree line to the east, and fast.

'Hit that damned propeller thing again and burn some air, hurry,' Exley ordered, and his men obliged. They might not have been able to stay in a steady hover, but they were able to propel the balloon towards the escaping riders easy enough. Exley lit another grenado as the fire heated the air in the balloon, and threw the explosive over the basket into the middle of the trees for good measure, laughing as it exploded; the trees now fully ablaze.

***

A breeze of fresh air – in comparison to the sewers – hit Longoss as he lifted his bandaged head above street level. Despite it being dark after extinguishing his torch in the mucky waters below, the shadowy street Longoss looked out onto seemed light indeed with the clear night sky's stars shining down.

'Is it clear?' Coppin asked. She had not long since had her first lesson in setting a trap for their pursuers, who'd unknowingly made themselves known by the sudden rush of rats that had swiftly and noisily entered Longoss' chamber, no doubt attempting to escape the large black rat Longoss and his companions knew nothing of.

Longoss only just heard her with his good ear as he scanned the shadows and rooftops. 'Doubt it lass, but we have no choice, we must move on.' He didn't mention the small boy he'd seen run off across the first roof he'd looked at. *Well, he's either a gang watcher or a Black Guild watcher. Either way, we're in the shit.* 'Come on,' Longoss said, climbing up onto the filthy cobbles. Rising to his feet, he drew his knife whilst continuing to check about him. He didn't turn to help Coppin out of the hole, because he knew it was time she started doing these things for herself. She had an aptitude for fighting and both Sears and Longoss knew it from what they'd seen. That was in a safe environment though. The real thing would be completely different and if she was to survive without them both helping her, she needed to use that strong independence he knew she had and start fending and thinking for herself, rather than relying on either of them.

'Gods that's fresh,' Sears said, taking a deep breath and pulling himself to his feet, before drawing his sword. *I never thought I'd say that about Dockside.* 'Where now?' he asked Longoss, his own eyes darting from shadow to shadow. He'd put his maille hauberk back on before they left the sewer chamber, but hadn't had chance to clean or oil it, despite the barrel of oil they'd used on the floor for the explosive trap. His face matched his beard and hair from the rusting iron links, and Coppin couldn't help but smile to herself as she looked upon the serious, orange face of the big man.

'We make a stand here,' Longoss said, surprising them both.

Sears rounded on the former assassin, a question on his lips. He stopped short of asking that question as his eyes followed Longoss' to a rooftop, which now revealed the silhouettes of several figures. Those figures moved to the edge of the roof and looked down on the trio, weapons drawn. Sears took a deep breath and let it go heavily. 'I see.'

Coppin swallowed hard and licked her dry lips, the appearance of the armed men above finally distracting her from the awful smell coming from her and her friends. 'We can't run?' she said finally.

Longoss shook his head.

Before another word was spoken, the street-assassins dropped down from the rooftop to face the trio.

'They're meant to hold us here until someone with my mark arrives, I'm sure of it,' Longoss said, moving out to the right as Sears moved to the left, leaving Coppin in the middle brandishing a long knife Longoss had given her back in the chamber.

'Then let's go!' Coppin said desperately.

'Too late, lass,' Sears said, agreeing with Longoss.

'Think of Elleth when they come at us.' The former assassin pulled the bandage from his head and threw it to the ground. He cocked his head slightly to compensate for the missing ear as the group of street-assassins approached. Lopsided grins showed on the youngest faces, all of which were looking at the green haired girl in wet clothing.

'I will.' Coppin held the knife lightly like she'd been taught, but clenching her teeth tight.

As the first two – both of them teens – rushed towards Coppin, she ran left as Sears launched himself ahead and right, straight into their path. His sword plunged awkwardly into the lead boy's chest, crunching through ribs before being swiftly withdrawn. A gurgled cough of blood was the only sound that left the collapsing boy's mouth. His companion hesitated through shock, resulting in his head rocking back as Sears smashed his palm into the lad's face, knocking him unconscious.

Before the lad had hit the floor at Sears' feet, Longoss had charged into three others, all of which were seasoned street-assassins by his guessing, although he recognised none. Longoss led with his knife, which was easily parried by the lead assassin's blade, who grunted in surprise as Longoss jammed the palm of his other hand into the man's throat, stunning but not killing him. The next man fell swiftly from a heavy kick to the groin and instantly threw up whilst doubled in pain. Longoss barely evaded the third man's rondel dagger, which he saw pass close to his face. He used the close proximity of the man's arm as an opportunity to throw his head forward and crunch golden teeth into the flesh and bone of the dagger wielder's hand. The man cried out and pulled his hand in close, removing the threat of the dagger from Longoss and opening himself up to Longoss' right boot, which thumped between his legs, creating a similar response to the other street-assassin, minus the vomit. Moving past the three men swiftly, Longoss headed for Coppin who disengaged from the teenager who'd gone for her, opening him up to Longoss, who barrelled him off his feet.

Coppin ran to the three stunned men Longoss had been fighting. To Longoss' surprise, as he looked up from the unconscious lad beneath him, the woman thrust her knife into the first man's back, screaming in anger as she did so, tears streaking her face.

Sears had advanced across the street and was battling four men armed with a mixture of weapons. Coppin's scream turned him slightly and he received a glancing blow to his left elbow from an axe. The blade sliced across Sears' maille, the links giving way slightly and allowing the axe blade to slide clear, but the kinetic strike of the blow rang up Sears' arm. The impact on his elbow flashed fire up to his shoulder as numbness flowed down to his hand. Realising Coppin wasn't hurt, but was surprisingly yet aggressively finishing off the three street-assassins Longoss had injured, Sears used the sudden burst of adrenaline his pain and fear for Coppin had created and rounded on the man who'd struck him with the axe.

The axe hit the ground as the man fell back, crying out as he tried to stem the flow of blood from the stump where his right hand had been.

The blow Sears had dealt the axe wielder left the guardsman open to an attack from an old looking short-sword, which slid across his back harmlessly, his maille again saving him.

Before his luck ran out, Sears ran forward suddenly, away from the swordsman behind and into the other two men, who lashed out at him hastily, surprised at his sudden charge. Sears ploughed into the man on the left, who was the larger of the two, and smashed his forehead into the man's face, leaving an orange stain on the flattened nose. At the same time, Sears parried the other man's poor lunge with his short-sword. In the moment it took for the larger man to recover and the swordsman behind Sears to close in, Sears pulled his sword back from his parry and thrust it into the stomach of the man who'd lunged at him. Grunting in pain, the street-assassin fell to the floor as Sears pulled his short-sword free and turned swiftly, slamming the pommel into the already broken, orange nose to his left.

Longoss saw Sears turn on the street-assassin behind him, but missed what happened as a giant black rat leapt from the sewer hole next to him, latching itself onto his left arm and biting down hard. Surprising himself, Longoss cried out in pain as the long teeth scraped across bone. He flung his arm to the side, which took some effort with the size of the rat, and the animal flew from his arm and skidded across the floor, taking a chunk of Longoss' meaty forearm with it.

Almost dropping to one knee, Longoss raised his knife a fraction too late to fend off an incoming blow from a hafted-axe. Luckily, his defence wasn't needed, as green hair flashed past and the attacker cursed angrily, the long knife that had slashed across under his arm causing him to pull his blow and miss his target. Longoss took the opportunity and threw himself up and forward, knowing the hafted-axe was near useless at such close quarters. Biting down hard, Longoss took the man's cheek and spat it and the blood that came with it into his face, blinding him temporarily. At the same time, despite the immense pain thumping through his forearm, Longoss took hold of his attacker's testicles and squeezed, causing the man's eyes to widen as he screamed out in pain.

A flash of iron and a feminine scream ended the man's pain forever, before Coppin pulled Longoss off the man. Looking up at her blood-spattered face Longoss saw Coppin's eyes widen a split second before she threw herself to the side, taking him with her. A shout of rage and then metal on cobbles rang out as soon as Coppin's weight pulled Longoss from where he'd been. He turned swiftly to see Rapeel climbing back to his feet, a filthy axe in each hand.

'You're mine, Longoss!' the street-assassin shouted. 'And then I'll shaft the green bitch until she begs me to kill her too.'

Longoss spun and covered Coppin as a deep roar reached them from off to the side, followed by a rush of liquid fire that engulfed the dual-axe wielding street-assassin a moment after he charged them both. The resulting scream brought their heads back round as Rapeel dropped his axes and flung his arms about, his face contorted through the agony Sears' fiery breath had brought him. He stumbled backwards then, before disappearing down the hole to the sewers below.

Longoss looked around quickly, rolling over and pushing himself to his feet as Coppin looked to Sears. The big man's chest heaved as the light from his eyes slowly began to fade. The bodies of the street-assassins littered the floor, one of them being pulled at by a large rat wearing a chain collar.

Looking the opposite way to Coppin and Sears, Longoss took a deep breath and then let it out heavily. 'Hold that rage Sears, we're far from done yet.'

Both Sears and Coppin turned to look the same way as Longoss, whose eyes were set on the new arrivals; a line of true assassins stretched across the street.

'By the shitting gods of all that's something pissin' witty…' Sears' voice trailed off as he thought of Biviano. *Where are ye old friend? We need ye now more than ever.*

Longoss took a couple of steps back, his eyes not leaving the line of assassins as he crouched, tucked his eating knife into his boot and picked up the hafted-axe lying next to him.

Seems they really have offered me up as a mark to all.

Risking a quick glance behind to his companions, Longoss' eyes widened further as he saw another gang of young street-assassins dropping down from the rooftops behind them. Sears met Longoss' eyes and nodded, taking Coppin by the arm and turning her to face the approaching youths, whilst Longoss stood and turned back towards the line of men and women in the opposite direction. Sliding his hands up and down the haft of the stinking axe he now held, he tested its weight and balance. The former assassin rolled his shoulders and head, his neck clicking as he stretched out his muscles; aches and pains suddenly forgotten.

With a thought of Elleth and, surprising himself, a final thought of Coppin, Longoss took a deep breath and lifted his head high. He walked towards the assassins with an air of such cold, calm confidence it seemed to radiate from his body. His usually assumed ungainliness was left behind to reveal the incredibly intimidating warrior he truly was. His head eventually dropped as he looked up through the tops of his eyes, a snarl pulling at the side of his bloodied, gold filled mouth.

'Ye wanted me, ye Black Guild bastards, ye've fucking got me!' Longoss' deep voice carried easily to the men and women facing him.

Gold teeth flashed as more than one assassin took a step back.

***

'Quickly!' Errolas' horse panted as he asked it to go faster. He was accelerating away from the others now as he headed for the Woodmoat as fast as his steed could carry him. Fal, Correia, Severun and Gleave were following him, digging their heels in and urging their horses on.

'What of the others?' Fal shouted, as another explosion briefly cast elongated shadows that stretched out ahead of the group.

'Starks and Mearson are looking after Sav,' Severun shouted back. 'His arrow was repelled and hit him in the shoulder. The balloon must have a rebound charm of some sort. We had no way of knowing.'

'But there were explosions in the trees as we left?' Fal had to shout louder as his horse rounded a lone tree, before coming back to the group on the other side.

'Grenados,' Gleave replied from the horse now alongside Fal's. 'All the balloons have them – gnome invention for mining, put to other uses by our lot.'

'They'll be alright, don't worry about that now.' Correia looked behind. 'The balloon's following us and that's what we wanted, now hurry. Let's just hope Errolas' kin don't finish us off.'

Errolas had pushed further ahead as the group raced on towards the growing black smudge of the Woodmoat. Fal turned and saw the burning light of the balloon as it rose slightly, following them. It had no chance of catching them whilst their horses ran flat out, but the animals were tired, they'd been pushed for hours that day and Fal feared one of them might fall in the dark. Errolas was getting smaller as he closed in on the Woodmoat and as Fal looked back again, his worse fear came true.

'Shi—' Gleave's horse tripped and fell, throwing him over its head to roll and land in a heap on the ground. Fal pulled hard on the reigns, as did Correia and Severun. Correia cursed and turned her horse to come back to the fallen rider. Once there she hopped down to join Fal as he tried to lift Gleave, the horse whinnying painfully in the background.

'Argh… don't!' Gleave grabbed handfuls of grass as he lay back. 'My leg…'

'Broken,' Fal said as Correia crouched besides them.

'Wimp.' She flashed a smile at Gleave, until she looked up towards the fast approaching balloon in the night sky.

Gleave cried out painfully as Correia prodded the leg. 'You bloody well fall off a horse at the worst—'

Gleave shouted several curses at the woman.

'Alright, alright, stop moaning. We need to get you on a horse,' Correia said as Severun dismounted.

'Broken leg,' Fal said to the wizard.

Severun winced. 'I can't do anything for that. We need to hurry though.' Gleave's horse whinnied again and Severun quickly ran over to it. The sound of a sword being drawn preceded the horse whinnying for the last time.

'Is there nothing you can do to the balloon?' Correia looked hopefully to the wizard as he ran back over to them. 'Gleave's not moving anywhere. He said his back feels funny?'

Severun closed his eyes and shook his head. 'Nothing, not with a rebound spell like that; It'll have been reinforced time and time again by the balloon's battle mage, and I've exhausted my powers for a while with the fight at Beresford. That last burst of energy from the trees took it out of me.'

'Then we make a stand here,' Fal said. 'I don't know how, but we've no choice.'

Gleave snarled. 'I'll bite the bloody bastard's legs if they come down from that damned balloon.' Fal believed it. 'You should all get on after the elf though, leave me to sort myself out. I'm a big boy, now you know.' Gleave's laugh turned into a groan of pain.

'I can maybe stretch to a basic defensive spell for Gleave, but not much more,' Severun said, clearly disappointed in himself.

Gleave waived that away. 'Don't be a fool, you three are fighting fit, don't be wasting it on me.'

'You're the fool,' Correia said. 'A flaming brave one though.' She grinned at him again as he grunted a laugh before wincing.

'Heads up,' Fal said, 'they're getting close now; watch out for crossbow bolts.'

'In the dark, aye, good luck with that,' Gleave said, winking at Fal.

Can't knock the humour from you can they, big guy. Fal smiled in return.

'I might be able to deflect the first of those,' Severun said, whilst turning his horse and standing behind it, 'but no more and no grenados.'

'That'll do,' Fal said. 'Correia mount up, we can try and get on that thing if it comes low enough—'

Fal stopped at the sound of a distant horn, a sweet ringing sound that carried across the flat fields from the dark line that was the Woodmoat. *Looks more like a fortress wall than a moat,* he thought, before climbing into the saddle of his horse and hefting his falchion high. 'Move apart, move apart,' he shouted to Correia, as he kicked his horse forward and towards the left of the balloon's flight path. Correia hopped up onto her horse with ease and drew her curved swords before urging her horse off to the right with her knees. Both broke into a canter to circle around the back of Gleave and Severun before coming back around, timed well with the oncoming balloon.

Severun concentrated on willing away any incoming crossbow bolts and felt his will assaulted as three glanced off the invisible barrier, much like the one protecting the balloon. The bolts barely missed him and his horse, and one landed close to Gleave. The downed pathfinder whistled as the bolt thudded into the earth nearby.

Fal and Correia circled the balloon as it dipped suddenly, and Fal attempted to reach up to it, falling short as an explosion erupted just behind him. His horse kicked and bucked away from it, almost throwing him clear, but he managed to hang on, although he dropped his falchion. Cursing out loud, he turned the frightened horse and headed back for his blade – back towards the balloon as he scanned the dark ground. A cloud of white smoke drifted gently across the grass from the most recent explosion, making it even harder to see.

Fal dismounted quickly when he saw his weapon, almost stumbling as he dropped from the saddle. Another explosion erupted nearby and he ducked as he saw Correia racing away from the patch of smoke and scorched earth. Fal's horse tugged on its reigns at the noise but he managed to hold the beast before climbing back into the saddle. He kicked the horse on and charged towards the balloon again as it got dangerously close to Severun and Gleave. It had dropped again as those on board were too concerned with reloading crossbows and throwing grenados overboard to think about maintaining altitude, and the only time the balloon got any lift was when the burner was briefly lit to ignite a grenado's wick.

Correia and Fal came round again, this time from behind the balloon as it reached an all time low, but just as Fal thought he might be able to reach one of the two ropes dangling from the large wicker basket, two crossbow bolts slammed into his horse's neck. The animal screamed before crumpling to the ground. Fal was dragged down with it and caught in the reigns, yet luckily he managed to move his leg out whilst the heavy beast fell. It kicked violently before eventually laying still. Fal mimicked the death in an attempt to stop the witchunters loosing any bolts his way, and only when a second explosion erupted, followed by the same horn he'd heard before, did he lift his head and look across the still body of his horse.

Correia had tried to leap for the dangling ropes below the basket as a grenado exploded near to Severun's position, sending the wizard's horse and therefore his cover galloping across the fields. Correia's horse kicked out at the same time and her leap failed as she crashed heavily to the ground just short of the dangling rope.

Pushing himself to his feet, Fal ran towards Correia whilst looking across to Severun, who deflected two more bolts under the moon's faint light.

Fal paused suddenly then as he saw something else in the sky, something that seemed to have risen from the dark fortress-like line of trees Errolas had ridden towards.

Just then, cutting across all the other sounds – the whirring, clicking propeller of the balloon, the distant whinnying of Correia's horse as it nuzzled her unmoving body and the stream of curses coming from Gleave's mouth as he lay propped up on one elbow, waving his sword around in the air – erupted a screeching roar that started high and ended with a guttural rumble that Fal felt in the pit of his stomach more than heard.

Fal stopped dead in his tracks and strained his eyes as he saw the distant fleck in the sky grow steadily bigger. He looked down then to the tree line, where more dark shapes were growing in size; shapes approaching from the Woodmoat.

'Riders,' Fal whispered. Over a dozen riders fanned out across the fields, heading swiftly towards him. He ran again then. Heading towards Correia, Fal sighed with relief through his heavy breathing as he saw her stir and then push herself up onto her knees.

The screeching roar split the night again and Fal looked back towards the source of the sound, which was obscured by the balloon reaching Severun and Gleave. A flash and a loud explosion threw Severun off his feet. At that moment Fal saw it. Correia pulled on his arm to stand and gaze, her whispered words confirming it.

'Gryphon.'

The beast appeared above the balloon suddenly. Cries of terror from the basket were almost drowned out by the guttural call of the mighty animal, half giant leopard half giant eagle. Mounted by an elf warrior, the beast lifted high above the balloon and twisted in mid air, before folding its wings and plummeting into a dive, its rider's lance reaching just ahead of the gryphon's huge, outstretched talons and claws.

Fal saw a figure jump from the basket as the gryphon struck the balloon. He was lucky to glimpse the black shadow of the man, who swiftly flashed across the dark background before landing on the ground. The man ran off to the right, away from the folding balloon as its occupants screamed.

The gryphon and its rider disappeared into the masses of canvas that made up the envelope of the balloon, before crunching into the basket and the witchunters below. Their screams ended as quickly as they'd begun and the gryphon reared up from the folds of sail like material, screeching into the night sky as the horse riders in the distance closed in.

Fal looked to the running figure then and after quickly checking Correia was unhurt, he took after the fleeing man towards a densely packed, but small wood to the south. Fal's muscles burnt with the day's riding and the recent fall from his now dead horse, but he pushed on as hard as he could, willing himself to catch the fleeing figure.

Another screeching roar was followed by the whoosh of air as the gryphon's powerful wings lifted the huge creature and its rider high into the sky. Fal didn't look back though, because his vision was fixed on the running figure ahead. He was closing fast and he hoped he would reach whoever it was before they reached the labyrinth of dark trees ahead.

Fal risked a quick glance behind as hooves pounded the ground. Some of the riders had stopped by Severun and had dismounted to help the wizard and pathfinder whilst the others, two of which had stopped by Correia, were heading towards the blazing trees in the distance where the rest of the group had been left.

Fal cursed as the running figure made the darkness of the trees before him and he swore to himself he would make whoever it was pay. As far as he knew, more than half of his friends and companions could be dead, or close to it, and whoever it was in those trees would pay for that. Nothing else mattered.

Chapter 40: Broadleaf Forest

A twig snapped in the overwhelming darkness to Fal's right, a sound magnified by the intense silence surrounding him, but he saw nothing. It was a gamble, but one he thought worth while. It was darker than dark, blacker than pitch, until the warrior opened his eyes after having them closed for a few moments. All available light – which wasn't a lot – flooded into his fully dilated pupils and allowed him to see easier in the dark. He swung his head in the direction of the snapped twig and saw a figure duck down behind a bush.

The quietest of clicks alerted Fal to the loading of a crossbow, and he jumped ahead and to the side, landing and rolling towards the bush as a louder click sent a bolt whistling past his ear. It thudded into a tree behind him and he leapt forward again, giving its owner no time to reload.

Swinging his falchion down in a shoulder breaking arc, Fal's hand and arm vibrated as steel connected with steel and a small spark flared for a fraction of a second. Fal's wide eyes took in a sudden image of a drawn, sneering face before he hopped back, barely missing the slicing swipe of the witchunter's rapier.

The bushes rustled and twigs snapped as the taller man came on, swinging and thrusting with the sharp blade as Fal hefted his heavier weapon in defence. More sparks flashed as the blades clashed, and each time, Fal's eyes caught a brief image of his attacker. Neither man said a word, all concentration thrown into the death match that spun and crashed through the undergrowth in the near light-less copse of trees. Although the wood they fought in was small, its size was enough to conceal the two men from any onlookers that might have been in the fields beyond.

A screeching roar drifted through the trees from far off as Fal threw a feint with his falchion, before shifting his weight onto his right foot and kicking out with his left. He connected with something hard, a knee or hip maybe, and the taller man grunted as he stumbled backwards into the trunk of a large tree. Wasting no time, Fal came on again, hacking down with his blade, the witchunter moving his head just enough to avoid the attack. Fal's blade stuck in the thick trunk then and he cursed as he tried to pull it free, ducking as his opponent's rapier slid along his weapon towards him. Fal had to let go and drop to the ground. Using the manoeuvre to his advantage, he lunged forward, wrapping his arms around the witchunter's waist, spinning the man and thumping him hard into the thick trunk. A sharp pain shot through the top of Fal's skull and his grip loosened slightly, allowing the taller man to bring up his knee, smashing the wind from Fal's stomach. Dropping to his knees, lost for breath, Fal still managed to throw a clenched fist up between his enemy's legs.

Horler Comlay cried out in pain and half doubled over before slamming his fist across the side of his attacker's head. The Witchunter General cursed as his knuckles broke with the impact and nausea swept through him from the pain in his groin. He stumbled sideways, tripping over something in the dark and landing heavily amongst the roots of the large tree. Horler looked up and saw the Orismaran pulling his falchion free from the trunk before swinging it down at his outstretched leg, which Horler moved just in time, kicking out with it immediately after. He missed in his hurried attempt to scramble away from his attacker.

A booted foot struck Horler's side as he attempted to get up. He sucked cold air through his clenched teeth at the impact, but managed to roll away, finally pushing himself to his feet. One hand still clutched his groin and the other throbbed with a dull ache from his broken, rapidly swelling knuckles.

Fal's head rang from the fist he'd taken to the temple, but he shook it away as best he could and launched another attack at the witchunter, who ducked left then right as Fal swung his weapon angrily.

Hooves thundered in the distance and then seemed to draw closer, the direction of the riders changing. Fal allowed himself a quick grin at the thought of the elven warriors riding to his aid.

Horler – his rapier lost to the darkness – reached for the dagger in his boot, just to find it too was missing. He turned then, narrowly avoided another swipe from the falchion, and ran through the undergrowth not caring what noise he made. His nausea continued and the knuckles on his right hand were throbbing terribly. The shorter, armoured man, the sergeant-at-arms he'd travelled all this way to kill, crashed through the bushes behind him. Horler ran all the harder, low branches and vines whipping his face. One left a painful red line across one eye as he cursed again and blinked away the blood and tears.

'Hold, coward,' Fal shouted, as he chased after the witchunter who'd attacked and maybe even killed some of his friends. 'Hold!' he shouted again, daring the witchunter to turn and face him.

Horler burst from the edge of the trees then and out into open fields. He cursed again as he realised he had nowhere to hide. Unarmed and injured, his companions almost certainly dead and a host of elves galloping across the fields on the far side of the small wood he'd just left, Horler risked a glance behind and saw the sergeant he'd been so hell bent on reaching, baring down on him, falchion in hand.

Something hit Horler Comlay then like a bull ploughing into him, one of its horns piercing his chest. His legs flew from under him as his momentum violently shifted backwards and down, slamming his back into the long grass and hard earth below. The pain screamed through his whole body… no, it was he who was screaming, up at the star filled sky as he grasped feebly at the long shafted arrow protruding from his chest. Horler's eyes struggled to stay clear, blood running across his right eye, tears filling both. They faltered and closed then, opening one last time to see two figures standing above him; the sergeant-at-arms and another, taller man, with a yew bow in hand and a bloodied bandage across one shoulder.

After managing to spit his own blood at the two men, the sergeant's falchion came down and Horler Comlay's pain ended, along with his life.

***

Moonlight danced from a dozen blades as Longoss weaved in and around his opponents, scoring shallow cuts and inconsequential bruising here and there and receiving the same in return. One near miss from a long, curved sword wielded by a richly dressed assassin actually opened up another man to the haft of Longoss' axe, which he used to successfully render the man unconscious, his hooded and cloaked form dropping unceremoniously to the filthy cobbles.

A sudden flash of pain stung Longoss' back as the crack of a whip reached his one good ear. He spun low, barely avoiding the claw like weapon of his closest attacker whilst receiving another stinging blow from the female assassin's second, barbed whip. She laughed as Longoss grimaced through the pain and rolled backwards, evading the oncoming claws of the small man close to him. One of those claws found purchase in Longoss' trailing leg and as the assassin used it to pull himself closer to his mark, Longoss did his best to ignore the pain long enough to thrust the head of the axe he carried into the face of the clawed assassin, breaking the man's jaw and subsequently knocking him backwards, which resulted in his claw tearing from Longoss' flesh.

'Bastard!' Longoss shouted, whilst rolling to the side, mindful of an Orismaran assassin leaping towards him, her tattooed face sneering as she punched out towards the back of his head, barely missing with her spiked gauntlets. Rolling back to where he'd struck the clawed assassin, Longoss brought the hafted-axe over one handed, using the weapon's weight and momentum to chop down through the tattooed woman's ankle. Her scream ripped through the night as Longoss leapt to his feet and struck her on the back of the skull, knocking her unconscious before skipping away from the oncoming sword of the richly dressed assassin.

The swordsman stopped as Longoss began to swing the hafted-axe in a defensive arc, keeping the man at bay long enough to assess the situation and locate his other attackers.

Laughing, the swordsman drew forth a flintlock pistol from his heavy wool coat and levelled it at Longoss.

'Very inconspicuous, Pietter,' Longoss said, nodding to the pistol.

The man laughed again. 'So says Longoss, who often takes marks out in broad daylight… well, who used to anyway.' Pietter squeezed the trigger and the flint hammer struck, but not before the whip wielding woman used one of her weapons to pull the pistol off target, giving Longoss an opportunity to charge the swordsman and plant his head into the man's face. The impact added more colour to the assassin's gaudy coat, moments after the loud crack of the pistol reverberated through Longoss' head. Pietter recovered well from Longoss' attack, flipping backwards and landing crouched, sword out to the

383

side and spent pistol in hand. Turning on the female assassin, he hissed and spat blood.

'Sorry, Pietter,' she said, shrugging and winking, 'but Longoss is mine.'

A crossbow bolt flew from the darkness and took Pietter in the chest, knocking him onto his back and killing him outright.

'Some things never change, Leese.' Longoss shook his head at the female assassin, who pursed her lips and frowned.

'I'm hurt you think so,' she said, whilst walking slowly towards Longoss. The young crossbowman from the shadows emerged to the side then, his ranged weapon replaced with an arming sword and dirk.

Longoss' eyes were drawn momentarily to the woman's swaying hips, before flicking back to her face. Full lips still pursed, she widened her brown eyes and stopped in front of Longoss, head tilted. He struggled to take his eyes from her, even though he knew her accomplice was moving around behind him. At some point in the fight, he'd manage to score a bloody line across her forehead with the blade of his axe, matting her long, dark hair.

'Why?' Leese said, shrugging slightly, her hands held behind her back – still holding the two barbed whips.

Licking his dry lips, Longoss' brow creased. 'Why what?'

'Why've you done this, Longoss?' she asked, blinking repeatedly, her every expression and her whole posture screaming an innocence Longoss was struggling to remember wasn't real. 'Why've you spoilt what you had, forced us to take you on? I can't understand it. None of us can?'

Longoss' head shook slowly as his eyes danced across the woman's features, soaking in the symmetry of her face, the shine of her hair. The blood had gone and the features were different now. As she approached, her body moving with such grace and confidence, Longoss almost choked as he realised he was looking upon Elleth.

'Why?' Elleth said, 'I don't understand?' She stopped an arms length in front of Longoss and he wanted more than anything to reach out and brush the black strands of hair from her brown eyes.

Brown? Longoss' face screwed up with confusion as he looked deep into those eyes.

'Shit!' he said suddenly, throwing himself to one side as Leese kicked out, a spike appearing from the front of her boot. She screamed in frustration as her illusion failed.

As Longoss rolled and came to his feet, Leese recovered swiftly, lashing out with one of her whips which tore through Longoss' shirt, ripping at his chest before returning to her side.

Linen shirt darkening with blood, Longoss rose to his feet and swung the hafted-axe around, connecting with the thrusting sword of Leese's companion, who'd dashed forward as soon as Longoss had dived to the side. Longoss used the whole of the axe in both defence and offence, connecting with his attacker several times, but not enough to knock the man off his feet as he managed to roll with each impact. Struggling to see where Leese was,

Longoss wasn't surprised when, like a shadow, the woman flitted across behind her companion.

Problem is, Leese, I know ye, and I know those whips aren't the real threat.

As Longoss thought it, the female assassin suddenly appeared next to him, lashing out with her spiked boot and plunging it into his upper right thigh. The painful impact caused the big man to falter in his defence against his opponent's dirk, which came in high and pierced the same shoulder he'd allowed to be stabbed by Blanck.

Longoss couldn't help but cry out, but the rage caused by the thought of Blanck and who that assassin had killed gave Longoss the anger needed to wrench his axe around the back of the man's lead leg. Hooking the curved axe head behind the young man's knee, Longoss pulled the leg from under the assassin, crashing him hard to the floor. Before either assassin could react, Longoss released his axe and drew his eating knife from his boot. He quickly sliced it around the back of the man's legs, hamstringing him much the same as he had Blanck.

The assassin screamed, as did Leese from behind, and Longoss rolled forward and over her partner and lover – for he knew that to be the case – turning as he came back to his feet just in time to see one of the female assassin's whips flashing past his face. The barbs of the whip ripped through his remaining ear, and when she pulled her weapon back, Longoss' ear went with hit, drawing forth a shouted curse from the big man.

'Ha!' Leese shouted, her eyes occasionally flicking to her partner, who was thrashing around on the floor attempting to press his hands to the back of his legs. 'You're a pretty sight indeed now, Longoss,' she continued, stalking around her lover, flicking in and out of Longoss' focus.

Breathing heavily, head swimming with pain, Longoss managed a golden, bloodstained grin at that. 'It's all the rage around here,' he said, 'but don't worry, Leese, I'll be sure to help ye join me in this bloody fashion before we're done here.'

Leese's seductive walk faltered and her eyes locked with Longoss', unable to look away as he held up his eating knife and pointed it towards her, mimicking the removal of both of her ears.

Licking her full lips, she suddenly smiled sweetly and despite himself, Longoss worried he'd be helpless should she attack him right now. His small knife felt incredibly heavy all of a sudden and his arm dropped as the woman moved forward once more, whips held behind her and trailing across the floor.

'Now now, Longoss,' she purred, 'you wouldn't do that to a girl, would you?' She stood before him suddenly, within striking distance, but no matter how hard he tried, he failed to lift his knife, or make any move whatsoever.

Leese dropped one of her whips and lifted her delicate hand to stroke across Longoss' bloody face. 'We had such a special thing you and I, once upon a time.' He closed his eyes briefly, remembering passionate scenes of the two of them, scenes he'd never remembered or thought of before now.

'There's no reason we couldn't have that again, just the two of us.' Her warm, scented breath brushed across his face as he felt her draw close. Anticipating the kiss to come, Longoss opened his eyes, wanting to look upon her face before their lips met.

Bitch, he thought suddenly, eyes widening in horror as he realised what she was doing to him. He willed himself to react, but his body refused to answer his call, every nerve ending crying out for the touch of her lips on his; her poisoned lips.

Longoss, ye stupid bastard…

As he roared inside, trying everything he could to pull his head back, to kick out or to fall to the ground, anything to stop those lips touching his, he heard what sounded like a distant female scream. Opening eyes he hadn't realised he'd again closed, Longoss saw Leese's beautiful face contort with pain and rage as a woman's open palm slammed into the side of her head, knocking her to the floor. Green hair flashed across his vision then and he saw moonlight catch on the blooded blade of a long knife, which slashed down and plunged into the chest of the female assassin at his feet.

'Leese!' a man further off shouted, and Longoss knew it to be her lover, moments before Sears appeared and finished the man with his blood slick sword.

Coppin gasped. 'Longoss…' She was stood in front of him now, her eyes taking in his multiple wounds in horror and her hands holding his face gently. 'Are ye with us?' she asked, staring into his eyes.

The first command his body responded to was a smile, a smile reciprocated by the woman in front of him, who pulled him close and held him tight.

All pain fell away then, all pain and all fear for her safety. They'd come through it, it seemed, and Longoss allowed a brief thought of Elleth before allowing Coppin and Sears to pull him from the centre of the street.

I think yer sister will be alright from now on, Elleth, whether I'm with her or not, I really do.

Despite that thought, Longoss knew he and Coppin would stay together for some time to come; he knew it was most likely his imagination, or the pain addling his brain, but he could have sworn he heard Elleth's voice telling him so through the throbbing of his ears.

***

The moon cast ghostly shadows around the edge of the small wood as Fal and Sav walked around rather than through it. A distant screeching roar and the thunder of hooves filled the area again. Fal struggled to support the weight of his tall friend, who'd almost collapsed after Fal had finished the Witchunter General.

The arrow Sav had taken to the shoulder, his own arrow rebounded by the charm on the balloon, had been removed and his wound bandaged. Drawing his bow, however, had taken immense effort and had no doubt damaged the scout's shoulder further. It had certainly sapped the last of his strength. Sav leant heavily on Fal now, as the pair slowly walked through the knee high grass and on to the gathering group in the middle of the large field, next to the crumpled outline of the destroyed balloon. Fal caught a glimpse of the gryphon and its rider in the distance, flying high over the line of trees that was the Woodmoat; a black shadow against the star-filled sky.

Hooves pounded the ground and Fal stopped, holding Sav up whilst looking back over his shoulder. Four elven riders approached with someone slumped over one of the rider's laps and a figure sat behind another, waving wildly. Fal lifted his free hand to show he held no weapon and the riders slowed their horses as they approached, lances and shields held high.

'That's my sergeant and the scout I told you about,' Starks shouted from the back of the lead rider, his bandaged face now visible.

'Hail, sergeant,' the lead rider greeted.

Fal smiled. 'Hail, master horseman. I don't suppose a lift is out of the question, to the others over there?' Fal pointed across the field towards the other group of riders and the destroyed balloon.

'Of course, sergeant, climb up,' the lead elf said. 'Here, we will take your scout.' The elf pointed forward and two of his riders brought their horses up besides Fal. One of them heaved Sav – who was almost unconscious – over his lap before Fal climbed up behind the other.

Fal looked to the body lying across the fourth rider's lap and his heart lurched at the sight. Mearson's face was almost unrecognisable. Starks' smile dropped as he too looked to the body.

Looking back to Fal, the young man's voice shook as he explained. 'He ran back to the camp for more supplies to help Sav, just after you all rode out for help. Another explosion struck close to us, burnt my face' – Starks pointed to the bandage that covered one eye – 'but Mearson… he didn't make it.'

Fal's stomach twisted and he felt physically sick as the news struck him. 'The bastards are dead,' he said angrily, more to himself than anyone else. *Not that it makes any difference to Mearson.*

Starks nodded and the riders set off, their proud mounts cantering ever so gently whilst bearing their injured guests. Despite the shock and his anger, Fal couldn't help but be amazed at how smooth the ride was, especially considering his steed's obvious power. He felt no need to hold onto the rider in front as the animal beneath him crossed the meadow swiftly, almost gliding as it went and hardly jolting him at all. Fal allowed himself a brief smile at the privilege of not only seeing the magnificent equine creatures, but riding atop one of them as well. Alas, his smile faded quickly as he looked ahead and saw two more figures lying on the ground. Correia and the elf riders, Errolas amongst them, crouched over the still figures that could only be Severun and Gleave.

Fal's heart skipped suddenly as he heard Gleave shout and curse, although no sound came from Severun's motionless form.

As they reached the group, Fal slid from the saddle and ran across to them; Starks close behind whilst the riders lifted Sav, and Mearson's body from the horses.

'How are they?' Fal said, and the group turned around to look upon him, their faces serious, but not grave.

'I've a bloody broken leg, how do you think I am?' Gleave shouted, his words turning into a yelp as a loud crack indicated the re-setting of bone. 'Flayed… shitting… argh… you bastard… that bloody hurt!'

'How about Lord Severun?' Starks asked as Errolas rose from the unmoving wizard.

'He will be alright,' Errolas said. 'He is unconscious, but our cleric here said Severun is strong and will recover. We need to get you all patched up though.'

'Bring the scout over here,' Errolas shouted lastly, and two of the elf riders carried the near unconscious and groaning Sav over to the group before laying him down beside Severun.

'Where's Mearson?' Correia asked. Fal looked down, then slowly up again to meet her worried gaze. She closed her eyes then and turned to Gleave, who was now looking at them both, his ashen face screwed up in disbelief.

'Dead?' Gleave's voice, barely more than a whisper, shook.

Fal nodded and the pathfinder cursed some more, punching the ground beside him before lying back in the grass.

'I'm sorry,' Fal said, sincerely.

Correia shook her head. 'He knew the risks. He was a brave one. Been with Gleave a long time and he'll be sorely missed, as will the others back at the cave.'

'I'm sure they will,' Fal said quietly, as he placed a hand on the woman's shoulder. 'Mearson was a good man and a great warrior.' Correia turned to him then, her stern visage faltering as she buried her head in his shoulder. Fal stroked her short, tangled hair and said nothing, knowing there was nothing more he could say.

Errolas looked to the ornately armoured rider who'd carried Starks. 'Lord Nelem, these people seek an audience with the council. We cannot delay too long, despite their injuries. Wesson has an epidemic and King Barrison has asked for aid.'

Nelem nodded and turned to his riders. 'Splint that leg and do what you can for the scout and wizard. The rest of you guard this area and bring them in when they are able to be moved. Errolas,' the elf lord continued, whilst looking back to the ranger, 'the rest come with us, but we cannot spare the horses, they are needed to defend this area. We have heard the rumours of a large goblin host and we cannot afford to let our guard down. We will travel on foot with the sergeant here and his two fit companions.'

'I'm fit,' Sav said, coughing as he pushed himself up onto his elbows. He winced as the weight pressed through his injured shoulder. 'I'm not missing

Broadleaf Forest. You said I'd see your home, Errolas, and I intend to.'

Fal moved over to and crouched by his friend. 'Sav, you could barely walk back there.'

'Very well,' Nelem said, surprising them all. 'Take this, scout, it will give you the energy you need, but you're to have no more, for a human could grow addicted to this far too easily.'

Sav's eyes widened and he managed to sit up, despite the pain, to swig the small glass vial the tall elf handed to him. The scout's eyes lit up further still and he licked his lips and smacked them at the sweet taste.

'What is it?'

'Never you mind, Sav,' Errolas said. He looked disapprovingly at the elf lord, who shrugged and headed off on foot towards the Woodmoat.

'What about Lord Severun?' Correia asked of Errolas. 'He is needed to explain what has been happening in Wesson.'

'He will be brought by horse when he is fit to ride, tomorrow hopefully,' Errolas explained. 'For tonight, let us make our way into Broadleaf Forest and hope the others can be with us in the morning.'

And so they did.

Fal, Correia, Starks and Sav followed Errolas and Lord Nelem across the fields, through the Woodmoat where a dozen Meadow Guard greeted them, and across the meadow into the elven realm of Broadleaf Forest, their emotions torn between grief at the loss of Mearson, and elation at finally reaching the elven realm.

***

It was the most relaxed Ellis Frane had felt in what seemed a long time. He sat back and let the white robed cleric's hands hover over and around his body. The warmth those hands released eased his aches and pains, almost making him feel like nothing bad had happened… almost.

'Will he be alright?' Biviano asked.

'Yes,' Morri said, although his expression didn't show it.

'Thank you for seeing us.' Biviano looked around the guardroom, taking in the other people being tended to by clerics. 'I know ye've had it hard this night.'

'Doesn't mean we'd turn anyone away, I'm just sorry your warning came too late,' Morri said, looking to Biviano with a sad smile.

Biviano nodded. 'Aye, me too.' *And if I hadn't forgotten Ellis Frane in the first place, we might've got here in time to warn ye of the attack.*

'Will ye be alright here, Ellis?'

The royal scribe turned to Biviano with a dreamlike expression upon his face and simply nodded.

'Good, because I need to call for reinforcements and then I need to go for Sears.'

The man nodded again and then closed his eyes.

389

'He'll sleep some time now,' Morri explained, 'it'll aid his healing. Well, his physical healing anyway.'

'Aye, there's not much cure for the other kind, I know from experience.'

'As do we all,' Morri said, gazing across to the wrapped corpses in the corner. 'Now go, you've seen this one is safe, do the same for Lord Stowold, and your friend.' Morri placed a hand on Biviano's shoulder and gave him a little shove, encouraging him to move.

Smiling with thanks, Biviano turned and made for the door. Reaching the blood stained, scorched corridor, he turned and made for the steps, almost bumping into two men as thoughts of Sears distracted him.

'Watch out, Sir Biviano,' a familiar voice said. 'Ouch!'

'You really are something you know that, Bolly?' Effrin shook his head at the man he'd just jabbed in the ribs.

Biviano looked up, clearly confused, but before he could open his mouth, Bollingham told him Lord Stowold had ordered them after him.

'So he just let ye follow?' Biviano said, wincing slightly as he scratched the inside of his left leg. His question had been mainly directed at Effrin – whose eyes were fixed on Biviano's scratching hand – knowing the cleric to be the trustworthy one of the two.

Effrin looked up and nodded. 'He did. He seemed torn with his decision to let you go, and as soon as you'd left, he pulled us to one side.'

'We thought he wanted us to call ye back,' Bollingham said, 'but oh no, he says whether ye don't wanna be a knight or not, ye have been one and he has to respect that, so sent us to assist ye.'

Biviano looked sceptical.

'He said he's sorry he couldn't send more,' Effrin said.

'And to hurry the hell up with the reinforcements,' Bollingham added, followed by a grin.

Smiling back at the both of them, Biviano nodded once. 'Well, what're we waiting for then, lads? Let's crack on.'

As the trio set off up the steps, Effrin staggered slightly, a sudden dizziness overcoming him.

'What's up?' Biviano asked, genuinely concerned.

I don't know, but whatever it was, it almost knocked me off my damned feet. Shaking it off, Effrin waved Biviano's concerns away and motioned for him to follow Bollingham, who was already away and up the stairs.

Chapter 41: Keep to the Path

A small clearing gave some relief from the intense, almost oppressive closeness the humans felt once they'd entered Broadleaf Forest. They'd walked into the forest from the meadow, following a barely visible path lit only by the ambient glow of the moon and stars above, which filtered down through the leafy canopy. The elves seemed to see just fine in the gloom, but at Correia's request, Errolas had agreed to use his star stone to give the humans some extra relief from the darkness. Now in the clearing, however, the moon's light was enough to not need the star stone as Lord Nelem stopped to talk to the group.

'Broadleaf Forest is unlike any wood or forest you are used to, even you, scout,' Nelem said, nodding to Sav. 'There are powers and ancient magics at work here, and it is unwise to anger the forest itself by disregarding or disobeying its laws.'

Sav now had a stupid grin on his face, which accompanied the glazed expression which had lingered since drinking the strange liquid Lord Nelem had given to him. He and Fal turned to each other and then back to Lord Nelem, in awe of the elf lord, whilst Starks looked around the dark clearing, his bandaged and burnt face a picture of confusion.

'Laws?' the young crossbowman asked. 'You mean your laws, Lord Nelem? Elf laws?'

Errolas and Nelem both smiled before Errolas answered the question.

'No, Starks, Lord Nelem means what he says. It is by the forest's own laws we elves live, not the other way around. We have lived here for millennia in the understanding that we follow the forest's laws and act as its protectors. It is hard to explain, because the laws are simple and yet complex at the same time. With us, however, you shall be fine. I am sure of that.

'There are a couple of laws I will tell you now,' Errolas said, 'but don't worry about any others, just follow us and follow our lead.'

The three human men closed in slightly to hear the two laws, whilst Correia stood to Lord Nelem's side, apparently aware of them already.

The reality proved somewhat disappointing to Starks, but with Sav being a scout, Fal coming from a land of thick forests and jungles to the south, and Correia being well versed in other cultures, even some elven it seemed, those three understood how important the two simple rules were.

'Do not stray from the path and do not light fire,' Errolas said, as seriously as any of the humans had ever heard him be.

'Is that it?' Starks blurted.

Fal frowned at the young man before turning to the two elves. 'Your forest's laws will be upheld by us, Lord Nelem, Errolas.' The elves nodded their appreciation.

'Then let us be on our way,' Nelem said, smiling sincerely. 'We have much distance to cover and we have no time to spare. We do not want your friends reaching the council before us unannounced, do we?' And so the group moved on, across the clearing and back onto the dark, narrow and winding paths of Broadleaf Forest.

***

The dark streets of Dockside were quieter than they'd been for some time and that worried Longoss, who again tried to shrug off Coppin's hands.

'I need to bind yer head, ye fool. Now be still,' she said, pulling the big man's bloody head down so she could wrap the cloth around it.

'It's too quiet,' Longoss grumbled, 'I don't like it.'

Sears shook his head. 'Samorl's bones, Longoss, ye lost both yer ears damn it? Course ye're finding it quiet, but ye're right, we can't hang about here.' Sears looked about the shadows and rooftops, whilst cradling his left arm, the wrist of which looked to be sat at a strange angle.

'Speak up, I've lost me damned ears,' Longoss said, irritably.

Not sure if Longoss was being sarcastic or not, Sears changed tack. 'We're lucky to have survived that,' he said loudly.

'I know, alright!' Longoss' outburst caused Coppin to step back. The former assassin's face immediately softened as he looked at the girl. 'I can't keep dragging ye about like this, Coppin. I need to go finish it; need to find Poi Son and—'

'Need to come to yer senses,' she finished, hands on hips. It was only then that Longoss realised she had been slashed several times upon her arms, although none looked serious.

'She's come a long way,' Sears said, standing behind her.

Longoss nodded his agreement. 'I know.'

Coppin held the big man's gaze as she spoke. 'Ye need to realise I'm in this for me, Longoss. I've seen and done things I never thought I would, or could, and I'm not sure it's all hit me proper yet, but I'm all the stronger for it, I know that much. I'm living my life now, not a life forced on me by others, and that's the way it's to stay.' She crouched down to check Longoss' other wounds. 'Sears is right though, we need to move on and we need ye to tell us where.' Coppin looked up into Longoss' eyes, which caused her heart to skip a beat, to her genuine surprise. Those eyes weren't those of a monster or killer, they were of a man who'd done what he had to do to survive, and one she now knew, somehow with certainty, would look after her and never harm her.

Nodding slowly, Longoss pulled his eyes away from Coppin's and looked up the street, towards the upper districts. 'I'm still stunned at the amount they sent after us,' he said eventually, as Coppin moved to check Sears' wrist – which caused the big man to curse repeatedly.

'I think that means ye're right about this mark the guild has,' Sears said through gritted teeth, as Coppin fashioned a makeshift sling for his left arm. 'It has to be something huge, to warrant this public display of violence in

392

order to stop us from talking.'

Longoss nodded. 'Aye, and the ones I faced weren't no street-assassins neither; they were true assassins. One of 'em almost had me, more than once too if Coppin here hadn't come for me.' He nodded his thanks and not for the first time since the fighting had stopped.

Coppin blushed slightly, as she had previously. 'I only did what either of you two would've.'

'All the same, lass,' Sears said, 'those were some brave moves. What we need do now though is make for the upper districts and the City Guard, and that means you two too, for surely they've no more to throw our way.'

Longoss was shaking his head before Sears finished. 'They'll arrest her and me, and I can't allow that, Sears.'

'They won't, I promise.'

'Really?' Longoss said, turning fully on the red bearded man. 'Ye can swear it, can ye? Because I don't believe we could know anything that's going to happen. Look at all this,' he said, sweeping his thick, bandaged arm about the body littered street and the dead assassins. 'They were my fellow guild members, some of which I've known for years. Not that I could've called them friends, but I couldn't ever have predicted this and ye can't predict the actions of yer captain or the magistrates, Sears, ye just can't.'

'Ye're right, I can't, but I need to warn them, although I still don't know of what exactly.'

As Sears spoke, there was a groan from across the street. Looking to one another, it was Longoss that ran across and crouched down beside the stirring assassin.

'I thought ye killed that one?' Sears said to Coppin, who looked back, confused.

'So did I?' *But I've killed a lot this day…*

They both looked across to Longoss, who looked back, gold teeth glinting in the moonlight.

'Well then,' Sears said, crossing the street, Coppin close behind, 'let's see what she knows.'

***

Long, smooth black hair cascaded down her pale skinned back, swaying gently from side to side as her hips swung gracefully. Slender fingers twirled the loose strands of hair that fell over her delicate shoulders as the sparse star light that managed to break through the canopy danced across her seemingly flawless form.

She wore no clothes and held nothing but her perfect posture as she sauntered seductively down the forest path, her pointed ears peeping through the black hair framing her cute, yet confident face. Bright green eyes gazed out beneath thick lashes, whilst her petite nose sat above dark lips. Her full, pert breasts gave way to a flat, toned stomach before her nakedness was fully revealed. The forest path's floor seemed to draw back away from her, vines and small nocturnal creatures darting back into the undergrowth, some of the latter peeking back out at the beauty that strolled passed.

There were men's voices ahead, human as well as elf and this intrigued her. She quickened her step ever so slightly and rounded a bend to see the back of a tall human male disappear around another curve in the tree lined path.

Leaving the path in a sudden burst of silent speed, the stunning woman ran effortlessly and silently through the trees before coming to a large ash leaning heavily across the winding path the group were travelling.

As they passed, she reached out and pulled the last of the human males through the bushes and behind the tree with surprising strength considering her delicate frame.

Sav, startled, moved for his short-sword, wincing as his shoulder cried out in protesting pain. Almost as soon as he'd felt the pain however, the same sluggish feeling swept over him that he'd been experiencing since Lord Nelem had let him swig the strange elven medicine. He looked up then, remembering he'd been pulled from the path. *Never leave the path,* he thought, swallowing hard. But all seemed well as soon as he looked into the bright green eyes looking back at him longingly. Sav's eyes wandered down, slowly, past dark lips – the bottom one of which was being gently bitten by the beautiful woman; the beautiful naked woman who stood in front of him, her head reaching only as high as his shoulders.

By all the gods above and below, I must be dreaming… or the elf lord drugged me. Aye, that must be it, I'm hallucinating.

Sav wanted to ask who she was, where she came from, anything to banish the apparition stood before him, but none of it seemed to matter as she reached up on tiptoes and brushed her tender lips against his, pressing her breasts to his chest and placing his hands around her back. His heart raced, his mind swirled and they fell together to the soft forest floor.

Oh, she's real alright. Sav felt her soft lips against his. He ran his hands across her smooth back and then down…

He began to leave all conscious thoughts behind as his mind swam with pleasure, the sound of running water close by a perfect accompaniment to the elven liquid again stealing away his pain and lucidity.

Suddenly, Sav's mind was torn away from the dreamlike state and the running water as the woman undid the cord of his braes and pulled them down.

I've died and there is a better place beyond.

Sav surrendered himself completely.

***

A tawny owl screeched and Starks jumped, then turned, awaiting Sav's laughter.

Sav was gone.

Shit! 'Sav?' Starks called gently, worried about getting the scout into trouble for leaving the path.

Both elves turned from the front of the group, their sensitive ears picking up the concern in the young man's voice.

'Where's he gone?' Errolas asked swiftly.

Starks turned back to the group and shrugged. 'He was here a second ago.'

Errolas and Nelem looked to each other and drew their curved swords. The humans copied their actions as the two elves pushed past them and ran back down the dark path, looking at the floor for tracks under the beam of light from Errolas' star stone.

Fal pushed past Starks then and ran after the two elves, the young crossbowman close behind after Correia had motioned for him to follow.

'I don't like this,' Starks mumbled, as they jogged on after the others. 'Can't see anything, we could be jumped on from right next to us and we wouldn't know a bloody thing until it was too late.'

'Hush!' Correia hissed quickly from behind. She scanned the blackness of the forest either side of the path. Her eyes were drawn to the beam of light from Errolas' star stone ahead as it suddenly pointed down.

Fal stopped when he reached the elves, and Correia pulled Starks behind her so she could press up against Fal's back to look over his shoulder. She ordered Starks to watch their back with a swift hand movement over her own shoulder, before taking note of the illuminated tracks on the ground in front of them.

Starks turned, loaded his crossbow and looked up, back the way they'd come. He whistled appreciatively just as the two elves pushed through the undergrowth and off the path, Fal close behind them. As soon as they'd disappeared into the blackness, Nelem re-appeared to shut Starks up. He looked passed Correia and down to the crouched crossbowmen, before looking over the young man's head to the naked, blonde haired woman who was practically skipping up the path towards them. She was clearly the target of Starks' appreciative whistle. Nelem ran his hand through his own long hair and laughed melodically.

Correia turned to see what he was looking at and screwed her face up as she saw the naked woman approaching.

'A nymph,' Nelem said. Correia rolled her eyes. 'There's a pool near here, they always stay close to water.'

'So that's where that damned scout is.' Correia's face screwed up in disgust and perhaps a little anger, or so the elf thought, glancing quickly at the Spymaster.

'Wow...' Starks said, as he lowered the loaded crossbow. 'Your elven women are beautiful... I mean, they—'

'What?' Nelem tensed suddenly. Correia saw the change in posture and turned fully, taking up a defensive stance with her swords.

'Your elven girls, they're perfect.' Starks laid the crossbow down and moved slowly towards the woman who was beckoning him forward.

'Elven?' Nelem asked, confused.

'Yeah, pointy ears and all that,' Starks said, unable to tear his eyes away from the beauty walking towards him.

'Get back!' Nelem yelled, and Correia lunged forward, pulling the young man back by his collar. Starks fell back onto his crossbow and the trigger clicked, launching the deadly bolt across the ground and slamming it into the naked woman's thigh.

Shrieking an otherworldly cry, the naked woman fell into a crouch, her delicate… no, her elongated clawed fingers wrapping around the protruding bolt as she ripped it out.

Starks shook his head, his mouth open in horror as the woman looked up, her eyes as black as the night, and her now obvious fangs exposed.

She screeched again, this time not far from the sound the owl had made just moments before, and Nelem realised then that it hadn't been an owl at all they'd heard, it had been a succubus.

Leathery wings unfolded from her back as she screeched once more. Her golden hair lifted on the black wings before falling back over her shoulders and breasts. Her feet were fully clawed now and pawed at the ground, the thick, black blood of her wound running freely down her leg as she beat her powerful wings. The wind rustled the trees and the deamonette lifted awkwardly into the air, hampered by overhanging branches.

Nelem pushed past the two humans and ran forward, his long, curved blade held out to the side as he leapt towards the screeching succubus.

Clawed fingers swept across in front of the succubus' chest and raked the elf's cheek before his sword tore through one of her leathery wings. He rolled as he landed and came back at the struggling creature immediately.

She landed badly, one wing torn and her leg unable to take the weight as the elf's sword came in again, straight for the throat. She managed to move just in time and thrust at the elf's groin with her sharp claws.

Nelem hopped back, the leather breeches covering his groin torn, but nothing more. He moved forward in a feint as the succubus turned to face an oncoming Correia, who lunged at the deamonette's back. The unnatural creature threw out an open palm and a wave of invisible energy knocked the Spymaster from her feet.

The distraction proved enough though, and as Nelem struck again, the strangely beautiful yet vicious head of the succubus fell to the ground, before being covered by the slumping, winged body.

Correia was pulled to her feet by a stunned Starks, as Lord Nelem ran past, back to where Errolas and Fal had left the path.

***

The dulcimer's strings hummed sweetly as two hammers struck them to create an eerily exotic sound. Pangan wasn't familiar with the piece, nor with the instrument his master was using to create it, but that wasn't unusual since the man stood in the corner of the dark, candlelit room seemed to have a different stringed instrument from one week to the next. All of which he was clearly able to play, although he often chose not to play them correctly, that much Pangan was sure when thinking back to some of the sounds he'd heard coming from the room in the past.

The assassin's eyes lingered on the trapezoidal wooden board and the strings stretched across it, all of which was sat on ornately carved wooden legs. The top of the instrument itself leaned away from the guild master, who used one of the hammers to strike two strings close together in the lower right hand corner, creating a low resonating tone. His eyes flicked up suddenly to Pangan, who matched the stare despite his fear, especially after the news he'd just delivered.

A sneer was the only warning Pangan had before Poi Son launched the hammer he'd used to strike the lowest cord. The hammer missed, barely, and Pangan wondered briefly whether it would've been prudent to let it hit him. Looking back to Poi Son, he saw the brief release of anger had lapsed already and the man was moving to the chair behind his desk.

'Tell me,' Poi Son said, 'how it is that three individuals can best our finest assassins and a number of street-assassins?' The guild master's eyes tracked Pangan as he walked across to the dulcimer and replaced the hammer thrown at him, which he'd swiftly retrieved.

'Honestly, Master Son?' the assassin said, turning to face his master before crossing back to where he'd previously been standing. 'I don't know.' He accompanied his words with a shrug of his slender shoulders.

'That much is clear.' Poi Son sighed heavily. 'He has sworn not to kill and yet still he wins out against all we send against him, as do his companions – a guardsman and a damned whore.'

'I think the mistake we made was allowing Blanck to kill—'

'Don't you think I know that now?' Poi Son shouted. He allowed himself a little satisfaction as the assassin in front of him looked to his feet after the outburst.

'Begging your pardon, Master Son, but I've never seen you this angry before,' Pangan said, lifting his head again.

Knuckles white, Poi Son shook his head. 'No, I don't suppose you have.'

'Would it have been better if I'd accompanied the assassins that faced Longoss?'

'Well, at least they might have been more subtle about their attack if you had, but no, there would've been no sense in losing you too. I need you more than ever, Pangan.' Poi Son reached into one of the drawers in his desk and drew forth a piece of parchment with a wax seal on the bottom right hand corner. It was impossible for Pangan to see what it said, both because of the light and the fact he couldn't read, but he strained to see the mark anyway.

'I have done things I don't like doing of late, and all because of one offered contract. A contract I have not yet accepted.' Poi Son's eyes remained on the parchment in front of him, and Pangan knew when to keep quiet and so did just that, allowing the guild master to continue. 'I ordered a personal hit on the new-found lover of one of my own assassins, albeit a whore. I then placed a mark on that same assassin's head and offered it to every man and woman of this guild, bar the other guild masters and their closest advisors.' Poi Son rubbed at the back of his neck and looked up to meet Pangan's eyes before continuing. 'And I even allowed you to offer a Dockside gang rewards on the mark of Longoss, thus creating multiple new street-assassins so as to assault him with numbers and people he could not know. All of this has resulted in nothing more than overt street fighting which could draw attention to this guild, at a time when that was exactly what I wanted to avoid.' Poi Son looked up at the ceiling and took a deep breath, before letting it out slowly.

'We knew he was powerful,' Pangan said, warily, 'but we couldn't have known how powerful.'

'You talk of Longoss?' Poi Son looked back at his closest advisor, who nodded. 'Yes, well it wasn't purely for that, that I wanted him to take this contract on. It was his bullish ways and the fact that once he'd given his word, I knew he would never have revealed our identity should he have been caught. In all honesty, I didn't think he was that good before all of this.'

'Gods,' Poi Son said, slamming his hands on the table, 'knowing now how damned dangerous and powerful the man is – and that's after swearing not to kill – makes me certain just how capable he would've been to take this mark on and succeed.' Pangan again nodded at his master, to show he was listening. 'But all it does now is lead me to another move I wanted to avoid.'

'Which is?' Pangan ventured.

Poi Son tapped the parchment with his right forefinger. 'To accept aid from a sister guild in Eatri.'

'But Master Son,' Pangan said, taking a step forward before his master held up his hand to halt him from both moving and speaking.

'I have no choice. This contract must be taken on and it cannot be linked to this guild and especially not to me in any way.'

To you personally? Pangan was suddenly suspicious and concerned as to why Poi Son would be talking about himself in such a way; a way in which he never had before with any other mark. He'd always talked about the guild as a whole, whether contracts came through him or one of the other guild masters, so why was this now about him? Pangan cursed himself as he saw Poi Son's brow crease.

'My reputation,' the guild master said carefully. 'After losing so many, Pangan, I cannot risk my position as joint master by making any more mistakes.'

'Of course,' Pangan said, not at all convinced at the explanation of Poi Son's self concern.

'If this contract is carried out successfully then our reputation not only in Altoln, but throughout all of Brisance will increase tenfold, and I cannot risk losing that chance.'

Still unconvinced of Poi Son's motives, Pangan asked what he intended to do.

Poi Son paused and looked down at the parchment on his desk, before looking back at his assassin. 'This mess with Longoss ends now. We've made open moves, despite my expressed wishes otherwise—' Pangan winced at the barbed tone, '—and so I expect you, Pangan, to stop at nothing now to ensure Longoss and his companions are silenced.' Poi Son held up his hand to stop the man's protests, knowing he would argue that he never took on a contract against Longoss like the others. 'Not you personally,' Poi Son added, calming the assassin, 'but I want you to put an open mark on Longoss and his companions' heads to any and all Dockside gangs.'

Pangan's eyes widened. *That has never been done in all my years.*

'Have them ensure the trio is dealt with using any means necessary, is that clear?'

Pangan nodded, reluctantly. 'Anything else, Master Son?' he asked, with no attempt to hide his sarcasm.

Poi Son couldn't help but smile, before realising what else he required. 'Yes,' he said, looking down to the parchment in front of him again and reaching for the goose feather quill and black ink pot on the side of his desk. 'Have this contract,' he continued slowly, whilst signing the parchment at the bottom, 'returned to the guild in Eatri whose seal is upon it.'

Pangan was leaning forward again, despite his inability to read.

'I am accepting their offer for their finest assassin to carry out the contract I shall now accept as our own.'

'And how, Master Son, will the completion of that contract raise our profile across Brisance if it is carried out by an assassins' guild in Eatri?'

'Very good question, Pangan, but leave the details to me. I am confident,' he said, handing the now signed and rolled parchment to the assassin, who'd stepped forward to receive it, 'that I have secured with the client of the contract I will now accept, a future where the Black Guild will sit atop the food chain, not only in the brotherhood of assassins' guilds, but of all human nations and their ruling powers within Brisance.'

Pangan's nerves fluttered as he took the parchment and looked into the cold eyes of his master. Nodding slowly he turned only to ask how he should have the message sent, considering the quarantined city and the insecurity of sending messenger pigeons over such distances.

Poi Son smiled wryly. 'My sources inform me that more than one group has left this city since the gates were closed to all, so I'm sure you will find a way.' Standing, Poi Son moved across to his dulcimer and picked up both hammers. He looked to his assassin one last time before the man left the room. Taking hammer to string, Poi Son prayed to any god below who'd listen that Pangan could stop Longoss leaving Dockside or especially from reaching the guild, because despite the grandest assassins being all about him within the building, the last thing he wanted was to explain to them why they were having to defend themselves against one of their own. It was all he could do to hide his own losses from them through all of this, and he could only thank his latest client for his assistance with regards to that. The thought of that client sent a shiver down Poi Son's spine and for the first time in many a year, he unintentionally struck a wrong cord.

I think client and yet I haven't even signed the contract yet… it is feeling more and more as if I am his servant, rather than he my client.

***

Sav was in his element, he'd never felt this way before; never had anyone made him feel this way before, not even the best whores he'd ever been able to afford. This elven woman seemed to know his every desire. The way she looked, smelt, moved… moved…

Why is she jerking back like—?

Sav cried out in shock and horror as the woman's head suddenly fell to one side in a spray of black, tar-like blood that covered his face. He scrambled to get from under the dismembered body despite his complaining shoulder, and finally managed to stand and draw his short-sword. Sav saw them then, as he wiped the thick, black blood from his stinging eyes.

Errolas and Fal both stood shaking their heads at him and pointing down towards the beautiful yet freakishly winged beast he'd been lying under.

Sav cried out again, this time at the sight of what lay before him.

Suddenly realising he was naked from the waist down – apart from his sword belt and scabbard – Sav quickly pulled up his braes and hose, stumbling as he did so and crashing down on top of the dead succubus. He was roughly pulled to his feet by Fal then, as Lord Nelem came crashing through the undergrowth, followed by a flustered and red faced Starks and a clearly disgusted Correia.

'What the…' Sav spluttered, as he looked back at the naked winged thing he couldn't get his head round.

'Succubus,' Errolas said.

'How did you know so soon?' Starks asked Errolas. 'We just encountered one on the path. Lord Nelem killed her… it. She was beautiful,' Starks continued, his eyes settling on nothing in particular, 'then…' the young man's voice trailed off as his gaze shifted to the one at his feet.

'We thought she was a nymph,' Nelem said, 'until your crossbowman here said she was an elf. You see nymphs appear to the one they are trying to seduce in the form of their own race, so that's how I knew, Errolas, because your friend here said she was an elf. But how did you know?'

'The wings,' Errolas explained. 'Since she already had what she wanted, she had relaxed her guard. Her wings were visible as she began to show her true form.'

Sav groaned, before bending double and throwing up.

Fal laughed. 'Serves you right you fool. You were told not to leave the path.'

'It is not that simple I'm afraid, sergeant,' Nelem said. 'Your man is not to blame here and he is lucky to be alive. Nymphs are one thing, they have lived in these forests as long as us and mean no real harm, but succubae, they are unnatural creatures, deamonettes from distant dimensions and times. Immense arcane magic is required to bring these forth and there has been none to my knowledge, in the north anyway, for…

'We must seek the council as planned,' the elf lord said quickly. 'There is more to this plague of yours than meets the eye I fear. It must be investigated further.'

'And stopped,' Correia said. The elf lord nodded his agreement.

After Sav managed to tie up his braes and wipe his face with his sleeves, the group set off back down the track with Errolas leading and Lord Nelem bringing up the rear, a black haired succubus head tied to his belt as evidence for the elf council. Sav walked along in the middle of the group, his head down and his pride the worst of his injuries, despite Lord Nelem's reassurances.

Chapter 42: Middle Wood

'It's alright,' Sears said to Coppin, who was berating herself again for failing to kill the female assassin at their feet. 'If ye *had* finished her, we'd have no one to make talk.'

'I stabbed her in the damned chest,' Coppin repeated, shaking her head and staring down at the bloody wound on the woman sneering back at her.

'She'll bleed out if left anyway, Coppin, and that's what we'll do if ye don't talk, Leese,' Longoss said whilst crouching next to the woman, a clump of her black hair held tight in his fist.

Eyes finally leaving Coppin's, Leese turned her gaze to Sears, her bloodied face softening as she looked upon the big man towering over her. 'Help me,' she managed quietly, although her voice caught at the end, resulting in a cough that brought blood to her lips.

Those eyes, Sears thought, *she's no threat… she just needs me to—*

A sharp pain in Sears' wrist – brought on by Coppin's prodding finger – snapped the man's attention back to the green haired girl, who glared at him.

'Stand guard, big guy,' Longoss said. 'We needs ye watching our backs, and looking at this one isn't worth the trouble.'

Leese managed a laugh, albeit short-lived as Coppin dropped to her haunches and jabbed a finger into the open wound on the assassin's chest. The resulting scream almost turned Sears back to them, but he held fast, his eyes darting about the street, making the most of the feint ambient light now coming from the rising sun behind him.

'Bitch!' Leese's chest rose and fell rapidly as she recovered from the sudden pain.

'Ye've seen nothing yet.' Coppin's lip curled as she looked the assassin up and down.

'Tell us who Poi Son's mark is, Leese,' Longoss said. The woman turned her head to him, or at least tried to, but the former assassin took hold of her chin and forced her head back to look upon Coppin and no one else.

'You won't kill me, Longoss,' she said softly, despite looking upon Coppin.

'No, but will,' Coppin said, holding her long knife in view.

A beautiful smile was Leese's response, followed by, 'You tried that already, girl.'

'This time I'll try harder.'

'Enough!' Longoss said. 'We've not time for games. The mark, Leese, tell us what ye know. There's something afoot for Poi Son to be throwing all this at me just for turning it down?'

Silence.

'Ye're right, Longoss, we don't have time.' Coppin reached forward with her bloody finger again and Leese pulled back, struggling against Longoss' vice like hold. As the finger neared the wound, Leese shouted, 'Alright

alright,' and Coppin stopped short, but left it hovering over the woman's chest.

'It's all Poi Son, the other guild masters know nothing of his mark or any of this,' she managed, her voice breaking here and there.

'Bollocks. He couldn't keep all this shit from them,' Longoss said, forcing the assassin's head around the street and holding it on her former lover's body.

'That was too easy,' Coppin said. 'She's lying.' Her finger plunged into the knife wound and Leese screamed again. Longoss threw a surprised look at Coppin and she withdrew her finger quickly, her emotions torn between shame and elation at the pain she'd caused the woman at her feet.

'Ye know what men are like around ye, Leese,' Longoss said, his eyes finally leaving Coppin's to look back at the assassin, 'and ye also know the effect ye have on women, so I suggest ye start telling the truth and fast, we ain't for waiting around here any longer.'

After the scream, Leese had fallen quiet and her breathing had turned from fast and heavy, to slow and shallow. Her eyes closed.

'No no no...' Longoss laid her head down on the muddy cobbles, shook her and then slapped her gently on the cheeks. 'Don't you die on me Leese,' he continued, shaking the woman and leaning over her.

Coppin looked from Leese to Longoss briefly, confused as to his motives for keeping her alive until he spoke again.

'We need answers, damn you!'

Her tear filled eyes opened suddenly and she sucked in a lungful of air, before screwing her delicate nose up at the pain.

Longoss leaned in close. 'Leese, tell us who the mark is and all this'll be over. The guild's not bloody worth it.'

She looked to Longoss, her brown eyes wide once more. 'I've told you what I know,' she whispered. 'It's all I know. I don't want to die, Longoss... I don't want to.'

'I know,' he said, nodding slowly, 'and ye don't have to, lass, just tell us all ye know.'

Leese shook her head slowly. 'He's telling no one who it is, I swear. I slept with him hoping he'd tell and still nothing.' Her voice was barely audible and Coppin had leant in to hear the words. She didn't miss the disgust on Longoss' face.

'With Poi Son?' he said, looking down on Leese, clearly surprised.

She attempted a nod. 'And still he wouldn't say.'

Coppin couldn't help but feel jealous as Longoss continued to look down on the woman he was now cradling. 'She knows nothing more, Longoss, let's leave,' Coppin managed, wanting to drag him away, wishing to see no more of the emotions he obviously felt for the woman who'd tried to kill him.

'You don't have to leave me, Longoss,' Leese said, lifting a hand to brush his face. 'There's always been something between us and you know it.' Her eyes half closed again and it wasn't hard to see the woman had to fight to re-open them fully.

'Longoss?' Coppin said, placing a hand on his arm. 'We need go, the sun's rising.'

He looked up then from Leese's eyes and noticed the lighting of the sky above the city. His eyes dropped back to Leese and he pulled his head back slightly, shaking it slowly as he did so.

'We need more,' Sears said, from behind Coppin, but Longoss shook his head all the more.

'She's told us what she knows and I believe her.'

'Because ye love her?' Coppin asked, trying to ignore the churning in her stomach.

'No,' Longoss said, laying the woman's head gently on the ground once more, 'because her allegiance is to her, not the guild and if she knew more she'd have told us, to survive.'

Sears cursed and faced away from the group again. 'Then we get out of Dockside, now,' he said, without turning back to them.

Coppin looked back to Leese and realised she was dead. The colour had left her cheeks and her hand had fallen from Longoss' face to lie at an uncomfortable angle on the floor next to him. Her chest had stopped moving too.

'I'm sorry,' Coppin said, unsure why, but she directed it at Longoss, who was looking down at Leese's still form. He looked up at her, brow furrowed.

'Why, because ye think I loved her? Ha!' He barked his laugh out and stood, grimacing as he realised again his multiple wounds. 'She thought she was playing me, so I let her Coppin. She didn't have the strength to sway me this time. There's never been 'owt between us two I promise ye that.'

Unsure where to look, her face flushing slightly, Coppin stammered something about it not being her business anyway and finally looked up the street, towards the upper districts and the rising sun.

'Why'd she not have the crossbowman shoot ye dead then?' she said eventually, without turning.

'Her lover?' Longoss shrugged despite Coppin not being able to see it. 'Because she wanted the price on my head to herself I expect, and the dope with the crossbow will have agreed to wound but not kill me if she batted her eyes at him.'

Coppin was about to talk again when she saw someone emerging from the shadows of an alley up the street. She hissed a warning and both Longoss and Sears swiftly moved to her sides.

'By all the dogshit I ever did step in, what The Three are they doing here?' Sears said, and his two companions both screwed their faces up, looked to one another in confusion and then to Sears, who was clearly no longer on guard, since he'd sheathed his sword. They looked then to the man who was walking towards them with a bloodhound at his side.

'Is he a guardsman?' Coppin asked as the man drew closer.

'Erm... yeah,' Sears said, although he didn't sound too convinced.

'And he's on his own this far into Dockside, at dawn,' Longoss said, pulling at the bandage wrapped about his head.

'Yeah, seems so.' Sears looked as confused as the rest.

As the seemingly unarmed Gitsham walked up to the trio, his dog at his side, he half-heartedly lifted his right hand in an attempted salute Sears' way, then looked to the other two and nodded, his face expressionless. 'Mornin'.'

Coppin managed a weak smile at the man. *He's not batted an eyelid at the bodies scattered about.*

'We're with Sears,' Longoss said.

'Obviously,' Sears added. Gitsham shrugged.

'What the hell are ye doing round here?' Sears asked, after realising Gitsham was offering no explanation as to why he was there or where he'd come from.

Coppin had dropped to a crouch and was fussing over the dog. 'What's his name?'

'Buddle,' Sears said, his eyes not leaving Gitsham's.

'Awe he's cute.' Coppin continued scratching under the hound's chin.

'Is this reinforcements?' Longoss asked, torn between amusement and despair as he thought about the situation they were in. '"Cause we need move and move fast, Sears, we've hung about too long.'

'No shit, big man,' Sears said, rounding on him, 'but we still have nothing do we? Apart from 'there's a mark and it's a big one' but nothing bloody more than that?'

Longoss held both hands up, palms forward. 'Alright, Sears, I know that and that's why I need to go for Poi Son.'

'Not this again,' Sears said, looking up and rolling his eyes. All the while, Gitsham made no move to offer any information as to why he was there or to ask them what they were talking about. He just looked on blankly as his dog had its ears scratched by an attractive green haired girl covered in cuts and far more blood than could be her own.

'Ye can't be running off there to die, Longoss. We'll go to Captain Prior and tell him what we know, and that's that.'

Longoss laughed. 'We don't know owt though do we? That's what ye keep saying and at the same time ye wanna take that lack of information to yer bloody captain.'

'Calm down, both of you,' Coppin said, standing and glaring at the two men. They both sighed heavily and Sears turned back to Gitsham.

'Well?' Sears asked, eyes wide as he leant forward. 'What do ye know, Gitsham?'

'There'll be no going to Captain Prior.'

Longoss grinned.

'And why's that?' Sears' annoyance was clear to see.

'He's got the plague. Lord Stowold's taken over for now.'

Longoss' face dropped as he thought of Sears running off to the Constable of Wesson, but before Sears himself could react to the news,

405

Gitsham went on.

'Been some trouble here, eh?' the man asked, finally looking about and taking in the bloody scene.

'Morl's bleedin' balls,' Longoss said, turning away from the man and shaking his head.

Ye'll think that a lot around Gitsham, Sears thought, before thinking of the sick captain.

'Longoss, that's rude,' Coppin said, placing a hand on Gitsham's shoulder and managing to draw his attention. When he fully looked at her, he seemed to rock back slightly, as if seeing her for the first time. 'What brought ye here, Master Gitsham?'

'Sears being in trouble,' he said, nodding towards Sears – who rolled his eyes and mouthed 'no shit' whilst running his good hand through his knotted beard. 'Buddle told me so.'

'"Course he did,' Longoss said, looking down the street.

'Actually...' Sears eyed the dog, which had moved and was looking like raising a leg behind Longoss' own.

'Alright,' Coppin said, unsure, 'so ye came to help Sears?'

'Aye.' Gitsham looked to Sears and nodded once.

Copping smiled. 'That's a lovely thing to do.'

'But ye didn't bring any reinforcements other than Buddle?' Sears asked, brow rising expectantly.

Coppin flashed Sears a dangerous look. 'Sears. Be grateful.'

Gitsham shook his head slowly. 'Nope, just us two.'

Sears noticed the horn on the man's belt. 'Ha! A horn. Why didn't ye say?' Sears reached forward and plucked the horn from Gitsham's belt. He took a deep breath.

Gitsham held his hand up and Buddle growled, all a split second before Longoss cried out and looked down upon his suddenly warm, wet calf.

'Ye can't say anything, Longoss, after all ye've done in those.' Coppin pointed to his groin.

'Maybe not lass, but I'd only just started drying from the sewer.' He shook his leg and bared gold teeth to Buddle, who bared his own teeth back. All the while, Sears had been holding the horn to his lips, awaiting an explanation as to why he shouldn't blow and call for aid.

'Too far in,' Gitsham said, eventually.

'In to Dockside?' Coppin asked.

'Aye, we're too far in to use that now.'

'Rubbish,' Sears said, lowering the horn only slightly.

'And I'm off whether ye blow it or not big guy,' Longoss added. 'I need to go for Poi Son, not have your lot drag me away.'

'They'd hear it from here and they won't arrest ye, Longoss, will ye be told.'

'Oh aye,' Gitsham said, 'they'd hear it, but it's too late for them to make it if ye blew it now anyway.'

'What do ye mean, Master Gitsham?' Coppin asked, a look of concern spreading across her face.

'Think we've dealt with the worst of 'em.' Sears nodded about to the corpses scatted here and there. Longoss grunted and Sears glanced sideways at him, not liking the sound or possible reason for the grunt.

Buddle growled and looked down the street. All eyes were upon the hound as Gitsham spoke next.

'He says a gang has found us, and that's what I was meaning by it being too late to blow the horn.'

'Flay me, Gitsham, ye need to learn to speed up when ye have news like that,' Sears said angrily.

The unmistakeable sound of ganger calls echoed off the walls of the buildings lining the street and it was hard to make out where they originated, but Buddle continued to snarl and look down towards the harbour end of Dockside.

'Time to move, now,' Sears said, suddenly setting out and heading towards the upper districts.

Longoss didn't budge. 'Sorry friend, but I'm for Poi Son, so I'll say thank ye and goodbye.'

Sears turned and looked to Longoss, despite being distracted for a split second by both Gitsham and Buddle, the former of which was staring at Leese's corpse whilst the latter proceeded to hump her leg vigorously. Shaking his head in disgust, Sears motioned for Longoss to follow. 'Come on, ye can't be attacking the Black Guild—'

Buddle yelped as Sears mentioned the guild, and the dog leapt off the leg he'd been mounting. At the same time, Gitsham took a step back and raised his hands to his head. His eyes closed momentarily before opening wide.

Coppin rushed to the man's side. 'What is it?'

'He figure something out?' Sears pointed to the dog, which had distanced itself from Leese's body.

Nodding, Gitsham looked from Coppin to Sears. 'Darkness, the darkness throughout the city, it's connected—'

'The darkness?' Longoss interrupted. 'Ye mean the plague?'

Gitsham nodded.

'Connected to what?' Longoss asked.

Gitsham looked back to the corpse and Buddle growled throatily.

'To her?' Coppin asked, confused. She looked to Longoss and he shrugged.

More ganger calls, closer this time.

'We all need to go now,' Longoss said.

'Gitsham, quickly!' Sears was getting more and more frustrated.

'To the Black Guild,' Gitsham said. 'Like pieces on a board, people are being worked, events played, it's all connect—

Gitsham almost dropped to one knee, but Coppin managed to hold him up and Sears lunged forward to assist.

'Sears…'

'Longoss, I know! Gitsham?'

'King Barrison,' the man managed. He looked suddenly pale and extremely weak.

Sears looked to Longoss whose eyes had widened. Longoss mouthed the question 'the mark?' and Sears' eyes widened too.

'Is the King the guild's mark, Gitsham?'

Buddle barked and then ran off up the street. Gitsham's eyes met Sears' and a single nod was all Sears needed to haul the man to his feet with his good arm, before letting him go and drawing his short-sword, pointing it after the bloodhound.

'Let's move,' Sears shouted as multiple men and youths rounded a corner lower down the street, a variety of weapons – makeshift and real – in their hands. Some pointed, others roared and shouted threats, but as one they ran towards the group in the middle of the street.

'Thanks to ye all and keep her safe, Sears,' Longoss said as he locked eyes with Coppin and smiled without the gold.

Sears nodded once, knowing there was no turning the former assassin from his path.

'I'm staying.' Coppin's eyes didn't leave Longoss' despite him shaking his head and his smile faltering.

'There's no time.' Gitsham turned and ran after Buddle, who was almost out of sight.

'Coppin?' Sears shouted, looking from her to the nearing gangers and back.

She turned quickly, looked at Sears and placed a hand on his heart. 'Ye can't change his mind, ye can't change mine. We're staying in Dockside. Now go. Go tell the constable. Go!'

Reluctantly, Sears nodded to Coppin and then to Longoss, who returned the gesture with a wink. Sears turned then and ran after the man and hound, willing his tired legs to carry him on all the way up the hill and away from the gangers. He forced the two he was leaving behind from his mind.

Longoss grabbed Coppin by the arm as Sears departed and dragged her after Sears briefly before turning off down a side street where he stopped suddenly to lift a sewer cover.

'Really?' she said, heart pounding as the sound of dozens of gangers grew ridiculously close.

'Ye wanted to follow me, lass.' Longoss pushed Coppin down the hole. *And for the life of me I don't know why.*

Longoss took a deep breath and dropped down after her.

***

The overlapping branches of the tall trees in full bloom created a tunnel-like passageway through the depths of Broadleaf Forest. A cool breeze gently rustled leaves and flowers, and flies, bumblebees and other insects hovered and flitted from plant to plant. The dawn chorus of a multitude of bird songs sounded sweet and uplifting, although rarely did the humans see any of the birds making the sounds.

As the sun rose in the east, its early morning rays shone through the forest canopy, splitting and spreading shards of light down onto the ground, where the mixed group of elves and humans walked. They passed through a large clearing surrounded by a wall of ancient trees, the foliage reaching up into the blue sky, creating a landscape fit for a dream. The grass they walked on was long and wild, with a scattering of pink and yellow flowers spread throughout. A shimmering border of blue ran around the clearing's edges as hundreds of bluebells swayed gently on the breeze.

Over on the far side of the clearing, a slender roe doe grazed, seemingly unconcerned by the group.

After briefly taking in the stunning sights, the group moved across the open ground, which finally caused the doe to move off into the thick undergrowth below the canopy, a flash of white from her tail the last the group saw of her.

Once passed the clearing and back on the forest path, Errolas stopped suddenly and held up his right hand. The group halted as one, although Sav continued to hold his head low from both embarrassment and disgust, even after hours of re-assurance from Lord Nelem behind him, that a succubus could seduce any human and most elves, and he should not be embarrassed by the incident.

Everyone in the group – except Sav – looked to the front where Errolas had moved forward, his head tilting as he listened to whatever it was he'd heard.

The elf ranger relaxed visibly and so did the rest of the group as a huge red stag strode onto the path in front of them, its thick neck supporting the weight of its impressive antlers. The huge animal, almost the size of a knight's destrier, walked up to Errolas and bowed its head towards him. The humans in the group feared the animal was going to attack the elf, until, matching the stag, Errolas bowed equally as low, before the two of them rose again to look into each others eyes.

'He's greeting us,' Errolas said, much to the astonishment of the humans who looked on. Fal turned to look at Sav, who finally looked up, mouth open as he stared at the stag in amazement.

'Greetings, my lord. What brings you to this area?' Errolas said to the animal, as Nelem moved past the humans to stand next to the ranger. The stag bowed its head again and Nelem reciprocated.

'Greetings to you too, my lord,' Nelem said. After a pause, the elf lord continued. 'You heard correctly, but the humans are with us. Although there have been other, more unsavoury, creatures in the forest. Ah,' Nelem continued, 'you already know that, of course.'

'He's talking to it,' Starks said to Fal, who hushed the crossbowman, intent as he was on the conversation seemingly going ahead before him.

'You travel alone?' Nelem asked. The stag shook his regal head, looking up into the trees.

Fal could have sworn the stag smiled.

A chattering high above the group drew their gaze up into the trees as a pair of red squirrels fell silent and looked back down at them. One threw an acorn which hit Starks on the head, before it hopped off across branches, chattering to its partner again with what seemed like laughter.

'Ouch.' Starks rubbed his head, although he had to admit, it hadn't actually hurt.

The rest of the group laughed.

Errolas nodded to the stag before turning to Starks. 'He offers his apologies, Starks. He says they meant no harm.'

Starks looked stunned, and merely nodded as the animal, and Errolas, turned to face one another once more.

'Indeed we did,' Nelem said, indicating the succubae head on his belt.

'He asks about our encounter,' Errolas confirmed to the humans, who continued to look on in awe.

Sav's head lowered at the mention of the deamonette. Fal struggled to hide his amusement.

Nelem nodded to some unheard comment or question. 'We… came across them by Birch Spring in the night, my lord. I almost mistook one for a nymph, until the boy back there said he thought she was an elf.'

Starks frowned at the term.

Errolas nodded. 'It is indeed troubling, my lord.' He looked ashen faced then, as did Nelem.

'Errolas, what is it?' Correia asked. It was Nelem who replied.

'Apparently the succubae are not the only creatures unnatural to the forest these past few weeks, and all since…'

'Go on,' Correia said.

Nelem frowned. 'Since the unseasonable storm on the western coast. The trolls on the Moot Hills have been bolder of late, and more so than he has heard tell of for decades. A group entered the Woodmoat no more than two days ago, until they were repelled by Meadow Guard.' Both Nelem and Errolas' heads dropped. 'Our kin lost five that night. He says we will hear more from the council.'

'You know our destination?' Correia asked of the stag, which nodded its head in answer.

'He says he hears much,' Errolas said to Correia. 'The forest talks to him. He knows of the plague sweeping your home and wishes your people a swift recovery.' Another pause before Errolas continued. 'Humans may not always play the finest role in the natural world, but your nation is an ally to Broadleaf Forest and his kin respect that.'

'Thank you, my lord,' Correia said. She bowed, triggering the same response from the large animal.

Nelem and Errolas smiled to the stag.

'He will be on his way now,' Errolas said, 'and wishes us all a speedy journey, and your city a fast recovery. There are things he must tend to.'

As Errolas finished speaking, the stag turned and disappeared back the way he had come, through low branches and tangled vines that closed around him as he left the path.

The things I've heard and then written off in the Coach and Cart Inn as tall stories or lies even, Fal thought once the group set off down the path again. *Would I have believed this if I'd heard it told by another? I think not, and yet I've just witness it, and it felt… normal? No, not normal, but natural for sure.*

It was another two hours until the group reached a large opening in the forest canopy. The path widened until the trees receded and a large glade opened out before them. A small river flowed through the centre of the sun drenched glade and a bridge crossed the river to one side. The bridge looked almost natural; a large and ancient oak lay across the fast flowing water, with a deep, wide groove cut through the length of the trunk to create a smooth path across. On either side of the bridge stood an elven guard in ornately formed armour that fanned out at the shoulders like large leaves of bronze and gold. Each section of their plate armour, from their greaves to their vambraces was decorated with intricate spiralling patterns carved into the unknown metal. The edges twisted and flared so each looked like leaves from various autumnal trees, matching the pouldrons on their shoulders and the sculpted helms which curved round to protect their cheeks before kicking out at the base to deflect blows from their necks. They wore fine silver maille – which shone in the sunlight of the glade – in-between the painted plates of armour.

In their right hands they held tall spears with shining, slightly curved blades at both ends. They rested tall, leaf shaped shields on the floor, holding the tops with their left hands as the shields leant against their sides.

As the group approached, the tall elves crouched, looped their left arms through the straps of their shields and hefted them to cover half of their bodies. They stood to attention then and held their spears lightly, clearly ready to use them if necessary. The movement of both guards had taken but a moment and Fal was impressed by their swift reaction to the group's sudden presence.

Both elf guards had long, chestnut brown hair that fell across their shoulders, the ends gently moving in the morning breeze, and as the group drew closer to the bridge, the closest guard called out to them.

'Hail Lord Nelem. What brings you away from the meadow and your retinue?'

'Our allies here.' The elf lord swept his hand to indicate Fal and the others who stood behind him. 'They seek an audience with the council. My retinue will be along today with more of their followers that were injured in an attack on the far side of the Woodmoat. They need swift passage to the council hall upon their arrival.'

'Very well, Lord Nelem, you may pass.' The two guards brought their spears close into their sides and took two steps each away from the bridge.

'Thank you my friends, oh... and beware. There are strangers to our lands besides our allies here. We encountered two succubae by the Birch Spring and the Great Stag told us he has heard rumours of yet more unsavoury creatures in our realm.'

The guard who'd spoken nodded and thanked Nelem for the warning. The group passed then and each of the humans nodded to the guards as they passed, stepping onto the ancient bridge, which only then revealed the spectacular spiral carvings and artwork covering every inch of it. The humans gazed in awe at the beautiful artwork as they walked across the ancient tree-bridge, the soothing sound of flowing water beneath them.

'Charms,' Errolas explained, as he noticed the humans' interest in the carvings. 'We don't mark without reason. This tree gave itself for our use and defence. It was old and had contracted a disease thousands of years ago. Our ancestors used it then to bridge this river, carving magical charms into it to keep it from rotting, and also to hinder its use by hostile creatures. Each carving means something different and they have been added bit by bit since the bridge was laid. As you can see, there is not much room for more, but the longer the tree lies and is used as a crossing, the stronger its defence to attack or unwanted crossing becomes.'

'Such beauty and such practicality all in one, it truly is amazing,' Fal said, and the others nodded, brushing their fingers across the finely carved wood as they crossed the bridge.

As soon as they reached the other side and stepped once more onto the lush green grass, without explanation, their hearts felt lighter, their minds clearer and the air so much sweeter. The sun kissed their skin and a warmer, yet still refreshing breeze flowed around them. Nelem's silvery hair danced in the pleasant wind, as did Errolas' as they set off across the beautiful glade, a glade that only now revealed groups of elven children playing by the water. They chased what looked like fireflies around and laughed playfully, a sound sweeter than anything the humans had ever heard before.

Errolas stopped then and turned to face them, realising they hadn't followed. He laughed and Nelem stopped just past him, turning to look upon the amazed faces of their human allies.

'I'm sorry, my friends.' Errolas smiled. 'I didn't think of the bridge crossing, it is something we are so used to.'

'This,' Errolas held out both his arms and swept them across the glade, across the playing groups of elven children and to the trees they were heading towards, 'is our home, the heart of our realm.'

'Oh Fal,' Sav said, his voice almost a whisper, 'we're here, we're actually here.'

Fal nodded slowly, his face a canvas to the joy and amazement he clearly felt as he took in the sights, the feelings and the sounds of the children's laughter.

A small group of young elves ran over to them, stopping just before the group and whispering to each other. They stared at the humans; the first they'd ever seen. Fal seemed to draw more stares than the rest, his tattooed face clearly of interest to the youngsters.

Errolas and Nelem chuckled as the group of humans and elven children stared and smiled at each other. Correia waved and the children giggled. The closest child held out her delicate, small fist before turning and opening it to reveal a beautiful pink and purple stone shining in the sunlight. She said something in a quiet, singsong voice none of the humans could understand. None, that was, except for Correia, which surprised everyone in the group, including Errolas and Nelem, who looked to one another, both wondering if the other knew she could speak their tongue.

'A star stone, for me?' Correia said in broken elvish, and the little girl smiled as she stepped forward with it. The other children giggled as Correia took the stone and thanked the little girl. She took a leather necklace from around her neck with a fan shaped sea shell attached to it that had previously been hidden down her top, and handed it to the small girl, saying something else in the child's beautiful language. The girl giggled and nodded, taking the necklace before running off past Errolas and Nelem, the rest of the children – including others from a nearby group – chasing after her, laughing and shouting.

Correia blushed slightly as all eyes focussed on her, something Fal or the others hadn't imagined possible from the stoic woman.

'Alright,' she said suddenly, her voice hard once more, 'on we go. We've a mission to be seeing through, so come on.' She waved them along as they grinned to one another. The two elves led the way and the group entered the forest once again, but this time, it didn't feel oppressive like before. Not that it had really felt bad before they'd crossed the river into the extraordinarily peaceful place, but there were no densely lined paths restricting their vision of the surrounding area here, and that made the humans feel much more at ease... more at ease than ever before. They even felt strangely at home.

They passed groups of elves who bowed to them as they passed, very polite yet clearly concerned as to why they were there. One elf, who looked young, most likely around fifty years old, Sav reckoned, but young in terms of elfkind, snarled as they passed, before turning on his heels and striding away from them as Lord Nelem hissed something to him in elvish.

'I'm sorry,' Errolas said, as Nelem glared off in the boy's direction. 'Some elves, very few in fact, but mainly those who lost relatives or close friends in the few skirmishes our people have had in the past, still maintain that we made a mistake when we signed the treaty with Altoln and its neighbours.'

'That was centuries ago,' Sav protested.

'That may be,' Nelem said, 'but the aftermath is still remembered by some and they still tell the stories, although it is frowned upon to tell them in any other way than in a historical, factual context.'

'What a shame.' Fal sighed and Errolas nodded his agreement.

Starks waved his hand around his head then, hissing 'psst' as he did so.

'Careful, Starks,' Errolas said, a smile visible in his eyes, 'that's no fly you swat at.'

Fal, Sav and Correia looked to Starks then, their eyes lighting up as they realised what Starks was trying to wave away.

'Fairies,' Sav said.

Errolas laughed. 'No, these are sylph; smaller than fairies and unable to use illusional magic like fairies, but very similar and very skilled in the art of healing wounds... should they choose to. They are cousins of fairies if you like. Sylphs are sometimes mistaken for flies or pollen even, when flying in large groups on hot summer days. Some even say they are invisible, as they can hear their whispers, but often cannot see them.'

The group listened.

There was indeed a sound akin to ever so faint whispering as more sylphs arrived, all of them floating around Starks' bandaged head, much to his annoyance. One stopped right in front of his good eye then and he could finally see that, although with tiny wings much like a bees, there was a very thin humanoid body, and a face only just visible. It winked at him, or so he thought, and said something in its whispering language before floating again noiselessly around his head.

'Starks, take off your bandage.' Nelem pointed to the dressing around the crossbowman's burnt face. The elf lord was clearly quite surprised as he gave the instruction, his eyes not leaving the multiple sylphs floating about Starks' head.

Starks looked to Fal, unsure, but Fal re-assured him with a nod, and the young crossbowman began to unwind the cloth, wincing with pain as he did so.

No sooner had the bandage been removed, the sylphs descended on Starks' damaged, red face, and he began to hop gently from foot to foot, wincing as if expecting something terrible to happen.

'Relax,' Errolas said, laughing along with Fal and the others when it was clear Starks could do nothing of the sort.

'It hurts,' Starks complained, 'like midges biting me all over. I don't like it.'

'Trust us Starks,' Errolas said again, 'you're an extremely lucky soul for them to want to help you like this.'

'Help me—

'Ouch!

'Help me?' he said through clenched teeth.

Nelem nodded. 'Yes, they're healing your face as we speak, now stop hopping around like a child.'

Starks stopped then, the realisation calming him as he looked to Fal and Sav, a grin – broken by the odd wince – spreading across his sylph covered face.

'Say Sav, maybe they can do something for your face too?' Fal mocked, to everyone's amusement, including the tall scout's, who'd began to point out there was nothing wrong with his face before catching on to the jest.

'Wouldn't have anything to do would they Fal? I'm near perfect as I am,' Sav said, grinning all the while.

Correia blurted out a short, sharp laugh, much to Sav's annoyance.

'It feels better,' Starks claimed, and the two elves pointed out that it looked fully healed as the small cloud of sylph finally moved away from his face, whispering to themselves all the while.

'They're so cute,' Correia said, and Sav looked at her amused and looking like he would say something, before she set her stern face again and turned away from him. 'No time to lose, come on,' she ordered, and both Fal and Sav laughed.

'Thank you,' Starks called out, as they left the cloud of sylph behind, their whispering increasing briefly in what Starks took to be a farewell.

The group passed more elves as they continued, some weaving, some turning wood on pedalled lathes, and a group playing strange looking instruments that made Correia and her companions want to sit and listen before Errolas and Nelem pulled them along.

A group of about two dozen elven archers released arrow after arrow into targets set over four hundred feet away down another long, narrow glade off to one side. Sav ached to take a closer look, but reluctantly followed the others, knowing they didn't have the time. The elven re-curve bows – much longer than Sav and Errolas' and more akin in length to an Altoln war bow – released long, perfectly straight shafts not just in a straight line, but in great arcing flight paths towards their targets, hitting buttresses of straw set at angles facing away from the archers loosing the arrows, but hitting dead centre almost every time.

After a long while of awe-inspiring activities alongside the path the group travelled, houses became visible both on the ground and high up in the great and ancient trees. The branches seemed to hold the wooden, luxurious looking homesteads with no nails or mortar-like bonding visible.

'The wood used to build our homes is given to us by the forest,' Nelem explained as he walked. 'The trees themselves understand we protect them and that we live by Broadleaf Forest's laws, and so here, in the Middle Wood, our home, they sacrifice limbs they know will grow back, whether it be for building materials, weapons or anything else we need. We do not take what we are not offered and the forest knows we make sacrifices to defend our home and so they do too. It is a symbiotic lifestyle that has worked well for millennia and I see no end to it as long as the balance outside Broadleaf Forest remains relatively the same.'

Elves young and old looked down from balconies and walked on rope bridges from building to building, tree to tree. Others climbed rope ladders or walked up spiralling ramps that climbed up the thick trunks of trees, held to the wood by giant, flowering climbing plants and vines whose lilacs, whites and blues twisted up the trees and around the elven homes, spreading their colours far and wide.

As the large trees on either side of the group thinned, they looked forward and up to the grandest, oldest and largest oak any of them had ever seen, or imagined even being possible.

'The Council Hall and Grand Palace,' Nelem announced, as he stepped to one side for them all to see and admire.

And admire they did, for the enormous tree held dozens of walkways, balconies, pulleys and what could only be described as natural, fungi-like fortifications, which grew out from the giant trunk of the tree here and there like elegant white drum-towers, all of which were manned by elven archers and spear men alike.

'We're going to that?' Fal asked, truly amazed.

Errolas smiled. 'Yes Fal, to it and up it, to the very top.'

Chapter 43: The Elven Council

The sun rose high in the sky as the warm spring breeze carried a mixed scent of freshly blooming flowers to the six humans who stood in the great council hall. The giant and ancient oak that stood in the centre of Middle Wood reached higher than the highest spire of Wesson's palace or cathedral. It was said to be the *first* tree, the mother to Broadleaf Forest and all other trees. Within its trunk – a girth that would take an hour to travel around on foot – lay the great council hall of both the elves and Broadleaf Forest itself. There were many chambers of varying sizes dotted around the natural passageways up through the trunk of the ancient oak, like a rabbit warren stretching high into the sky rather than down into the ground. In the very centre and close to the top of the sprawling branches sat the greatest of the chambers, the council hall.

The grand hall could hold a thousand elves, with intertwined branches forming banks of seating around a raised dais where the trunk of the ancient tree reached its uppermost point. The ceiling was awash with green as the tree's foliage created a gently moving, rustling canopy that allowed the sun's rays to pass through in parts to the hall below.

Upon the raised dais sat six regal looking elves in flowing robes that shimmered in the cascading sunlight, the colours of which none of the humans could quite describe. There were recognisable colours, those of the rainbow, and then other metallic greens, blues, gold and silver, and pearlescent colours that blended and swirled until no one true colour could be discerned. They were simply stunning, and it took Lord Nelem's introduction of the six humans to snap them out of their enthralled trances.

'My lords and ladies,' Nelem announced in a humble, yet commanding tone. The six council members shifted their gazes from the humans, to the speaking elf. 'I am proud to announce the arrival of King Barrison of Altoln's Spymaster, Lady Burr.' Correia curtseyed politely and the elf council smiled in return and nodded their acknowledgement.

'Lord Severun,' Nelem continued, 'formerly Grand Master of the Wizards and Sorcery Guild in Wesson.' Severun bowed deeply, but didn't miss the strained smiles that greeted him from more than one of the council members.

'Sergeant Eppe Scoppus of Tyndurris, personal protector and guard of the aforementioned Lord Severun.'

How in all the realms do they know my name?

Fal bowed, his face flushed as he noticed every other human except Correia glance his way in surprise. Fal had never told anyone his Orismaran name and had been known, even by his parents once they arrived in Wesson, as *Falchion* or *Fal*. Sav looked upset despite being announced to the council by Lord Nelem. He was clearly affronted that he didn't know his best friend's true name, and Fal didn't look forward to the inquisition he would certainly receive once they were alone.

'May I also announce,' Nelem continued, 'Sergeant Gleave Picton of King Barrison's own Pathfinders. And last, but by no means least, Godsiff Starks, crossbowman of Tyndurris.' Both men bowed low, although Gleave struggled slightly with the wooden crutch he'd been given on arrival to the Middle Wood no more than an hour before.

Errolas stood at Severun's side, his hand hovering as if ready to catch the wizard should he sway. The elves outside the Woodmoat had treated Severun and Gleave as best they could, and when an escort had arrived some hours later, they'd been brought on horse drawn stretchers to the Middle Wood, where they'd received further treatment from skilled elven clerics. Severun had suffered extensive magical exhaustion and had been given a potion to take slowly over the next few hours to revive him and his magical reserves. He'd been advised to rest, but had insisted, along with Correia, that their meeting with the elf council could wait no longer.

Gleave's leg had been splinted and a light healing spell cast over it to speed his recovery. He too had insisted on being present at the council meeting. Both men had been lifted to the highest level of the tree via a system of pulleys, whilst the rest of the group, led by Errolas, Nelem and a troop of eight impressive council guards, had climbed up through the centre, a feat which took them quite some time indeed, especially with all the questions it brought from Fal, Sav and Starks along the way.

'Your people don't do things by half do they?' Starks had said, much to the amusement of the elves escorting the group.

One of the council members, a tall – even for an elf – male with long, bright red hair rose from his ornately carved chair, the markings of which were similar to those covering the bridge to the Middle Wood. The male elf held his arms out wide and smiled.

'Welcome friends. Welcome to our home.' He lowered his arms and sat back down, looking from side to side as the other council members nodded their agreement. 'Who will be speaking to us this fine morning, will it be you Lady Burr, or Lord Severun?'

Correia looked to Severun and then stepped forward, seemingly very calm under the probing eyes of the elf council. 'I will, my lord,' she answered humbly.

'Very well, Lady Burr, continue if you please.' The elf lord's voice was as if from a dream, and mixed with the rays of sunshine and the gentle breeze that kissed the faces of those present, the humans could easily have mistaken the whole experience for just that. Fal was impressed further still that the council were speaking Altolnan and not elvish, especially since it was the humans who were guests in the elves' own council chambers. A courtesy he was sure other nations or races would not receive in his own King's court, despite King Barrison's good nature.

'My lords and ladies,' Correia began, ensuring she made eye contact with them all. 'First of all, I want to offer our sincere gratitude for your aid in our quest. Whether you know it or not, your ranger, Errolas, as well as your

Meadow Guard, especially Lord Nelem here, have aided us greatly in reaching you.' Correia continued to explain the arduous journey the group had taken to reach the council and how important it was they delivered their message swiftly and in full.

Correia went on to tell the council about the plague and the terrible grip it held on Wesson. She also explained that King Barrison had ordered the city quarantined as soon as was possible, but how he and his advisors believed it wouldn't stop the plague for much longer. She told them the King feared the plague could spread outside the city and further a field, perhaps even towards Broadleaf Forest itself.

Before Correia could mention Severun, the eldest female elf spoke, her voice sounding tired, but no less sweet and soft than any of the elves the humans had encountered thus far, save perhaps for the child Correia had spoken to by the bridge.

'Lady Burr,' the old elf interrupted, 'my name is Lady Frewin and it is a pleasure to meet you at last. We have heard much of your travels in years past, and I have said many times to Lord Anthral here,' she gestured to another elderly elf who sat next to her, 'what a pleasure it would be to finally meet you in person.'

'Thank you, Lady Frewin. It is a genuine pleasure to finally visit your realm.' Correia gave the most sincere smile any of the humans had ever seen her give.

'My concern, Lady Burr, is the origin of this plague your city is suffering. We lost contact with Errolas whilst he was investigating arcane magics within Wesson and since then—'

The tall, red haired elf who'd greeted the group spoke then, his eyes fixed on Severun.

'Since then, your plague has appeared, and I say your plague, because it is in our mind that the plague was created by you, Lord Severun. Am I right?'

Everyone in the room turned to the wizard then, whose head lifted slightly as he took a step forward. The eight council guards, their ornate bronzed armour similar to those who stood guard by the bridge into the Middle Wood, took several swift, almost silent steps forward before being waved back by Lady Frewin.

'You are correct in your assumption, Lord..?' Severun's voice shook ever so slightly, and so Errolas took a step forward to steady the wizard, who Fal now thought looked older, much older than before.

'Lord Errwin-Roe,' the red haired elf replied. 'And it is no assumption.'

Severun conceded the point with a single nod. 'Lord Errwin-Roe, I did, it seems, create, or at least release, the plague that now sweeps and destroys my home—'

'Please,' Correia interrupted, but Severun held up his hand and the Spymaster held her tongue.

'I do not wish to be defended, Correia. I have held court with my own peers and have received my punishment; death as far as the masses are concerned and banishment from my former life, from Wesson and Altoln itself once the plague has been dealt with. That is my punishment.'

Both Fal and Sav gasped, and looked at each other before realising how loud they'd been. They lowered their heads whilst Severun continued.

'It is not me that we are here for, although I would accept any further punishment readily, knowing as I do, that I have done a great wrong to my own people. It is those people, alas, who need your help now, my lords and ladies. I have released something our mages cannot cure, at least not in the grand scale that is needed, if at all. King Barrison calls on you for aid, to honour the treaty and to help prevent, if nothing else, this plague from spreading further still.'

'Lord Severun,' Anthral said. 'We are not here to judge you. As you so rightly say, your own King has done that as he sees fit, and it is his place, not ours. What you and your people have come to ask us for is aid, whether it be medical, magical or otherwise, aid is what you need. It is not for any one of us, however, to decide on that matter alone. You must understand we need to discuss this in private. We have many things to discuss, and that succubus head our Lord Nelem is carrying there is one such thing. So please, if you all will allow it, let us have our time to discuss matters. You may wait in comfort and we shall call upon you when we are decided.'

'Lord Nelem,' Errwin-Roe said.

'Yes, my lord?'

'We wish you to stay here. Errolas escort our guests to a waiting chamber and have food and drink brought for them. We will try to be as swift as the situation will allow.'

'Yes, my lord,' both Nelem and Errolas replied at the same time.

Errolas escorted the humans across to a side door, the hinges of which were living branches that opened the great leaf-covered door as they approached. Inside were jutting pieces of wood covered in lavishly embroidered cushions, all of which created comfortable seating areas and tables. As soon as they'd all taken their seats, another door opened and several elves swept through. They carried bronze platters of exotic looking fruits and silver chalices of crystal clear water.

Correia snapped at Gleave when he asked if they had ale, and the group managed a laugh between them, although the atmosphere was tense. Gleave was clearly struggling with Mearson's death and everyone thought it wise to give the man some space, which after the brief laugh about the ale, meant no one said a word for quite some time. Eventually, Sav broke the silence by asking what Fal's name meant, and why he'd never told him before. Fal's face reddened again, but before he could answer, the main door opened once more and Lord Nelem strode in, inviting them back into the council hall.

The group looked to one another and rose in silence, their hearts pounding in anticipation at what the council had decided. They followed Nelem and Errolas out and back across to the centre of the hall to take place in front of the council members.

They soon noticed one of the council members, a pale skinned black haired male who'd been sat on the far right of the dais, had disappeared. The remaining members looked tense.

Lord Errwin-Roe stood again and so did the other four council members, their swirling robes shimmering in the rays of sun filtering down through the leaves above. Their movements were accompanied by the chirruping of a goldfinch flock. The small, red-faced birds flitted about the hall regardless of the seriousness of the scene below them.

'The council has discussed these matters and has come to a decision,' Errwin-Roe announced, a frown upon his angular features. 'A decision I'm afraid not all of our members were pleased to hear.' The atmosphere was almost palpable as no one in the room dared look to the empty chair on the far right.

Looking to each human in turn, Errwin-Roe continued. 'Lord Salkeld has, unfortunately, left the hall due to our decision. He is unhappy due to the cause of the plague in Wesson, as well as other things that do not concern you as a group.'

The elf lord's eyes seemed to linger on Correia longer than she would have liked, and a cold, unpleasant shudder ran through her.

'As for King Barrison's request,' the red haired elf lord continued, 'we grant that request in the form of both medical and magical aid, to be sent to Wesson as soon as some much needed information is passed on to us from Lord Severun regarding the arcane magics that were used.' Severun nodded several times and everyone in the group breathed a sigh of relief, although they still feared what else was to come.

'Lord Severun,' Errwin-Roe said, 'if you could follow Lord Nelem, he will escort you to our clerics, who have been asked to gather for your arrival.'

'But of course,' Severun agreed, before being led by Nelem, who held the weakened wizard's arm gently, across the hall and through the main doors.

'Lady Burr.'

'Yes, Lord Errwin-Roe.'

'It has been brought to my attention that Altoln as a nation has been using black powder weapons for at least test purposes, and who knows what else? We wish to hear your comments on this please. I do not need to remind you of our military treaties regarding such substances do I?'

Correia stood straight and tall before answering, although Fal felt he couldn't look upon the elf council's accusing eyes. 'I'm afraid, my lords and ladies, that this isn't a subject I am at liberty to discuss without my King's knowledge. May I most respectfully suggest that your advisors seek an audience with him on their arrival to Wesson?'

Both Fal and Sav glanced at each other quickly, and Fal noticed Starks swallowing, rather obviously. He was clearly nervous with the whole situation, as were they all.

You've done grand, lad, nothing for you to worry about. I just wish I could tell you that right now, although I'm not sure whether we have anything to worry about or not myself at this point, if I'm honest.

Lord Errwin-Roe looked annoyed, but didn't answer. To Correia's surprise, the answer came from the back of the room.

'Seek an audience with him? Are you serious, human?'

Everyone in the room turned to see the council member who'd left during the decision making process. He stood by the main door, two armoured warriors by his side, their skin pale and their hair as black as their armour. The council member's hair matched his warriors', although his was tied high in a ponytail. His colourful robes had been replaced with a black cloak and sleek, form fitting dark green armour that accentuated his muscular torso. A black leather wrapped sword hilt protruded from behind his right shoulder; a two handed grip to a large great-sword strapped diagonally to his back.

Anthral visibly shook with rage. 'Lord Salkeld, you chose to leave this discussion before it had ended, do not presume you can walk back in and resume your side of the argument after our decision has been made.' Anthral's ancient form rose slightly in his chair as the dark featured elf at the back of the hall laughed.

'Quiet, you old fool. I'm not here for lectures on history so I need not listen to your ramblings.'

'Enough!' The beautiful council member to Errwin-Roe's right shouted in place of Anthral, who looked too stunned by Lord Salkeld's outburst to make comment himself. She stood as she shouted, her pale face flushing red with anger as she glared past the humans stood before her, to the armour clad councillor by the door. Her blue-black hair, hanging almost to the back of her knees, spread out lightly, dancing with static at the tips as she took a step forward. The wood at her feet visibly darkened as she did so. Her fingers flexed, almost contorted as her beautiful features hardened into something fierce.

Briefly turning to look at the elf councillor behind him, Fal saw the confident air about Lord Salkeld falter under the she-elf's fiery gaze, but the elf lord managed to go on despite his obvious fear of her.

'You cannot expect to run to their aid after they play with dark powers they know nothing of, and use black powder they cannot understand? It is folly is all I say. Now calm yourself, sister, I apologise for my outburst, to you and to Lord Anthral, but I foresee great sorrow with the continuation of their kingdom. It has moved against us before. Who, or what, will stop it doing so again?'

'You act like a child, brother,' the elegant elf maiden replied, her face softening slightly and the wood at her feet lightening in colour once again. 'You always see the pain and despair in things, never the joy or hope. These aren't games we play, there are hundreds, possibly thousands of humans… living beings, dying in Wesson, and they need our aid, Arrlo. Would you have us abandon them for the errors of a minority centuries ago, or the errors of one man who is now meeting with our clerics to end this disease before it spreads beyond their city walls?'

Arrlo Salkeld's shoulders dropped slightly, his stance relaxing as his eyes searched the floor at his feet for answers.

'I'm not happy with the black powder, it needs dealing with,' he said, finally looking back to his sister, yet avoiding eye contact with any other council member.

'It will be,' Errwin-Roe assured Arrlo, 'but diplomatically and with King Barrison himself, not our guests here. They deliver a message and ask for aid and we shall honour our treaty, even if their King does not.'

Fal felt cold at those words and the hairs on the back of his neck stood on end. Turning once again, he noticed Lord Salkeld's sly grin. The dark armoured elf bowed low then, his long pony tail falling forward across his left shoulder, before he turned and left the hall, his two warriors close on his heels.

'I must apologise for my brother's behaviour, it is most embarrassing, but he is young. In fact, he is the youngest ever to be placed on the council. Sometimes I wonder why he ever… well, let us not press the matter, we have much to organise.

'Lady Burr. If you wouldn't mind, we would like to discuss the return journey with you, and what supplies and aid we can offer.'

'Very well, my lady.'

'Please, you must call me Serra, I insist.'

Correia smiled sincerely as she was guided from the hall by Serra Salkeld.

'Sergeants, scout and crossbowman,' Errwin-Roe said, his smile returning sincerely. 'Lord Nelem tells me of your bravery outside the Woodmoat, as well as the tales Errolas has told him of the fight to defend Beresford from a vile goblin horde. You all look tired and your equipment in need of repair. Let our artisans take care of your equipment while you rest and await your return to Wesson. Follow me and I will have it all taken care of for you.'

'Thank you, Lord Errwin-Roe,' Fal said, beaming as he and the others bowed low to the tall, red haired elf lord.

'Oh, enough of that. You are guests and the formalities are over, the council has made its decision and you cannot leave for Wesson until all has been arranged, therefore, we may as well enjoy ourselves in the meantime. What say you?'

Fal, Sav and Starks grinned and looked at one another before voicing their agreement. Gleave looked tired and made no comment or expression other than a swift nod towards the elf lord. They followed Errwin-Roe across the hall as the two older council members fell into discussion once more. Fal overheard Lord Salkeld's name mentioned, but nothing else.

The group passed through another leaf covered door into a room similar to the one they'd visited before, but much larger and much more lavishly decorated, although they hadn't thought that possible. Elves appeared almost immediately and took their weapons and armour, assuring them they were in good hands. More food was brought forth, the smell coming from the platters reminding everyone present of fond memories, some of which they'd forgotten until that moment.

How is it a smell can trigger such recollection of memories I forgot I even had? Fal scooped up and took in the scent of an unusual fruit, its sweet aroma reminding him of his father and the games they used to play when he was very young, growing up on the Orismaran coast.

Wine followed the food, much to the delight of all, and Fal was pleased to see Gleave lighten up slightly after consuming some of the crimson liquid. Despite the laughter, merriment and the sun still being high in the sky, Starks fell asleep after one glass of the elven wine, much to the mirth of all – Sav especially.

Once the food had been eaten and the few remaining scraps taken away, Errwin-Roe encouraged the three of them to tell him about the plague, and when that topic was exhausted, they told him about the fight with the monster in the cave and their amazement and joy at seeing his dream worthy home. After that, the three men heard stories centuries old, both from Errwin-Roe's own experience and from what Lady Frewin and Lord Anthral had told him. For the two elderly elves had witnessed the battles against Crackador and his Naga, being they were the oldest elves still alive in Broadleaf Forest.

As the stories continued throughout the afternoon, Sav and Gleave – through near exhaustion and injury – fell asleep where they sat. Fal took the opportunity to talk of Orismar and the meaning of his name, to which Errwin-Roe smiled, patted Fal on the shoulder and motioned for him to wake the others.

'It is time for us to entertain you on the forest floor,' the elf lord said, smiling and moving to the door. 'It is rare indeed we welcome visitors, and there will be plenty of others who wish to hear your tales and tell you their own.'

If Wesson wasn't in such grave danger, I'm not sure I could force myself to leave this place. Fal smiled and nodded, before waking each of his friends.

Chapter 44: Threats and Promises

'I've told you this is a mistake,' Arrlo Salkeld argued, as he paced from one end of the treetop balcony to the other.

His two, black-armoured guards respectfully averted their eyes from their lord's beautiful sister, who tried to calm her angry brother.

'And I've told you, brother, it is the council's final decision to help the humans.'

'Am I not a member of the council, Serra? Is it not my decision also?' he replied through clenched teeth.

A gust of wind blew Serra's blue-black hair across her face and she sighed as she brushed it away with her delicate fingers. 'You gave up your say on this matter when you stormed from the hall like a child.'

Arrlo hammered his armoured fist down onto the wooden rail of the balcony, before hanging his head low. His sister winced at the aggressive action and silently apologised to the great tree, whose branches had grown in such a way as to create the living balcony they stood on.

The elf lord let out a slow, controlled breath. 'I fear for our realm, our people... Brisance in general at the hands of these humans. Is that such a bad thing?' He looked back towards his sister, who returned his look with soft eyes and a gentle smile.

Arrlo continued, holding his hands out to the side imploringly. 'They are a young, rash race that thinks nothing of the living world that exists all around them, sister. They kill and burn and destroy with such blatant disregard for anything that is not of value to them. I see them as nothing more than a cross between dwarves and goblins.'

Serra gasped at the statement and rushed over to her brother, placing her pale hands on his ornate pouldrons.

'Surely you cannot believe such a thing of them, Arrlo? Perhaps they bear similarities to the dwarves regarding their lust for power and wealth, but the goblins?' She shook her head. 'No, I will not believe you truly think that.'

Arrlo sighed again and looked deep into his sister's eyes, smiling briefly before turning to rest on the rail he had struck. 'I don't know what I believe of them. They scare me, I know that much.'

Pulling her head back slightly in surprise, Serra said, 'I never could have dreamed you would fear anything or anyone?'

'Nor could I. I do not fear the dwarves; they do not threaten us and even if they did they are predictable, as are goblins, trolls... even demons like the succubae Lord Nelem encountered... in his own forest! I dread what might be lurking in *our* forest at such a time. But these humans, they are unpredictable, unreadable. I do see good in some of them, Serra, I truly do, but it is the rest I fear. They grow and change, adapt and seek out more land, more ways in which to grow and expand... much like this plague of theirs.'

'Oh, Arrlo... don't say such things. That's worse than your comparing them to goblins.' *My dear brother, how you've changed... you were once full of such innocence and wonder.*

Arrlo ran both of his hands through his long, black hair which was now hanging loose, his eyes tight shut as he clenched his jaw repeatedly before replying. 'Why does it seem I am the only one that can foresee the dark places their expansion and ambitions, greed and warmongering could lead us? Even these so called goodly humans in our midst have meddled in the arcane.'

Serra frowned at her brother's frustration and again placed her hands on his pouldrons.

'Even our greatest seers cannot foresee the future with any great accuracy, Arrlo, so I don't see why you choose to try to do so. We have no idea what the future holds, for any of us, so I see no reason to worry about it. We have a chance, here and now, to help the humans rid their city of a plague that, if what our mages believe is true, has been thrust upon them on purpose, and not by the wizard Severun. If you want to worry about any possible future, worry about that, for whoever would wish such a horror upon a people can only have the darkest of hearts, and such a being is a natural enemy of ours. That alone should be reason enough for us to help the humans in their struggle, even if that struggle goes beyond this plague.' She moved her left hand to her brother's chin and pulled it gently round to face her. 'This action on our part, right now, could secure our alliance with them far beyond its current state, thus warding off any such future you fear from our neighbours.'

Arrlo nodded his head half-heartedly and his sister moved her hand back to his shoulder.

'Let us hope this alliance can be strengthened then,' Arrlo said finally, 'on their part, because in my mind, they have done nothing but break it up to now.' Arrlo Salkeld looked back out over the forest again before continuing.

'Whatever evil they are seemingly facing with regards to this plague, it has no place in the future I have in my head. That future is one in which the humans themselves, their new found dwarven black powder in full use, will become that very black-hearted evil you mention.' He turned to Serra then, his unblinking stare confirming the conviction of his following words.

'And I swear to you now, sister, should the humans so much as glance our way with those weapons in hand, then I shall bring at the very least the full might of the Evergreen Glades upon them, ideally of Middle Wood too. And I would treat them no differently than any of the evil creatures I have slain in my life.'

'Arrlo...' Serra closed her beautiful eyes and hung her head low. She pulled her brother in close as the two of them fell quiet, listening to the peaceful sound of the forest.

The trouble is, brother, I have had the very same fears. I just cannot allow myself to believe they could come to pass. 'King Barrison is a good man, I am sure of that,' she said soothingly.

'Yes, that may be so, but is his heir, the Black Prince? Or *his* heir, or the next?' Arrlo Salkeld let the question hang in silence, unsure whether to be pleased or not with his reasoning when his sister failed to answer back.

***

Hours had passed since Sears, Gitsham and Buddle had left Longoss and Coppin. Most of that time had been spent hiding here and there, knowing that to outrun the gangers pursuing them was impossible. In fact, if it hadn't been for Buddle's nose, sniffing out ambushes ahead and finding safe – albeit for short periods – hiding positions within Dockside, then they would already have been caught and killed, Sears was sure of that. He knew he didn't have the strength or energy left to fight such numbers, nor did he have Longoss or Coppin with him.

I've killed enough as it is, Sears thought heavily, whilst the three of them huddled behind a small outhouse overflowing with excrement. The lay house it served rose up beside them, its window shutters closed and its door marked with a black cross. *I see their faces now, some of them not far into their teens and I struck 'em down...*

Buddle growled and Sears turned to look at the bloodhound, its drooping ears lifting slightly.

Ye've saved us time and time again now, dog. I owe ye me life tenfold.

Gitsham's head tilted and then he leaned over and whispered into Sears' ear. The big man's eyes widened.

'How many?' Sears whispered the rhetorical question whilst looking from the hound to Gitsham and back. 'He can know that, specifically?'

Gitsham shrugged and climbed to his feet. Sears followed.

'We're close to the edge of Dockside though, that's what ye said when we stopped here, right?'

Gitsham nodded, before starting to bite the filthy nails on his left hand.

Screwing up his face and prodding his broken left wrist, the sling long since lost, Sears dared a look around the side of the outhouse. He pulled his head back quickly as he saw several youths milling about on a corner, weapons in hands.

'They're really close,' Sears whispered, his mind drifting for a moment to the vial in his pouch. Alas, he knew the contents of the vial would knit the broken bones of his wrist swiftly whether set right or wrong, and he had no idea how it was at the moment. Coppin had helped him with it as much as she could, but the following cat and mouse game they'd been playing with the gangers had taken its toll, and the joint felt worse than ever. Whilst gently running his fingers over the swelling, he looked back to Gitsham, awaiting the next plan of action.

Nothing...

Gitsham dropped slightly as Sears toed the back of the man's knee, which resulted in him turning to face Sears, who raised his eyebrows in anticipation.

'We blow the horn now and then run to the right.'

'Ye're bloody kidding me here, Gitsham?' Sears stood straight and looked

427

up to the sky, shaking his head before looking back at the man. 'Again and again ye say the horn will do no good, and now, with 'em as close as they've ever been, ye want me to blow it?'

Gitsham shrugged. 'Aye.'

'And then… run, just run?'

'Aye.'

'By the ragged baps of the witch god of I don't know what or where nor do I give a shit anymore—'

The horn rang out long and loud and then again twice more as Sears blew hard, his eyes tight shut.

What had been fairly deserted streets, what with the black crossed doors and the gangers on the prowl keeping everyone else indoors, suddenly grew noisy with the calls of gangers.

Sears opened his eyes and saw both man and dog had gone.

'Shit!' He ran out from behind the outhouse and turned right, glancing only quickly to the left, enough to see the swiftly approaching – and now increased – mob of youths and men running his way.

More ganger calls and taunts followed Sears as he ran after Gitsham and Buddle, who weren't far ahead of him. His lungs burnt as he sucked in as much air as he could. Several aches and pains resurfaced and his wrist throbbed painfully with every pounding step he took.

The noise grew louder as the trio passed an unusually tall house for Dockside. Sears looked through the windows incredulously as he realised the residents were having what looked like a party… no, a blatant orgy.

'They think… it'll keep away… the plague,' Gitsham shouted from in front, his breathing as ragged as Sears' own, 'by pleasing… the Loving God.'

Sears shook his head as he ran. *Any excuse. I didn't even know there was a Loving God?* Sears suddenly realised what the large house meant, however, and the realisation put a smile onto his red bearded face. *Houses that big only lie on the edge of Dockside—*

A crossbow bolt skidded across the cobbles by his feet.

'Not far now Gitsham, keep running,' Sears shouted. *As long as I don't take one of those bastards in the back of the head.*

We need to pass what we know to Stowold, Sears thought suddenly, as stones landed here and there about him, *and if that means Gitsham is the only one to make it, I'll damned well make sure that's the case—*

The big man grunted as a stone thudded off his left shoulder. Although it wasn't large, it hit hard enough to cause Sears to stumble slightly as he instinctively twisted away from the impact. Cursing, he righted himself quickly and risked a glance behind.

'Shit! Gitsham, they're close!' Sears finally drew his short-sword with his good hand.

'Blow… horn… again,' Gitsham managed.

Buddle barked from up front.

Gods' sake! Sears re-sheathed his sword – which wasn't easy whilst running

428

– and pulled free the horn, biting the end to stop it clattering across his teeth. He took in as big a breath as he could manage, the cold air burning his lungs. *I hope Longoss and Coppin fare better.*

The horn sounded pathetically and Sears winced as another stone struck him on the back. The sound of footsteps followed him now, extremely close, and as he took in another burning breath to blow again, Buddle howled long and hard. Sears lowered the horn and looked around Gitsham, who was slowing to a jog in front of him.

What's the fool doing slowing… oh!

Sears hadn't thought he'd ever hear himself laugh again when he'd heard the footsteps close behind him just then, but as he saw a familiar face round a corner up ahead, flanked by half a dozen city guardsmen, he burst out a torrent of uncontrollable laughter; that, along with the line of men now stretching the narrow street, caused the footsteps behind him to falter. Not wanting to risk complacency now, Sears threw all he had into one last sprint towards the line ahead, where Buddle lay flat out and Gitsham stood double, hands on knees and reddened face gasping for air as a white robed cleric held a hand over him, searching for serious injury.

The ganger calls behind Sears increased despite the men now approaching; weapons drawn, heater shields held high and two crossbows being aimed. Those crossbows clicked and launched bolts either side of Sears as he finally slowed and barrelled into the face he'd been locked onto since he lowered the horn.

'Biviano,' he half said half laughed between gasps. His mouth was so dry his saliva felt like a thick paste in his mouth, but none of it mattered now. He'd made it.

Angry shouts erupted as the crossbow bolts found their marks.

'Reload,' Bollingham shouted, whilst moving past Sears to hold a line just behind the big man. 'Here they come!'

'The horn worked?' Sears asked, incredulously, his breathing slowing but a little.

The cleric, Effrin, laughed. 'No, Sears, the dog! Damn well nearly made me sick when he *contacted* me and told me where to head to.'

Eyes wide at the revelation, Sears looked back to Biviano. 'We need to move, matey.' He held his friend out at arms length. *Damn, he looks rough, sick even.*

'Yeah yeah, I look like shit. Yer eyes say it all, ye ginger get. Now face up, soldier, ye're not running no more.'

'What?'

'You angry, big guy?'

A crossbow bolt thudded into Bollingham's shield and the man cursed, before shouting, 'shoot at will for 'morl's sake.' The two crossbowmen pulled their triggers and two more gangers dropped, including the one who'd shot at Bollingham. 'They're closing, form up!'

'Ye need get Gitsham outta here, he has important news for Stowold,'

Sears said, shaking Biviano slightly. 'And get yerself out too, we'll never hold these. There'll be more on the way.'

'There's more here.' Biviano looked past Sears, who turned and looked down the street.

Sears cursed. *So that's why the little bastard gangers hung back at the end.*

Over three score gangers emerged from doorways, alleys and further back down the street as Sears looked on, the closest ones – the original chasers – whooping and hollering as they darted forward here and there, throwing all sorts of missiles at the small shield wall of the patrol stood in front of Sears.

'Like I said, are ye mad, Sears?' Biviano looked to his friend and grinned.

Sears nodded. 'Aye.' He fought back a tear, overwhelmed that after all he'd been through, no matter what happened now, he'd made it back to Biviano.

The wiry guardsman shook his head. 'Not angry enough, ye ain't hit me yet.'

Laughing despite the situation, Sears punched Biviano on the shoulder with his good hand, but the man just laughed.

'What in Samorl's crusty arse was that? Ye fat sack of shi—'

Biviano nearly went over sideways as Sears threw his back into his good fist and smashed it into Biviano's maille covered shoulder.

'Bastard!' Biviano's face screwed up with pain as he attempted to roll his deadened arm. 'That's it, big guy, I need ye really pissed off for this lot.' He pointed his sword past Bollingham. Sears turned just in time to see a throwing axe spin through the air and glance off the farthest shield bearing guardsman to his left. The man ducked under his wooden shield, but not before the blade of the axe cracked off his kettle-helm. Luckily, he survived the impact and re-raised his shield and sword, shaking his head angrily.

Sears roared and his eyes flared.

'These bastards murder and rape for fun, Sears, and this is our chance to pay the shites back, what say you?'

Sears roared again.

'What say all of you?' Biviano shouted.

As the shield wall roared, the gangers charged.

Despite the sound of dozens of booted feet, screams of rage and the single howl of a bloodhound, the sound of clattering hooves suddenly filled the street... many hooves.

Sears' burning eyes took in the hate filled faces of the large number of gangers closing rapidly on them. He also noticed the sudden shock in many of their faces as they met the shield wall and a horn rang out, along with a familiar upper district accent.

'Make way, make way, make way!'

Weapons clashed and voices cried out in pain as Sears grabbed Biviano and yanked him roughly to the side of the street. They took cover where Effrin, Gitsham and Buddle were, as the two crossbowmen loosed their final bolts and dove, along with Bollingham and the other shield bearers, out of the way of the heavy cavalry pounding down the street.

The charge was led by a rider in green livery and blued plate, the latter decorated in ornately carved battle scenes. Closing swiftly on the gangers, the heavy trapper of the large destrier under that rider took a crossbow bolt through the serpent's eye of the displayed heraldry. The bolt scored but failed to pierce the warhorse's flank as it charged on, and from behind the maille aventail of the open face bascinet worn by the horse's rider, spewed the most horrendous curse imaginable.

Bagnall Stowold and his personal retainers, three of them knights, smashed into the panicked mob of gangers with literally bone crunching force.

Men fell beneath hooves whilst others fell from the blow of the Earl's war-hammer. Others were skewered on lances carried by the outer edge riders whilst more where hacked down by sword and axe. Over two dozen heavy horse continued on down the street, hacking and slashing as they went, Stowold's curses mixed with the screams and shouts of dying men and boys alike.

A knight wielding an axe was pulled from his horse as he slowed and drew close to an alley, a flurry of blows and a bollock dagger through his great-helm's visor finishing him. His bay destrier turned and lashed out at the attackers, its hooves crushing more than one skull before it bolted, chasing after the continuing charge.

Most of the gangers fled, running down tight alleys or deftly climbing up onto rooftops to escape across the broken tiles and thatch of the buildings about them.

One, however, a large man carrying a pole-axe, turned on a mounted man-at-arms to Stowold's right, and swung the weapon in the manner it was designed for, to unhorse riders.

The intended target managed to duck away from the weapon's hooked blade in time, although it sliced a bloody line through his upper arm, which was protected by his padded gambeson, but not armoured. Cursing, the Earl's man swiftly drove his horse on to chase down easier prey.

'Try me, whore son!' Stowold shouted, as his destrier reared, its front hooves lashing out at the ganger. The heavily built man took a blow to the shoulder, but surprisingly shrugged it off, whilst bearing a row of sharpened teeth and hissing at the constable and horse.

Constrictor gang calls sounded here and there as the large man swung the pole-axe in a figure eight motion.

'Have I made the acquaintance of a gang master?' Stowold's voice sounded slightly muffled behind his maille aventail.

The gang master spat at Stowold and then charged.

'Seems so.' Stowold turned his destrier with his knees whilst using his heater shield to deflect the first blow from the long weapon. The impact caused the Earl to grunt in pain from the injury received previously in the cathedral assault. The pole-axe blade scratched across the shield's coat-of-arms as if decapitating the serpent it depicted, and the gang master grinned as he withdrew, readying himself to lunge again.

Before he could recover, the large warhorse jumped – despite the armoured man on its back – and kicked out with all four legs, knocking back a short, wiry ganger who was running in from the alley opposite, crushing his ribcage with the impact. The other legs connected with nothing, but kept the gang master at bay long enough for the experienced constable to shift his position in the saddle, ready for the following – rushed – aggressive lunge by the gang master.

More constrictors called from the rooftops as gangers started to rally to watch their leader fight. Renewed fighting also tied up Stowold's retainers further down the road, as gangers rushed them from all sides. The Earl's liveried men swung and hacked and turned their horses in unison to keep the attackers at bay.

As the long weapon came in again, Stowold leaned down and towards it, dropping his war-hammer to hang by the leather thong attaching it to his wrist. He deflected the main brunt of the attack on his shield, allowing the remainder of its force to slide up and across his right pouldron, the bladed hook slinking across the maille of his coif.

If it weren't for the maille protecting his neck, Stowold knew the hooked blade would have sliced him a fatal blow, but he knew how armour worked and he knew what it could take. He also knew that whilst maille would allow a slicing blade to run across its metal links harmlessly, the hook of the pole-axe, once pulled, would pierce through those links and into his neck, pulling him down and out of his saddle.

The risk Stowold had taken was a calculated one though, and as the gang master's lunge reached its farthest extension, Stowold reached across with his now free hand and took hold of the wooden shaft below the pole-axe's blade. Holding the wood firmly, the constable gritted his teeth and pulled hard on his reigns with his painful shield arm. Stowold's well trained destrier reared back and up at that, the sudden movement and force of it yanking the pole-axe from its wielder's hands.

The gang master's face twisted into a snarl as the experienced constable pushed the pole-axe further back out and around, away from his neck, ensuring its hook didn't snag on his maille coif. Continuing the smooth manoeuvre, Stowold brought his attacker's weapon swiftly across in front of him and threw it to the floor on his left, all before his horse's front hooves returned to the muddy cobbles.

Surging forward, seax knife now in hand, the gang master launched himself at the mounted noble, just in time to receive a skull crushing blow from Stowold's war-hammer, which came down in an overhead arc from left to right and ended in an explosion of blood, bone and brain.

The large gang master dropped heavily to the floor, and the faces on the rooftops disappeared as swiftly as they'd re-appeared, whilst Bagnall Stowold, fresh curses on his lips, scanned the scene for his next target.

'Lord Stowold will drive them off,' Effrin said. 'We need to get you out of

Dockside.' The cleric was fussing over Sears' wrist, but the big man – mouth still open from the unexpected cavalry charge – pulled his arm away and turned on the cleric.

'Not before ye see to him.' Sears pointed at Biviano, who rocked back, surprised.

'Me?'

'Aye, you, ye know ye're sick, so stop ignoring it ye fool, we need to get ye sorted more than me.'

'He's right.' Gitsham walked over to the small group as the shield bearers once again set up a defensive line across the street.

'What do *you* know?' Biviano said, disliking all the attention.

Gitsham shrugged. 'Nowt, but him…' he nodded to the bloodhound at Biviano's feet. Buddle growled when he sniffed Biviano's leg, and Sears couldn't help but smile.

'Oh, ye're mates now eh, you and the hound?'

Sears winked in return.

'Dick,' Biviano said. *But by the gods, big guy, it's good to have ye back.* Biviano had hardly finished the thought when he collapsed.

Sears grimaced at the pain in his wrist as he caught his falling friend. 'We need get him to an infirmary, quickly.'

Effrin was shaking his head as the sound of fighting died away and Lord Stowold approached; armoured legs and war-hammer slick with blood. 'We need to get him to Tyndurris,' the cleric said, his eyes moving nervously to the man looking down on him from beneath the blued steel of an aventail covered bascinet.

Stowold nodded. 'Aye, but take him by horse, with an escort.' He directed the latter to the two men-at-arms by his side, both of whom nodded. One of them reached down and Sears and Effrin helped lift Biviano up and over the man's lap.

'I'm going with him,' Sears said, motioning for the second rider to dismount as the rest of Stowold's men arrived back from down the street, led by his two remaining knights. All of them brandished bloodied weapons and one of them carried the body of the knight who'd been killed. More than a few of the others looked to be injured, although none of them seriously.

Stowold shook his head and pointed his war-hammer at Sears. 'Like pissing stones you are, man. You're going to Lord Yewdale, with the gormless one and his dog. If what Biviano told me is true, you need to report whatever it is you've been doing whilst gallivanting around Dockside, and report it quick.'

Reluctantly, Sears looked from the unconscious form of his friend to the Constable of Wesson. Finally, he nodded. 'Aye milord.'

'Meanwhile, ladies, I'm back off to the cathedral. Can't leave Jay Strawn and my squire running the place, or it'll end up a bloody brothel. Ha, what!'

'Cleric, you and Bollingham take Biviano to your guild. You two,' Stowold pointed his war-hammer to two of his men-at-arms, 'take Sears and Gitsham

433

to the palace and quick about it, the hound can follow.' Buddle let out a long, low wine.

'Suck it up, dog,' Stowold said. 'You're of the guard, not a pet.'

Buddle's head rose slightly and he turned towards the palace before heading off that way. Sears and Gitsham were pulled up behind their two riders. Sears' eyes shifted back to Biviano as soon as he'd settled behind the saddle.

'We'll see he gets the best care,' Bollingham said, and Effrin nodded.

'See that ye do or ye're both answering to me.'

Both men nodded and climbed up behind a rider each.

'Oh and thanks, all of you,' Sears said, looking about all the men and settling on Bagnall Stowold, whose face was still covered by his aventail.

'Soft shit,' the constable said as he spurred his destrier on towards the cathedral, the majority of his retainers following. A lone bay destrier rode amongst them, the reigns of which one of the two knights had taken.

With final looks and nods between the Earl's remaining men, they set off with their passengers, splitting up and heading to their separate destinations only when they needed to.

***

Glass vials, bottles and tubes with a multitude of coloured liquids and gasses bubbled away in the clerics' chamber of Tyndurris. A dozen clerics stood in silence, awaiting the confirmation they all feared, as they and Orix – his head wrapped in a bandage – looked to Ward Strickland.

The magician's deep purple robes stood out in bright contrast next to the surrounding white of the clerics', and he took in all of their weary faces before saying what he'd come to say.

'We have all been through a great deal of late. We have lost friends and loved ones and have seen, for the first time since its creation, a direct attack upon and within this very tower.'

All of the clerics nodded and some fought back tears as they thought of those lost.

'You have all worked,' Ward continued, looking to every one of them as he spoke, 'so very, very hard to combat this plague and discover its origins. It is now clear to us that the suspicions some of you have had, are indeed true. With great regret, but at least a little relief for Master Orix here, it is up to me to announce to all in the guild that this plague was indeed attached, for want of a better word, not to Master Orix's potion, but to Lord Severun's arcane spell. Unbeknown to him I might add.'

Several in the room gasped, whilst others nodded their heads knowingly; after all, it was their own theories and discoveries that had led to that very conclusion.

'How are you sure Severun didn't know of the plague within the spell?' a young male cleric asked, which resulted in fierce looks from several others in

434

the room, including Orix.

'You have my word, Nikoless,' Ward said, 'and that is all you should need from your Grand Master, despite all that has happened.' Everyone in the room nodded their agreement, including the young cleric.

'My apologies, Lord Strickland,' Nikoless offered. Ward acknowledged the apology with a nod and a genuine smile before continuing to address the clerics as a whole.

'I make a promise to you all today, that we as a guild will continue to work to our very limits to cleanse Wesson of this plague. Once that has been achieved, we shall continue in an effort to trace the spell and disease that has struck our city, thus rooting out those behind it.'

The clerics voiced their agreement as one, clearly determined to find those responsible for the tragedy aimed at both their city and kingdom.

'Do we have any leads at all regarding the origins of the magic; of who instigated this attack on Wesson?' Morri asked from the corner of the room. 'Or could it be,' he continued, 'the plague attached to the arcane spell used by Lord Severun was in fact a co-incidence, something added much earlier perhaps, and so not at all aimed towards Wesson specifically?'

Orix smiled at Morri's hopeful thinking.

'I wish I knew,' Ward said honestly. He shook his head as he went on. 'But there is no way to be sure... yet.'

'We'll find out, one way or another,' Morri said, and several clerics voiced their support and agreement.

Ward smiled. 'Thank you, my friends. With our guild working together, I have no doubts we can prevail not only now, but in the future, whatever it may throw at us.

'Now, I will let you return to your work whilst I go do mine.'

The clerics thanked their new Grand Master and moved off to continue with their various tasks.

'You did right to take on the role you know?' Orix said, as he accompanied Ward into the corridor outside the room.

'Perhaps,' the magician replied, clearly unconvinced. 'You do know that if the council's decision hadn't have been unanimous, I wouldn't have taken it,' he added, with a genuine smile.

The small gnome beamed back up at him. 'I do know that, because you have done just that in the past. You are who they want though, whether you like it or not, and that's what's best for this guild. Our members are amongst the most brilliant minds of our century, if not our millennium; they know what they are doing. You weren't chosen as part of a popularity contest, you know?'

'I'm hurt,' Ward mocked.

Orix tutted in response. 'You know my meaning. They chose you because you're what the guild needs. You're the mage for the job, and no one knows better than me personally.' Orix winked at the magician.

'Bah,' Ward blurted. 'You would have done the same for me should I have been carried off over someone's shoulder.' The two shared a heartfelt laugh, the first either of them could recall for some time. Once the mirth had passed, however, Ward's face darkened as he crouched and looked to the gnome before him.

'I may not have admitted it in there, Orix, but I'm sure there is some force behind all of this, as is our King. It was no accident or co-incidence there being a plague attached to the scroll that found its way to Wesson and into Severun's hands. And we will discover those behind it. You know and trust me in that, don't you Orix?'

'Oh, I both know and agree, especially that we will figure it out. After all, you have *me* working on it.' With another wink, the old gnome turned on his heals and headed back into the busy clerics' chamber beyond.

I hope you and I are both right there, Orix, for although we know this plague was no accident, the motive still eludes us, and that's something we need to remedy, quickly, before the plague's creators make their next move.

***

As the night drew in on Broadleaf Forest and its Middle Wood, several elf musicians played pleasant melodies that seemed to reach in and massage the very soul; the sweet sound flowed around the boles of the trees, spreading far and wide like the spring breeze enjoyed earlier that day. The light of the moon now cascaded down through the branches of the tall trees, and the laughter of humans did little to sour the elven voices that suddenly joined the exotic instruments, sharing harmonies that sounded as natural as the dawn chorus the group had heard that morning.

A magical fire – the colours of which seemed to change with the mood of the music – crackled in the middle of a clearing, where intricately woven blankets of various pastel colours covered the floor, atop them cushions filled with feathers softer than anything humanly imaginable.

The group of humans had been led there by Lord Errwin-Roe, and invited to relax and unwind. Their return journey would not set out until the following day and so they were to get some much needed rest and recuperation.

The elf musicians sat on low branches all around the clearing, playing instruments none of the humans, bar Sav, had ever seen before.

'Some of the elf scouts play at our camps when on patrol from time to time, but this, this is truly heavenly,' he'd said, as he'd dropped down onto the cushioned floor surrounding the colourful firelight.

Errolas, Nelem and many other elves had come to join the visitors, and Fal smiled both physically and inwardly as he took in the scene. It was how he'd always imagined life with the elves, better even, apart from the odd jibes and looks he and his companions had received upon their arrival to Middle Wood.

It's not like I don't get that back in Wesson though. In fact, I'm far more used to it than the rest of the group, he'd thought to himself earlier that day. Despite that and the outburst from Lord Salkeld, Fal was genuinely elated to have had the opportunity to experience the wonder that was Middle Wood. Looking around at the rest of the group, he could well imagine the rest of them were thinking along similar lines, all apart from Correia perhaps, who'd seemed pre-occupied and lost within herself, down even, since the council meeting with the elves. Gleave had asked her what was wrong at one point, just to be told to go and enjoy himself, so no one else had thought it prudent to approach her with the question. Fal sipped the sweet wine he'd been given and thought about asking Correia himself, not wanting her to miss out on the joy they were all experiencing.

Suddenly, the music took on a fast pace and both humans and elves alike cheered as a group of dancers ran, jumped and swung down from branches into the clearing and around the magical fire. Fal's train of thought was lost completely as the performers began to move in harmony with the uplifting music.

The male and female dancers wore hair of all colours tied up in high set pony tails, with streamers of bright silver and gold following their hands and feet as they leapt and spun around the fire. Their heads and hair snapped to and fro with the music as they rolled over one another and jumped from feet to hands and back. The males of the group propelled the scantly clad females high into the air where they danced across branches before falling back into their partners' arms.

The seated humans and elves alike spoke and laughed as wine and fruit was passed around. The wine was served in silver goblets and the fruit on beautiful wooden bowls that looked as though they'd grown that shape, rather than being carved.

Starks sipped the clear elven spirit he'd been given and his watery eyes let a tear roll down his cheek as he gazed longingly at a particular rare, red haired she-elf, who spun past him with sparkling silver streamers swirling about her like a metallic, star-lit zephyr. She stopped still just long enough to throw the young crossbowman a smile and a wink, and he looked – eyes wide and tears streaming – at Fal before whimpering something about being in love and then passing out on the cushions behind him. A broad shouldered elf sat to Starks' right swiftly took the goblet from his hand before it spilt over the now snoring young man. Fal looked at the elf who laughed and shrugged, pointing at the recovered goblet of spirit and then to Fal, before passing it across and motioning for him try some.

Fal hesitated after the effect it'd had on Starks, but Errolas appeared by his side then and assured him it was safe. That was good enough for Fal, and so raising Starks' goblet in a toast to the on-looking elf, Fal took a tentative sip and rocked back at the sweet yet extremely potent drink, much to the amusement of both Errolas and the elf by Starks' side, who smiled and downed a goblet of the same in one.

'That's some strong stuff,' Fal said, laughing.

Errolas nodded his agreement and then pointed to Sav, who was already up and dancing with a particularly cute, dark haired elf who seemed to be finding the lanky scout's awkward movements highly amusing.

Nelem sat down then, in-between Fal and Gleave. 'The scout's no terpsichorean is he?' Both men agreed with the elf lord, neither wanting to admit they didn't know what he meant. Smiling politely, they clapped their hands along with the elves around them and laughed at Sav's continued attempts to match the elf-maiden's steps.

Correia scoffed at the sight, downed her goblet of wine, which seemed to have no effect on her whatsoever, and left the clearing, heading back to the ground house the group had been given to sleep in.

Gleave rolled his eyes and managed to push himself to his feet, much to Fal's surprise considering the man's recently broken leg.

Taking two elf dancers by the hands, Gleave linked arms with them and shouted for more to join in. 'Mearson would've loved this,' he shouted, and before he'd finished, almost all within the clearing were on their feet and linking their arms to form a huge circle around the colourful flames of the camp fire. They danced around and around, supporting Gleave and kicking their legs out awkwardly in imitation of the pathfinder. All present laughed loud and long, and on it went, dancing, laughing, eating and drinking, long into the night.

The next morning seemed to come too fast for Starks, who awoke with a start. He opened his eyes and then closed them again as he saw both Sav and Gleave's grinning faces just inches above his own.

'Morning, sleepy head. You feel rough?' Sav said, and Gleave chuckled to himself as he wandered out of the room shaking his head.

'What happened?' Starks' eyelids slowly closed again.

Sav laughed all the more. 'You passed out after crying and declaring your undying love to Leiina.'

Starks' eyes flicked open again. 'Who?'

'Don't listen, Starks, you did no such thing,' Correia said as she entered the room, glowering at Sav.

'Spoil my fun why don't you? Just because you're moody doesn't mean—'

'Sorry, Sav? You seemed to be speaking a little too quietly for me to hear then?'

'Nothing, *my lady*.' Sav flashed what he thought was a winning smile. 'Just missed you during the dancing last night is all. I thought you would've been eager to share a few steps with me?' He winked at the unamused woman who feigned a look of disappointment.

'Oh, but you already had a partner didn't you, Sav? How could I compete with a vixen like that young, or should I say old, elf you were swooning over.'

Starks shook his head in total confusion, realising it must have been early in the night indeed when he apparently passed out.

'Jealousy doesn't become you, my dear.' Sav shook his head in a pitying manner.

'Oh please,' the Spymaster said as she repaired swiftly to the other room.

'You'll never win her over like that you know,' Starks said, 'even I can see that.'

Sav screwed his face up in what Starks knew to be feigned disgust as he too strode out of the room, but not before telling Starks to get his lazy behind out of bed.

The morning brought the smell of fresh flowers, grass and all the *green* smells of the forest, accompanied by the sound of animals, birds and elves at play.

Fal stood under a low branch in nothing but his linen braes as an elf slowly poured cold, fresh water over him. He gasped and rubbed his face as the water cascaded over his head and olive skinned body.

Correia made an appreciative noise, clearly enjoying the scene as Sav stormed past her and off towards a group of female elves who'd been present the night before. They all turned as Sav walked over, cheering and mimicking a few of his dance steps from the previous night. He gleefully re-enacted his steps to the apparent appreciation of the group, who flocked around him to the disbelief of Fal, who was watching and shaking his head.

The rest of the group left the quaint little house then, and Gleave pointed out a red haired elf maiden to Starks, whose face flushed with recognition. She looked across and giggled as she waved to the young crossbowman, who gingerly waved back whilst receiving a playful prod in the ribs from Gleave.

'She's so, so perfect,' Starks said, with an appreciative sigh, and Gleave laughed as he walked across to the group, dragging Starks all the way.

Fal wandered over to Correia then. He pulled his linen shirt over his head, sat on the ground and pulled his hose and boots on before looking up at the woman to ask her how she was.

'I'm fine,' she said before Fal could say a word, and he merely nodded, knowing full well it wasn't the time to press her.

'Where's Lord Severun? He wasn't with us last night, nor have I seen him this morning,' Fal asked. The Spymaster pointed to the great oak sat like a fortress of wood and leaves in the distance.

'He's been with their clerics and mages doing, well, magical things. I'll leave that stuff to him.'

'What're we to do then, if they're not ready to leave yet?'

'They'll leave when I say so,' Correia said, eyes on Sav and the elf maidens before realising Fal meant the elf mages. She sighed and ran her hands through her hair. 'I'm sorry Fal.'

'No need, Correia, no need.'

The woman pulled him to his feet and he patted her on the back, before pulling her off towards the mixed group of human men and elven women.

The she-elves took the humans on a tour of the Middle Wood, showing them artisans of all types. Some wove the same blankets that had been used to cover the ground the night before, whilst others carved ornate and elegant ornaments using wood they explained was donated by the trees to be used in the construction of necessities. Others beat metal with hammers in a style none of the humans had seen used before, creating weapons, armour and various other tools and implements.

By the time the group had reached a large orchard where elves picked a wide variety of ripe fruit, a whole host of children had gathered to follow the humans. They pulled on their arms to ask questions and laughed at Sav's dancing.

'What The Three is that?' Starks blurted, and the whole group, children included, followed his gaze along his outstretched arm to the tree line at the edge of the orchard.

'Aw, don't worry, it's harmless,' Leiina said. She took Starks' hand and skipped across to the creature emerging from the undergrowth, her red hair dancing behind her in the breeze as Starks – almost skipping himself – ran by her side.

The rest of the group followed, several of the elf children hanging off their shoulders or pulling on their hands as they walked.

As they got to the edge of the orchard, the undergrowth parted fully to reveal a huge, fleshy bodied creature on stump-like legs that shuffled its bulbous, orange form out into the sunlight of the orchard.

'Gods above,' Starks said, his jaw remaining low as he took in the creature before him. His red haired companion giggled and pulled him in close for a hug. Gleave pictured the young man as a fluffy bunny in the arms of an intrigued child. It was the only way he could make sense of it. He shook his head and grunted a laugh to himself, before thinking again of Mearson. *Damn, brother, you'd have loved it here.*

Sav looked mortified, mouthing 'why him?' much to the amusement of Fal who saw his friend's reaction, as did more than one of the remaining elf maidens, some of whom deciding to wrap the scout in a hug of their own.

All human eyes, apart from Sav's and Starks', were fixed completely on what was now fully appearing from the undergrowth. Fal thought it was one of the strangest things he'd ever seen, apart from the sight of the not so pretty Sav wrapped up in the arms of several stunning elf maidens.

'What is it?' Fal asked. The reply came from Errolas behind him, which made him jump.

'It's a *pandorus sphinx.*'

'A what?' Gleave asked, and only then did Sav look out from the cluster of girls to take in the slowly moving form of the creature. Starks was also clearly interested, despite the dreamy look plastered across his face as Leiina placed her head on his shoulder, her red hair cascading down his chest and back.

Sav laughed in amazement and everyone turned to him. 'It's a moth larvae… like a caterpillar, but huge.'

The giant larvae slowly shuffled towards the group, all of which moved out of its way as it lumbered past. Great circular eye-like patterns ran down its side as its small – compared to the rest of it – head bobbed up and down, consuming the grass and plants it passed over. A large horn-like tail sprouted from the back end of the creature and waved from side to side as it moved past the group, slowly shuffling off towards the centre of the orchard.

'That's truly amazing.' Fal locked his hands behind the back of his slowly shaking head. The rest of the humans nodded their agreement.

Leiina looked from the larvae to Fal. 'Not everything in the Middle Wood is as you would normally see it elsewhere,' she said to him, before turning back to Starks.

'Well, you're bloody right there,' Gleave said, staring and nodding towards the attractive elf playing with Starks' hair. The whole group laughed, apart from Starks who positively beamed back at the burly pathfinder.

The high spirits and happy mood of the group lowered suddenly as new arrivals appeared in the orchard. From the far side of the fruit trees came seven riders on proud, black steeds. Some of the slim yet powerful looking mounts pawed at the ground as their riders stopped by the small crowd. Several of the children seemed to lose interest in the group at that point and ran off back the way they'd come, whilst the others quietened down and looked to the elf maidens for direction. One of the she-elves put her finger to her lips and the kids nodded, whilst the pale skinned, black haired riders looked on with dour expressions.

'Can we help you, Lord Salkeld?' An elf maiden asked. Her golden hair hung in a long plait across her left shoulder, revealing what looked like a feint tattoo of an elven rune on her right. Fal had to pull his eyes away from that tattoo, to look back at the lead rider.

The elven knight – for surely that's what they were – to the elf lord's right snorted at the question. 'It seems you are already helping the humans.'

A couple, but not all, of the girls let go of Sav and looked to their feet.

'We're being hospitable, nothing more, my lord,' one of the girls who'd let go of Sav said. Several of the others nodded their agreement, eyes still lowered.

Starks glanced sideways to Leiina, who remained defiantly by his side much to his relief, and so he puffed his chest out just a little more.

'I hope there isn't a problem with us being shown around, Lord Salkeld?' Correia asked confidently. The dark green armoured lord seemed to almost snarl at Correia's words.

'Of course not, Spymaster Burr. You are our guests and our home is your home. I wouldn't dream of upsetting you or your little party... while you are here.'

The elf knights fingered the hilts and pommels of the long-swords that lay in their saddle scabbards, and Fal didn't miss the intended threat for what it was, and neither did Errolas it seemed.

'Whilst those kind words are welcome in my home, Lord Salkeld, I would apologise for cutting this pleasant conversation short. I have come to retrieve our friends and allies and so must bid you farewell. I wish you a pleasant journey back to your home in the Black Forest.'

Fal tried to hide the smile that pulled at the corners of his mouth. He cringed as he noticed Sav had failed completely to hide his.

The elf lord's knights bristled then, their mounts growing restless. Arrlo had to raise his hand as two of the armour clad elves half drew their elegant swords.

'Of course, ranger, and I bid you all a pleasant journey back to your city.' His eyes shifted back from Errolas to Correia. 'I do hope you find it as you left it.' Arrlo Salkeld nudged his horse with his knees then and trotted regally passed the group, his sneering knights close behind.

Several of the elf maidens made their excuses and swiftly left the group along with the remainder of the children, whilst the handful left tried to apologise for the elf lord's behaviour.

Correia and the others wouldn't hear of it. They assured the elf girls they'd sincerely enjoyed their time with them and considered each and every one of them a new friend. The elves assured the group they felt the same, especially Leiina, who turned Starks by the shoulders and embraced him in a passionate, lasting kiss that stunned everyone in the group, human and elf alike.

***

The iron-studded oak door crashed open as two panting men burst through and into the sparring chamber of the palace.

From a circular arena filled with a thin layer of sand came a strained groan and then a dull thud as Will Morton, bare from the chest up and sporting several silvery scars across his shoulders and chest, slammed a much younger but equally stocky knight down onto his back. Sand lifted into the air and a squire off to the side called a point to the Lord High Constable, who finally looked over to the two men attempting to stand to attention in the open doorway.

Offering a hand to the prone knight without looking, Morton heaved the man to his feet and shoved him off to the side before walking across to the edge of the arena, his bare feet making no sound on the sand beneath him.

It wasn't until he reached and sat on the wooden barrier, twisting to look at the intruders, did he notice an equally out of breath and panting bloodhound at their feet.

'What?' Morton said simply, as he brushed sand from the palms of his hands.

Sears glanced sideways to Gitsham, who merely shrugged, and so clenching his teeth before taking a deep breath, Sears explained the information they'd discovered in Dockside.

After a moment's pause whilst Lord Yewdale climbed over the barrier and proceeded to brush his braes and hose down, the man finally straightened, looked back at the two men and asked again, this time with incredulity. 'What?'

Sears looked again to Gitsham, but the man was too busy staring at his feet.

'Sire, it is our belief—'

'I heard you damn it, it was rhetorical.'

Sears swallowed hard and maintained a straight back, eyes front.

Pacing now, the Duke turned to the knight and squire. 'Leave.' They both nodded and left the room swiftly through a second door on the far side of the chamber.

'You claim the Black Guild has placed a mark on King Barrison's head?'

'Yes, sire,' Sears said.

'Aye,' Gitsham said.

'And the dog?'

'The dog, sire?' Sears asked, confused.

'The dog told you this?'

'Not me, sire, him.' Sears jerked the thumb of his good hand to Gitsham.

'Ah… that's alright then.' Morton rolled his eyes and rubbed the back of his neck. He moved across to a bench and picked up a blood-red linen shirt, before pulling it on over his head. He then dunked his head in a cold bucket of water and thrashed it about, spreading droplets all about him.

Buddle whined.

'Thirsty boy?' Morton said.

Buddle barked.

'Go on then,' the Duke said, motioning for the dog to drink from the bucket which he placed on the floor. Buddle raced across the room and lapped at the water as Morton crossed back towards the two men, but not before picking up and strapping on his belt, which held his ornately sheathed bastard-sword.

With the sound of Buddle lapping up water in the background, Morton rubbed at his face and stared into the eyes of Sears, before asking who else knew of this.

'Lord Stowold, sire, and some of his men.'

'And?'

Sears paused, but under the scrutiny of the Lord High Constable, easily caved. 'A former whore called Coppin and a former assassin called Longoss.' Sears didn't miss the flash of recognition when he mentioned Longoss' name, despite the Duke hiding it swiftly. He turned to look upon Gitsham, whose head was still pointing to the ground, suspiciously like he was sleeping.

'And you, Gitsham?' Morton asked, surprising Sears that he knew the man's name.

Nothing.

'Is he asleep?'

'Erm… it appears so. It's been quite an experience, sire.'

'I suppose it has, travelling through Dockside with assassins and gangers on your heels, whilst a dog talks to you in your head.'

Buddle wined over by the bucket.

'I already know much of what you say.' Morton looked back at a surprised Sears. 'Somehow, Stowold received a message that you needed assistance in

443

Dockside and that you had important information, of what I had no idea and nor did he. He did inform me, however, that Gitsham here could speak to that magical hound of his, or visa versa.' Morton pointed back towards Buddle, who was now lying down next to the bucket, his eyes slowly closing. 'Although I must confess, I'm struggling with that part. Anyway, I digress. If I am to take your word for it about this mark, and it seems that by your word, we in fact mean the word of a former assassin of the very guild you are saying has placed a mark on our King's head. Then I must conclude the Black Guild, for some reason, has let you escape to bring this information to me. Why?'

Sears almost rocked back on his heals. 'Why must ye assume that, sire?'

'Why?' Morton laughed. 'I know of you and your partner's success within Park District, Sears, but please. There's no way you survived Dockside alone, with not only riots, gangers and a plague ripping through the damned district, but with a bloody assassins guild on your arse as well man? No, it's my thought that Longoss is still working for the Black Guild and for some reason, they wanted you to get this message to me.'

Sears was shaking his head as the Lord High Constable spoke.

'You don't agree? You thought it was your skill as a soldier that got you through it, do you?'

'No, milord, I don't think that, but nor do I believe Longoss was still part of that guild—'

'Friends now are we,' Morton said, voice rising dangerously, 'you, the assassin and his whore?'

Sears had to check himself from swinging for the man as Coppin's battered and bruised image popped into his head. *She's more than ye'll ever be, ye bastard.* Breathing deep, Sears thought of Biviano and managed to calm himself, although from the sudden yet brief look in Lord Yewdale's eyes, Sears thought his own eyes may have just betrayed his anger.

'If they wanted that, sire, why did they not just tell me the King was the mark? Why not tell me and let me walk out of Dockside?'

'If it was that easy, would you've believed it?'

'It was Buddle who sniffed it out. I fought assassins, all three of us did before Gitsham and Buddle arrived, damn, we near never made it out and Longoss wounded them all—'

'But didn't kill them?'

'No, he swore never to kill again. He did all he could without breaking his word.'

Morton laughed knowingly, for reasons Sears couldn't understand. 'This rot gets better.'

'Listen to me!' Sears shouted, becoming animated at the same time. Morton took a step back and placed a hand on the hilt of his sword. Both Gitsham and Buddle jumped awake. 'I might as well have gone through The Three in there along with that girl and Longoss! We ran, we hid, we crawled through fucking sewers and fought numerous bastards to bring ye this information! They killed Longoss' love and they near damned killed us too! If it weren't for Gitsham and Buddle here, I'd still be hiding or dead and none of us would know who the damned guild's mark was, they certainly didn't tell me! The only reason we got out—' Sears pointed to Buddle, Gitsham and himself, '—was because Biviano and Lord Stowold came for us in force—'

'And who'd you think authorised that, you dumb bastard?' Morton's eyes locked on Sears.

Stunned, Sears closed his mouth and glanced sideways to Gitsham, who made a point of not looking at the big man. *Ye could've told me that before I went off on one at a pissin' Duke, ye shit,* Sears thought, knowing Gitsham had known that fact by the lack of eye contact.

'Sire—'

'Sire nothing, Sears,' Morton said, hands on hips and a wry smile spreading across his lined face. 'I had to know you were serious, because news like this is serious business. I can't just take it in easily and not probe. Anger brings out all sorts, including the truth often enough.

'The King though… 'morl's reeking corpse Sears, I never thought that, not the most bloody benevolent ruler we'll ever see.' He looked back up into the red bearded face of Sears and sighed long and hard. 'You've done well soldier, damned well and the King will hear of your efforts, mark my words.'

Sears was still stunned and a little confused. *Was all that really necessary? Flay me but these nobles aren't right in the head.*

'There's going to be a lot of planning to do now, to work out how best to combat this news, and that's whilst we're still trying to figure out this plague and all the shit it's stirred up.' Morton rubbed at his bristled chin and began to pace again.

'Can we not just assault the Black Guild, milord? They've taken heavy losses—'

'From you and your new friends?' Morton asked. Sears didn't know if the Lord High Constable was being sarcastic or not, but answered seriously anyway.

'Aye, a little,' Sears said, nodding, 'but mainly because of the plague, sire. As have the gangs around Dockside. We might've fought like demons and believe me, sire, we did, but there's no damned way I'd be stood here now if this had happened a couple of weeks ago.'

Morton continued pacing, although he'd nodded at Sears' answer. 'No,' he said eventually, 'we can't assault them, as much as I'd like to. We don't know where the bloody guild is for starters.' Stopping suddenly, he turned to Sears. 'The assassin, Longoss, you didn't bring him in did you?'

'No, milord,' Sears said, unsure as to the Duke's motives for wanting the former assassin beyond asking him where the guild is. *Why didn't I ask him that?* Sears silently cursed himself.

'Shame,' Morton said, almost to himself, 'could've done with questioning him…' He trailed off as he headed to the far door of the sparring chamber.

Sears, Gitsham and Buddle all tracked the Duke until he reached the far door and opened it. Before he walked through, he turned to all three and nodded. 'Good work lads, now back to your business,' he said, before leaving the room.

'Well shaft me sideways, what the hell was all that? It was hardly necessary,' Sears said, turning to Gitsham to find him sleep standing again. Looking across to Buddle, he could have sworn he saw the bloodhound shrug.

Chapter 45: Return To Wesson

Several thick plumes of black smoke rose into the cloud-filled afternoon sky and drifted lazily across the city. The temperature had dropped slightly and the air felt damp with anticipated rain as the column of horses and carts trundled towards the coast. Wesson's walls looked dull and foreboding as the smoke rose behind them. The banners on the large eastern gatehouse hung limp in the cool breeze that gently ushered the forming clouds in from the sea.

The roads to and from the small bridge across the River Norln to the south of Beresford – the only passable place for miles around without going through the contested town itself – had been empty of merchants, farmers and travellers in general. The elf council had sent clerics, mages and warriors to aid King Barrison, yet no one gathered to watch the elves pass. Correia and Severun largely keeping to themselves along the journey, and everyone else remained similarly quiet, thinking about what awaited them in Wesson. Lord Nelem and Errolas had also accompanied the group at their own request, as did Lord Errwin-Roe, who was eager to speak to King Barrison, a man he claimed he'd not seen since the reign of Barrison's father. But even *their* presence hadn't lightened the mood of the travellers along the way.

Beresford, Fal thought heavily, eyeing the columns of smoke rising high from the walls of Wesson before him. *Does the town still stand? Even if the goblins pulled back from the west side of the town, they could've continued on through farms and villages with little to no resistance. Is that why the roads have been so quiet... or has the plague escaped the city's quarantine?* Fal grimaced at the thought of either outcome.

'There she is,' Sav said, unwittingly wrenching Fal from his thoughts as he pulled his horse alongside and nodded to the city. 'She doesn't look too clever, Fal. I'm not looking forward to walking through her gates.'

Fal shook his head but didn't answer, instead, he nudged his horse forward again and the group followed, the elf contingent with their carts bringing up the rear.

They walked their horses down a slight decline, following the stone road leading to the eastern gatehouse of the capital city, untended fields stretching out to either side.

Fal took in the empty ridge and furrowed fields. *The farmers are too scared to come close... or worse.*

He fingered the hilt of his trusty falchion, a weapon re-sharpened and oiled by the elves of the Middle Wood. It had been a wonderful surprise to hear what the skilled rune-smiths had said when presenting the group's weapons back to them. His mind easily slipped back to the dreamlike Middle Wood as he thought about the events that day. He wanted to escape his surroundings and think upon it one last time before Wesson revealed its potential horrors.

***

Along with Sav, Starks and Gleave, Fal felt honoured to be attending a training session hosted by the council guards who'd been their escorts whilst in the great oak. The skill, speed and strength presented by the council guards were truly awesome as they sparred with one another in front of their human guests. As they moved, their weapons seemed to shimmer, whilst others glowed like the depths of a roaring fire. After an impressive series of routines, the elves encouraged the humans to try out their own returned weapons, to see what they thought of the work the rune-smiths had carried out.

As Fal, Starks and Gleave looked on, Sav eagerly stepped forward and drew his returned bow. He grimaced due to his injured shoulder as he pulled the cord back. Fal told him he should wait until he was well, but Sav insisted he had to try out his returned weapon.

The scout stood almost completely side-on to the target at the end of the range, a range of almost four hundred yards. He shook his head slightly at the impossible distance, knowing a war bow would struggle to make the range, let along his hunting bow. He shifted his weight forward onto his front facing left foot, determined to see what the rune-smith had done to his prized possession.

At the same time as shifting his weight forward, Sav pushed with his left hand which gripped the now rune carved bow-stave, whilst drawing with his right hand's index and middle fingers on the hemp string until the back of his thumb was resting comfortably on his right cheek. He took a deep breath and blocked out the pain. Almost as soon as his hand had reached the side of his face, he slowly let out his breath and relaxed his fingers, releasing the string and its carefully selected arrow.

The arrow sprung elegantly from the yew bow and flew straight, hardly faltering as it cruised towards the seemingly impossible target, turning ever so slowly as it did so, which was to be expected due to the arrow's goose feather flights.

As the arrow reached the point where Sav expected it to dip, bringing it down into the long grass of the archery range, the scout's face lit up. The arrow continued straight and level, turning once more before connecting with the centre of the target buttress and releasing a loud thud that reached the humans' ears a brief moment after the arrow's impact. The elves, of course, had heard it a split second before the humans, and had already turned to congratulate Sav, increasing his elation.

Sav turned to Fal first, a smug look upon his face and then to the rest of them, kissing his bow and cheering along with the growing crowd of onlookers.

'You required the bow to reach the distant target and with your will, skill and strength all working together, the bow obeyed,' the rune-smith bowyer explained. 'Should you require an angled shot, within reason of course, then

448

the bow should obey those silent commands too. Try it,' he urged, motioning to an angled target about one hundred and fifty yards away and facing off to the left. Sav looked sceptical, before recalling the elf archers he and the others had witnessed training in this very technique the day of their arrival.

If this works, I think I'll actually cry.

Sav drew another broad-headed arrow from his quiver.

'Just imagine the arrow striking the centre of the target,' a female archer said in her sing song voice. 'It takes some getting used to, but...'

Sav loosed. The arrow seemed to briefly head in the same direction the front of the target was facing, before arcing rapidly and thumping into the upper left hand side of the buttress. Sav whooped and the others laughed.

'I love it!' he cried, and the elven children who'd gathered around his feet giggled and cheered. 'Thank you so much,' he said to the rune-smith bowyer, 'I don't know how I can repay you?'

The elf laughed and waved the comment away. 'Use it against our enemies. We are allies and friends I hope, and I know you will use it wisely.' The elf bowed before stepping back so Starks could move forward. His crossbow had been beautifully carved down each side of its stock and now had what looked like a gold laced string. He had also been presented with a quiver of heavy looking bolts, of which he'd been told to use wisely and sparingly, although the elf who'd presented them to him had encouraged him to use one. He claimed it was so Starks could truly see what they were like, as words would do them an injustice, but Fal thought it was because the elf wanted everyone to see his craftsmanship, and why not?

Leiina clapped her hands excitedly and blew Starks a kiss, much to the amusement of most and envy of Sav.

Starks knelt and spanned his crossbow with such ease his face dropped slightly. *They've reduced the draw weight?*

He imagined the probable lack of power such an easily drawn cord would offer, but fitted one of the heavy looking bronze tipped bolts none the less. His eyes widened and a smile pulled at the side of his mouth as he looked upon the rune engravings along the bolt's shaft. Lifting the crossbow so the stock was resting on his shoulder, Starks looked down the weapon, levelling it towards a target half way down the range; doubting the new string's effectiveness.

Fingers resting on top of the stock, he pressed up on the cold metal trigger under the weapon with his thumb and the bolt seemed to lurch from the string, dipping slightly before taking off at a tremendous speed towards the target. A fraction of a second before it reached the straw buttress the bolt exploded into a ball of orange flames which engulfed the target, reducing it to ashes in seconds before dissipating into nothing more than a cloud of white smoke.

Sav burst out laughing and looked in astonishment to the elf who'd worked on the crossbow. The elf nodded, smiled and motioned for Fal and Gleave to step forward.

Starks had to be moved out of the way as he stared, mouth open at the destroyed target ahead of the group, but he soon composed himself again as the red haired elf maiden bounded into his arms once more.

Both Fal and Gleave drew their weapons and hefted them, feeling the weight in their hands and trying to work out if there was any difference to their weapons' balance. Gleave stood with one hand on a crutch, his injured leg splinted, and he bobbed his hand axe up and down in his free hand whilst Fal sliced his falchion through the air.

Two of the armoured council guards stepped forward, their curved swords held high in defensive positions. Fal looked to Gleave, confused as to what they were supposed to do.

'Just try a simple dodge, Sergeant Falchion, when they attack you,' Fal's rune-smith said, and so he nodded his accord.

The two elves switched stances and came on as one, moving swiftly at Fal. They came from two directions and he failed to see how he could dodge without parrying a blow, but he tried all the same, assuming hopefully they would pull their blows should he fail. As he shifted his weight and lurched to his left, attempting to leave the reach of one elf and pass dangerously across the front of the other, he found himself where he'd wanted to be before the closest elf had reacted.

That same elf ended up stumbling past Fal and looking round at him in surprise. The elf looked slightly embarrassed then, but joined in when his comrades erupted in a hearty laugh at his expense.

And here I was thinking they'd be far faster… are they playing with me?

'That was your leather armour, sergeant,' the rune-smith said, his green eyes sparkling. 'We decided on improving that instead of your weapon, I hope you do not mind? I assumed you hadn't seen the subtle markings I added to the inside of your greaves and vambraces, so thought I wouldn't tell you until you tried them for yourself.'

Fal was thankful but shocked. *I don't recall them even taking my armour? Well, I'm certainly not going to complain.*

'So I can move much faster in this armour?' he asked, slightly confused.

'Oh no, sergeant, not at all, your armour, or rather the runes I placed upon your armour are illusion runes that simply leave a slight image of you as you move. Therefore your attacker mistakes your movement, fails to anticipate it correctly and gives you a momentary chance to dodge, parry, counter-attack or whatever the situation requires.

'Be careful not to start relying on it, though,' the rune-smith added, his forefinger held up to mark the warning, 'but it will certainly prove helpful, I am sure.' Smiling broadly, the rune-smith bowed low.

'That's amazing. I'm so very grateful,' Fal said sincerely, returning the bow. Standing straight again, he looked at the other humans, beaming at them all. They all grinned back at Fal, clearly excited for him as well as themselves.

'Don't think I'm in a state to try mine out,' Gleave said eventually, and all around agreed. He looked pale and the injury to his leg, although healing, was clearly taking its toll, especially after his antics at the gathering the night before. 'I notice fancy runes, though, on the blade.'

One of the rune-smiths, an old looking elf with silvery hair plaited down to the back of his knees, nodded slowly before walking over to and opening his hand to retrieve the axe. Gleave placed the weapon in the elf's slender hand and stared, awaiting the revelation of what the weapon could do.

With a wry smile, the silver haired rune-smith whispered to the weapon which... disappeared.

Eyebrows raised and eyes wide, Gleave looked from the empty palm of the elf to his companions and back, taking a step – almost stumbling – backwards when he saw the weapon was back in the rune-smith's hand.

'Where'd it go?' Sav asked, stepping forward and staring at the weapon.

'Nowhere,' the elf announced, his smile broadening, 'you just couldn't see it, but I could.'

'Fuck off,' Gleave said in amazement. Fal squeezed his eyes shut and Sav stifled a laugh. Several elven intakes of breath later, Gleave quickly apologized and explained he'd meant it as an exclamation of excitement, not as an insult. Still unsure, the silver haired rune-smith stepped in close to the now red faced pathfinder and whispered to him the word required to activate the weapon's runes.

'Even better,' Gleave said, after the elf explained Gleave would still be able to see it. The large man lifted the axe to his lips and whispered. Again the axe disappeared, but it was clear to all Gleave could still see it in his hand as he waved it about, his eyes not leaving the space above his fist. 'I can't say how useful that could be,' he said, half stunned and still looking at the invisible weapon, which only re-appeared when he willed it to.

I wonder what they'd have done for Mearson if he were here... Gleave smiled tightly and nodded his thanks to the rune-smith, who nodded in return.

It had been an exhilarating day and all in the group were overjoyed by their gifts. It was then that Correia re-appeared and so they assaulted her with stories of what they'd been up to, until she announced it was time to leave, which caused a subtle sadness to descend upon them all.

Although she had received runes on both her swords, Correia was clearly in the same awful mood that had come on after their encounter with Lord Salkeld, and so the other members of the group decided to keep their distance and certainly didn't asked her what the rune-smiths had done to her weapons, despite all of them wanting to know.

Severun, returning with Correia, was quiet too, and simply shook his head when Fal had asked if he'd received any gifts from the elves.

When the group finally left the Middle Wood, not long after the training session, the children threw white petals from the branches of trees all around the edges of the glade where the bridge crossed the river. The snow like effect added to the beauty and magic the group had witnessed since their arrival, and proved a fitting backdrop to their tearful farewell.

Starks had to be dragged away by Fal and Sav as both he and Leiina sobbed, not wanting to be parted. They swore they would meet again in the future and Sav thought he saw a tear on Correia's cheek, but for once decided not to taunt the Spymaster.

Elves cheered and handed the group food and gifts as they passed. They wished them luck and bid them a fond farewell. Musicians played music that pulled at the group's hearts, causing turbulent emotions that swung between regret to be leaving, to joy and happiness to have been there in the first place, all whilst their column of horses and carts crossed the decorated, ancient bridge.

As the group left Broadleaf Forest and entered the meadows between the forest and the Woodmoat, Fal looked back one last time. He smiled as he met eyes with the Great Stag who was watching them leave. The noble animal bowed low and Fal reciprocated as best he could whilst turning in his saddle. A great sadness overcame him then, and he feared he would never see Broadleaf Forest again. *I'll forever relish the memories, but a part of me will never again be whole after leaving this place.*

Once past the Woodmoat, Gleave showed the group where they'd buried Mearson the morning after the fight with the witchunters. Being Mearson's closest friend, Gleave had decided Mearson should be buried within sight of the Woodmoat, and the elves that had looked after him and Severun throughout the night had agreed. He said they'd also sworn to keep their eye on the grave marker, which Gleave himself had calved from a fallen branch.

The group paid their last respects and Fal felt lower still at losing a man he was sure would have become a great friend. 'I feel proud to have fought alongside you,' he whispered, before leaving Correia to say her goodbye.

Mearson... Correia mouthed the words running through her head. *It was a pleasure and an honour to have known and fought along side you. You were a true friend to us all, especially Gleave... I'm not sure how he'll be without you? Not the same, that's for sure.* Correia fought back a tear as she remembered times the three of them had laughed together. Other Pathfinders had come and gone and each one lost was a knife in her heart, but Mearson had been with her for years, and she knew his loss would be felt keenly by her and Gleave especially. *Rest easy, soldier, and we shall see you again one day, when it is our turn to fall.*

***

Calls and bells rang out as the mixed human and elven column neared Wesson's eastern gatehouse. Fal looked up to the figures above, the calls bringing him back to the present. *So few walk the ramparts?*

It took a long time after Correia announced herself and the elven lords before anything happened, but finally, Will Morton arrived. The Lord High Constable looked down upon them, his face lined and weathered, his expression sour and his mood equally as bad.

'Open it,' the Duke said to a sergeant-at-arms by his side, his low voice barely audible to the elves below.

'But sire, the King's order—'

'Open it for pity's sake, man! They're here to help.'

Swallowing hard, the sergeant-at-arms nodded and rushed out of sight. Morton also disappeared, before his distinctive bellowing of orders drifted over the ramparts to the elves below.

Hold who back? Errolas thought, glancing briefly to Lord Nelem at his side.

The great wooden gates creaked terribly as they slowly swung inwards and the drawbridge, hardly ever lifted, came crashing down, lifting dust and dirt high. The column's horses clattered across the wooden drawbridge once the dust and dirt had settled and then echoed as they passed under the great stone arch, the fire wrecked Coach & Cart Inn on sad display in front of them as they entered a crowded square.

Gods above... Fal struggled to drag his eyes from the scorched ruins of his favourite tavern. So many memories he had of that place and yet now, now it looked as if a giant had put a foot through both of the turret roofs and smashed the joining bridge to pieces, the remains a jumble of smoking blackened timber and piled rubble.

'Clerics and mages to Tyndurris, any dignitaries to the palace,' Morton shouted, snapping Fal from his reverie. The Lord High Constable looked down on the column as it entered Wesson's cobbled streets.

'Can you hear me, my lords?' Morton's voice was low, but not too low that the elves below missed it, despite the growing noise from the gathering crowds of people.

Lord Errwin-Roe looked up then and nodded almost imperceptibly. What he and his kin heard next nearly turned their blood cold. He looked to the nearest cleric and mage, who looked to one another, pained expressions upon their angular faces. Nodding his understanding when they whispered their replies to him, Errwin-Roe looked up to the Lord High Constable and shook his head solemnly. Morton's face dropped when he saw the answer and an almost overwhelming feeling of sorrow hit him from the elves below. He recovered quickly and nodded his understanding and thanks to the elf lord.

Correia caught the brief, seemingly silent connection between the elves and the Duke, but when she looked to the man above, he broke eye contact with her, his face once again set to his usual grimace.

'Clear a path,' Morton shouted to the stretched line of city guardsmen now trying to hold back the gathering people. 'Make way for our saviours!'

People pushed and shoved to see the only people to enter the city since the quarantine started. A thin row of ragged and ill looking guardsmen pushed them back with shields, whilst holding a variety of swords, axes and war-hammers high.

Fal swallowed hard at the sight of weapons rather than cudgels in the hands of the guardsmen. *I dread to think what they've been through. Fighting their own whilst dealing with the plague's effects on them and their own families...*

'Help us,' a woman cried out, her face a mess of buboes.

The group winced as two guardsmen, scarves covering their faces, dragged her from the crowd and pulled her away as more people began to shout.

A fist was thrown and a guardsman went down heavily, his nose flattened. Before he could recover and climb to his feet, several feet came in kicking and stamping as many others took the opportunity to run towards the open gates.

'Close it, close the gate!' the sergeant-at-arms shouted from the ramparts above.

The last carts of the column had only just entered the gatehouse as people rushed towards them, their feral looking eyes set on the perceived freedom beyond Wesson's walls.

'No one escapes,' Morton shouted.

Fal manoeuvred his horse along with the elven warriors – who also drew their curved weapons – to protect the carts from the sudden rush of people as more guardsmen went down under the press of bodies.

'Hold,' Nelem shouted, to several elven warriors who'd begun to advance. They reluctantly walked their horses back to protect the carts.

Screams joined the shouts of fear and anger in the crowds as those guardsmen still standing began hacking wildly, doing all they could not to go down, knowing it would be their end.

Sav, bow swiftly strung and arrow nocked, fought a war within himself as he saw one guardsman hacking down a sick looking woman who'd lashed out at him, the falchion flashing once, twice and blood arcing back as he hit her a third time. She crumpled to the ground. Next to that, Sav saw a different guardsman being kicked and beaten on the ground, a flash of iron silencing him finally.

There's no target, Sav thought, his heart pounding as he began to panic. *I can't shoot any of them, they're not an enemy. None deserve this…*

The rumble of metal on stone alerted everyone to the slow raising of the drawbridge, but no one could free themselves to close the large gates some people were now nearing.

'Correia, orders?' Gleave shouted from the back of one of the carts, his leg now splint-less, but still of little use in such a situation.

Correia hesitated, looking frantically about for an answer as her own people tore themselves apart. *We need to get the elves out of here.* She turned to Lord Errwin-Roe and noticed him flashing rapid hand signals to his warriors and mages.

A sudden rush of air erupted from one of the richly dressed mages, causing horses to shift nervously and one cart to roll backwards despite its driver's best attempts to have its horses hold steady. That wind gained strength and as the front runners for the gate reached parallel to the inner opening of the large stone archway, they tumbled sideways, away from the closest cart and away from the open gates.

The drawbridge was now half closed, and following more directions from the elf lords, several of their warriors dismounted and rushed to the large gates, heaving them closed.

'Protect the gate crew,' Correia shouted. Fal, Sav and Starks turned their horses and rode into the gatehouse, turning them to create a line alongside the remaining mounted elves.

As the shouting and screaming continued, Sav noticed the occasional arrow or bolt whipping down from the gatehouse into the crowd around the few remaining guardsmen. Their well placed shots cleared a path for the men to back swiftly towards the column in front of the gatehouse. *They'll close on us fast now and what then? Will I kill whoever comes close or will I fall, unable to cut down unarmed people who have been through so much.*

'We need get the carts out of here,' Fal shouted, as the gates behind him finally thudded shut. He felt the tall elves that had closed it and remounted press their steeds along side his and his companions to form a solid line. 'Simulate a charge,' Fal said, 'they may break!'

'And if they don't?' Sav was now several elf riders away to the side.

Fal shook his head. *I don't know...*

'Severun!' Correia shouted suddenly, and all eyes moved to the hooded figure rushing out into the narrowing gap between the column and the crowd. The wizard passed between two running, injured guardsmen and then stopped dead. He threw his arms to the side, white staff held out horizontally, and then lifted his chin high.

Silence...

The whole square fell silent and the oncoming crowd faltered and then stopped just short of the hooded wizard, who broke the silence with a voice filled with malice and hatred, a voice that carried to every man, woman and child present. 'I am Lord Severun, burnt at the stake by this city for my crimes, but here I stand again before you now! Who here shall challenge my revenge? Who here will share in the pain I felt upon that pyre?'

Those closest to Severun tried to back away, but the crowds behind them stopped their retreat.

'Who here, shall burn?' he shouted, and as his voice echoed from the buildings, his arms ignited, sending thrashing flames up and all about him.

The resulting ripple of fear that swept through the on-looking crowd acted like the ripples of a cast stone on the surface of a lake. After a brief delay from those behind the terrified people at the front, the whole crowd surge outwards from the burning wizard.

As the crowd spread out and away from the gatehouse, the heavy clatter of hooves on stone alerted everyone in the square to the arrival of eight heavily armoured knights riding muscular destriers. Colourful thick trappers covered the horses as the knights cantered up the street from the direction of the palace, the Duke of Adlestrop at their head atop a particularly richly caparisoned horse.

The added threat of the Duke and his retinue dispersed the crowd even faster, many dragging off the injured and dead they knew.

As the rapidly approaching riders looked upon the inferno that was Severun, the lances of those in front lowered as swiftly as the crowd departed, and with a roar, the first three – Rell of Adlestrop at their head – spurred their mounts on; powerful legs thrust the snorting beasts forward as their riders leaned into the attempted lance strike upon the blazing demon that had assaulted their city.

'Hold,' Morton ordered from the ramparts above. 'Hold, damn you!'

Adlestrop and his two knights couldn't possibly hear the order through their padded caps, maille coifs and great-helms as they charged.

The remaining knights formed up to turn their own lances on the elves at the gate.

'Hold, you bastards!' Morton shouted, waving his arms wildly. This was followed by a swift burst of motion from two horsemen below, as Nelem and Errwin-Roe sped swiftly across the cobbles towards the now dying fire that was Severun. As soon as they'd left the arch of the gatehouse, Fal, Sav and Starks followed on their own mounts, unsure as to what they were going to do, but not wanting to leave Severun or the elf lords on their own.

The *illusionary* flames all about Severun had all but gone when he turned upon the sound of rapidly approaching horses. Just as his eyes met the black steed, rich yellow livery, polished armour and deadly lance point of the Duke of Adlestrop, Severun felt the impact strike him. His feet left the ground and the air left his lungs as, along with the magical exhaustion and fear the inferno illusion had brought on, Severun lost consciousness. Lord Nelem had scooped Severun from the ground with his armoured arm and threw him over his saddle a mere heartbeat before the lance would have reached its mark.

Adlestrop rocked back in his tall saddle at the speed of the elven mounts. His lance missed the demon by a breath. He screwed his eyes up and braced himself, convinced he was going to collide with the riders crossing his path. As his destrier continued, Adlestrop opened his eyes and realised he'd somehow passed the riders unscathed. He heaved on his reigns with the hand of his shield arm and turned his steed swiftly, noticing through the slits of his great-helm two of his knights milling about back where he thought he'd surely connect with the elven riders. Their destriers were just settling as Adlestrop realised they'd pulled up at the last minute, and when he looked across to the gatehouse he realised why. A flush of anger welled within him.

Will Morton touched down lightly, his breaths coming quick and fast as the elf mage who'd magically lowered him to the ground smiled across at him. The row of knights who'd begun to charge the elves were turning circles, trying to calm their aggressive mounts as Morton glared at them all. None removed their great-helms as they finally settled, finding anything but the Lord High Constable's eyes to look at.

'What's the damned meaning of this, Yewdale?' Rell Adlestrop's voice sounded muffled but strong through his highly polished great-helm as he addressed his fellow Duke. Adlestrop's black destrier trotted proudly towards Morton, its yellow trapper bouncing and distorting the black bend and two black hounds' heads displayed there, which was clearly emblazoned on the yellow field of his surcoat and shield too.

'See to the injured,' Morton shouted, as he strode across from where he'd been placed down. He headed straight for Adlestrop. Several of the elves took the order well and ran over to the surviving guardsmen, dragging them back to their own clerics. Those that had survived were mainly battered and bruised, but many hadn't been so lucky and their bodies littered the square, along with those of a dozen or more civilians.

'Lord Adlestrop,' Morton said, followed by a curt nod as he stopped in front of the Duke. 'Or should I address you as Earl Marshall now?' Morton added with a poorly hidden smirk, referring to the man's latest title.

'Address me how you please, Yewdale, but I'd much rather address the fact the gate has been opened, against my *uncle* the King's own orders, and when I arrive to investigate I see a damned blazing demon in the square?' He planted his lance in its holster on the saddle, and lifted his great-helm free, revealing a smaller – equally as polished – open faced bascinet beneath. His maille coif was of an old tegulated design which was rarely seen in Altoln, but the face that looked upon Morton was far younger than was expected by many of the onlookers.

'That demon, Lord Adlestrop, is none other than Lord Severun, former Grand Master of the Wizards and Sorcery Guild, and you nearly ran him through.' Morton's hands rested firmly on his hips and he held his head high as he awaited an apology.

Several of Adlestrop's knights bristled, their helms turning towards the unconscious wizard, who'd been laid out on one of the elven carts.

'If I'd bloody well known that, I wouldn't have missed,' Adlestrop said, teeth bared.

'Enough!' Correia walked her horse forward. 'These carts need moving, now, before the crowds return. We've been through enough shit to get the elves here and they've been good enough to come, I'm not having them welcomed this way, Rell, you hear me?'

Fal, Sav and Starks, all three of who'd been somewhere in between the gatehouse and the spot where Severun had been picked up by the elves and nearly skewered by Adlestrop, now flanked the Spymaster as she addressed the suddenly embarrassed Duke.

'Spymaster Burr,' the young man stammered, 'I… I didn't notice you there.'

Someone's got an admirer, Fal thought, despite still trying to take in all that had happened.

'No, you were too busy charging in, trying to be a hero. Now, as has been said, we need to get these carts moving. The elves have come to *help* us, Rell, not invade us.'

Nodding quickly, Adlestrop's reddened face turned from Correia and glanced about to his knights, all of which were looking to him. 'As Spymaster Burr said, we need to move.'

'As I bloody well said too, if I recall, you jumped up shite,' Morton said under his breath, before turning to the elf lords, who couldn't help but smile at his comment. 'Follow the Earl Marshall, my lords, and he and his knights will guide you.' The elf lords bowed their heads and Morton saluted them, before stalking off towards the gatehouse's door to the ramparts. He failed, however, to avoid Correia's eyes as he passed her.

I know that look. That's not a good look, Correia thought, as she shouted for the column to hurry after the already departing knights; Lord Adlestrop at the head of the new column.

Falling in behind the heavily armoured retinue, every human and elf in the column gazed about at the surrounds and people – for many had already returned, this time looking on in silence at the elves passing through their city.

After traversing streets filled with black crossed doors and smouldering pyres, a handful of elves including Lord Errwin-Roe, accompanied by Correia, headed off towards the palace whilst the rest entered the heavily guarded and opening gates of Tyndurris.

The armed and armoured guards opening the gates looked grim, their faces dirty and strained. They perked up a little when they saw the elves, but it was clear it would take much more to lift their spirits after the death and destruction they'd witnessed.

'Sergeant Falchion, we thought you were dead?' one of the men at the gate said, his face lighting up a little more.

'Dead, Hale, why?'

'After the prison fight, Sarge,' Hale said, lifting his kettle-helm slightly to take in the healthy looking sergeant. 'The Castellan and his guards were killed in a fight with Samorlian witchunters, as were many of the inmates. You didn't know?'

'They assaulted this bloody tower,' another guard explained, before Fal could answer, 'through tunnels under Tyndurris itself!' He was surprised Fal didn't know. 'How come you're riding in with elves anyway, Sarge? That's pretty impressive in my book.'

'I'll explain another time, Sedge. Is everyone alright?' Fal was worried now.

'No, Sarge,' Sedge said, whilst Hale shook his head solemnly. 'A few of us didn't make it, some mages too.'

Fal shook his head, clearly stunned. He'd never heard of tunnels under Tyndurris. He reeled at the thought of what the Samorlian witchunters had done since the plague had set in. *How long have they been waiting to strike this very tower? It doesn't matter how long; to take advantage of this plague which has killed so many as it is, they were supposed to be our protectors as much as the City Guard and those knights, but they've been nothing but the enemy within. And after what I did, releasing this plague… am I any better?*

You were unwittingly involved Falchion, so yes, you are far better than they.

Fal jumped in his saddle and cast his eyes about, quickly noticing the gaze of the female elf mage, Feliscine, who'd accompanied them. She smiled sympathetically and then turned away, her long golden hair lifting slightly in the breeze.

A sudden calm despite all he'd seen since entering the city washed over Fal as he looked upon the elf mage. *I don't know if you'll hear this, Feliscine, but thank you.*

Hale and Sedge looked at each other in confusion, clearly unsure as to why their sergeant had just visibly jumped and then looked to one of the elves, although they both agreed she was incredibly attractive and certainly worth looking at.

The elven carts were still passing through the gates. They creaked as they rumbled across the courtyard to the stables on the far side of the courtyard, where more of the guild's men were guiding them.

Fal climbed down from the fine white elven steed he'd ridden back from Broadleaf Forest, and Sedge held the animal steady – not that it was required, the horse was well trained.

'Tell me about it all when I have announced the elves to the guild council,' he said to the two guards. 'Who's in charge at the moment?' Fal remembering that Severun was no longer the guild's Grand Master, nor was he permitted to enter Tyndurris, and so was currently en route to the palace with Correia and the elven lords.

'Lord Strickland is Grand Master now,' Sedge said, 'and Master Orix is inside, still working on the cure for the plague.'

'You have a cure?' Fal said, surprised. The two men nodded eagerly.

'It's in its basest form apparently; experimental, or something like that?' Hale said whilst closing the gate behind the last of the column. He offered a half-hearted shrug. 'Not ready for distribution anyhow. I guess the elves are here to help with that?'

'That's extremely positive,' one of the elf clerics who'd overheard the conversation said. 'The sooner we can see what they have, the sooner we can complete and assist in distributing it.'

Fal nodded his appreciation and asked Sedge to take his horse to the stable.

'Starks me old mukka,' Hale shouted, as he noticed the young crossbowman hopping off one of the elven horses. 'Where the heck have you been?'

Starks returned his friend's smile, albeit half-heartedly, his mind still clinging to Leiina and the knot in his stomach that hadn't left him since he'd left her. As well as that, upon seeing the destruction during their entry and journey through the city, his mind had also been on his family and whether or not any of them still lived.

'He'll tell you when he's rested,' Fal said, knowing the young man was in no mood to talk. 'Go get some sleep, Starks, and we can discuss everything tonight. I need to get inside with the elves, introduce them to Master Orix and leave them to get everything sorted.' Fal directed the latter to the gate guards as Starks disappeared quietly into the tower.

'Very well, Sarge,' Hale said. 'Speak to you later and glad to have you back.' He saluted and smiled to Fal, before heading across to his post, his companion leading Fal's horse away after a friendly salute of his own.

'Thanks, lads,' Fal shouted, as he made his way over to the elves. *Although*

I'm not sure if I'm glad to be back with Wesson in this state, I hardly recognise the place.

'This way, master cleric,' Fal said to the lead elf cleric, who followed both him and Sav into the tower, the other clerics and mages in tow. The remaining elves helped the stable hands tend to their horses and supplies, whilst the receding sound of heavy hooves on cobbles announced the departure of Lord Adlestrop's remaining knights.

***

Further south in the city, a short while later, Correia and a hooded, exhausted but conscious Severun led Errwin-Roe, Nelem, Errolas and two of their elven guards into King Barrison's Palace, as Lord Adlestrop and his knights moved on to the stables to dismount.

Adlestrop had attempted to engage Correia in conversation during the journey through the city. Alas, upon seeing the sadness in her face at the destruction and death all about them, he hadn't pressed her when she didn't answer.

Once within the palace, with its huge pillars of marble reaching high to hold up the impressive ceiling, Correia Burr, Spymaster of Altoln, swallowed hard as she heard the news awaiting them.

King Barrison had contracted the plague and it had taken its hold swiftly. The royal clerics had admitted they were unable to do anything but ease his swiftly approaching death.

'How did it find him in here?' Correia had demanded, unable to control her anger and confusion. *This is why Morton wouldn't talk or even look at me, coward.* 'And why isn't Master Orix here?' she had added, before the clerics could answer the first question.

They told her the King had insisted on walking the streets to offer comfort to those who were suffering, to tell them his finest clerics were working on a cure and help was on its way. No more than two days later he'd fallen ill and had been forcibly put to bed by Will Morton and two of his knights. The King was stubborn and insisted he should be able to take the throne in his court and hear the pleas of his people. He also wanted to visit Tyndurris after the Samorlian attack and offer his condolences for the mages and guards lost. Will Morton and Hugh Torquill had disagreed, however, and so there the King lay when Correia walked into his chamber. He looked incredibly old and weak to the Spymaster, as if all his years had caught up with him at once.

'My King?' Correia said quietly, to no response. Softer still, as she approached his side, she whispered, 'father?'

Barrison's eyes flickered and opened slowly, a wretched cough tearing from his cracked lips as he curled up in pain before looking up at his illegitimate daughter.

'Corrie?' he said with a gravely voice. 'You're back? Did—' he coughed violently, 'they come... the elves?'

'We did,' a smooth, melodic voice said from the doorway.

But you can't help him can you? Correia thought helplessly, not taking her eyes from her father. *That's what Morton was asking you at the gatehouse... he's too far gone.*

'Errwin?' Barrison smiled as he used Correia's arm to pull himself upright. She did her best to hide her horror at the state of her father; his bloodied fingers and the torn skin about his neck where he'd clearly been scratching at the numerous buboes infesting him.

'Hello, Barrison. I'm surprised you remember me, you were very young last time we met.'

'How could... I forget,' Barrison said, followed by a chuckle, a chuckle that turned swiftly into a spluttering cough. 'Back my child... you're not to come close, now back.'

Correia took a couple of steps back, her eyes glazing over as she did so.

Those eyes suddenly widened with hope. 'But father, the *caladrius*, why haven't you let it in here? I shall call it.'

'You have a caladrius?' Nelem said from the doorway, laughing in disbelief. 'I thought your coat-of-arms to be symbolic,' the elf added, referring to the King's well known caladrius emblazoned livery.

Correia looked to her feet as her father glared at her.

'They are rare indeed,' Errwin-Roe said. 'A bird of such pure soul they come second only to unicorns for sure.'

'A gift, a long time ago...' Barrison's eyes half closed before re-opening fully, a sudden burst of energy taking him as he looked upon Correia once more. 'A gift from the ruler of Sirreta at the time, when I was but a boy, but no, I shall not use the bird, that is why I have had it locked away from me, for I know it would either die to rid this plague from my body, or show me my death before I am ready to realise it.' He held his bloodied finger up to stop Correia's protest. 'That bird is best left for the young, for you dear, or your brother.'

Correia gasped. 'Edward has the plague?'

Barrison shook his head. 'No, he is aboard his ship, but if he were to contract it and I had used the caladrius—'

'But the elves are here now,' Correia interrupted. 'The end is in sight and Edward doesn't have the illness, you do. So use the damned bird, father, I beg you.'

Errwin-Roe stepped closer. 'Correia is right, King Barrison. There is more to this plague than we yet know. We don't believe it was created by your wizard here,' the elf lord said, gesturing to the hooded Severun who kept his eyes down, unable to look upon the King, 'but we do believe his spell carried it and I fear it was intentional.'

Barrison sighed heavily. 'We have begun to suspect the very same.'

'It may well have been used as a weapon,' the red haired elf lord continued, a look of disgust briefly flashing across his face. 'There are strange happenings afoot in your lands and ours. We need you as much as you need

461

us right now. There is increased troop movement to the south and yet we have received no messengers from Sirreta. Have you?'

Barrison shook his head, his mind slipping into thought. *No, Errwin, we haven't, but we* have *learnt of the Black Guild's plans for me. My daughter doesn't need to hear of that right now. I imagine all of this is enough for her as it is and I think the Black Guild will be too late anyway.*

'Father, the elves wish us to send a group to The Marches, maybe even into Sirreta, to investigate. We need you strong and on the throne, where you belong. The plague will be cured now, I am sure of it, but there is much rebuilding to be done and if this plague was indeed intentional, it could only be meant to weaken us.'

'But by whom?' Barrison's hand rose to scratch at his neck until he caught his daughter shaking her head. He lowered his hand and despite his best efforts, his eyes started to close.

Correia and Errwin-Roe glanced at each other, their eyes meeting but for a swift moment.

'There is something more we must discuss,' the elf lord said, looking back to the King. 'I need you fit so I can have it out with you about your use of black powder…'

Correia's second glance to the elf was filled with incredulity and anger, yet her father's eyes opened suddenly as he looked back to the red haired elf stood before him.

'It feels wrong to berate you while you lie in bed, so call the caladrius. It will hurt my heart to see the bird die, but you are needed, by far more than your citizens alone, and far more than you know.'

Barrison looked from the elf to Correia and back, another long sigh leaving his lips. *I am defeated by my father's old friend and my daughter.* 'Very well, Errwin, have my chamberlain call for the bird, it seems we have much to talk about, you and I.'

Correia moved back to her father's side, brushed the matted hair from his clammy forehead and smiled. 'Thank you, father, you're doing the right thing. I have something for you, for when you have recovered.'

'You are so thoughtful, my dear, always have been. Is it one of those local recipes you always manage to find for me?'

Correia laughed. 'Am I so predictable?'

***

Strong incense burnt in Tyndurris' guardroom, which seemed different somehow to Fal. It didn't take him long to realise the reason for the smell and bright, magically enhanced lights. *It's become a makeshift infirmary.*

Several bunks were occupied with guards and mages alike, all suffering from varying stages of the plague. Casting his eyes about the people in the room, Fal was drawn to a bed surrounded by guardsmen not of the guild. He recognised a couple of them as he approached, including the patient. Whilst looking on, the largest guardsman, who was sitting by his smaller companion's bed, looked up to Fal. The red haired man's eyes widened as he saw Fal watching them.

'Ye're back,' Sears said, hopefully.

Fal was confused. *No one knew we'd gone?*

'Are they here, the elves?'

Fal nodded. 'Aye, they came in with us not long ago—'

'We need them here, now!' Sears surged to his feet. 'Biviano's got nothing left, he's all but gone, where are they?'

Holding his hands out to calm the big man, Fal stepped forward. 'They're talking to Master Orix upstairs—'

'Flay that! Go get 'em, quick.' Sears became increasingly animated then, almost pacing besides the bed.

'Sears,' a cleric close by said, 'calm down. I shall go talk to them, but Master Orix has done all he can for everyone in here, to keep them as long as possible.'

'I know that, Effrin, but the elves, they can help.'

'I'll go talk to them, but only if you calm yourself,' Effrin said.

'He's right, big man, ye need to calm,' another guardsman said. He was stood by the bed closest to Fal. 'Ye been sat there since ye got here two days ago, ye need to rest—'

'Shut it, Bolly! Effrin, I'll calm down if ye get a move on.'

'Alright, I'll see what I can do,' the cleric said, before rushing from the room.

'You all look like you've been through The Three,' Fal said, motioning to the recently healed wounds on Bollingham and the poorly healing ones on Sears.

'He won't let them touch him; says he'll let them heal him when they heal Biviano.'

Sears glared at Bollingham, who shrugged back. 'It's the truth.'

'Not done him no good though has it.' Sears nodded to Biviano's still form, the man's neck, arms and face scratched raw.

'They're doing all they can,' Fal said, hoping to re-assure the big guy, although he knew little would do that. 'Did you guys assist in the tower's defence?' he asked, unsure as to why they were in the tower and not an infirmary.

Sears shook his head.

'Nope,' a flat voice said, startling Fal. He turned to see a dead pan expression on the man standing behind him and then looked down to see a drowsy looking bloodhound at the man's feet.

'Morl's balls, Gitsham. Where'd you two appear from?' Bollingham asked.

Gitsham shrugged. 'About.'

Bollingham shook his head and turned back to Fal. 'They were knocking about Dockside, fighting assassins and gangers, whilst us two,' Bollingham pointed to Biviano and then himself, 'were taking on the Samorlians at their cathedral.'

Fal filled his tattooed cheeks with air and let the breath out slowly.

'Aye,' Sears said, finally sitting back down besides Biviano, 'ye summed it up there, sergeant.'

'I'm still unsure as to how you knew I was coming in with the elves?'

The dog whined as it began wagging its tail.

'The dog,' Bollingham said.

Fal looked confused.

'I'm not explaining it more than that; not that I could if I wanted to,' Sears said, eyes not leaving Biviano. 'Wouldn't do owt to make it any clearer, sergeant, but aye, the dog; somehow it's always the dog and we owe him a lot for that.'

Buddle crawled under the bed and sat by Sears, resting his head on one of the big man's worn boots.

Shaking his head slowly with continued confusion, Fal turned finally to the sound of approaching voices.

Sears' head whipped round a moment after Buddle's, and Bollingham followed suit. Gitsham however, was now sleep standing, and failed to react to the sudden activity about the bed next to him.

Two elf clerics, the elf mage who'd somehow *spoke* in Fal's head in the courtyard, and Master Orix had appeared with the young cleric Effrin, before swiftly moving into the room and around Biviano.

Sears had willingly stood and backed away, followed by Buddle and Bollingham, all of which moved across to Fal to give the clerics and Feliscine room to work.

Biviano never stirred as those working on and around him talked quickly, using words none other present understood, apart from perhaps Buddle, who seemed to have perked up more than any of those who knew the hound had ever seen.

Gitsham remained asleep, standing, but asleep.

Several balms, ointments and unguents were brought forth and applied to Biviano's tender flesh, as well as a strange gas that moved around and finally into Biviano's nose and mouth.

Heads shook here and there and the clerics and Feliscine muttered to themselves and each other from time to time.

Sears didn't miss Effrin's worried glances his way, and after a good while that seemed to have only made Biviano look worse, the red bearded guardsman finally stepped forward, eyes locked on Effrin. 'What's going on Effrin?'

Fal felt the tension build and Buddle growled; the look of surprise on Feliscine's face when she turned to look at the bloodhound was unmistakeable. After a brief, stunned moment, she finally pulled her gaze from the animal and looked back to Biviano, ignoring Sears' question, as did the clerics, bar Effrin, who stepped away from the bed and walked round to Sears. Fal didn't miss the glance the cleric gave Bollingham.

'They're doing all they can to save him, Sears, but—'

'But what?'

Effrin looked nervous and Bollingham placed a hand on his sword, much to Fal's surprise.

What's going on here? Fal thought nervously.

Effrin continued carefully. 'He's close to the end, as you know, Sears. There's no cure yet formulated—'

'Then what the hell are they doing to him?' Sears' voice rose towards the end, and the elf clerics looked worriedly over their shoulders at him.

Swallowing hard and steeling a glance to Bollingham, who slowly stepped back out of Sears' eye-shot, Effrin continued. 'They're testing their possible cures on him.'

'He's not a bloody experiment!' Sears shouted, pushing Effrin to one side and stepping forward.

Fal winced briefly at the word, remembering the last experiment he was part of, before rushing forward, along with Bollingham, to grab Sears' thick arms and haul him back away from the working clerics, who, despite the sudden threat, calmly continued their work about Biviano.

Although they managed to pull him back slightly, Fal froze when a pair of burning red eyes turned on him. He flew through the air as Sears lashed out, the big man turning then on Bollingham, who released the arm he held a fraction before it swung around, attempting to fling him off. He ducked quickly, but received a knee to his chest which flipped him backwards and slid him across the stone floor.

Righting himself quickly, Fal drew his falchion and rushed in, waving it in front of Sears before dodging about him, egging him on.

Sears grabbed left and right, determined to take hold of the sergeant before he had a chance to use his falchion on him. Every time he thought he had the tattooed man however, he'd already moved.

Before anything else happened and despite Effrin's shouts for Sears to calm down and Buddle's sudden barking, the elf mage, Feliscine, stepped back and shouted in surprise.

Everyone stopped.

'What is it?' Orix looked across the bed at the elf mage from the stool he stood upon.

'I... I don't know,' Feliscine said, her head tilting as she looked at Biviano's still form.

'What have ye done to him?' Sears shouted, as Bollingham warily stalked back across the room towards the big man.

'Nothing and nor will we be if you don't control yourself,' Orix said, pointing a small finger at Sears. 'We need a workable cure from the experimental ones we have and your friend here is close to dead. We need try the ones we have and if we spend any more time discussing it then he's dead anyway. At least this way he has a chance.'

In that instant Sears' glowing eyes faded and his breathing calmed. He looked to Fal and Bollingham, his expression one of regret and shame.

Both men nodded there understanding, although Sears couldn't help notice Bollingham's laboured breathing.

Oh shit, I broke his ribs…

'He's…' Feliscine started.

'He's what?' one of the other elves said, looking to his companion and friend as her eyes scanned Biviano.

Feliscine shook her head. 'I'm not sure, but…' She reached over and pulled the nearest elf cleric towards her, whispering into his ear quickly.

The cleric's eyes widened and he nodded. 'Possibly,' he said, looking down to the still form lying on the bed. He reached out with a syringe and plunged it into Biviano's arm.

Sears stepped forward, but Orix held his hand up high and the big man stopped, face reddening.

'What is it?' Orix asked Feliscine.

'I can't say *what* or *who* he is, but from what I've felt when I try to contact him… he has great resolve, both mentally and… I don't quite know… his soul?' She looked at Buddle then, who barked once, tail wagging.

'Let's see then shall we,' the elf cleric said, after taking a sample of Biviano's blood. 'The potion you hold,' he added, motioning suddenly to Sears, 'let's have it.'

'I tried this and it didn't work,' Sears said, taking the small flask from his belt, confused as to how the elf cleric knew he had it.

'We can tell one has been used on him already, recently and several times, was it that one?' the other elf cleric asked.

Sears nodded. *But how could ye know?*

'Where's it from?' the same elf said.

Sears shook his head. 'I don't remember. I truly don't. I've had it years, it refills itself.'

Fal looked to Bollingham who nodded and shrugged at the same time, seemingly to confirm the story.

The elf held out his hand and Sears passed it to him. 'Like I said, I tried it.'

Removing the stopper from the flask and sniffing it, the cleric's eyes widened, before passing it to the cleric with the needle. 'It's ancient, but powerful, much more powerful than I've ever smelt.'

'Try tasting it if ye think it smells bad,' Sears said, scrunching up his nose.

The elf with the needle looked to his companions, all of which, including Master Orix, nodded. With a nod himself, he plunged the needle into the flask and deposited a drop of Biviano's blood.

'What are you hoping for from this? A cure?' Effrin asked, as confused as the rest.

'We shall soon see,' Feliscine said, winking at the human cleric. She placed her hand on the potion and blood mix and closed her eyes tight. The air in the room grew thick with static and the tips of the mage's golden hair danced lightly as she hummed gently to herself. The pleasant sound continued, as did the pressure in the room. Buddle's tail wagged harder than ever and almost everyone in the room's ears popped suddenly as the mage stopped humming. Her beautiful eyes opened and she nodded to the cleric who'd taken the blood, before removing her trembling hand.

The flask was shaken thoroughly then, before being added to a larger container and its contents brought in by the clerics and mage. With a quick stir of the now mixed potion by Master Orix, a long handled silver spoon was dipped into the viscous liquid by one of the elf clerics and gently brought to Biviano's lips. Without any help from anyone, Biviano opened his mouth and the liquid was poured in.

He swallowed, Fal thought hopefully.

Sears pressed his hands to his bearded cheeks and rocked slightly back and forward, as all in the immediate vicinity held their breaths.

After several moments, the first breath to be released, heavily, was Biviano's as his eyes slowly began to open and his skin immediately began to improve.

'By the gods,' Master Orix whispered, before shouting out with joy, 'we've got a cure!'

A cheer erupted from those present then as Biviano's eyes finally opened fully, taking in the angelic features of the elves looking down on him. Despite the beauty of the female elf by his side, Biviano couldn't help but settle on the red bearded face of the man who appeared next to her.

'Sears,' he managed slowly and quietly.

All fell silent as Sears leaned closer to hear his friend speak.

'Ye're a dick, ye know that?'

The elves' eyes widened as Sears stood straight and roared with laughter, followed by Fal, Bollingham and Effrin.

The laughter continuing as the elf clerics rushed about the room with the gnome, administering the cure to the other patients there, the large container already replenishing itself as they'd hoped it would after adding the bearded guardsman's ancient potion.

After several tense moments passed, it became clear to all that the potion they'd created didn't hold all the answers.

'None of them are responding?' one of the elf clerics said, clearly confused.

'I don't understand?' Orix shook his head slowly. 'It worked on the guardsman over there?'

With a heavy sigh, the elf cleric who'd taken Biviano's blood placed a delicate hand on Orix's shoulder. 'Clearly we have more work to do, Master Orix, as much as it pains me to admit.'

Orix was nodding before the elf finished and he finally agreed, knowing many more would die with every moment wasted. 'We should take blood samples of all of these patients then and repair to the clerics' chamber.'

Solemnly nodding their agreement, the elves set about alongside the old gnome. They swiftly took samples and resigned themselves to the fact that some if not all of those around them would surely pass before a true cure was created using what they'd already discovered.

Across the room, Biviano had fallen asleep once more, a peaceful look upon his face as Sears finally allowed Effrin to tend to his wounds.

Fal's stomach churned and bile rose in his throat as he looked about the faces of the clerics. *We thought we had it, so swiftly, so simply. Gods below, how long will it take them to find an answer to all of this?* Rubbing the weariness from his face, Fal moved across to Master Orix, offering his services to the cleric, although he didn't know how he could help.

Bollingham assisted Effrin with Sears, none of them paying any attention to the elf mage, who'd drifted to the side of the room, her eyes locked on Biviano.

Who or what is he? Feliscine asked.

I don't know. I have my suspicions, but I can't be sure, Gitsham replied. His eyes remained closed as he stood in the middle of the room, multiple clerics moving around him to various beds and their suffering occupants.

Nor can I, Feliscine thought. *Thank you though,* she added sincerely, *for pointing out the big man's potion. It would have taken us a long time to produce enough of a cure to go around without it, and many, many more in this city would have been lost.*

I'm glad I could help, Gitsham replied, whilst remaining motionless. *Although it seems we're yet to find that cure?*

No, but we have the means to distribute one now. And we do have the guardsman's blood and the combined knowledge of all who are here, so I'm sure it won't be long until we have a cure.

I can feel that you sincerely believe that, and that warms my heart.

Feliscine nodded subtly, despite the pain she felt as she cast her eyes about the room at the few souls already slipping away from their broken bodies.

They're both intriguing, these two, she thought finally, looking back to the closest bed. *It's rare indeed to find such beings, and rarer still to find them together.* She smiled warmly as her eyes moved from the recovering Biviano to briefly stop on Sears, before settling finally on Buddle. *Mind you, friend, you're quite extraordinary yourself.*

The bloodhound's tail wagged so vigorously his back end shook from side to side where he sat; looking up at the beautiful elf he'd just spoken to. *It's nice of you to say so, Feliscine, and even nicer that you noticed!*

The elf mage winked at Buddle, before moving to assist her companions.

With a departing slap to the back from a wincing Bollingham, who thought it was time he got out of everyone's way, Gitsham was startled awake. 'What did I miss?' the dog handler said flatly, genuinely; completely confused.

Buddle turned a full circle at that moment, dropped to the floor, yawned and fell asleep.

***

A proud peacock-sized bird of the purest white, with a similarly long and beautiful tail, walked slowly into the King's bed chamber. It cocked its head sideways as it saw the King, and then hopped, surprisingly delicately for its size, onto the end of the grand bed where the sick man sat up, looking into the bird's eyes.

'I'm sorry it has come to this, my old friend,' Barrison said gently, as the bird slowly padded up the large bed to stand directly in front of him. Correia had opened the beautiful, tall stained-glass windows and a strong breeze blew in, a hint of smoke detectable from the pyres burning throughout the city. The caladrius' feathers ruffled slightly as the window opened, as did Barrison's hair.

The elegant bird cocked its head again and leaned forward, its neck extending further than it looked possible, until Barrison looked almost cross-eyed into the bird's bright blue eyes.

The King looked sleepy then and his eyes drooped as the bird pulled its head back, releasing a beautiful yet mournful cry. It turned swiftly, leapt from the bed and unfolded its angelic wings to soar effortlessly out of the window and across the city. It beat those wings once, twice and then up, up it went into the clouds above. Its call slowly faded as it vanished into the thick, grey clouds that suddenly unleashed a torrent of cold rain.

After a moment's silence in the room, with nothing but the sound of torrential rain outside and the heavy beat of her heart, Correia spoke. 'What now?' she asked simply, her voice little more than a whisper as she stared at her father.

Barrison's eyes had closed.

'It will continue high into the sky, higher than it or any other bird can go,' Errwin-Roe explained sadly.

'Higher than it can go?' she asked, confused.

The elf lord nodded. 'Until it burns up in the atmosphere of this world, along with the sickness it has drawn from your father.'

A sickness I caused. Severun finally looked upon the deathly form of his King.

Correia's eyes suddenly widened and she moved to her father's side. His cheeks had flushed and his eyes ran with tears, but all signs of the plague had vanished.

My eyes never left him, Correia thought, gripping his hand tightly, *yet I cannot recall* seeing *the plague leave him?*

'I feel ten years younger,' Barrison said, his glazed eyes opening as he turned them upon his daughter. His voice was shaky, but grew stronger as he continued. 'Yet there is a part of me missing; a sadness I feel will never pass.'

'The caladrius will never leave your heart then, or your memories. That is a good thing King Barrison, a good thing indeed.' Errwin-Roe turned and left the room, a tear rolling down his cheek.

***

Three wrecks lined the opening of Wesson's walled harbour, nothing more than masts and the tips of fore and aft-castles breaking the rippling waters. Citizens and sailors alike were talking about thunder with no lightning just off the coast on the nights the ships had made a break for open water, yet no one linked it with the actual destruction of the vessels. Even when a large ship was occasionally spotted out to sea – a ship much larger than any normally seen in the King's fleet – there were no rumours it was that ship that was responsible for the thunderous sounds or the three wrecks.

Lord Errwin-Roe made his argument to King Barrison, once the King had been bathed, fed and was ready. The two fought verbally over the use of black powder, although the elf could not deny its effectiveness against the ships that had tried to break the quarantine. A warning was given by the elf lord and heeded by the King, but the subject was left largely unresolved as the conversation turned to more pressing matters.

Whilst the King and his advisors spoke to the elf lord and his advisors about what the continuing plague and all that had followed meant for both Altoln and its neighbours, mages and clerics from Tyndurris, as well as their elf counterparts, worked with a myriad of concoctions and potions; trying to work out how their combined ingredients had worked on one man, but no other.

A flash of emerald and a burst of static that lifted the hairs of everyone present filled the clerics' chamber of Tyndurris.

'Any luck?' Orix asked. Dark bags hung under his eyes and his stomach growled for food as he stood on a stool next to Feliscine, eagerly awaiting a hopeful answer.

She turned to him with a tight smile, but shook her head. 'Not this time, Master Orix.'

Sighing hard and rubbing at his face, the old gnome nodded. 'It was worth a try,' he said through his hands.

'We'll keep on until we have something,' she said to him, encouragingly.

'I know, and we're forever in your debt because of it.' He lowered his hands and managed a weak smile up at the beautiful elf.

'There's no debt owed here,' one of the elf clerics across the room said, and Feliscine nodded her agreement.

'Well then,' Orix said, stretching his arms out to the side, 'let us continue. Falchion?'

'Yes, Master Orix?' Fal walked across from the doorway where he'd been standing watching the occasional flashes of magic and plumes of coloured smoke.

'How fares the guardsman, Biviano?'

Fal nodded. 'Very well, actually. You'd hardly think he'd been sick at all. The other patients however…'

Orix nodded and Fal could see the weight of it all wearing the gnome down.

'Is there anything you need me to do, to help?'

'No, thank you, Falchion, but knowing you're there should we need you is more of a help than you realise.'

Fal nodded to Orix and bowed low to Feliscine, who smiled in return, before he moved back to the doorway.

Another colourful flash of magic lit the chamber, followed by a hollow pop that rang through Fal's ears as he turned back to face the room. *Please let whatever that one was work,* he thought, before seeing the human magician who'd enacted the spell shake his head regrettably.

Chapter 46: Distribution

A whole week had passed since the elves had arrived in Wesson. In that time, it was said over three hundred more bodies had been burnt on the continuing pyres about the city, and that was just the ones declared or found. Many more, it was thought, would be locked up behind black crossed doors.

And so it was, with an immense sense of relief, that on a clear spring day, Fal, Sav; Starks, Errolas and the other elven warriors, along with Lord Adlestrop and knights of his and the King's own retinue, escorted elven and human clerics through the streets of Wesson.

They eagerly began distributing potions from six large carts, all laden with the plague's cure; discovered the day before by altering not the combined potions that saved Biviano's life, as they'd been attempting to do since his recovery, but by removing and replacing his blood from that original potion.

It was discovered Biviano's blood itself, along with a little help from Sears' potion and one of the elves' own, had in fact destroyed the bacteria infecting his system. It was also discovered, however, that the potion containing Biviano's blood – that hadn't had the required effects on other patients – wasn't strong enough to work outside of his own body, or rather away from his own immensely strong soul, as one of the guild sorcerers had put it.

The breakthrough came from that discovery, when an elderly female wizard named Yanosh, along with Feliscine, managed to magically re-create the effects of Biviano's own blood and enhance it further, thus destroying the plague's bacteria in any subject. This allowed the remainder of the original potion – which included Sears' own from his flask – to assist patients' own immune systems in a rapid recovery.

The whole guild, along with the elven clerics and mages, had worked throughout the night to perfect and test the new cure on several patients in the guild – unfortunately none of them the original men and women that had shared the room with Biviano – so it could be distributed as swiftly as possible across the city the following day, without any further problems or failures.

After a week that had felt like an eternity, it was clear to all in the guild, if not all in Wesson, that without the aid of the elves and their ancient knowledge of magic and healing, the process of developing a workable cure for everyone could have taken months if not years.

People flocked to the main squares as the carts rolled in. The bodies piled high on the pyres at the centre of the squares increased still, as more of the dead were thrown on by city guardsmen, men-at-arms from the palace, as well as those from several volunteering guilds and noble families, all of which had been affected in some way by the plague.

Some soldiers wore elongated, beak like plague masks, which were thought to keep the plague away from the wearer's nose, despite the plague not being pneumonic. Alas, those masks did more in the way of scaring the sick populace further still, rather than anything else.

As the people gathered in large numbers, knights and more soldiers from various organisations and households controlled the crowds as best they could, so the potion could be distributed as evenly and safely as possible.

Any disturbances were swiftly and aggressively suppressed by the soldiers, knowing it to be the most effective way of preventing further riots through recent and grim experience.

General healing spells were also released over the crowds by a large group of human mages, using spells including those brought by the elves. They knew it would take days, but it was a start, and a relief to know the plague would finally be beaten back.

Despite the discovery of a cure, the city was still held under strict quarantine by King Barrison, and would remain that way until both the elves and human clerics agreed it was safe to open the gates.

Morri smiled as he administered the cure to a young child with buboes marring her neck and face. Tear streaked dirt smeared her raw cheeks, yet she beamed up at the cleric after he poured the sour liquid down her throat.

The sorceress, Cullane, crouched next to Morri and placed her hand on his shoulder as she looked out over the lines of people. 'It's all going to be alright,' she whispered, for him alone to hear.

'I hope so, Cullane, I really do.' *I just wish I could've saved Midrel.* Taking a deep breath, Morri administered the cure to the next in line and smiled at the nod of appreciation he received.

Orix rode on one of the carts along with Elloise. They distributed and administered the cure to citizens whilst under the protective gaze of Fal. The gnome hadn't received any serious injuries in the attack on Tyndurris, but others had lost their lives and for that, both King Barrison and Lord Yewdale were furious. They swore the Grand Inquisitor and his order would answer for their crimes, and had put up posters pardoning Orix and releasing him from his house arrest, much to his surprise and gratitude.

And quite right too, Fal thought, looking to a nearby post displaying one of the pardons, and knowing, as he did, the genuine heart of the old gnome in front of him.

Accepting the plague would be cured and the citizens could start rebuilding their lives had allowed Orix to at least find a little comfort in his participation in creating the cure they were now distributing. It would take a lot of hard work, he knew, but it gave him – gave them all – more than a little hope for the future of Wesson. He did his best not to think about where the plague had originated, for that wasn't for him to worry about. He knew his duties and that was what he would concentrate on. *There are far better people than me to work out that mystery, and far better still to deal with the answers that are revealed.*

***

Longoss pressed his broad shoulders against the underside of the cold stone slab. Clenching his golden teeth, the big man groaned and heaved, pressing with his legs to lift the piece up, before managing to bring his hands up enough to shift the weight bit by bit to the side. He finally managed to rest it back down and slide it – with the dull scrape of stone on stone – to one side, creating enough room to pull himself up and into the cellar above.

Before the former assassin could turn and offer his hand, the green hair of Coppin appeared from the darkness below, and the woman nimbly followed Longoss into the smoky, lamp lit room.

'Ye're sure he'll not mind?' Coppin asked, whilst brushing herself down.

Oh, how ye've changed in such a short time, lass. Longoss admired how she took everything in her stride; unfazed by spider webs, rats or the continuous flight through Dockside's underground. The two of them had even managed to reach the administering of the plague cure after they'd both developed buboes, and all without being caught by the gangers pursuing them. *And all without any complaints from you.*

'No, he'll help us, lass, I'm sure of it.' *Well, pretty sure…*

Longoss looked about the room. His stomach churned and growled as he saw salted meat hanging from hooks, and barrels of ale and wine stacked opposite. Mouth beginning to water, he licked his lips before noisily sliding the square stone back into place. The resulting bang of the slab dropping back down lifted a cloud of dust which caused Coppin to cough, followed by a wooden creak outside the door at the top of the stone steps that ran along one side of the cellar.

'Well, we'll soon find out anyway,' Longoss said, eyeing the door whilst blinking away the dust. He rose to his feet and pulled Coppin behind him, missing the smile she gave at his act of protection.

The old oak cellar door, which had multiple iron studs and bars holding it together, suddenly swung inwards, revealing a large, greying man holding a well kept crossbow. The weapon pointed down into the cellar. Upon seeing Longoss and his companion – for Coppin was peering around her protector's shoulder – the man with the crossbow looked confused for a heartbeat, before taking a deep breath and releasing it long and slow.

'Do I even want to know, Longoss?'

Gold teeth showed and the two men laughed.

'I'm not sure ye will, Keep, but I'll be telling ye anyway.'

'Aye lad, I expect ye will, but first,' the innkeeper said, whilst removing the bolt from his crossbow and relaxing the string, 'introduce me to yer lovely friend there.'

Coppin, feeling Longoss' posture fully relax for the first time since she'd met him, stepped out from behind the big man and waved awkwardly. 'I'm Coppin,' she said sweetly, despite her heart racing at the thought of trusting anyone other than the man stood next to her.

'Well, lass, it's a pleasure to make yer acquaintance for sure. Now get yerselves up here so I can throw some food and drink down yer throats. Ye both look like ye've taken on The Three and survived, although Longoss has clearly come off the worse. Ha! I never thought that face could get uglier.'

Coppin didn't know who 'The Three' were, but after all her and Longoss had been through, she was quite sure she would never want to find out. She looked to Longoss, who hesitated after a bark of laughter at the man's insult.

'Is it clear?' Longoss said in all seriousness, nodding upwards.

'Of who? Patrons?' Keep asked.

'Of the guild?'

Coppin didn't miss the look on the innkeeper's face before his swift recovery at Longoss' question.

'Aye, I think so, boy.'

Boy? Coppin thought, suppressing a smile. *He's hardly that.*

'I don't need think so, Keep, I need know so. So how's about we stop down here for now, if that's alright by you?'

Rubbing the bridge of his nose and sighing hard, the innkeeper nodded. 'Alright, let me square stuff away up here, then I'll be down and ye can tell me what's going on, because the rumours I've been hearing have scared the living daylights out of me, Longoss, they really have.'

Longoss' eyes narrowed ever so slightly. *Square what away? Perhaps I should've left the stone off the hole...*

'And help yer selves to what ye need down there,' Keep added, addressing Coppin, 'any friend of the boy there, is a friend of mine.' With what Coppin was sure was a sincere smile, the innkeeper turned and left, closing the door as he went and locking it, from the sound, behind him.

Coppin turned to Longoss, who'd regained some of his tension; she could almost *feel* it even though they stood apart. A little bile rose in her throat and she swallowed it down, holding her expression neutral as Longoss looked her way.

'Who is he, this man who calls ye *boy*?'

'He trained me,' Longoss said, smiling without the gold.

Coppin's stomach lurched. 'He's Black Guild?' she said, not even attempting to hide the shock.

'No, lass, he *was*. He retired long ago, which is a rare thing I might add.' Longoss moved across to a barrel, held a clay pot he found under it and pulled the cork. He took in the familiar scent as the dark liquid sloshed into the pot. Replacing the cork quickly, he lifted the pot to his mouth and drew in another deep breath through his flat nose before downing the contents in one.

'And ye trust him, fully?' Coppin hadn't moved, except to place her hands on her hips as she stared at Longoss' back.

'Eh?'

'You trust him?' she said again, this time louder.

''Course I do.' Longoss repeated the process at the barrel, but turned to offer her the second pot of ale. He rocked back ever so slightly when he saw her stance and expression.

'We've not known each other long, Longoss, but after what we've been through… together, I thought I deserved the truth from ye, and I think I deserve yer trust.'

With a tight smile, Longoss placed the pot down on the side and walked across to the green haired girl in front of him. He nodded once and took up her hands in his. 'Ye do deserve it lass, and ye *do* have it.'

'Then be honest with me, always,' she said, looking up into his eyes, *because I trust ye with all I have.*

Longoss nodded again. 'Keep trained me in the guild. He was my mentor, but unofficial like. He took me under his wing, not because he had to, but because he said he saw himself in me and he wanted to keep a little of the old honour he once knew and restore it in me. It was that man who drilled into me the importance of me word. I trust him as much as I could anyone, Coppin, but that doesn't mean I trust him with yer life, because apart from you, there's no one I trust that much.'

Coppin felt her eyes moisten and she pulled Longoss in close, wrapping her arms around his waist and pressing her face against his linen covered chest. His thick arms wrapped around her as he rocked her gently from side to side.

'I gave Elleth me word, to save ye, and although I failed to save her, I won't fail you in anything ye ask of me. I give ye me word on that.'

'I know,' Coppin whispered, before turning her head so he could hear and repeating it for him a little louder. *And I've never felt safer.* She pulled out from his embrace and looked back up at him, a thought coming to mind.

'What of the guild? Will he help us attack them?'

'I need to admit to myself we can't attack them outright,' Longoss said, although he clearly found it hard to say out loud. 'Sears was right there and Keep will only tell us the same. We can, however, disrupt them and I'm hoping he'll help us. If we can cause enough trouble, combined with the Constable of Wesson and his peers knowing of the mark on the King.' *If Sears made it that is. By the gods, I hope he did,* 'then hopefully we can scupper their plans enough to drive them into the ground and destroy them that way.'

Coppin nodded. 'I'm glad ye've come to that conclusion, finally.'

'And ye agree?'

'Aye, Longoss, I agree. I want to make them suffer as much as you do, for Elleth, but there's no sense in throwing our lives away needlessly in the process.' *And I want no more street fighting and killing, not unless it's necessary.*

'Then we shall continue yer training, with Keep's help.' *For I know ye well enough now lass, to know ye won't settle for anything else.*

'Who was she?'

Longoss' confusion to the sudden question was clear. He looked down at Coppin and frowned. 'Who's who?'

'The one ye trained, yer old apprentice, since ye're feeling all truthful with me?' She smiled sweetly and he laughed.

'What does her name matter? It was years ago and I don't see why it's relevant.'

'Was it Leese?'

Longoss laughed again and shook his head. 'No.'

'It's relevant because she's Black Guild and I need to know all I can.'

'She's not Black Guild.'

'She's not?'

Longoss shook his head.

'Ye didn't train her for the Black Guild?'

'No.'

'Then who?'

Longoss paused for a while before answering. 'The King.'

Coppin's eyes widened and she pulled her head back slightly before replying. 'King Barrison? Honestly?'

'Yes, lass, I'm being honest. That's the point of this isn't it?'

'But,' Copping said, hesitating and looking about the cellar for a moment, as if her questions would be answered that way, 'why were ye training her for the King?' She looked back to him for the answer.

'Because he was told I was the best at what I did.'

Coppin nodded, knowing that made sense. 'You are.'

'Were.'

'Are!'

'I might have been, some might've said. Until her…'

'She bested ye?' Coppin looked unconvinced.

'She never *did*, but she could.'

'I don't believe it,' Coppin said, shaking her head.

'Leese nearly did, and she's not a patch on her.'

'*She* didn't take ye on one-on-one; ye'd been fighting and running continuously for Samorl knows how long. Anyway, ye had me, so there's no bother there.'

Longoss laughed. 'Yes, I did, didn't I?'

Coppin blushed slightly and then continued, albeit hesitantly. 'Could I be better?'

'Than Leese?'

She was shaking her head as he spoke. 'Than *her*?'

Longoss gave the most sincere smile she'd seen yet. 'Ye know what, lass, I think ye could.' *And I bloody well mean it too.*

I'm not sure I'm ready for that answer. Coppin's head spun. *I don't want to kill anyone else. We've hardly stopped running since this all began and in truth, I'm afraid to. I'm scared all the faces I've killed will return to haunt me; I've heard that happens… but if it meant being able to protect myself from anyone, being able to protect Longoss…*

'What's her name?'

Longoss looked up and sighed hard. 'I still don't see why ye need it? Why it matters?'

'It matters to me. To know there's someone out there who ye trained, like ye've been training me… damn Longoss, because *you* matter to me and I want to know you.'

He looked long and hard at the woman in front of him and he couldn't deny the flutter in his belly and the skip of his heart as she smiled up at him. *Only one other has melted me with a smile like that... and that was such a short time ago. Am I such a monster that I could feel this way again so soon?*

'She loved us both, Longoss. In her short time with us,' Coppin said, 'Elleth loved us both, as we did her.' She smiled again at the look on his face and couldn't help the tear that rolled down her cheek.

Longoss' face flushed and despite himself, he felt tears of his own. He'd never felt so vulnerable, so open, even with Elleth, and yet he'd never felt so safe. He would give Coppin everything he had, he knew that at that moment. *Watch over us Elleth, wherever ye are, and I give ye me word once again, I will stand alongside yer sister for as long as she allows.*

'Correia Burr,' Longoss said eventually.

'What?'

'The woman I trained – her name is Correia Burr.'

***

After more meetings between King Barrison and the elves, contingents of soldiers were ordered to patrol Dockside to dissolve any further riots by the various gangs ever present there, thus allowing the continued distribution of the cure throughout the lower district.

Whilst that happened, the King's navy, along with the Wizards and Sorcery Guild and the Guild of Engineers, started working on ways to move the wrecks from the harbour.

It had raged for just a handful of weeks, yet the Great Plague of Wesson had claimed over a third of the city's population from both its own grasp and that of the chaos it brought along with it. Many buildings had been destroyed by riots, looters and fire, and the Lord High Treasurer knew that to rebuild what had been lost, the King would have to raise far more funds than he currently had available. On top of that, the King and his lords, along with the elves, were now sure the plague had been unleashed on Wesson intentionally.

There were more questions than answers regarding the plague now, and both the elves and King Barrison swore they would do all they could to find those answers together. They wanted to know who and where the plague had come from, and more importantly, why. And since Severun seemed to be losing the memories of the arcane spell he'd enacted, they knew finding answers to those questions would take time; something both parties believed they were short of.

Barrison now needed to raise funds, and fast. He sent petitions for aid to the dukes and earls of Altoln, but he also had what he now believed to be enemies within, and if not enemies, then hindrances at the very least, although the Black Guild could hardly be classed as the latter. Archbishop Corlen, however, could, and so he was dismissed from his position as advisor to the King. It was also announced that the Samorlian Church was no longer recognised as a national religion. It was not banished or ordered to disassemble, but it would no longer have any voice in court, nor any jurisdiction in the kingdom; its order of witchunters were ordered to stand down and disband.

City guardsmen had remained on the doors of the Samorlian Cathedral, and Bagnall Stowold ordered to remain there with his own men until further notice by Will Morton, thus deterring any return by a witchunter backed Grand Inquisitor, who was still at large in the city, despite the joint efforts of the various lords of Wesson to have him apprehended.

Fal was pleased to hear the news about the Grand Inquisitor and his witchunters' official disbandment a few days later. As was Sav, who decided it was finally time for a drink to celebrate their successful mission. Fal had declined at first, his mind and heart torn between the horrors his actions had released on Wesson and the wonders their mission had led them to witness. Despite it having been the worst time any of them could have imagined; living through pain, suffering and hardships, they'd found new friends and a new family of sorts. And so, when Sav insisted upon that drink, Fal finally agreed, knowing the scout well enough to realise he wouldn't let it go, for which Fal allowed himself a genuine smile.

The final remnants of the plague had finally been brought under control and the city's gates opened to trade once more, although none was expected for some time, for much of the city was still in ruin and the fear of the plague still strong in the minds of the surrounding areas. The riots and fires had gutted whole sections of even the most wealthy of districts, and many inns and taverns had been used as makeshift infirmaries. The Coach and Cart Inn, however, as seen by the group as they'd entered the city with the elves, was no more. In front of the old inn now stood a large canvas marquee where a makeshift welcoming tavern had been prepared for any who dared enter the re-opened gates of Wesson. It was here the group of friends now sat.

Fal felt humbled by the whole experience. He'd seen things he never thought he would, made new friends he knew he would cherish for years to come, and had come to realise that, although he loved Wesson dearly and thought of the grand city as his home, he wouldn't be satisfied any longer unless he was travelling and exploring a world full of wonders.

His stomach churned; there was more to it than that.

I cannot sit back and continue as if nothing has happened; look daily upon faces in a guardroom and give them orders knowing my actions caused the deaths of their friends and in some cases, families…

He thought hard about Franks Heywood again. Upon returning to the city, Fal had attempted to visit Franks' family, only to discover they too had fallen to the plague. That had struck Fal harder than almost anything else, but good news followed bad, and it pleased him to know Starks' family had survived. The young guard had spent a lot of time with them since his return, but his place was, in his own words, by Fal's side, wherever that may lead. *And I'm glad of that, for something is coming, I can feel it. The Lord High Constable may not wish to tell us yet, but I'll be flayed if I'm sitting by and waiting for whatever it is to happen.*

Fal looked around at his friends and wondered where their thoughts took them. They didn't have the horror Wesson had been through weighing on their shoulders, but Fal hoped wherever he went, they would all be by his side.

If nothing else, I shall go to Beresford, for that town needs help removing their new residents, and I hear Lord Adlestrop's father is riding back to attempt to relieve his town with what little men he has left after the plague. They'll certainly need all the help they can get.

It had been reported the goblins and hobyah that had assaulted the river straddling town, despite losing their strange red-skinned chieftain, were still embedded on the west bank. The massively reduced forces of Wesson were unable to send extra men with the Earl of Beresford to re-take his town, whilst similar incursions throughout the north of Altoln were tying up border forces and village militias, causing many lords to look to the defence of their own lands, keeps and villages.

I have to look forward now, but not forget. Put what has passed behind me and concentrate on the future. We were successful in our mission and we assisted in bringing about an end to the plague. Whoever planned this, I hope you know that you failed. Wesson is still here, Altoln is still here and whilst there are people like those beside me, you will not prevail.

He smiled tightly to himself and took his tankard of ale in hand, to propose a toast to the end of the plague, knowing his friends deserved it for all they'd done.

Alas, before the much anticipated ale began to flow, the flap of the makeshift tavern was thrown aside. A hard-faced, black haired women with a rough looking soldier wearing black, hard leather armour and a dark green gambeson strode into the canvas covered space, plunging the few patrons there into a stony silence.

'Sergeant Falchion,' the women said, hands resting on the two sheathed swords hanging from her belt.

Fal stood up and nodded once.

'You and your companions are to come with us, no questions... and hurry.'

Fal looked to Starks and Errolas, and Sav, who sighed heavily and slammed down his full tankard of ale. Without another word, the four of them followed Correia and Gleave from the makeshift tavern and out into the dark city beyond.

Epilogue

The dark gardens of Wesson's Park District smelt wonderfully fresh to the large man who walked slowly down the winding, moonlit path surrounded by heavily shadowed bushes and trees. The pleasant sound of running water close by and the hoot of a little-owl in the trees not too far away only enhanced the perfect evening. The smell of the pyres still clung to most of Wesson, but not here, not now at least, and the walk was proving a brief but well needed reprieve following the squalor the man had been forced to endure since his flight from the Samorlian Cathedral.

The Grand Inquisitor fingered the jewelled rings on his fat fingers as his companion babbled on besides him about the injustice shown by King Barrison. The Grand Inquisitor grunted his agreement, avoiding the plants at the side of the path so as not to soil his richly adorned robes.

I thought he said he'd been 'slumming' it whilst in hiding? Corlen thought, finally taking note of the Grand Inquisitor's spotless attire. *He's probably in a large house in Park District, just not as large as usual. Samorl forgive me, I shouldn't think that way.* Despite the chilled night air, the Archbishop used the handkerchief clutched in his left hand to dab at the sweat beading his brow, before making the sign of Sir Samorl's Lance in the air with his right hand. His thoughts swiftly returned to the dire situation the church had found itself in. *I must know what the Grand Inquisitor plans to do.*

Stopping suddenly, the Grand Inquisitor squinted into the darkness ahead as the Archbishop began to ask a question. He grabbed Corlen's arm to silence him and the man jumped, looking to the Grand Inquisitor before facing forward.

'What is it? I don't see anything,' the Archbishop said, his voice quivering slightly despite seeing no threat.

'Shhh…' The Grand Inquisitor took a couple of steps forward and drew a sharp rondel dagger from his belt. Palms damp and heart quickening, he squeezed the wooden handle of the dagger tight and set his jaw firm.

A figure shrouded in a black hooded cloak emerged from the darkness ahead and moved slowly, silently towards them. The figure's features were hidden under the heavy hood, but two piercing orbs of sapphire began to glow by his side, drawing the eyes of the two men opposite. The Archbishop backed away slightly but the Grand Inquisitor puffed out his broad chest and snapped at the figure.

'Be gone, scoundrel. You will find nothing but pain here.'

'It is you, Grand Inquisitor, that is the scoundrel,' the hooded figure said, his voice carrying just enough for the two men to hear. 'Your so called *law* and your protection from the King has finally come to an end. It was that protection alone that had stopped me from doing this a long, long time ago.' *Though I know not whether I would have had the strength to do this before now. Alas, after all that has recently happened…*

'So you know who we are?' Corlen said, from behind the Grand Inquisitor. The Archbishop's voice grew with confidence, yet he remained well behind his larger companion. 'You must realise the punishments this man could put you through for merely talking to us in such a manner.' Corlen took a step forward then and pointed to the Grand Inquisitor, his handkerchief still in hand. 'Well, do you?'

They couldn't be sure of course, but both men could have sword they *heard* a smile in the tone of the hooded man's voice when he replied.

'Oh no, Archbishop, that is where you are mistaken. For I no longer officially exist, and you… well, you no longer hold any authority in Wesson, or anywhere in Altoln for that matter.'

The Archbishop bristled, but the Grand Inquisitor held up his hand to halt the man from speaking further.

'And you do?' The Grand Inquisitor's eyebrows rose in anticipation.

'My orders, as sweet as they are, come from the King himself. For I am his new right hand, that moves in the darkness to seek out and destroy those whom he does not wish to be seen dealing with himself.'

The Archbishop began to tremble as he backed further away, his head shaking in disbelief. *This man's confidence…* Corlen's stomach knotted. *I've not seen the like in the Grand Inquisitor's presence in all my days.*

'So, the King finally has the courage to do something dark,' the Grand Inquisitor said, a snarl pulling at his top lip, 'to accomplish something he deems necessary. I never thought I'd see the day.'

'You won't,' the hooded figure whispered. The sapphire orbs to his left flared as the ground beneath the two Samorlians rumbled. They both looked down with a mixture of fear and confusion as the ground began to liquefy and suck at their feet.

The Archbishop cried out as he fell backwards, expecting his head to connect with the hard surface of the stone path, but it didn't. As the large man reached the ground, arms flailing and handkerchief flying out to the side, he disappeared below its surface, consumed by the bubbling mass of tar that had replaced the stone.

Corlen didn't resurface, and the thick, sucking tar continued to draw his companion down to meet him.

The Grand Inquisitor roared and threw his dagger uselessly at the hooded figure as the bubbling liquid drew him down. His rage fell away quickly and was replaced by fear as he realised with horror his shoulders were already fully submerged.

The cloying black liquid began pulling at his fleshy neck.

'I may be following orders, you evil wretch,' the hooded figure said as he stepped forward into the moon's light and pulled back his hood with his free hand, finally revealing his hate filled eyes, 'but this is revenge, for me, pure and simple. Revenge for my parents and all those your inquisition has wrongly tortured and burnt alive… or thought you did!'

One last word was just about audible through the bubbling, spurting mess that erupted from the surface of the tar as the Grand Inquisitor disappeared beneath its surface. The onlooker wasn't surprised to hear the word spat as a curse. In fact, it pleased him more than he'd have thought possible.

The onlooker had caused the deaths of thousands, and that fact, he knew, would haunt him until the end of his days. But this death... this death would not, and he played the hate filled word over in his mind as he set out into the park, striding triumphantly over the solidifying ground that only he would recognise as the Grand Inquisitor's tomb.

Yes, you bastard. Severun.

The former Grand Master of the Wizards and Sorcery Guild rubbed under his replaced hood, at the throbbing ache behind his black eyes. *Although, I'm not sure I'm the only one in here any more... and I'm quite sure it wasn't King Barrison alone that wanted that bastard dead, but where the other order came from... I can't quite remember?*

***

Far to the south of Wesson, in the forest borderland known as The Marches, all manner of creatures ran for cover, and flocks of birds ascended high into the sky as a commotion erupted through the forest's thick undergrowth.

The usual, constant but melodic noise of the forest gave way to the snapping of twigs, rustling of bushes and the heavy breathing of a desperate duo.

J'iak could just about see his companion to the front and right of him as she hacked through a thin, low branch with her sword. She ran on and he followed, not daring to look back as they pressed on towards the border.

A parakeet screeched above and the hairs on the back of the armed and lightly armoured man rose, but still he didn't look back. He kept his eyes on his companion as she ducked under a thicker branch and crashed through a thorn bush, making no sound despite the pain as the needle like thorns tore into her flesh. J'iak followed her through, equally as quiet apart from his heavy, ragged breathing.

His hand axes had started to feel heavier the longer he ran, although their pendulum motion propelled him on as it had for hours. Sweat matted his short black hair to his head and his heart thumped in his chest. He ducked under another low branch and leaned forward into his run again, never taking his eyes off his friend and the rough path she was creating with her sword.

Don't hesitate, keep running for queen's sake.

All manner of creepers came close to snagging J'iak's booted feet, and he had to keep part of his mind attuned to his surroundings so as not to trip and fall as he kept pace with his nimble partner.

Another creature cried out from behind this time, although what it was he didn't know, nor care. He swallowed hard, trying to keep his thoughts away from that which pursued them.

J'iak pushed on even harder, noticing his companion pulling away a little.

Despite his lungs burning with the exertion, as did his thighs, J'iak didn't falter as he forced himself ever onwards.

More low branches, large bushes and a sudden copse of tightly packed trees caused J'iak to lose sight of his friend for a couple of racing heartbeats.

No no no... where is she?

She looked back at her partner for the first time in a long time as she crashed through the densely packed foliage.

J'iak was gone, and she knew what that meant...

Tears in her eyes, sweat on her brow and a white knuckled grip on her slender sword, the woman continued, ever onwards towards a border and a kingdom she feared she would never see; towards Altoln.

***

Cheung sat, legs crossed on the dusty ground of the rooftop garden, all manner of potted palms, succulents and cacti surrounding him, as well as delicate orchids of varying colours. Henna tattooed arms out to the sides, with black bladed, bone handled kamas in his hands and his black robes folded carefully next to him, the Eatrian assassin concentrated on the small palm leaves of the potted plant opposite him. He mimicked the slow movements of the swaying leaves with his arms, the slightest corrections required – whilst holding his weapons at arms length – burning at his rope like muscles that flexed then relaxed under his pale skin.

He'd been in the same position all night as he re-read the letter passed to him in his head. That letter had come from the Black Guild in Altoln's capital city, Wesson, via his own guild masters.

The politics of the letter held no interest for Cheung, and he knew his masters would scrutinize that side of things. He'd admitted to himself upon his initial examination of the document, however, that it was interesting to learn the large assassins guild in Wesson was, for an undisclosed reason, unable to carry out the contract they'd been presented with. He didn't believe it was inability on their part or fear of the mark's position within their kingdom, and so willingly removed it from his mind, knowing it bore no importance to the fact the mark was now his, not theirs. It would only prove as a distraction, and he never suffered any of those.

With no obvious trigger to anyone who may have been watching, although that was highly unlikely without Cheung knowing about it, the assassin rose suddenly and effortlessly to his feet, stretched in several different ways, and then donned his robes in an impressive manner considering his kamas never left his hands.

He took one last look around his rooftop garden then, much of which he knew would wilt without his attention over the coming weeks if not months of travel, target acquisition, elimination and then return travel.

Taking a deep breath and freeing his mind of his plants and everything else

484

but the mission, the assassin walked backwards slowly. Reaching a certain point he couldn't possibly have seen, Cheung hopped lightly off the side of the building, setting out to find a suitable method of transport to cross the inhospitable and dangerous leagues between him and his latest target: King Barrison of Altoln.

***

Fal patted the neck of the proud white elven steed he'd been given by Lord Errwin-Roe, and took one last look behind him at a city he hardly recognised. The elegant horse trotted through Wesson's eastern gate, its head and tail held high as it followed the black mare of Correia Burr. Sav, Errolas, Gleave and Starks followed behind on their own proud steeds; each were armed, armoured, carrying saddle bags and wearing the dark green of a pathfinder; setting out on a mission to the south none but Correia and Errolas knew about.

***

Fransys wasn't happy. His big sister had forced him to cut off his shoulder length hair because hers was short and brown like Mamma's and she was jealous, and now she said he looked like Old Man Mickel the farmer, albeit blonde, not grey.

'Well I'm not old, Meya, I'm only bloody eight.' He took another handful of dirt from the road he sat on and threw it back at the door to his family's cottage, praying to Sir Samorl for Meya to come out just at the right time. Looking back over his shoulder, he frowned to see it hadn't happen.

'Useless bloody god,' Fransys said to himself, before looking back up the road which led out of Hinton. Fransys' eyes widened and his breath caught at the sight before him. Licking his dry lips, he struggled to think what to do. He wasn't even sure if what he saw was real or a trick of the light. He'd heard that could happen, especially when tired or upset.

'Dadda,' Fransys called softly.

Nothing.

'Dadda!' he shouted, as the dirty-white caparisoned horse and armoured rider he saw on the road drew closer. The black hart on the blood and dirt soiled white trapper, heater shield and surcoat was clear to the boy's young eyes.

'What now, lad?' Hjefroy said as he came to the door of the cottage, his left hand scratching at the stump where his right had once been. Hjefroy frowned as he noticed his son's shorn hair, which had mirrored his own earlier that same day. Sighing hard, he turned to shout for Meya, knowing it would be his daughter's doing.

'Dadda look!'

Hjefroy couldn't miss the fear in his son's voice. He tensed as he turned

485

and looked back out the door, following his boy's frightened stare up the road to a loan rider, whose horse aimlessly walked to and fro, picking at the patchy grass by the side of the road. *Baron Brackley? Not like you to travel alone…*

Hjefroy's gut lurched as he realised the reason for his son's understandable fear. He walked slowly out into the road to stand in front of Fransys. 'Go inside lad, this ain't for yer eyes,' he said, unable to take his own from the sight before him.

'Is that the Baron of Ullston, Dadda?'

'Aye, lad, it is. Now go I say.'

'But his head… it's gone, and he's still riding his horse?'

Hjefroy closed his eyes tight for a brief moment before turning and dropping to crouch in front of his son. He rested his left hand on his son's shoulder, whilst tucking his stump into his shirt as was his habit. 'The Baron's dead, my son. He isn't riding, the horse is walking itself, I promise you that.'

Fransys' blue eyes were wide as he tried to look round his father. 'But how does he not fall off and who killed him?'

'If I tell ye, will ye go indoors and send yer mother out to me?'

Fransys nodded.

'What did the Baron do for us, Fransys?'

'He built us this cottage.'

'Aye, that he did, but what else, for everyone in the area?'

'He holds the summer fete at his hall.'

Hjefroy smiled despite the situation. 'And what did I used to do with the Baron, lad?' He wouldn't have thought it possible, but his son's eyes widened yet more as he remembered.

'Fight thieves and goblins and monsters.'

Laughing, again despite the situation, Hjefroy nodded. 'Aye son, we did, and I think that's what Baron Brackley went to do recently. He went to fight off some nasty goblins—'

'But they killed him?' Fransys cut in, solemnly.

Hjefroy nodded again. 'I think they did. It's an old wicked trick for goblins to tie a lord or knight to his horse and send that horse on its way, to frighten people like us, but that's all that's happened here lad, ye see?'

Fransys' eyes welled with tears as he nodded, his head hanging low at the end.

'But we won't let 'em scare us will we, son? The Baron deserves a proper Samorlian burial and that's what yer mother and I will give him, but I need ye to go get her for that, and then I need ye to be brave and go stay with yer sister, make sure—

'Ah-ah, Fransys… I know what she's done to yer hair and I'll be talking to her for it, but ye need to be with her and stop her—'

'Dadda,' Fransys said suddenly, whilst again looking past his father.

'What?'

'The Baron, Dadda… he just drew his sword.'

Hjefroy's heart almost stopped as he heard the words and saw the genuine fear returning to his son's face. Turning round slowly whilst remaining crouched, Hjefroy looked upon his former liege lord's armoured corpse, as it lifted its blooded broadsword high and turned its mount to face the two of them.

'Morl's bloody balls,' Hjefroy said whilst breathing out heavily. He grabbed his son with his good hand then and ran for his cottage. 'My sword,' he shouted, 'Sasha! Grab me my fucking sword!'

Hooves pounded the earth behind them.

***

With a swirl of thick, acrid smoke and a scream a spoilt child would be proud of, a fleshy red sack of bones with yellowed teeth and black eyes appeared on the moss covered ground. Steam poured from that flesh, flesh that slowly rolled over revealing a curled up, howling goblin, whose scrawny limbs, bald head and torn ears shuddered violently.

Finally, the red-skinned creature's shudder slowed to a tremble as he began to stiffly unwrap himself from his self hugging fetal position. He looked about himself and painfully stretched his thin but tightly muscled limbs, the trembles falling away to a growing confidence that spread a sharp toothed grin across his pointed face.

The Red Goblin's howling screech had fallen to a mumble, which now transformed into a rasping chuckle, before developing into an all out manic laugh. Forcing himself to his feet, the goblin chieftain stretched his arms and legs completely, his naked and toned form disgusting his observer.

Bowing low in an almost mocking gesture, without even looking upon the recipient, The Red Goblin spoke his first coherent words since re-awakening. 'Your wards worked, just like your emissary Dignaaln said they would.' He slowly waved his hands in front of his face, before checking his legs and torso, making sure all had returned in tact. He finished by taking a hold of his cock and balls and giving them a good tug.

'Indeed,' an unamused, bass-like voice said from within The Red Goblin's head. 'Did you doubt that fact, goblin?'

The goblin snarled. 'Chieftain!' He released his package to pick at his right ear. 'And not at all, it's told your power is unmeasurable.' The Red Goblin sucked the product of his ear picking from his clawed finger and looked up high, into his observer's eyes.

'You'd do well to remember my power. You are naught but a servant to me. Your title means nothing here goblin.'

'I was chosen by a bloody god!' The Red Goblin's defiance was apparent through his balled fists and wide stance.

The voice in his head roared, dropping him to his knees.

'You were born of a mortal mother who bled to death as your father had you tattooed red at birth, by a shaman he later killed.'

The Red Goblin rocked back at the revelation, his eyes darting around, focusing on nothing as he tried to find a way to disprove the facts unfolding in his head.

'Do not mistake that with being chosen by a false god you fool. If you hadn't murdered your father the first chance you had, you might have learnt that yourself.'

Taking in deep breaths to calm his beating heart, The Red Goblin looked at the skin of his arms. He shook his head slowly and tried but failed to climb to his feet; his legs refused to work for him.

'You may not have had the beginning you believed, goblin, but you do have power. You have my backing, after all, and there's nothing more you could ever need to fulfill your ambitions.' The voice had lowered, but its every syllable continued to resonate throughout the chieftain's skull. 'Now tell me what I wish to know, and we shall talk more about the great things I can do for you.'

Licking his thin lips, The Red Goblin finally stood. He straightened his back and lifted his head, before revealing what he knew the being before him had been waiting to hear since his arrival.

'The north is in disarray and the kingdom as a whole has been weakened as you desired... master.' The Red Goblin had uttered the latter with reluctance whilst struggling to push the new found truth about his origins to the back of his mind. Visions of future glory, power and wealth won out in the end however, and he grinned as he locked eyes with the creature towering over him. 'From what I've done and seen, I believe now is the time for the humans to witness your return.'

The look The Red Goblin received caused him to step back, and although he would never admit it, even to himself, the goblin chieftain almost felt sorry for the humans of Altoln and Sirreta, for what was to come... well, it didn't bear thinking about, even for him.

So ends the first book from the tales of the Black Powder Wars.

Thank you for reading
Black Cross
First book from the tales of the
Black Powder Wars

Online reviews are mandatory.
Well, maybe not, but they're more than welcome.
Please also feel free to contact me on the following social media sites:
Goodreads, Facebook, Twitter
@JP_Ashman
#BlackCross
#BlackPowderWars
#SPFBO

J P Ashman is currently working on:

Black Martlet
First short story from the tales of the
Black Powder Wars
(Due for release late 2015)

Black Guild
Second book from the tales of the
Black Powder Wars
(Due for release 2016)

Biography

Born Lancashire, England, J P Ashman is a Northern lad through and through. His parents love wildlife, history, fantasy and science fiction, and passed their passion on to him. They read to him from an early age and encouraged his imagination at every turn. His Career may be in optics, as a manager/technician, but he loves to make time for writing and reading every day. Now living in the Cotswolds with Wifey and their little Norse Goddess Freya, he is inspired daily by the views they have and the things they see, from the deer in the fields to the buzzards circling overhead.

Writing is a huge part of his life and the medieval re-enactment background and tabletop gaming lend do it; when he's not writing the genre, he's either reading or playing it. He plans to keep writing, both within his current series, and those to come, whether short stories or epic tomes.

Biography taken from the SPFBO Author Interview by,
Mihir Wanchoo.
www.fantasybookcritic.blogspot.co.uk

14460203R00286

Printed in Great Britain
by Amazon.co.uk, Ltd.,
Marston Gate.